A Life Singular
Book 4

I0566414

Lorraine Pestell

Other books in the "A Life Singular" series:
Book 1 – A Life Singular
Book 2 – A Life Found
Book 3 – A Life Entwined
Book 5 – A Life Tested
Book 6 – A Life Loved
Book 7 – A Life After

For Jenny,
whose eagle-eyes and objective feedback are always invaluable

The author supports two not-for-profit organisations which provide invaluable assistance to Australian children in need:

EdConnect Australia (formerly the School Volunteer Program)
(http://EdConnetAustralia.org.au) *"We're harnessing the wisdom and skills of older generations to enrich the learning experience of young people who are at risk of falling by the wayside in an often over-burdened school system."*

The Smith Family *(www.thesmithfamily.com.au).* *"The Smith Family is a children's charity helping disadvantaged Australian children to get the most out of their education, so they can create better futures for themselves."*

Prologue

Freya stood in line for the reception desk at the Qantas Lounge, nervously flicking the corner of her boarding pass. The young man behind the counter was doing his best to deflect a barrage of insults from an oversized businessman who had missed his flight, and the sensitive artist smiled in sympathy whenever she caught his eye. She presumed it hadn't been the airline's fault that the aggressive traveller had arrived late, and most certainly not within the clerk's sphere of control. It never ceased to disappoint her that such verbal abuse was so often directed at the least deserving.

The eighteen-year-old rehearsed her pitch while she waited. Her bag weighed heavily on her shoulder, stuffed to bursting with samples, testimonials and a number of photographs taken at her recent Brisbane exhibition. She felt confident in her ability to sell herself, although with no idea how stiff the competition might be for next year's endowment scholarship for The Good School.

Mid-sentence however, the irate passenger at the front of the queue fell silent as the sliding doors parted and a tall, slim figure with a mass of sleek, dark curls entered. A wide smile and a pair of enchanting eyes met each turning head before waving to the man behind the counter, who immediately excused himself from his current customer and picked up the telephone.

The lady in the tailored suit and high heels diverted towards a leather couch and deposited her two bags on the floor beside it, preparing to sit down. Instead of checking her voicemail messages, as she had obviously intended, Freya could hardly believe her eyes when the new arrival made a bee-line for her.

'You must be Freya,' the graceful celebrity assumed, extending her right hand towards the star-struck young woman. 'There aren't too many of us with such unruly mops of hair! I'm Kierney Diamond. It's so good to meet you.'

By now, half a dozen people were waiting for attention, all of whom gaped in astonishment at the unremarkable bystander who had been greeted like a long-lost friend by the famous United Nations ambassador. The Queenslander lifted the satchel containing her portfolio off her shoulder and placed it awkwardly between her feet, almost overbalancing in her haste to accept Kierney's handshake.

'Yes. Thank you,' she stammered. 'Yes, I'm Freya Gunarwardene. It's a real honour, Ms Diamond. I wish my hair looked like yours!'

The thirty-six-year-old beauty smiled. 'Thanks, and please call me Kierney. Come out of the line. There's a meeting room booked for us inside, and I expect someone'll show us through in a minute. How was your flight?'

A beaming Qantas staff member appeared from the office behind Reception right on cue, ready to usher their VIP visitor inside the lounge. Her expression altered momentarily, not knowing who the second guest was and struck by the similarity in the two ladies' physical appearance.

'Step this way, please, Ms Diamond. It's lovely to see you again. Is this your guest?'

'Hello, Hannah,' Kierney replied. 'Yes, Freya's my guest. Fleeting visit today. I'm booked on the five-fifty to LAX. Please could you send someone to call me? What time's your flight, Freya?'

The youngster followed the others into an area reserved for First Class passengers, unable to remember when her return flight departed. She fumbled around in her handbag, feeling anxious and inadequate, while the scarlet-lipped employee held the door open for her. Unfolding her itinerary and scanning it quickly, she provided the requested information, and the dark-haired pair were duly left on their own.

'Sorry,' the older woman frowned. 'I didn't mean to put you on the spot. Please sit down. I've been really looking forward to meeting you ever since we spoke. Would you like tea or coffee? It's just outside. I'm dying for a coffee. I left Melbourne before six this morning. Oh, is that a copy of "ALS"?'

True enough, Kierney had spotted the distinctive top right-hand corner of her parents' autobiography as her interviewee opened her bag and began to extract the collateral she had brought with her. The unmistakeable emblem of two initials formed into its singular number caught both sets of eyes at once, embarrassing both women with its power.

'I always carry it, wherever I go,' the teenager nodded. 'It's like a lucky charm. My friends tease me that it's my comfort blanket, and it's become known as "The Book" in my family.'

Wondering if her words might come across as too sycophantic, Freya's voice trailed off. She had drawn quotation marks in the air, a habit which annoyed her in others, but to her relief Kierney was laughing.

'That's funny! We call it that too.'

'It cheers me up when I'm down,' the young leader admitted, 'because it's full of such hope. And I couldn't think of anything more wonderful than to meet someone like your father.'

The famous ambassador for peace felt tears springing to her eyes at these words, fortunately distracted at that moment by her mobile telephone ringing on her lap. 'Do you mind if I answer this, please?'

Shaking her head, Freya waved a feeble hand, amazed at even having been asked. Why did she feel so revered by such an impressive international figure? There was nothing girlish about this tall, dark-haired celebrity, and yet the difference in their ages appeared negligible, sitting opposite each other in the small space.

Trying not to look as though she was eavesdropping, the artist gazed around the room, realising fairly quickly that Kierney was speaking to someone very important. Being left alone with her thoughts, insecurities frightened her, punishing her for being so forward with her idol.

'That was my boss,' the part-time musician apologised. 'He likes to know where I am at all times.'

Only the Secretary General of the United Nations, Freya gulped.

'It's embarrassing. He calls me "Ms Next-in-Line", which is amazingly flattering,' the human rights advocate continued. 'It's at times like these I wish *Mamá* and *Papá* could hear him.'

Both beset with the same romantic notion, two pairs of moist, shining eyes met again.

'I'm sure they can,' the younger woman hazarded.

Their meeting officially underway once coffee had been served and sampled, Freya began to relax. The person in whose hands her fate lay listened carefully, interjecting every now and then with an insightful question. Her demeanour was exactly how the youngster had expected: compassionate yet commanding; authoritative yet amiable. An adolescence spent immersed in the pages of "A Life Singular" now stood the applicant in good stead, feeling totally at home in this stranger's presence. There was an odd air of mutual respect laced through their conversation, rendering the meeting less like an interview and more like two firm friends chatting in a laneway café over a glass of wine.

'The committee will be making its final decision about the award next week,' the renowned lawyer explained, returning the candidate's written submission and moving to examine one of her drawings in great detail. 'We're down to a shortlist of three, after my brother discounted one applicant yesterday. It's always a difficult choice.'

'I can imagine,' Freya nodded. 'I can't believe I've got this far, to be honest. And I was really thrilled to hear you wanted to meet me. Thanks for paying for my ticket to Sydney. I'm not a very experienced traveller, as you saw earlier. I felt like your dad when he was going to New Zealand for the first time.'

Kierney chuckled. 'Not quite so hyperactive, I hope.'

'Oh, I'm not so sure,' the artist's eyes dropped for a second, before correcting their manners in such exalted company. 'I was on my own. I'm sure I would've been very excited if I had someone to share the experience with. I even went to the Stones Road at lunchtime. On a kind of pilgrimage, I suppose.'

'Did you?' her distinguished lookalike appeared pleased to hear this. 'Wow! What did you think?'

'Some sort of pride, I think,' the eighteen-year-old answered, unsure of herself again. 'I'm not sure why. It didn't really hit me until I was back on the train, but I felt proud that I pay so much attention to your parents' advice, and that I'm serious about doing my best to change the world.'

'For your own father?' Kierney asked, seeing a faraway look in the candidate's eyes. 'To honour his memory?'

'No, not really. More to honour your parents' memory. I feel so connected to them,' she paused, catching her breath. 'Oh, sorry! That's inappropriate to say in front of you. I'm sorry if I'm getting too close. I worried about how much of a fan I could be during this interview process.'

The older woman smiled. 'Don't apologise, please. It's always nice to hear how much people loved them. Ryan and I've become quite adept at partitioning that aspect of people's applications. We always debate whether being a fan of Mum and Dad should be a selection criterion, which I won't go into now for obvious reasons, but at some point it'd be nice to share some more memories with you.'

The bemused young painter nodded, stoked that there would at least be more contact with this surprisingly gentle and encouraging role-model. 'OK. Thank you. I'd love to hear more. How's your son, by the way. It must be hard to be away from your family so often. Behnam, isn't it?'

Kierney nodded. 'It is, but I'm never away for more than a few days at a time. Ben, we call him. We were all in Melbourne this time, but Arka flew back with him this morning. Here... I've got an up-to-date photo'.'

Their two heads of long, black hair came close together, scrolling through pictures on the diplomat's mobile telephone until they reached a cute portrait of a small boy offering a spoonful of his breakfast to whomever had been snapping away. The teenager gasped, overcome with an atypical rush of love for the little tyke.

'Oh, he's adorable,' she whispered, unable to stop her fingers from stroking the surface of the screen.

Ready to put the handset back into her bag, the busy mother again made eye contact with her young interviewee. A curious reaction indeed. And the strongest signal yet...

'I think you know my other reason for wanting to meet you in person,' Kierney said, her voice slightly hushed.

'Yes,' the humble painter responded. 'I hoped we could talk about that.'

It was clear that both women had been doused in the same foreboding ambiance. Leaning back and smiling, Freya was frozen in her seat, desperate to resist a completely unexpected urge to hug her interviewer, who twisted a heavy ring which she wore on the middle finger of her right hand. The avid reader had recognised this striking piece of jewellery when they had first introduced themselves, now shivering at the sight of its four inset stones.

The famous daughter broke the silence, slapping a palm on each knee decisively. 'Your date of birth caught my attention, and I was interested in your comments when we spoke last time. Ryan thinks I'm nuts, and we're inundated with cranks claiming to be our parents. I have no real confidence in the whole concept, and he has even less. Almost none, in fact. But your reaction to Ben's picture just now was acute, and I feel creepily like I already know you. I hope you don't mind me telling you this.'

'No,' the younger woman said, her spine tingling. 'I've always had a weird feeling about it, as I mentioned when we talked before. And there's so much in your dad's book that I think I understand. If that makes sense?'

Jeff Diamond's gipsy girl had tears in her eyes, daring to believe she were a step closer to solving the mystery of her parents' long and hopefully continuing journey. This sweet-natured and persuasive artist, half Australian and half Sri Lankan who had accomplished so much in her eighteen tender years, evidently had a head-start when it came to appreciating the messages in the revealing best-seller.

Ryan and Kierney had certainly been taken by the biographical details documented in this young woman's application for The Good School's scholarship, telling how her deceased father had been a sufferer of Post-Traumatic Stress Disorder and of how their family had been torn apart by its effects. However, as the compassionate lawyer secretly vowed to confess to her older brother, it was truly a mammoth leap between empathy and reincarnation.

Freya struggled to maintain her smile too, knowing there was one more vital statistic as yet unimparted which was likely to bring this surreal encounter to an unsatisfactory conclusion for both women. Even if she were who Kierney hoped she was, there was one aspect of her personality that would surely be a showstopper.

Flying Away

Kierney Diamond watched her brother put down the weighty hardback and issue a long sigh. The student siblings had paid a fleeting visit to Melbourne for their grandparents' combined sixty-fifth birthday celebrations and were now back at the airport again, one returning to Sydney and the other bound for Heathrow.

'Where are you up to?' the eighteen-year-old asked, her dark eyes alighting on the familiar tome.

'Leaving for London,' Ryan replied.

'Are you enjoying it?'

'Yes and no,' the young man scoffed, the well-worn expression igniting both hearts. 'I can't believe how many revelations it contains. Even for me.'

'Us,' his sister assured.

'Cool. But there are *so* many things I didn't know. Page after page of the stuff. Was it like that for you?'

Kierney nodded. 'For a family who talked all the time, a good deal still obviously went unsaid. To protect us, I suppose. It's nice. Comforting in a way.'

'Or maybe they just forgot,' Ryan countered. 'Things too painful to remember; that you'd rather put out of your mind, so after a while you just do. I guess it must've all come flooding back when Dad was forced to sort everything into sequence.'

The law student sighed. 'I think you're right. Gerry told me the other day about a very emotional conversation he had with *Papá* while he was writing. He said he hadn't understood the reason why *Papá* was so obsessed with certain memories, and that it was only after he'd read about *Papá*'s decision to have kids that everything made sense to him.'

The tall, blond sportsman shrugged and chuckled, heaving himself to his feet. 'Ha! That'd be right,' he teased. 'The master of the blindingly obvious strikes again! Gerry never has been one to pick up on the subtleties of life.'

Kierney smiled. 'He's getting better, I think. We need to remember that the vision was only clear to *Mamá* and *Papá* at that point. Still forming, which means they probably hadn't discussed it with anyone else. Not where it was all leading, you know… Oh, I'm getting a lump in my throat just thinking about it. It's just so magical, seeing their dream come together. You'll enjoy the next few chapters. Practice makes perfect…'

'Practice makes perfect?' Ryan echoed. 'I assume that's a reference to sex. Thanks, sis'. That actually freaks me out a bit. I'm not sure I want to be reading about our conception on a 'plane full of ogling eyes. Perhaps I'll leave it 'til I get home. I'll be too self-conscious to read it in public.'

The Sydney University undergraduate shook her head. 'Why? How will anyone know what you're reading about, you idiot? Hide the book in a magazine or something. I love the part where he tells the newborn you that you're the perfection they were practising for. "*Ergo*," *Papá* says. Like a foregone conclusion.'

'Yeah. He said that loads of times. "You are practice made perfect, guys." Right before they gave us some other shit about working harder or something.'

His sister couldn't help but laugh. The impersonation of their father's dark-brown voice was accurate enough, but the sarcasm was overblown. She sensed the cricketer's discomfort as he struggled with his own emotions. Their parents had never missed an opportunity to tell their children how important and wanted they were; a lesson learned the hard way by one and never to be repeated by either.

'"Exquisite sex begat two perfect beings,"' the romantic teenager quoted. 'The hierarchy of drugs thing is interesting. You'll get to that bit soon, if you're where I think you are. And then there's the hint about Nick.'

Ryan blanched. 'Shit! Yeah. Bloody Nick! D'you believe there's any truth behind his claim? Really?'

'Who knows?' Kierney shrugged. 'Another indication that blood's not thicker than water if there's no love in your family. *Papá* didn't care much when Granddad dropped the bombshell, and much, much less last year. Unsurprisingly… I just wonder if they'd have pursued it more if *Mamá* had still been alive to meet him too.'

'Jeez. Rollercoaster or what!' the young man exclaimed, now with more interest in reading further.

'I know! You'd better get ready,' his sister said, checking the clock on the wall. 'They'll be coming to get you in a minute.'

Nodding, Ryan disappeared to the restroom before his flight was called for boarding. While he was gone, the younger Diamond prodigy lifted their father's substantial autobiography from the table and opened it up to the page where a tatty Cambridge University Press bookmark had last been inserted. She had read the intricate web of stories from start to finish twice already, yet still found it disconcerting to uncover facts and observations about her own life through the farsighted but worn-out eyes of her beloved *Papá*.

Leaving for London, Kierney reminded herself with a sigh. How thrilling it must have been for the young stars to be free to live life in their own way. The independent teenager attempted to put herself in her mother's shoes, back in the mid-nineteen-seventies, thinking how exciting it would be to embark on the journey her mysterious boyfriend had envisaged with such clarity. It surely was a veritable leap of faith for the privileged high-society child. Her daughter remembered fondly the stories both parents used to tell of their ambitious plans and how Jeff's wild ideas were painstakingly shaped into a set of achievable milestones by Lynn's pragmatic and level-headed management. They had truly been a partnership made in heaven, the sentimental student had long realised.

Leafing back a few pages from her brother's marker, Kierney felt tears welling up as she ran her fingers over the embossed rendering of the simple but stylish tattoo her parents shared, which over the years had become almost as famous as their names and faces. These tiny inked icons heralded the relationship's true magic, Jeff had reminded his children on many an occasion. She and her brother had not quite understood the significance of his wondrous statements at first, but once the young woman had lost herself in early chapters of the book, their full impact had gradually begun to unwind.

Ryan would be turning twenty in the next few months, having left the boisterous Jet behind in a triumphant wake of sporting success, and the willowy gipsy girl herself was these days officially an adult too. Nevertheless, it was difficult to imagine either of them setting off on quite such a life-changing adventure as their parents had begun at similar ages. When the eternal couple had boarded that flight *en route* to London early in the New Year of nineteen-seventy-five, would they have had any real idea who they were to become and how much they would change the way people behaved towards their fellow man, woman and child in years to come?

Yes, Kierney insisted to herself. She believed they did.

It was now fifteen months since their father had gone in search of his dream girl all over again, and both Diamond children had been pleasantly surprised at how their lives had carried on without upheaval or excessive grief, just as the wise man had projected during those last, frantic weeks together. The dreamy songwriter replaced the marker and closed the book, tilting it to see from the top how far through the large volume it was located. Approximately halfway, she contemplated in wonder. The life she had known with her parents hadn't even begun, and yet her *Papá* had spent almost as long articulating the incredible campaign up to this point as he had in documenting the rest of their life singular.

Ryan returned to gather up his belongings in preparation for departure, attracting the attention of a group of girls travelling together. Kierney rolled her eyes at his casual but confident wave, being drawn into the throng along with him. After they had signed each person's boarding pass and posed for a few photographs, the *débonair* cricketer held his hand out for the book.

'Hang on a sec'. Look at this...' Kierney invited, turning the upper edge into her brother's line of sight and flicking the top of the bookmark. 'Almost fifty percent of the way through, and they're not even married yet. That's amazing really.'

'Is it?' the final year student replied. 'Why? Isn't that just following the normal exposition, climax and *dénouement* thing?'

'Well, yes. I guess so, but he obviously considered the process of becoming one as much of an accomplishment as all the huge things they did together, as one, in the next twenty years.'

Ryan shrugged. 'Yeah. Maybe. I never thought about it like that. It's going to be surreal reading about our births. I'm almost tempted to skip that part.'

His sister laughed. 'Ew, yes. Especially the blowjob in the shower!'

'Oh, shut up, for God's sake!' the young man grimaced, shoving the book into his hand luggage, folding the flap over and fastening the clip. 'That's enough from you. Dad told me he wanted to steer clear of what was already in the public domain, 'cause people already know all that stuff. Maybe that's why the second half covers so much ground.'

'*Muy buen*'. That's a good explanation, brain-box,' the dark-haired teenager smiled. 'Plus, maybe that's our story to tell. Later. You know... Do you think we'll ever know their next incarnations?'

The young man scoffed. 'What? Don't even go there. Needles and haystacks, *pequeñita*, don't ya think?' his father's sarcastic intonation replicated again. 'I'm more worried about all the loonies who'll make that assumption about themselves or their kids and plague us in a few years' time. "Hey, Ryan, my daughter used to be your mum. Don't you remember her?"'

'Hmm... That has crossed my mind a few times too. And how the hell would we know if one of them really was the genuine article? They might be born anywhere in the world, which I suppose is why we sometimes never meet "The One" in our whole lifetime. That's kind of sad, isn't it? I don't want to wait until a future incarnation to find the happiness they had.'

'Whatever...' her brother replied, dismissing his own secret and shared disappointment. 'I've got to go. Are you going to be alright here?'

Brother and sister embraced warmly. It would be six months until they next saw each other, but neither was afraid of the separation. Both young lives were busy with study, playing sports, making music and spending time with friends, and the technology their parents' timely investments had made possible always kept them well in touch.

'Yes, I'm fine,' Kierney replied, kissing his cheek. 'I'm glad we came home for "G" and "G"'s party, but I'm looking forward to getting back to uni' too. I feel like I'm leaving Melbourne behind, just like *Papá* predicted.'

16

'Me too,' Ryan agreed. 'He was a wise, old man, after all. I honestly didn't believe him, did you?'

'Not really. Not so soon anyway. Should have, evidently. Safe flying, Jetto.'

'*Adiós, chica.* Onwards and upwards.'

***

'What's this?' Jeff asked, watching the smiling blonde pull out paper and pens from her flight bag and place them on their tray-tables.

'Homework,' Lynn answered. 'But we have to do it on our own.'

'What? No cheating or collusion?' chided her handsome travelling companion, instantly intrigued. 'Can't I even sneak a look when you're asleep?'

The young woman gave him a stern glare. 'Definitely not.'

The flight was not yet twenty minutes in the air, and already a sense of impending boredom was encroaching. How well Lynn could read his mind these days, and how grateful the healing rock star felt that she took the time to do so. The twenty-four hours leading up to their departure had seen the line on his happiness chart break all previous records as it whizzed up into the distortion zone.

His dream girl had come prepared for mania however, having finished reading Doctor Diamond's Law of Compensatory Addictions and plotting a course to smooth the extreme peaks and troughs just enough to strike the perfect balance between stability and impulsiveness. After strictly controlled intervals of forced solitude and combined excitement, the pair had coasted past her parents' awkward farewell, through Passport Control and all the way to their current location, high above the clouds and heading in a north-westerly direction at a rate of knots.

Jeff turned the blank pieces of paper over and over again. 'Are you going to give me any clues?'

Lynn laughed. 'No!' she kidded. 'It's an exercise in telepathy. Of course I am. A normal life. We both independently need to write down what a normal life means to us.'

Her boyfriend's eyes widened. 'Ah, OK! I can tell you right now that I'm gonna need way more paper than this. Is it a thesis you're looking for or a song? And who's going to mark it? Philosophical arguments for and against or a checklist of practical instructions? There are just so many ways to tackle it.'

The nineteen-year-old smiled and lifted herself up off her seat to kiss his cheek, tucking her legs underneath her to make herself comfortable.

'*¡Excelente!* It'll stop you from getting bored then. We're going to mark each others'. And write whatever you want in whatever format you want.'

'Can't I just watch the movie and tell you later?' Jeff requested, leafing through the in-flight magazine to find the Entertainment section.

'If you like,' Lynn shrugged. 'But you won't, will you?'

The swarthy intellectual cocked his head and dealt his fellow passenger a heart-stopping wink. The family goodbyes at the airport had been cheerful, and only a few tears had been shed. Marianna and Bart had seemed relaxed and in love themselves, waving to their elder daughter and her ambitious and *avant garde* suitor as the automatic doors into International Departures opened for the famous musicians. Jeff had put his arm around Lynn's shoulder while they both looked back, their free hands high in the air until the doors slid shut. Once through the baggage security checks, they had found a couple of seats in a dark corner of the air-side bar and settled down for their final two hours on Australian soil.

'Well, gorgeous,' the chart-topping performer had declared, wondering if the broad smile on his girlfriend's face was as genuine as it looked after saying goodbye to her family for another year. 'This is it. We're finally alone. It's all up to us now. Are you ready?'

'Yes, very,' came the tennis champion's immediate confirmation. 'You?'

The twenty-two-year-old musician had raised his beer glass to his beautiful best friend. 'You bet. To us!'

'To us!'

And now, flying First Class on Qantas to London, here they were on the opening night of their new life singular. As usual, the flight attendants had fussed around the stars when they first boarded, so much so that they had to request the noise be kept to a minimum to spare the other passengers from the disturbance.

To uphold her elevated position in Australia's pseudo-aristocracy, Lynn had been brought up with strict flight manners, which the pretender from Sydney's western suburbs had also magnanimously assumed. The golden rules instilled in the Dyson children from a tender age were one, to always dress smartly, as befitting their privileged status; two, to not behave in a drunken and disorderly way in front of staff or fellow travellers; three, to not leave the cabin in a total mess like a lot of spoiled passengers seemed to; and four, to keep themselves to themselves.

Rule number four was the one the young lovers were looking forward to the most. The initial eight-hour flight took off in a southward direction at ten-thirty at night, circling Melbourne's city centre and Port Phillip Bay before veering towards the Northern Territory, bound for Singapore. The former child-star had waved her birthplace goodbye from the window seat without a trace of regret.

The seasoned travellers had struck a deal that Jeff would swap to the window on the second leg of their journey, since he hadn't been motivated to see London's extensive metropolis from the sky on any previous flight. The opportunity cost of this deal however, as he watched enviously while his girlfriend arranged her pillow against the wall, was that no sooner had he taken his last mouthful of complimentary *Shiraz*, than a lipsticked, tight-skirted stewardess appeared at his side to refill his glass.

'No, thanks. I'll wait for dinner,' he declined most uncharacteristically, putting his hand over the tumbler and smiling at her overenthusiasm.

Of course, the attentive woman had not planned on leaving the vicinity of her favourite singers in a hurry and proceeded to bend over the good-looking star, reaching into the seat pocket to retrieve a menu card. Lynn briefly opened her eyes to check out the amusing scene, understanding exactly how beguiling the entire female population found her red-blooded boyfriend.

'Have you checked the options for dinner, Miss Dyson, Mister Diamond?'

Accepting the card from the brunette's hand, Jeff pretended to scan down the culinary choices, using a gratuitous few moments to study her uniformed figure far more closely. There were worse ways to while away the hours on a long-haul flight than to take in the view from the aisle seat, but it was becoming clear that this particular painted lady had definite designs on him that could escalate to irksome now that he was flying as half of showbusiness' newest item.

'Can we swap seats?' he joked, after the brazen stewardess had given up. 'These flirt attendants are going to drive me insane.'

'Mister Popular,' Lynn teased, giggling at yet another new descriptor he had defined. 'Flirt attendants? Take your medicine. You love the attention really, don't you, Mister Diamond?'

The playful man rolled his eyes, knowing full well how little he could hide from the astute Miss Dyson. Putting on a surly tone, he read out the meal selection, more out of spite than curiosity, before retrieving the blank sheets of paper that Lynn had given him and commencing his dissertation. His pen drew lines to divide one page into four quadrants and gave each a title: "J thinks L wants", "L thinks J wants", "L wants" and "J wants".

Out of the corner of his eye, the diligent passenger could see a certain inquisitiveness brewing beside him. Being left-handed though, it was easy for him to mask his writing. With a haughty flick of her hair, the spurned onlooker poked fun at his secretive behaviour and returned to her book. Observing him with a better informed eye, her heart suddenly overflowed with love for this emotional powder-keg of a man on whose wild ride she had decided to tag along.

The first theme Jeff's mind offered was "Freedom". Lynn would want time to herself. And he hoped he would too, once things began to settle down. Did she think he knew that? And did she know he thought that? The happy man closed his eyes and imagined themselves in the new apartment they had seen only in photographs.

Freedom to come and go, freedom of thought, freedom to experiment and learn and freedom from nightmares and phobia. They would both be busy, separately studying in different parts of the sprawling city, meeting their own new sets of friends and becoming involved in their respective university activities. It would be healthy for the devoted *duo* to keep as many distinct interests as possible, as long as they reserved sufficient time from their professional schedules to spend in each others' company.

The second theme descended on the prolific thinker before he had finished dealing with the first: "Routine". He knew Lynn craved routine. In fact, in his opinion, she craved it too much, and their relationship would benefit from more spontaneity than she would introduce alone.

This was shaping up to be a fascinating exercise, Jeff thought, and he couldn't wait to share their results. He looked across at his beautiful best friend and smiled.

'This is a great idea.'

'Good. Thanks,' she replied. 'I'll do mine after dinner. Do you mind? I just want to read for a bit.'

'Sure,' her boyfriend leaned over and kissed her. 'Anything you like. It was your idea. Enjoy the peace and quiet.'

The philosopher meandered lazily from topic to topic, blocking out the sound of meal trolleys being prepared. Hopefully, his next glass of wine was not far away. He stood up to stretch his back and legs, glancing towards the curtain which separated their rarefied atmosphere with that of the rear of the aeroplane, willing some second-hand smoke into his nicotine-starved lungs. As it turned out, these quadrants weren't proving at all useful to categorise the attributes of his normal life, so the creative addict sat down again to transfer his semi-random thoughts onto a new piece of paper under each theme instead.

Forget the cravings, he urged his overactive mind. Lynn had designed this endeavour with the specific purpose of overcoming them, and he would damned well make sure the structure of his argument impressed her.

However, midway through the transcription process, the musician was suddenly overtaken by a rush of lyrics. He had been toying with a few profound phrases for the past couple of days, but nothing substantial had materialised until now. He felt tears stinging behind his eyes as the poetry surged out of his heart in a veritable torrent.

The stunning woman to his left had fallen asleep, still with her book open on her lap. Her boyfriend picked out a fresh piece of paper and captured the subliminal messages this burst of energy had set free. Where had this guardian angel come from? She, who had proven her worth in her own right a thousand times, now gave him her love so unconditionally and in return only took his breath away.

The song which proceeded to write itself on the tray-table beside a fresh glass of red wine would promise that its composer would be everything his *Regala* could ever desire. And much more, if she were to allow it. No matter the price, he intended to repay her dedication a million times over. This she must know, and he would tell her every day.

***

After dinner, Lynn placed a blank sheet of paper on her tray-table and wrote "A Normal Life" as a heading across the top, underlining it with a flourish. The intensity of the songwriting process had rendered her man tired and sentimental, necessitating a welcome romantic and carefree exchange to lighten his mood.

'Don't show me yet,' Jeff warned, drinking in the meditative air which had gathered above their seats.

His neighbour gave him her endearingly familiar questioning look. 'Not much to show! I've set myself a challenge now. My brain won't think.'

'Doesn't matter. Leave it then,' the empathetic intellectual shrugged, sensing a more serious, even melancholy mood engulf her. 'Is something wrong?'

The nineteen-year-old sighed. 'No. Not really. Just a stupid, nagging idea that's playing on my mind.'

With a half-smile, her boyfriend leaned over, prised the pen from her fingers and lifted her right hand to his lips, kissing the soft skin of her wrist. 'Oh, yeah? That's my trick. *Digame.*'

'I suppose you're already in the Mile High Club?' the veteran jetsetter asked, heavy-hearted and slightly embarrassed.

Taken by surprise, the rocker with the party reputation paused before indicating in the affirmative. He felt full of remorse, even though he had nothing to be ashamed of. He understood that his past unshared did not sit well with Lynn, but there was little either lover could do about it.

'Yes. You suppose correctly.'

The young woman stared straight ahead. 'I thought so.'

Jeff figured he had two ways to go with this: he could make light of the topic or he could make excuses, neither of which seemed appropriate at the start of their union's brand new episode. He saw no value whatsoever in admitting that scarcely a flight had gone by without coercing a stewardess or a nearby passenger into the confines of the lavatory for a thirty-thousand-foot copulation or two.

The notorious sex-god began with the first option, concluding that it would only serve to buy him time to come up with something better. 'I'm sorry. Do you want to join too? I'd be delighted to perform your induction.'

Lynn smiled, which required more effort than she expected. 'Thanks. I don't know. Not today, I think.'

'Sure. Maybe another time. Just say the word,' her boyfriend replied, feeling like a rat. 'You know, it was really, really bad, to be honest. Tacky, extremely clumsy, a bit painful and not worth it, except to be able to say I'd done it. Just a tick in the box, if you know what I mean.'

The compassionate man looked away, letting the subdued beauty beside him digest his comments and gripping her hand less tightly. He didn't feel any better having voiced them, so had no reason to believe she would either, having heard them.

After a minute or so of silence, he dutifully checked in again. 'Are you OK?'

'Yes. Thanks,' the dignified teenager responded. 'Sorry. I know I can't expect to share every new experience with you. It just takes me a while to come to terms with things, that's all.'

'Why did you mention it?' Jeff asked. 'If you'd already guessed the answer?'

'Because I'd rather know for sure. Why *didn't* you mention it?'

The patient man's expression changed to one of dismay before he had the chance to check his reaction, annoyed that his partner had turned the problem around to be his fault when he was trying so hard to repair the damage.

'No reason,' he responded curtly. 'It never even entered my head. I'd forgotten all about it. Certainly not to hide it from you. It just wasn't that memorable, and that's the truth. And I'm not saying that just to make you feel better, although I do want you to feel better.'

'Would you have suggested it, if I hadn't brought it up?' Lynn persisted, feeling confused.

Jeff sensed her insecurity and recognised it well. His refined girlfriend needed to be asked, and clearly it was his job to do the asking. That was fine. He could handle this mission...

'Ah, yeah! Damned sure I would've done at some point. I'm just not *that* much of an exhibitionist,' he smiled kindly, gesturing around the aircraft at the fact that they were surrounded by fellow travellers. 'But all it'd take is one look at your exquisite body sitting so close during a quiet, unlit moment to start my sexual time-bomb ticking. Just you wait, lady...'

The thankful young woman dearly wanted to believe what her worldly companion was telling her, leaning over to kiss him. How the tables had turned in their two years apart! Jeff Diamond's previously sparse catalogue of life experiences had leapfrogged that of Lynn Dyson in the time it had taken for her to complete her Californian degree.

'Shhh! Thanks. I'll get over it in a minute. Will you nominate me, please?'

'Absolutely,' the handsome playboy replied with a lecherous grin, relieved that the issue appeared to be resolving itself. 'It'll be my pleasure. I'll spring it on you one day, so you can't say no.'

'Hmm…' his girlfriend murmured, picking up her homework again. 'I don't know about that either.'

Focussing back on the growing list of ideas for a normal life, Jeff gave the girl next-door a suitably suggestive wink and reverted to the theme of routine *versus* spontaneity. *More work required*, he smiled to himself. A hook for another song was drifting in and out of his head, and he shut his eyes tightly to prevent it from escaping.

"Simplicity". The simple life was what he was seeking, despite the wealth of opportunities ahead of them. As an antidote to the hype which would continue to follow them wherever they went, he guessed. It was a conundrum to the millionnaire that, as he had become more affluent and influential, his desire to live the high life was diminishing. After the initial surge of excitement to buy the car of his dreams and to participate in the whole gamut of rich men's pursuits, the fulfilment he sought was not to be found in material possessions and expensive indulgences.

So what exactly did he want from a normal life? What was simplicity? To be who they wanted to be. That was a type of freedom too. And how about simplicity as opposed to opulence or luxury?

The boy from Canley Vale cast his mind back to his gorgeous schoolgirl's apartment at Dyson Administration, where she had spent the majority of nights since she had started senior school. It was no bigger than his lowly, rented flat in Richmond, although better appointed and infinitely less dilapidated. Before that, the pre-teen had been a weekly boarder at the junior school for Melbourne Academy and had regaled many a story about living in a dormitory environment. It had lacked privacy and was fairly basic, but plenty of communal fun was had nonetheless.

No, Jeff affirmed. Neither he nor his ravishing concubine needed opulence. A comfortable space with a few labour-saving amenities was all they required. Moreover, luxury and simplicity could definitely coexist, because luxury could be synonymous with enjoyment without necessarily being expensive. The multi-millionnaire pondered what his dream girl's idea of luxury living might be. True, she had spent her weekends and holidays in the enormous expanses of Benloch, both the house and the farm, and was familiar with the world's most highly-starred hotels. London may turn out to be claustrophobic for her if they didn't spend a fair amount of time in the open air, and it would hardly be extravagant to while away an afternoon on Hampstead Heath every now and again, British weather permitting.

Momentarily distracted from his task by another new message commanding to be expressed, the poet pulled out a fourth piece of paper and began to scribe yet more new verses. Jesus! Why was his brain producing folk songs lately?

This mental renaissance he was undergoing was unleashing some real surprises.

Jeff's next theme was "Diversity". By now, it was close to one o'clock in the morning in the part of the world they had recently left. He considered taking a cigarette break or settling down to watch the movie, but this exercise he had been set was firing up his imagination nicely. London, for him, was the perfect place in which to surround themselves with every conceivable type of acquaintance: old and young, cosmopolitan and stereotypical; various nationalities; homo- and heterosexuals; religious zealots and refuseniks of all persuasions; political animals and party animals.

The twenty-two-year-old, still ever hungry for knowledge, yearned for long, stimulating and challenging conversations with people whose points of view were poles apart. Not wanting to be outdone by his sleeping partner on key performance indicators, the ambitious world-changer had set himself the lofty goal of bringing opposing parties together in at least two world conflicts over the next five years. He had a number of case studies in mind for his doctoral thesis and was impatient to enlist his intellectual role-model and new overseeing professor, John Francis. To achieve this objective, it would be necessary to develop a circle of open-minded, tolerant humanitarians, pragmatists not dogmatists, who could help him formulate an action plan for making the world a better place.

Pausing, the young man pressed his head back into the leather seat and took a few deep breaths to stave off advancing sleep. Maybe his last train of thought wasn't quite what Lynn had in mind when she had asked him to describe a normal life. Smiling, Jeff put brackets around these most recent notes. They represented the very abnormal life he was hoping to cultivate alongside his beautiful best friend in their new home as the months went by. He would love her to come along for what promised to be an exhilarating ride, but this was altogether her choice. Her priorities had been directed elsewhere before, he realised, but hopefully less so these days.

Hey! This was something worth writing down: a solid foundation on which to build individual ambitions. Yeah, that was good. With a pang of longing, the lost boy knew he would still need his dream girl to come home to, or at least on the other end of the telephone after a hard day on the road. This was the dependence he doubted he could relinquish, and didn't much want to anyway. The knowledge that Lynn was ever there waiting for his return, both physically and spiritually, was fundamental to who he wanted to be. He had told her a long time ago that she was his lighthouse; a role which would never change for as long as he lived.

This brief brush with insecurity led the old soul to yet another theme. What about health? They had to do whatever they could to stay healthy, both corporally and cranially, if they were to accomplish their long list of achievements. He looked across at the Olympic athlete beside him, who had fallen asleep with her reading lamp illuminating her youthful face. Her tanned skin was clear and radiant, her hair shone, and she was as strong and fit as she had ever been.

Jeff turned off the light above his partner-in-crime and set about observing every fine, feminine detail in the dimmed cabin. Christ, she was so beautiful. The British winter weather would be cold and wet for their first couple of months, with more than a fifty-fifty chance of regular snow. He added fitness *régime* to his list, unable to recall noticing any facilities for keeping fit and healthy when he had visited London before. Then again, his lifestyle at the time had hardly called for it! Plus, he felt sure this pre-requisite would already have been well researched by the Dysons, so it was time to move on from physical health.

Furthermore, bodily fitness wasn't what he meant by healthy. His tired mind referred to something quite different. After writing down "Drugs and alcohol", Jeff closed his eyes and inhaled deeply to stem a wave of nausea as he remembered the periods of debauchery he had enjoyed the last few times he had been to London. There was no way he would allow himself back into that sordid way of life, no matter what temptation came their way. Europe was a paradise for the experimental, but he had played those games before. Such excesses were well and truly out of his system, and he did not plan on exposing his squeaky-clean, unsullied girlfriend to the seedy underworld which lurked down many a dark London alley.

Therefore, their normal life would include far fewer cigarettes, less alcohol and only the occasional spliff. This time around, he wanted his *sojourn* in the northern hemisphere to consist of taking pleasure from illicit substances to enhance a good time, rather than relying on them to manufacture one. A respecting relationship with his old vices, rather than using them. That old theory still held, the rock star figured with a sly nod.

"Entertainment" was the next entry on the songwriter's list. Four words found their way onto the page: "Movies – get over it." He and Lynn had rarely spoken about this, but he knew she liked the occasional visit to the cinema because it was a leisure activity that she could enjoy anonymously and uninterrupted. Not that she had put pressure on him to go, knowing the unpleasant memories the prospect conjured up, and indeed they had had precious few free evenings lately.

Nevertheless, watching the latest box office hit on the big screen was very much a part of most people's normal life, and they would be living on the doorstep of the West End, within walking distance of one of the richest arrays of theatres, cinemas and art galleries in the world. They simply had to make time to immerse themselves in *cosas artísticas*, he decided, before adding *y sportivas* for good measure.

"Learning". Their formal studies of course, but also wider. Technological advancement was key to the farsighted man's ambitions for better universal communication, and Paragon Holdings was already incubating some exciting breakthrough products. As its reluctant Chief Executive, he needed to find some way of keeping on top of the latest developments while he was in the UK, but how should he do this? More a topic for discussion with Gerry and the luminaries at MIT, the passenger concluded this heading was too complex to mull over so high above sea level and with his eyelids beginning to weigh very heavy.

Rubbing his forehead and straightening his spine, Jeff added "Travel" to the list, simply followed by the word "heaps". He was dangerously drowsy and scanned the First Class cabin, which was almost full. The last time he had been on a long-haul flight, albeit in an uncomfortable Economy seat, the famous musician had struggled valiantly to stay awake for fear of spooking everyone with his nightmares. He wasn't confident enough yet in his newfound sleeping skills to allow himself to doze off without his trusty slumber monitor being aware.

The young man caught sight of another male passenger on the other side of the cabin, chatting up one of the tight-skirted flight attendants. He wondered how long it would be before the pair found themselves in the cramped confines of the toilet together, as he had tried a year or so ago. At least the First Class facilities were likely to afford horny passengers a little more comfort! He cringed at the unpleasant conversation earlier about the Mile High Club. Yes, those impromptu encounters for physical gratification had given him a much-needed thrill at the time, but he had absolutely no desire to revisit them anymore.

Best of luck, buddy, the sober and satisfied new man sniffed in derision, while the sleaze-bag across the aisle groped the buxom, heavily made-up woman eagerly and with no inhibitions, presumably after more than his fair share of free alcohol. He wondered what the Qantas employees' expectations were from customers who could afford a seat in the Jumbo's nose... Was a quickie with a First Class passenger a better experience than the Economy equivalent? Was it like calling oneself an escort as opposed to a prostitute? It all came down to the same act in the end.

Rising to his feet slowly while trying not to disturb his peaceful girlfriend, Jeff stretched his six-foot-four-inch frame and made his way up the aisle to the galley and some superficial but attractive female company to pass the time. The remaining high-flying waiter and waitresses were chattering merrily when the superstar appeared in the doorway to the cramped, sterile kitchen, cutting their conversation short at coming face-to-face with their famous passenger.

'Hi,' his deep voice opened, watching all three swoon. 'Please could I have a beer?'

'Certainly, sir,' replied the tall brunette whose name badge read "Jacqui".

She flicked open a can and poured some amber liquid into a glass, excited to be in such close proximity to her favourite pop icon. Her hands shook as she held the drink up to his waiting hands, and he took hold of both can and glass quickly.

'It's Jeff, not sir, by the way. Thanks, Jacqui.'

In the galley, there was another ginger-haired female of ample proportions and a slim, young man, who switched into flirtation mode as soon as they realised who was in their presence. The handsome rock star leaned casually against the wall and let them carry on, continually amused at the effect he had on people.

'Are you going on to London?' asked the well-coiffured man labelled "Philip". 'Work or play?'

'Bit of both, I expect,' the musician answered. 'We're going for a year, to study mainly. One-way ticket.'

'Study?' Jacqui shrieked. 'Why do you need to study? And Lynn Dyson? You guys are megastars. Are you really boyfriend and girlfriend?'

Jeff chuckled. 'Yes, we are. And we don't *need* to study. We want to. It'll be awesome. Good to feed the brain now and again.'

'So aren't you going to make any more records?' whined a glum Melanie, the redhead who had outgrown her uniform.

Their delectable diversion refilled his glass with the rest of the beer from the small tin, and three hands instantly shot forward to relieve him of the empty vessel and toss it into the rubbish bin. All three tittered, as if they were party to some incredible secret.

'Sure we are. Nothing'll change,' the traveller confirmed, raising his drink to Melanie in thanks. 'Just where we're living. Get away from the parents... You know how it is.'

The flight attendants burst into raucous laughter. To think that even pop stars had rows with their parents was just too funny!

'Shhh!' Jeff urged, glancing out into the cabin to see if anyone had noticed the disturbance. 'What time do we land?'

Jacqui, who appeared to be in charge, consulted her flight plan. 'Singapore, oh-six-hundred hours,' she recited. 'That's six in the morning. You two make a great couple. I saw you do that stage show in Japan. "Everlasting" blew me and my friend away! I love that song. It was fantastic! You're both so amazing-looking and talented.'

The performer thanked her for educating him and for the compliments. 'You guys are looking after us very well. When do you get off duty?'

Melanie and Philip giggled to each other. 'Are you going to join us? We're going to a nightclub on Bugis Street. You should come too. It'd be fab'.'

'Love to,' Jeff responded, 'but we've got another 'plane to catch. I'd better get back to Sleeping Beauty over there. Nice talking to you. Thanks for the beer.'

'Ooh! Wait a minute! Can we get a photo' before you go?' Melanie squeaked, jumping up and down like a child. 'Please, Jeff?'

Posing with each ditsy employee in turn, the celebrity smiled for the camera. As soon as he could, fearing the commotion would wake everyone up, he requested two glasses of chilled water and returned to his row. Slotting his tall frame back into the seat caused Lynn to stir, not entirely accidentally on his part.

The young woman smiled, groaning softly. 'Hi. What time is it?'

Jeff's watch read two-thirty. 'Three and a half hours to go. You OK?'

'I'm fine, thanks. I need to get up though,' his neighbour stretched and pointed to the glass of water on his tray-table. 'Is this mine?'

'Yep,' he answered, passing it to her.

'Ahh... Perfect,' the grateful passenger said, drinking it down. 'Have you slept at all?'

Her boyfriend shook his head. 'No. Not yet. I was waiting for you. I didn't want to fall asleep without you knowing. Just in case. You know...'

Lynn climbed over his long legs, pausing for a kiss when his large hands ensnared her waist. 'OK. I'm sure you'll be fine. Slide into the window seat, and I'll sit here while you sleep.'

Good idea, the tired man agreed. He made himself comfortable with the pillow and blanket, leaning against the aeroplane's cool inner wall. By the time his saviour returned, he was out cold, and her heart glowed. Already this flight was so much more manageable than having to babysit her oversized, highly-strung toddler.

It was time to do her homework, the young songstress decided, happily declining another glass of champagne from Philip. She resisted the temptation to read through Jeff's notes, which had been stuffed untidily into the seat pocket in front of her. A normal life, she mused. For as long as she had known her hyperactive boyfriend, they had been riding an erratic rollercoaster, mostly at a rapid pace and frequently out of control. With butterflies in her stomach, Lynn thought back to their first night at the theatre, where her friends had been sitting next to an empty seat not fifty metres away. Where would she be now, had she turned him down and seen "A Streetcar Named Desire" with the school group as planned?

On that day in February nineteen-seventy-two, something had compelled the sixteen-year-old Melbourne Academy student to find out more about this exotic-looking stranger who had appeared out of nowhere to ask her for a date. Their very first conversation had foreshadowed a connection the like of which she had not encountered before or since. It was as if this man had placed her under a powerful, intoxicating spell. As their relationship had developed, in equal parts enthralling and frightening, she had found it completely impossible to break free from this fascinating, supernatural incantation.

Lynn had not been brought up with any Christian observances or allegiances but was reasonably well educated about religion nonetheless. Since the rock star sleeping next to her had begun to notch up hit records and acclaimed concert performances, several commentators had mocked and questioned him about the religious themes he often used, not to mention the fact that Gerry's father had even dubbed him the second Messiah.

The impressionable youngster knew her humble intellectual's personal view was that there was no supreme power as such. However, he had also told her that he was happy to be proven wrong, in which case he presumed God was more likely to live inside one's imagination, taking whatever form made sense to that person, rather than the representation of a single, omnipotent being. Her own view was similar, but her idea of religion was less like the worship of a deity and more centred around earthly, moral values and goals which motivated people towards positive and constructive ends.

However, the mysterious notion which Australia's darling thought to be favoured by her mystery man was that somehow he had been selected to do good for the human race, and with his meteoric rise to stardom over the last two years, she now felt inclined to believe it too. People flocked to Jeff Diamond everywhere he went. She had seen it on the television, and more recently first-hand. Females of course, since he was so good to look at, with charisma and an engaging personality as well. But males too, which was more unusual. Jeff had an enormous number of friends, these days in all corners of the globe, and most people he met were keen to stay in touch.

Take Gerry Blake, for example, the young woman continued to ruminate, still not having put pen to paper. Why on Earth had a high-achieving, private schoolboy with the world at his feet and plenty of connections from the same social demographic become inseparable from the self-described worthless manchild of impoverished parents in Sydney's western suburbs? Had the academically-gifted and sporty grammar school student subconsciously recognised something in the thirteen-year-old ragamuffin which had caused him to follow the younger boy's lead on practically everything? At Christmas, Gerry had confessed to adopting his friend's sexual mercenary lifestyle unwittingly. Having now met the Blake parents, Lynn had the definite impression that they were not the type to raise a son who would dive into bed with any woman crossing his path! Therefore, he must have been convinced to behave that way by some other force.

Lynn stared past the dormant Adonis, out of the window at the darkness. So had she seen the same something in Jeff that Gerry had seen? Was it an aura of greatness or the work of an extraordinarily skilful confidence trickster? Her own father had been suspicious, especially when he had investigated the pretender's family background. True, the driven tearaway had been manipulative and persistent while pursuing her, but since she had agreed to be his life partner, he had backed right off. So far, he had given her no reason to distrust him.

Where was she going with all this deliberation? Ah, yes, the nineteen-year-old remembered. She had been asking herself what normality would have looked like if she hadn't renewed her membership to the peculiar but compelling club of Jeff Diamond upon her return from California. In fact, she knew exactly what it would be like, because she had lived for two years without him, unable to forget how powerful an influence he had been on her. Although she had thrown herself one-hundred percent into her UCLA studies and into the movies she had made, the medals she had won and the hits she had recorded, there had remained a huge void in both her heart and her mind where this beautiful black stallion used to hang out. Other men of standing had moved in and out of her life during this period, yet none had inspired her or enthralled her the way Jeff had done, and now did again.

Yes, there was no doubt that the teenaged sporting celebrity was under the Pied Piper's spell, but she absolutely loved it to bits. Jeff made her insides jump every time she picked up the telephone or saw him for the first time after an absence, no matter how short. He was the love of her life, of that she was certain. She was willing to absorb the flak which Gerry launched her way for pandering too much to the dark-haired control freak's neediness. *You can talk, Mister Indomitable*, she smiled inside. Her willingness was so all-consuming because this imaginative young woman so wanted her man to be happy and to achieve the ambitions he held so dear. She was utterly convinced that, rid of the effects of his childhood trauma, Jeff Diamond would turn out to be the perfect man. And he had been. For the whole nine days since Boxing Day anyway!

What would a normal life do for the troubled soul sleeping next to her? It would bring him a clarity of mind he hadn't previously known, at last allowing him to concentrate without the interference of past calamities and present anxieties. Lynn had studied the paper he had published with Sarah Friedman in great detail, focussing on their analysis of Maslow's Hierarchy of Needs and how it related to mental illness and dependency. The privileged youngster found it inexplicable how the tortured teenager could have had such a strong grasp on the more sophisticated of self-actualisation needs when some of the most basic ones had gone unmet at the more fundamental levels during his formative years.

When his curious girlfriend had questioned him on the topic, the intellectual had maintained that for each need that was overlooked, he had introduced a compensating addiction into his life; some subconsciously, some not. For example, the absence of the basic physiological requirement for sleep had been compensated for by his addiction to sex, being another bodily need the supply of which he could better control. She had no difficulty in believing this particular scenario!

Next, to substitute for the unsatisfied safety and belonging needs, namely the love and protection of a family, and the lack of a basic moral framework in his childhood, Jeff had become completely obsessed with the idea of the love, protection and stability that Lynn herself could bring him. How this concept had coalesced in his youthful mind was still a complete mystery to the singer. And then, knowing he couldn't realise his own ambitions via the highest level of needs without sufficient credibility or esteem, the nobody from Canley Vale had set about engineering various using and respecting relationships which would build his self-confidence, fuel the mutual respect of like-minded people and ensure he achieved everything he wanted to achieve.

Jeff Diamond had fashioned his own, phenomenal life from virtually nothing. His approach was almost Hitleresque in those early years, Lynn remembered him admitting warily to her one night when they had sat up talking for hours. This sinister comparison had scared her, and more so when she found out that the prolific author was also writing a novel about social engineering loosely based on Joseph Mengele. He had even likened her own father to Mengele, which had fascinated both lovers even more as the two most important men in her life went head-to-head over her.

The romantic but realistic young student concluded that her man of intrigue couldn't possibly be a God, nor even a second son of God. There was nothing remotely divine about Jeff's passage through life. Yet despite this, each step on his perilous journey had been taken quite deliberately, designed to teach him how to meet his own needs on the highest tier of the hierarchy. Indeed, the more she thought about it, the more she found it hard to name anyone with higher moral standards... once adjusted for Jeff's self-fashioned slant on morality, admittedly... and who was more creative, spontaneous and broad-minded. His superior intellect and ability to accept facts and apply them in myriad ways had turned him into a hugely successful businessman and a philanthropist without prejudice.

Unlike his childhood role-models, the man they called The Australian Elvis was entirely motivated by good, while also having grown up with an acute awareness of evil. How powerful could that be? He possessed all the alluring qualities and uncanny acumen of a born leader who was intent on making the world a better place for some of life's most neglected minorities.

This was why Lynn Dyson was happy to help her man realise his dreams, even if it meant slipping into the background while she watched people fawn all over him. It felt almost perverse that Jeff's ability to satisfy her desires had turned out to be the ultimate ticket to his success, since her position in society gave him a springboard to mass exposure, leaving her wondering why she didn't feel as affronted as Gerry by being used in this way.

Was her simple answer to this question too naïve for words? Was she being suckered in on a rampant and romantic scam, in danger of coming to a devastating end as soon as her boyfriend had got what he wanted from her? No, Lynn smiled, remembering their twin tattoos and the deep-seated emotional reaction they had elicited. Their love would stand the test of time, and ostensibly through the ages too...

Her sexual poet had described his role as her passionate, parasitic front-man, yet there was nothing parasitic about their future relationship as far as his dream girl was concerned. There was as much for her to gain from being with him, both behind closed doors and in the public eye.

Hence, suckered in or not, this young lady's idea of their normal but singular life should be one of balance. Jeff had grown up as a man of extremes, a manic depressive who had spent years lurching back and forth between crisis and euphoria. Her role was to shave the tops and bottoms off these extremes, but not so far as to stifle his creativity or dampen his enthusiasm. Neither star could contemplate becoming lost in mediocrity. No self-satisfied fat cats allowed! She had learned enough about her enigmatic stranger to know that he valued the destructive lessons almost as highly as the constructive ones, because they were all instructive. They all contributed to building this incredible strength of self-actualisation he coveted and which he was intent on passing on to others too.

Lynn continued to write about balance. Stability with excitement, the basic functions of life with outrageous experiences, absence with togetherness and intellectual pursuits with simple pleasures. Her list grew steadily: study; anonymous travel, weekends away; living frugally, with one day a month where they spent no money; liberal doses of steamy, desirous sex; long dinners at home... "Learn to cook!" she scribbled next to this last item. "Trips to the library, attend concerts (all types), festivals (Knebworth, Glastonbury, Fringe, not Glyndebourne); teach Jeff how to go to the movies."

Through her concentration, the young woman sensed the engines ease off, and the nose of the aeroplane immediately dipped forwards. They would soon be arriving in Singapore. A series of loud clicks spluttered through the intercom' system, followed by a disembodied voice informing them that they were about to commence their descent into Changi Airport. This remote *reveillée* was duly softened in person for those in First Class by the cabin crew, who were preparing to serve breakfast before landing.

Against the window, the contented scribe's handsome travelling companion took a deep breath then slowly exhaled, coming to after two hours of undisturbed sleep. Her heart skipped a beat on spying a cheeky grin that told her how pleased he was to see her. He reached over, brushing an avaricious hand across her back, and pulled her close into his waking body. The pair lay together for a few minutes in silence, until they became aware of the perky, flame-haired flight attendant appearing in the aisle.

'Good morning, Jeff, Miss Dyson. We're going to be landing in an hour.'

'Right,' a deep, croaky voice replied, still half asleep. 'Thanks, Mel.'

'Mel, Jeff and Miss Dyson?' Lynn repeated coquettishly once the young woman had delivered their trays. 'Hmm... Something's wrong with this picture. You're very familiar with each other.'

Her incorrigible boyfriend smiled at his clandestine fraternisation. 'Yeah, well... I got bored. They gave me a beer and wanted to take some photos. It passed the time.'

Dark eyes assured the green-tinged nymph beside him that there was no point in raising even a half-hearted objection, hoping his girlfriend's jealousy would be fleeting. A smile and a resigned shake of the head confirmed this to be true. As they consumed their watery portions of bacon and scrambled egg, she confessed to needing to get used to the adoration that would continue to be lavished on him. The world loved the man whose life she now shared, and he derived energy from the attention.

'It's no different the other way round,' Jeff commented, blowing her a kiss through steam rising from his coffee cup. 'I feel the same whenever blokes melt at your feet too. We're even, I hope.'

***

'How did you go with your homework?' Jeff asked, after they had stretched their legs and swapped back into their original places in preparation for landing. 'Did you cheat?'

He winked in response to the look of disdain on his girlfriend's face, fishing into the seat pocket and retrieving his assignment, which had become somewhat crumpled over the last few hours. As if to prove him wrong, Lynn brandished a single sheet of paper covered with neatly-aligned paragraphs.

'No. Stop with your cheek, Einstein! Mine's here. I thought a lot but didn't write much.'

'Sometimes less is more,' the kind man responded, inviting her to look outside as the aircraft banked to counter her hesitation. 'I have to remember that myself. The city looks just like any other in the dark, doesn't it? At least we'll see more when we take off again.'

Sipping on orange juice, the songwriter strained to see out of the window as the pre-dawn lights of the busy South-Asian trading hub came into view. His quiet and very sexy neighbour nodded and kissed his stubbly cheek, nourishing the morning erection that throbbed undetected in his lap. Flying with his beautiful best friend was an order of magnitude more enjoyable than enduring the endless monotony in the company of strangers.

'How long are we on the ground for? Not long, I hope,' the teenager mused.

'*No recuerdo*,' Jeff responded, shifting position to ease his predicament. 'Couple of hours maybe. I'd rather get going straightaway. I just want to get there now.'

Lynn kissed him again. 'Same here. Still… Nearly halfway.'

Soon, their long, buffeting descent was finally over, and the big bird bounced twice on the runway before the engines screamed into reverse and the aeroplane slowed to taxi speed. The other passengers were ushered out of First Class, while the celebrity *duo* was invited to meet the pilot and co-pilot. They posed for one last photograph with the animated bunch of Qantas employees before succumbing to the familiar assault of perfumed humidity which seeped into the Singapore terminal building in spite of the air-conditioning.

Even though the airport was virtually deserted at this hour of the morning, the tall rock star's senses fought against the opposing forces of human traffic and the mechanical droning of enormous condensers overhead. He was reminded of the last time he had strode through these same corridors, his ears still blocked from the recent change in air pressure and gripped by uncertainty after his dream girl's cry for help. How their life had changed since that day! And because of that day, he admitted with a certain pride.

'Did you want to buy anything?' the seasoned traveller asked, looking up at his smiling face while they passed the long line of arrival and departure gates towards the shopping plaza.

Jeff shook his head. 'Nope. Maybe a bed? Or failing that, a quiet coffee somewhere. We're going to get another breakfast soon anyway. Weird, huh? You'd think, with the number of people flying two legs between Australia and the UK, they'd figure out a better feeding system.'

Lynn laughed and pushed the sex-mad companion sideways, flinching as his arm circled around her shoulders. 'Stop thinking! You're in transit. You don't have to think.'

'Ouch! Sorry,' he chuckled, remembering her tattoo. 'You haven't mentioned it. How was it to sleep on?'

The slender athlete took her favourite man's hand and continued walking, blonde hair a stand-out in their present location. Heads turned continually, but the famous performers had long since perfected the art of pretending to be invisible.

'It's not too bad. Just when you scrape the surface,' she smiled.

The layover hours passed relatively quickly, and before too long the couple found themselves seated at their new departure gate. Boredom was beginning to give way to excitement for the final leg of their journey, especially when more and more British accents gathered to chatter around them. The pair's anonymity was well and truly blown by some Australian holiday makers who had spent several hours in the bar, and they were forced to dodge some fairly intrusive questions. The aircraft was fortunately soon ready for boarding, meaning that the First Class passengers were free to occupy their seats whenever they wished.

Not normally one to take advantage of such privileges, Jeff took the decision to board straightaway in order to save his precious angel from any further annoyance. The group of boisterous travellers had invaded their privacy a little too much for her liking, and he had sensed her patience was wearing thin.

'*¡Dios sea loado!*' the musician exclaimed in frustration, slumping down into seat 2A. 'What arseholes! Are you OK?'

Lynn had seated herself cross-legged in seat 2B, assuming the lotus position with her eyes closed. She began to chant, but burst out laughing instead.

'What was it you said then? God what?'

'Praise the Lord,' Jeff translated, amused at her unusually gregarious reaction. 'You OK? It's not like you to want to let off steam. You're turning me on, lady. Just so you're aware.'

'What's arsehole in Spanish?' the young woman asked, shrugging off his advances with a grin. 'I think I'm going to use it frequently.'

The linguist chuckled. 'I'm not teaching you such vulgarities. Try *hueco de culo*. Or maybe *cretino*. It's less profane but equally offensive.'

'*Bueno*. Nine o'clock,' Lynn announced, adjusting her watch. 'What time is it in London now? Seven hours behind?'

'Yeah. Think so. There's a long way to go until you need to know.'

The pretty teenager laughed again at her boyfriend's nonchalance. 'That's funny!'

Jeff gave her a quizzical stare. 'Why is that so funny? You've breathed in some dodgy fumes or something. You're behaving very strangely all of a sudden.'

Before the normally sedate Olympian had a chance to compose a suitable reply, the senior steward arrived to introduce himself to his new batch of First Class passengers. Lynn Dyson and Jeff Diamond shook his hand, once more launched into their official capacities, and politely exchanged pleasantries over a glass of champagne.

'This is the last thing you need right now,' her man teased. 'What's got into you, angel?'

'Nothing,' Lynn answered, enjoying the cool bubbles in her mouth. 'I'm just happy to be on the 'plane and heading to London with you. You handled those *huecos de culo* masterfully. I don't know how you didn't hit that tall, skinny, rat-like one.'

'Thanks,' Jeff smiled. 'It did get a little out of hand towards the end. I was glad to hear the boarding announcement, that's for sure.'

Only two other patrons occupied the First Class cabin for this flight, and they had been strategically seated on the other side of the broad fuselage, affording ample privacy to everyone. There was a definite advantage to this *élite* mode of transport, the thrifty, left-winged radical reluctantly admitted. With fourteen hours of flying ahead of them, the studious couple surrounded itself with books and magazines. Jeff found a crossword puzzle in the Straits Times and settled down to solve it, watching out of the corner of his eye as Lynn flicked through the photographs of their new apartment for the umpteenth time.

'Anything changed since you last looked at those?' the comic enquired. 'They'd better be the real deal, or you're going to be very disappointed.'

'Ha ha,' his girlfriend scoffed. 'Of course they are. Oh, look! Breakfast, take two.'

Another female flight attendant introduced herself and talked them through their service at great length. Jeff slid a glance sideways as if to say "Get these people out of my face." To his surprise, he received an empathetic smile in return. Two identical meals in such quick succession wasn't high on the young musicians' agenda, but they felt obliged to accept with diplomatic appreciation nevertheless.

Once breakfast was over, the nineteen-year-old reached into her bag to retrieve her homework. 'Shall we compare notes?'

'Hmm. OK,' Jeff agreed, trying to remember where he had stashed his. 'How do you want to do it? Read each others' and come back with rebuttals?'

'Yes. That'd be a good start,' the happy teenager giggled. 'Have you still got yours?'

The disorganised millionnaire stood up and rifled through a folder of paperwork under his jacket in the overhead locker. How could the front-end of their fabled pantomime horse possibly be expected to be systematic as well as mesmerising and charismatic? Filing ought to be the job of the back-end henceforth, he concluded, knowing such a sexist opinion was probably not best verbalised in his current position.

'Somewhere... Hey, look! You can have my HSC certificates instead, if you like. Here it is...'

Lynn took the four sheets of paper that were being fanned out before her eyes, momentarily distracted by the scruffy blue dossier that was slotted into the seat pocket. Not that she doubted for a minute that her boyfriend had earned the many qualifications he claimed, but her curiosity leaped at the chance of seeing the proof and setting her suspicious mind to rest.

'Four pages!' she exclaimed. 'You worked hard. Gold star!'

Jeff took a bow, then slumped down like a dead weight. 'Yeah, but remember, less can be more. It'll put you to sleep.'

The beautiful blonde kissed him. 'No, it won't. You're gorgeous. You're so relaxed. It's great.'

'Why, thank you,' he replied. 'I do feel good, I have to admit. Come on... ¡Leerlo!'

His fellow passenger picked up the first page; the one that had been divided into four quadrants. The same word had been written in each box: "Freedom." She turned towards him, pouting.

'So explain this one, please. It looks like you never want to see me again.'

The young man strained to see over his playful girlfriend's shoulder and laughed aloud. 'Oh, yeah! Ignore that page,' he advised. 'I was going to be a smart-arse and do it from four perspectives, but it didn't work. That could be Part Two of this exercise.'

He helped himself to the sheet of red herrings which obscured his best efforts, screwed it up into a ball and bounced it off the back of the empty seat in front.

'What's smart-arse in Spanish?' Lynn asked, smiling at his antics.

'*Genio*,' the quick wit answered, straight-faced.

'Liar! That sounds like genius.'

Jeff feigned disbelief that she should doubt his word. 'Just read, woman! Jesus!'

He sighed heavily, feeling a wave of emotion course through his veins. Freedom was right on the money, he thought. If this teasing, kittenish side to his dream girl was the result of their break for a new frontier, he was about to redefine his own happiness all over again. Doing his best to suppress a fresh urge to rip her clothes off, the intellectual clicked the end of his ballpoint pen and frowned, making her giggle again.

With the backdrop of darkening skies as they were propelled anticlockwise around the planet, the pair made themselves comfortable, and each set about digesting the plans the other had written for their impending normal life. With Lynn's missive being so short, her examiner soon began to make notes and doodle all over it. Every time she attempted to see what he was doing, he made an extravagant effort to hide it from her.

'I feel ashamed,' the songstress lamented, reaching the end of the learned gentleman to her left's submission. 'It was my idea, and you've given me heaps more than I gave you.'

'This is great though,' Jeff dismissed her concern. 'Who cares? Don't worry about it. I'm glad you gave me the challenge.'

'So you think I need more surprises?' Lynn asked, flipping back to the section on spontaneity.

'Yes, I do. Shut up and think about it for a while, then we'll talk afterwards. I want to wallow in this dream for a bit, knowing how soon we can make it come true.'

His obedient girlfriend relaxed back into her chair, swooning at another Pied Piper phrase. They sat in silence for a few minutes. The songwriter noticed she was chewing on her lower lip, as if fighting with her emotions and longing to express herself. She looked very cute, and it aroused him again. He felt his penis swelling under the tray-table, fantasising that Lynn's fingers were about to unzip his fly and lean over until her mouth made contact.

Snapping himself back to reality, the twenty-two-year-old fixed his eyes back on to the sheet of paper covering his lap and diverted his attention to Lynn's words instead. This long journey was proving to be a veritable endurance of *libido*-suppression which was rapidly exiting the enjoyable stage.

Surely an opportunity would present itself, with their latest artificial night-time soon to be induced as part of the cabin staff's regular routine.

'Hey! Isn't this interesting?' he exclaimed, nudging his girlfriend's arm, very happy with what he was reading.

'There's nothing here that I don't want, and yet the only real duplicate is going to the movies. How weird is that? It's fascinating how differently we express the same ideas. I love it!'

Lynn nodded. 'They're actually two very complementary lists, I agree. Exactly as you put it originally. What did you say? Philosophical arguments or a checklist of practical something? We need to stick to what we're good at because the combination is powerful. Don't you think?'

'Absolutely, angel. So you're going to learn to cook, and I'm going to learn to go to the movies,' her partner summarised, leaning over to kiss her tempting mouth. 'And you mentioned sex when I didn't, so what does that tell you?'

'That you omitted it intentionally?' the intelligent woman suggested after a few seconds' pause.

Jeff smiled wryly. 'Damn! Got it in one, baby. You can see straight through me. But seriously, I love the whole idea of balance. That's exactly right. We need to find that middle ground. And I really like the idea of a day when we don't spend any money too. The "make do" day, because we don't have to.'

The tennis champion snuggled against her handsome intellectual's arm, the warmth of proximity causing her heartbeat to accelerate. 'And I like the long conversations over dinner. I have a lot of learning to do too, and there's only so much we can absorb from reading and attending classes. That's why I need to learn to cook, otherwise we'll be meeting people in restaurants and getting thrown out at closing time, just when you're getting fired up.'

'Maybe,' he responded, 'but there are plenty of restaurants in London that are open all night, trust me.'

'I've had an idea,' his fellow passenger announced, sitting up straight and changing the subject abruptly, 'for creating a school for people like you.'

The long-haired rock star looked at her in amazement. 'What d'you mean? What kind of school?'

'A senior school for positively-charged empaths,' the re-energised woman explained. 'Gifted kids who have that leadership quality and drive to do good things. Those who have what it takes to turn knowledge into wisdom but haven't got the right connections or enough money to bring their dreams to fruition. It'd be the job of this school to create a stream of young adults who want to change the world for the better, just like you do.'

'Isn't that a bit *élitist*?' her boyfriend asked, intrigued and highly flattered by this new concept. 'I don't want us to create another Dyson movement.'

'It *has* to be *élitist!*' Lynn insisted excitedly. 'Listen! Sometimes you're too egalitarian, mate. How many people like you are there? Not many. It wouldn't be a big school.'

The cool philosopher stared straight ahead, plunged into a delightful mental turmoil of conflicting ideals. How could he rationalise his beautiful best friend's tangential proposal? He believed that everyone should be offered the same opportunities, but her assessment was perfectly correct. Some opportunities were wasted on some people. Indeed, he would have leaped at the chance to attend such an institution, with progressive teachers and the ability to mix with like-minded students and potential investors while they developed their individual projects.

'I guess so. What would we call it?' he asked, raising his hands and drawing a banner in the air. 'The Good School? Hey! Did you go to a good school? No, I went to *The* Good School!'

Lynn laughed, stoked that her mastermind had taken the time to consider her not-so-left-field idea. 'The Better World School. Sounds a bit wanky.'

'The Wanky School?'

The former private school student feigned alarm. 'Yes! You've got it. We'd get a lot of interest for that one.'

'Is it really a whole school or just a program to offer to certain students?' her boyfriend offered. 'You could align it with a university, like an MBA program but for kids.'

The young woman beamed, preferring this idea to her own. 'Actually, that does make much more sense. Yeah... Much better. I'd been wondering about the feasibility of keeping a whole set of teachers across all subjects, but a program would be much more focussed and easier to fund.'

'Right, and this type of kid wouldn't need to be asked twice to attend, so you'd have no problem getting them there outside school hours,' Jeff added.

This might work, the information-hungry technocrat figured, thrilled by the energy generated by their high-altitude brainstorming session. They hadn't even landed in London, and his *Regala* was already sharing his vision and even building on it. This year out of Australia would be the making of them, without a doubt.

'Residential'd be good too,' Lynn suggested. 'That way it could be like immersion, like your long conversations over dinner. It's no good when you just get started and then your mum turns up.'

Caught off-guard, the songwriter let out a bitter chuckle. '*If* your mum turns up.'

'Sorry,' the compassionate teenager smiled, knowing she had hit a raw nerve. 'I didn't mean...'

'Stop right there,' Jeff kissed her contrite lips. 'Don't indulge me, angel. It's my fault for being so sensitive. I know you didn't mean anything. It's an open wound, that's all. Like our tatts.'

'How is yours, by the way?' the smiling songstress asked, fondling the sexy dip in the centre of his chest where the older tattoo had already healed nicely.

'Can hardly feel it,' he answered, touching the new one gingerly. 'Well, no... Now you come to mention it, it is pretty sore.'

'Mine too,' Lynn agreed, 'but dull rather than sharp. Easily tolerated.'

The happy man chuckled at her turn of phrase. 'Sounds like you're talking about a person. He's dull rather than sharp, but easily tolerated. That wasn't a Freudian slip by any chance, was it?'

'Absolutely not!' his dream girl yelped in jest. 'I'm talking about the pain. Now you *are* being oversensitive.'

'Well, whatever... I love the idea of The Good School,' her dark-eyed stranger proclaimed, settling back into his wide, comfortable *élitist* seat and closing his commoner's eyes. 'We should sleep on it and see what it's turned into by morning.'

'OK. Thanks. Are you tired?' his girlfriend asked. 'It's like you flicked a switch all of a sudden. High energy one minute, no energy the next.'

Jeff smiled without opening his eyes. 'It's this backwards time travel,' he moaned. 'It fucks with my brain.'

Soul-mates were very observant, the drowsy man's mind registered, and he jumped when loving lips touched his, kissing her hungrily. Was it his imagination, but had their relationship already taken on a richer aspect? The multitude of dimensions he had described for their normal life were taking hold as they sped further westwards, unleashing a liberating form of combined creativity which filled his contented heart with joy.

And as if this wasn't wonderful enough, it seemed to be having a most amorous effect on his travelling companion.

'Did you want to join that club now?' Jeff asked, seizing the opportunity.

'No. Not yet,' Lynn shook her head, sounding tired too.

'Shame,' her man murmured, lifting her hand and tugging it towards his crotch, only to divert at the last minute and bring it to his lips. 'Later then. *Dors bien, mon amie.*'

London Town

Two hours before landing at Heathrow, the flight attendants began to rouse their four First Class passengers. It was still dark outside the little portholes, with only the faintest stripe of sunrise behind them. Craning her neck to take in the magnificent view without tripping over her sleeping partner's legs, Lynn decided against waking him for a while longer. He looked at peace, and it gave her time to take him up on his invitation to leaf through the folder of official documents he had produced earlier.

Sure enough, it contained all his examination certificates; an impressive collection gained gradually from the age of thirteen at Fairfield High School until his Bachelor's degree in Computer Science. Butterflies churning in her stomach on recalling the time when her handsome nobody had cornered her in the corridor of RMIT and asked her out for the very first time, and the young woman let out quiet gasp after quiet gasp at the full extent of her rock star's academic achievements.

She was already privy to the regular battles Jeff had faced at school to obtain permission to take the some of the easier tests in advance of his age group, so that he might concentrate on excelling at other subjects. His graduation from RMIT had also been with High Distinction, which was news to the Melbourne Academy *alumna*. And here was evidence of the Masters he had recently completed, the certificate still in its envelope.

What was this? A birth certificate. Lynn suddenly felt guilty for prying into something so personal but was simply unable to resist. There were the names of his parents, she drew a sharp breath again. Father: Paul Diamond, Mother: Luciana Maria Diamond *née* Moreno, Date: 2nd June 1952, Time: 10:30am, Place of Birth: Parramatta Hospital.

Next in the pile was a rather succinct letter from the New South Wales Department of Social Services, addressed to Pavel Diament at their Stones Road address, dated February nineteen-fifty-seven. It made reference to a prior report into the welfare of his children, informing him that social workers had raised serious concerns about their declining health and sanitary conditions, followed by a comment concerning the ability of his wife to take sufficient care of their family.

Lynn counted the years in her head, hoping she was reconstructing events chronologically. Luciana had died when her son was fourteen, and the spellbound young woman was fairly sure she remembered Jeff's father being imprisoned when the boy was twelve or thirteen. February nineteen-fifty-seven, she re-read the letter. Her boyfriend would have been nearly fifteen by that time. What a poor example of State Government record-keeping... No wonder he had seen fit to keep hold of this item of ill-timed correspondence! She tried to imagine what it would have been like for the troubled adolescent to receive such a letter, and pictured him swearing profusely and tossing the useless piece of paper across the room with all his strength.

There followed a death certificate, immediately sending shivers down the caring singer's spine. Tears welled up in her eyes while she read the details: "Accidental death due to an overdose of amphetamines and alcohol. Lacerations to arms and upper body leading to significant blood loss." Lynn was about to turn the page when she noticed the date of death in the top right-hand corner. The unfortunate woman had met her doom on her son's fourteenth birthday. The reader stifled an involuntary sob, jamming her hand across her mouth, determined that Jeff must not wake up to find her crying.

Quickly and with trembling hands, the ashamed *voyeuse* closed the folder, replaced it in the seat pocket and reached her toiletry bag down from the bulkhead compartment. Putting on a smile for the flight attendants and obliging them with an autograph each, she disappeared inside the lavatory to freshen up and to recover from the shocking information her piece of detective work had unearthed. Poor, poor Jeff. Was there no end to the tragic details which would unfold about her perfect stranger over time?

Some minutes later, another announcement crackled over the loudspeaker, letting passengers know that they were about to be served with their latest meal. The musician opened his eyes to the sight of his gorgeous co-conspirator sitting to his right, reading a novel and looking radiant for her arrival in their new hometown. He checked his watch. Fantastic, he thought. Little more than two hours to go until they landed at Heathrow. He must have slept for a good stretch. Another benefit the touring rebel would do well to acknowledge about flying in the front rows.

'Morning,' his husky, rock star's vocal chords sprang to life. 'Did you sleep?'

Lynn greeted her boyfriend with a broad smile. 'Good morning! Nearly there, finally. Yes, thanks. I slept well until about half an hour ago. How are you feeling?'

'Don't know yet,' Jeff answered with a grin, twisting round in his seat. 'Fucking breakfast again? I'm boycotting breckies for a week once we get there.'

Lynn chuckled. She was looking forward to disembarking and couldn't wait to see their new living quarters. Her roguish bad-boy had sought to dispel his default morning blues by staring out of the window, rather than by goading her into the usual physical gratification. Delighted by another good sign, she jumped when he suddenly reached his right arm backwards and tapped her knee.

She followed his gaze and his pointing finger to look outside and share the view which had impressed him so much. 'Wow! That's amazing!'

The sunrise was spectacular. Thick, lumpy clouds covered the ground thousands of metres below, with a layer of fiery orange icing. Next, seeming to rest on the orange, was spread a light blue layer where the sun was emerging over the horizon. The blue became progressively darker the further west and high in the sky the couple looked, and there were stars still clearly visible at the top, way above the aeroplane.

The young woman knelt down in the footwell next to her partner's legs, resting her left arm across his knees. 'Beautiful, isn't it?'

'Certainly is.'

The pair stayed gazing at the scene in silence for a good few minutes, lost in their own thoughts of London.

'This is a picture of us,' the romantic teenager ventured, eyes shining as they turned to meet their encouraging, brown counterparts. 'All that cloud down there's the confusion and chaos we're going to have when we first arrive and while we're figuring out what's what. Every now and again, we can see clearly down to the ground. See?'

Lynn continued her imaginative description. 'The orange stripe is our excitement at starting our new life singular; meeting people, starting uni', loving each other... Gradually burning off more gaps in the clouds of confusion. Does that make sense?'

The excited woman giggled self-consciously at her tentative attempt at sensuous composition, glancing across at her reticent boyfriend. A tear was making its way down his face, rolling slowly from his right eye. She paused, squeezing his thigh to see if he was alright.

'Don't stop,' Jeff urged without turning his head, his voice cracking. 'I want to hear the end of the story.'

The happy teenager took a deep breath. 'The light blue's your new self and the dark blue is what's left of your old self. And the stars are your flashes of inspiration: the songs; your ideas... You know... The creative stuff that you don't want to let go of. We need to make the light blue stripe bigger without hiding the brilliance of the stars.'

Her black stallion sniffed back more tears, overcome by the powerful allegory his dream girl was painting. 'Christ,' he whispered. 'You're amazing, Lynn. I love you so much. That's exactly what I want to do. It's so unbelievably good that you understand.'

The Olympian stood up, leaning over to kiss the corner of his right eye, surprisingly enlivened by the taste of salt on his skin. 'I love you too,' she replied. 'We're going to have so much fun.'

Long arms reached around Lynn's hips and pulled her down onto his lap in the half-light of the cabin. The flight crew remained ensconced in the galley, preparing to serve another meal. As far as Jeff could see, the other passengers were still asleep. He slotted his hand through the gap between the seats in front and drew an unused blanket deftly towards him. A passionate kiss smothered her mouth while his hands unravelled the folds and threw the layer of tartan weave roughly over themselves, beginning to fondle her breasts and abdomen underneath her clothes. The breathless woman could feel his erection pressing against her buttocks and longed to feel it inside her after the anticipation of being so close for so long.

'You have to let me induct you into the Mile High Club,' the ardent lover hissed in her ear. 'You've turned me on so much with your picture of us. I am so horny that I'm not gonna make it off the 'plane.'

'Won't someone see us?' his furtive partner hissed, fighting her own arousal. 'It sounds exciting but dangerous. What if we get interrupted?'

Jeff's teeth nipped the back of her neck, his breath warm on her skin. 'That's the whole idea. Not just anyone gets admitted into the Mile High Club. *Il faut du courage, mi amor.* They won't interrupt us,' he assured her. 'They're used to it. We hardly need to move. I'm so ready to blow. I need to be inside you right now.'

'OK,' Lynn agreed apprehensively. 'If you're sure.'

The surreptitious superstars undressed as far as necessary under the blanket, their eyes still fixed on the ever-lightening skies. The sunrise was following the young woman's plan to the letter, and the light blue of the day had begun to stretch upwards into the darker and starrier night.

'Let's live dangerously,' she affirmed, feigning confidence.

Her lover's expert fingers worked their magic as she sat on his lap, finding her moist and ready. He shifted her weight slightly until he could slip his engorged penis inside without causing her to cry out in shock. However, after a few moments, they both agreed that the friction on their twin tattoos was too painful, desperately trying not to laugh too loudly while they switched chairs and faced into the cabin.

'This is way too exposed!' the young woman whispered. 'What if I make eye contact with someone?'

'Close your eyes then, you chicken,' the sexy baritone voice vibrated against her cheek. 'I'll keep a lookout. One of us has got to be brave around here.'

Slow movements under the blanket, combined with his caring hands inside her shirt stroking her breasts and back, built a sensation that was exquisite in the extreme, mixed with the excitement and the odd twinge of discomfort from their touching tattoos. The warm walls of her vagina flooding around him, Jeff opened his eyes to see tears of rapture in those of his beautiful best friend.

'You can guarantee I won't ever, ever remember my previous Mile High experience now,' he assured her, kissing her neck and feeling her body sink further into his embrace. 'This is unbelievably sexy, angel. You are the absolute best.'

The euphoric young woman could feel a great man's heart thumping against her back, and rapid breathing gave away his imminent climax. She couldn't help herself as his fingers brought her to orgasm for a second time, and she let out a low moan.

'Shhh!' Jeff panted, laughing softly. 'You're supposed to be being quiet. Oh, Jesus! This is all your fault...'

Three or four slow and subtle thrusts of his hips against which Lynn resisted flagrantly, and her lover's long-awaited nirvana surged forth. Checking quickly that they had not been rumbled, he did his best to prolong their heavenly, hushed hiatus until the screaming inside receded. His right hand emerged from the top edge of the blanket and guided the blonde head gently into the crook of his neck, stroking her hair and kissing her blazing cheek. The serene stars sat linked together in the same spot for several minutes, basking in the erudite pleasure of having done something so imperceptibly shameless.

'We have to move,' the teenager murmured soon afterwards. 'We'll get sprung.'

'OK,' the patient man answered, still languishing in an inner glow. 'We're fine, but if you're scared... You go.'

The long-legged nymph slipped out from under the blanket and made her way gracefully to the lavatory. It felt impossibly childish not to be able to wipe the grin off her face when she walked along the aisle, such was the exhilarating experience, and then again upon her return, since her fellow passenger was now fully dressed. The blankets were folded, and he was reading the in-flight magazine as if nothing untoward had taken place.

'Where've you been?' the comic asked. 'It's been so bloody boring here. I wish something worthwhile would happen for once.'

Lynn was embarrassed by how loudly her boyfriend was speaking and slid into her seat, almost unwilling to look at him. Amused but sympathetic to her blushes, he grinned and helped himself to the toothpaste and his toothbrush from her toiletry bag and dropped them cockily into the breast pocket of his shirt.

On the way to the bathroom facilities, he stopped in at the galley and attracted the attention of one of the flight attendants. 'Hi, Alison. I'm Jeff. Do you guys still carry postcards of the 'plane?'

'Yes, sir,' the slim, fair-haired woman replied, reaching into a high compartment in the kitchen and pulling a few out. 'I mean, Jeff. Sorry! We do. How many do you want?'

'Cheers. Just one. Perfect. Could I borrow a pen too, please?'

'Certainly,' the stewardess' face reddened.

Their famous guest had one more request. 'Also, please could you bring us a glass of champagne each with our food?'

'Of course. We'd be glad to. I'm such a big fan of both of you. It's amazing to have you flying with us, and together...'

Armed with a pen and his postcard, the charmer thanked the gushing woman, disappeared into the tiny space and locked the door. He reappeared a few minutes later, climbed over the stunning passenger in his row and made himself comfortable again in the window seat. No sooner had he sat down than their breakfasts arrived, along with two bubbling flutes.

The celebrity princess looked a little surprised but accepted graciously, guessing this to be part of some scheme or other. Her suspicions were confirmed when her handsome partner winked and thanked the flight attendant before raising his glass to his beautiful best friend.

'Here's to us and to our colourful London life,' he toasted with a smile so sincere that it warmed her heart.

Lynn clinked glasses and echoed his words. 'Did you arrange this? You don't even like champagne...'

From his shirt pocket, Jeff produced the postcard and held it out. 'Lynn Dyson, it is my great honour and extreme, orgasmic pleasure to welcome you into the Mile High Club.'

The young woman gazed open-mouthed at her latest award, leaning over to kiss her smiling *paramour*. 'Thank you! Mine too. What *is* this?'

She chuckled under her breath as she examined the innocent picture of the Boeing 747 aircraft on one side, and then turned her makeshift certificate over to read a message written in her boyfriend's handwriting.

"Mile High Club Entrance Exam (Score out of 10):

1. Tacky   0
2. Awkward   2
3. Painful   4 (extenuating circumstances)
4. Sexy   20
5. Memorable ∞ (room for improvement)

ALL my love,
Jeff"

'Room for improvement!' Lynn laughed aloud. 'Is that an infinity symbol?'

Jeff cocked his head, happy to elicit such an unaffected response from this amazing woman.

'Thanks! You're so sweet,' the delighted woman said, still grinning from ear to ear. 'I couldn't have done it without you.'

'I'm glad to hear that! Let's hope it's the first of many. I love you, angel. And see this...' his left-hand index finger pointed to the three-letter word above his name. 'These glidesmaids, and everyone else I might flirt with... They mean nothing, Lynn. It's all an act. Part of the show.'

The blonde teenager put a hand over his mouth to silence her perfect stranger. 'I know, Jeff. It's the same for me. You have all my love too. Let's eat, and try to pretend it's not eggs again.'

The couple ate their third breakfast in a row amid cheerful discourse about how close they were to landing and what their plans were. A car was to pick them up from Terminal Three and take them to meet the real estate agent, who would in turn take them to their accommodation. With Dyson Administration's assistance, the sportswoman had arranged every single detail for immediate occupation, even down to a full refrigerator of food, a case of *Rioja* and some European beer.

The captain announced that they were about to commence their descent into London Heathrow, followed by the usual requests to prepare the cabin for landing. The flight attendants rushed to clear away breakfast and provided arrival cards for the four passengers in their special care.

'What's our address?' Jeff asked his efficient sidekick, reaching this box on the form. 'I suppose I'd better start trying to remember it now. And please could you throw over my passport?'

Lynn recited the address she had already memorised and skimmed her man's passport through the air in his direction, scoring a direct hit on his nose.

'Cheers, darling,' he mocked. 'I didn't mean literally, but thanks anyway.'

The weather over London was predictably murky, making it difficult for the excited musician to identify many famous landmarks on their way down. The pilot had been directed to approach the runway from the south-west, flying over Windsor Castle. The collection of turrets and courtyards dating back to the eleventh century suddenly came into view as the aeroplane dropped beneath the cloud-cover and tracked southwards. It then banked steeply over the expanse of Windsor Great Park, which was shrouded in a layer of fog leading all the way down to Virginia Water, eventually straightening into its final approach.

Appeased at last, Jeff traced the winding path of the Thames as far east as he could see, until the mist obscured the bridges beyond Hammersmith. He had hoped to be able to point out the three-way split in the Grand Union Canal near their new flat, where he had spent many happy hours while on tour. After describing the area in words and hand gestures instead to his eager concubine, they were also surprised to see how heavy the traffic was, especially seeing that it was still very early on a Saturday morning.

'Jeez, I never knew there was so much water around London. This is fantastic,' the twenty-two-year-old turned to his lover, taking her hand. 'It's so different to home, even from up here. From the air, it's so much easier to see everything all so squashed up together, but low-rise, like Paris. Not like Manhattan at all.'

Lynn tried to catch the view, but the First Class seats were too wide. All she could see was more grey sky. The aircraft touched down in light January rain, taking a long while to wind around the complex web of taxiways and come to a standstill at the gate. Within a few minutes of unlocking the doors however, the celebrity passengers had said goodbye to the flight crew, crossed onto the aerobridge and were soon in the terminal building, ready to be whisked through Passport Control on the double.

***

Sure enough, reunited with their luggage, the young stars emerged through the doors into a noisy arrivals hall and spotted a man in uniform carrying a sign saying "Victoria", their agreed code word. The driver recognised them immediately and shook their hands with vigour.

'Welcome to London, sir, miss.'

Jeff helped the short, stocky Englishman to load their luggage into a waiting Jaguar and in no time at all had struck up a conversation about cars, as if the two men had been mates forever. He moved to open the passenger door and jump into the front seat, before remembering that riding up-front in a taxi was a peculiarly Australian thing. Besides, as Lynn's questioning look reminded him, this prestige vehicle was slightly more refined than one's average Hackney cab.

'Hey, pretty lady,' the larrikin started, climbing in beside his beaming girlfriend. 'D'you mind if I share your cab? Where are you going? Christ, it's easy to pick up beautiful women in this town! I've only been here five minutes...'

The driver laughed as the stunning blonde hit the clown next to her.

'Shut up!'

The car dropped its famous passengers outside a nondescript real estate agency in Maida Vale. The pokey office was a hive of activity, which then further erupted with excitement as soon as the couple opened the door and set off a tinkling bell reminiscent of a British situation comedy show.

Jeff couldn't help but suspect that most of these people didn't usually work in this tiny branch, and especially not before eight o'clock in the morning on a Saturday! The new arrivals were pounced upon with cups of percolated coffee and biscuits, while a woman who introduced herself as Rita fussed around them.

'Have you had breakfast?' the office manager asked, supervising as they were signed the various lease documents.

The couple stifled their laughter.

'Thanks, but you wouldn't believe how many breakfasts we've had over the last thirty-six hours,' Lynn shared with the confused woman. 'The coffee's great though.'

Formalities complete, Rita led her good-looking celebrity clients outside, through the back of the office, where the same driver was waiting. They all piled into the back of his luxury car, rendering it a far tighter squeeze than before. The songwriter sneaked a sideways glance at his blonde beauty and grinned. It was actually very welcoming to be among friendly people who were failing miserably at treating them like VIPs and thereby meeting their every expectation of a normal life rather well.

The Jaguar soon pulled up in front of a four-storey apartment building behind tall security gates, set back from the road in mature gardens. Rita clambered out of the car with difficulty and punched a combination of numbers into a keypad, starting the gates rolling open. Once inside, the young couple could make out a double set of glass doors between lines of rose bushes.

How very English, Lynn thought, genuinely impressed with their new surroundings. 'This is beautiful.'

They followed the talkative agent up to the second floor in a rickety lift; one which still required a concertina grille to be pulled across before it would function. The entrance hall was lined with mirrors, and there were flowering plants on small tables on each landing. Flat Six was at the rear of the building, and Jeff was almost disappointed to find that the front door was made of obscured glass. His girlfriend touched his hand, which was immediately covered by a covetous warmth.

Rita opened the door, inviting the couple to enter. The chivalrous gentleman stood back and let his lady go in first, following closely behind. The building was fairly old, with high ceilings and narrow corridors. There was plenty of light though, and they soon found themselves in a large, airy living room with a view over a small quadrangle. The *décor* was warm and cosy, tastefully furnished and with a white baby grand piano waiting to be put through its paces.

The real estate agent was anxious for their approval, wringing her hands as her clients gazed around quietly. 'Do you like it?'

'It's fantastic,' Jeff responded, looking for his partner's endorsement. 'Thanks very much for arranging everything.'

Lynn nodded to the relieved woman. 'I agree. It's perfect. Thanks, Rita.'

They completed the tour and were given thorough instruction on how to operate the various appliances and the central heating system. The kitchen was newly modernised, as was the stark, tiled bathroom. A second bathroom had been created *en suite* to the main bedroom, which left both quite small, but it didn't matter. Everything was fresh and clean, and the whole set-up fitted superbly with the stars' ambitions to live frugally and in a minimalist style.

'Happy?' the young man asked, hugging Lynn close.

'Really happy, yes. Rita, it's lovely. Thanks so much.'

The driver had brought their luggage up in the lift and was waiting patiently on the landing. Jeff left the two women discussing the arrangements for maintenance and went to help to bring everything in, dumping it all in the hallway.

'We'll sort it out later, thanks, mate,' he told him. 'Can we offer anyone a drink? Do we even have the technology for that?'

Rita declined. 'Thank you. That's very kind, but I'll leave you to it. Give us a ring if you need to know about the area or anything. Your bank is just a few doors down from our office on Elgin Avenue. There's a Post Office there too. You'll easily get your bearings, won't you?'

'Yeah. Thanks. We'll explore later,' the imposing musician assured her.

The awestruck woman was dying to ask for autographs but decided it was too unprofessional under the circumstances. Instead, they all shook hands again, and the newly-installed man of the house closed the door once the estate agent and their driver had entered the lift.

Smiling and yawning at the same time, Lynn wrapped her arms around him. 'Do you really like it?'

'Of course I really like it,' her boyfriend answered. 'You're here, and it's just like the photos. What more could I want? You've done a great job of getting exactly what we were looking for. I love it. Just think of the long conversations over dinner we could have in that dining room, and the piano looking out the window... It's exactly what we need, angel.'

The nineteen-year-old was ecstatic that her flatmate was as taken with the place as she was. She picked up one of the suitcases and began to lug it towards the main bedroom. Jeff grabbed another, and within minutes, they had everything open and items strewn all over the carpet. Pausing to stretch his back and feast his eyes on his beautiful partner, his gaze alighted on the bed with a beseeching look on his face.

The comic heard a deep sigh. 'I'm just kidding,' he grinned, throwing a stray T-shirt at her. 'I made you a promise and I'll keep it, OK? Besides, I met this brazen mile-high chick earlier. She gave me one hell of a good time.'

Lynn laughed in relief. 'Good. Shall we make some tea?'

'Why not? How jolly English of you,' The Australian Elvis joked. 'That would be splendid. Ring for the butler, m'lady.'

Climbing over the obstacles on the bedroom floor, the couple made their way back into the kitchen and opened each cupboard in turn, searching for the wherewithal to make tea. Before too long, they had assembled everything required and paused to take in their surroundings in a little more detail.

'That's right,' Jeff observed. 'They put their washing machines in the kitchen over here. I remember someone telling me that a while ago. Odd, but strangely OK.'

While the kettle was boiling, the songstress left her man pushing buttons and twisting knobs in an attempt to master their new appliances, intent on checking out the far less complicated features of the polished, black piano. A few bars rang out of a tune that her collaborator didn't recognise. He poured water into the very English teapot and stirred the leaves vigorously before joining in the early morning jam session.

'That sounds good,' he approved, sitting down beside her on the wide piano stool. 'This looks brand new.'

Lynn agreed. 'Yeah. I think it is. The keys are very stiff. Have a go.'

Jeff slid across and began to pick out a melody for one of the songs he had written during the flight. It was the first time he had tried to piece it together, and he quickly gave up, falling back to an old favourite. "Shelter" was not only one of his girlfriend's favourite ballads but was also perfectly apt for their new circumstance. The sound echoed loud beneath the low ceiling, prompting his flatmate to flatten the damper pedal to the floor, her arms reaching around the romantic soul at the piano.

'We're going to have to be careful for the sake of the neighbours,' she rued. 'What was that you started playing?'

The songwriter tried again, and the new song took a little better shape the second time. 'Just something that came to me on the 'plane,' he answered. 'It needs more work. Not a big enough idea to stand on its own, but we'll see. I wonder when the guitars'll get here.'

'Probably a couple of weeks. They have to be cleared by customs and everything, so it'll take a while. We could buy a cheap one to tide us over.'

'Yeah,' her minstrel shrugged. 'I'll cope. So what day are we going to have as our thrift day?'

'Hmm... We probably need to see what our spending patterns are first, in case we pick a day that doesn't work.'

The philanthropist scoffed. 'That's not the idea! Poor families can't just pick a day that works.'

'Sorry. I know,' Lynn hesitated, clearly ashamed. 'OK. Pick one.'

'Don't be sorry. You're probably right. We'll see how the land lies first. I'll get the tea.'

Fending off a conciliatory hug, the blonde musician continued to play softly, looking out over the trees and beyond to the rows of rectangular, white-framed windows in the distance. Every building appeared to be a block of flats exactly like theirs. How many interesting people must live around here? She was beginning to understand why her boyfriend was so keen to base themselves in this area. It was intriguing to contemplate other people's lives proceeding in parallel behind each identical brick wall.

Within a couple of minutes, the young man returned with two china cups and saucers. 'I bloody well hope you're not expecting to use these god-awful tiny things when our stuff gets here,' he moaned, placing them gingerly down onto the coffee table. 'It's just not us, is it? I mean, two mouthfuls, and it's gone.'

Lynn smiled. 'Thanks. My dad would say they were "twee".'

'For once, I can't help but agree,' the comic rhymed. 'What d'you want to do now? Our first adventure. What time is it?'

Jeff looked at his watch and answered his own question. 'It's still not even ten o'clock. Jeez! I wonder how long before we feel adjusted to the time. It feels like mid-afternoon to me.'

'Breakfast?' the happy woman joked. 'It was so hard to keep a straight face when Rita asked. How about showing me one of those Little Venice cafés for a less twee cup of coffee?'

Jeff clattered the fine Royal Doulton piece down onto its chintzy saucer. 'Tremendous idea, old girl! I'll probably get us lost, but that's half the fun. What's our address again? I need to write it down and keep it in my wallet, in case I need to get a taxi home.'

His ever-organised flatmate lifted a sheet of paper from the top of the pile of documentation which Rita had left on the piano and pointed to the address on their paperwork, before picking up the plastic envelope of odds and ends that went with the flat and delving inside.

'There are three sets of keys,' she said, dangling one towards her boyfriend. 'We'll hide the third set somewhere.'

'Downstairs in the garden, you mean?' he chuckled. 'Along with everyone else's? I don't need all these to carry round. Which one's the front door?'

The lovers proceeded down the hallway to test out the locks. They agreed it felt peculiar to have supplanted their life to a brand new location, peering down the landing to see if any other residents were spying on them while they attempted to figure out which key was which. And how long would it be before the other flats' occupants cottoned on to their famous neighbours in Number Six?

'You're disappointed the door's glass, aren't you?' the nineteen-year-old remarked.

'You bet! Now I can do solid doors, I want a solid door to practise on.'

'Too bad,' Lynn quipped, pecking his hairy cheek. 'Look at how fast this grows! You've grown a real beard in the time it's taken us to travel halfway across the world.'

Again, the young woman was gathered into loving arms, and her face was brushed by the softening stubble on the tall man's jowls while they kissed. She was almost disappointed that he made no mention of the other body part growing between them. The keys sorted out, the happy pair put their winter coats on and left their new home, buzzing themselves through the security gate. They checked the combination against the number which Rita had given them, and thankfully it re-opened first time.

'So much to learn after such a long journey,' the tired sportswoman moaned to her companion.

Jeff put his arm around her non-tattooed shoulder, and the couple strolled down the street. He took stock of where he was: in London with the girl of his dreams and looking forward to a year of blissful happiness in the old city. The temperature was cold, but with virtually no breeze. He found the old canal easily, and they made their way down to Little Venice within five minutes.

'*¡Aquí está!*' the guide cried out with aplomb. 'Browning's Pool. Looks very different at night, I remember. Let's go over there...'

The teenager's gaze followed his pointing finger to see a longboat which had been turned into a café, complete with tables on the canal bank. 'It's a bit like the Melbourne laneways crossed with Amsterdam.'

'Yeah, but colder,' he agreed, hugging her close. 'If it's too cold to sit outside, we can go in.'

They took their seats, buttoning their jackets to the collar and shoving their hands in their pockets to warm up. A smartly dressed waiter soon came out to take his new customers' order. Before he had even reached their table however, a broad grin had spread across his face.

'Jeff Diamond, *c'est vous?*'

'*Marcel, oui. Bien sûr, c'est moi!*' the francophone replied, springing to his feet and embracing the waiter enthusiastically. '*Comment ça va?*'

The two men kissed each other on both cheeks, the very French way. What a perfect start to their outing, Lynn thought, as she waited to be introduced to yet another long-lost friend whom the Pied Piper had encountered so soon into their stay.

'*Marcel, voilà mon amie,* Lynn.'

Standing up, the tall blonde allowed the flamboyant, moustachioed waiter to kiss her on both cheeks too. Twice, in fact.

'*Mademoiselle Lynn Dyson. J'suis enchanté à faire votre connaissance enfin.*'

'*Merci, Marcel. Enfin?*' the young woman enquired.

At last? Neither man reacted to her enquiring tone, so she continued the introduction, hoping she had chosen the correct form of address.

'*Et le vôtre aussi, Marcel.*'

'*Ah, très bien, mon brave,*' the Frenchman gushed. '*Une beautée qui parle français en plus. Magnifique! Bienvenus, tout les deux. Qu'est-ce que vous voudriez comme boissons?*'

The pair ordered coffee in accordance with their master plan, *cognac* to heat them up and *croissants* because it seemed *de rigueur*. Sitting back down at their table close to the canal, Lynn shot a warm smile towards her proud boyfriend.

'You're loving this, aren't you?' she said. 'What did he mean by "*enfin*"?'

'Loving it? It's bloody fantastic! I don't know what he meant. We had many a drunken conversation about you, so I guess he remembered. D'you mind?'

'No,' the kind celebrity responded. 'Not at all. It's lovely. I only hope I can continue to come up with the goods, French-wise.'

'You'll do fine. He speaks perfect English. The Lucky Pierre accent's all part of the show.'

Jeff fetched a copy of The Guardian newspaper from a nearby table and lit a cigarette, stretching his long legs and letting out a long, contented sigh. 'My first London ciggie,' he proclaimed. 'D'you want one?'

Lynn shook her head and watched him drag hard and swallow the smoke, only to breathe it straight back out again. A long tubular plume formed as it mixed with the chilly air. This man was certainly the sexiest smoker she had ever seen, and how he knew it!

Their drinks and *croissants* arrived *tout de suite*. The young woman grabbed a section of the thick Saturday edition, and the twosome settled down to enjoy the peaceful setting. A family of ducks trailed a gentle wake behind them in the dirty, brown water of the Grand Union Canal, and people on bicycles courteously made way for each other on the narrow towpath.

'I thought we moved to London,' she thought aloud, breaking off a corner of her *croissant* and covering it with *beurre blanc* and *confiture d'abricôt*, 'but somehow we've ended up in Belgium.'

Jeff smiled and sniffed his approval without looking up from the newspaper, setting butterflies in flight again in her stomach. Who cared? This was an extremely good adventure to kick off their new life singular, she concluded, reaching into her handbag and bringing out a pen and notepad. She began to write down details of various West End shows which were advertised in the entertainment pages.

'I wonder where the sports centre is,' Lynn changed the subject, not really expecting her boyfriend to know the answer. 'It's supposed to be near the tube station.'

Again, the Sydneysider's finger drew a confident arc, pointing beyond the café and to the other side of the waterway.

'The tube's in that direction. We can go there after this, *si tu veux*. Someone's bound to know. We'll pick a fit-looking person in the street and follow him or her. I could do with a burn actually, now you come to mention it. Along the canal'd be good. Tomorrow, nice and early. Why don't we aim to go in the morning and then come back here for breakfast?'

'Breakfast?' the Olympian exclaimed. 'No. Not again! What about your boycott?'

Grinning, Jeff caught Marcel's eye and shouted. *'Encore des cafés, s'il vous plaît*, mate.'

Having acclimatised to the temperature, the pair settled down to read for a while longer, the damp English weather gradually seeping into their southern hemisphere heads through foreign nostrils and clearing the stale aeroplane air from their lungs. Lynn's eyelids were desperate to close, so she encouraged them to remain open by staring down the canal at the rows of houseboats moored against the stone wall. She recalled her learned friend speaking about people living in them and felt a shiver run down her spine as he rolled his shoulders.

'Aching?' the sympathetic woman asked.

'Yeah. Really,' he replied. 'I'll be alright after a few nights' sleep.'

'Will you?' Lynn didn't believe him for a minute. 'I forgot to tell you... I did some research on the topic of neck and shoulder tension with our sports *masseur*. He says the problem will eventually go away but it could take months.'

Jeff listened absentmindedly. 'Ah, yeah? You didn't tell me you'd been discussing my body with other people.'

'I haven't,' the mischief in his playmate's voice was accompanied by a suggestive smile. 'I didn't mention any names. I was just talking to him about long-term muscle injuries, cramping and prolonged contraction. It was a theoretical, hypothetical discussion, that's all. He didn't ask any questions, so I didn't have to give him any details.'

'Good,' the songwriter responded, feeling a little self-conscious. 'So what's the prognosis? Are you going to shoot me?'

His lover giggled. 'If you were a horse, I might.'

'I thought I was.'

'Oh, yes! So you are! Oh, well...' she shrugged, taking his hand across the table but stopping short of any further flippancy on the subject of murder. 'He suggested getting regular deep tissue massage and neck manipulation by a physio' to undo the knots that cause the pain and cramps. The reason I didn't mention it before is that it'll probably be fairly overwhelming. Like when we were in Queenstown...'

'What d'you mean by overwhelming?' the patient asked. 'Painful? I don't care about that, if it's going to fix the problem.'

Lynn shook her head. 'No. Well, yes. It would hurt too, but mainly because the physical effects are inextricably linked with the emotional effects. Don't you remember how you reacted in New Zealand, that night before Gerry and Suzanne interrupted us? It's why, as your emotional side gets better, the physical side will eventually too. But in order to speed up the physical, we'll most likely need to speed up the emotional.'

'I'm not sure I understand why you're looking so worried though,' Jeff looked confused. 'I can handle it as long as you're around.'

'I can't explain it,' the concerned nineteen-year-old continued, smiling. 'It's a gut feeling, I suppose. I just think it'll bring back all the painful memories when they work on your muscles.'

Her boyfriend shrugged, draining the last of his coffee. 'Well, you know I believe in gut feel, so who knows? I'm willing to give it a shot, whether it fucks with my head or not. I'd pay a high price to get rid of these headaches and the concrete shoulders.'

'What I was going to suggest was learning about it together,' Lynn ventured, looking him directly in the eyes. 'I'd love to be able to work on you, if you know what I mean. Then if my gut feeling ends up being right, it'd be a safe environment at least. *Do* you know what I mean?'

'Yeah. Sure I do. Thanks. I appreciate it. So where do we have to go? A faith healer? Witch-doctor?'

The sportswoman laughed. 'Yes. Sort of. Not a sports *masseur* anyway. This guy suggested someone who's more into holistic medicine. Mind, body and soul. So, yes, faith healer's pretty close. Spiritual healing.'

'Are there drugs involved?'

Images appeared in Jeff's head of the famous music festivals of the late nineteen-sixties, in the era of free love and all manner of other stimulants. He tried his luck with his conservative helper, but predictably, she shook her head with true Dyson disdain.

'Can I at least have an out-of-body experience?' he pushed a little further. 'I've always wanted one of those.'

'As long as you come back,' Lynn laughed, relenting somewhat. 'No. I can't imagine it would involve drugs. I'll do some investigation when we get set up. That's the other thing we need to find... Where the nearest decent library is.'

Her bad boy sighed. 'So much to do. Shall we make a move then? Thanks, by the way, angel. It sounds great, drugs or no drugs.'

The young singer stood up and reached her wallet out of her handbag. 'You're welcome. I'll get this.'

Jeff lit another cigarette and watched the stunning vision enter the café to pay their bill. There was another item to add to their normal life's checklist: he must force Lynn to think of herself once in a while. Did she really have nothing to focus on which wasn't already completely under control? Maybe this was the root cause. Being Lynn Dyson was too easy. Everything was so straightforward in her world; she made a decision to do something, found out how to do it and then did it. Her whole life had been one long stretch target, and it was now up to him to supply new challenges. This would not be difficult!

'Marcel says we have to come in for dinner soon,' the nineteen-year-old blonde told her boyfriend as they waved to the waiter standing in his doorway.

'Sure. I'm up for that. It's great at night here. All the trees are lit up, and the houseboats. It's magical,' the thoughtful man explained. 'And the beauty of it is we're just a few minutes' staggering distance from home.'

'Provided we can remember the code to get back in,' Lynn giggled.

***

Six weeks had gone by in a flash since Lynn Dyson and Jeff Diamond first arrived in London. They had settled in well to their respective university courses and had resumed hectic travel schedules in earnest. Free of the restrictions of her MAC contract, the popular singer was now able to work with whomever she chose. She had complete access to recording studios at the Royal College of Music, which gave both performers ample time to develop new musical ideas, either separately or together. They had also booked a fortnight's holiday in the Caribbean over Easter and were looking forward to jetting out of the damp, grey days of early spring.

Gerry and Heather's baby was due at about the same time, sending Celia Blake into overdrive. Fortunately, she and the mum-to-be got on famously and schemed together to ensure that the nefarious dad-to-be stayed on the straight and narrow. He had arranged to come out to Britain in June to play with the rally car which he and his distant business partner had bought and was safely garaged somewhere up north, in the Lake District.

Jeff had reacquainted himself with Professor John Francis, and they had struck up a close working relationship which regularly spilled over into their social lives. Staying true to their pact, the famous new arrivals had hosted several successful dinner parties and they were soon receiving return invitations to a host of interesting events all over the country.

By dint of London University's solid reputation, in addition to the city's general level of curiosity, the PhD student also found himself with access to many great thinkers in the world of politics, anthropology and economics across Europe and in the United States. He was stoked to be finally able to explore issues of discrimination and injustice in all parts of the world and all walks of life with people who had real, practical experience.

The swarthy rock star was in his element, even going so far as to precipitate an unexpected stir with an off-the-cuff comment which hit a raw nerve in the academic community for its obvious simplicity. He had been arguing one day with a group of students and lecturers about the causes and effects of discrimination.

'You want to talk about discrimination?' he had asked of them. 'You should try being left-handed!'

All of a sudden, there had been research papers commissioned on the breadth and depth of learnings from everyday difference and discrimination in society, and the outspoken celebrity had been interviewed several times on the radio and television. He had been amazed by the response to what was merely an observation on one of the more regular but always overlooked instances of discrimination to which he had fallen victim his whole life, and the disproportionate reaction fuelled by his public profile gave him a perverse kick.

It was only just beginning to dawn on the intellectual just how influential he had become, solely from having sold a few albums and making an appearance on the Michael Parkinson Show. Or was it also due to the fact that his name was these days officially linked to the great Australian dynasty? Not entirely comfortable with the possibility, he could scarcely discount or even devalue this factor, since this had been his *modus operandi* all along.

With this level of sway over serious opinion, and moreover, on people he hardly knew, came a huge weight of responsibility too. The chart-topping musician realised that from now on he would need to be particularly careful what he put on public record. His stunning and suitably taciturn sidekick was not shy in mentioning that on occasion he was known to express some less than mainstream views which, in the wrong hands, might be twisted and used against him.

For example, if the star were to advocate, as he often did, for the castration of all brutal sex offenders, his newfound hold over the nation's pop culture may catapult this irrevocable punishment as a serious contender for legislation in no time. The wise young man understood this concept only too well, since if this were to happen, he would lose all control over the debate. And furthermore, he might be forced to live with the consequences of whatever those in power chose to make of his grandiose statements.

Therefore, the new Jeff Diamond vowed to practise the art of circumspection, as his beautiful and judicious best friend advised him. Politics for politics' sake had always irked him, yet he had to learn to accept it as a necessary evil now that he was mixing with the big end of town. Reluctantly, the pretender bowed in humble deference to Bart Dyson, who was these days a master of the political stage after learning these same lessons as a hot-headed twenty-something with similarly big ideas.

Behind the scenes however, the lovers' steady progress in smoothing out the troubled soul's rough edges still occasionally fell foul of circumstances. Neither Lynn nor her pragmatic nobleman was especially surprised when the first mind-numbing wake-up call mounted a debilitating assault on their UK happiness. It happened one evening, in a crowded Circle Line train, when the couple had synchronised their return home from classes with the plan of visiting the gymnasium before grabbing dinner at a favourite restaurant.

Watching more and more people squeeze onto the train and cram their way inside the packed carriage, Jeff's attention was transfixed by the sight of several smaller passengers being jostled and knocked off their feet as they attempted to keep hold of the rails and dangling, coiled spring handles, for the first time in over a month fearing the onset of a panic attack.

'Are you OK?' his girlfriend asked, herself squeezed up against the wall at the far end of a carriage. 'You look terrible.'

The songwriter, who had managed to shield himself and his precious companion from detection on the crowded platform, inhaled as nausea threatened to rise from his stomach. He could see from the look on Lynn's face that she had guessed the boy from Canley Vale's return was upon them, and her disappointment both saddened and reassured him. He had rejoiced in the dependency's retreat over the last few weeks but now found his mind full of compulsive hallucinations.

'I need to get out,' he hissed, looking around with crazy-horse eyes and hoping they weren't far from the next station. 'I can't deal with this. Can we?'

Mercifully, the brakes had already begun to squeal, and the lights of a Baker Street platform flashed past. Beads of sweat had formed on Jeff's forehead, and by the time the train had come to a stop and the doors had opened, he was struggling for breath. The stars fended off eager advances as they forced their way through the sea of commuters, who were all amazed to catch sight of the newest A-list local residents.

The young man's legs had turned to jelly, obsessed with the prospect of dropping to the ground and being humiliated in front of so many wide-eyed people, and it took the athlete's entire strength to stop him from overbalancing.

After two interminably long switches of escalator, the couple finally reached street level and flashed their passes at the uniformed ticket collector. Spying fresh air up ahead, Lynn guided her spaced-out boyfriend through the exit and scanned the pavement for somewhere to sit down. There were no seats, so she took hold of his elbow and practically dragged him to the nearest tree, against which he threw his weight in relief.

'Wow!' the shocked teenager exclaimed. 'Are you OK? You never told me your tube phobia affected you that badly. Do you want me to get some water or something?'

'There's Lynn Dyson!' the pair heard from a male voice over their shoulders.

'Jeff Diamond!' another shouted.

Within next to no time, an excited throng had gathered around the ancient elm whose gnarly roots had lifted the paving slabs at the stars' feet. The twenty-two-year-old sucked in another lungful of air and prepared to don his crowd-pleasing mask once again, although his insides still churned. These fans would surmise he was drunk again, or high on drugs, and tomorrow's newspaper headlines would drag Lynn's name down with his if he didn't set the story straight as soon as possible.

His girlfriend had jumped to the same conclusion, judging by her own fake smile, and the two musicians gamely answered a barrage of questions and agreed to sign autographs on any piece of paper thrust towards them.

'We have to go now,' the caring singer raised her voice at a suitable lull in proceedings, gesturing across to a dimly-lit Greek restaurant on the corner of the next side-street. 'We're meeting friends for dinner. Sorry, everyone. Have a good evening.'

Jeff's eyes shouted his thanks as the lovers joined hands and walked calmly away from their spellbound admirers, letting themselves into the nearby restaurant and requesting a table. Colour was returning to his face, and he was forced to admit that the onslaught of impromptu adoration had actually done him a favour.

'You told a barefaced lie, Miss Dyson,' the dark-haired superstar whispered, their heads coming together as they sat down at the small table. 'That must be a first. You're going to join me in hell after all.'

Lynn smiled. 'Too bad... I hear heaven's not all it's cracked up to be.'

'Who told you that?'

'I seem to remember an enigmatic stranger saying something similar when he drove me back from a convent a few years ago. Are you feeling better?'

Love beamed from his guardian angel's face, and Jeff was at once hit with an extreme sense of gratitude and a raging rush of sexual energy. 'Yeah. Much better, thanks. You were fantastic. I love you so much. Can we go to a hotel?'

'A hotel?' the nineteen-year-old held her hand over her mouth and scanned the faces of the other diners in the quiet restaurant in the hope that no-one could overhear them. 'No. We can't walk out now.'

'We can,' her boyfriend smiled. 'I'm too turned on to think about eating. Come on. There's bound to be one close by.'

'Jeff! No! Are you serious?'

The boy from Sydney's west took a deep breath, knowing he shouldn't succumb to the old urges so easily. His saviour had come to his rescue again, engineering a most ingenious diversionary tactic. The least he could do was buy her dinner before he assuaged his bestial needs. But, Jesus! His psyche hadn't slipped this far out of whack for several months, and the pull towards an easy conquest to restore his equilibrium was staunch in its persistence.

The handsome man's mouth was about to respond when the waiter arrived at their table with the wine list and two menus. Taking one folder politely and seeing the other two handed to her dinner date, the dignified aristocrat heard a soft chuckle emanating from the opposite side of the table, followed by a half-smile and a long sigh.

'Yes, angel. Let's have dinner. *T'as faim?*'

Lynn's face reddened as she fought back tears, just as her lover's leather boot edged forward and made contact with her own shoe. She always knew when he was sorry, even though she had forbidden him from uttering the word whenever she came to his aid. When he spoke to her in French, it was meant as a call to her soul. This much she understood.

'Not really,' the beauty answered. '*Merci*, my perfect stranger. Are you going to tell me what hit you so hard?'

'*De nada, Regala.* Sure, if you want to know.'

Of course Lynn Dyson wanted to know. And Jeff Diamond absolutely needed to tell her.

Waiting for their meals to arrive, the couple enjoyed their wine while the story of a young boy being suspended from rough, thorny leather straps hanging from the ceiling of a train bound for Cabramatta was unravelled into words for the first time. It was more troublesome to listen to than to vocalise, the grown man acknowledged, noting looks of horror exchanged for gasps of disbelief in equal measure. He recounted how his drug addict mother had ignored his pleas to be helped down to the floor, and how he could still feel the drop's depth reverberating through his knees whenever he thought of that traumatic episode.

The contrast of the irresponsibility shown by the child's cackling witch of a parent and the kindly but inaccessible solace offered by an elderly man across the aisle brought tears to his girlfriend's eyes again. How could one's flesh and blood be so cruel? And how powerless that elderly gentleman and his fellow passengers must have felt... Why hadn't someone spoken up? This was another reason why she oughtn't to silence her world-changing boyfriend when he aired his opinions. He spoke up when no-one else dared.

'I love you, Jeff,' she raised her chin and said aloud, much to her partner's surprise.

Both diners refused dessert on the house, as offered by a proprietor who recognised the drawcards currently attracting attention towards his modest establishment. Lynn was restless, worried about missing her workout. Her boyfriend paid their bill and shook the restaurant owner's hand as they passed through the door which had been expansively held open for the famous patrons.

'Are you up for getting back on the tube?' the young woman asked. 'It won't still be crowded. We'll get a seat.'

'Yeah,' Jeff agreed. 'I feel like walking, but I know you're in a hurry. No point prolonging the fear of getting back on the horse either, I guess. You're a hard taskmaster, gorgeous, but we should.'

The songwriter felt strong, slender fingers grip his hand tightly, rejoicing once again at his ability to do the right thing despite the nagging desire to claim his prize for actions already completed. This learning process was edifying in its own way, and he felt sure he wouldn't be denied his pleasure for long.

'I have to train,' Lynn repeated. 'The French Open's only a few weeks away.'

'Train tomorrow,' he quipped, lifting her hand to his lips.

'I have to train tomorrow too.'

'Sure you do. Train, train, train. It's all you ever do. You never have time for me anymore. Are you sure you're not having an affair?'

The champion giggled. 'With the handle of my tennis racquet?'

'Christ Almighty!' her boyfriend yelped. 'I did not expect you to say that! That's actually a pretty erotic fantasy, baby. Are you sure you need to go to training right now?'

Clattering down the steep wooden slats of a deactivated escalator, down to the Bakerloo Line platforms, the laughing pair was relieved to find itself two of only a handful of other travellers. By the time they had alighted at Warwick Avenue and surfaced into the tree-lined boulevard, the sportswoman's peculiar *peccadillo* had morphed into a smutty song which her entertainer had vowed to fashion into something significantly more respectable while she was at the gymnasium.

After walking for a few minutes towards Blomfield Road and the canal, Lynn hesitated for a second at the opening of a narrow lane which led behind the houses, as if disconcerted by a noise or having spied a person in the shadows. Her protective chaperone scanned the darkness but drew a blank.

'What's up?'

The teenager's hand suddenly tugged on his own, pulling him around the corner. 'Take me in the park.'

'What?'

Jeff had heard her correctly, he was sure. In the course of the last two hours, their very normal evening had turned decidedly abnormal after his uncontrollable trip to the dark side. Yet whether it was the unconventional re-purposing of sports equipment or suggesting sex in the park, his conservative golden princess was already showing promising signs of a daring and altogether less straight-laced adulthood in which his presence appeared to figure prominently.

The dumbstruck rock star took no persuading, letting himself be led towards the blackness of Little Venice Gardens, not even confident that they could gain access after dusk. Sure enough, the determined teenager dragged him through the nearest gateway. She pointed into the obscured depths within, past a children's playground and beyond the pair of tennis courts where the celebrities had hammed it up with a crowd of locals a couple of weekends ago.

'Are you sure about this?' it was his turn to ask.

'Yes, I am. Come on. There's no-one here.'

The young man was not so certain of this fact, given that the evening was not too cold and the area was known to be inhabited by a number of vagrants. Mildly concerned for their safety, his carnal instincts deterred him from issuing the naïve woman some sort of warning before throwing caution to the wind.

'You're going to have to let me take a piss first,' he joked, kissing the appealing mouth of his partner-in-crime. 'You plied me with too much alcohol.'

Lynn shrugged, standing firm. 'If you have to.'

'Jesus, Lynn! Please don't stop making my dreams come true,' Jeff shouted, lowering his fly and turning to face into the bushes. 'I have to, and with you loitering right there, it's going to take a bloody long time to hit the ground.'

The young woman wandered around the small, secluded piece of lawn, selecting a spot where they would be the least conspicuous. 'You're an animal,' she responded with a hearty laugh.

'I am,' her boyfriend affirmed, running up behind her and grabbing her waist, and the couple whipped round in a circle and crumpled into the wet grass. 'And you love it, don't you? Tell me you do.'

'I love it. I really love it, and I love you, Jeff. Is this spontaneous?'

'Pretty much,' his mouth uttered through a fevered kiss.

Blissfully happy at the end of their most unusual evening, Lynn and Jeff had returned home from the sports centre just before midnight and tumbled straight into bed, exhausted and unable to deny the huge high that lingered from their brief, fumbling encounter in the gardens.

The songwriter lay in the dark and listened to the regular breathing of his sleeping angel, an erection rock hard under the covers. His troubled mind refused to slow down, and his body responded with its habitual craving for power. Forcing himself to channel this energy into a new lyric or melody, he stared at the intricate rose from which the lampshade hung above their heads and willed his heart to beat more quietly.

'You're like a fish out of water, aren't you?' his bedfellow said out of the blue, having woken a few minutes earlier in the midst of his gargantuan struggle.

'Yep,' the frustrated man affirmed. 'Sorry.'

'Don't say sorry. No more sorries, we agreed.'

'You agreed…'

Lynn hitched herself up onto one elbow and pouted. 'What? I don't think so…'

'I didn't agree to anything,' Jeff shrugged, unable to resist her lips. 'You told me that was how it was going to be. I didn't make any promises.'

'Damn!' the beautiful woman laughed. 'That's true.'

Her strung-out stallion hugged her and planted a big kiss on her furrowed brow as she flattened onto her back and pulled the covers back up towards her chin. 'Sorry, angel,' he whispered directly into her ear. 'Got you on a technicality. Go back to sleep.'

Obediently, the blonde singer closed her eyes and turned her body away from the heat radiating on the other side of the bed. She felt sorry for this man who was trying so hard to please her in every possible way, remembering the extreme symptoms which had thrown their world into chaos earlier that day.

Two steps forward and one step back, they had agreed during dinner, in itself much better than the other way around. There was no deadline on his path to reparation, was there? It wouldn't harm their progress if she were to give in once in a while, particularly since he was due in New York in a few days' time to fulfil some pre-tour promotional obligations. The sympathetic musician shifted a little, knowing this would offer sufficient rope for her drowning man to seize onto if he needed to.

'I can't sleep.'

'Can I help?'

Jeff's heart soared. 'D'you wanna help?' he dared to cough suggestively, with a smirk hidden in the nocturnal shadows.

'I always want to help. You know that,' Lynn whispered.

'Yeah, but *that* kind of help?'

'Oh, I always want to help.'

'Then yeah, I want some help.'

Tangling arms and legs moved in a bonded, sensual dance, awakening the passions of Jeff's sleepy therapist. He loved how her fingers immediately encased themselves around his aching penis, guiding it towards her vagina and meandering it around for her pleasure. Groaning softly, his own fingers worked until he was able to push his size inside her, feeling her come within seconds.

An owl hooted in the distance, from the direction of Little Venice Gardens, making them chuckle in shame for their *al fresco* interlude under the bird's watchful eye. The poet teased his tired muse that they had received a score of two hoots earlier, which was bound to indicate room for improvement, and was chuffed to hear no objection to a return match for the purpose of eliciting a higher score.

Instead, the young woman climaxed again, holding his body so tightly that he could do nothing to prevent himself from following her lead. Lying together in the warmth of their exertion, no words were spoken until Lynn heard her relaxed lover's breathing change.

'Will you put your hand on my back, like you used to?' she asked, moving to her right and curling her back.

'Like this?' his voice croaked, her generosity overwhelming him again.

'Yes. Thank you.'

'Does it feel good?' he sniffed, stroking her hair with his free hand.

The nineteen-year-old sighed. 'Yeah. It's perfect.'

'Different?'

'No. Just the same. Exactly how I hoped it'd feel.'

A tear rolled down the millionnaire's face, safe in the knowledge that the word "hoped" had been chosen over "expected" for a good reason. 'Sweet. Like I'm glad I'm not always him anymore.'

'It's OK. It doesn't matter how long it takes,' Lynn sighed.

Jeff kissed the delicate skin of his Regala's shoulder, where their two initials were etched side-by-side into her flesh. 'G'night, angel.'

'Goodnight, mercenary.'

'Former mercenary,' her old soul reminded her.

'Forever angel,' she returned. ''Night.'

***

'Did my dad really become demanding after he'd had an anxiety attack?' Freya asked her mother out of the blue.

'Pardon?' Alison Gunarwardene looked up, shocked to hear her daughter raise this topic.

'Dad,' the schoolgirl clarified. 'When he'd had an episode of rage or whatever. Was he... you know... Did he force you into anything?'

The *divorcée* flinched, perturbed to have been reminded of a past she had put behind her. 'Why are you asking? Have you been reading that damned book again?'

'Yes,' Freya sighed. 'Please don't call it "that damned book", Mum. It's an awesome book. It's my Bible, and nothing you say's going to make me stop reading it.'

Unbeknown to her mother, the seventeen-year-old was making her way through Jeff Diamond's bestseller for a fourth time, and this edition actually belonged to her. Already having downloaded it onto her Kindle, she had requested a hardback copy from her grandparents as a present for passing her examinations with flying colours, and it had immediately been elevated to her most treasured possession.

Alison frowned. 'I'd rather not talk about how your dad behaved towards me when he was angry,' she said. 'I've read the book too. I can only guess you're trying to tell me I wasn't kind enough to him.'

'No!' Freya leaped to her own defence. 'That's not at all what I was going to say. I know you tried to help him.'

'Well, you shouldn't go drawing so many parallels with Jeff Diamond purely because he and your dad both had PTSD. Your dad was a violent man; couldn't control his temper. He had a mean streak, Freya. Something you know very well, so pull your head in a tad.'

The young woman bit her lip. She did have a habit of speaking her mind, even though she always tried to do it as tactfully as she could. It was inside her. She could often see things so clearly that it unnerved her, frustrated not to be able to express herself around adults who always claimed they knew best.

She also hated the fact that she had become so curious about sex. All her friends were too, some already having lost their virginity in all manner of embarrassing ways. She couldn't bear the thought of being touched by a man, especially after the abuse her father had put her through before he took his own life. Yet how amazing it would be to fall in love with someone like Jeff Diamond, who seemed to know everything and was so sensitive to the world's needs... Just like she was, in fact.

'Sorry, Mum. You don't need to keep reminding me. You're supposed to be helping me forget.'

The older woman's gaze met that of her daughter, having inadvertently grasped the barb on the olive branch that had been proffered. Her intelligent little girl was turning into a feisty adolescent, eager to exert her authority over the rest of her family while she tested her wings. These were the words the psychiatrist had used at any rate, not that the mother's frame of mind had been open to understanding them. Ten years of denial hard to shake off, she too had read between Jeff Diamond's superbly crafted lines and learned lessons too late to save her marriage or the life of the Sri Lankan refugee whom she had married in a fit of pity.

Unfortunately for Freya too, the feeling of apathy which surrounded her Australian parent at that time had only intensified when it came to her creative but scarred eldest child. Her younger brother didn't seem to incur their mum's wrath to the same extent, and the daughter struggled to come to terms with this perceived favouritism. These doubts compounded her own unease, wondering if distancing herself from her family was the right thing to do. The counsellors had advised against it, but her instincts told her to flee. She longed for "A Life Singular" to send her a signal that would help her make this life-changing decision.

Picking up her copy of the Diamonds' autobiography, the student tucked it into her schoolbag. Her fingers flicked the edge of a large white envelope which had arrived in the post that morning. Freya knew what it contained. She asked her mother to call her when dinner was ready because she planned to spend the next few hours painting in her studio, hardly able to stand the suspense of climbing the stairs and vanishing behind her door with the secret packet silently screaming to be opened.

With any luck, the artist's eighteenth birthday would be celebrated in another city, on another continent and with people who knew her worth.

From Strength To Strength

As weeks turned into months, the superstars' life continued to develop exactly as they had planned during the long, northward migration. The peaceful co-existence which had begun in Melbourne at the end of nineteen-seventy-four had deepened between the two lovers, to the point where each felt free to engage in student activities and professional engagements. Precious little remained of the prior compulsive dependence which had hung over them like a fire blanket poised to descend at any moment and spoil their fun.

In fact, Lynn had deliberately avoided discussing the state of her boyfriend's mental health for as long as she could, to give him the maximum opportunity to adjust to their new life on his own terms. He seemed content enough, brimming with enthusiasm for his research and inspired by the intellectual heavyweights who continued to form an orderly queue at his door.

Both to Jeff's credit and his dream girl's relief, the rapidly healing man had been on his best behaviour ever since they reached their chilly destination. Their shipment had arrived a week after they did, and their apartment was these days filled with a mix of familiar items which made them both feel much more at home and new purchases that evidenced their shared future. They were totally relaxed around each other, and the pressure and reliance she had previously experienced as he oscillated between high and low and back again had almost completely been eliminated.

Their social lives intersected on occasion, each proud to show off the other. Nothing had given the teenager more of a thrill than to spy her rock star sitting in the third row of the stalls at the Royal College of Music's first orchestral concert of the year, during which she had been invited to conduct several pieces in the programme.

Even when Lynn had been forced to cancel a return flight from New York owing to a last-minute television appearance, there had been no fireworks to speak of. She had telephoned home with considerable trepidation, choosing to couch her change of plan in terms of their reunion being rendered extra-sweet by the wait.

The philosopher had laughed at the sought-after singer's attempt to plead a case for delayed gratification, accusing her of some pretty tenuous reasoning. Moreover, he had remained unruffled by having to survive an extra day on his own. Another significant step forward had been made, and the patient young woman concluded that it was time to talk openly again about his recovery.

Walking home from dinner on his girlfriend's first evening at home after her trip, Jeff had suggested calling into a quaint, old public house in Covent Garden. He had ordered Drambuie for himself and *Kahlúa* for his beautiful best friend, and they had secreted themselves at a small table in the rear of the building that dated back to the seventeenth century. The weathered beams overhead were barely high enough for the tall rock star to stand upright without coming in contact with the ceiling, and the pair had chuckled shamefully at his pretentious concept of being giants in a tiny world.

'So tell me...' Lynn began, taking his hand across the table. 'How are you? You know... Inside your head?'

The smiling man's eyes flashed at her question, as if it was one he had been longing to hear. As usual however, his mouth feigned coolness.

'Which of me are you talking to?' he joked, looking around at imaginary people sitting on either side of him.

'All of you,' the beauty replied, keen to convey the seriousness of her enquiry. 'It's been ages since we had a good talk about your happiness chart. I want to check where your line's been going.'

Jeff twisted his chair to one side and crossed his legs out into the narrow space between the tables. There followed a pendulous silence, while he drew a long, slow intake of breath into his lungs. His fingers drummed on the table, but his stare never moved from her blue eyes until he expelled the air out through his nose. He was well aware of the effect this silent statement had on his exquisite partner.

'You know, angel... My first reaction is to light a cigarette as soon as you challenge me, but I'm not going to do it.'

'I don't mind,' Lynn's response was not entirely truthful, since she was thriving in the reduced amount of pollution her flatmate's new clean-living self brought as a side-effect. 'Have one if it helps you think more clearly.'

The anxious musician coughed, his fingers having ceased their percussive accompaniment. 'I don't think it does, to be honest. It's only a habit.'

'Oh, OK. That's good,' she said, watching him take a large gulp of his whisky and crunch the ice-block in typically sexy fashion.

'Yeah. I'll just switch to another vice, and hey, presto! I'm fine!' he let forth a caustic laugh at his own expense.

'You're avoiding the question,' his inquisitor giggled, 'but I'm enjoying it!'

'No, I'm not,' he winked, before turning more defensive. 'I'm just thinking about where to start. You're right. It's been a while. You don't know how hard it's been to wait for you to bring this up. I was determined to outlast you, and I made it.'

The pretty musician felt guilty, reaching forward and pressing down on the back of his hand to still it's nervous twitching. 'I'm sorry. It wasn't supposed to be a contest.'

Jeff fixed his lover with a grateful gaze. 'I'd be lying if I told you there weren't times when I feel on a knife-edge. You know how I love a good crisis. But I'm happy with how things are going. Don't know if I could be any happier, frankly. It doesn't feel natural all the time, but it feels right all the time. Make sense?'

Lynn nodded, her heart overflowing at the measured understatement. His honesty was refreshing, especially after one of her new college friends had recently detailed some cheating of spectacular proportions by her longtime boyfriend. The news had elicited a strange reaction from the blonde celebrity, feeling simultaneously sympathetic and smug because the frequent white lies told in jest only amused her, safe in the knowledge that she remained the epicentre of Jeff's universe.

'It makes perfect sense. I know how hard you've been working on things and I'm really loving the result. I just want to know if you're stressed out and only not telling me because you made me a promise.'

'Fuck, angel! Stop exposing me for who I am, for Christ's sake,' the complex character complained, flicking a beer mat at his *confidante*. 'I'm not stressed out. I'm good as gold. Just occasionally, I get scared you're slipping away and I'm desperate to bring you back under my control. It's tough because I know it's all in my imagination even though it doesn't feel like it. But then whenever I reach for you, you're always there, so it's no drama. It's getting easier every day.'

'Oh, that's so good to hear,' his girlfriend said with genuine admiration. 'I'm glad you feel that way.'

Lynn's voice trailed off. It was almost impossible not to come across as patronising in this situation. She hoped her tortured soul-mate knew she was happy for him to reach for her whenever he wanted to, but that was actually the opposite of what he needed. Why was human nature so counterintuitive sometimes?

She pressed him further. 'What about when I had to cancel my flight? I thought you'd be angry but you seemed OK.'

'Yeah,' Jeff sighed. 'Not surprised. That's what I mean by getting easier every day. When I heard you tell me, I was waiting for the fuckers in my head to taunt me that you're never coming back, that you've met someone else and don't want to see me again. But it didn't happen this time. I surprised myself, but I was damned if I was going to mention it!'

'Excellent,' the teenager smiled. 'Stubborn, but excellent. I'm really thrilled for you. Do you think it's permanent yet? Or still a work-in-progress?'

The philosopher dealt a heart-stopping wink, reaching for her empty glass. 'I hope I'll always be a work-in-progress, angel. And you too... The secret to our success is to always leave room for improvement. Didn't I tell you that already?'

Shaking her head at the mocking tone, the young star stuck to her quest for information. A boisterous group of people had arrived at a table close by, which caused her to become self-conscious on her man's behalf. Without speaking, their eyes met across the table, and she received the subtlest of signals to put her mind at rest.

'Can I ask you another serious question, please?'

'Of course,' her handsome lover answered, grinning at her coy expression. 'You've been saving them up, haven't you?'

Lynn was nervous, she had to admit. It was pointless to pretend otherwise, and foolish to expect that the perceptive soothsayer across the table wouldn't sense it.

'Yes. Oh, Jeff, I really need to know if you still think about committing suicide every day,' she blurted out, her fingers picking at a knot in the ageing tabletop.

'Whoa, angel,' the twenty-two-year-old groaned, clasping her clammy hands in his. 'Slow down. It's OK. This is probably not the best place to have *that* conversation. D'you want to go?'

'No,' his girlfriend answered, forcing a brighter tone. 'I'm alright. I was really scared you wouldn't be able to stay calm, but look at us! You're fine, and I'm a blithering wreck!'

Jeff smiled. 'You're not a blithering wreck. Well, maybe a one on the blithering wreck scale. You make me fine, *Regala*. And I'm doing a lousy job at reciprocating, evidently. I'm sorry. From now on, I'll give you more regular updates instead of leaving you to worry. Not every day, no.'

Lynn's face opened up into a broad grin. 'Really? That's fantastic! Some days still though?'

'*Oui. De temps en temps*,' the boy from Canley Vale admitted. 'It's involuntary. I certainly don't wake up every morning and think, "What the fuck is there to live for today?" Nowhere near like I used to. When you're there next to me when my eyes open, or when I hear you up and about already, my mind doesn't even try that shit anymore, for some reason.'

'Yay!' the young woman swooned. 'That's perfect.'

The compassionate man could sense the healing properties of his words and gave the entranced blonde a little more. 'I seem to have convinced myself that each morning's another day to spend with you, whether we're going to spend it together or not. As long as our invisible elastic connection's slack, I'm positive. Totally at peace. For the most part, I guess.'

70

'*Excelente*,' the celebrity murmured under her breath, also not kidding herself that this assessment reflected the whole story. 'But when I'm not there?'

Extending his left hand to stroke her flushed cheek, Jeff exhaled. 'Baby, I don't want to put all this pressure on you again. My mind's nowhere near as destructive as before, but I'm not going to lie and tell you that waking up alone's easy. It's not, and half of me hopes it never will be…'

'Room for improvement again?' his muse responded with the most welcoming smile.

'Yeah. Jeez, you're gorgeous! Sorry I didn't tell you that for a while. Sure, there are always those first few minutes when Gravity convinces me something terrible's just around the corner and that we'll never see each other again. Sometimes I jump out of bed straightaway, and by the time I'm out of the shower, I'm ready for action. But other times, it takes longer to rid my brain of the compulsion to end it all, and I can't even get the soles of my feet on the floor. It's happening less and less though, so please don't worry too much.'

'Do you want me to do anything differently?' the young beauty asked.

'Nope,' Jeff replied. 'Definitely not. You're perfect, Lynn. Just perfect. It's me who's still screwed up, and there's nothing you could do that you're not already doing. Just more of the same, if that's alright?'

The music student leaned over the table and kissed him. 'It's very alright. If you're sure.'

'Oh, I'm damned sure, angel,' her dark-haired mystery man swore, crossing his heart and pressing his hand over his tattooed chest. '*Encore une, mon amie?*'

Seeking to close the conversation, Lynn's dashing, bohemian lover scraped his chair across the floorboards as he stood, picking up their empty glasses. From their dark hiding place, she observed him share a joke with the staff and customers at the bar. For someone so confident in himself and his ability to win the admiration of strangers, it must be a relief to know that his deeply-held insecurities about losing those closest to him were also subsiding at last.

Two tall, Scandinavian-looking women immediately headed for the recognisable superstar and began to flirt blatantly with him, unaware of the fact that his girlfriend sat waiting for his return. The equally famous Australian watched him raise his hands to signal that he was not interested in their advances, at first to no avail. Butterflies took flight inside her when, before collecting their drinks, he ended up pointing towards her. Whatever he said must have done the trick, since the giddy girls retreated with whines of disappointment.

Jeff ran his hand across the nineteen-year-old's shoulders on his way back to his seat. Two full *liqueur* glasses were placed onto the table, and the giant squeezed himself back into the small space.

'It's dangerous out there. *Skål,* baby!'

Lynn gave a knowing nod, clinking her glass against his. 'Oh, yes. Poor thing. I saw how awful it was. How can you possibly cope?'

'Come on... That's not fair!' the ham cried out. 'Like it never happens to you... Anyway, in response to your question about the new me being permanent: yes, it is definitely permanent. I couldn't be more sure of it. It's exactly who I want to be and how I want us to be with each other. What about you?'

'Oh, I'm rapt to hear you say things like that. God, I love you so much! The old you and the new you,' his dream girl replied. 'But the new you is so much easier for both of us to live with. I hope you agree.'

'Sure, yeah. Without a doubt.'

'I get insecure too. Like just then, with those two girls... I know you're going to give them the flick, but there's always some risk that one day you might not. I wouldn't want to lose that feeling of jealousy though either. It'd mean we were taking each other for granted, or worse still that we didn't care anymore.'

The palms of Jeff's hands slapped the table, causing their glasses to shift sideways on the varnished wood. '¡*Exactamente!*' he shouted, grinning from ear to ear. 'See what a fine line it is? I'd hate for us to trust each other a hundred percent, because that would indicate we didn't respect each other for being human or for being our own boss. It's like the discussions I've been having at uni' about trust in negotiations. If you constantly treat the other party as benign and compliant, two things result: one, you get complacent and stop watching your back; and two, the other party'll get pissed off with constantly being used and end up doing something impulsive and out of character. That's what I don't want to happen to us.'

Leaning forwards, Lynn sighed in delight. 'It's great to see you so fired up again. The stars are out tonight.'

The passionate intellectual was on a roll, energised by an undeniable sense of renewed freedom. 'Angel, you have to understand...' he exhorted. 'I still carry a lot of guilt with me all the time. Can't shake it, and I can't work out why. Part of the reason I've kept quiet since we've been here is for payback. I know I still owe you so much. I need to feel like the scales are balanced before I can really lay it to rest.'

His girlfriend was curious to uncover more about this interesting angle. 'So how will you know when the scales are balanced?'

'Fuck knows!' Jeff leaned back in his chair and let out a loud laugh.

'But what if I were to tell you they're already balanced?'

The Sydneysider shook his head, reaching for his packet of cigarettes on autopilot and then putting them down again. 'No. That wouldn't work,' he answered. 'I'd have to feel it.'

Lynn shrugged. 'Well then, I can't help you.'

Jeff shrugged back and blew her a kiss, mostly to draw this particular conversation to a close. '*No. Está la verdad, Regala. ¿Caminemos?*'

The rock star rose to his feet while swallowing his last mouthful of liqueur, seeing his blonde companion do the same. He was showing off a long, slim cigar which had been procured at the bar along with their last round of drinks.

'This looks good,' he smirked. 'To top the evening off?'

The ecstatic pair walked through Leicester Square and stopped at an ice-cream van parked kerb-side just before the station. Jeff gallantly attempted to avoid blowing cigar smoke over his pretty date's cone, resulting in a peculiar *polka* along the street as both the wind and the pavement frequently had them changing direction.

'The other thing that's helping,' the songwriter added, putting his arm around his favourite friend while waiting for a set of traffic lights to turn red, 'is that I'm no longer solely dependent on you for intellectual stimulation.'

Lynn huffed at the apparent rebuff. 'Thanks! Were you ever? I'm not sure I'm giving you any anyway.'

'Come off it!' the ambitious student disputed her self-deprecation. 'What've we been doing for the last three hours? All that talk over dinner about DCF and the charities? And there, in the pub? Don't do yourself down. You sound like the old me.'

'OK,' Lynn acquiesced, lovingly taking his hand. 'Maybe.'

'It was beginning to feel like we'd exhausted all the possibilities for good information in Melbourne. But here, it's a whole new world. Do you know I unwittingly coined a new phrase the other day?'

'No. What was it?'

Jeff chuckled. 'I was talking to this openly gay, extremely camp guy at uni'. He remarked that he hadn't met anyone else straight who he could have a deep and meaningful with. You know, about people... The frailty of human nature and all that stuff. I told him I was "heterogenius." How's that for arrogant, eh? But he loved it, and now everyone's using it.'

'I dare you to make that the title of your next album,' his girlfriend suggested, rolling her eyes.

'Jesus! I don't need that pressure, thanks all the same,' the songwriter declined. 'How are the plans for the US tour coming along, by the way?'

Lynn realised this was the first time the discussion had turned to her side of their life singular for quite some time. She didn't care, loving the fact that the unstoppable conversationalist was so enthusiastic about life at last. It had been he who had changed direction, hadn't it? She could have done the same at any point. Balance, she thought.

'Oh! Really well, thanks,' the cheerful musician answered. 'The dates are confirmed for August, before Flushing Meadow. During the summer holidays and probably when you'll be up north, driving the rally car with Gerry. The set's going to be very corny, I think. I need you to help me change my style. Would you? In the studio, please?'

Lynn Dyson's fan *Número Uno* stopped dead in his tracks and fixed her with a dazed look. This was far too good an opportunity to miss. He seldom had the chance to sing her praises, not only for payback purposes but also because he loved her so much. He needed as many better ways to tell her as he could snaffle.

'Change your style? What the hell's wrong with it?'

The former child star looked pensive. 'Nothing's wrong with it, except that I've outgrown it. The stuff I'm writing for other people is what I'd like to be recording myself, but so far I haven't. I need to lose the cute girl next-door image. We can't be talking about establishing "NGOs", charities and education programs... you know, all that grown-up stuff... if I'm swanning around Disneyland or rowing boats across the lake in a white dress, can I?'

'Fair point!' Australia's very adult entertainer exclaimed in mock consternation. 'Take a speed boat out in your bikini, then strip off on the bow. That'd get my vote. I'd move next-door to you in a heartbeat.'

'Hey, thanks! I don't want you moving next-door!'

Jeff shrugged. 'Metaphysically speaking, you minx. Your fans'll never let you get away with it though. They love you the way you are. But not as much as I do.'

'I know,' Lynn sighed, accepting a tender kiss. 'I'm not that person anymore. You said it yourself... You're in a different headspace from the music of the past, and I feel the same way. I need to change gear and do something more sophisticated.'

The adoring man hugged her close. 'Angel, you *are* sophisticated already. Maybe you just don't realise how sophisticated you are. Christ, Lynn. You're hot! Let's talk more at the piano when we get home.'

'Thanks.'

'Although getting out from behind that big, black chastity belt'd be a good start,' her boyfriend added, 'if you're hell-bent on being sophisticated. But that'd be a damned shame for the band because it's sexy as all hell to watch you play the piano too.'

'Thanks,' Lynn repeated, encouraged and content to wait until later for some more image counselling from Mister Communication himself. 'Just need a balance again, I s'pose.'

The talkative pair had arrived at Oxford Circus tube station and managed to lose their identities in the seething mass of people who were filing down to the Central Line platforms. In an effort to stay hidden, the eternally grateful young man embraced his dream girl and kissed her long and hard until the train arrived. And also because it felt good, of course.

Lynn knew that it had been a wise move to initiate the conversation about her healing friend's mental state. It had brought about a kind of redress since Jeff clearly could still benefit from a certain amount of validation to maintain the momentum of his recovery. Despite his outward arrogance, she wasn't about to have him go it alone completely. Probably never, she suspected with a puzzling element of relief.

Once safely secreted inside their cosy flat, with the heating on and large mugs of coffee in hand, the singer tested a few of her aforementioned new songs to the willing, infatuated audience of one who had stretched out on the couch. They sang together, echoing each other phrase after phrase, with tears rolling down both their faces, until they were joined at the hip on the piano stool. Highly charged after their discussions, this was a perfect *prélude* to the unbridled passion that was to end their long day.

'I'm going to have to give you co-writer credits on this one,' the pianist told him, signing off with a multi-octave *arpeggio* and a final, crashing bass note a semi-tone off key.

Jeff shook his head. 'No. It's yours. It's beautiful, and so right for where we are now.'

The composer sighed and leaned heavily against him. 'Will you take me to bed, my perfect stranger?'

'Err... Let me see? Will I?' he quipped, wasting no time in fondling her breasts. 'OK. If I must.'

'I love you so much, Jeff Diamond. I'm sorry I put off speaking to you. It's still quite stressful in our new stress-free life, isn't it?'

Her lover kissed her pouting mouth, peeling her clothes off while she stood in front of him, swaying back and forth as his hands caressed her bare skin. With his tongue heading steadily over her abdomen and on towards her vagina, he unzipped his pants and pushed them down past his knees. Giggling at the contortions they were both putting themselves through to avoid losing contact, Lynn stepped away, grabbed the ends of his trouser legs and tugged them all the way off, one at a time.

Within no time, the couple was completely naked, the sophisticated blonde superstar sitting astride her dark, sultry rock god with their mouths locked together. Moving rhythmically inside her and feeling her writhe in pleasure, the intellectual wordsmith was unable to hold his poetic tongue.

'Maybe that's what makes us so special?' he suggested, eliciting an involuntary sigh that made him laugh. 'The healthy tension. Listen! My job is to keep it healthy and not stray back into the unhealthy, and your job is to slap me down if I do.'

'OK,' Lynn agreed, playfully enacting his instruction. 'Take that, you bounder! But let's not have any no-go topics though. If you want to say something, just say it.'

'Sure. I want to say, "I love you."'

Their eyes met. These three words were all the man needed to say, and the aroused teenager in his arms burst into tears as she came.

'I love you too,' she sobbed. 'I want you to feel as good as you make me feel.'

Jeff thrust into her, trying to prolong the blissful sensations for as long as possible. 'Oh, don't you worry, angel. I feel damned good.'

'You've changed from "I love you because I need you" to "I need you because I love you" now, I think,' Lynn whispered, laying on top of his breathless body and wrapped in blazing hot, covetous arms.

'Hmm?' came a drowsy, satisfied reply. 'Have I? That's good, isn't it?'

The young woman brushed a soft kiss onto his tattooed chest. 'It's amazing, Jeff. I love it.'

'*Bueno. Te amo* too.'

'I don't think you knew which side you were on when we first got back together.'

'Not sure I do now either,' her beautiful black stallion tried to make light of his emotional reaction.

'But you will,' Lynn continued. 'I'm willing to bet that by the time we come back from London, you'll be in the "need because you love" camp all the time. Like I am.'

'Yeah, angel. Hope so.'

***

Michelle England, Lynn's best friend from their school days, flew to London for Easter, after which the generous hosts had booked a fortnight's vacation for four on the beautiful island of Antigua. A suitable male chaperone had been identified for the ginger-haired law student from among their many university friends, leaving the celebrities disgruntled to hear that she had met someone special in Melbourne not two weeks before departure. They placed differing bets as to how long her oath to remain faithful during her holiday might last, given the exotic location and endless supply of cocktails on offer.

On the morning before their guest was due to fly in, Jeff rolled over and smiled, pulling the quilt up over his chilly shoulders. 'So what are we going to do today, gorgeous?'

'Well, I can tell by the recent change in your breathing what you'd like to do first,' Lynn replied, her eyes dancing but her voice prim and proper.

'Yeah? Am I that transparent?'

The young woman shrugged and looked away, rifling on the carpet to retrieve the travel book she was reading. She knew how her sporadic displays of indifference drove her red-blooded lover wild.

'Jeez! I don't even need my dick to give my evil thoughts away these days. You've got me sussed, as we Brits say.'

Giggling, Lynn feigned disinterest, this time much more overtly. 'Persuade me then...'

'No,' her boyfriend teased. 'Make me wait.'

'Make you wait?' she echoed, dumbfounded. 'Is that in my interest?'

'Yep. I'm sure it is. Tell me about Antigua.'

'I don't know anything about Antigua yet,' his efficient entertainment coordinator answered, walking her fingers up his tight abdomen until they reached the "JL" tattoo, where they stopped.

'So tell me how you imagine it.'

The beautiful body reclined sexily on the mattress, stretching her legs and angling her face upwards as if lying on a comfortable beach lounge and baking in the Caribbean sun. The magazine she had grabbed from the floor slipped back out of sight like a guilty lover. Her kissable mouth let out an extended moan of contentment, and expressive hands curled their fingers above her head like a dancer.

Closing her eyes, Lynn gathered her long, blonde hair up and let it fan out behind her. The mime artist heard her lustful bedfellow's breath accelerate a little more while he drank in the sights and sounds of their combining fantasies.

'Gentle waves lapping on the shore,' she began, 'fruity drinks with colourful, little paper umbrellas and the sound of a steel band...'

Jeff coughed in jest, unable to keep his hands off the tanned breasts which mesmerised him with their undulations. 'Yeah. That old *cliché*. What else?'

'Coconuts dropping on the heads of unassuming sunbathers,' Lynn continued, keeping a straight face. 'But it's OK. We'll be wearing our hard hats.'

'Hard hats and bikinis,' the amused young man joined in the fun, rolling on top of her and pinning the irresistible body to its imaginary sun-lounger. 'That's a good look. I can be fine with that.'

Later that same day, families filled Heathrow Airport to bursting point in their quests to get away for the Easter school break. Busy terminal buildings were frustratingly dangerous for the famous new Londoners since their presence in the UK was now common knowledge. Security staff ushered the superstars behind the scenes, where they waited in a plush office for Michelle's flight to disembark.

'Lynn!' the excited traveller exclaimed as soon as the door opened.

Jeff remained seated and looked on happily as his special lady greeted her friend with equal enthusiasm. He knew how much she had been looking forward to showing their first international visitor the various facets of her new life: the flat in Maida Vale, the limitless shopping opportunities of Oxford, Bond and Regent Streets, not to mention Knightsbridge, and the many eclectic bars and restaurants that the pair had explored and sampled in the three months so far. He hoped also that the redhead's arrival would serve the athlete as a short respite from steering him through the uncharted waters of normalcy.

The females' effusiveness left the young buck itchy for the impending bachelor party with his manager. He didn't have long to wait, thankfully. Plans for Gerry Blake's trip were also in the offing for later in the year, once the older man had become a father. And what grand plans they were shaping up to be too!

'Mish, you remember Jeff,' Lynn joked, proudly turning to her boyfriend, who stood up and took the full force of the woman's embrace.

'Hi, you handsome devil!' Michelle gushed. 'Great to see you. You look so happy, both of you.'

'Cheers,' the young man smiled and put an affectionate arm around his dream girl. 'I am, and this stunning creation puts up with me. It's great to see you too. Shall we go?'

The Ford Granada the famous *duo* hired at the airport whisked them back into the city with their guest. Jeff felt like a *chauffeur* as he transported the gabbling girls sitting side-by-side on the back seat; all he needed was the peaked cap. Every now and again, Lynn's reassuring right hand would reach forward to stroke his neck, at once propelling him into wild fantasies of their upcoming trip to paradise. Although he was content to slink into the background over the next few days, preparing for an important meeting with a high-ranking United Nations official and having a doctoral paper to be written thereafter, every little gesture from his beautiful best friend nourished his spirit.

After having put Michelle's rented boyfriend on notice that his after-dark services may not be required after all, the foursome met for dinner in the Hard Rock Café at the western end of Oxford Street, overlooking Marble Arch and the expanse of Hyde Park. The wait staff and fellow diners gaped incredulously at the good-looking celebrities drinking cocktails and tucking into the restaurant's renowned burgers.

Initially, Lynn had reported when the two women returned to their flat from lunch and sightseeing, every second sentence her friend had uttered had been about Ian, the final-year law student with whom she had fallen head over heels in love. With a hushed voice, surrendering to her hard-working flatmate's eager embrace, she mimicked the redhead's endless praise: how funny Ian was, what a good position Ian had secured with one of Melbourne's most prestigious legal firms and, of course, how fantastic Ian was in bed.

Not wishing to be outdone in the "World's Greatest Lover" league, Jeff chanced his arm and placed a bet with his protective girlfriend that distance and a few drinks would soon change the fickle filly's inclination towards faithfulness, granting her one night's grace in the long, narrow spare room across the hallway. The loyal nineteen-year-old had voiced fervent objections, accusing her former sexual mercenary of pinning his own loose morals on her longtime best buddy, in response to which he reserved the right to merely smile, wink and send her away.

Of course, temptation was rife for the impetuous visitor, since the carefully selected sporty, blond International Relations major's ready wit and lazy Texan accent had weakened her holiday resolve within the first few hours. The golden-haired sportswoman leaned into her lover's warm body on the bench seat of their booth, wrapped up in his arms and watching their tourist laughing along with the American's easy style. Every time the confident and entertaining rock star's teasing "I told you so" eyes met hers, she would pout her disgust and resignation at once more coming off second-best in judging human nature.

By dinner time on Michelle's third day in London, all thoughts of remaining true to the wonderful Ian had flown out of the window, and the triumphant Scott was invited back to the Maida Vale apartment after a night at the theatre, complete with cheesy grin. The drunken pair's clumsy foreplay in the taxi had been almost embarrassing to witness, leading Lynn to wonder if her boyfriend's shaking head disguised a longing for the shared steam of their first few dates.

'Are you jealous?' she asked, climbing exhausted into bed after a full day at university on top of a strenuous early morning training session.

'No! What of? Those two?'

'I mean, do you miss all that groping in cabs? You know, when the journey can't go quickly enough?'

The relaxed twenty-two-year-old shook his head. 'Ah, maybe a bit. Do you? Groping can be done anywhere. Here... Let me demonstrate.'

Squealing at the speed with which her man's wandering hands made their way under the hem of her short nightdress and found her bare buttocks, the teenager acquiesced, kissing his broad grin and making a grab for his naked genitals. Long, slender arms and legs, now losing their tan deepened by an Australian summer immediately following her last Californian one, wound around the heavy-breathing mass of arousal which her question had awoken. She stared into the loving authenticity in his eyes and succumbed to the pleasure on offer.

'Are *you* jealous?' Jeff's deep, insistent voice spoke directly into her ear, his mouth kissing the sensitive skin on the side of her neck, eliciting a quiet groan that gave him his answer.

'Not really,' his lover replied through her unrestrained climax, strong hands on his hips ramming his tumescent penis inside her to prolong its effect. 'Oh, you're amazing! How can I be jealous when you make me feel like this? Even though I'm as angry as hell that you know my friend better than I do.'

The sexy songwriter chuckled, slowing the pace to buy more time in this latest visit to heaven and immediately sensing a ceding response. 'Benefit of the doubt,' he murmured, rolling sideways until the breathless beauty loomed overhead, his eyes never once disengaging from hers. 'You're just being a good friend. It's nice. Gropeworthy in itself, but I know where you pop princesses need to draw the line. Take it from me, lady... I'm mentally groping you.'

Lynn kissed his chest and ran her finger over his tattoos. 'That's lovely, if a little creepy. Thanks, Jeff. I love you. I bet your loyalty to Gerry wouldn't run that far.'

Hungry lips swallowed her truism before it could be fully spoken, and the young woman relished her perfect stranger's stubble smiling against her face. She revelled in the crystal clear emotions which transmitted sensually between them, and felt another orgasm quickly gathering momentum while their pubic bones ground together. How could she ever be jealous of Michelle and her agreeable but banal all-American boy? The familiar intensity of this red-blooded male sent her into raptures time and time again. There was no thought further from her mind, hoping he knew to believe her too.

In their anonymous flat on the edge of London's busy West End, Jeff often found himself unable to fall asleep straight after sex like he used to, now that his demonic nightmares were under control. These days, his well-rested brain was too active, too inspired to stock up on more sleep. Tonight was no exception, and he could tell Lynn was struggling to remain conscious after their heady corporal intoxication.

'Are you going to leave your knee up like that all night?' she muttered, her hand reaching out of the covers and attempting to push on his thigh.

'That's not my knee,' the comic sniggered. 'And yes, probably.'

His girlfriend gulped. 'I'd be terrified if that wasn't your knee. Go to sleep.'

Smiling, the contented superstar slid his foot further down the sheet until both legs were straight. 'There. Satisfied?'

'Thank you. Now what I really meant is, "What's keeping you awake?" because it's making me feel like I have to stay awake too.'

'You don't have to. I'm fine. Just not ready to fall asleep, I guess.'

'Are you sure?' his caring girlfriend persisted. 'What's eating you? Your head's too busy. Turn it off.'

Jeff rolled to his right and planted a kiss on her frazzled forehead. 'I can't turn it off, angel. Just ignore me. Pretend I'm asleep. Do you want me to make snoring noises?'

'No,' the nineteen-year-old burst out laughing. 'That'd be worse! I need to find a way to make your mind shut down. Switch sides and lean into me and try to breathe slowly.'

Grateful for the endless patience of his resident, nubile therapist, the restless intellectual made a one-hundred-and-eighty degree turn and settled his left side into the mattress. Lynn Dyson's arms surrounded his torso in a wholly unfamiliar *volte face*, causing a new supply of sexual urges to spring forth in an instant. Fighting his instincts, he pressed his back into her relaxing embrace and attempted to focus on following her lead.

'This could work. I already feel more relaxed, if only above the waist.'

'Shut up,' his bedfellow whispered.

'Is counting sheep the same as making me aware of my breathing?'

'Kind of, I suppose,' Lynn answered. 'It's to make you unaware of everything else that's been on your mind, which has a similar effect as being aware of your breath.'

'Don't leave me.'

The Olympian sighed at the customary rush of despair accompanying her boyfriend's attempts to let go, thankful that this reaction was at least becoming rarer as the months went by. 'Of course I won't leave you. I like it here.'

'Good.'

'If you can reduce your resting heart-rate down to less than seventy beats per minute,' his girlfriend teased. 'I'll let you grope me in the next taxi we catch.'

'And if I can't, will I have to keep my hands to myself in public for the rest of our life?'

'Yes.'

'Oh, shit,' he groaned and raised his right arm to cover his eyes.

'Put your arm down, you idiot. Your heart's having to work harder with it there.'

'Fuck,' the comic feigned a huff, by now having lost the battle with his erection. 'Not half as hard as something else.'

'Stay calm.'

'Stay fucking calm, you mean,' Jeff laughed in exasperation. 'I'm sorry. I love you, Lynn. You're the absolute best, and I'm OK. I'm just not sleepy, and this is turning me on way too much for either of our goods.'

The pair settled into silence, spooning and regulating inward and outward breaths until they became too warm. Kissing her man's shoulder, the young woman rolled away and drifted off to sleep straightaway. Her boyfriend's brain was still awash with ideas, churning and bubbling around. Why did he most want to change the world in the middle of the night? Surely, it could wait until the morning.

A few minutes later, the sleepy blonde to his right turned around and tapped his bent knee again.

'It's not my knee, I tell you,' the insomniac sighed, rolling over and pulling his long-suffering partner into his body. 'It's comfortable.'

'For an awake person.'

'Maybe I am an awake person tonight. Do you want me to leave you in peace?'

Without moving, Lynn's voice became more insistent. 'Breathe!'

'Yeah. I'm sorry. I'm driving you crazy.'

'No. I just want you to relax. It'll only take a few minutes. Think of Antigua again. The waves lapping around the sides of the boat or something.'

Her hopeless case let out a soft moan. 'It's too warm.'

'It's not too warm, Jeff. You're generating heat by moving. Keep still and relax.'

'And leave you in peace. I like it here too, by the way.'

***

The Australian *trio*'s two weeks in the West Indies were a huge success. After such an industrious start to their year in the action-packed British capital, the hard-working celebrities revived under the sun, left on their own for long periods by Michelle and the fun-loving Scott. Whether relaxing by the pool or languishing in their king-sized bed overlooking the beach, an abundance of latent ideas, songs and charitable projects was unearthed and fashioned into marketable material through connubial collaboration.

Better still, Jeff hadn't suffered a single nightmare since the middle of February, and their search for faith healers had yielded some interesting evening classes run by an ageing hippy whose slow and often aimless sentences were peppered with the words "man" and "far out". The entertainment value alone was worth the price they paid for these brief but therapeutic *exeats* from their hectic schedules.

Nothing could stand in the young couple's way now, it seemed. Concrete shoulders and their resultant nagging headaches were proving stubborn, but Lynn's skills as a no-nonsense *masseuse* were increasing along with her orchestration and record producing prowess, not to mention her propensity for clandestine lovemaking under the stars in Kensington Gardens on the way home after either type of class.

At the end of April, the well-prepared and reinvented singer-songwriter took off again for her first solo tour of the United States. With former band-mates Richard Kerr and John Betts adjusted to their New York natives lifestyles, they were delighted to be asked to join their childhood friend for gigs across the wide country, from her old stomping ground of Los Angeles, through the mid-West and Chicago, down to Florida and Nashville before ending up in the Big Apple itself, where Jeff Diamond was also due in early June.

To kick-start her concert series, the stunning blonde fulfilled a longstanding engagement at Sir Bradley Morrison's behest to appear in a Disneyland family television special, where she went through the motions with a wide smile on the outside, while hiding much internal teeth-gnashing at the sheer childishness of the set.

A few nights later however, Australia's whiter-than-white princess was filmed strutting her stuff on stage in skin-tight leather pants and belting out some of her more recent compositions in svelte, revealing evening gowns, both to the vociferous appreciation of her audiences. With an exit from her teens plainly on the cards, by the time she landed back at Heathrow and launched herself into a pair of welcoming arms, her metamorphosis was apparently complete.

'You mean to say neither of us has to get up and go anywhere this morning?' Jeff grinned, lifting the bedclothes to join his beautiful best friend.

Both successful transatlantic trips over, the couple was reunited in London with two whole, uninterrupted weeks at home together before the Wimbledon Grand Slam championship. It was a cool, early summer's morning, and they showered and jumped back into bed with their coffee after having already endured a run along the towpath, marvelling at the exotic symphony of wild animals greeting the dawn behind the high fences surrounding Regent's Park Zoo.

'No,' Lynn smiled, sensing happiness radiating from the other side of the bed.

'¡Fantastico!'

The strong Spanish accent fairly growled from his throat as he confirmed his state of mind. Dark, solicitous eyes drilled into the shimmering pools of blue beckoning from the opposite pillow, and the impatient man inhaled deeply when a graceful, slender arm floated through the air.

'Can we?' he asked.

The compassionate superstar put on a comical frown, always taken aback when her boyfriend made such a request, as if he still didn't deserve her. Often occurring at the most unlikely juncture, these rare moments of insecurity from this intellectual powerhouse were genuine enough, and yet she knew her lover was also wise to their evocative power.

'Did you fill in the form?' she responded, backing away but ensuring her hand remained in contact with his cheek.

'Yep. A hundred times,' Jeff nodded with a half-smile, 'and I've even got one of those home photocopiers on stand-by.'

The young woman's sunny laugh was smothered into a kiss, and their bodies moved closer together. Saturday morning in London with no place to go for several hours except to paradise. The jet-lagged pair had risen before first light, running at a cracking pace beside the canal, past the houseboats and over Primrose Hill before sweeping in a jagged loop around Camden Town and back along the waterside again.

'Aren't you tired?' Lynn teased.

'Nope,' her boyfriend shook his head, caressing her breasts and abdomen while his fingers worked some meticulous magic elsewhere. 'I'm dosed up on endorphins, adrenaline and a whole lot of testosterone, I'll have you know. You do that to me, angel.'

'Natural stuff,' the athlete gasped, arching her back and moaning in pleasure. 'I love you.'

'All natural, baby,' Jeff affirmed. 'My new hierarchy of drugs...'

'Thanks. That's amazing.'

The attentive lover kissed her lips hard as he felt her orgasm begin to take flight, carefully pausing and letting the fever subside. 'Lynn at the top, always my drug of choice.'

'Oh,' his girlfriend sighed, breathless and clawing at his sides for more. 'Don't stop.'

'Don't stop? OK. I won't stop. Cigarettes do instant stress relief, and alcohol boosts my happiness score. But you, my saviour soul-mate, send me higher and higher every day.'

Lynn overflowed with tearful joy as her climax engulfed her, feeling his length penetrate her to magnify every single sensation until she screamed for him to spare her. Gradually, he slowed the pace and basked in her rapture, searching for her tongue and fixing her eyes with his.

'You said, "Don't stop." Now you want me to stop. You have no idea what you want, do you? You like me *au naturel*? D'you know if you want more?'

She nodded, being rapidly transported to a better place once again by the insistent motion. 'Much more.'

'And a fucking great dose of love into the bargain,' the expert added, drinking in the pleasure on his dream girl's face and buoyed by her responsiveness to his every touch.

'Is that natural too?' the gorgeous woman giggled, panting with pent-up desire.

'Naturally, ma'am. Feel good?'

'You bet,' Lynn murmured, kissing his chest as he lay down beside her. 'You?'

'You bet.'

Jeff's throbbing penis lingered way too long in the opening of her vagina, its tip brushing her clitoris just subtly enough to keep her heightened sense of arousal at fever pitch. After making her wait until she cried out and clasped his balls tightly, he let out a roar and sank inside, dropping his weight down onto her like a favourite winter blanket.

'Oh, God! You are so, so gorgeous,' the teenager whispered, kissing his mouth and smearing beads of sweat off his brow. 'And you're so menacingly calm.'

'I know,' her boyfriend hissed. 'Menacingly calm? I like that. Calm before the storm. I can give you that, angel.'

Immediately, he upped the pace, catching his pre-orgasmic partner by surprise and triggering a huge rush of sensation. There was no stopping him now, and their fevered thrashing quickly built to its thundering crescendo.

'No way!' Lynn cried out. 'This is fantastic! I feel like we're so in tune. So together.'

Jeff sensed the end was nigh and rolled his dream girl back onto the mattress, grinding without mercy and closing his eyes to concentrate on the ecstasy in her voice. Finally, he straightened his arms until his head looked directly down over the beautiful face, slowing almost to a standstill as he climaxed inside her. He saw her smile as she noticed the change in his eyes, as she always did, and felt her twist to maximise the resistance against his erection.

'Jesus, Lynn,' he smiled. 'I love it when you say things like that. You make it bloody difficult to do calm, I can tell you.'

'But you love the challenge,' his girlfriend appended, possessive arms claiming her replete lover and lips kissing a mouth which moved to protest. 'Calm is good, but I don't need you to be calm all the time! I love you, Jeff. Really love you.'

***

'So is that when you grasped the whole brand thing?' Gerry asked. 'In London?'

Paragon Holdings' Chief Financial Officer puffed out the first mouthful of cigar smoke, leaning back into the cream leather driver's seat after accepting a light from his Chairman. He and Jeff were spending a lazy November Sunday aboard the older man's luxurious motor yacht, *Cairdeas*, which had been a Christmas gift from his client over twenty years earlier.

'Yeah. Probably around that time,' his mate nodded. 'Not in those precise terms. People didn't really talk about branding back then, did they? It was more about image, rather than brand. Image was the here and now, whereas I think we cottoned on to the whole idea of investing in what we'd become while we were there.'

The widower sighed heavily, recalling another poignant conversation he and his dearly departed had shared at the piano in their compact Maida Vale flat. Those had been heady days. They didn't seem to be able to put a foot wrong, no matter how impulsive or casually-conceived their ideas were. For the first time in either career, the world beyond popular culture had begun to take the young couple seriously.

'We learned to capitalise on everything in its own way,' Jeff continued, dragging hard on his own mellow Havana and peering through his sunglasses at the sun sinking towards the horizon. 'People must've figured that Lynn's aristocratic background... you know, coming from sound stock, old bean...'

'Move on,' the former private school boy scoffed, recognising a sly dig when he heard one. 'I left my violin at home.'

His friend sniggered. 'Fuck you! Lynn's aristocratic background coupled with the articulation of passionate but intelligent solutions to serious problems were worth a punt. We didn't know we were building a brand as such. More like perfecting a formula.'

The celebrity mimed a mixing bowl being stirred, dipping his finger into the magical concoction and tasting the imaginary sweetness. Gerry smiled. His biggest client had eagerly accepted his invitation onto the boat for a blokes' day out and had been sharing the latest chapters in his upcoming autobiography. It hadn't taken long before the pair started to rehash memory after bittersweet memory of their meteoric rise to corporate hegemony.

'We became an institution, Lynn and I,' the superstar shrugged.

'You did, mate. Though you say it yourself!'

'Though I say it myself,' Jeff acknowledged the conceit in his previous statement. 'Humility is a wonderful thing, but arrogance gets you noticed. Bart Dyson said that to me, y'know.'

Gerry's eyes widened at his mate's uncharacteristic doff of the cap to his distinguished father-in-law. 'Did he? You're very charitable towards him these days.'

The rock star who had fought his way into favour with his dream girl's parents all those years ago, twisted his chair around and rose to his feet, gathering his thoughts while checking out Fiona's two female galley-hands who were sunbathing after serving the two men their lunch. He turned back, cursing his unrelenting *libido*.

'Charitable? Yeah. Guess so. He said it at Jet's eighteenth birthday party. Lynn berated Jet for some smart comment or other, and good, old Grandpa came to his rescue yet again. Could always rely on those two ganging up on us.'

The businessman chuckled. 'And here endeth the charity... Go on, mate. What were you saying about institutions?'

'Chapter sixteen, verse three,' Jeff took a deep breath. 'We learned so much during that year in London; about life, about each other and about ourselves. From all sources, but mostly how to make it all work together. And by the end, we'd turned into teachers. Preachers, almost. We talked about it all the time. So-called stardom had taken on a different purpose. Was it right?

Who were we to hold the patent on common sense? On rational thought? But we did, somehow.'

'Did you turn that thing on?' his manager interrupted, suddenly remembering the voice recorder laying on the table between them, relieved to see the red light flashing regularly. 'Good man. I forgot.'

A tear edged its way out of the forty-four-year-old's sentimental eye, deftly brushed off his cheek with the heel of his left hand. The move had been disguised as a flick of ash into the breeze, and he smiled internally to see that he had got away with yet another falsehood. This life had gone on too long now. It was wearing thin on everyone.

'Lynn was so fucking masterful back then, as she was right up 'til the end. She just always knew what to do to help me out, whether it was covering up for my insecurities or boosting my ego enough to clinch that next deal. And it was religion, strangely enough, that really ignited the flames of inspiration.'

Gerry frowned. 'Your wife? Religious?'

'No,' the grieving husband sneered. 'Religion, not religious. We both recognised the power of religion, even though neither of us ever truly understood what makes people believe. That's why we always felt so conflicted about becoming pseudo-preachers. As if we'd stolen someone else's ideas and were now making money hand-over-fist off the back of ancient inventions. Jesus!'

Seeing his old friend gripped in a painful vice of loss, the accountant stood up and put a supportive hand on his shoulder. From this more elevated vantage point, he too spied the lounging ladies on the deck below and let out an ear-splitting wolf-whistle. The women looked up and screamed in chorus, frantically clasping their nude breasts and pulling towels over their exposure. Jeff shrugged and shook his head, claiming no part in the lecherous disturbance, while having no issue with sharing the gratuitous eye-candy.

'Apologies, ladies,' the buffoon yelled from the bridge, 'As you were. Don't mind us!'

The two men turned their backs on the view and paced across to the leeward side of the majestic launch. *Cairdeas* had seen considerable active service since its refit in the mid-nineteen-seventies, having slooped after the famous family and their indomitable manager as a floating refuge from marauding fans in many a cosmopolitan coastal city.

'Is the book covering our ruminations behind the scenes?' Gerry asked, perching on the low wall of the aft deck. 'All that stuff with John Francis? Is that going to interest people?'

Jeff nodded. 'Yeah. That was my point yesterday, mate. I've compiled all the facts and figures around how we went from javelin throwing to guided missile precision with our messaging, but my challenge now is to make it interesting. Compelling, even...'

'I'd read that stuff,' the successful investor pouted, 'but I guess I'm not representative of your target audience.'

'Shit, yeah. You are so my target audience, Gez! Everyone's my target audience, which is why it's so bloody difficult to pitch it right. It's about love and wisdom, at the end of the day. Love and wisdom. Everyone wants those things, but how I go about selling that message to all and sundry is a minefield of trial and error. I need to experiment on a wide spectrum of people, but I haven't got time.'

The author heard a disgruntled sigh from the man on his left but refused to turn around and acknowledge it. Instead, he stared out into the bay. The realist in him acknowledged he was unlikely to win the staunch Irish conservative around to his ethereal commitment to Lynn, and yet he longed to hear a few words of support for his choice from the man who had known him the longest.

'From those last few months in London,' the rock star's deep, lionhearted baritone continued, 'we set about institutionalising positive change led by ordinary people, by taking the rallying power of organised religion and supplanting it fairly and squarely into the secular world.'

His manager let out a stiff chuckle. 'Amen. God be with you, my son.'

'God can go fuck himself,' Jeff whispered, staring the lapsed Catholic down. 'You can't hold this against me now. You got filthy rich along with us in those days, and I never forced you to compromise on your beliefs. Don't close your mind at this late stage, mate.'

Gerry capitulated, extinguishing his half-smoked cigar and downing a glass of iced water. 'Sure. OK. Carry on.'

'What worked for us in the corporate world... scale, innovation and the pooling of many different and complementary skills... could just as easily be directed towards social justice and equality, individual by individual, from minority to majority group. We figured this out over dinner with John and a wide variety of local anti-establishment student heroes of international relations. People who've supported us for all those years since, and who've taken nothing from what we achieved. That's what the book needs to redress. All the love and wisdom generated in that little Maida Vale flat, and on the damp grass of Hampstead Heath, smoking pot and dissecting economies and political landscapes until they were skin and bones.'

Again the orator glanced over to make sure the Dictaphone was registering his thoughts for future regurgitation into the computer. 'So then, in bed of a weekend morning, once all those brains had sloshed into taxis and left us to bonk the rest of the night away, we'd explore every avenue until we stumbled upon the link with religion.'

The gregarious businessman sat with his eyes fixed on the horizon, the fingers of his right hand twisting the cord of his swimming shorts as if he were missing a string of rosary beads. This reconstruction of a pivotal time in his clients' outstanding careers, waxed so lyrical in its understated pathos, owing of course to the untimely demise of their fortune's beautiful co-architect, stirred powerful memories of his own youthful vigour.

'A brand based on our singular tattoo would unite followers and practitioners equally well as could a crucifix or a star of David,' the celebrity espoused. 'It was being in that environment which gave us the concept of combining ordinary company processes and religious ethos to address Maslow's entire pyramid, making sure each need was aware of all others, and more importantly their interdependence.'

'Yes, indeed,' Gerry sighed. 'I remember you talking about that on the 'phone. Something about not wanting to alienate anyone because somewhere in that triangle would be the hook for every person.'

The songwriter laughed at the "hook" reference. 'Genius, mate,' he replied generously. 'The music was always part of it too. That's exactly right. In fact, everything's part of it. You've given me a good idea with that, so thanks!'

His friend smiled, surprised that a spark of intelligence had slipped out without him even noticing. 'Welcome, mate. What did I say?'

'Hook. Every good speech... or song... needs a hook. And in order not to alienate those turned off by mass fervour of any kind, our music and sporting triumphs would also contribute to the brand, ensuring the message was universally applied, complete with a stack of memorabilia to keep the mission front-of-mind. And that was before we had kids. The kids gave us yet another kick forward because kids make people hopeful. Even you, no?'

'Bastard,' the older man cursed under his breath, his aversion to minors ever a bone of contention between the childhood friends. 'I suppose so, if you force me to admit it. But don't tell Fiona. I'm under pressure to build a relationship with her lads.'

'Shit! Don't let Kizzy hear you talk that way either then,' the billionnaire chuckled at the erstwhile confirmed bachelor's airborne quotation marks around the fateful words "build a relationship." 'She's quite good friends with John, I think. She has very strong views about how you should accept them into your new married bliss.'

Reaching into the mini-bar built into a white, circular table that reflected the midday sun, Gerry pulled out two tins of beer and tossed one to his sparring partner. 'Oh, really? And I wonder where she got such strong views from, pray? So the religion thing was only another hook? Isn't that a bit blasphemous?'

Jeff cocked his head and frowned. 'Only if you're a believer, I guess. It's hard to blaspheme against something you don't subscribe to in the first place. But I get what you mean. I've always been a hypocrite. You know that!'

A mouthful of frothy lager spurted from the executive's mouth as he struggled not to choke. 'I couldn't possibly comment. My client a hypocrite? No way, Your Honour. Fuck me!'

'New ideas must be framed in such a way as to make them instantly familiar and therefore attractive,' the intellectual justified his earlier postulation. 'Whether it's a tune that seeps into your head and drives you crazy, consistent role-models who look good and sound friendly and non-judgmental, to whom most people could relate... It couldn't fail...'

Again Jeff caught his breath, feeling the tattoo over his heart constrict in a sweet, burning sensation. 'But Christ Almighty, the sex was good! So unbelievably deep and meaningful.'

Gerry smiled in sympathy. 'I know it was, *Maiastra*. I think I finally get that. Same with Fiona. It took me a hell of a lot longer to find out, but I got there in the end.'

The world's greatest lover sighed, hearing the reluctant expression of regret in the Irishman's tone. 'Make the most of it. All you need are love and wisdom, mate. Make the fucking most of it.'

An Earthly Destiny

As London's spring slipped indiscernibly into summer, with temperatures rarely above fifteen degrees Celsius and only the occasional dry day, Lynn witnessed her magic-man's continued transformation amid quiet, unobtrusive joy. Nightmares were virtually a thing of the past, solid doors opened peacefully, and his compulsive paranoia had given way to a nonchalant and good-humoured equanimity. Charming and chivalrous as ever, he held true to his word and spoiled his beautiful best friend with lavish attention and generous latitude, always seeming to know when she needed which. Her time was divided between the stimulating lessons in composition, orchestration and recording techniques and her unrelenting sporting commitments.

For the dashing doctoral candidate, their chilly new home was proving his intellectual making too. His thesis, under the friendly supervision of Professor Francis, fulfilled his world-changing desires on the macro level and still left him with ample capacity to assist his girlfriend's more tactical efforts to improve life for disadvantaged families. No longer forced to waste so much energy on modifying his own behaviour or compensating for an debilitating lack of sleep, the full power of his jubilant mind was discharged unfettered to tackle some of the modern age's most burning issues.

Whenever Jeff satisfied the demands of his music career, his elevated status also empowered him to capitalise on each travel opportunity to spend time with many influential global players: politicians, representatives of non-government organisations, venerable statesmen and academics.

The champion tennis player successfully defended her Wimbledon singles title in late June, joining her family in the house they rented every year near the All England club. The tournament had not been without drama however, when she had come close to being knocked out of the semi-final by her kid sister, Anna, who had grown up even faster than their prophetic father had expected. During the fortnight away from their Maida Vale home, she took perverse pleasure in listening to a raft of lame and decidedly normal boyfriend excuses for staying out late drinking with friends and taking advantage of his temporary freedom.

The happy party boy had broached the subject of the unexpected near-miss on Lynn's return, nervous to discover whether either coach or father had been angry. Big D had the perfect opportunity to blame her close call on the pair's decadent lifestyle, yet the blonde sportswoman had merely confessed to being frustrated with her own performance. She was at pains to let him know that her call to account had been short-lived, dissolving quickly as she described the couple's many projects to a line of appreciative familiar faces. Like their music, it seemed, sport was set to become a conduit for their more serious goals and no longer an end in itself for the golden girl.

Every day brought new learnings for both Australians, and with their close circle of friends, they fulfilled their plan of discussing and working in collaborative enclaves to solve the world's problems over long, lingering dinners. Indeed, wrapped in each others' arms on such evenings, sharing every nuance and nourishing their mutual fascinations, the passion evident between them never failed to draw envious comment from their *cadre* of contemporary *cognoscenti*.

Material wealth meant little to either superstar student, except for the comfort it gave them of not being required to focus on sustaining themselves while striving for other, loftier objectives. Wealth for Lynn Dyson and Jeff Diamond was to be found in emotional fulfilment, strong friendships and steadily amassing assets for the various not-for-profit businesses they were developing. Gerry and his growing team of specialised empire-building accountants had established the Diamond Celebration Foundation on the celebrities' behalf. Along with Paragon Holdings, which continued to plough money into technology innovation, the two successful organisations attracted altruistic and entrepreneurial investors from all walks of life.

The boy from Canley Vale was often struck by the sight of his own image in the old-fashioned, three-way mirror on the bedroom dressing table of their furnished flat, mystically conjuring up a different man from each viewpoint. The face on the left belonged to his old self; the troubled soul cursed with the scars of mistreatment, whereas the face on the right revealed the respected and powerful leader he was well on his way to becoming. Completing the fascinating picture, with Lynn's hands on his shoulders and her smiling face reflected above his, the character in the centre acknowledged that he and his beautiful best friend had reached a crossroads, manifesting itself in their new musical directions but also more subtly in the way they approached every other aspect of life.

Nevertheless, not a day went by when the young man didn't pinch himself to make sure he wasn't dreaming. Their life singular was creeping unerringly close to the vision his imagination had painted, way back in his old bedroom, overlooking the depressed outer-suburban street below. His special lady was equally aware of this turn of events, often voicing her continued wonder at how accurately her mystery man had forecast his future and how happy she was to have been able to help make it a reality from the outset.

And Lynn Dyson *was* undeniably happy. Her boyfriend no longer harboured any doubts on this score and had even given up asking if she was sure.

'This is working, isn't it?' Jeff smiled, tired and stoned after yet another late night after-party but keenly anticipating a slow release of the pent-up sexual energy he had been storing in reserve during another spectacular sell-out concert.

'What's working?' asked the stunning, long-legged blonde who was undressing seductively as he spoke. 'Us, you mean?'

'Yeah.'

'It's perfect, yes,' she affirmed, jumping onto the bed and grabbing for her lover's arm to drag him down towards her. 'So perfect that we hardly need to talk about it anymore.'

The rock star kissed his forever groupie, pulling her close into him with a demanding left hand on her hip. The older and more worldly this woman became from her experiences gained in his company and elsewhere, the more expressive and assertive she was in the bedroom. Such erudition was only to be encouraged, he had insisted. It appeared his dream girl had taken him seriously when he had described them looking over the edge of the world and trapping anything that took their fancy. She clearly felt very safe and uninhibited, which was gratifying to the boy with the history of violence and an unusually persuasive turn of phrase.

Hungry eyes watching on as fingers with painted nails moistened her vagina in preparation to receive his full length, the Machiavellian sex-god trusted he was in step with his dream girl in this regard. Nothing about her receptiveness and her unbridled physical responses hinted otherwise.

'Don't you want to talk about it?' he played devil's advocate again, kissing her waiting lips and taking her right breast firmly in hand. 'You got something else on your agenda? What shall we talk about instead?'

'Yes. Same as you,' she laughed in return. 'I love you, Jeff Diamond. Make me scream like those girls in the front row.'

'Correct answer. What girls?'

Without missing a beat, the couple combined mind, body and soul until both were overflowed and sated. Another busy day would be fast upon them, Lynn's scheduled to the minute and Jeff's a higgledy-piggledy collection of loose arrangements, controlled occasionally by Cathy in Melbourne or arranged *ad hoc* around business meetings and his teaching obligations.

'I can't begin to tell you how much I love you,' the aroused songwriter said, turning over to the prostrate, nude and totally irresistible temptress in his bed.

'You don't have to. I can feel it.'

'That's good,' he murmured, kissing her warm and swollen just-loved lips. 'It's important.'

Slender fingers appeared from under the sheet to stroke his prickly chin. 'Can *you* feel it?'

'Oh, yeah,' her boyfriend breathed heavily against her cheek. 'Still can't quite believe it, but I can feel it.'

Gentle laughter sent shivers running down both sets of limbs, which instinctively entwined yet closer, their kisses increasing in intensity as fire ignited once more. Through their drowsy contentment, somehow the energy boiled up between them, making them instantly greedy again, and their united bodies moved slowly until both came to orgasm locked in each others' arms.

'Now do you believe it, Jeff?'

'I'm taking it on advisement.'

'I'll send you a memo,' nodded the gorgeous blonde with her legs wrapped tightly around his hips, 'sir.'

'You do that.'

***

Jeff had arranged a long weekend in Edinburgh for the occasion of Lynn's twentieth birthday. For the first time in a year, he needed a plan. Their calendars were filling up well into the future, and it was becoming difficult to arrange anything remotely surprising. The date itself was the day after her upcoming defence of the US Open tennis singles title, and the doubles final, if she and her partner were to make it through, was on her actual birthday. She had been working for the last few months on building a solid doubles partnership with Great Britain's own ladies' star, so her boyfriend had to believe there was more than a fighting chance that the birthday girl would be fully-occupied and celebrating triumphantly that evening.

Making the reluctant but right decision, the young man decided not to crowd his gorgeous tennis champion. Instead, they had settled on a long weekend away at the Fringe Festival to immerse themselves in alternative culture before driving further north to Gleneagles for some golf lessons. John Francis had introduced his *protegé* to the Professor of Economic History at Edinburgh University, and the eager student had arranged to fly up a day before his dream girl was due to arrive back from New York, to soak up the renowned academic's wisdom along with a dram or two of rare fire-water.

Life couldn't get much finer. Since returning from a brief Antipodean fly-past, he and Lynn had talked regularly, openly and enthusiastically about their future. They had set various initiatives in motion to realise The Good School concept and had mapped out their plans for procreation. Both thought that sooner rather than later would be best for producing their offspring. Given the nature of their respective careers, interwoven itineraries were unlikely ever to be stable or light, and most probably, there would never be a sensible point at which to take time off. They were in the fortunate position of being able to hire plenty of help however, leading them to hatch a grand scheme involving a string of international nannies who would teach their children other languages and cultures at their most impressionable ages.

The pair drew up a detailed five-year timeline using large sheets of manuscript paper from the budding conductor's stock. Jeff spotted a gap emerging where his beautiful best friend could give birth to two babies in relatively quick succession between the Montreal and Moscow Olympics. How crazy, they had laughed. Was family planning now an Olympic sport? It seemed an absurd necessity, but a necessity nonetheless. This meant that their two children would need to be conceived and born somewhere between September nineteen-seventy-six and January nineteen-eighty, to give Lynn's body sufficient time to recover and return to full fitness for the following September. Two gold stars were duly adhered to their project plan, charged with high expectations.

Yet there was an item missing from their agenda, wasn't there? The step the Sydneysider's tortured soul had rebelled hard against for so long. He cast his mind back to the soul-searching he had inflicted upon himself over Gerry's unplanned fatherhood before the lovers left for London. Why did he resist it so fiercely? Was it a perceived loss of independence? Or freedom? Or simply the archetypal fear of commitment for which men were frequently criticised. Did being officially linked to another person compromise his ability to be himself? Had he inherited an irrational antipathy from his own father?

All these excuses were superficial and ultimately ridiculous, the songwriter cogitated. What had he advised Gerry while Heather was pregnant? Do the right thing by the child and then split up later if family life didn't deliver the happiness he sought. The divorce rate was increasing steadily with the advancing century, especially in showbusiness circles, and the stigma of second or third marriages was lessening in the modern age.

Regardless, Jeff hardly wished such a fate on his dream girl, nor on their children. Come to think of it, he didn't fancy putting himself through that particular ringer either... Was there even the slightest risk of this happening to them, after everything they had experienced together and with the glory of their master plan beckoning enticingly from the future? Even in his most pessimistic frame of mind, the failure of their relationship was but the remotest of prospects.

No, the wise man decided. The time had come. His painful past was these days firmly consigned to the far reaches of his memory, set apart from the man he was today. And despite her progressive attitude towards most things, Lynn was quite traditional when it came to affairs of the heart. He wouldn't want it any other way, he made his silent confession. Perhaps it was the control freak in him, or maybe, for once, he ought to admit to being a closet traditionalist too. His refined girlfriend would never be brazen enough to bring up the subject with him, but surely she must be wondering, with all this talk of children...

The apprehensive musician had already selected the song. In fact, there had been a shortlist of three, but one stood out so far above the rest that it had featured several times in his dreams. He had even awoken with a start one morning, hoping he hadn't sung it in his sleep and thereby given the game away. This moment had to be so special; the perfect proposal for his perfect partner from her perfect stranger.

Ring? What to do about an engagement ring? Jeff couldn't presume to know the sophisticated woman's taste to this extent and for such an important symbol that would hopefully be cherished for a long, long time. She had never passed comment on anyone else's jewellery, leaving him with no clues as to her preference. She must pick out her own, he decided, and after the fact. This was on the presumption of a "yes" vote, of course...

But what if his dream girl didn't want to get married? What if he had read her wrongly, and her genteel brand of progressive feminism had renounced the need for a legal seal of approval? The lovers had their tattoos as testament to their togetherness, but her empathetic boyfriend suspected she would want to make things more official than this. Her family would definitely expect it, but that may also be a good reason not to bother.

Only one way to find out!

Practical things first, the romantic schemer needed to be confident of finding a piano in a reasonably private place. Normally unfazed by onlookers, the consummate performer didn't relish the idea of proposing in front of an audience, even though asking the question to top all questions in public would be an awesome stunt which the press and their legions of fans would lap up. Again, depending on the answer.

Shit! The boy from Canley Vale marvelled at the fact that he hadn't become a total wreck over these deliberations. A year ago, he undoubtedly would have. He congratulated himself on how far he had come, with a caution that a rejection would surely set him back again by a long way. Oh, well... That was the chance he had to take. What was his *credo*? Do the right thing and face the consequences? Like so many times before in this life both cursed and blessed, if he were to drive it forwards in the direction of his choice, no alternative option existed.

The girl of his dreams wouldn't politely decline, would she? Where might that put their ongoing relationship? Fears of abandonment chased each other around in circles in his head, and it irked the philosopher that he had taken this long to uncover the subconscious reason why he had avoided the issue so determinedly up until now. The new Jeff Diamond was still under construction evidently, in spite of an apparent lack of lingering symptoms.

Lynn Dyson arrived at Edinburgh Airport on Friday morning, triumphant with her US Open wins and after a trying week of press conferences, television appearances and exhibition matches. She and her favourite late-night caller had spoken on the telephone the night before, and she had been full of excitement for their weekend in Scotland. Still feeling sluggish and hung over from his protracted dinner with Professor Stephenson, the excited student drove their rental car back out to Ingliston just as his girlfriend's flight touched down in the grey, windy city.

It was raining heavily outside. The multi-millionnaire stood leaning against the wall, holding a dripping umbrella. His eyes watched the love of his life move through the arrivals hall and shake a short line of hands before she emerged through the doors into the baggage collection area. It reminded the thoughtful man of the first time the pair had made eye contact, through the computer room window at RMIT, when she was but a sixteen-year-old schoolgirl and he but a tortured and penniless undergraduate. Her presence had mesmerised him then, as it did now.

The celebrity looked stunning. Tall, slender and graceful in a cream leather coat, a long, flowing skirt and high-heeled boots. Jeff's heart still skipped several beats every time he set eyes on her, not to mention the other inevitable and embarrassing side-effect. Acting as cool as ever, he pushed himself lazily off the wall and strolled over to meet her. They kissed tenderly, laughing as he wrestled the cabin bag from her ever-independent hands.

'Is it still raining?' the traveller asked, pointing to the wet umbrella. 'It was pretty bumpy coming down.'

The couple waited for the athlete's suit carrier and tennis holdall to trundle around on the carousel, exchanging news from the last few days. Jimmy Connors had won the Men's Singles, and the champion told her boyfriend how both winners had danced clumsily together at the tournament ball. The intellectual then gave his eager apprentice a flavour of the conversations he had shared with Don Stephenson about the inner workings of European politics and economics and how they contrasted with the US from so many aspects.

The twenty-three-year-old was infuriatingly restless, feeling nervous about the evening's elaborate plan. If Lynn detected any odd behaviour, she chose not to say anything. She couldn't help but notice his bloodshot eyes while in the car driving back to the city, jumping to her ordinary and totally plausible conclusion.

'Did you have a big night last night or didn't you sleep?' she asked, unsure whether to be amused or concerned.

The driver clutched at his temples and grimaced. 'Bit of both,' he admitted, grateful for her compassion, even though his suffering was entirely self-inflicted. 'I seem to be feeling worse as the day goes on. My fault though. A dram or two too many single malts. I'll get over it fast now you're here though.'

The couple soon arrived back at their hotel on the eastern end of Princes Street, cast in shadow by the ancient castle. Dumping Lynn's bags at the foot of the bed, they embraced and fell onto the old-fashioned eiderdown. She could tell her man was in dire need of some tension-releasing therapy, and they were soon in the throes of their usual passion.

'I missed you heaps,' Lynn told him. 'This feels so good.'

'Me too,' her lover gasped. 'Jeez, it's so good to be close to you. It feels like ages since we've done this.'

An interval of afternoon delight relaxed the tormented soul a little, for which he was grateful. It meant the pair would be afforded an easy few hours, relaxing over a late lunch followed by a *matinée* comedy show. With any luck, his smiling partner would suspect nothing. Before heading out into the damp air, Jeff made a big fuss of opening her birthday presents.

'I can't believe we've known each other for over three years and I still haven't managed to share your actual birthday with you,' her man lamented.

After the theatre, they walked along Rose Street hand-in-hand until they came upon a cosy jazz club the songwriter had unearthed, down a narrow alley between two shops, through a closed door and up a winding staircase with holes in the carpet. Lynn wondered how he had known it was here, to which he responded perfectly truthfully that he had found it by chance the previous afternoon while wandering the streets, choosing to go in and share a beer and a few stories with the locals. The pertinent information left undisclosed was that he had arranged to have the place to themselves for an hour before the Saturday evening patrons began to file in.

Jeff ordered a bottle of the best *Tempranillo* grape varietal he could find on the wine list while his famous girlfriend made herself comfortable at a table near the stage. He loaded the tray with two large goblets and took it over to where she had moved to take up residence at the piano, responding to the bartender's request. They toasted her birthday, her wins and being in Edinburgh together.

The stunning woman licked her subtly-painted lips in delectation as the deep flavour bit at the back of her throat. 'Mmm... That's superb,' she said, savouring another mouthful. 'This place is really nice.'

The musical *duo* sat and messed around with various song ideas for half an hour or so. Such creative outpourings were habitual for them, and still Lynn was none the wiser to her man's nefarious intentions. Her face was alive with simple pleasure, celebrating her birthday belatedly, and he glowed inside knowing how all the more sublime her innocent shock would be once she realised why they were here.

'Here's one I prepared earlier,' the songwriter announced, taking advantage of a natural break in their animated jam session. 'From me to you.'

'Thanks. You're really spoiling me. Another birthday present?'

'Not really, but you're welcome anyway,' he shrugged, blood pumping through his temples. 'Does there have to be a reason?'

The blonde beauty had stood up to refill their glasses, giving her partner the perfect opportunity to slide into the centre of the piano stool. The chords rang out under the low ceiling, and the raised volume signalled to his handpicked audience that this was a composition she was supposed to take seriously. She leaned on the side of the majestic, black instrument and gazed at her gorgeous minstrel.

Nerves jangled in Jeff's head, rendered fuzzy by this latest concentrated ingestion of alcohol. Yet as he began to sing the opening lines of "No Point Fighting", any apprehension soon evaporated, and he found his spirits soaring while he sang into his dream girl's eyes once more.

The song penned during his recent fortnight of solitude spoke of safety and security where there had been none, new directions for his lonely course, and clarity born out of love. Lynn's smile gave only her adoration away, her eyes filling with tears which held their descent in abeyance until the whole lyric was unveiled.

Still the power ballad swept both lovers away on its *arpeggios*, the rock star's voice mellow from wine, yet sharpened by the morning's dozen cigarettes. His own emotions were also in check, but barely. He sang about closing in on something unavoidable, after which there would be no turning back. He asked her to imagine places they would only find together, with his lighthouse as the most precious gift he feared he had lost and would never hold again.

Before the familiar baritone voice had finished the chorus' closing lines, the young woman had already begun to clap. There were tears falling from both pairs of eyes by now, and the sustain pedal remained lowered under the pianist's heavy shoe for several seconds while the rich sound hung in the air.

'That's beautiful,' she enthused, grinning and wiping her eyes. 'Thanks again. That's going to be a huge hit.'

Finally lifting his foot and leaning back slightly, Jeff Diamond's deep brown eyes drilled into Lynn Dyson's shining blue gems, with two special words on the very tip of his tongue. Two words that he still couldn't quite believe he was about to utter.

'Marry me?'

The plain, unornamented question took its time to reach its recipient, and the world stood still in its honour. The singer watched as his Number One fan's expression changed from professional appreciation to rapturous disbelief in a split-second.

'Are you serious?'

Her handsome entertainer nodded, smiling at her innocent response. 'Never more so.'

Letting out a dignified whoop of joy, the twenty-year-old celebrity flew around the piano like a tornado and enveloped her waiting boyfriend in a strong, euphoric embrace. He stood to absorb the impact, and they kissed as if they never intended to stop.

'Yes!' she cried. 'Yes, please. Oh, Jeff! I'd love to marry you. Yes! ¡Sí! Oui! Yes in every language!'

The humbled superstar exhaled over his *Regala*'s head and closed his eyes, feeling relief course through his veins as her energetic hands continued to grip him tightly, all ten Olympian digits clubbing together to send sharp pain radiating from his upper arms up into the base of his skull. He hadn't dared project forward to an acceptance, nor the form in which it might present, but this uninhibited joy was better than any fantasy. His mind flooded with an optimistic serenity the like of which he had never known before.

'Thank you, angel. Whoa! I love you, but you gotta let go before you starve my brain of oxygen!'

Lynn laughed apologetically, releasing his arms and taking hold around his waist instead. The barman's tiny jazz club unusually full of tearful mirth, he guessed what must have happened between the two striking musicians and brought over a bottle of champagne and two glasses.

'Congratulations are obviously in order! *Slange var,* as we say here. Can I offer you this on the house?'

Jeff turned towards him and waved a sincere apology for the commotion. 'Thanks. That's very kind.'

The emotional blonde accepted with wide eyes, and the couple sat down at the piano again while their chuffed host popped the cork and filled their glasses with boundless effervescence. After swallowing a mouthful from his overflowing glass and toasting his girlfriend's strident endorsement, the songwriter began to replay the same chord progression, his heart jumping to feel her lean into him.

A stray tear traced its way from Lynn's left eye and on down the crease of her nose as she sipped her drink, being brushed away before it had a chance to mingle with the bubbles. The long-armed pianist removed his right hand from the keys and laced his arm around his beautiful best friend, continuing to play as well as he could with only one hand.

'I didn't think you'd ever want to get married,' the young woman ventured after a few minutes of silent reflection. 'Whether you even believed in it, you know... I sort of avoided the topic.'

'Me too,' the rocker with a reputation chuckled. 'Up until a year ago, I didn't see the point of marriage at all. Even when I was speaking to Gerry about his baby dilemma, and he asked me what I'd do in his situation, I said I'd only do it to make you happy. Then when we got the tattoos, which are much more permanent than wedding rings or even a signature on a register, the whole concept became somewhat moot.'

The wise man felt his lady's head nod against his collarbone, his heart brimming over with love at her understated response. 'But since we've been in London and things have got so, so amazingly good, even down to the fact that we've been talking about having kids soon, it just seemed like the perfect seal of commitment on our relationship.'

'It is. Very perfect.'

Jeff's lips pressed a kiss into her hair. 'I guess I severely underestimated what a good idea it was, judging by your reaction and the way I feel right now. I love you, angel, and I want you to be completely happy.'

Lynn angled her head back to peck his cheek, sniffing as he wiped a new batch of tears from her eyes. 'Oh, I am already completely happy. And now you've made me even more completely happy.'

'So you want to get married? I wasn't sure how you felt about it either. I was agonising over it last night, which is why I looked like death warmed up this morning.'

'You didn't look like death warmed up!' his girlfriend countered, frowning at the peculiar English expression. 'You look fantastic! You are the most handsomest man in all the world. I couldn't believe it when the song ended with "Marry me." It just never entered my head, but I'd be so proud to marry you.'

The twenty-three-year-old musician felt lightheaded from a sudden dip in blood pressure. It was his turn to fight back tears as his brain absorbed her words and gave itself permission to believe them.

'*Magnifico*,' Jeff murmured, running his hands over the keyboard again until they had reprised the verse of his poignant ballad. 'That's settled then! It was meant to be a total surprise. I didn't want to give you any clues, but I was sure my body language and my nerves were dropping hints left, right and centre. Oh, and by the way, I'm never going to say those two words to anyone else. This is forever, baby. Or longer, if possible.'

Customers were beginning to drift into the piano bar for the early evening cocktail hour, and the noise level rose around them. The self-effacing celebrities clinked their champagne flutes together and shared another chaste kiss, content to merge into the background and finish off both bottles. They began to discuss the logistics of when and where and music and guests until it all became too complicated for their tired, alcohol-infused minds to process.

'Let's get some dinner,' Lynn suggested. 'Where did you eat yesterday?'

Last night's soused intellectual couldn't remember. 'Somewhere the far side of the castle,' he replied. 'On the Royal Mile, I think. We were so deep in conversation that Don could've taken me anywhere. I just followed him like a pissed-up puppy.'

The pair forbade each other to speak about weddings at dinner, which they found easily a little further down Rose Street. They chose Italian cuisine, and the heavy *pasta* dishes left them very sleepy on top of their wines.

Next morning, the elated young man put in a call to Bart Dyson. He didn't intend to ask the big man for his daughter's hand in marriage, but he definitely wanted to be the one to break the news. Annoyingly, they were unable to get hold of him either at Benloch or Admin, so Jeff had to be content with leaving a message for him to ring when they were back in their flat in Maida Vale. Lynn was disappointed by the delay, since she was itching to tell her mother the happy news, but her man remained adamant that everything should be done in the proper sequence.

Departing Edinburgh on a typically cool summer's morning, the delirious pair drove northwards through the Trossachs and on to Auchterarder, where they practised their best guttural Scottish accents as the mist gradually lifted. The luxurious hotel welcomed its special guests with a lone piper on the steps of the entrance, followed by a flamboyant Highland Fling and a whisky tasting on arrival, unaware of their private celebrations.

'You didn't put them up to all that fuss, did you?' Lynn asked, wondering if the right royal reception had been all part of an elaborate, extended proposal.

'No way,' her boyfriend groaned. 'So much for a quiet weekend. If we weren't so tired, I might've claimed it as my own idea though.'

The room key opened the door on a suite fit for a king and queen. Its *grandeur* was almost overwhelming for the boy from Canley Vale, whose priority now they were officially on holiday was to concentrate his full attention on one thing only. He slipped a gentlemanly arm around his one thing and led her to the window, and they stood gazing out over the fourth fairway soaking up the silence.

'I'm glad you didn't get down on one knee,' the young woman admitted out of the blue, leaning back into her suitor's muscular body and joining all four hands together in front of her. 'I think I would have burst out laughing.'

Jeff looked sideways at her, smiling. 'Yeah? I thought about it.'

'What changed your mind?'

'The image of you bursting out laughing, I expect,' came his dry reply. 'The mood would've been ruined.'

Lynn laughed. 'It was perfect just the way it was. Really special.'

The grateful songwriter stepped to one side, drawing the curtains across the bay window. To his delight, he turned back into the room to find his favourite lady unzipping her knee-high boots. He hoped she wouldn't stop there, crossing the room to alter the lighting to a more subdued setting.

'So what are you going to say to Dad when you eventually speak to him?'

'Too bad, she said yes?' the comic quipped, with a playful winking.

Lynn slapped his arm. 'That's not fair. He likes you these days.'

Moving in to assist with further disrobement, the arrogant pretender apologised for his sarcasm. 'OK. It wasn't fair, I'm sorry. What'd you like me to say?'

'I'm not going to help you,' his lover teased. 'Just something conciliatory but forthright.'

'Conciliatory but forthright?' Jeff laughed. 'What the hell does that mean? You're right. That definitely doesn't help me!'

'Oh, for God's sake, just tell him! Then I can ring Mum and be excited.'

Her boyfriend felt guilty, slipping his hand under her top and pulling her close for a deep kiss. 'Sure, angel. I'll think of something. Don't worry. I won't enflame the situation again. I'm over all that. Come here. Let me soothe our souls.'

The Gleneagles Hotel turned out to be every bit as sumptuous as its five-star reputation suggested, and the couple made the most of the facilities; Lynn in the spa, Jeff in the library and both in the well-equipped gymnasium. Their golf lessons provided welcome light relief as well. Neither had played seriously before, and the instructor was patient as they took their well-honed racquet sports techniques and adapted them to the long club and dimpled ball with varying degrees of success.

***

Still immersed in a surreal trance, the celebrity pair flew back to London on the Monday afternoon, ready to return to normality and the next day's classes. The hour was too late to telephone her parents by the time they reached their flat, forcing Lynn to wait another day. She negotiated permission from her resident control freak to call Michelle instead, leaving Jeff to eavesdrop and rejoice at how happy the women's conversation sounded.

All signs indicated that it had been a stonkingly good idea to take this extra step, and not only for his dream girl's benefit... No matter how modern and progressive the students considered themselves to be, it appeared that a sort of retrograde mystique now surrounded them, casting their minds into the time when marriage had been the only form of commitment available.

The musical sportswoman made her excuses first thing the following morning, escaping the flat in order that Jeff might speak to her father unencumbered. She also had an idea for a new song to thank him for his proposal and was keen to lock herself in the studio to rehearse and record it.

At eight o'clock, or five o'clock the same afternoon in Melbourne, the songwriter picked up the telephone to his future father-in-law, strangely not anxious in the least. Confidence boosted by his lover's overt happiness, he wasn't seeking an approval or a blessing. Lynn's mind wouldn't change if neither was forthcoming, but with her screams of joy still ringing in his ears, he was determined not to spoil anything for her now.

'Bart, it's Jeff,' he said, on hearing the big man's booming voice. 'How're you going?'

'I'm well, Jeff, thanks. Sorry to have missed you yesterday,' his girlfriend's father sounded cheerful. 'What can I do for you? Is everything alright over there?'

'Yes. We're fine too, thanks. Sir, I have some news for you,'

'News? Good news, I hope.'

The younger man smiled at the words coming down the line, unsure how to interpret a subtle defensive overtone. *That depends*, he thought.

'Hope so. It is for me,' he answered, his heart in his mouth once again. 'This weekend, I asked Lynn if she'd marry me, and I'm happy to report that she accepted. I wanted to make sure you heard it first, sir. Well before it hits the press, *et cetera*.'

Silence greeted the rock star from the other side of the globe. Had he come to the point too quickly? He thought he noticed Bart take a deep breath and braced himself.

'Well... That's great,' Lynn's father responded after quite a delay. 'Congratulations to you both. I'm very pleased for you. When? In London?'

The cool, almost indifferent response caused Gravity the troll to stir from his prolonged hibernation, catching his host unaware. 'Thank you,' Jeff replied, doing his best to ignore the knot in his stomach. 'In Edinburgh, actually. We went up there when Lynn got back from the Open, for the weekend. We're still reeling, if you'll forgive the pun, and she can't wait to speak to her mum.'

'Good, good. Marianna'll be excited to hear all about it, I'm sure. And thanks, Jeff, for doing me the courtesy of letting me know,' Bart continued in a less officious voice. 'It's a big surprise, I must say, but it's great news. I know we've had our differences in the past, but the past is the past. I respect Lynn's decision and I'm happy for you both.'

'Excellent. Cheers, Bart. It crossed my mind that you might want me to ask your permission first.'

The elder statesman laughed aloud, also seeming to relax at last. 'Now that's Marianna's father you're talking about. I concede I may not be particularly liberal in my views, but I certainly wouldn't have expected that. Especially not from you, of all people.'

'You'd be right there! That would've been somewhat of a sell-out,' the traditionalist *nouveau* agreed, with a sturdy chuckle to match his opponent's good grace.

It was reassuring to hear his girlfriend's formidable father comparing similar experiences, and the musician felt a little ashamed at having ambushed him. Being so far away, little could have been done to avoid it, but no wonder he had taken a while to warm to the idea. It wasn't every day someone rang from another time-zone having just proposed to one's daughter!

'Absolutely,' Bart acknowledged. 'You're your own man, Jeff. And I wouldn't want anything else for Lynn, to be honest. And by all accounts, you're both doing some remarkable work over there.'

'Thanks very much. That's kind of you, sir. It's good to hear you say that.'

The Olympic stalwart sounded genuine enough, his voice recapturing its usual potency. 'So have you thought about when this wedding will take place?'

Jeff smiled, detecting a modicum of excitement creeping in too. 'Whoa, wait a minute! Not yet, no. We've hardly got our feet back on the ground. That's Lynn's end of the bargain anyway. I only do the easy stuff. All I know is that our schedules are ridiculously crowded, so we need to pick a date fairly soon or we'll be retiring before we get hitched.'

'That sounds familiar,' the older man replied, amused to hear the pretender's comments ring true. 'Marianna and I had only four or five weekends to choose from the whole year after we got engaged. I'm just glad you left off popping the question until after the Slam. Lynn would've been too distracted for words.'

Give me some credit, for Christ's sake, the twenty-three-year-old muttered under his breath, holding the receiver away from his mouth. He had hoped that by now the sporting hero no longer expected him to sabotage his daughter's career. The millionnaire intellectual gave his old adversary the benefit of the doubt. The comment was most likely meant as a joke, albeit poorly delivered.

'Out of interest, sir?' Jeff had to ask.

'Mmm?'

'Would you have given your permission?'

Again, a pregnant pause jammed the telephone line, and the young man cursed his own stupidity. Why did he continue to test people out when invariably it only served to challenge his own burgeoning resilience?

'Good God, yes, Jeff!' the booming voice returned. 'Of course I would. You've proven yourself a hundred-fold over the last year. And Marianna will be thrilled to bits, believe me. She thinks you two make a wonderful couple.'

'Thanks, sir. That's very cool.'

The boy from Sydney's west felt a lump in his throat and tears stung in his eyes. Clearly, Lynn's parents' approval was more important to him than he had imagined.

'Listen, Jeff... I have to go,' Big D announced abruptly. 'I'm sorry to cut this short, but let's all talk again sometime over the coming weekend. I'd love to hear from Lynn but I'm going to be in Canberra until Friday, so let's arrange to speak on Saturday morning, Melbourne time. We'll both be at the farm. Does that suit you two?'

Sighing the tension out of his lungs, the strung-out songwriter drew a complete blank concerning the contents of his diary for Friday evening. No matter the potential conflict, he would move it if he had to. He needed to get past this point as soon as possible, to permit his beautiful best friend to relieve him of the baton of mounting hysteria.

'It's fine by me,' he assented. 'Lynn's not here at the moment, so I'll check with her, and we'll ring you back if necessary.'

'Good show. Thanks again for the call, Jeff. Say hello to Lynn for me. Bye for now and congratulations again.'

'Thanks, and you're welcome, sir. Have a good trip.'

The line went dead, and Jeff Diamond went to jelly. Deed done! It wasn't yet eight-thirty in the morning. Not even he could justify a whisky this early!

***

Lynn returned late that same afternoon to an empty flat and a scribbled note.

> 'Spoke to your dad. All good. They want to talk Friday night (our time). Gone training. Ring tomorrow... Jx'

Ring tomorrow? That would certainly be a long workout, his girlfriend smiled. Her unfailingly romantic flatmate must be referring to the purchase of an engagement ring. How nice! She already had a pretty good idea which style she would choose. In truth, marriage had been on her mind for a while; ever since they had started to talk about children.

The young woman had been in no real hurry to discuss it though, because Jeff's interests seemed to lie in more symbolic, pagan gestures of commitment that eclipsed the superficial institution of civil marriage. Neither celebrity would have entertained a religious wedding, leaving Lynn to resign herself quite happily to a *de facto* relationship in which to raise a family.

Yet since accepting her mystery man's simple proposal, a distinctly feminine force had consumed every fibre of her being, and the idea of a colourful and musical affair, complete with long, flowing gown and some sort of ceremony with family and friends, had begun to ignite her imagination. Better still, the excited twenty-year-old felt goosebumps all over, folding the note and tucking it into her purse for safekeeping. Now her perfect stranger was even talking about a ring!

Did this mean that Jeff Diamond was her *fiancé* instead of her boyfriend? What an old-fashioned term to apply to someone who wanted to supplant the old ways! Lynn was sure her cool bohemian would balk at being classified as such, and the complementary label with its extra "e" did nothing to inspire her either. But marriage... This age-old tradition was a whole different, grown-up

106

ballgame, and one that had sent her head spinning while her heart continued to sing with an uncontrollable *joie de vivre.*

In return for Jeff's generosity, there was also a design forming in the sportswoman's head of a symbolic ring for him. She was keen to speak to a jeweller and find out how long it would take to craft the object in her mind's eye. The only piece of jewellery she had ever seen on him up until this point was the stud earring for which he had opted a year earlier, less than a day in advance of the couple's grand reunion.

Lynn sighed again, remembering those fraught few hours while she wrestled with her conscience and her feelings, finally making the most fortuitous and astute telephone call of all time. Jeff would wear her ring, wouldn't he? Wild horses wouldn't stop her wearing his! She grabbed a piece of paper from the coffee table and sketched a signet ring shape with a black background and a flat surface to inlay four diamonds, but only over time.

The Four of Diamonds, the whimsical musician mouthed, putting the final touches to her drawing. Her man, of course, was the Ace of Diamonds, as he would remind her from time to time in his oh, so irresistibly arrogant way. With one stone in place, her beautiful black stallion could wear the ring straightaway, but with the promise of more to come.

After they were married, she would add the second as his wife; the Pair of Diamonds. The dreamy singer caught her breath. Would she change her name? Wow! Another factor they hadn't considered as yet...

'Lynn Diamond,' she stated out loud.

Or Lynn Dyson Diamond? To hyphenate or not to hyphenate? Would her progressive old soul expect her to change her name? He might not even want to share his. They had their professional *personæ* to consider too...

So many questions, none of which were for answering unilaterally in this never-ending paradise that they had moulded over the last few months. The young woman felt sure her *fiancé* would absolutely adore the concept of their future children being represented by absent gemstones for the Three and Four of Diamonds respectively. Was it tempting providence to be so prescriptive about their intentions? *Act like a winner*, she scoffed at her father's overused edict. Everything would go according to plan.

Lynn lifted her eyes to check the clock: too late to go shopping now. Feeling settled, she decided to wait and ask Jeff first. There was no point in having a ring made if he were never to wear it. Busying herself with dinner preparations instead, she was unable to keep the grin off her face. Loud music blasted from the stereo system as she danced around the kitchen, from the refrigerator to the sink to the stove of her Cloud Nine, W1 "des-res".

On his return to the flat, the tired songwriter could hear the upbeat sounds from the lift lobby. He opened the door and let himself in silently, finding his beautiful best friend hard at work. He sneaked into the bedroom and jumped straight under the shower. Combing his hair in front of the mirror, he checked himself out. His muscles were pumped up and aching from a long training session. He had gained more than five kilogrammes of brawn over the last couple of months, in a deliberate effort to beef up for the coming Australian summer. Now he had committed to a closer link with the Dyson family, his ego simply wouldn't allow him to present as the skinny, dark-haired poor relation among the tanned, blond heavyweights.

And the result was not so shabby, the tall man smirked. Lynn had complimented him many times on his physique. He crept into the kitchen under the cover of blaring rock'n'roll, causing the singing cook to jump out of her skin when she noticed the refrigerator door open out of the corner of her eye.

'God, Jeff! You startled me!' she gasped, hand on heart. 'When did you get home?'

The intruder was bent double laughing at the priceless reaction. 'Sorry, angel! I couldn't resist. You were so engrossed in what you were doing and in the music. I just wanted to see how long I could be here without you knowing. I'm sorry.'

Hugging close, the lovers kissed passionately. Jeff could feel her heartbeat against his chest, and it turned him on.

'Did you like my note?' he asked, spying it still sitting on the kitchen table.

Lynn nodded, her eyes dancing. 'Mmm, thanks! I wasn't sure what you meant by "Ring tomorrow." It sounds as if you were going to stay at the gym' all night.'

'*Bueno*,' her *fiancé* replied, kissing her again. 'That was the whole idea. D'you have time to go shopping tomorrow?'

Those same blue eyes lit up. 'Oh, I think I could squeeze it in! Why wouldn't I? How did it go with Dad?'

Jeff poured his intended a vodka and tonic before sitting down at the table with a can of Danish beer. Through a growing fixation on the delights beneath her clothes, he forced himself to focus on the conversation he had shared with this gorgeous creature's father.

'I'm sure I could squeeze it in too. OK, considering...'

The blonde shook her head and groaned. 'What do you mean by "considering"?'

'I took him by surprise. At first, I don't think he knew what to say, so it was a tad awkward. I told him I'd asked you to marry me over the weekend and that you'd accepted. He sends his congratulations and said your mum'd be overjoyed.'

'That's good. So why "considering"? What about his reaction?' Lynn pressed. 'Was he happy or not?'

'Yeah. He seemed happy enough after a while. He said some nice things about me. And I checked if he thought I should've asked his permission, to which he said no. He joked about your mum's dad being like that and said he certainly didn't expect me to do it. "Of *all* people…"'

The All-Australian daughter was relieved, giggling at her boyfriend's impression of the rambunctious patriarch. 'So we're supposed to have a four-way call on Friday night, Saturday morning?'

Jeff nodded, tipping his head back to coax the last few drops out of his tin of beer. 'Yep. They'll be at Benloch. He asked me if we'd set a date already.'

'We need to,' Lynn affirmed without hesitation. 'You know what our diaries look like.'

His flatmate dished their dinner onto large plates and placed them on the table. The impatient young man picked up his cutlery and stood both pieces on end, tapping them on the Formica surface and fixing her with a stare.

'Soon,' he declared. 'I don't want to be in this weird *fiancé* limbo for long. It doesn't serve a purpose for me, and you know what the press'll do with it. Sorry to be so unromantic, but it'll be a nightmare, won't it? All that endless hounding… *Whaddya* think?'

'Well! That's pretty definite,' his girlfriend replied, astonished at the assertiveness he had displayed. 'I agree actually, now you come to mention it. We're not naïve virgins, moving from the shelter of our parents and out into the big wide world. The whole engagement concept doesn't really fit with our ethos, does it?'

'No. Ethos? I've never heard you use that word before.'

The twenty-year-old smiled at the intellectual's approval. 'Do you like it?'

'Yeah. I do. You're gorgeous.'

'Thanks!'

'But betrothal,' Jeff winked, changing the subject and grimacing as if the word tasted revolting. 'What's with that?'

'Engagement's like having you on lay-by,' the stunning woman teased. 'No-one else can buy you.'

Her boyfriend's eyebrows raised in doubt, unable to resist such a tempting opportunity to exert some light-hearted dominance. 'No-one else can buy *you*, you mean, my presumptuous little luxury item. You move from "Property of Bart Dyson" to "Property of Jeff Diamond" during this betrothal phase. You realise we're going to have to come up with a whole set of new rules about how you behave around me?'

The gold-medal superstar scoffed. 'Yeah, right! We both know what that deserves. "Ring tomorrow," I think my reply would be.'

Her partner laughed too. '*Excelente*. I like it. So when?'

'What about New Year's Day?' Lynn had obviously been giving the date some serious thought, judging by how naturally it had rolled off her tongue. 'It's a Thursday, but that won't matter. Everyone from my side'll be in the same place.'

Jeff stopped mid-mouthful. 'Well, shit! That's pretty soon!' he exclaimed, swallowing his food down. 'You don't have to take me *that* seriously. That's only three months away. Can you organise it that fast?'

'Don't know,' she replied with a shrug. 'I haven't organised a wedding before. What could be hard about it?'

'Oh, *nada,* I guess. Piece of cake. Hey, listen to this…'

Smiling, the young beauty looked up at the unexpected diversion. Her relaxed dinner companion had rested his knife on the side of his plate, now reaching for a book which sat face-down on the kitchen table. As it was lifted and opened, she could see it was "*L'Etranger*" by Albert Camus. He had mentioned during their stay at Gleneagles that he planned to retrieve a quote about marriage from this novel, and she was pleased he hadn't forgotten.

'This is the extract I wanted to find for you,' the *connoisseur* of French literature continued, pulling out the tube ticket which had been used as a bookmark. 'This is Merseault, *l'étranger* himself.'

'So does the title mean stranger, or is there a different meaning?' Lynn interrupted.

'Outsider, *je crois*, in this context. Someone who feels strange compared to his surroundings. Camus writes in the first person, and it's pretty powerful. The feeling of isolation. Listen… You'll get what the title means from his voice. It's all also one long paragraph, which is striking in itself.'

'Did you write this too?' A shiver ran up the singer's spine as she spoke.

'No,' Jeff smiled. 'Not this time. Camus only died in nineteen-sixty! *C'est impossible, ma chérie. Alors, écoute un peu:*'

"That evening, Marie came to see me and asked if I wanted to marry her. I said that it was all the same to me and that we could get married if she wanted to. Then she wanted to know if I loved her. I replied as I had once before that that didn't mean anything, but said I was pretty sure I didn't love her. 'Why marry me, then?' she asked. I explained that it was of no importance whatsoever but if that was what she wanted, we could get married. And besides, she was the one asking and I was happy to say yes. She then remarked that marriage was a serious business. I said: 'Not at all.' She said nothing for a moment, just looked at me in silence. Then she spoke. She simply wanted to know if I would say yes to any other woman who asked me, if I were involved with her in the same way. I said: 'Of course.' She then wondered if she loved me, but there was no way I could know anything about that. After another moment's silence, she murmured that I was very strange, that she undoubtedly loved me for that very reason, but that one day she may find me repulsive, for the same reason. When I said nothing, because I had nothing more to say, she smiled, put her arm through mine and said that she wanted to marry me. I said we could do it as soon as she wanted. Then I told her about my boss' plan and Marie said she'd like to get to know Paris. I told her that I'd lived there for a while and she asked me what it was like. 'It's dirty,' I replied. 'There are pigeons and dark courtyards. Everyone looks pale.'"

Et voilà! So *whaddya* reckon to that?'

The *raconteur* lowered the book a few centimetres so that he could see his pupil's face. Raising from their fixated position on the front cover, her eyes spoke volumes, and the *chagrin* moved him to tears. Mission accomplished, his old soul rejoiced.

'Wow. So hollow,' she whispered. 'The way she... Marie, was it? She didn't like what she heard but still wanted to get married anyway. Perhaps she didn't really love him? Just liked the idea of getting married.'

'Yeah. Kind of leaves you cold, doesn't it? His strangeness is appealing to her now, but she expects it'd repel her in years to come. And neither character gives a toss about that either.'

The woman whose passion appeared boundless nodded sadly. 'Like a business deal, or buying some boring essential item you need but don't really care about. And then he just changed the subject, as if Paris being dirty and full of pale people were just as important as getting married.'

'*Exactement, Regala.* Not exactly what happened last Friday *arvo* with us, eh? But that could've been me, angel. When I read it for the first time, at about seventeen, it was as if I were reading my own narrative.'

His girlfriend extended her hand and placed it on his hairy forearm, squeezing slightly as tears welled up in her lover's eyes too. 'I can imagine. It's not anywhere close to how we feel now though, thank God. I'm glad you don't relate to him so much anymore. Is that what you're trying to tell me?'

'Sort of,' Jeff shrugged. 'I suppose I figured I'd only ever be getting married if I got someone pregnant. Same as Dad, and most people round our way. People never married for love in real life, as far as I knew. I could never see myself excited at the prospect of spending the rest of my life with the same woman. It'd only mean boredom and routine and endless years of keeping my mouth shut and fucking around to get my kicks.'

'Oh... That's awful,' Lynn agreed. 'Like you didn't deserve to be happy? I've heard of people marrying for money or an easy life, so that's pretty loveless too. I feel very special. Lucky, more like... We've got the real deal.'

Her perfect stranger dropped the book all the way to the table-top and slid his chair back. He invited his empathetic saviour to stand too, embracing her strongly. There was no self-pity in his eyes, she registered with relief. This was a man whose self-esteem had been rebuilt and who now felt fully empowered to go after what he wanted.

'You are very insightful, Miss Dyson,' the emotional storyteller praised. 'The indifference and apathy sprang out of the pages back then and slapped me in the face, like I was denied the right to anything intimate. But then I went back and read this book again when we found out Gerry'd slipped it to

Heather, and that same passage scared me to the core. It reinforced in my mind that I didn't want to compromise on anything where we were concerned. You and I exist to make each other happy, so that's what we're bloody well going to do.'

'Amen!' his dream girl laughed, struggling out of her lover's arms and flexing her feet and ankles until her lips could reach his. 'That should be in our wedding vows: "Do you, Lynn Dyson, promise to bloody well make Jeff Diamond happy?"'

The songwriter chuckled. 'So do you?'

'I do,' she giggled, kissing him again. 'No, sorry. I bloody well do.'

'And I, Jeff Diamond, promise to bloody well make Lynn Dyson the happiest woman in the world, in this lifetime and in all future lifetimes to come.'

With a potent fervour heating the air, Jeff's expression changed to a worried frown. 'Fuck! I should try and get hold of my bloody sister,' he sighed. 'She needs to know, I s'pose. And Gerry too. Celia'll go crazy.'

Lynn did feel pity this time. For her, the prospect of imparting her news to anyone prepared to listen was a chance to share her supreme excitement. Yet for the man whose family was fractured and who was only recently coming to grips with friendships that delved deeper than swapping football scores or bodily fluids, she realised how stressful this immediate aftermath must be, everyone absorbing their news while tainted by each individual context.

'I'm sure Madalena'll be happy for you,' she offered, knowing how strained relations were between the millionnaire musician and his thoughtless and unschooled sister. 'I'd really like it if she'd agree to be a bridesmaid, along with Michelle. But that's up to you.'

A fresh batch of mixed emotions surged through the western suburbs native, guilt instantly bubbling to to the surface. His beautiful best friend reached her arms around him again, and he hugged her tentatively.

'Jesus,' he murmured. 'Lena a bridesmaid? That's some offer. You don't even know her. She's feral, angel. I need time to think it, but on the face of it, it would be amazing. I just don't know if she'd do it. She has no clue what our life's like, and there's a good chance she'll say or do something totally inappropriate. I'd hate her to ruin anything for you or your folks.'

Wiping his eyes, the tall, dark man cleared the table, pouring the remaining wine into their glasses. He gulped down a glass of water and refilled it from the tap. His flatmate continued, seeing the old Jeff struggle with an idea that the new Jeff liked a great deal.

'OK. Give it some thought and let me know. I likely won't get to meet her beforehand at this rate. That is if New Year's Day works out.'

'New Year's Day will work out,' her boyfriend assured her. 'I have every confidence in your organisational ability. Just tell me what I need to do when and where, and I'll be ready, armed and waiting.'

'Thanks. Armed? What with? I hope that's not necessary,' she laughed. 'What about music?'

Slotting himself back into the corner at the small kitchen table, Jeff leaned his chair back against the wall, crossing his legs and settling down with this new and much more interesting topic.

'Hmm... Not "Donna Jade", methinks,' he chuckled, referring to one of his biggest hits which had been the subject of legal action from his former girlfriend, a Sydney television reporter.

'No. Probably not,' the pretty singer aired her indignance.

Her headstrong and playful stallion flashed a wide grin. 'I'm sorry. That was mean. But funny though!'

Lynn had already moved on however, familiar with his trademarked mix of compassion and contrition laced through the dead-pan humour. She reserved judgment on whether he had been entirely truthful in insisting that she had inspired this particular song her despite bearing his old flame's name. There was no point in worrying about it these days. He hadn't proposed to Donna Watts, and she had lost count of the number of songs written solely for her.

'I've had an idea for a wedding song,' the blonde musician pushed on, 'based on a theme from a Saint Saëns' symphony. I've worked on it at college for the last couple of days and I've thought of a lyric I think you'll love. I'll play it for you later on. See what you think.'

Jeff nodded, in no doubt that the occasion was in good hands. 'Sounds great. I'm sure I'll love it. I've only got about twelve songs so far,' he replied with a smug wink.

His collaborator-in-chief giggled. 'Only twelve? Doesn't surprise me. We could release a corny wedding album and make *squillions* for Childlight.'

The charity the couple had established in Australia for victims of all types of child abuse was about to become a reality in the UK too, staffed by equally committed psychologists and backed by other well-known celebrities who had been eager to jump on the bandwagon. The first few promotional events were due for their official launches the following week, giving the two stars an exciting sense of achievement as their tour of duty in the northern hemisphere entered its final quarter.

Lynn had been a student in California when the burgeoning philanthropist had announced the original Childlight concept as a spin-off of The Fellowship, which had in turn been all but adopted by its former and now extremely rich client. The young woman sometimes felt guilty that she had taken over the management of the not-for-profit organisation since her return. This loss of control was of no consequence to the new Jeff however, who saw his dream girl's involvement only as another sign that their life together was melding nicely.

'That's actually not such a bad idea,' he responded. 'Even a single or an "EP" would be enough. Let's do it. For Christmas too, along with some sort of fundraising appeal.'

The lithe frame on the chair opposite suddenly sprang to its feet again. 'Come on! Go into the lounge, and I'll bring coffee. I have to sing you my response to your proposal.'

The enthusiastic young woman took her boyfriend's hands and dragged him out of his comfortable corner. Once in the living room, he stationed himself by the rear window, standing with his wine glass and a cigarette, full of loving anticipation. The blonde pioneer thought how bohemian he appeared, dressed in his customary black; long hair shining under the eight candle-shaped bulbs in the room's ornate light fitting, with three or four days' growth on his chin and so devastatingly self-assured that she scarcely remembered the old Jeff these days.

'You look amazing,' she smiled, beginning to play the introduction of her special, celebratory offering.

Lynn asked him to close his eyes and picture themselves at Coldwater Creek, the idyllic location at her family's homestead in central Victoria. This her audience had no trouble in doing, for it was a popular destination for many of his best loved fantasies. The song told him how happy its singer was to be fulfilling their destiny, and no matter what life may throw their way in the future, she would remain at his side.

'That's awesome,' her handsome intellectual said, coming to sit beside her at the piano while she cycled through the chorus for a third time. '*Gracias, mi amor*. It's perfect. Sing it again, please. You really know how to feel me, don't you? Can we put this on our corny but lucrative wedding album too?'

***

Kierney stole into the office at the rambling house near the northern bank of the Yarra River, having returned from a busy day at Melbourne University to find Frank Sinatra's voice broadcasting at full blast throughout the ground floor. Sure enough, the culprit and his trusty, four-legged sidekick were sitting on the verandah outside the French windows, sharing a pizza but not the accompanying cigarette.

The seventeen-year-old's heart skipped a beat. Her father must have started writing about the wedding, and she couldn't wait to read the next few chapters of the maturing autobiography. The plan for Gerry's own nuptials were now in full swing, with only three weeks to go until the Byron Bay *extravaganza* that Jeff had been coordinating.

It had taken almost twenty-one years for the two friends' roles to reverse, and in another bitter twist of irony, both men had been decidedly single at the other's marriage. The Ole Blue Eyes' classic ballad which had held such significance for her parents at the tail end of nineteen-seventy-five was now set on repeat in the CD player, presumably being mapped into some ceremonial choreography for December nineteen-ninety-six's return match.

Undetected, the willowy teenager sat at the computer and scrolled through the open document, eager to find out how far the author had progressed since her last update. There on the desk next to three empty coffee mugs and a full ashtray was the famous lyric, marked up with various hieroglyphics which must have translated into some magical code for Gerry and Fiona's Big Day.

'For once in my life, I have someone who needs me,' Kierney sang along quietly when the track looped again. 'Someone I've needed so long. For once unafraid, I can go where life leads me, and somehow I know I'll be strong.'

How very appropriate these words had been for her beloved papá, marrying the woman who had saved him from the horrors of his childhood. As the verse continued, the youngster recognised each uncanny line in the undulations of action brought back to life through her parents' romantic memoirs. Going from boyfriend and girlfriend to husband and wife, Jeff Diamond could now touch what his heart used to dream of, and yet nothing in Act Two so far suggested to its potential readership that their relationship was new.

'For once in my life, I won't let sorrow hurt me. Not like it's hurt me before,' the youngest Diamond sang on. 'For once, I have something I know won't desert me...'

Indie had picked up on the new voice in the house, so her cover was blown. Jeff looked round to see what had caught the dog's attention, springing to his feet when he saw it was his gorgeous daughter. The pair hugged, completing the line in unison and staring into each others' big, brown eyes. Lynn had deserted them, as it turned out, and the grief-stricken father was shortly to do the same to the two newest precious stones depicted in his black signet ring.

'For once, I can say, "This is mine. You can't take it,"' they both yelled into imaginary microphones, accompanied by tuneless barking loudly rendered by their canine backing singer. 'As long as I know I have love, I can make it. For once in my life, I've got someone who needs me.'

The dark-haired *duo* danced together until the music faded, Kierney's cheek pressed into her dad's T-shirt by a large, loving hand. They broke apart, and the widower exited the study to switch off the stereo or at least change what was playing and turn the volume down to a level less likely to crumble the foundations.

'I'm sorry, *pequeñita*,' the guilty man said, walking back in to see his younger child seated in his chair again. 'Are you OK?'

'Yes, Papá,' she answered. 'It's fine. I know how you feel. Have you written anything about the wedding preparations yet? Or were you playing that song just because of Gerry's?'

'Mostly Gerry's, but I'm gearing up to it,' the billionnaire affirmed. 'It's going to be easy writing. Really easy. But it'll be time-consuming too because I've got to sequence it all properly. There was a lot going on at that time, and much of it was done by your mamá without my knowledge or involvement. Fortunately, her records are flawless, as you'd expect.'

Kierney sighed. 'Hmm… What about her diary? Is there much in there that surprised you this time?'

'Yeah. Always.'

'Nice surprises?'

'Yeah. Always,' the grieving husband chuckled, resting his hands on his daughter's shoulders and leaning down to kiss the top of her head. 'Not so much in what she wrote about, but more in the words she chose and how much more deeply she contemplated things than I realised. I guess I always assumed she was telling me everything, but there was so much that she didn't directly express that I'm only finding out now.'

The teenager twisted round and gazed up into the forty-four-year-old's eyes. 'Oh. Does that make you sad?'

'No, baby. Not at all. It makes me feel better, like she saved something for me. To help me out even after she's gone. Just like the song says. How was uni' today?'

'Awesome!' his daughter answered, spinning around in the chair and jumping to her feet. 'We're ready to send out the proposal to government agencies in nine countries. We're really rapt with it. All the numbers stack up, and the benefits section you helped me with was approved without any amendments, so thanks for that!'

'Awesome!' Jeff mimicked the beaming teenager. 'That's fantastic, *pequeñita*. You make sure your name's on the cover. You've put a lot of energy into that thing, and I'm proud of you. And so's Mamá, I'm sure. So, so proud of you.'

'Thanks heaps. I'm proud of me too, and I don't feel like the baby of the team anymore. At least, they never act like they're carrying me. Do you want some dinner?'

The matching pair of Diamonds made their way through the hallway and into the kitchen, swapping their news. Kierney was genuinely happy in her circumstance these days, nine months after Lynn's death, and the widower acknowledged with great relief that she had endured her own grief cycle with few, if any, long-term regrets. He knew she and Ryan still missed their mother, yet they now spoke of her in the past tense quite naturally.

'D'you want me to stop congratulating you on Mamá's behalf?' he checked, being directed to take a seat while the youngster chopped some vegetables.

'I don't need you to, if that's what you mean,' she replied.

'OK. Yeah. I s'pose that is what I mean. I'll stop then.'

His gipsy girl turned towards him, sharp knife in hand, and he backed closer to the wall in jest. She burst out laughing, apologising profusely and issuing a request for her father to transfer the rest of yesterday's steak pie from the counter into the oven. He obliged, skirting around the busy kitchen-hand, muttering under his breath about the lack of safety measures observed in his own home.

'Shut up,' Kierney sighed. 'It's not your own home. You don't own anything anymore, as you keep reminding us. Anyway... I don't want you to stop sending me messages from Mamá if it makes you happier. I don't need them, but I like receiving them. I know she'd be proud of me, and I hope she can see what I'm up to every day.'

Jeff ran his fingers across the seventeen-year-old's shoulders. 'That's a great response. As confusing as all hell, but I think I get it. Keep doing what I'm doing, but you've got your own thing going on with her. Red or white tonight, Ms Diamond?'

'White, please,' the independent student requested. 'Do you remember your official engagement speech? The one in the restaurant? Did you write it down?'

'Yep, cubed. Word for word.'

'That's great. I'm so looking forward to reading that passage as soon as it's ready.'

The widower reached into the pantry and pulled out an aged Shiraz which had been left behind by one of Gerry's business colleagues after a raucous buck's party planning session. Popping the cork and setting it on the kitchen table, he crossed the floor to extract a bottle of Sauvignon Blanc from the refrigerator. He slotted the white wine into a cooler and set it down alongside its red companion, distracted by his mobile telephone buzzing in his pocket.

'Sure thing. It won't take me long to get through that part,' he told her, chuckling at the screen that looked so tiny in his hand. 'Your brother sent me an epigram. *Assez drôle*, I have to admit. Sorry, Kizzo. The restaurant speech... I rewrote it the other day, in preparation for adding a whole slew of new rising action around the lead-up to our wedding. I recited it to your mamá again many times, over the years; usually when I'd had too much to drink.'

Kierney chuckled, tutting in comic disapproval. 'Or when you were stoned? What's an epigram?'

'Dry humour,' her father answered, taking two loaded plates from her outstretched hands and placing them on the table. 'He's practising for some stand-up comedy night he's entered. What are you trying to say? I didn't have to be off my face to come on all romantic, I'll have you know...'

The pair sat down to eat. Jeff picked up his glass and toasted his flourishing housemate, tears brimming in his eyes when his brain conjured up a smiling image of the pretty flatmate to whom he had proposed across a polished black grand piano in Scotland.

'To romance and sex. May you and your clown of a brother have a great deal of both, *pequeñita.*'

'Thank you,' the young woman smiled. 'To romance and sex for us all. You write about it, so I can read about it, until you and Mamá can go at it again.'

'Go at it?' the widower screwed up his face. 'That doesn't sound particularly romantic. But alright, if you insist. We'll send you a picture.'

It was the teenager's turn to scowl. 'Ew! No, thanks. Nor a tape. So when you say that humour is a defence mechanism, is this what you mean? It's like you're forcing yourself to be funny to counteract the sadness.'

'Yeah,' Jeff shrugged. 'I am, I suppose. It distorts the pain, anxiety, fear so far that it puts a temporary distance between whatever the issue is and me. It allows me to take a break from myself. It's the best I can do, baby, and it makes people relax around me. Plus maybe, it can remind us not to take life or ourselves too seriously.'

Kierney nodded, swallowing a mouthful of the delicious pie and taking a sip of wine to chase its heat down. 'That all makes perfect sense. I hadn't thought about it from that angle. I didn't think you'd do it to belittle the situation.'

'No way. Keep eating. *Pero digame...* How do you know about me quoting my own speech back to Mamá when I was stoned? That wasn't too long ago. Just after her fortieth, I think. I'd come back here after one of those cheesy Crown gigs, having shared some sweet *ganja* with the band.'

'She told me,' the young woman giggled. 'The next morning. She said you were gorgeously incoherent for about twenty minutes, then you recited her proposal word-perfectly before descending into gobbledygook again.'

'Mmm... I remember that night only too well. She surprised me. I expected to come home to an empty apartment.'

'I know. She told me that too. I really want to read about that. I've got goosebumps just thinking about how fantastic it must've been to find her in bed waiting for you.'

'You bet it was! She was on fire. And I was on fire too, in a mellow, stupefied sort of way. I'm pretty sure she knew those lines by heart too.'

'She must have,' the eternal couple's daughter agreed. 'She wrote the song for "King of Hearts" from it.'

Jeff dropped his knife and fork onto his plate, suddenly breathless. Kierney gasped at the clatter of metal against china, her eyes catching him clutch his left pectoral muscle and rub it hard. After a few moments of stunned silence, both returned to their meals.

'I can be pretty bloody predictable,' the handsome former rock star smirked. 'But you knew that already.'

'Are you talking to me?' the seventeen-year-old wondered aloud.

'Yep. To both of you. Sorry to scare you.'

'That's OK. Well, whichever memories you decide to recount, I can't wait to read those next few chapters. I want the full-length feature version, Papá, including all the bits that end up on the cutting room floor.'

'*Bien sûr, pequeñita.* Blow by blow?' the playful writer enquired, exhaling again as another fitting memorandum stung his chest.

Kierney shook her head. 'Please! That's Jetto's birth you're talking about now. I want kiss by kiss.'

'Slurp by slurp. Tongue on tongue. Orgasm b…'

'Enough! We're eating. There you go again with your defence mechanism. Cut it out.'

Jeff winked, doing as he was told. 'Right you are, Your Worship. Every last kiss shall be thine, I promise.'

It's Official

Jeff awoke first the following morning. It was six-thirty, or one-thirty in the afternoon on Australia's east coast. He lay watching the gorgeous blonde in serene slumber for ten minutes or so before getting up to make some coffee. Deep in contemplation, he began to rehearse the telephone conversation he was shortly to share with his sister. Madalena ought to remember he was living in the UK, but there was no guarantee. She had shown scant interest when he informed her of their move. London might as well be another planet to someone whose universe had a radius of no more than thirty kilometres.

And Gerry required notifying too. The big-mouthed musician was resigned to copping an ample serve of grief from his manager, having moralised at him a little too much and a little too often. He expected the accountant would be spoiling for retribution, therefore prepared to take any feedback about his news on the chin.

Lynn stretched and opened her eyes as soon as the domesticated millionnaire returned to the bedroom with two full mugs. The morning's chill had penetrated her consciousness while he had been gone, as demonstrated by the quilt tucked around her neck. He chuckled as her fingers hastily tried to counteract the strangling effect of her twisting body.

'Good morning, *chica bella*,' he said, sitting down on the side of the bed and leaning over to kiss her chilled forehead. 'Can you breathe in there? You were singing our new song.'

'Was I?'

'No. But it's a nice thought.'

'Argh! I fall for it every time,' the young woman giggled, frustrated at her enduring gullibility in the face of her flatmate's quirky sense of humour. 'You'd think after all this time, I'd have learned to be suspicious of everything you said to me first thing in the morning.'

Jeff gave her a flash of his mischievous eyes. 'Yep. You'd think so. I can't help it if you're dumb in the mornings.'

His *fiancée*'s lightning strike of a fist hit him in the chest, nearly sending his mug of coffee flying. 'Bastard!'

'I'm going to try to ring Lena,' the twenty-three-year-old announced, snaffling his indignant bedfellow's hand on the rebound and bringing it to his lips to curb her cheerful fury. 'D'you want to talk to her?'

Calming down at the uncertain tone in his voice, the sportswoman nodded, unsure of what she might say. Madalena was soon to be her sister-in-law, even though the pair knew next to nothing of each other. Her mind assembled a collage depicting a woman about as unlike herself as possible and with whom the only thing she would have in common was the handsome man who had re-joined her under the covers. Looking to her left to respond more civilly, she noticed that his demeanour had predictably reverted to the dazzled rabbit of old.

'Of course. Come on,' she dealt him an encouraging smile. 'It won't be that bad. Do you think you'll get hold of her?'

'Sure. Can but try,' he answered, picking up the telephone and leafing through his address book. 'I'll try my grandmother's if I can't find her on the number she gave me last time. Be prepared for some abusive language. I'll do my best to keep it to a minimum or use words you won't know. Wish me luck.'

Accepting a cute peck on the cheek, Jeff dialled his sister's last-known place of residence. After a few clicks and whirrs, a string of beeps from the international exchange sounded. A female voice answered, but it wasn't one he recognised.

'Hullo?'

'Hi. Is Madalena around, please?' his deep, smoky Pied Piper timbre caused Lynn to swoon, so practised was he at hiding every *iota* of anxiety.

'Yeah. Hang on,' shouted the woman on the other end. 'It's for you!'

The caller's eardrum felt the vibration of the receiver hitting a hard surface, raising his eyebrows and nodding expectantly to the blonde beauty. Stealing another kiss for moral fortitude, he broke away when he heard someone arriving.

'Who is it?'

'*Olá, Lena. Es Jeff. ¿Qué tal?*'

'Jeff? Aren't you in London?' Madalena shrieked. 'Jeff-*chico*?'

'Yes, of course Jeff-*chico*. I'm in London right now, *en cama*,' her brother confirmed. '*Es a las siete de la mañana aquí. ¿Como vas?*'

'Good,' Lynn could just about make out the other woman's words. 'Why ya ringin'?'

Her patient boyfriend sighed on encountering the usual resistive attitude, alarmed by its familiarity after so long. He could feel the hairs on the back of his neck rising, wondering whether Gravity the troll might be hiding nearby. His dogged rival wouldn't be far away since he could already taste the fear mounting as his jaw began to seize up.

'*Porque tengo algunas noticias para tí,*' he answered, his voice wavering.

Lynn slid her hand into his, fairly certain she had understood so far: he had some news. That was a distinct understatement, evidently required under the circumstances. She cuddled into his tense body, and he swapped the receiver to his left ear to put his arm around his favourite confidence booster while they waited for a response.

'What?' Madalena seemed interested at least. 'You comin' to Sydney?'

'No,' Jeff replied. 'Christmas maybe. Lynn and I are getting married, Lena. *Sólo quise decirle antes de lo ves en la televisión.*'

A coarse scream from the twenty-five-year-old shot through the airwaves and echoed around the snug London bedroom, causing her brother to extend his right arm comically. The western suburbs accent with which he had grown up was now repellant, in stark contrast to the feisty but refined morning greeting he had received from his sophisticated lover.

'*Gracias,*' the supplanted Sydneysider replied. 'Is that a good scream or a bad scream?'

'*¡No te creo!*' his sister screeched. 'Getting married? I can't believe it. *Es bueno, chico. Muy bueno. Soy jelosa.* Lynn Dyson gonna be related to me? I can't bloody believe it!'

Jeff laughed. Madalena had combined the English word "jealous" with the Spanish *"celosa"*, and the result was childlike, evoking yet more painful memories. Australia's darling had heard her last comment plainly enough and read her boyfriend's mind as he was thrown back in time.

'*Sí. Está aquí ahora.* D'you wanna talk to her?'

'*¡Aí!* I dunno what to say,' the older woman objected.

'Neither does she,' her brother responded, becoming calmer and even somewhat supportive, handing the telephone receiver to his *fiancée* and blowing her a kiss. 'Here she is...'

'Hi, Madalena. How are you?'

'Hi. I can't believe it,' the harsh accent repeated.

'It's nice to talk to you and I'm looking forward to meeting you soon,' the gracious diplomat continued, ridiculously discomfited considering how accustomed she was to making small-talk with people of far higher standing.

'Yeah. Me too,' came the reply. 'Why d'ya wanna marry me baby brother?'

Lynn laughed. 'Why? Because he's gorgeous and good in bed!'

'*¡Aí!*' Madalena cried out again.

Jeff was stoked to hear his girlfriend's ringing endorsement, pitched at the right level for its intended audience as usual. She paused before carrying on, leaning back onto his chest in a deliberate attempt to line up their tattoos. She knew such an intimate act would cheer her stressed-out lover.

'I've got a question to ask, if I can…'

'Yeah? What question?'

'I'd love it if you'd be a bridesmaid at our wedding. Please?' Lynn asked. 'We'd like to get married on New Year's Day. It'd be great if you could come to Melbourne and play a part in the ceremony.'

'*¡Aí!* What?' the telephone spluttered for the third time. 'Bridesmaid? Shit, yeah! Are you sure? You don't even know me.'

'That's what *I* said!' her brother yelled from above Lynn's head, loud enough for the older woman to hear properly.

'Arsehole!' Madalena was as articulate as ever.

The songwriter sniffed and reclaimed the receiver. 'Thanks a lot! You don't have to decide now. There's a shitload to organise, so we'll let you know what's going on as soon as we know ourselves. *¿Lena, dirás a nuestros abuelos? No quiero dirigirme a ellos.*'

'OK, *chico*,' his sister agreed to relay the news to their family. 'They won't come though, *ya sabes.*'

'Yeah. I don't give a fuck,' the young man told her, kissing the back of Lynn's neck and feeling her snuggle closer. '*No son importantes para mí. Pero por verdád, me gustaría tu estar allí.*'

'*Gracias.* Me too!' Madalena responded, sounding genuinely keen.

Jeff asked one last question. '*¿Has tenido noticias del papá, Lena?*'

'*No. Nada, nada.* Are you gonna tell him?'

'Don't know,' her brother replied, the thought only having occurred to him these last few seconds. '*Veremos.* Anyway… *¿Qué sigue con tigo?*'

He heard a man's voice in the background and sensed some distraction on the other end of the telephone. A customer, he assumed. Had he come to pay Madalena a call, or was he her flatmate's client?

'*Oh, nada.* Nothing much. Same, same.'

'D'you need anything?'

'A million dollars,' the gold-digger wasn't joking. 'Send me a million dollars.'

Lynn picked up this message loud and clear, twisting round and giving her man a sympathetic smile. *What would you do with a million dollars, Lena?* She could almost hear the words running in circles around his head, as he had described on several occasions.

'Some things never change,' the musician let out a caustic laugh, seeing no point in hiding his frustration. 'I'll send you something. We'll talk more when you come to Melbourne. OK?'

'Yeah. Good. Whatever. New Year's Day, right? Send me a ticket? Fuck, *chico*! I still can't believe it,' Madalena rattled on. 'First I get a rock star for a brother, and now he's getting married to Lynn Dyson. It's unreal!'

Jeff laughed. 'It is unreal alright! *Hasta luego, Lena.* Be good.'

'You too,' his sister replied. 'Nice to talk to Lynn too. Say 'bye from me. You still in bed?'

'*Sí,*' the proud man confessed. 'She's butt-naked. Life's good, eh? *Adiós.*'

'Disgusting! *Adiós, chico.*'

The line disconnected, and the young man breathed a sigh of relief. His girlfriend motioned to him to cuddle into her under the covers, which was just what he needed. The heating system had taken the worst of the chill from the air, but being cocooned in the dark with the girl of his dreams soon dispelled the gloomy remnants of the siblings' strained discourse.

'Jesus Christ,' he groaned, feeling the tip of his penis pressing into soft skin. 'It's too taxing on the nerves, getting married. Maybe we should call it off.'

'Alright,' Lynn acquiesced with a carefree flick of her hair. 'If you want.'

The couple made love, exchanging light-hearted banter while the clock's hands ticked ever on. It seemed as though their senses learned to give and take a little more every time they succumbed to mutual carnal satisfaction. Despite now knowing each other so well, raw energy ebbed and flowed on an autonomous path, leaving them breathless and elated at their final climax.

Over bowls of cereal, Jeff's gorgeous and resolute blonde conscience reminded him of his plan to ring Gerry too. She had emerged from the bedroom in full make-up and with her hair blown dry in a sleek, straight style which suited her increasing sophistication, skin-tight pants and a billowing cotton blouse finishing off a most attractive package.

'Christ almighty,' the rock star grumbled, craning his neck to plant an approving kiss on her cheek. 'Do I have to? I've got no energy for all these serious conversations.'

Picking up her bowl, Lynn wasn't about to tolerate such a lame excuse and waved her spoon in the air menacingly. 'You have so! You are the patron saint of serious conversations. Which language are you going to talk to Gerry in?'

'Expletives, I expect,' her boyfriend replied, shrugging in appreciation of her gentle helping hand. 'You're right. I need to do it. Better get it over with. Can't we just do this without anyone knowing?'

Breakfast over, Jeff sat down in the living room and dialled his manager's number, having been left alone with his duty while his sexy taskmaster busied herself with her own preparation. The executive's personal assistant answered the telephone brightly.

'Blake and Partners. Gerry Blake's office.'

'Paula, hi. It's Jeff Diamond,' the client announced, trying his best to sound enthusiastic.

Madalena's answer to his ill-timed question about their father had knocked him for six, and it annoyed him to think he was still so susceptible to distraction. The past was never that far buried after all. These first few days of their engagement should be joyous, and the last thing he wanted was to spoil Lynn's happiness by dragging them back into those dark times.

'Is the great man around, please?'

'Hello, Jeff! How are you? I'll put you through.'

Two clicks later, the ebullient accountant's voice sounded remarkably like Bart Dyson's except cruder. 'Diamond? What the fuck does he want? Oh, sorry, mate. Is that you?'

His old friend smiled. 'Good to talk to you too, Gez. How are things?'

'Good, good,' his manager replied. 'You chasing money?'

'No! Bloody cheek! Although I did get the August summary in the post the other day. Forty-three songs last month. That's gotta be worth something.'

'Fuck, yes! We deposited close to five-hundred grand yesterday. You might like to tell me where you want it to go, before I truck it off to my Swiss bank account, never to be seen again. I hear Hawaii's nice this time of year.'

Chuckling, the successful songwriter considered his options for a second or two. For the briefest of moments, he wondered if he ought to take any of these idle threats of embezzlement seriously, before chastising himself for such merciless thoughts. Gerry had many dubious leisure habits, but when it came to loyalty and staying above the law, there was none straighter.

'Half in Childlight UK, for the launch,' he decided on the spur of the moment, 'and the other half in a new account, please, mate.'

'New account for what?' the older man asked. 'What have you gone and started now? For Christ's sake, I can't keep up with you guys. Did you know Steph's leaving?'

'No. Why?'

The distant employer couldn't remember if he had ever known who Steph was in the first place, or what she looked like, but recalled he had spoken to her on the telephone several times. One of the charitable trust tax specialists, he surmised.

'She's pregnant,' the frustrated boss explained. 'Damned babies. They screw up everything. I was hoping for great things from said Stephanie.'

'Are you referring to Jenna?' Jeff interrupted, smiling ruefully. 'How are she and Heather?'

'Yeah. Good, thanks. All well. We've actually been getting on pretty well lately. The nanny idea was a good one.'

The multi-millionnaire was thrown for a moment. 'You got her a male nanny? You weren't supposed to take me that seriously!'

Gerry scoffed. 'No dice, man. You should know me better than that. There aren't any. I checked all over Melbourne. Straight blokes just don't do that kind of work, and I'm not sure I want to subject my bloodline to any bi-sexual fuckery. Surprise, surprise, really, eh? We ended up finding someone she really gets on with, and now they're inseparable. Lives in and everything. Enjoys a glass of white wine of an evening. Bitch about me behind my back... Bloody perfect, mate. It's taken the pressure off, so I do owe you a drink or two for the original idea.'

'Cheers,' the musician replied. 'You're welcome. Glad to be of service.'

Nonplussed, the businessman brought the focus back to the purpose of his client's call. 'So what's up in ye olde London towne, me old fellow?'

His longtime friend cleared his throat. He had never envisioned this situation occurring between the pair of fun-loving men-about-town. For some strange reason, it felt a hundred times more awkward telling Gerry than it had been asking Lynn in the first place.

'Mate, I've got news.'

'You're getting married,' the accountant beat him to it, knocking the wind out of Jeff's sails in one sardonic blast of indomitability.

'Yes, we are! How the hell did you know?' Jeff shouted down the telephone.

'Well... This is all very Daylesford, you know, but I dreamed it. Exactly this cryptic, circular conversation. A few days ago.'

'Fucking hell!' the celebrity cursed.

Hearing her partner's raised voice, Lynn rushed into the lounge to see what the fuss was about. He cupped the mouthpiece with his hand.

'Gerry dreamed we were getting hitched.'

Her jaw dropped. 'Really? Did he will it to happen?'

Smiling at her mock consternation, the songwriter lifted the receiver back up to his mouth. 'Lynn says, "Did you will it to happen?" Does this mean it wasn't my idea after all? For fuck's sake!'

His girlfriend giggled and left the room again, casting the well-known theme song for "The Twilight Zone" on the airwaves as she departed.

'Who knows, mate?' Gerry responded. 'You're the one who believes in that kind of mumbo-jumbo. So tell me all about it. Was it all gushy and hearts and flowers? No. On second thoughts, don't tell me about it. I'll speak to the lady myself, if I may. Did she say yes? I should ask first, just in case.'

Jeff couldn't help but laugh. 'D'you think we'd be having this discussion if she didn't? I should let her tell you. You'll enjoy her version better than mine.'

'Good point,' his manager admitted. 'Jolly good show! Is she still there? Just humour me and say she's got no clothes on.'

'Yep. I never let her put clothes on anymore. House rule. Although your salacious fantasies are banned from now on. Hang on, mate. I'll get her. She's in the other room.'

Leaving the receiver on the cushion, the happy man stood up and went to the doorway, calling his beautiful best friend back. 'Hey, angel. Gerry wants to talk to you.'

Gliding gracefully along the short corridor to re-join him, Lynn took the receiver from her insatiable lover as he pulled her down onto his lap on the couch.

'Hi, Gerry! How are you? You've been dreaming, so Jeff tells me.'

'My maladjusted darling, what have you done?' the pompous clown asked. 'Have you taken leave of your senses?'

'No.' Giggling, the twenty-year-old cringed at this melodramatic phrase. 'I'm perfectly lucid. Tom's a wonderful man.'

A hearty guffaw bubbled out of the telephone's earpiece, and Jeff threw her a dejected look. She apologised by connecting her open mouth with his and grinding her backside hard into his aroused lap. His tongue caressed hers, growling in pleasure. Breaking away, she stroked his unshaven chin.

'Excellent work,' the man in Melbourne continued, blind to the adults-only action taking place on the London sofa. 'So was he very romantic? Did he get down on one knee?'

'No. It was at a piano in Edinburgh, in fact,' Lynn clarified with a casual air, by now astride her lover and having fished his penis out of his shorts, soon stroking him in a regular motion. 'But yes. It was very, very romantic.'

'*Auch, aye, the noo*,' Gerry attempted his best Scots accent. 'Was there haggis involved?'

The woman laughed. 'Yuck! No, thankfully. But there had been a substantial amount of whisky consumed the night before, I suspect, judging by the bloodshot eyes and the scratchy voice.'

'Aha! So you got him at a weak moment,' her boyfriend's best mate deduced in triumph. 'Good on ya, Miss D. Congratulations indeed! Did he give you a big rock?'

'Not yet. That's today's job,' she informed the Irishman, whipping off the modest blouse she had donned for their shopping spree and whispering a dirty comment about other big rocks her hands had tracked down.

'No wonder he asked for money to be transferred to a new account,' Gerry chuckled. 'Get the biggest one you can find. He can afford it. Go the whole hog.'

Lynn chuckled, playfully resisting her lover's thumb as it tried to rub her clitoris through the fabric of her knickers. 'I might just do that. Here's Jeff back. Talk soon, Gerry. Say hi to Heather and Jenna for me.'

Pouting, the dark-haired Adonis took the telephone back, breathing heavily, and his gorgeous siren wrestled free of his tight, desirous grip. Collecting himself, he focussed back on his good-natured manager.

'So, mate... Would you do me the honour of being my best man?'

The accountant glowed inside. Best man? The thought hadn't even crossed his mind, but of course he was the perfect choice for the job. His dream hadn't uncovered this part of the story.

'I would,' he replied without hesitation. 'My honour entirely, sir. Fantastic! Cheers, mate. It's a pity you're so far away. I can't even get you to buy me a beer.'

'Take it out of my new account,' Jeff joked, playing aimlessly with his abandoned genitals. 'So, yes. Can you set us up a wedding account, please? It looks like New Year's Day's the favourite. Don't know where yet though.'

'That part's out of your control, I'm guessing,' quipped the freewheeler who knew nothing about weddings.

His famous friend sniffed. 'Yeah. Totally. But it's much better that way. I'm just going to do what I'm told.'

'Not a bad idea, mate. New Year's Day, did you say? As in under four months away?'

'Yep,' Jeff confirmed. 'Soon, isn't it? Nothing's arranged yet, but that's what we're aiming for.'

'Is she...'

'No, she's not,' an angry voice cut Gerry's impertinent question short.

The former Sydney Grammar head boy whistled. 'Ooh! Sensitive, aren't we? Just asking, for Christ's sake!'

The songwriter couldn't shake his annoyance that his proposal had been pre-empted. He didn't like the idea of the supercilious executive somehow controlling his actions, even though he knew better than to read anything into it. Just because most of their mates had been obliged to get married, it didn't mean that Gerry should automatically jump to this conclusion. He was marrying the girl with whom he had always maintained he would end up and had suffered the Blakes' sustained mirth for all those years as a result.

Occasionally people get married because they love each other, you bastard... 'Sorry, mate,' he responded, regretting his impulsive reaction.

'So how are you going to split the cost of this shindig between you and the new pa-in-law?' the thick-skinned businessman enquired as if neither offence had ever been committed.

'Jeez, mate! No idea,' his old friend answered. 'We haven't got to that yet. I spoke to him yesterday. That was weird.'

With genuine admiration, Gerry laughed. 'Did you ask him for her hand?'

'No. I announced it as a done deal. He was shocked at first, but warmed up after a while. And I rang my sister earlier today too. Lynn wants her to be a bridesmaid, which is gutsy and more than a little misguided. You'll have to decide who you're going to favour, Michelle England or her. You met Michelle, didn't you?'

'Redhead? Studying law?'

'Yep.'

'I know her, yes. Who has the most honour?'

'Ha!' Jeff laughed at the eternal party boy. 'Who d'ya think?'

From the couch in Maida Vale, the younger man heard a buzzer sound from the prestige Collins Street corner office which he could picture clearly from the other side of the world. The busy company director's next appointment must have arrived.

'Gotta go, mate. Might work on a threesome. Anyway, many congratulations again. Sincerely, mate. I never doubted you. You make a handsome pair. And yet more marketable, I don't doubt.'

'Cheers, Gerry,' the songwriter sighed with a wry smile. 'Talk soon. *Adiós.*'

His list of calls checked off, Jeff slapped his knees and pushed himself to a standing position. He found Lynn lying on the bed, surrounded with books and working on an assignment. She smiled sympathetically when he walked through the door to find her, and he slumped down onto the mattress, head in his hands.

'I'm fucking knackered! Where'd you go? My big rocks are missing you. I hope that sort of disgustingly distracting behaviour's not going to stop once you're my wife...'

'Of course not! I'll make it my business to disrupt as many important 'phone calls as I can. Are you OK? You look like you've run out of petrol. Things'll settle down soon.'

The young beauty swung her legs off the bed and paced around to her haggard partner's side. Her hands bent on restoring his energy level, she encouraged him to stand up and hugged him tight. 'Celia'll be on the 'phone soon, I expect. Shall we go out before she rings?'

Jeff smiled and gave his saviour a heartfelt kiss. 'Jesus! You're right. Fantastic idea. But let me finish what you started now, please, wench. Then I'll fetch my cheque book, and this Diamond's going to buy you some more.'

***

On the way into the West End, keeping a safe distance from prying weekend shoppers' eyes, Lynn began to explain the design she had conceived for Jeff's black ring. Joggling along in an almost empty southbound Bakerloo line train, the handsome rock star had been hypnotised by the tale of this custom-made piece of jewellery's gradual evolution.

'That's such an original idea,' he said, dealing her a surreptitious kiss. 'So individual to us. This is supposed to be your shopping outing, but. Not mine.'

'What's mine is yours,' his girlfriend joked at the wordsmith's uncharacteristic use of the popular Sydney emphatic conjunction. 'Isn't that how it goes?'

Trumped again, the twenty-three-year-old raised his eyebrows. 'Yeah. Of course,' he acceded. 'Sure. Let's do it. Thanks, angel. It's an amazing idea. I've never worn a ring before, so I don't know how long it'll take me to get used to it.'

'It's not for a wedding ring,' Lynn insisted. 'It's separate. It's like the original signature tattoo. Just from me to you.'

The intellectual put on an air of confusion. 'OK. So I'm going to have two rings, like you? What's this one for then? Engagement?'

'No. Not really. Just for us and our family as it grows. Something unconventional, Jeff. Can you handle it?'

His girlfriend's blue eyes sparkled, offset today with dark brown mascara and a light dusting of eye shadow. Their affectionate teasing raised her man's blood pressure yet again. Turning twenty away from home, amid her first taste of true independence, had transformed the privileged princess into a confident seductress with a flawless grasp on almost every reality. She not only read him like a book these days, but frequently played the most vital role of a world-changer's offsider by testing his own integrity in the safest of environments.

Said world-changer rolled his eyes. 'I can handle it. It's you I can't handle when you unmask me like that. The battle of the control freaks once again. I adore you for it, but it's excruciating.'

'Sorry. I mean one ring now, unconnected with engagements or weddings or anything. For here,' the happy woman grinned, pointing to the middle finger on his right hand, 'and the second one's on your wedding finger.'

Checking around to make sure they weren't being overheard, her boyfriend raised his large, piano-playing hands in front of his eyes and twisted them back and forth, almost as if he didn't altogether recognise them.

'Jesus! This is all too complicated,' he ribbed his lively shopping companion, before dropping his hands back into his lap and twitching the provocative middle digit of his left hand. 'And this is my wedding night finger...'

'Shhh!' Lynn's eyes widened in embarrassment, and she frowned. 'That's disgusting.'

Alighting at Oxford Circus station, faced with scores of inquisitive fans eager to catch sight of the popular pair, they managed to escape and head towards Green Park. Neither Australian superstar knew where to buy jewellery, and it would have caused a huge scene if the question had been put to an autograph hunter, ever hungry for scandal. They remembered the Burlington Arcade on Bond Street being suggested somewhere along the line, either by an advertisement in the newspaper or by one of their dinner party guests.

They soon arrived at the glittering *cul-de-sac* of long-established gem specialists, marvelling at the many thousands of pounds' worth of precious stones and metals contained in this concentrated area of the city. Hand-in-hand and deep in conversation as usual, they gazed down the never-ending line of windows.

'It's lucky you're here,' Jeff said, after following his partner's lead. 'You're making this very easy for me.'

The dual-stone diamond and twenty-four carat gold engagement ring Lynn chose in only the second shop glittered in the bright lights above the counter. It sat proudly sparkling on her long, slender finger. The staff had made an outrageous fuss of their clients, until every last one... including a few from next-door, they guessed... had cooed over the exquisite piece. The restless rocker endeavoured to contain his impatience with their exuberant brand of customer service, eager for this experience to be as memorable as possible for his dream girl.

'Do you like it?' he asked. 'Are you sure this is it?'

'It suits you so perfectly, Miss Dyson,' the assistant gushed, placing the plush red cushion beneath Lynn's hand and spreading her fingers across it for the umpteenth time.

Like this makes all the difference, the cynic cursed inwardly. There was no disguising his special lady's happiness however, and enduring this arduous process for just a while longer was a small price to pay.

'Jeff, it's gorgeous. I absolutely love it. Do you?'

'Yes, I do,' he agreed. 'You look fantastic and very happy. You're glowing, so this must definitely be the one.'

Without further contemplation, the ring was boxed up, purchased and shoved straight into the inside pocket of the dashing millionnaire's leather jacket. Outside on the street, his excitable girlfriend kissed him, vainly trying to distract him while she picked his pockets.

'You're not getting it yet,' he insisted, fighting her off. 'Pick somewhere nice for dinner, and we'll do it properly.'

The couple sauntered back to The Ritz Hotel for a celebratory drink and a bite to eat. Lynn scanned the faces of their fellow diners, mostly wealthy Bond Street power-shoppers partaking in a spot of luncheon while the swipe strip on their credit cards cooled down. Some seemed to recognise her, more likely from an issue of "Horse and Hound" or "Woman's Weekly" rather than from the "Rolling Stone" or the "New Musical Express". A few made eye contact and smiled sycophantically, but most looked down their noses as the youngsters strolled through the luxurious lobby.

'Snooty bunch, aren't they?' Australia's darling whispered with a smile.

The richest and most authoritative long-haired philanthropist in the world ordered a whisky and dry ginger for himself and a glass of wine for his dream girl, taking the menu back to their table in the bar. They toasted their first purchase of the day. How significant a month September had become for their relationship... Three years ago, Lynn had left for the US, and just last year the lovers had reunited after her birthday. And now here they were in September again, preparing to marry in only a few months' time.

Lynn Dyson was in the process of becoming Jeff Diamond's *fiancée*. What a splash this news was about to make in the printed media and on the many entertainment programmes around the globe! It was fortunate indeed that they were so far away from home, otherwise they might be obliged to relinquish every last vestige of privacy until their legions of fans adjusted to this high-profile *liaison*.

'Please could I see it again?' the elated singer pleaded with her relaxed and fulfilled chaperone, again lunging for his jacket pocket.

'No,' her boyfriend scolded in no uncertain terms. 'It's gone. I lost it already. Sad but true.'

They compared notes on their favourite dinner places as suitable locations for a ring presentation. Nowhere in Chinatown was considered sufficiently secluded, and those in Knightsbridge and South Kensington were all too formal. There was a tiny Nepalese restaurant in St John's Wood which the musicians had tried on a whim one night a few months back after a late session in the studio. The food had been tasty, and the service low-key. They decided to return after dark that evening.

Back out in the street after lunch, the couple set about choosing a different jeweller for their quest to find Jeff's much more progressive piece. Not convinced that any of the stores they had visited earlier would offer a truly made-to-order service, they ventured upstairs in the old arcade. Behind a wooden door with the most unassuming of signs, they found an elderly German by the name of Werner to whom the empathetic *duo* warmed straightaway.

Lynn explained her idea carefully, building an imaginary structure on her partner's finger, and Werner began to sketch a design on his blotter. A square with the corners rounded off, with a solitaire diamond in one quadrant. He suggested a heavy gold signet ring style with black jet-stone for the base of the inset. He showed them some samples of the semi-precious material, and between the three of them, a visualisation of the desired end result soon took shape.

'So this masterpiece'll be a few years in the making,' Jeff told the master craftsman, man to man.

'Unless you have twins.'

'Wow! Oh, I hadn't thought of that,' the young woman exclaimed, momentarily horrified by the jeweller's dry wit. 'But that's OK. It'll just mean the last two are added in together. So you think it'll look good?'

'Yeah. It'll be fabulous,' her boyfriend nodded, already quite attached to the unique idea. 'Although having twins is a scary prospect, I agree.'

Werner provided the stars with a price quotation and an estimated timeframe of ten business days. All three shook hands, and the Olympian put down a deposit to secure the transaction. For the second time today, the elated philosopher sensed her soul radiating a newfound power. Lynn Dyson was coming of age, and not purely in this current lifetime.

The intelligent aristocrat had learned a great deal from the former street-kid, including how to negotiate her preferred outcome. Having spent her childhood and adolescence doing either her father's, coaches' or musical director's bidding, it had seldom entered her head that she could dictate matters herself until she met her enigmatic stranger. Jeff was such a masterful mentor in this regard, and she studied his methods fastidiously whenever she had the chance to witness his magnificence in full flight.

The trick was in the diversity of both the vocabulary and the body language the communicator expressly selected, as the sportswoman had divined. The skilful combination of various facial expressions, hand movements, posturing... even down to when he stood up or sat down, leaned forward or back... all triggered different emotive reactions in people. And the tone of his voice would change subtly during the course of a conversation, becoming more or less insistent depending on his objective or how willing the other party seemed to be.

A useful double act was emerging as well. The ambitious partners had talked about it several times over recent weeks: persuasion to the power of two, Jeff had coined it, scrawling "P^2" on an unused paper napkin one night over dinner. Their *modus operandi* would see him advance alone into a situation of conflicting opinions and adversarial positions, working his mesmeric magic to diffuse the emotion until the other party or parties demonstrated a desire for accord.

At this point, the front half of their famed pantomime horse would transfer them to Lynn for the compassionate and systematic patience she employed so naturally, in order to map out an achievable solution to the problem. The impetuous arbitrator had little tolerance for distilling the detail, and the rear-end of the pantomime horse lacked the brazen courage to go in with all guns blazing. It was a match made in negotiation heaven, he had been at pains to tell her.

'Did you want to wait until yours is ready and do a single ceremonial ring thing?' Lynn checked, as they walked along Oxford Street hand-in-hand.

'No,' his reply was most emphatic. 'I'm itching to see you wearing yours as soon as possible. Mine we can do over another dinner, because it's not linked to weddings, *comme t'as dit.* If I play my cards right, I'll get four dinners out of this one piece of jewellery. And with any luck, four mellow, post-dinner mega-fucks.'

'Unless we have twins,' his dream girl giggled, shaking her head at his crudeness.

'Mmm... Indeed. That would've been the mega-fuck right there! Perish the thought.'

'For you or me?' the slender celebrity queried. 'Why the anguish? It means you'd get both of your children at once. That wouldn't be so bad, would it?'

'No. I'm only kidding. Primarily, I'm authorising the thoughts to perish on your behalf,' the tactful philosopher answered, once more taking the coward's option.

'Right answer!' Lynn grinned. 'God! You're easy to wind up these days. I love you!'

The two star students parted ways at the northern end of Regent Street, the sportswoman on her way home and then on to the gymnasium for a cardio' training session, and the lecturer to the university to tutor a late class. Resigned to putting their enchanting adventure on hold and settling back into the reality of their normal life, the pair agreed to meet later at the unassuming Nepalese restaurant on the Edgware Road.

As soon as his dream girl was out of sight, Jeff opened the small box covered in red velvet and stared at the engagement ring he had purchased. It hadn't been too expensive, but that scarcely mattered to him these days. No-one could ever accuse his beautiful best friend of extravagant tastes. Material things were almost as unimportant to the wealthy former child-star as to the former poor boy from Sydney's south-west. The stunning, simple design she had chosen, with its cluster setting of two independent stones was the perfect allegory for their relationship. He so looked forward to threading it onto her finger tonight.

Jeff Diamond, engaged? He felt dizzy as another burst of emotion rose from deep within. What a turn-up for the books! This street urchin from Nowheresville, New South Wales, had acquired a diamond ring in London's swankiest district and was soon to use it to claim the hand of Australia's most eligible young woman. He hadn't stolen it, and neither would he be repaying a loan shark five dollars per week for the rest of his life. Despite having joined the millionnaire's club almost two years ago, still the progressive unveiling of the fairy story his adolescent Pied Piper self had woven in the silence of his mad, old world never failed to catch him by surprise with its spooky accuracy.

Striding up High Holborn towards The Aldwych and his tutorial, waving and smiling to every double-take on his path and politely declining any further contact, Jeff's thoughts turned again to his father. He wondered how much information the prisoner would have gleaned about the life of fame and fortune his unwanted son now enjoyed. He was inquisitive to find out and undoubtedly it would be perversely pleasurable to be able to gloat in the old man's face, yet obstinate pride remained strong. Why should he give the bastard the satisfaction? Paul Diamond had never helped his family, so why should his son feel any inclination to make him happy? Moreover, remembering the many blatant and ignorant biases from his childhood locale, the Polish immigrant would most likely show contempt at Jeff marrying into the archetypal White Anglo-Saxon Protestant clan.

The lost boy's good news would have made his mother happy, the nostalgic philosopher mused with some confidence. She had understood and appreciated romance in her more reasonable moments, when she hadn't been ripping down treasured posters from her son's wall in a fit of drunken rage.

Towards the end of her short, disappointing life, Luciana Diamond had been unable to stand the sight of attractive women, most likely due to her ground-down sense of self-worth. It had torn the teenager's heart to shreds each time he had been left to restock the Lynn Dyson tribute gallery on his side of the bedroom to the sound of his sister's derisive jeers. Oh, yes. He understood the desire to sabotage other people's happiness only too well.

Perhaps enlisting Madalena as a bridesmaid was a bad idea after all. She wouldn't know how to behave in Lynn's circle. The distant brother could hardly renege on their offer, in spite of the calamity he was now beginning to dread. Rather than transfer his fear to the excited bride-to-be, he vowed to request chaperoning services from Michelle. The forthright solicitor would make sure the tramp stayed out of trouble. He couldn't help but smile... This insurance policy would protect his sister and the Dysons' embarrassment, with the added benefit of ensuring the safety of any male guest who presented as a likely soft touch.

The more he pieced together memories of the dark-haired street-girl, the more Jeff felt his attitude soften towards her. He who held so much compassion for other unfortunate individuals had long struggled with a deep-seated resentment born out of her closeness to their parents. In later years, this animosity had been exacerbated by her inclination to leech off her younger brother, most probably not even aware of the guilt he bore.

Only today, straight after their telephone call, he had begun to write a cheque for a large sum of money, intending to post it on their way to the tube station. It had been torn up and tossed into the rubbish bin at the last minute after more soul-searching with his flatmate, wherein they concluded that the Sydney prostitute would only fritter the cash away on drugs and booze, or buy tarty clothes or other frivolous items. A home of her own might be a better investment. At least then she would have a roof over her head for the rest of her life, provided the naïve woman wasn't pressured into signing it over to her pimp in exchange for some special treatment.

The boy from Canley Vale found it more disturbing to picture the men who ran prostitution rings in their old neighbourhood. Indeed, he had studied their techniques carefully when he sought to hone his own powers of persuasion. They were simply out to make easy money at the expense of the less astute. What was the difference between these blokes and the high-rolling commercial criminals at the top end of town? He had heard enough tales of woe from Gerry's clients having fallen foul of professional confidence tricksters. The musician squirmed at the thought of his own easy money falling into such hands instead of funding positive change.

And the Jaworskis... The lost boy shuddered to think what the surviving relatives of his father's victims might think of his rise to stardom. They would know exactly who he had become: a prime target for blackmail and extortion, always a lucrative sideline for the Polish gangland bosses. In fact, it was a wonder that the prominent celebrity hadn't already been contacted with a timely reminder of those whom his father had wronged.

The next generation of the powerful underworld family was a few years older than Jeff, and there had been at least four sons. Maybe more. How much strife might he bring into the Dysons' lives by becoming the human interface between crime-lords such as the Jaworskis and their associates and the fine, blue-blooded, all-Australian family? From his new position as future son-in-law, he now had a much less subjective viewpoint into why Big D had been so keen to investigate his daughter's boyfriend's past. There was a real and present danger lurking there which he had denied fervently until recent times, having interviewed representatives from both sides of the Northern Ireland conflict as part of his doctoral thesis.

A sudden panic attack enveloped the young star. The first in a few weeks. Jesus Christ! Perhaps they oughtn't to return to Australia at all... Breathing deeply and willing his eyes to focus, he paused and lit a cigarette, leaning against a tree. He must have looked particularly ill, he realised, for within seconds, he became aware of a lady shouting directly into his face, having stopped to ask if he was feeling alright. Anxious not to be recognised, the student waved her gratefully away before she had a chance to peer more closely. The surge of anxiety passed after a few minutes, and he continued on to the Politics faculty and his lecture.

Back in the austere university building, the reality of his overflowing in-tray was a welcome change, and Jeff soon immersed himself in the topic of the afternoon's session. His postgraduate students were animated, and they quickly divided into polarised groups, arguing each other against the metaphorical ropes. The class adjourned after ninety minutes to the union and shared a few beers with their famous, well-respected and ultra-cool lecturer. An all-male contingent, the language and discussion topics soon became bawdy and lewd, since the Australian star in their midst had come to revere the British sense of humour and loved to egg them on. Their opinions were irreverent and often brutal, conjuring up imagery which never failed to entertain him and supply its share of song ideas.

The intellectual expected that settling back into the down-under way of life would be a challenge after the surfeit of stimulation at his brain's disposal during their UK stint. Lynn was looking forward to being back home in Melbourne with her friends and family, and he had no intention of derailing her plans due to his reticence. Instead, he had resolved to spend as much time as possible overseas, in these ancient, culture-rich cities, surrounded by people with a deeper understanding of life than the typical *ocker* descendent of eighteenth- and nineteenth-century migrants.

His *Regala* had unwittingly described his dilemma to perfection when they had been setting up The Good School. His cultural home was among those who possessed the wherewithal to convert information into knowledge and knowledge into wisdom.

Adding further fuel to the argument, the old soul tirelessly chased this wisdom of ages and found great inspiration from being steeped in the complex civilisations which had evolved over many centuries. His beautiful best friend was very much the product of the pioneer way of life, as were her siblings and most of her close friends, yet her partner had turned out to be a throwback to times of persecution who identified inexplicably strongly with Europeans.

His theory had not met with dissent from his clever soul-mate, as he had initially feared when expressing his need for greater history than modern-day Australia could supply. Neither's northern hemisphere ancestry drove them to an affinity with the native aboriginal traditions, much to their regret. No question that both backgrounds instilled a strong work ethic. However, Lynn's pioneers were driven by the narrower survival needs of their immediate community, whereas the struggles of Jeff's inheritance emanated from a much broader context. This type of wisdom he wouldn't find in mainstream Australia, nor even in New York's robust money-making machinery.

The thoughtful analyst didn't have time to go home after their post-class drinks, with darkness descending on the autumn London evening. His plan comfortably galvanised over a few pints of beer, he jogged along Tottenham Court Road to Euston, then down Marylebone Road until he reached the St John's Wood section of the Edgware Road. He was keen to arrive in advance of his dinner companion, not wanting to find her already sitting alone in the restaurant, fair game for any determined fan. He had worked up a considerable hunger by the time he got there and was shown to a quiet table against the wall.

Excelente. The gorgeous and eminently sensible creature knew not to be early. Relaxing at last, Jeff sat with a beer, some *papadums* and a notepad, waiting for his dream girl to grace him with her presence. A bottle of red wine was delivered, opened and left to breathe on the table, and the ring box began to burn a hole in his jacket pocket. Should he get down on one knee and embarrass her this time? Maybe!

Two students in for a cheap, early dinner accosted the approachable superstar for his autograph. Glad of the distraction, he ordered three more beers and asked them to join him when they revealed they were studying at the

Business School nearby, where he had taught some undergraduate classes earlier in the year. The *trio* swapped stories until his guest arrived and threw the lads into total confusion, causing their tongues to hit the table simultaneously.

Anticipating such a reaction, the Sydneysider took a good look at the other two men, less than five years his junior. They behaved like teenagers; boisterous and selfish, and he contemplated the eternity rapped up in this modest age difference as the refined, elegant young lady sat down opposite him as his future wife.

Lynn obliged the speechless pair with her autograph too, smiling as her handsome gentleman issued a blatant hint that it was time to make themselves scarce.

'Hi,' his girlfriend said, finally alone with their menus and glasses of wine. 'Good afternoon?'

'Yeah. Not bad.'

'You look tired,' she mentioned. 'Is there anything wrong?'

The young man sighed. 'Only that I've been thinking a lot about my family today. You know... After I asked Lena those questions about my dad. It scares me to think that I might be putting you and your family in danger.'

Lynn's eyes were full of compassion rather than concern. 'Why now and not before?'

'Good question. I suppose I was kind of in denial about the types of people who know me,' he explained, pleased that the previous angry reactions no longer magnified his response when he was put on the spot. 'Everyone's going to know about our wedding shortly, and I don't want to create targets of you all for anyone who might be holding any grudges.'

'But don't you think they'd have done something by now, if they were going to?'

'Yeah. Possibly,' her boyfriend replied, pushing back in his chair and painting on a broad grin. 'I expect I'm overreacting, given what's going on. Let's forget it. It's not why we're here tonight. How was your afternoon, angel?'

Lynn sensed these worries were troubling her man deeply but trusted his decision that further deliberation could wait. Love swelled her heart, admiring the sensitivity shown by the man she was to marry. Keen to lighten his mood, she told him about her training session and also that Celia Blake had left a suitably slushy answering machine message for them. Jeff chuckled, cottoning onto his perfect partner's nefarious plan.

The diners placed their order with the waiter above the overtones of whispering all around, and their *entrées* arrived within minutes. The eager music student wondered when and how this maker of many statements intended to present the ring, or whether he had arranged for a special show of some sort, or even if he had changed his mind. As usual, nothing about his demeanour gave him away.

Their plates were soon empty and cleared away after the first course. Anticipating an equally fast turnaround for their main meals, Jeff seized the moment. Lynn was midway through another funny story from the day before, chattering fondly about friends who hoped to visit them in Melbourne next year. While she spoke, he deftly retrieved the bevelled, velvet cube from his pocket, his fingers turning it over and over out of sight while he collected his thoughts and prepared something significant to say to mark this most inconceivable of occasions.

Lynn glanced up in sudden expectation, the atmosphere having become turgid and highly-charged. Their invisible elastic connection felt at its slackest, and the handsome pretender could sense his dream girl's heart-rate quickening with every jangling nerve. Taking a deep breath, he slipped the red box out from under the table, still weaving it through his fingers, and fixed her with an adoring and unyielding stare.

'You might recognise this,' he opened, teasing her by dragging it across her line of vision like a hypnotist's fob watch.

The dazzled twenty-year-old nodded, smiling and coughing in surprise. 'Yes, I do. You're making it dizzy, spinning it around like that.'

Jeff exhaled, chuckling at the childish insinuation. His gaze intensified, drilling into her aquamarine eyes with his trademarked, sexy half-smile on his face.

'I'm making myself dizzy,' he admitted, cocking his head slightly and winking.

The stunning singer reached for his hand and squeezed it, picking up on her boyfriend's heightened emotional state. She remained quiet however, realising their special moment had arrived.

'It's been a long, long time for you and me,' the smooth baritone voice stated, closing his eyes. 'Loving you is the most important task I have ahead of me, angel, and I'm going to do it well for the rest of my life.'

Lynn gulped and knew she would cry if she opened her mouth to respond, such rarity having descended on the modest Himalayan restaurant.

'Thank you,' she whispered. 'Me too.'

The orator continued. 'No, angel. Thank you, a thousand times. By loving you, I mean I'm going to make it my life's work to understand you inside and out. I want to know your every wish and every aspiration, and help you make them come true. I want to see you fly higher than anyone's ever flown before. All that I hope you've already heard from me.'

His dream girl's eyes were shining with tears. More than ever before, the boy from Canley Vale felt certain it wasn't the first time their two souls had found themselves in this situation. He was also positive he would never again see something so beautiful.

'But, Lynn,' he continued, 'you know I love you the most when I'm completely helpless in your arms, skin-on-skin, hearing each others' heart beating.'

Jeff refused to blink, not wishing to miss a single second, even though his pulse was thumping in his temples and his eyes stung trying to fight back his own tears. With both hands clasped together, still clutching the little, red box, he pressed them against his heart.

'I want to hold you forever, angel. So close. I want us to learn how to touch each other differently every day, and not just on the outside. I need to breathe you in, I need to taste you and feel your energy flowing through my veins for all the years to come.'

The romantic soul watched as his girlfriend's chest rose and fell as she listened intently to his words. 'And see these eyes? Behind these beautiful blue eyes... In there are our children,' he told her, pointing with two fingers of his left hand. 'I can see them so clearly that I already know them. That's our destiny, my angel. In there. You had the vision too. Our four diamonds. *Te amo, Regala. Et je t'aimerai toujours.*'

Apart from emitting a barely audible, involuntary sigh, the spellbound woman remained quiet. She was entranced, never giving the handful of other diners any thought. Their little corner of England's capital stood frozen in time, desperate to hear how the story would end.

About to bring his incantation to its zenith, Jeff sat straighter and cleared his throat. 'So... Victoria Lynn Shannon Dyson, will you do me the greatest honour of becoming my wife?'

The blonde and several onlookers gasped as one at the pure intensity of the moment, swept away by the poetic sentiment. Her face had stolen a march on her decision, and Jeff's big, brown eyes begged her to put her thoughts into words.

'Yes, Jeff. I will. Thank you. That was so beautiful, and I've never been more sure about anything. *Je t'aimerai toujours aussi*, magic-man.'

Beaming from ear to ear, the nobody who had fought the odds and turned himself into a nobleman flipped open the box and removed the ring from its cradle, holding it up between their faces and letting it catch the light. Excited chatter echoed all around the unassuming restaurant, mesmerised as the famous tennis champion extended her left hand towards her outspoken rock star. He slipped the twin-stoned golden band onto her finger before bowing to kiss it in a poignant welcome to its new and permanent home.

'I love you, Lynn,' he whispered. 'This is it, gorgeous. For all to see. You are absolutely perfect.'

Both lovers stood up and stepped away from the table, taking care not to knock over the glasses. They held each other in a long embrace, ignoring the many pairs of eyes currently fixed upon them, for a moment not even noticing that a round of applause had broken out.

'Oh, Jeff,' the ecstatic young woman replied. 'That was such a wonderful speech. I love you so much. We're going to be so happy. I promise you too.'

***

That same night, safely back in their St John's Wood love nest, Jeff brought the house down with his screaming; the first nightmare in over two months. He had predicted it might happen in his heightened emotional state, abandoning his *fiancée* as soon as she fell asleep and closing the bedroom door in an effort not to disturb her and spoil their momentous day. Despite best endeavours however, he had succumbed to fitful slumber, and Lynn awoke to a pandemonium of yelling and swearing in at least two languages. It was just like the old days.

She ran into the lounge to rouse her drenched *fiancé*. He had kicked their solid, wooden coffee table out of position with his bare feet, scattering books and magazines across the carpet in the process, and hadn't woken despite the fact that two of his toes were bleeding. The young woman shook his sweating chest hard and stared directly into his face. His fists were clenched with rage, and his long limbs spasmed madly.

'Jeff!' Lynn shouted, grabbing his wrists and pulling him up to a sitting position. 'Wake up! It's OK. There's no-one here. Wake up!'

Finally the pattern broke, and the dreamer recognised the strident beauty crouching on the floor in front of him. Cursing in Spanish, a familiar repugnance was written all over his face. To her relief, his features gradually softened, and he slumped against the back of the couch, exhausted.

'Welcome back,' his flatmate said, stroking his trembling knees. 'What were you dreaming about? You looked absolutely disgusted about something. I forgot how deeply asleep you are when this happens. I couldn't wake you.'

The tormented man didn't respond at first, frightened by lingering images behind his eyes but unable to express the anger he felt towards himself and his mysterious sparring partners. He drank from the glass of water Lynn had run in with before thrusting his fingers into soaking hair and pushing his head backwards against the cushions again. His chest was heaving in and out with a mechanical urgency, presumably to bring his heart-rate under control.

'Was it what we were talking about over dinner?' his girlfriend asked. 'About your dad and the gangs from the Stones Road?'

Jeff nodded and sighed, holding his hand out for her to join him. He was longing to speak to her, but his mouth refused to function. Scowling a little at the feel of his damp skin against her naked shoulder, she nestled under a heavy arm and rested a hand on his thigh.

'If you think it's a real threat, we should seek some advice.'

While the healing songwriter remained in such an unstable state, the sportswoman didn't much care to link her proposition with the investigation her father had commissioned the previous year. However, it was a logical leap she was sure this intelligent man would make of his own accord. Sure enough, he uttered a long moan, tensed his abdominal muscles and dragged his torso upright, twisting to face her. Lynn giggled as she fell sideways, suddenly deprived of her slippery bolster. With his forearms on his knees, he stared at her from under a furrowed brow, still shell-shocked but smiling a little at her antics.

'You're probably right,' he answered after a lengthy pause. 'Whatever happens, I'm not going to try and contact my dad about the wedding. I don't want to risk anyone finding out that I'm still... and therefore you guys are... connected with him in any way.'

'OK,' his *fiancée* agreed without drama.

This hypothesis sounded sensible under the circumstances, and the middle of the night was hardly the best time to start dissecting the pros and cons of such an unpleasant scenario. Lynn shivered, wrapping her legs up underneath her in an effort to keep warm.

Jeff slapped his knees with his hands. 'Fuck it! Let's go back to bed. I'm sorry, angel. I'd hoped all this crap was behind us.'

'It's been a stressful day. Go easy on yourself. Look what you gave me today...'

The proud tennis star held her left hand out towards him, the faintest sparkle still visible from her new ring even in the darkened room. The man who had bought it re-joined her on the sofa and jogged the side of her shoulder playfully.

'*Merci, ma fiancée. Je t'aime.*'

'*Je t'aime aussi, mon amour,*' she replied. '*Voulez-vous coucher avec moi?*'

The dark-haired gipsy grinned, keen to leave his troubles behind. '*Bien sûr!* Take me. I'm all yours, baby, nightmares and all.'

The lithe twenty-year-old led her boyfriend into the bathroom, sitting on the side of the tub while he soaped the layer of perspiration off his skin. Once back in bed, they held each other close until all ten senses had been satisfied.

Lynn fought to remain awake long enough to allow her worried man to drift off first, but things didn't happen quite as she planned. The contented lover watched tiredness overtake her, stroking her upper arm in a slow rhythm and planting the odd kiss on her neck as her breathing slowed. When he was certain she had fallen asleep, he pulled his right hand out from under her body and rolled onto his back.

'I love you,' he whispered. 'Thanks again.'

The most beautiful woman in the world murmured something incoherent and tugged the covers a little higher to ward off the chill. Jeff smiled on hearing her well-meaning nonsense and lay staring at the ceiling for half an hour or so, going over the events of the day. Somehow it seemed that for every step he took into the future, there were always new challenges to face.

No big deal, the philosopher concluded. He was still terrified, but his dream girl had a plan. He needed to believe he was in good hands. It was time to relinquish control, or at least to learn how to share it.

***

At Lynn's request, her parents published a dignified, unassuming announcement in Australia's three most popular daily newspapers: The Australian, The Sydney Morning Herald and The Age. She and Jeff had managed to convince everyone at their management company that the words "*fiancé*" and "engagement" should not be used in connection with their wedding plans, given the fact that they had been living under the same roof for the best part of a year, making it unmodish and hypocritical to regress along traditional lines at this stage.

The ballroom in the Dyson Administration building, where the budding songwriter had made his tentative, secret *début* in front of his Number One fan, had been booked for a New Year's Day ceremony and reception, and invitations were designed, ordered and dispatched around the world in record time.

The guest list grew and shrank according to the mood of the day. Neither celebrity wished to invite people for purely political reasons, preferring to keep the whole thing as intimate as possible. Of course, Bart and Marianna Dyson had other ideas, adamant that the occasion demanded the participation of the large number of individuals who had been instrumental in their elder daughter's success. Each camp had compromised a little, agreeing that the ceremony's congregation be restricted to eighty while the reception numbers would top out at a hundred and fifty.

Jeff Diamond's side of the ledger remained necessarily lean. Without hesitation, he invited Madalena, the Blakes, Suzanne and Steve and Professor John Francis and his wife, adding a few university mates, his band and record company staff and the majority of his management team.

An obligation towards blood relations was noticeably absent for the Sydneysider, going to great lengths to persuade the Dysons that there was no mileage in sending an invitation to his grandparents. He felt sure their most polite and least likely response would be to decline. Fortunately, the elders of the sporting dynasty were sympathetic to his reticence surrounding other members of his family. Like many in their own wide circle, they would only attend out of curiosity or to brush elbows with the *glitterati*. They supported the alienated relative in his mission to discourage any gratuitous snooping into the swanky world he had penetrated, familiar with the gold-digger phenomenon. Above all, as Lynn had offered, why give them the idea that he wanted them to share their joy?

His *fiancée* attempted to keep her list of significant personages to a minimum too. For her part, she shared her parents' debt of gratitude towards those who had helped raise and educate her. The songwriter appreciated this sentiment to a certain extent, especially when he thought back to the small number of farsighted teachers who had given the rogue scholar a chance when all else seemed lost. Nevertheless, it would be somewhat hollow of him to invite them, having not maintained contact otherwise. He had cultivated precious few respecting relationships during those self-absorbed and survivalist days and was content to keep it that way.

The bulk of the remaining guests were usual suspects from their country's high society: politicians, families of good standing, even the Governor of Victoria and the Governor General. There were representatives from Melbourne Academy, from the Australian Olympic Committee and from the entertainment industry.

The excited superstar was in her element arranging every last detail, spending hours on the telephone in the evenings, as soon as Melbourne opened for business. Her college workload was coming to a head, with exams commencing in November, and the busy pair had shared their concerns that she mightn't have enough time to fit everything in. Yet as had been the case throughout her short life, somehow the puzzle pieces soon slotted together.

Both playing to their strengths, Jeff was content to leave the project management to Lynn's tireless organisational skills. Every now and again he would receive a status report and a few allocated tasks to perform, but largely he was surplus to requirements and luxuriously left to saturate his senses in the last weeks of their London *sojourn* in whichever ways he saw fit. This process comprised impassioned, alcohol-fuelled debates, accompanied by much table-thumping and throwing back of chairs in dissent.

Bureaucracy insisted on hindering the impatient man's progress across many of their initiatives. He often found himself in insufferable, fruitless meetings with well-intentioned but dis-empowered government officials, whose worlds turned so much more ponderously than he needed. It was a tough exercise in tolerance, increasingly aware of the difficult and delicate diplomacy required to accomplish anything involving the alignment of multiple parties, each of whom had its own poorly-understood agenda.

The empathetic genius' childhood habit of asking why until there were no more plausible "becauses" had earned him a reputation for unearthing many outdated and plain stupid regulations and procedures which had evolved over the years, yet the extent of inertia prevalent around effecting change remained unfathomable to the ambitious renegade. His beautiful best friend would simply smile and nod whenever he vented his frustrations, persuading him that they had no alternative but to let certain matters take their due course.

On a high note, the world-changer's ring had been delivered, complete with its first, sparkling stone. It was taking him ages to get used to wearing it, despite having fallen in love with its promise. Lynn laughed at him constantly playing with it, twisting it around his finger and flipping it in the air.

'See how hard it is for you to adjust?' she teased. 'That's what it's like for all these people whose lives you're shaking up.'

The clever woman was quite correct, as always. It was a timely corollary which Jeff swore never to forget. Henceforth, every time his attention was drawn to the ring, not only did it make his heart jump at the thought of their future together, but it also reminded him to permit each scheme to evolve at its natural pace. The Olympian from pioneer stock with whom he was to share the rest of his life had absorbed some "old culture" ways after all, which filled her *fiancé* with joy. It would make settling back down-under so much easier if she understood both perspectives.

'OK. I get it,' her humbled partner smiled. 'But I've got to keep the pressure on or nothing'll ever change. Just think how fidgety I'm going to be when I've got a ring on each hand... I won't know which to fiddle with first.'

Lynn giggled. 'True. It might even help with giving up smoking, 'cause you'll have plenty to do with your hands.'

The fashionable couple's social life stepped up into an even crazier gear during December as the lines blurred between their professional commitments, hosting and attending functions and dinner parties, participating in Christmas events and appearing on television and radio almost every day. Their stay in London was drawing to a close, and with it a large number of tasks remained to finalise various projects and relocate their multi-dimensional life back to Melbourne. They were also eager to maintain the many newly-forged friendships after their departure.

Lynn needed little encouragement to go home, with the pull of family and her ingrained sporting patriotism. It was a far different story for Jeff however. Without question, their big day was helping to entice him back, yet he already felt a distinct pang of longing every time he caught himself wondering how he would fill his days with such rewarding work once the excitement of the wedding and honeymoon was over.

In spite of these reservations, there had never been any other option but to return to Australia, no matter how much the bohemian songwriter hankered for Europe's cosmopolitan diversity. Both lovers knew he would never ask his golden girl to raise their children anywhere else. His *fiancée* was grateful for his silent understanding, even recording a cover of "Midnight Train To Georgia", the Gladys Knight hit from two years earlier, to let him know she appreciated his sense of loss. She remembered how closely he related to the line, "I'd rather live in her world than live without her in mine."

'Why don't you do a specific Spanish or French album?' the compassionate beauty had asked one morning. 'You've done the odd crossover thing before, but you'll reach such a different market by doing a Europe-only version. You could tour in those countries with a different band too. It'd give you a whole new following to build.'

The more Jeff Diamond considered exploring every corner of the world, the more Lynn Dyson became content to take a background role in their master plan. Their pantomime horse analogy was holding true. Organising meetings and researching different opportunities from their comfortable Melbourne apartment would allow her to keep her training *régime* for the Montreal Olympics on track, record her own music and concentrate on developing their charitable foundation.

It was as if the stars' individual lives were reversing their focus. The singer-cum-sportswoman had spent much of her childhood on the move and no longer looked forward to long flights and living out of a suitcase, whereas the romance and magic was yet to wear off for the boy from Canley Vale, who hadn't ventured beyond Sydney's outer limits until three years ago. The world was truly his oyster, and as everyone knew, this good-looking rock star traded on aphrodisiacs.

'Do you mind me preferring to stay at home while you travel?' the young woman had asked. 'I mean, we'll be spending a lot of time apart. We'd planned to do everything together originally, but that doesn't feel right anymore. We've kind of outgrown that, don't you think?'

Jeff had considered her comments for a good few seconds before responding. 'You're right,' he agreed with an element of regret. 'Even a year ago, if you'd suggested I travel alone, I'd have been mortally wounded; like you didn't want to spend time with me. But now I'm cool with going our separate ways to get things done more efficiently, apart from the obvious lack of nocturnal stimulation.'

'It makes sense though. If we're going to have kids, that is. Constantly carting children around the world would be pretty arduous for all of us.'

'And just think of all the frantic reacquaintances we'll have on a regular basis,' her boyfriend winked. 'Not to mention all the discussions we've had on kids needing a stable environment.'

The grinning musician leaned forward to accept a kiss. 'Just as long as we're both getting what we need from our life singular.'

'Absolutely, angel. We just need to keep talking. It'll work itself out.'

In the third week of December, with all exams finished and final papers submitted, the two students stood gazing around at their stripped out Little Venice apartment after checking the furniture for any personal items they might have forgotten to pack. All was as it was when they had first arrived in January, save for the tinge of sadness which replaced their eager anticipation.

The car was due any minute to take them to the airport, and they had agreed with the estate agent to leave the keys in the kitchen.

The philosopher hugged his star pupil. 'It's been an amazing year, angel. Thanks for inviting me.'

'Yes, it has. You can say that again,' his *fiancée* replied in typical English fashion. 'You're welcome. Thanks for sharing it with me. I am sad to go. Really, I am. This little flat has really felt like home to me.'

'You never got a chance to make my apartment feel like home, did you?' Jeff guessed, confident of her answer. 'When we get back from the Canaries, we should fix that. We could even move if you want. I don't mind. To be honest, I've almost forgotten what my place is like.'

'But what would I do to it? I love your apartment the way it is. Let's just see how we feel when everything settles down. You're OK with that, aren't you?'

Her handsome man kissed her forehead, grinning. 'Yep. It's all good. I learned a Welsh word from a fellow student a few days ago: *hiraeth*. It means longing for what was; a void or even nostalgia, I suppose. And I'm full of it.'

His wife-to-be chuckled. 'Indeed you are.'

'You know, gorgeous...' he continued, kissing her again. 'We came here as two people wanting to be together, and we're leaving as one solid unit intending to be apart a lot of the time. What happened to our dream? How did this year change us so much?'

Lynn looked into his eyes. 'Probably because we have total confidence in us now. Do you remember that first afternoon after I moved into your apartment, and Gerry and Vanessa were coming to dinner? We were so scared of invading each others' space for those first few days.'

'Ah, yeah,' the young man affirmed, lifting his hands to his head at the awkward memory. 'Not wanting to lose our independence. One not wanting to piss the other off. Anxious to make it work but not really knowing how... Stressful, huh?'

'But now we don't care if we piss each other off,' his girlfriend laughed. 'We'll adjust to whatever works. I really respect your ambitions to travel, and I know you respect my wish to stay at home. It's perfect.'

The intercom' buzzer sounded, dispersing the reflective atmosphere. Jeff moved their luggage into the lift while Lynn informed the driver that they were on their way down. They were stopping off in Los Angeles on the way home to perform in a Christmas concert and a television special, which meant their homeward journey consisted of two long flights with a hectic three-day break in between.

***

A night flight across the Atlantic gave the lovers the opportunity to discharge their grief in an intense, blanketed mile-high experience, under the cover of First Class darkness. The rock star's American agent met them at the airport, and they spent a jet-lagged morning signing merchandise and answering questions at a press conference.

The whole world wanted to know every intimate snippet of information about the couple's wedding and honeymoon plans. Despite the insatiable showbusiness gossip boring them senseless, they graced each question with as much detail as they felt appropriate. They kissed on demand for the cameras, Lynn smiling sweetly while her *beau* complained at having to repeat the process over and over and attempted to change the subject to no avail.

It was as though all the meaningful and positive things the popular celebrities had set in train during their year away had been placed on hold while they got married. Their fans' priorities seemed all wrong, but there was nothing either of them could do about it except be thankful for the multitude of good wishes.

'Baby, please take me home!' Jeff exclaimed, falling onto the bed in their hotel room on Sunset Boulevard. 'I can't stand being a fairground attraction any longer.'

'I hear ya,' Lynn replied in her best American accent. 'Not long to go now. I'm beginning to catch you up on the "over it" stakes. What do you want to do now? We've got four whole hours to ourselves.'

'How about seeing a movie?' the young man suggested. 'Something to get our minds in a completely different place.'

They decided on "Dog Day Afternoon", which had been released a few months prior and had earned its director and stars a veritable catalogue of accolades. Having been so busy, the couple had never got around to seeing it at the time and rejoiced when the hotel's *concièrge* discovered it still showing in a tiny dive of a picture house on the other side of the city. Taking full advantage of their brief transformation into everyday people, they bundled into a taxi, loaded themselves up on popcorn and drinks and slipped anonymously into the theatre.

The movie was violent and quirky, and the youngsters were nervous that the plot may trigger some of Jeff's old fears. With only a handful of fellow cinema-goers around them in the smoky gloom, no distracting symptoms surfaced, and they wallowed in their enjoyable interlude. They were both huge fans of Al Pacino, whose performance was inspiring as the unfortunate Sonny with his transsexual wife.

That evening, the refreshed pair spiced it up together on the Johnny Carson Show and fielded yet more invasive and puerile questions about their relationship with their smiliest faces painted on. The interview bored the mischievous, dark-haired rocker, who pinched, nudged and kicked his dutiful girlfriend incessantly behind the desk while she searched for different ways to express the same, tired information for the tenth or eleventh time. She didn't miss a beat, which only made him try harder.

'You utter bastard!' Lynn yelled, climbing into the *limousine* at the end of the night and fending off his amorous advances. 'Man, you're going to pay for that tomorrow!'

And Jeff was already sorry. Something told him the sportswoman was deadly serious, and he wondered what kind of retribution she might hatch for their live show the following night. No amount of cajoling or apologising could soften her determination, much to his overt amusement and inner glow. He had brought this sublime agony on himself, he lamented, and could hardly wait to receive his punishment.

The next day's rehearsal went off without a glitch in a studio that resembled a huge aircraft hangar at Universal Studios. The show's production team had enlisted a cast of thousands, and holiday spirits were high among some of the music business' brightest stars. Jeff Diamond had done the Australian contingent proud, strutting his way through a loud and raunchy version of "Santa Claus Is Coming To Town", and the producers were pleased with it, despite their fear of crossing the line for a family show. The young man made a politely noncommittal promise when asked to tone it down for the real thing that evening.

Of course, the consummate showman had no intention of doing so. His dream girl assisted him in his quest, dancing across the stage looking invitingly sexy in the shortest skirt Santa Claus never wore. Every time the expert dancer made an attempt to grab or kiss his stealthy partner, she slipped out of his grasp by a whisper. It drove him crazy and made their opening set into a sizzling, seductive spectacle. The audience was spellbound, swinging their arms above their heads, cheering and stamping their feet throughout, leaving the director dazed and open-mouthed in the wings as he watched his show sail perilously close to that invisible line of decency.

Breathless, Jeff grabbed Lynn round the waist as they left the stage and refused to let go. 'Don't you *ever* stop doing that,' he panted, sweat on his brow and the broadest smile on his face. 'If that's me paying for it, then bring it on, lady. You were awesome. Hotter than hot.'

The director was walking towards them, holding his hands up and clapping. 'You guys are on fire! I think that's the first time we've featured foreplay on a Christmas show. It's going to be impossible to top that next year. Thanks a lot, you two.'

'The girl next-door grew up, Mike,' the handsome star replied, a hand firmly attached to his beautiful blonde temptress' hip.

Critics and public alike were raving about the CBS Christmas Special when the following morning rolled around. Lynn read the newspaper reviews aloud at breakfast and turned the page round for her co-star to see the photographs. They were tired, hung-over and keen to leave for the airport and then board the aeroplane bound for Sydney. Only one more stop before they would be back in Victoria and safely ensconced in one place until New Year's Day.

Australia's princess had secured premium tickets for the Blake family to attend "Carols in the Domain", where the superstars were also appearing. They and their esteemed manager were to spend Christmas Eve in the city before driving to Mosman for lunch the next day.

After a few post-show drinks, the group said their interim goodbyes at the door of the Intercontinental Hotel, which had been selected for old times' sake. Lynn hadn't gone as far as to request the same room, yet it had been a moving experience for the pair to share a nightcap alone in the small library bar where some fifteen months ago a certain millionnaire from the western suburbs had seduced an attractive television star in a red pencil skirt with a vodka and an interesting book.

Although Lynn and Jeff were totally wiped-out, it was great to be with their friendly hosts again for the festive season. The outrageous intensity of the previous Christmas had long vanished, and Gerald and Celia could scarcely believe the difference in the dynamics of the young couple's relationship after their year out of the country. Their pseudo-son was no longer the desperate, needy attention-seeker they had helped to bring up through his dangerous teenaged years, and the stunning blonde had clearly staked out her territory. With no less *chutzpah*, the handsome tearaway had matured beyond recognition under the Olympian's balancing influence.

Most conversation at the table concentrated on Jacinta's own engagement, which had been announced a couple of weeks prior. The stars had pleaded with the family not to let the topic drift to their upcoming event, reminding everyone that they had answered every possible question at least a hundred times already.

Predictably, the veteran troll hiding in the back of Jeff's mind put in an appearance in the early hours of Boxing Day morning. Gravity and Miss Irony, who had long been relegated to the sidelines, could still be trusted to save their best for occasions when happiness and optimism had dominated during the day. The characters in the ensuing nightmare had been vividly crafted from the shadows of his past, reigniting the fear that they might one day emerge in the forefront of their life singular.

Lynn listened patiently while her forlorn *fiancé* voiced his concerns. 'Everything's going to be fine. We're well protected these days.'

'I hope you're right,' he sighed. 'Let's never move to Sydney, eh? I'd be a nervous wreck twenty-four seven, waiting for something to happen to one or all of us.'

Homecoming

The next morning, the young man was on the road early, heading for Fairfield to collect his sister. His beautiful best friend had things to do in town, she had said. Secret things, no doubt deliberately arranged to make the next few days run more smoothly for him. Her first, sensible suggestion was that the groom-to-be should spend a few private hours with Madalena before he introduced them face-to-face, to test how she might react and to warn her about the Dyson family and what was required of her over the coming days. Having rented an ordinary Holden sedan, he cruised across town *incognito*, marvelling at the events which had come to pass since the last time he had made this journey.

After accepting a supporting role in her brother's wedding ceremony, Madalena too had been paid a number of house calls. She had been measured for a bespoke dress by a *chic* dressmaker whose name she had never heard, much to the seamstress' annoyance. She had also been visited by Michelle England to shop for shoes and by Celia Blake to deliver her dress and to check that it fitted properly.

Jeff had asked the two women if they wouldn't mind making sure his wayward sibling was ready for the occasion. Their oversight was important not only to help her look the part, but as much to give the naïve woman some gentle advice on how to approach being a bridesmaid to the country's most glamorous of brides. And then to report back to a nervous groom on her readiness.

'*¡Chico!*' came a crude yell from a window above his head. 'Up 'ere!'

Madalena and another woman were hanging out of a first-floor window in a dilapidated block of flats. Her brother climbed the stairs and was transported back in time. His head span faster the closer he got to her door, pausing for a moment and leaning against the wall before he rounded the final corner and came face-to-face with the animated pair.

'Where'd you go? This is Zoe, my housemate.'

Zoe, the millionnaire felt sure, was in the same line of work as his sister. Her denim skirt was one size too small and barely covered her backside, and there were bruises all over her thighs and arms. *Tasteful*, he thought, revolted by the rough treatment to which these women must be subjected every day.

She was friendly enough however, excitedly offering the superstar a beer from a battered, thrumming old fridge. He accepted, even though it was not yet ten o'clock in the morning.

'*¿Estás lista?*' Jeff asked, looking around for some evidence that Madalena had packed.

'*¡Sí!* For more than a week!'

Jeff had no memory of his sister's emotional responses, strangely edgy around such explosive excitement. '*Cálmate,*' he urged, as much for his own benefit as hers.

The feisty woman was bound to be hard to handle on the aeroplane. It was fortunate that Lynn would be on hand to offer assistance, and the anxious musician dared to believe Madalena would be better behaved in front of her.

'Speak English, you guys, for fuck's sake,' Zoe whinged, puffing on a cigarette. 'I don't know what I'm missing out on.'

His nostrils picking up the smell of smoke, the visitor retrieved his own packet from the back pocket of his trousers, flicking it open and offering it to his sister. She fished one out and accepted a light from the imposing figure, who dragged hard on his own cigarette to settle his nerves.

'Sorry,' the linguist replied. 'It's a rude habit. It just feels natural to talk to her in Spanish. Hey, I need you to calm down, Lena. Where are your bags?'

Madalena led her brother into her bedroom. It was bare, with no curtains and a worn raffia mat covering several cracked floor tiles. There was a suitcase next to the bed which looked too high-quality to be hers, and over it hung a suit carrier from David Keith, the Dyson family's exclusive Collins Street tailor. At least she hadn't forgotten her dress, Jeff thought.

'*Muy bien,*' he said. 'Have you got everything else? Shoes? Shit, I don't know. What else d'you need to be a bridesmaid?'

Madalena screamed, jumping up and down like a five-year-old. 'Bridesmaid! My little brother's getting married!'

Before he knew it, she had kissed him on the lips. 'Hey!' he yelped, recoiling. '*Basta, Lena, basta.*'

It was also too late to avoid a bear-hug from the excitable woman. The former tearaway who had become so sophisticated and urbane over the past few years was suddenly confused, unsure how to deal with this primitive bundle of energy. He didn't remember ever having hugged his sister before. Was this even right? Sensing he was uncomfortable, the twenty-six-year-old drew back.

'What?' she laughed at the shocked expression on his face. 'It's been so long since I had a brother. I forgot all about you.'

Jeff looked at the woman with long, dark, unkempt ringlets and eyelashes coated in sticky, black mascara, about the same height as Lynn but as skinny as a rake.

'*Te pareces a la madre, Lena.*'

'I know,' she nodded. '*Abuela* says that every time I screw up, and pissed-up old men think I'm her in the bar. It's *crapola*.'

Jeff inhaled sharply, not fancying a dip into the deep and meaningful before they had even hit the road. The images his sister's words conjured up were particularly disturbing.

'Come on. Let's go, *Señorita Crapola*,' he smiled, tucking the suit carrier under one arm and curling his fingers round the handle of her case.

'You got me ticket?' Madalena asked, straightening herself out and hurriedly applying another layer of bright red lipstick. 'What time's the 'plane? You know I never went on a 'plane before? Neither's Zo'.'

'I guessed as much. One o'clock, I think. The tickets are back at the hotel.'

'Ooh!' chirped Zoe from the doorway. 'The tickets are back at the 'otel. Get how posh 'e is now, Lee!'

The boy from Canley Vale rolled his eyes. 'We're all the same. Come on. Move your arse, *chica*!'

Almost hysterical, the housemates embraced. Zoe whispered a few choice sentences into the other woman's ear before pushing her through the doorway. Madalena followed her brother down the stairs like a bewildered puppy. They both waved back up to from the pathway leading to the road, and then again when they drove away.

The thin waif glanced around the rental car. 'This isn't very flash. It's just a Holden,' she sneered, two fingers raised to signal for another cigarette.

Jeff chuckled. 'It's rented for five hours. What do you expect? Jesus, Lena! I'm not going to hire a fucking Ferrari to pick you up. Where are *your* smokes?'

His sister wanted to know everything about her stay in Melbourne. Pummelled with question after question, the famous songwriter answered the first few with extreme reservation. However as they both relaxed, he began to let his guard down. This was the first adult conversation he had ever shared with his closest relative, and he found he actually quite liked her. She wasn't stupid by any means; simply plain ignorant. Despite having learned next to nothing in her quarter of a century on this planet, the little she knew appeared well understood.

'*¿Llevas algunas drogas?*' the driver asked, looking to his left to gauge her reaction.

'No. Only weed.'

'Weed is drugs,' Jeff snapped. 'Fuck, Lena. *Lo sabes.*'

'OK. Yeah,' his sister admitted.

'If they find it on you at the airport, we'll all go to jail,' he threatened. 'And I don't want Lynn to have to get married in prison. That OK with you?'

'What about me?' Madalena bleated. 'I don't want to go to prison either.'

'Or you,' the angry man added, flicking the indicator on and pulling the car into the side of the road. '*Ninguno de nosotros.* Dump it, Lena. Get out, and we'll chuck it away.'

The street-girl knew she shouldn't object. Her little brother was the boss these days.

'It cost me a week's wages,' she complained.

Jeff was rapidly losing patience. 'Yeah. And that's important?' he blurted out, biting his tongue as a shard of guilt stabbed him in the gut. 'I'll get you some in Melbourne, I promise, if you have to have it. But we can't fly with it. Christ, I'll have some myself once we get home.'

'Rock stars all do drugs, don't they?' the pacified woman joked, climbing back into the car after extracting two small packets from a pocket in the side of her suitcase.

She watched agog as the tall, good-looking man emptied the clear plastic bags into the bushes at the side of a bus stop. Was this really her brother? She hardly recognised him in his expensive clothes, shiny shoes and with well-groomed hair. Where had the lanky teenager gone? What had happened to the sullen, book-obsessed boy who had lived in tracksuit pants and an assortment of second-hand T-shirts, playing the guitar and singing to himself in the corner of their shared bedroom?

The small-town prostitute vaguely remembered an adolescent who had sported many more black eyes and cut lips than acne pimples, and whom she had chosen to disown once he became the talk of the school after passing so many examinations. So this was who that oddball kid had turned into. *Not bad*, she nodded to herself.

'Yep. They do!' Jeff replied with a wry smile, changing the subject. 'So you met Michelle?'

Madalena nodded again. 'Yeah. Lynn's best friend. She was OK. We got the same size feet.'

The intellectual took this is a sign to back off, forcing himself to calm down. 'Ha! *Bueno. ¿Grandes, no?*'

'*¡Culo!*,' his sister yelped, thumping his arm.

She was friendly at least, the young man thought. In fact, it was somewhat like having his dream girl beside him in the car, but with all her smooth edges rendered sharp and abrasive.

'Lynn's looking forward to finally meeting you. You'll like her, I'm sure. She's just normal. She cares, Lena. About everything.'

'Why?'

'What do you mean, why?' Jeff retorted, surprised by the response.

'Why does she care about everything?'

The superstar's mighty brain was duly stumped. How did one answer a question like that? Evidently, Madalena didn't understand the value of caring for anything. He didn't even know where to start. Much like himself twelve months ago, she had a long road ahead, and was this even a journey she would be interested in taking?

'*No importa,*' he said, shaking his head.

'Are you in love?' Madalena asked, after a minute's silence for the abandoned conversation.

Jeff nodded without looking away from the road in front of him. 'Of course. More every day.'

'Like you were with your posters?' the playful passenger teased him. 'Wankin' windows, you called 'em.'

'Did I? That's funny, but I don't remember saying it. *¿Estás segura?*'

'Yeah, I'm sure!' his sister asserted. 'Remember I caught you once? *¡Que fue vergonzoso!*'

'Probably,' the young man frowned. 'It happened a lot, so not surprised I got caught a few times. Have you ever been in love?'

The career hooker cackled. 'Na. Never! After what happened to Mamá? Just use 'em up and spit 'em out, that's what I say. No-good fuckers, all of 'em. Except you, *chico.*'

Jeff shook his head. 'Except me? You don't even know me, but thanks anyway. That's a bloody shame, Lena. I'm sorry you feel that way. Shit, isn't it?'

The tormented boy's left hand reached across from the gear lever towards his passenger, whose right hand was fiddling with the bottom button of her jacket. She let him take it, uncomfortable with his pity.

'Do you hate him like I do?' he asked. '*¿El papá?*'

'Fuck, yeah!' Madalena shouted, pulling her hand away. 'And those bloody Jawos. They're all a piece of shit. They're all the same. Pimps too. Fuckin' scumbags.'

A turgid hush descended from the roof of the car, enveloping the pair in its numbing cloud as they sped eastwards towards the CBD. Jeff cranked the radio up loud, just in time to hear his own latest single finishing. The young woman shrieked when his name was mentioned between songs and took great pleasure in expelling some choice expletives to let him know how often her friends teased her for having a famous brother.

Jeff was glad someone in his family felt excited by his success, and it improved his lacklustre mood. He was also relieved that their destination was in sight, catching glimpses of the dark structure of the Harbour Bridge between the buildings.

'Is that Sydney over there?' Madalena asked.

'Yeah. You've seen the harbour before,' her brother reminded her. 'We were here a couple of times when we were kids. The bridge is around the next corner.'

'No. Not me. I never come here.'

The woman was wrong, but her driver didn't push his luck. He wasn't surprised she had selective recall. It had likely served her well, as it turned out.

'Well, you're here now,' he said instead, as they lurched round a sharp corner and drove down beside Circular Quay. 'There's the Opera House. You've seen that too.'

'Yeah. On telly.'

'Right,' Jeff replied, smiling. 'Our hotel's just a few minutes away. Be nice to Lynn, *por favor, chica. Es muy importante para mí. Comprendes?*'

'*Sí, chico. Comprendo,*' Madalena nodded. 'You're in love and you want your wedding to go well. I get it, mate. That lady Celia told me. She was posh. Much posher than Michelle.'

Jeff let out a genuine laugh this time. 'Yep. Celia is posh. I'll grant you that! *Pero es muy simpatica también.*'

The siblings had reached the entrance of the hotel's underground car park. The Holden pulled up to the barrier, which stuttered and shook its way up to a near-vertical position in front of them. The awestruck woman whooped to see it move especially for them. Her brother found the first available parking space, opened the boot and removed her luggage, while she twirled in circles. Her joyous lack of inhibition would have been cute if she wasn't three years older than him and about to take part in his marriage ceremony, in Lynn Dyson's bridal party and in front of both the Prime Minister and the Governor General.

Jeff motioned to his sister to walk through a door to their left. 'Call the lift, please. Press "L".'

'"L" for lift,' Madalena chanted.

'"L" for lobby, actually,' her brother corrected her, amused by another childish response.

Without warning, his brain was awash with lyrics as he experienced a flashback to his dream girl's heart-stopping "Please wash me" remark. A pleasant sensation swirled around him like a cool waterfall. Fortunately, his charge was too busy staring around the mahogany and marble vehicle in which they were ascending to notice what had come over him. As they crossed the enormous entrance vestibule, everybody turned and stared at the striking celebrity and the thin woman who resembled him so closely.

The Catholic Argentinean Polish Jews saw a couple pointing, easily able to overhear them saying, 'That's Jeff Diamond, isn't it?'

The handsome star grinned but kept walking, grabbing Madalena by the elbow. Tugging his hand, she looked back, almost tripping over as she twisted round. 'They all *reckonnise* you. That's fuckin' amazing! What's it like?'

They had reached the lifts next to the main reception area.

'Great, most of the time, but it can really slow us down. Press "6" for six, please,' the young man teased.

His sister giggled, lunging for the bank of illuminated digits. 'OK, boss! What room are you in? Is it flash?'

'Six-oh-four,' Jeff replied. 'Yeah, it's flash. Huge bed. *¡Podría caber seis personas!*'

'*¿Seis?* Serious?' she exclaimed. 'Here we are. Six-oh-four. Can I open it?'

'Sure!'

The healing star flinched, having answered one of his questions. Unlike him, Madalena hadn't developed any door phobia. He had been carrying the key in his mouth since they exited the lift, now motioning for her to remove it.

However before the hapless woman had determined which way up the key needed to be inserted, the door opened for them. Lynn Dyson stood there, looking casual, radiant and extremely happy to see them.

'Hi!' she said, reaching to help her boyfriend with the baggage.

'It's OK, thanks, angel. *Entrar, señoritas.* Did you hear us?'

'Yes! Something about the bed being big enough for six people?' the pretty blonde laughed.

Jeff sat his sister's belongings down in order to give his saviour a re-energising hug. He needed it badly, she soon realised. Her eyes looked into his for answers, but none was forthcoming at present. She turned to the new arrival with open arms.

'Hi! It's so nice to meet you.'

A new Madalena had appeared; a demure, shy, overawed Madalena. Jeff took a moment to absorb the transformation while the two women stood eye-to-eye, still a metre apart. His diplomatic *fiancée* tried again. She walked closer and held her hands out.

'Thanks for coming to Melbourne,' she welcomed the stranger in their midst, casting her mind back to the odd passage her man had quoted from Camus' novel. 'I'm so excited to have you as my bridesmaid.'

The older woman allowed herself to be hugged, stiff and awkward. 'Hello. I can't believe it,' she stuttered, turning round to her brother for support. '*Chico*, it's really her. Just like on telly and in mags. He had your pictures on the wall in our room.'

Jeff smiled from under a furrowed brow at his gorgeous lady. 'Yeah. A bit older now though, and multi-dimensional.'

The older woman's expression suggested that this last adjective had gone over her head. Lynn looked from one to the other, eager to make friends.

'You look so alike. Same smile. We'd better get going. You're later than I thought.'

Her boyfriend looked at the alarm clock by the bed. 'Jesus! You're right. I'm an idiot. We should've left your luggage in the car, Lena. Not thinking straight.'

The nervous rock star passed their extra passenger's suit carrier to its owner and picked up his case, along with hers. Lynn carried her own bags willingly, stuffing their three tickets into her handbag. Door closed for the final time, they loaded everything onto a waiting trolley and made their way back to the lifts.

'"L" for lobby,' Madalena whispered under her breath, unable to take her eyes of the stunning superstar in the company of her little brother.

Once more in the car, the dark-haired stray sat quietly on the back seat, open-mouthed and staring out of the window. The same inexpressible thought occurred to her temporary guardians, each seeking to confirm what the other was thinking. While Jeff navigated the one-way system and drove towards Kingsford Smith, Lynn tried once more to break the ice.

'Madalena, it's my hens' night tonight. You're welcome to come, even though you won't know anyone.'

'Hens' night?' the shrill voice echoed. 'I danced at plenty of bucks' nights but I never been to a hens' before.'

This her brother didn't find at all hard to believe! He hadn't ever attended a hens' night either, but was willing to bet the dancing on this particular occasion would be slightly more sober and restrained. He rolled his eyes and muttered under his breath.

His girlfriend was more conciliatory however, censuring him gently. 'We'll be dancing too. Michelle'll be there. You met her a few weeks ago, didn't you?'

'Yeah. OK,' the hesitant bridesmaid agreed. 'Sounds good.'

The driver issued a silent prayer for the calming effect his beautiful best friend was having on his wild sibling. '*Excelente.* My bucks' night's tomorrow,' he added. 'Christ knows what Gerry's got in mind for me. I hate to think what sort of a headache I'll have the day after.'

The two young women alighted from the rental car at the Departures terminal while their handsome chaperone returned it to the depot. Lynn took charge of her overwhelmed future sister-in-law, seeing traces of the old Jeff in almost every trait.

'This way,' she invited, pushing the trolley with their bags piled high upon it.

'Here... Can I push that?' Madalena asked, suddenly full of enthusiasm.

'Certainly. Thanks!'

The slender, graceful celebrity walked beside her boyfriend's gangly sibling, gently steering her and their baggage trolley towards the check-in counters.

'I never been to the airport before,' the Sydney native began to open up.

Lynn Dyson was kind, she thought. Not full of herself like other pop stars she watched on the television. And quiet. Posh but not over-the-top. In fact, not at all how she had imagined her to be. What had her brother said? "Lynn cares about everything." Come to mention it, that kind of made sense now.

The superstar chuckled politely at the simple remark, which sounded as if their wide-eyed guest thought there was only one airport in the whole country. 'And I've been to way too many airports,' she countered. 'Especially in the last few weeks. We haven't been on the ground for more than three days in ages. I can't wait to get back to Melbourne.'

'So where d'you live?' Madalena asked, gradually feeling braver. 'With my brother?'

'Yeah. He's got an apartment in the city, on the top floor of a sixteen-storey block. You'll like it, I'm sure. We're going there today. But then on Tuesday, I'm going to my parents' farm to get ready for the wedding. I'm not sure what Jeff's got planned to do while you're here.'

Her *fiancé* caught them up in the queue for check-in, more relaxed for his few moments alone. They had taken the decision to book three Economy tickets from Sydney to Melbourne, given their new companion's unpredictability. Now finding her feet a little, she constantly shifted her gaze from Lynn to her brother and then to her colourful and noisy surroundings. She was no longer quite so uncomfortable, merely a little bemused at having been thrown into such a foreign world.

There wasn't much time to waste in the airport, thankfully. The first-time air traveller marvelled at the conveyor belts which whisked their luggage away behind the scenes. Making their way to the departure gate, they passed a cafeteria with an empty table in a secluded corner.

'Who wants coffee?' Jeff suggested, receiving exuberant nods from both women.

'Another coffee addict?' Lynn asked her boyfriend's sister once they had sat down.

'Shit, yeah. Not as much as him though. He always drunk heaps o' coffee. Used to sneak whisky in it from Dad's stash. He was always pissed too!'

'Really?' the young woman smiled. 'What a surprise!'

The butt of their humour arrived back to see the two conspirators laughing. 'What's so funny? I see it's going to be "Embarrass Jeff Day" from now on.'

'Your sister told me you used to put whisky in your coffee when you were a kid,' his *fiancée* updated him, eyes flashing with affection.

The grateful songwriter basked in the warmth, and not only from the coffee. 'Hmm… That'd be right,' he nodded. 'But did she also tell you I used to put it in hers too?'

'Shut up, *culo*,' Madalena grimaced.

Lynn laughed. 'Hey, I know what that means! He refuses to teach me the bad words.'

'Ha! I only use the bad words now. I hardly talk Spanish ever. No-one talks it round our way. Mostly Arabs now. Hey, *chico*! D'you know 'bout Alberto? He got locked up for keepin' immigrants in 'is club.'

'Yeah. I heard that,' Jeff confirmed. 'I saw him last year, just before he was charged. How long for, do you know?'

'Aw, not long,' his sister shrugged. 'He's out now. Layin' low.'

Their flight was announced as soon to commence boarding, so the threesome gulped down their coffees. Madalena began to show signs of nerves for her first ever take-off, clinging on to her brother's arm. Jeff saw Lynn's gaze alight on the red-painted talons clenched around his elbow and winked. From every direction, people pointed and shouted their greetings and good wishes.

Their frightened fellow traveller's mouth was by now permanently open in amazement at the attention her brother and his famous girlfriend drew. Young children were sent to request autographs by shy parents, and not-so-shy parents sidled up for a chat in the queue. Everyone wanted to hear about the wedding of the decade, leaving the stars no alternative but to answer the same old questions again and again while patiently shuffling towards the entrance to the aerobridge.

'How do you stand all this *scandolo*?' Madalena asked. 'I'd be like, "Fuck off, you bastards? I'm gettin' on a 'plane."'

The dignified couple looked at each other, unable to prevent themselves from laughing, before shooting apologetic looks at those still waiting for their chance to say hello.

'Thanks for that, Lena! We'll be sure to try that next time. It's *escandolo*, by the way,' the songwriter responded, stressing the first syllable missed by the uneducated woman.

The Fairfield nobody stuck her tongue out. 'Smart-arse! You always tried to be smarter than me.'

Lynn was forced to turn away, not wishing to encourage the blabbering woman and noticing that her cool intellectual had also let this one go through to the keeper. Finally past the desk and clutching their boarding pass stubs, the *trio* made their way to their seats. Frustrated and relieved to be on board, Jeff ushered their guest into the window seat.

'Are you scared of heights?' he asked.

'Dunno,' she answered. 'Ain't never been up 'igh yet, 'ave I?'

162

Smiling again, the sportswoman perched on the edge of the aisle seat and watched her boyfriend's six-feet-four-inch frame squeeze in between them. 'Do you want to sit here?' she offered.

'No. This is fine, thanks, angel. Just don't expect me to breathe.'

Madalena sniggered. 'Don't breathe! You'll be goin' to your funeral not your bloody weddin'.'

'Funny, funny,' Jeff groaned. 'Put your seatbelt on, please. *Eso aquí.*'

He handed his sister the two ends of her belt straps and showed her how to fasten the buckle. It clicked into position, and he received a satisfied grin from a crooked but reasonably clean set of teeth. Her face was pretty, he concluded, if a little weathered from years of smoking. With the services of a good make-up artist and hairdresser, his sister would scrub up fine for the wedding pictures. He sighed at the thought of the myriad magazine articles and news bulletins he expected to feature the photographs and other footage, wondering if his own face muscles would have the stamina to smile for so long.

'How long is it to Melbourne?' Madalena asked, lifting her bottom off the seat cushion to stare around the aeroplane. 'Do I get any food?'

The celebrity couple exchanged the same thought again; a veritable glimpse into their future.

'Yes. We'll get lunch after we've taken off,' Lynn confirmed.

'*Excelente,*' the young man responded, thumping his armrests like a spoiled child. 'I had a beer on an empty stomach. I need food now!'

Busy staring out of the window to her right, his sister jumped as the aircraft shunted backwards, away from the gate. 'Shit! We're movin'.'

'*Si, hermana mía,*' Jeff said in a supercilious tone. '*Se necessito.*'

'*Chico,*' Madalena whined, 'I'm not that dumb.'

The rock star overheard someone in front of them laugh and felt guilty for teasing the virgin jetsetter again. 'Sorry, Lena. Just wait until we're taking off. You'll be impressed.'

The passengers sat quietly while the aeroplane taxied to the end of the runway, some paying attention to the safety demonstration being carried out in the aisle while the rest carried on reading or snoozing. The flight was full, and the sound of chatter soon carried on around them.

'This is exhausting,' the drained man whispered into his stalwart companion's ear, taking the opportunity to nip her delicate skin with a quick kiss. 'Why is everything we do so bloody hard? I want to retire.'

Lynn leaned into his arm. 'No, you don't. She's lovely, Jeff. Sweet.'

The exasperated musician couldn't altogether agree with his girlfriend's generous, rose-coloured impression, despite being prepared to admit that his view was a little tainted. After a final turn, the engines roared, and the aeroplane lurched forward. Madalena's hands gripped the armrests, and her neck and jaw muscles became taut. Her brother left her alone, ready for any sign of panic. The ground was left behind within fifteen seconds, and the jets strained to push the buffeting aircraft through the coastal breeze.

'Fuck!' the amazed woman mouthed to her brother.

He smiled, putting his finger to his mouth to make sure she didn't say this word again or louder. 'You OK?'

Waiting until he had made sure his sister was comfortable, Lynn tapped Jeff's arm, fluttering a piece of paper she had been reading. 'Look at this,' she said, clearly excited. 'We've got the freehold for the building in Hawthorn. I talked to Admin while you were collecting Madalena, and they faxed me the paperwork through this morning.'

'Whoa! *Fantastico!*' her man replied. 'That's great news. We can kick that thing off properly now.'

This particular building was to be the new headquarters for the Australian arm of Childlight. The charity had been a huge success in the UK and had attracted substantial donations, exactly as it had in their home country. As his partner-in-crime had hoped, this nugget of good cheer re-energised the philanthropist sufficiently to turn back to his sister and fulfil his entertainment obligations.

'Hey, *chica.* D'you like your dress for the wedding?'

'Yeah. It's cool,' Madalena replied, looking past him to Lynn. 'I got another one too. Dunno what for... What's yours like?'

'Shhh! I can't discuss it in front of the groom,' she laughed, tapping the side of her nose with her index finger. 'I'll tell you later.'

'Oh, yeah. That woman, Celia, told me that,' the bridesmaid looked sheepish. 'I'll shut up about it.'

'That's OK,' the gracious singer smiled. 'The other dress might be for the hens' night. Oh, here's lunch.'

The flight attendants fussed around their star passengers, taking their drinks orders and lifting plastic trays over their heads. Jeff needed to demonstrate how to release the tray-table, and his sister's dropped down suddenly, taking her by surprise.

'It don't smell too good,' Madalena complained, wrinkling her nose at the aroma drifting through the cabin. 'What is it?'

'Pot luck,' her brother scoffed. 'Even if they told you what it's supposed to be, you'd never recognise it.'

His sarcasm was lost on Madalena. Their nearby neighbours evidently enjoyed it however, judging by the tittering from the seats in front. Bewildered again, she peeled back the foil lid, steam scalding her fingers and making her swear again. Inside was *lasagne*, purportedly, with a few peas and carrots. The *pasta* was curled up at the edges and crusted on to the container, yet edible nonetheless.

'Nice,' she changed her mind, scoffing it down.

'Hey! Slow down,' Jeff warned in a low voice. '*Tienes que comer más lentamente. Nadie lo tomará de tigo.* You're going to get fat before you go home.'

'*¡Ai!*' Madalena exclaimed. 'I can't get fat. I have to...'

The smiling superstar cupped his hand over his sister's mouth, knowing she was about to make reference to her profession. 'Leave it out, Lena. Not here!'

From the left-hand side of her struggling *fiancé*, the sympathetic blonde rested a hand on his arm. This fish out of water was a handful, not unlike her brother had been before his rapid recovery. The memory of his first flight to New Zealand was at the forefront of her mind, and she breathed a sigh of relief for how much easier their relationship had become.

The next few days promised to be a challenge for them all. Both bride and groom had a great deal to do before the big day, and Madalena did not appear to be in the least bit self-sufficient. Lynn knew Jeff had put Cathy on notice that his sister may need caretaking, but his team was bound to be busy too, and Gerry would be far from tolerant of such *bogan* behaviour. They would manage, she assured herself. They had no choice.

The hour-long flight passed quickly. Jeff hadn't spoken to his sister about anything substantial, owing to the array of inquisitive ears tuned into the famous couple's every word. She asked about his concerts, and his abridged account skirted round the whole truth for fear of sounding conceited. He enquired about friends he remembered from their teenaged years, frequently needing to cut her replies short before she publicised something his reputation would prefer not to have in the public domain.

The engines cut before too long, and the aeroplane began to drift in towards Tullamarine. At first, Madalena wasn't brave enough to look out of the window, yet curiosity got the better of her after a while. The city looked enormous stretched out to her left and underneath the fuselage, having no idea which landmarks to watch out for. Her kid brother was holding Lynn Dyson's hand, she noticed, watching them kiss out of the corner of her eye. They did go well together. Moreover, this boy she had never understood was quite obviously someone very important these days, and by some miracle, he was marrying the girl of his childhood fantasies.

Landing in Melbourne was strangely cathartic, and the Europhile realised he was pleased to be home after all. Catching up with his surrogate family in Sydney and seeing how excited they were to see him and his gorgeous *fiancée* had left him guilt-ridden for his selfish desires to leave them all behind. Life was all about balance, he replayed his *Regala*'s sound advice. Lynn and he were in the fortunate position of being able to be anywhere they wanted to be simply by manipulating their schedules, so there was no basis for his complaint.

'Home,' the grateful young woman sighed, as the wheels bounced on the tarmac. 'It seems to have taken an eternity to get home.'

'Sure has,' her boyfriend agreed. '¿*Lena, qué tal? Estás blanca como la blanca.*'

Madalena was speechless. She stared out of the window and watched the airport terminal building coming towards them. As soon as the aircraft came to a standstill, their neighbouring passengers jumped up out of their seats and started collecting their belongings, anxious to get on with their days.

Jeff attracted his girlfriend's attention as they watched a Business Class flight attendant struggling against the tide. He reached their row at last, breathlessly asking if they wished to be taken off first.

'No, thanks. We'll wait 'til the end, if you don't mind,' Lynn assured the smartly-dressed man. 'Thanks a lot for thinking of us. We're not in a hurry.'

So much for travelling anonymously among ordinary folk! Anyone who hadn't noticed their famous travelling companions up to this point now knew for certain who they were, and a renewed wave of excitement rushed through the cabin. The noise level spiked as everyone tried to talk to, at or over the much-loved celebrities. The handsome comic closed his eyes and rested a heavy hand on each woman's forearm.

His *fiancée* made eye contact with the man's confused sister in the window seat and mouthed "Shhh", tilting her head towards him. Madalena rolled her eyes. He was such a spoiled brat now!

Eventually, the aircraft was empty enough for the threesome to walk out in a dignified manner. The two stars sandwiched their nervous fellow traveller between them until they emerged from the aerobridge into the main terminal. Their driver was already waiting at the gate, with a sign which read "DDD".

'Nice touch, angel,' Jeff winked at his girlfriend, kissing her fondly.

'What?' Madalena asked, clueless again.

'Normally when we arrive places, they just have "DD",' Jeff explained. 'And it doesn't mean ginormous tits, if that's what you're thinking. The third "D"'s for you today.'

'I'm not "D". I'm "M",' his sister corrected them. 'I'm not Lena Diamond no more. I go by Moreno.'

'Since when?'

Jeff tried to disguise his shock, feeling at once dejected and confused. This was probably a wise move on reflection, given the fears he currently harboured. Perhaps he should have done the same a few years ago. Too late now, judging by the extreme amount of attention the newly-arrived passengers were receiving.

The crowds waiting around the celebrities' arrival gate were overwhelming. How people ever got wind of their travel plans beggared belief, with all the decoys Cathy and the staff at their management company threw to the press. Security guards had been drafted in from all over the airport to help keep the throngs of well-wishers from mobbing the happy couple and their mystery companion. It wouldn't have taken a genius to work out that this tall woman with Mediterranean features must be Jeff Diamond's sister. The resemblance was striking.

After their long journey, neither musician was inclined to pause and sign autographs. Both launched a slew of innocuous sentences into the air in response to the ceaseless questions. They were ready to scream by the time their luggage had been retrieved and they were ready to make their way to the waiting car.

'Hey! Have you got door keys?' Lynn asked of her exhausted boyfriend, a look of dread on her face.

With the car's engine running and a full load on board, the thought suddenly occurred to her that she had overlooked this small necessity while they were packing. From the front seat... the Australian way... Jeff leaned back and shoved his hand into his pants pocket, pulling out a familiar key ring and brandishing the jangling collection over his shoulder.

'Oh, thank God for that!' the twenty-year-old sighed in relief. 'I'm glad one of us was thinking.'

'And it ain't normally me!' the young man chuckled, notching up a score in mid-air.

It was more than a little weird to pull up in front of their city apartment building after so long. And even more weird to have his six-year-old big sister with them, tugging on their metaphorical coat-tails. Between them, they transferred their luggage into the lift, and Jeff pressed the combination to get to the top floor. The lift doors closed, and they glided towards the roof.

'Penthouse!' Madalena chortled. 'Like the mag'. You live in the fuckin' penthouse.'

'Yep. The fucking penthouse,' the self-made millionnaire repeated, slightly sickened by the scornful connotation. 'We live in the fucking penthouse, don't we, angel?'

Lynn thought better of joining in. She saw Jeff was annoyed, but this wild woman was not yet her responsibility. She caught her lover's eye to check if he wanted her to open the front door, only to receive a definite "No." Her tired heart jumped for joy. Confidence was all he needed. Their time in London had given him all the confidence he would ever need.

Truth be told, the lost boy transformed did feel uneasy approaching the solid door with which he had battled so often during his darkest days, yet he wasn't prepared to let it beat him. He lifted the key and slid it into the lock, taking a deep but noiseless breath. It resisted at first, stiff after an idle year, but he gripped the key harder and applied a little more force.

A sharp click signalled the latch snapping out of its housing, and the door swang away from him, cracking and spitting its objections. The owner's heart rate quickened in anticipation of visiting demons, but none made itself known. He stood back and gestured to the others to walk on through.

'Home, sweet home!' he shouted triumphantly, pulling his guardian angel into his body and kissing her.

As she voiced her half-hearted objection to being manhandled so roughly, she broke away, eager to hear his verdict.

Reading her mind, Jeff paused to whisper in her ear. 'Welcome back to the fucking penthouse, gorgeous. Too easy.'

'Fantastic,' she mimed back, ecstatic. 'Welcome home. I love you.'

The cream marble flooring and the cool pastel colours on the hallway walls and ceiling appealed to their visitor. She paced all the way to the end with her bag as if hypnotised by her circumstance before wheeling around to find out where the others were. She caught sight of them sneaking a kiss in the doorway and carried on walking. The lounge was the quite biggest room she had ever stood in. And the view! As far as the eye could see...

Her brother followed her in, leaning on the back of the couch to watch their transfixed guest absorb the scene. He allowed a humble sense of pride to surge through his veins. He had earned every square metre of this beautiful home, fair and square and after tax. It was, he had no choice but to admit, very nice to be home.

'You can see Sydney if you look hard enough,' the joker suggested, seeing his sister's nose pressed into the sliding glass door. 'I'll open them in a minute.'

'Fuckin' 'ell, *chico*,' Madalena yelped. 'This place is bloody amazing. Did you buy it?'

'Yep,' Jeff answered. 'Cool, no?'

'Heaps more than cool! And look at the piano. Not like *Bubshka*'s. Grand piano?'

Lynn had disappeared into the bedroom, preferring to leave the siblings to themselves for a few minutes. At last inside the apartment they had shared for such a short time, the lost boy felt desperately lonely for his dream girl right at this moment, but issued her a silent vote of thanks for doing the right thing as usual. He was trapped with this erratic firecracker of expletives whom he hardly knew but was beginning to want to know better.

'Yeah. Baby grand. Smaller than a full grand. Open it,' the songwriter invited, pointing to the lid of the polished black instrument which had seen no action for almost twelve months. 'Can you still play anything?'

'Na!' Madalena snapped. 'Course not. You play somethin'.'

Yes, Jeff thought. He would play something. This was a good idea. He lifted the stool back, sat down and adjusted its position until his feet were in line with the pedals. Opening the lid, he caught his breath, once more hit by an incisive humility. He scarcely remembered this piano, in spite of the number of chart-topping songs it had helped him to write. A few expansive chords tested the acoustics in the room, and the composer knew at once that Lynn must have had it tuned last week. Such things happened around him like magic.

'This one I wrote about you and me,' Jeff Diamond told his older sister without pathos.

He played one of his earliest hits as fluently as if he had been practising it all morning, his rich baritone caressing the lyric after rasping and cracking into life. He had smoked half a dozen cigarettes since disembarking from their long flight without having sung a note for twenty-four hours, and the gradual smoothing gave the plaintive phrases even greater solemnity.

Madalena was riveted. She had heard her brother's distinctive voice on the radio countless times and had seen him perform on television, even once live. This was totally different though... The man they called The Australian Elvis was singing to her in his swanky apartment in Melbourne.

'Did you really write it about me?' the woman asked. 'Play it again.'

Jeff nodded without breaking the flow. The hardness in his ragged sister's expression was fading like a watercolour left out in a shower. He willed his heart to react more strongly to the occasion, but it couldn't. Why? It was so unlike him not to feel anything. His senses habitually tipped too readily into overload, needing to hold back.

Convinced there was an emotion inside somewhere, the singer started again from the top. While he reprised the first verse, he sensed his dream girl enter the room behind him. He begged her telepathically to give him permission to feel; a sanction to bond with this blood stranger they had brought to town.

As if she were reading his mind, Lynn's loving hands alighted on his shoulders before the end of the chorus. The storyteller sang louder, a rush of sexual tension rising within him. The love of his life leaned forward, pressing against his back and with his head poised in front of her breasts. The sensations became more vivid the louder he played and the more she touched him. He could hardly tell which pair of hands was causing the spell to work, putting the wise money on hers rather than his.

'Play "Rain On Tonight",' his biggest fan requested. 'That's a good one for Madalena too.'

Exhaling deeply, the showman tipped his head back and settled into her cleavage, eliciting an affectionate chuckle from both lovers. His girlfriend kissed the top of his head, and his concentration was instantly shattered. Shaking his head while his sister looked on in typical confusion, it was a stretch to think back to the opening bars of a song he seldom played.

The homecoming rock star looked over at the woman on the far side of the room, with her dark, wavy hair and stick-like limbs, and sang without inhibition. His heart beat faster, and his eyes began to sting. It seemed as though the magic was gradually infiltrating the space between them, but the long-hidden familial link was disinclined to show itself too soon.

It was a hard ask, Jeff realised. Were it not for his upcoming special occasion, he and Madalena may never have spoken again for the rest of their lives. Why was he always so impulsive? What had he been expecting? He pulled back and promised himself that he would rekindle some sort of sibling bond before they flew apart again.

'That's enough,' he declared, thumping a loud final chord twice for good measure. '*Gracias por venir, Lena. Es buen' qu estás aquí.*'

'We should have a drink to celebrate getting home and having you here,' Lynn suggested, breaking the tension. 'How about some wine?'

'Drink? OK. Have you got beer? I don't like wine,' their guest countered. 'Can you do "Go Down Easy" now? That's my fave of 'em all.'

'Christ! On my own? Not at the piano,' came Jeff's gruff retort. 'That one wouldn't work without the band. Let's open a bottle of wine, angel. Thanks.'

The mellowing rock star looked around for his twelve-stringed guitar, riddled with guilt for having dismissed the request so readily. Remembering their collection of instruments was still on its way back from London, he picked out a few chords anyway. A blues version might work, although this hard-edged clubber was then unlikely to recognise the monster hit from nineteen-seventy-three which he invariably saved until his first *encore*.

'Oh, yeah. I forgot,' he smirked. 'No guitars here yet. I'll give it a go. The faster songs need the guitar, y'see?'

While the entertainer sought to satisfy his critical audience, the lady of the house returned with a bottle of red, three wine glasses and an ice-cold beer to cover all bases. In an effort to add more depth to the driving beat from the bass octaves, she provided some backing vocals and pounded the top of the couch's cushions as a makeshift drum-kit. Even with all these improvisations, the variation on a theme didn't work too well.

'Sorry, Lena,' he laughed, pulling a throat-cutting motion. 'I'll figure something out before you go.'

'Try some wine,' Lynn invited. 'It's much stronger than beer.'

She had hit Madalena's hot button, not exactly by chance. Their ill-mannered visitor's attention was diverted, for which Jeff gave his future wife a knowing, grateful nod. She was an expert at getting the best out of people, setting them a challenge too tempting to pass up.

'Can I smoke?' Madalena asked, her eyes darting from one host to the other.

'Sure. Good idea,' her brother answered, standing up and pushing the piano stool to one side. '*Momento.* I'll find the keys for these doors.'

Madalena walked towards the picture windows which ran the whole width of the living room. '*Madre de Dios!* Is that yours too?' she asked, pointing outside.

'The northern suburbs?' the young man scoffed, walking over to toast his *fiancée*'s able assistance. 'No. Not yet.'

'Na!' his sister whined. 'The fucking balcony, you dick.'

Shrugging, one of the richest men in Australia located the keys from a drawer in the coffee table, where they had been taped out of sight while the apartment had lain vacant. He beckoned Madalena towards him, removed the cellophane from a new packet of duty-free cigarettes and flicked it open for her. She took one out eagerly and stood waiting for him to offer her a light. The sexy smoker put a cigarette in his mouth and fished into his trouser pocket for a lighter.

'Yes, Lena,' he hissed in annoyance, unlocking the door and sliding it across. 'The fucking balcony belongs to this dick and that beautiful angel over there. You got a problem with that?'

Leaving the dark-haired *duo* together again, Lynn drank in the wonderful sight of Jeff smoking, seeing him offer his sister a seat in the open air. His left foot kicked idly at the table leg as they talked, clearly signalling a great deal of hidden animosity between them, bubbling away beneath the surface.

Cigarette finished and squashed into the floor under her foot, Madalena sauntered with her wine glass to the far side of the tiled terrace to gaze out over the rooftops of Carlton and Fitzroy. Having reached the railing, she turned and screeched at her brother.

'Jesus! What floor are we on?'

Jeff followed her to the edge, allowing her to grip his arm and gaze all the way down to the street below. 'Sixteenth! Higher than your flat, eh?'

The amused songwriter led his sister back to the table, bidding her to join him. She obeyed, twisting her chair to face into the sun. Downing the rest of his wine, he took another two cigarettes out of the packet and lit them both, sitting with his back to the stupendous view of his adopted city.

'Take it easy, will you, please?' he urged, blowing smoke into the cool early-evening breeze. 'We've got heaps to do over the next few days and we need you to help out a bit. I'll give you some 'phone numbers for our friends, so you can call them if you get lost in town. And whatever happens, don't bring any drugs back here. Please? I know you think I'm an arsehole, but we can't afford to take any risks. *¿Comprendes?*'

The sullen woman nodded, picking flecks of ash from her tongue with painted fingernails and smearing saliva along the edge of the glass table-top. 'Yeah. I understand. I'll be good while I'm 'ere. I don't know no-one anyways, so how can I get drugs?'

Taking a hundred dollars out of his wallet and handing the notes to his sister, Jeff shrugged. 'I don't know. I'm just asking, so you know.'

'Cheers, *chico*,' Madalena said, snatching the money as if it were from a client she couldn't wait to get rid of. 'I won't make trouble for you. I like Lynn. She's good for you.'

Her brother smiled. 'You're not wrong. She's so bloody good for me. She accepts me the way I am.'

'You're completely different to before, but. Relaxed and laid-back. I never remember you bein' laid-back before.'

'Maybe,' the happy man shrugged. 'I only ever saw you when something shit-house was going on. No wonder that's all you remember. How are the old folks, anyway? Still bitter and twisted?'

Madalena chuckled. 'Only about Dad and you. I never knew what you done though. Sometimes I stuck up for you, but they don't listen. What did ya do?'

'¡*Nada!*' Jeff answered in defiance. 'You know I called in there last year, looking for you? Did she tell you?'

'Na. What'd ya want?'

The millionnaire rock star hesitated, weighing up the risk of being honest. This was his sister, after all. Did she still hang out with the same set of aimless locals who bore malice toward everyone better off than them, not even smart enough to be disillusioned? Lynn had been right to suggest making his own enquiries, and Madalena's photograph would be in all the newspapers in a few days' time.

'I needed to find out what was happening in Fairfield and on The Stones. Lynn's dad was snooping around, and I wanted to know who was still on the patch and what was being said. I wanted to know if you'd heard anything.'

'Shit!' Madalena cried out. 'There ain't nothin' to know, chico. Them blokes aren't hangin' round me like a fart no more, if that's what ya mean.'

Sniffing in derision, she stubbed out her cigarette on the glass table and brushed the ash onto the tiles, gazing past the side of his head. Her first had been tossed onto the gleaming tiles and squashed by an equally angry foot a few minutes earlier, leaving an ugly, damp smear. Jeff's expression didn't change. It wasn't worth the energy. She would be gone soon.

'No-one cares about that stuff anymore,' his sister continued. 'They forgot about it for a bit, then it started again when you got famous. People askin' questions. But now it's all stopped again.'

None the wiser for his sister's confused version of the truth, the tired superstar ushered her back into the lounge room. His beautiful best friend patted the cushion beside her on the couch, requesting them to join her while she sifted through a pile of letters and other items. Their guest made herself comfortable on the second sofa, kicking her shoes off and stretching along its full width.

'Make yourself at home,' her brother shook his head at the contented sigh emanating from Lady Muck herself.

'Put a record on,' Lynn suggested, jumping up to hand round refilled wine glasses. 'Then we could listen to "Go Down Easy" the way it's supposed to sound.'

'Now why didn't I think of that?' Jeff grinned, blowing the gorgeous woman a kiss. 'Good idea. We can listen to me all night. What could possibly be better than that?'

Madalena groaned. 'Is he always this big-'eaded?'

The blonde singer laughed out loud. 'Yes!'

'Hey!' her boyfriend objected. 'Whose side are you on? Christ! That's not fair.'

'No. It's not,' his girlfriend nobly rescinded her previous answer. 'He's only joking. We hardly ever listen to our own music.'

The full-bodied Shiraz slipped down the visitor's throat rather nicely, to her surprise. 'Ooh! This is pretty good. I never 'ad red wine before. It bites all the way down 'ere,' she observed, running a finger from her neck, all the way through the gap between her breasts.

'Why don't you show Madalena to her room?'

Jeff stood up, pleased to expend some more nervous energy. 'Good idea again. You're on the ball today, angel. *Sígueme, Lena, por favor.*'

From the hallway, the brother and sister with different surnames heard the introductory strains of his massive early hit fill the apartment. He had forgotten how powerful his music system was, having become accustomed to a stereo of inferior quality in London. Madalena turned round briefly too, starting to sing along, but changed her mind. Her eyes had already caught a glimpse of the bedroom into which Jeff was pointing.

'*¡Puto, chico!*' she exclaimed, her jaw dropping again. 'This is a fuckin' palace. Is this where I'm sleepin'?'

'Yep. It's just a bedroom. The bathroom's here.'

The young woman whistled again when she clapped eyes on the sumptuous, glistening marble and polished brass tap fittings. She made straight for the set of soft, inviting towels, pulling one off the rail and wrapping herself in it.

Her brother continued from the doorway. 'Our room's over here, and the kitchen's next to the lounge room. Just help yourself to anything.'

Madalena cackled, appreciating an unintended irony in his words. 'You think I'll steal stuff, don't ya?'

'No,' answered the boy from the western suburbs, 'but I know you'll be thinking about it.'

'Why did you write so many sad songs?'

Jeff was taken aback by such a sensitive question out of the blue. 'Jesus, Lena! I don't know,' he replied. 'I write what I feel. Sometimes I feel sad or angry, so I write sad or angry. Sometimes I write happy. It depends what I'm thinking about at the time, and what I can make out of it.'

His answer met with his sister's approval. The people's poet remarked inwardly that a truly caring person would have enquired about what made him sad before recalling in whose presence he was. The abuse she had suffered at the hands of so many awful men and at such an early age had rendered her heartless and indifferent to suffering, whether someone else's or her own.

'I wrote a few poems once,' she blurted out, suddenly blushing. 'Yonks ago, when I lived at *Abuela*'s. And then when I got pregnant.'

'*¿Verdad?*' he asked, amazed both by the news and by her reddened complexion. 'D'you remember any of them?'

'Na!' the skinny woman scoffed. 'They were *crapola*.'

Her brother shook his head and smiled with compassion. 'Nothing from the heart is *crapola*. You should try and remember them. You might be a successful songwriter waiting to be discovered too!'

Madalena laughed again, childishly dismissing her famous host's comments. After a brief circuit to take in the rest of the apartment, the pair wandered back into the lounge room, passing by the master bedroom, wherein Lynn had begun to unpack. Once he realised she had dodged them, her *fiancé* returned to fetch his *Regala*, leaning in for a long, hard kiss to take advantage of their handful of seconds alone.

'I love you so much,' Jeff told her, fondling her engagement ring between the thumb and middle finger of his right hand. 'You're great with her. She's putty in your hands.'

The sophisticated woman shrugged. 'I had the best teacher.'

'Yeah? Thanks, but that couldn't possibly have been me. She drives me absolutely berserk,' the frustrated man confessed. 'She needs a bloody babysitter. D'you think she's up to the responsibility of walking down the aisle?'

'It'll be fine. Michelle'll look after her,' the smiling goddess assured him. 'She'll calm down after a while.'

'*Digame*, angel... When we were in the car going to the airport, did that look you gave me mean it was like we had our own kid in the back seat?'

'Yes!' Lynn exhaled, goosebumps raising the skin on her arms. 'I wondered if that's what you were thinking too. She's so dazed by the whole thing. A bit like you were when we flew to Queenstown.'

'S'pose so,' Jeff reluctantly agreed, not welcoming the comparison but admitting a fair likeness. 'Come on through with us, baby. We can take care of all this later.'

***

Jeff's eyes invited his dream girl to drink some more wine. Most probably to stop Madalena from polishing off way more than her share. The neck of the bottle hovered over her glass, so she obliged although she didn't really feel like any more. There was so much to do tomorrow, and drowsiness threatened to consume the *trio*.

The telephone rang on the table behind Lynn's ear. It was the first time they had heard its distinctively Australian ring-tone since they had returned from overseas, at first not registering where the noise was coming from. Lynn twisted her arm around to answer it, handing her glass to her *fiancé*.

'Hello?'

'Lynn, hi!'

'Welcome home!'

'Mish!' the happy woman exclaimed. 'Thanks! How are you?'

'Great! And you guys? Is Jeff there? When did you get back?' Michelle asked, excited to hear her close friend's voice. 'Can I come and pick you up?'

The sportswoman sighed, pulling a face for her quizzical boyfriend. 'Yes, definitely. We've only been back here for a short time. Is half an hour OK?'

The pair had arranged to get together to check out their outfits at the first opportunity. Lynn's wedding dress was at the redhead's flat, and the young bride couldn't wait to see it and touch it for the first time. Their favourite tailor had put the finishing touches to the design by correspondence over the last few weeks, and she had received some Polaroid photographs just before they had flown out. She adored what little detail she could make out and could hardly wait to try it on.

Jeff had switched on the television in an attempt to distract Madalena. He looked at his wits' end, nervous of each and every ill-conceived comment. His girlfriend decided to rescue him again. She knew she oughtn't to and could imagine Gerry's warning finger tapping on her conscience, but her tired lover wouldn't be expecting it. This was justification enough in her mind.

'Jeff's sister'll be coming with us,' she told her maid of honour. 'I'll get her to bring her outfit too, and we can all get kitted out together.'

Michelle was happy with this idea. It would be good for the bridesmaids to get to know each other better before the day. 'OK. Great! We'll come back here to get ready for tonight, so you can bring her then too. Might as well all go from here together and leave cars at home.'

The deal done, Lynn put the telephone down and re-joined the others. 'That was Mish,' she announced. 'She'll be here in a few minutes. We'll leave Jeff on his own for a few hours, Madalena, while we try our dresses on together. Is that OK?'

The young man looked from his sister to his partner and back again. The offer was tempting indeed, but surely he couldn't burden the two close friends this way. His eyes travelled to the skinny girl who had never grown up and felt drained by a bewildering shame at not being better equipped to entertain his own sister. Was he game to stare at this gift horse's tonsils?

'Thanks, angel, but it's OK. Lena and I can look after ourselves. You go. You guys haven't seen each other for so long.'

'No. We're fine. It'll be great!' his girlfriend insisted. 'I'm excited to see what we all look like together. Is that alright with you, Madalena?'

The startled guest was excited to be part of the preparations, but apprehensive too. 'Yeah. I don't care. I haven't put the whole kit on before. Where're we going?'

Are you sure? Jeff looked at Lynn again, and her eyes gave him permission.

'Just to Carlton. A bit north of here. It's only five minutes' drive,' she told their visitor.

'OK. Cool,' Madalena shrugged at her brother. 'Is the hens' party still tonight?'

'Yes. But we'll come back here beforehand to get ready. You might want not to be here!' Lynn instructed her flatmate with a cheerful grin.

'Hmm...' he agreed. 'I forgot about that! Perhaps. Hey, Lena. Do yourself a favour...'

'What?' his sister's voice was laced with suspicion.

'Don't go on about what you do for a living tonight, please? Lynn's mates don't want to hear about that stuff. They won't take it too well.'

Madalena simply shook her head, showing no emotion. 'I know.'

Neither musician had the faintest clue as to the meaning behind their visitor's response. They would just have to wait and see. The singer took charge of her new *amigo,* and they migrated to her bedroom to sort out what she needed to take to Michelle's. Jeff was in the master bedroom when his *fiancée* returned to fetch her own belongings, walking open-armed towards him. They kissed for a long time, making the most of another unforeseen slither of privacy.

'Are you sure about this?' he asked. 'You don't have to. She's my responsibility.'

'It'll be fine,' Lynn assured him, seeing the relief her man was doing his best to hide. 'I want to get to know her. It'll be much better than going out tonight cold, not knowing what to talk about. Are you staying here?'

The world's most fortunate man thought for a second, looking at the clock. 'I might give Gerry a ring and catch up on some boring bureaucracy,' he smiled, still scarcely believing his lucky break. 'He's got the tickets for The Canary Islands too, so I may as well get them from him now. Christ! I'm so hanging out for some time on that boat!'

176

'Me too. Hey!' the young woman whooped as her feet left the floor, being swung in a circle.

'Three weeks of sun, sea and sex. Can't fucking wait, *chica*!'

'And no press conferences,' Lynn added. 'Hopefully anyway. If anything happens this afternoon, I'll 'phone here or Gerry's office. If you're going to go anywhere else, please could you ring us at Michelle's?'

Jeff nodded. 'Yep. No worries. Thanks, angel. I really appreciate you doing this. I owe you. Again.'

'No. You don't owe me anything,' the smiling beauty replied, stroking the hair on his chest and kissing him a fond farewell. 'We're in this together, remember?'

The couple returned to the lounge room, where Madalena was already standing next to her luggage as if she were waiting for a bus. A buzzer sounded in the hallway, making the baffled guest jump out of her skin.

'Jesus! What's that?'

Lynn ran out into the hall to answer it. 'Hi, Mish! I'll be right down.'

From his seat at the piano, the songwriter had snatched an opportune moment to write down one of the new songs that were taking shape inside his head. He heard the door click shut behind his dream girl and got up to see if his sister was alright. He stared in amazement at the funny scene, handing her a piece of paper listing various telephone numbers and the address of their apartment.

'Have fun this *arvo*,' he said. 'Just ring this number if you need anything. The girls'll take good care of you, I'm sure.'

Lynn arrived back with her longtime friend, deep in conversation.

'Hi, Jeff! Hi, Madalena!' Michelle yelled, running to hug the good-looking hunk of manliness. 'Welcome back! And congratulations, face-to-face at last! You look great! Thank you for proposing to my bestie. What a fantastic excuse to get dressed up!'

The groom-to-be accepted her vociferous greeting with enthusiasm. 'You're welcome! Tough gig, but someone had to take her. Couldn't have Lynn Dyson left on the shelf, could we?'

The ginger-haired solicitor squeezed his biceps. 'Ooh! You feel good too!' she squealed. 'Lynn told me you'd been working out. Mmm... Very nice.'

Jeff's sister looked on in silence as the affectionate scene played out. She watched her brother hug the new arrival and kiss her cheek, jealous of his newfound happiness. She had never had a male friend. Her grandfather and uncles had looked after her well enough, but every other man in her life paid in cash.

Michelle turned and extended her hand to Madalena, who smiled and issued an awkward wave.

'Let's go!' Lynn announced, picking up her bags.

She kissed the amused songwriter, still glowing from the gratuitous compliments. He grabbed her in close to him, joking that there were so many bags, boxes and other bits and pieces heading downstairs that it looked like a shopping spree in reverse.

Two of the three women laughed.

'Enjoy yourselves,' he called after them. 'You'll look stunning, all of you. And if I'm not here before you go out tonight, don't get into trouble.'

'Can we say the same to you tomorrow?' his girlfriend turned and asked.

Feigning indignance, Jeff put his hand on his heart. 'Oh, ye of little faith! I'll be a paragon of virtue,' he boasted.

'So we'll be able to play loud music on Wednesday morning then?'

With a deep groan, the young man raised both hands to his head, already imagining with zero degrees of difficulty how bad his hangover might be after the huge binge his best man would likely be planning. 'Yeah, well... Maybe not quite that virtuous...' he cautioned. 'But you won't be here anyway, you fox, so you'll never know.'

The threesome left, giggling like naughty schoolgirls; Lynn and Michelle sharing news while Madalena followed close behind, still not knowing quite where she had ended up. Back on the sixteenth floor, Jeff stretched out on the couch, immediately sleepy. He had no idea what time his body-clock thought it was, and a few hours with no sister-minding duties were a stupendously welcome bonus.

After fifteen fleeting minutes, the tired traveller shook himself awake. This was not a good use of his time, given how much there was to do. Breathing deeply to force oxygen into his brain, he lifted the receiver and called his manager's office at Blake & Partners.

'Mate!' he shouted, when he heard his old friend's voice come on the line. 'We're back!'

'I saw, for God's sake!' Gerry replied. 'Did you really think you'd be able to sneak across the border? You're all over the TV. Sorry I didn't come down and scream at you with the rest of the city's population.'

The VIP client laughed. 'Yeah. It was manic. Lena was like a frightened rabbit.'

'Jesus, Mary and Joseph! I forgot your sis' was flying down with you,' the affable executive said. 'She'll probably think it's like that all the time.'

'Very funny... Listen, mate,' Jeff cut to the chase. 'Can I drop by this afternoon and catch up on some of the outstanding stuff? There must be a bloody enormous pile of correspondence to deal with, some of which has got to be pretty urgent by now. I'm waiting for three contracts to come through for DCF, and a whole bunch of new shit from South Africa. I don't want to leave any of it hanging over until we're back from holidays.'

'Sure thing. We can open a few beers, you lucky bugger,' the businessman scoffed. 'I wish I were off to The Canary Islands with a leggy, blonde athlete. Your tickets are here, by the way.'

In Gerry Blake's sumptuous, newly-refurbished corner office, a level below the original space that his company had long since outgrown, the multi-millionnaire and his accountant sat smoking with a stubbie of beer each. The first item to be passed across the desk was a bulging, white envelope, opened and re-sealed. Jeff tore into it again and tipped the contents out, scanning the names on the itinerary.

His heart jumped for joy. 'Fantastic, thanks,' he said, bundling everything back into the envelope and tucking it into the inside pocket of his leather jacket. 'Come with us. Lynn wouldn't mind. Perhaps not for the first few days because I don't anticipate seeing daylight for a while. But the second or third week... We'll be up for receiving visitors by then. It'd be huge.'

The older man shook his head. 'It's not customary to gatecrash one's mate's honeymoon, old boy.'

'Bullshit! Customary, *schmustomary*. Come on,' his friend teased. 'Since when have we done anything customary? It's not as if Lynn and I are going to need a fortnight to figure each other out. We already know who we are. We'll be getting bored with each other by then.'

'It's tempting,' Gerry confessed. 'But who would I bring? I couldn't bring Heather and the baby on your honeymoon.'

'No. Probably not,' Jeff agreed, noticing that the party boy still didn't refer to his child by name. 'Just yourself'd be fine. There are women on them there islands, I hear tell. You could have fortnight of free lovin' as your equivalent of a holiday romance.'

'I could indeed! I'll think about it,' his manager replied, picking up a whole stack of papers and fanning through them. 'Meantime, look at all this shit. You are scalding hot property, Jeff Diamond. We have to seriously look at restructuring your set-up, otherwise you're going to have a tax bill bigger than Australia's GDP.'

'Fuck! What's going on? You're supposed to be my accountant. Aren't you paid to stop this happening?'

'Mate, gimme a break,' Gerry joked. 'I am stopping it happening. Get this... I looked on the ASIC register the other day. You earned twenty times more than Bart Dyson last year. I might drop that into my speech...'

The modest chart-topper rolled his eyes, allowing himself to feel smug for a fleeting moment. 'Nice. Inappropriate but nice,' he grinned.

The two men worked through the accumulated paperwork, arguing and debating each decision. It was much more efficient to be back in the same town instead of conducting their business over the telephone, the musician realised, and he had missed Gerry's light-hearted irreverence. The Irishman was a true-blue antidote to the *cadre* of left-leaning comrades with whom he had surrounded himself in London.

There it was again: balance.

'It's Lynn's hens' night tonight,' Jeff mentioned over their third beer. 'She's taking my sister. It'll be interesting to find out how she fits in. If she fits in, I should say…'

Gerry nodded. 'Mum told me she went to the wild, wild west to drop off her frock. A bit of a rough area? Mum quite liked your sis' though, I think.'

'Ah, she's OK, I s'pose,' the former lost boy groaned. 'And your mum's a sucker for lost causes, let's face it. It's just that we have no connection, Lena and I. Her world's so unbelievably narrow. She only sees men as sex objects, meal tickets or pimps.'

His manager laughed out loud. 'It wasn't so long ago that someone else was none too different about females.'

Jeff kicked his chair backwards, uncomfortable with the blatant veracity of his friend's observation. 'Bastard!'

'And me too,' Gerry added. 'But I took your lead, remember?'

'Sure you did,' the superstar moaned. 'Must be my fault. Fuck off!'

He had spent a year without people blaming him for things and had grown to quite like it.

Things To Do, People To See

The rest of her guests were already seated at the table when Lynn, Michelle and Madalena reached the top-notch restaurant for the hens' party. To celebrate their friend's exit from single life in true Melbourne style, everyone had dressed up to the nines and was ready for a night to remember.

The chief bridesmaid had arranged tickets for a *risqué* cabaret show on King Street and had let the rest of the hens in on the surprise in advance. Jacinta and Tamilla Blake had flown down from Sydney after Christmas, only a couple of hours later than their famous friends, happily introducing themselves to Janice Siegel, Lynn's school friend and fellow MAC vocalist whom they instantly recognised.

Then, having also made friends with sisters, Jane and Sarah Markham, the extroverts were quick to discover that all except Janice had shared a bed with the handsome groom at some stage in their pasts. It was embarrassing to think they were all here now to celebrate his marriage, and they made a collective vow not to mention it to the bride!

Also, there were team-mates from the Australian Olympic equestrian squad and Lynn's favourite tennis coach and practice partner. The table's animated conversations divided down music and sporting lines, with Jacinta and Tamilla in the middle, as the newcomers to the Melbourne circle.

Everyone screamed with delight when the guest of honour arrived. Milling around the table, there were hugs and kisses all round. They each had a veritable catalogue of news to impart after her lengthy absence and couldn't wait to hear how her year in London had gone; especially now that it had culminated in a proposal.

'Sorry we're late,' Lynn said, beaming at the sight of all her closest friends in the one spot.

Australia's most eligible young lady spoke to her assembled friends one by one, posing for photographs and accepting hugs and kisses. Cocktails arrived before the threesome had had a chance to take their seats, causing great hilarity when it was suggested they should shoot them down their necks as fast as they could to make up for their tardiness.

'The taxi took ages,' the blonde singer made their excuses. 'I guess you've all met by now?'

The array of made-up faces nodded and urged her to sit down, shuffling round to free up three adjacent seats along one side of the table. Waiters and waitresses buzzed around taking drinks orders, and question after question flew in the direction of the blushing bride about her preparations for the big day: her dress, their vows... It was a lively scene, and the wandering star was overjoyed at being back in Melbourne, despite the lingering jet-lag.

'Everyone...' the star guest brought the table to attention. 'This is Jeff's sister, Madalena.'

A *frisson* of intrigue rippled round the table at meeting the stranger who bore such a strong resemblance to the exotic-looking rock star. The dark-haired woman endeavoured to follow Lynn's introductions, quite sure she would never remember who was who.

'Just call me Lena,' she suggested, mainly to her brother's girlfriend. 'That's what everyone calls me, 'cause Madalena's so long.'

'OK. Thanks,' Lynn smiled, sweeping her gaze along the expectant faces. 'That is certainly easier. Lena, everyone!'

Madalena sat demurely between Lynn and Michelle and felt safe, albeit intimidated by the noisy bunch. She had heard Gerry Blake's name before in connection with her brother, and sort of knew he had two sisters, but that was about it. Michelle had been fascinated during the afternoon by Jeff's sister's graphic descriptions of her *clientèle* and the types of acts they often asked her to perform, which in turn had helped the outsider to open up and enjoy herself. She had also told them that most of her clients hailed from Lebanon or other North-African countries, in answer to her future sister-in-law's question about her ability to converse with their taxi driver in *pidgin* Arabic on their way to the restaurant.

The Sydneysider explained to her companions that these men often already had two or three wives, yet continued to visit for "real sex." The flabbergasted private schoolgirls had no idea what this might have meant, but chose not to push for details. The amazed legal eagle had been full of questions about this unsavoury line of work, and Lynn had been happy to let the conversation meander freely in order that the two bridesmaids might bond a little before the ceremony, all the while thinking how hard it would have been for Jeff to listen to their conversation.

'Is it true they ask you to pee on them?' her curious friend had asked.

'Yeah. Some do,' Madalena had answered with a wicked smile. 'And sometimes they piss on me.'

'Ew, yuck! How revolting!' Michelle shrieked, glancing sideways at the sophisticated blonde celebrity and grimacing as though nauseated by the concept. 'How the hell do you do it?'

The skinny woman chuckled. 'That's nothing. One guy always takes a shit when he gets to my place and gets me to lick his arse clean.'

'Oh, my God! Madalena, that's gross!' Lynn had cried in dismay. 'Poor you. Can't you say no? Do something else instead? How often does that happen?'

As the girls within earshot exchanged horror-struck glances, she noticed that her *fiancé*'s victimised sister scarcely reacted to the other women's display of emotion and revulsion, merely rubbing her thumb and fingertips together to signify that the objectionable activity generated a reliable revenue stream for her.

'It's disgustin', so I always spit it out on 'im after,' she stated, before letting out a maniacal cackle. 'It really gets the old fucker goin'! Some of 'em need a lot of 'elp to keep it up.'

Looking back at the afternoon's revelations, it had crossed the Australian princess' mind several times how many parallels existed in the matching pair's attitudes to sex, clearly resulting from their unusual upbringing. They had grown up surrounded by sex, used as a commodity to be bought, sold or otherwise traded. Perhaps Madalena was cleverer than she appeared, exaggerating her experiences for her naïve and very proper audience of posh young ladies? Or perhaps not... It was highly probable that these stories were more authentic than her own, romantic ideal of uniting two people in love.

Champagne corks popped at both ends of the table, and wine and water flowed steadily during dinner, none of the party keen on getting too wasted too early. Nevertheless, the discussions soon became freer of inhibition. The girls were determined to enjoy themselves, and no topic was off limits.

'What's your favourite part of Jeff Diamond?' Michelle asked the table, for a quick ice-breaking game.

Everyone screamed. One by one, they gave their answers, giggling and watching the guest of honour's reactions. Her vote was for his eyes, to which the others uttered an emphatic "ahh," before she added that on second thoughts, the rest of him was equally attractive.

Madalena chose his wallet, which made the group roar with laughter.

After their *entrées*, Lynn's best friend pulled out a piece of paper from her handbag. Unbeknown to the singing sportswoman, she had telephoned the stars' publishing company that afternoon to solicit answers to twenty secret questions for the purpose of testing the bride's knowledge of her husband-to-be.

As the maid of honour explained the rules, also not omitting some of the laughs she had shared with the groom in the process of gathering the salient facts together, Jane wailed in horror. 'Oh, Lynn! I hope you do better than I did at my hens'! Sarah made my questions so hard that I didn't even reach the pass-mark.'

Her school friend chuckled. 'But they still let you get married?'

'Yes,' the elder Markham sister shrugged.

'So what's the point of the test, Mish? Just to humiliate me?'

'Of course! Why else?' the lawyer affirmed, seeing Madalena's face full of wonder. 'I hope you can answer the ones she misses, Lena.'

'No chance in 'ell!' Jeff's sister scoffed. 'I dunno nothin' about 'im.'

The whole table burst out laughing again, with no idea how true her statement was. Michelle did her best to hide the piece of paper from Lynn, who prepared herself by swigging down a large mouthful of champagne.

'OK. I'm ready,' she announced. 'Do your worst.'

The ginger-haired woman took a deep breath, but instead of reading the first question, dissolved into a fit of giggles.

'What?' Lynn smiled, craning her neck to read the scrawled handwriting.

'Oh… Just something your beloved said.'

'Tell us!' Jacinta screamed. 'Don't keep it all to yourself!'

'Nothing,' Michelle became the picture of discretion. 'Lynn Dyson. *Nisi Dominus Frustra.* Question One.'

The bride-to-be shook her head at the irreverent use of Melbourne Academy's school motto. She signalled she was ready by sitting up straight in her chair, hands in her lap and feeling surprisingly nervous.

'Easy one to begin with: what is your *fiancé*'s full name?'

'*¡Ai!* Even I know that one!' Madalena piped up, watching Lynn rest her index finger against her cheek and stare at the ceiling.

'Um… He probably said that I don't have a *fiancé*, but otherwise it's Jeffrey Moreno Diamond.'

'Yes and yes,' Michelle nodded. 'Excellent start, Miss Dyson. He did say exactly that, although he was keen to substitute the word as "love-god", in which case he would qualify. Two points. Are you ready for Question Two?'

The celebrity shook her head, having no trouble imagining these words being breathed down the telephone by her impish black stallion. Perhaps it was his mix of humility and arrogance that she loved the most of all?

'Hang on…' Tamilla piped up. 'Why don't you have a *fiancé*?'

'Jeff hates the term,' Lynn responded. 'It is pretty archaic, isn't it? He is my love-god though, just for the record. Next question, please.'

Michelle rolled her eyes. 'Question Two: where was said love-god born and where did he grow up?'

'Parramatta Hospital and Canley Vale, both in New South Wales,' Lynn reeled off, visualising the birth certificate she had sneaked a look at on their flight to London, almost a year ago now.

Madalena swallowed a mouthful of her drink. 'Jeez! Did 'e really say that? He was s'posed to be born at 'ome. Complications with mum, I think, and they went to 'ospital in a rush.'

'Bonus point to Lena. And I need more information, Lynn,' Michelle goaded the dignified woman beside her, remembering it was part of her responsibility as chief bridesmaid to keep Jeff's sister from opening her mouth too often. 'That's not the full answer.'

'Oh, OK. Stones Road, Canley Vale, New South Wales. I don't know the number. Flat Four is all I know.'

Michelle shook her head, her pen poised to mark a big cross against the question on her sheet of paper. 'Well... Lucky for you, he didn't tell me a number either,' she smirked. 'Full marks again.'

A polite round of applause circled the table, and the centre of attention took another sip of wine.

'Right,' the question-mistress continued. 'Question Three is what's Jeff's favourite animal?'

'Favourite animal?' Lynn responded. 'Wow! I don't know. Dogs?'

'Horse,' Gerry's elder sister countered, shaking her head. 'We all know how much he loves horses.'

A collection of disappointed sighs were uttered from the equestrian end of the table when Tamilla gave her sister's deliberate spoiler away. The dog was the right answer, of course, and the maid of honour moved on to the fourth question.

'If he could live anywhere in the world, where would Jeff live?'

'Paris. In the Latin Quarter,' his girlfriend guessed. 'How specific was he for this one? The third turning on the left after the *café* near the Sorbonne where they serve *cognac* on ice?'

'Show-off!' Sarah teased. 'What's the answer, Mish-mash?'

'Just Paris,' the solicitor replied. 'And where did he say he thought you'd like to live in all the world?'

Lynn hadn't been expecting this question and needed a few moments to think it through. She tried to picture her gorgeous man, probably sitting in Cathy's office, talking into the telephone that afternoon. What would he have said?

She smiled. 'The arrogant sod probably said anywhere that he was!'

Michelle opened her mouth to respond, but Lynn hadn't finished.

'Or Pellegrini's,' she laughed. 'We often say we like it so much there that we might move in.'

'Your first answer is the only one I can accept,' her officious friend cut her off, before coming clean. 'And it was correct. That's what I was laughing at earlier, except he described himself as an arrogant arsehole. Our conversation began to get rather silly at this stage. He asked me how hard I wanted to make the questions, and I said, "As hard as you like." You can just imagine where that went...'

Madalena again voiced her objections, beginning to enjoy the posh girls' company after all.

'I've no idea what you mean,' the blonde superstar assumed an innocent air. 'He knows I like a challenge.'

The redhead fanned her face with the question sheet before carrying on. 'Okey dokey... Moving along! Question Six. No. Wait! I'm going to skip a few because our main course'll be here soon. Question Thirteen, unlucky for some...'

'What is Jeff's favourite part of your body?' Michelle asked, seeing Lynn frown and steel herself for further humiliation.

Madalena sniggered. 'You said, "Movin' along"!'

'Ahem,' coughed Jacinta, urging the bride to provide her answer.

'Either my left shoulder or my heart,' came the reply.

Certain of the girls cooed with jealousy, while others demanded to know why she had suggested her left shoulder. For the benefit of the few who hadn't shared a sports centre changing room with the Olympian, she suggestively lowered the strap of her dress until the "JL" tattoo exposed itself. Again her friends swooned, learning a little more about the famous couple's dedication to each other.

'Both are correct, but the wrong way round,' Michelle sighed. 'One point. You're too damned good at this. Question Fourteen: when getting up in the morning...'

Lynn's eyes widened. 'Oh yes? Back in the gutter again!'

Her excited girlfriends cheered and clapped. This was the type of question that interested them, having missed out on a year of regular gossip. Until tonight, very few of them had had any idea the sixteen-year-old schoolgirl had met her mystery man so long ago. The convoluted story met all the criteria for a romantic fairy tale, except it was she who played the Princess Charming role and he was no longer the penniless pauper.

Michelle began again, tutting like a schoolteacher. 'When getting up in the morning, does Jeff clean his teeth or shave first?'

'Oh, boring!' shouted Sonia, the tennis coach. 'Can't you give her more options that shaving and cleaning teeth?'

The bride-to-be laughed. 'Yeah! I agree. First before what?'

'Lynn Dyson!' her maid of honour scolded, failing to control the *fracas* which had broken out around the table. 'You're not taking this seriously. Not before anything. You're not married yet. You shouldn't know about these things. Clean his teeth or shave?'

'Sorry. I forgot. I've been out of the country. Of course I don't know about any of *those things*, whatever they are,' the contrite young woman replied, drawing quotation marks in the air and looking alarmed. 'He cleans his teeth, definitely.'

'Correct answer.'

'And then he comes back to bed, and much later he might shave.'

Peals of laughter erupted, and the unruly rabble raised their glasses to their grown-up friend again, attracting a great deal of attention from other patrons. Up until this point, only the staff had been aware of whose hens' night was being celebrated.

Once the excitement had subsided, Michelle tried again. 'Question Sixteen: where did you touch him on your first date?'

'What?' Lynn yelped along with everyone else. 'Touch on our first date? I was a good girl, I assure you. And this time, I'm not lying! Hands? Lips? We did kiss, I confess. That's obviously not what you're looking for...'

'No. Not lips,' the redhead taunted, striking the piece of paper so hard with her pen that she punched a hole through it. 'One more try?'

Then came an idea in a flash of inspiration. 'His watch!'

'Oh, my God! That's right!' her friend exclaimed, mouth dropping open. 'I can't believe you got that. I was sure this one'd catch you out. Jeff didn't though. You nearly didn't get it.'

'Watch?' Tamilla cried out in disbelief. 'Wristwatch? How disappointing!'

'You have to explain that one,' Jane laughed. 'What were you doing? Finding out what time it was? Sounds like you were desperate to get away.'

'I was really nervous,' Lynn remembered, butterflies fluttering in her stomach as the memory reconstituted itself in her mind's eye. 'He was standing behind me with an arm on either side, with his hands resting on the rail of a tram-stop shelter on St Kilda Road. We were coming home from the theatre, and we stopped for a while before crossing over and going back into Admin. I had absolutely no clue what to do, so I reached out to hold onto his hand. I didn't realise he was left-handed and wears his watch on the right wrist, so I ended up grabbing hold of the watch instead. It's so like him to remember something quirky like that.'

The girls were very amused by the naïve account of the night that had started the whole, complicated love affair. Their main courses were in the process of being delivered, forcing Michelle to hunt through her list for one last question.

'OK, Lynn. Lucky last,' she declared. 'What's his favourite present of all the things you've given him?'

The alcohol well and truly having its full effect, several rather unseemly items were suggested by various hungry hens, most of which would figure prominently in Madalena's service catalogue. Lynn put her finger to her mouth, requesting decorum and glancing around to make sure they hadn't upset any fellow diners.

Torn between so many significant gifts her humble *beau* had accepted, the bride had one of two likely answers from which to choose, breathing in deeply to prolong the suspense.

'Either his jet-stone ring or his leather jacket,' she offered, staring at her friend in anticipation.

'That's amazing!' Michelle shouted, showing the piece of paper to Sarah, on her left. 'Completely, word-for-word correct! "Either my jet-stone ring or this leather jacket." I'll dock a point for an erroneous possessive pronoun, just because I can.'

Everyone clapped. They came to the unanimous conclusion that a surfeit of knowledge about her handsome specialist subject had been demonstrated, leading Michelle to declare that the wedding could safely proceed. Lynn gave a shallow bow and instructed them all to eat their food.

For the rest of the meal, as hard as she tried to divert her guests away from the wedding, the homecoming celebrity was unable to sustain another topic of conversation with her friends. Her thoughts drifted to her partner, who was to succumb to Gerry's mercy tomorrow night too, and wondered if any of his raging bucks would even mention the big day. The ladies around her table were more obsessed with this wedding than she was, all eager to know the most intimate details about her relationship with Jeff, what her dress was like and where they were going on their honeymoon. She admitted defeat and soon found herself lost in the dreaminess of the occasion too.

Lynn was pleased to see her future sister-in-law chatting happily and joined in with a humdrum analysis of the current fashion in shoes for a few moments before turning the other way and putting her arms around Michelle. She thanked her good friend profusely for such a well-organised evening, whispering that she was also grateful not to have been presented with a cake in the shape of male genitalia, as one of her Olympic team-mates had suggested. When dinner was over and desserts had been summarily rejected in favour of dancing, the glitter of glamorous girls piled into taxis to travel the three kilometres from the South Yarra restaurant into the city for their cabaret experience.

Madalena smiled when she reached the King Street club. This was familiar turf for the seasoned night-bird, but seldom as a consumer! She caught the bride's eye, and they shared a secret laugh. The show was highly entertaining, beginning with a smutty but clever comedian who made the girls cringe more times than they smiled.

The male strippers gyrated and lunged through their dance routines, artificially tanned and hairless, sweating buckets under the stage lighting. As all three visitors from Sydney had predicted, the body parts Lynn had feared she may need to cut, slice and consume proved to be disappointingly small and unerotic once the men's clothing was shed. This was of no real consequence to the joyous friends, beyond a few derisory remarks and surreptitious pointing, and the whole party rushed onto the dance floor at their earliest opportunity.

Michelle made sure no-one was left out, fending off ardent fans for the blonde singer and trying various creative ways of drawing in the sparse male contingent for those who were still single.

At one o'clock, the wilting guest of honour began to think about calling it a night, hoping she wouldn't meet too much resistance. The Markham sisters had already left. Jane had a baby at home, and Sarah agreed to share a taxi after much tipsy deliberation.

'Are you tired, Lena?' Lynn asked.

'Yeah. A bit.'

'Me too. Shall we go?'

'Sure. I was up early today.'

Linking arms with the gangly gipsy, the twenty-year-old signalled to her chief bridesmaid across the busy dance floor. 'We're going to head off soon. We're exhausted.'

Michelle made a sad face and looked at her watch. 'Already? It's still early!'

Lynn said goodnight to the Blake sisters, who were keen to party on with Michelle and the others. She and her sister-in-law-to-be were escorted by security guards through the doors, where scores of clubbers were still hoping to gain entry, down the steep steps and out onto the street to find a taxi. It didn't take too long before one stopped for them, and they hopped in with great relief at being able to take the weight off their *stiletto*-clad feet. Within five minutes, they pulled up at the door of their apartment building.

'It's cool to live this close to the CBD,' Madalena said.

It was the first time Jeff's sister had initiated a conversation all night, and the young star smiled. 'Yes. Pretty handy. Thanks so much for coming tonight. Did you have a good time?'

The guest nodded. 'Yeah. I 'ad a great time. Didn't think I would when I got there, but the food was good and I got to sit in the audience at the club. I ain't never done that before, and it's yonks since I went on a girls' night out. I love dancin'.'

Her host nodded. 'And you're a good dancer. That's one thing, apart from hair-colour, that you've got in common with your brother.'

The furtive pair eased the front door open and tiptoed into the hallway. Lynn removed her shoes to prevent the heels from clicking on the tiles, and Madalena followed her lead after a not-so-subtle request. Walking past the door to the master bedroom, Lynn noticed the bed hadn't been slept in, and the only light in the apartment was in the eerie form of blue, flickering shadows from the television. Turning to her companion, she put a finger up to her lips.

Jeff had fallen asleep on the couch a number of hours ago, judging by the stilted slapstick of an old black and white movie which he would have flicked past. His sprawled-out form was surrounded by beer bottles, a three-quarters full whisky bottle and a tumbler containing the cloudy liquid residue of melted ice blocks. The scene of destruction was completed by a variety of empty Chinese takeaway containers strewn over the coffee table.

'Look what a slob I'm marrying,' she chuckled to Madalena, who was staring at the spectacle as if she didn't recognise its centrepiece.

The millionnaire had changed out of the smart, dark crimson shirt and black pants he had worn on the aeroplane into an old, faded T-shirt and a pair of shorts that hadn't made the journey to London, their flimsy fabric unsuited to the English climate. To his glowing girlfriend, he looked like the old Jeff again; the pre-London, pre-bohemian Jeff. She was overcome by his reassignment as the common-or-garden variety Aussie student she had met three years ago, seeing how easily he could switch into the ordinary man with whom she had made love outdoors at the dam on her parents' farm.

Lynn felt like crying. She was so full of love for this lost boy who had been intent on snaring her at any price. During a quiet moment that afternoon, she had plucked up the courage to ask Madalena if she experienced nightmares after their mother's death. The question had been met with a blank stare and a disinterested, monosyllabic dismissal, which left the young star wondering if the abused woman could possibly have been spared.

The bride-to-be slipped her hand onto an exposed knee and rocked Jeff's leg from side to side, trying to wake him up without startling him. A book on Basque architecture slid off his chest and fell onto the floor. He stirred, feeling its weight shift sideways, and his reflexes made a grab for it. Sensing he was being watched, he opened his eyes to find his dream girl and his sister gazing at him with bemused smiles on their faces.

'Oh, Jesus,' he whispered, putting his hands over his eyes. 'How long've you been there? I'm being visited by angels. What time is it?'

Madalena laughed at his reaction, backing up and sitting on the edge of the sofa. Lynn crouched down by his head, having picked up the book and placed it on the coffee table.

'A bit before two,' she answered, kissing his sleepy mouth tenderly. 'You look like you've had a good time.'

With a theatrical groan, Jeff heaved himself up to a sitting position and surveyed the mess. 'Hmm... Yeah. Sorry. We went for a few beers when Gerry finished work, and then I got hungry walking home.'

Ruffling his messy head of long, black hair, his flatmate stood up and started to clear away the *débris*. He tugged at the hem of her dress, urging her to leave the carnage until the morning, when he would see to it. In anticipation of an amorous reunion, their third *amigo* had disappeared to the bathroom, leaving the tall man free to struggle to his feet and envelope his bride-to-be with loving arms.

'Hullo, hen,' he put on his best Scots accent. Did you have fun with all the chickens?' he asked, with a concerned expression. 'Did she behave herself?'

Lynn nodded, eager for more kisses. 'Yes, thanks. We had a great time. Lena was fine. A bit quiet to begin with but she warmed as soon as we all got to know each other. She's a great dancer, just like you, and she's got comic timing too.'

'Timing? Was she giving a speech or something? Thank Christ,' he muttered under his breath. 'That's a relief.'

His sister returned, plainly embarrassed to interrupt a private moment. Spying their guest out of the corner of her eye, Lynn broke away from her lover's grip and continued to pick up the containers and bottles.

'Hey, stop! Leave all that, angel,' her guilty boyfriend repeated, slumping back down, slightly bilious at the sight and smell of the leftovers as they were disturbed. 'I'll take care of it tomorrow.'

'It is tomorrow,' his lover giggled.

'Yeah. Smart and sexy. You don't have to remind me. I mean daylight tomorrow. Let's go to bed. How're you doing, Lena? Lynn likes how you dance.'

Madalena smiled, making no attempt to stifle a yawn that revealed several missing teeth. 'Can I go to bed too? I'm fucked like a duck. I had a good time, Lynn.'

'You're really welcome,' the superstar responded. 'It was a good night, and I'm fucked too!'

Chuckling at his foul-mouthed female flatmates, Jeff hauled himself back off the couch and grabbed his *fiancée* playfully. He wondered whether his sister ever said "Please" or "Thank you".

'You will be…' he threatened, growling into her ear.

Madalena screamed. '*¡Ai!* I don't wanna hear you guys talk about sex! Me 'ead's full o' male strippers and shrivelled-up cocks. It's my night off, and I'm goin' to sleep.'

'G'night, Lena,' her brother laughed at the uncharacteristically descriptive outburst. 'Put your earplugs in. I'm bloody horny, and this woman looks like she needs fixing up. *Duerma bien.*'

The *trio* kissed each other goodnight and went their separate ways in the hallway. Once behind their bedroom door, Jeff undressed quickly and climbed into bed on the promise of a tantalising striptease quite unlike those witnessed earlier, any last vestiges of inhibition wiped out by the residual champagne in Lynn's system. After admiring the way her black, lacy *lingerie* complemented her svelte body for as long as his *libido* would allow, he wrapped his arms around her, their tattoos connected, and they made love with hushed passion.

'Thanks for taking such good care of Lena,' the breathless man squeezed out between voracious kisses. 'You've made things very easy for me. I owe you.'

'No, you don't,' Lynn objected again. 'You've got to stop saying that. It was nice to have her there. She spiced up the evening. She was really amazed that there were five people around the table who'd slept with you.'

The young man's conscience filled with shame, and he lost all momentum for a while. 'Shit! Yeah. I guess that does look pretty bad. Sorry about that. That wasn't too nice a thing for you to hear either,' he moaned. 'Was that Jack or Tammy?'

'Jack, I think, via Lena. It's OK. I don't mind,' the cheerful woman responded, twisting her hips to goad him into action. 'I'm long over that. In fact, I probably shouldn't admit it, but I'm very proud to have won you over them.'

The former "Love 'em and Leave 'em Kid" kissed her mouth hard, coming inside her with a huge rush inspired by her words of love. Trusting their visitor across the landing would be fast asleep by now, both lovers cried out as the pleasure overtook them.

'Jeez, angel. You should go out with the girls more often! That was fast and furious. But anyway, I'm not sure the fact that I've slept with half of your close friends is grounds for pride, but I feel slightly easier about it.'

Lynn smiled, squirming out from under his heavy weight. 'Whatever. A man'd be proud if the situation was reversed, so why can't I be? Wouldn't you?'

'Fair point,' he admitted, straightening his arms and making the spirited woman stretch further to make contact with his lips. 'I have only slept with one though. There was no sleeping involved with any of the others. Except with Lena as little kids, of course. Was she one of the five at least?'

His dream girl reached up to take hold of his broad shoulders and tried to tempt her man back down onto her chest, lifting her head to kiss their tattooed insignia glistening on the damp flesh of his chest. Jeff arched his back instead, his tongue caressing the delicate skin around each of her raised nipples before dropping down to rest on top of her, satisfied and ready for more sleep.

'No. Six then! You know what I mean,' she smiled. 'We weren't worried about semantics during our conversation. By the way, Jack and Tammy are taking Lena out tonight for more dancing. She can really move!'

'Really? Christ! I totally forgot about that. Yeah. Gerry told me,' Jeff replied, opening his eyes and rolling onto his back with a heavy sigh. 'Thanks a lot. You're life-savers, all of you. It completely slipped my mind that I'd need to find something for her to do. Good that you're all onto it. What did they think of her?'

Lynn shrugged, swinging her legs off the bed and heading towards the bathroom. Her boyfriend did the same, anxious to hear how his sister had been treated by the opinionated, well-to-do siblings who had teased him so heartlessly as teenagers.

'They were a bit condescending at first, but as they all got drunker, they warmed to her. Michelle was transfixed this afternoon, hearing about all her Arab customers and what they ask for. It's quite revolting actually. I'm glad it's not me having to do those things. I don't think I could, no matter how much I needed the money.'

'What sort of things?' the brother was curious, although his gut advised him otherwise.

Against her better judgment, after initially insisting he find out for himself after the wedding, the young woman gave in and recounted some of the dubious services the ins and outs of which the two Melbourne Academy girls had learned earlier that day. Jeff listened with interest for the first minute or so, yet his curiosity didn't last long. Without warning, he darted across to the toilet, leaving his partner with the unpleasant sound of vomitting to add to her lengthening list of spilled bodily fluids.

After a while, the retching stopped, and all became quiet. She filled a glass with water and moved to one side to give the poor man some space. Groaning, he splashed water over his face, as pale as a ghost.

'I'm sorry,' she said, placing a loving hand on his back and reeling from the heat in his shoulders. 'Wow! You're so hot! I shouldn't have gone into such graphic detail. It was gross.'

'That's "real sex"?' the angry man hissed, spinning round to face his gorgeous partner. '"Real sex." That's what she said her customers come to her for. Stuff their wives and girlfriends refuse to do because it's demeaning and downright ugly, more like. Fucking hell! I feel sick enough imagining that kind of perverted debauchery with faceless people, let alone my own bloody sister.'

'I'm really sorry. I shouldn't have told you.'

'Yes. You should've,' the musician countered. 'I need to know, even though I don't want to know. I'm glad you told me. It might not sound like it just at this moment, but I am. And I damned well need to do something about it.'

The two lovers returned to the bedroom, and Jeff swallowed an entire glass of water in a single gulp. Lynn lay down and sleepily pulled the sheet over her, realising that her worried philosopher was now wide awake, leaning up against the headboard, frowning and deeply disturbed.

'Angel,' he murmured, placing a heavy hand on her shoulder. 'You can rest assured I'll never ask you to do anything like that.'

'I know,' his beautiful best friend replied, stroking his twitching thigh in return. 'It's another world, isn't it? I was thinking that earlier. Sex is really a product to be bought and sold for Lena. She just thinks about the money, Jeff. She even said sometimes she has to pee on people.'

The disgusted brother grimaced, burying his face in his hands. 'What? Fuck, Lynn! That I don't wanna know! This is my sister we're talking about.

193

That's not sex by anyone's definition. For Christ's sake! I've got to get her out of that life somehow.'

'But she's happy,' the refined young lady told him, hoping he would believe it was the right thing to say. 'It doesn't seem to bother her, and most of her friends are in the same game. They support each other, I reckon. And she looks healthy enough, don't you think?'

Her *fiancé* was forced to agree. 'Quite possibly, but it still bothers me, angel. What does it mean for her future? She's going to turn into a lonely, fucked-up drunk, just like our mother.'

'I hope not,' Lynn shook her head. 'I don't think she considers she's being taken advantage of. It's just a job to her. What do you want to do? Move her to Melbourne? He who never used to think about the future…'

The compassionate man shrugged. 'No. But I do now, and I need to plant a few seeds in her head, like you did for me. I don't know what'd be best, but there's got to be something better than that shit. Here's me embarking on a so-called normal life, after everything that happened to us. Wife and two kids, staying out of the police's way, working somewhat regularly…'

'That's a stretch,' Australia's darling interjected, giggling kindly.

'Yeah, well,' the chart-topping world-changer leaned forward and kissed her. 'Don't spoil my rant with home truths, *s'il te plaît*! Lena deserves normal too, doesn't she? If I can sort myself out, I have no choice but to do the same for her. She'll never do it for herself.'

'Alright,' Lynn agreed, turning away from him and snuggling under the sheet. 'Let's talk to her when we get back from the holiday. You could invite her down again, without the pressure of the wedding hanging over us.'

'*Gracias*, angel. Enough of this awful crap. Let's get some sleep. Dream magical wedding dreams, gorgeous.'

Jeff slid down the bed and draped a long left arm over his bride-to-be, spooning close and kissing the matching tattoo on the back of her shoulder. The pair lay in silence and lost themselves in pleasant thoughts of the days and weeks to come.

'This is the last time we'll sleep together in this bed in sin,' the young woman muttered, just as her lover was drifting out of consciousness.

Shifting his weight onto his right elbow, he moved his head to check the expression on her face. She was smiling, and her eyes had an extra glint shining in them.

'*¿Bueno, no?*'

Lynn leaned over and kissed him on the lips. '*Sí. Muy, muy bueno. Te amo.*'

'*Te amo* too. You're so fantastic. I'm glad the girls gave your sins a good send-off. You'd better not still be considering joining that cult you mentioned in the early days. D'you remember that?'

Lynn took a moment to make the connection to a flippant comment she had made during the couple's first dinner with Gerry and Suzanne, when the innocent sixteen-year-old had announced that she belonged to a religious sect which forbade sex after marriage.

'Oh, yeah!' she laughed aloud. 'Wow! You've got a good memory. I'd forgotten that stupid remark.'

Jeff closed his eyes, remembering his own mortifying mistake from that very same date. 'Hmm...' he murmured, realising how close he had once come to subjecting his dream girl to exactly the type of aggressive sex that nobody deserved, whether prostitute or dream girl. 'You're not the only one who was stupid that night.'

The episode in question had delivered a salutary lesson indeed; one upon which he vowed to reflect long and hard in the coming weeks, while he made up his mind how to deal with his sister.

'Go to sleep,' Lynn said, tapping her beautiful black stallion on his furrowed forehead. 'Stop thinking.'

'Both good ideas, angel. G'night.'

***

Lynn was up early the next morning, excited to be setting off for Benloch to make the final preparations for Thursday. She also wanted to spend some time with her family before driving back on the morning of the wedding to rehearse the music for the ceremony and reception. Her mother had complained that it was unlucky to see the groom before the procession, but there had been no other chance to practise with the full contingent of musicians. She would deal with the bad luck if it were ever to eventuate.

It had been lovely to wake up in the large, airy apartment after the confined spaces of their London flat. There was no sound from Madalena's room, and the couple enjoyed a leisurely coffee on the balcony in the morning sunshine. Jeff looked delicious, bare-chested and dressed only in pyjama trousers, and his silk-clad *fiancée* couldn't keep her fingers from playing with the hair on his forearm as they talked through the Order of Service to made sure nothing had been forgotten. No detail had been left to chance, and the happy man felt confident that he simply had to follow his running sheet to make the whole day perfect.

After leaving a note for his sister, the songwriter accompanied his dream girl through the city to Dyson Administration, where she was collecting a car for her long drive up to the farm she had been missing. The city bustled with tourists, supplemented by commuters who were unable to escape the daily drudgery for the festive season. On a familiar trail, they tried hard to dodge the crowds and avoid the inevitable delays and intrusive questions from well-wishers.

Refusing to be dropped back outside the apartment building, the handsome chaperone hugged his charge tightly.

'Enjoy tonight,' she said. 'After all the talk last night about meaningless sex, I want you to know that I'm OK with it, if you want to have some last-minute fun tonight. For old time's sake, or however you might view it...'

Jeff stared at his partner in wonderment, a corrupt sense of adventure alerting his body to forbidden pleasures that had been buried with his past. Those days as a sexual mercenary were now a dim and distant memory; something he no longer needed. Or did he? For old time's sake, or however he might view it?

'Whoa! Are you sure? It hadn't even crossed my mind, but I'm pretty sure it will later, once Gerry's got me tanked up. Not fair on you in the slightest, but it's a fine, fine offer. *Merci beaucoup, Regala.*'

His *fiancée* kissed him, once again knowing she had done the right wrong thing yet again. 'It's up to you. Do whatever you want. Custer's Last Stand, or whatever it is! I believe you're sincere in how you feel about us and the future we've planned, and I already know my love for you is strong enough to cope with it, so go for it!'

The enigmatic stranger of yore leaned into the kiss, hoping she could taste his gratitude and brimming with Machiavellian respect. 'That's amazing. I'm not sure what I'll do with yet another bonus gift of generous proportions, but it means so much, let me tell you. I won't abuse it, that's for sure, and I can't wait to see you on Thursday, angel. That's the understatement of a lifetime. It's getting close, isn't it? Singularly close.'

The soul-mates embraced one final time, and Jeff leaned over to open the car door for his wife-to-be. Closing it firmly and hearing the engine fire, he was unable to stop a wave of emotion from engulfing him. He tapped the car's roof twice, and the girl of his dreams pulled away, waving cheerfully from the window. He stood and watched the car until it disappeared around the corner, tracking westwards towards the main thoroughfare due north and out of the city.

To shake off the instantaneous onset of the doldrums, the solitary man sprinted back through the city, his baseball cap pulled down low over his face. So low, in fact, that he could hardly see where he was going. The remaining jet-lag in his veins conspired to slow his legs down, and his lungs felt as though they needed to expand for an hour or so to blow out the residual high-altitude air. He didn't have the luxury of an hour on this occasion however, on account of his sleeping sister back in the apartment. As a compromise, he took the long way home to the east of the city and back along Victoria Parade.

The warm summer's day presented a stark contrast to the dark, cold London mornings in which he and Lynn had been running over recent weeks. Jeff was pouring with sweat by the time he reached his apartment building, after stopping to buy the morning newspapers and some milk. When the doors opened for the celebrity at ground level, his neighbour from the other side of the top floor was already in the lift, coming up from the basement car park.

'G'day,' the famous musician said, breathing hard. 'Pete, isn't it?'

'Yes. Morning, Jeff,' the wealthy businessman replied, surprised to see the superstar whom he had rarely encountered during the two years they had been living across the hall from each other. 'You're back from overseas then? When did you arrive?'

The red-faced runner leaned against the wall, his long hair sticking to his face. 'Sorry about this,' he gestured to his drenched T-shirt. 'Just been for the first warm weather run in quite a while. We got back yesterday. How've you been?'

'Great,' replied Pete. 'You guys are getting married, aren't you? On New Year's Day? I'd better not have that wrong after all the press!'

The lift opened on the sixteenth floor, and the two men stepped out onto the landing. The portly property investor had come home with the same items, and they both chuckled watching each other juggle their handfuls to fetch keys from their respective pockets.

Jeff nodded and issued a long sigh. 'Yep, we are. It's bloody crazy! We're looking forward to some time to ourselves, I can't deny. Hey, mate... It's my bucks' night tonight. If you're not doing anything, you're very welcome to join us. Lynn and I never managed to get you round for drinks in all this time. It'd be great if you could.'

'Wow! Thanks a lot!' his neighbour accepted, somewhat awestruck. 'I'm not doing anything tonight. Are you sure? That'd be amazing. Where are you going?'

'Excellent,' the friendly star said, happy that he had finally made contact. 'No fucking idea where we're going! D'you know Gerry Blake of Blake & Partners? He's my best man, so who knows what he's cooked up?'

Both men laughed. Of course Peter Bourke had heard of Gerald Blake Junior. Who hadn't? He had a formidable reputation in Melbourne business circles. It crossed Jeff's mind that the last time he had confronted this bloke on the landing, he had also been hot and sweaty, but for a much different reason.

'We're meeting at Rosati's on Flinders Lane, seven sharp. D'you know it? Suit and tie, I gather, neither of which'll last long if I have any influence on proceedings.'

Pete smiled. 'Rosati's? Certainly do. I'm there all the time when I'm in town. See you at seven, Jeff. Cheers.'

The investor shook the athlete's hand and let himself into his apartment. Jeff did the same, and easily too. Fantastic, he thought. Life was good!

The shower in the main bathroom was in full swing, and the radio had been turned up so high that the whole place pulsated with the bass beat. The millionnaire's hurriedly scribbled note was screwed into a ball on the kitchen counter. Cooling off a little, he put on a fresh pot of coffee and shut himself into the *en suite*, realising his sister was singing along to the music. Well, it almost passed for singing, he smirked.

What would he do with Madalena today? He had some time this morning to give her a short tour of the Victorian capital, but it would have to be on foot because he had made the decision not to open the container and start his beloved Aston Martin until they returned from their honeymoon. He fleetingly regretted relinquishing so much control to others, soon concluding that uncaging and re-caging the beast wasn't worth the bother for a few hours at most. After lunch, he would need to leave them both to their own devices while he took care of the remaining odd jobs he had been assigned before the couple flew out again and withdrew from society.

For Christ's sake… The star chastised himself at the way his mind reacted to more air travel when so many people would leap at the chance of flying high to faraway places. He had had enough for a while, and so had Lynn. They should have booked a cottage on the Great Ocean Road or somewhere along the Pacific Highway, instead of jetting off overseas again. Still, it would be paradise once they arrived and settled in. Tenerife, one of the Canary Islands off the north African coast, was becoming a trendy hotspot.

The guilty man smiled to himself as the shower's cool water gushed over him. He had forgotten to tell Lynn that he invited Gerry on their honeymoon. He hoped she wouldn't mind. Freshly-shaven and enlivened by anticipation, Jeff strode bare-chested into the kitchen to find a thin-framed woman with long, dark, curly hair sitting on the balcony and smoking.

He poured two cups of coffee and headed out to join her. '*Buenos días,*' he opened gently, trying to gauge if she was still a little fragile. '*¿Com' estás?*'

'Hi, *chico*,' his sister stared at him open-mouthed before issuing a brutal wolf-whistle. 'Jesus! You look good! Where'd'ya get the six-pack? I never knew you were so cut.'

Jeff sniffed, embarrassed to receive such a carnal reaction from his own flesh and blood. Nevertheless, such admiration was always acceptable, since he worked damned hard to keep himself in top physical condition. It was almost a non-negotiable for marrying into the Dyson clan.

'Hung over?'

'Yeah, na. Not too bad,' Madalena replied. 'Lynn made us all drink water, so that 'elped. You got any Panadol?'

Her brother left his cigarette burning in the ashtray, returning inside to fetch some painkillers. 'D'you want any breckie? Eggs, bacon… Toast?'

'Yeah. Good. I'm starving. Where's Lynn?'

The man of the house strolled back into the fresh air, having rustled up a selection of tablets and two glasses of water. He watched the visiting stranger swallow them and light another cigarette straightaway. Shaking his head in disconsolate recognition, he re-lit his own and made himself comfortable with his coffee and the newspapers. Such bad manners warranted a short delay to breakfast delivery.

Madalena looked across in anticipation. 'Where's Lynn, I said?'

'Sorry. She's gone to her parents' place to catch up with her family. They're having a New Year's Eve party. She'll be back on Thursday morning. I hope! I'll make some food in a minute.'

'OK,' his sister shrugged. 'What we doin' today?'

Jeff examined the young woman more closely, wondering what he might do to improve her life. She had dressed in a short skirt and a skimpy top which looked as if it had been worn so often that the fabric had stretched until it barely hid her pink push-up bra. Straggly, wet hair shone in the morning sun, every now and again drawn back by bony fingers.

Madalena's legs were shapely enough and less bruised than Zoe's, with a few fresh nicks from this morning's razor, and bright red toenail polish had cracked and chipped on equally bony toes. She had the skeleton of a fifteen-year-old covered by the skin of a thirty-five-year-old. Not too dissimilar to how he must have looked a few years ago, the healing soul reckoned, before his guardian angel had taught him how to wind back time.

The patient brother shrugged. 'I thought we'd do a bit of sightseeing this morning. Walk around Melbourne? Check out some of the normal tourist spots. Then I've got some work to do this *arvo*, so I'll have to leave you at the shops or somewhere.'

Madalena's eyes lit up at the prospect of being shown around the city. From what she had seen from Michelle's car and their string of taxis yesterday, there was a lot to see. Driving through the prosperous inner suburbs of Victoria's capital presented a much different *vista* than the dowdy streets of south-western Sydney.

'Yeah. Sounds great,' she agreed. 'I wanna see the MCG. Everyone says 'ow big it is. And shoppin'. Yay! Lynn bought me a heap of cool clothes on Chapel Street yesterday.'

Jeff looked up, momentarily stunned. 'Did she? OK. *Muy buen.* I didn't know about that. She did say you're going dancing with Gerry's sisters again tonight. Jacinta... Jack and Tammy.'

His sister let out a horrible, raspy sound that doubled as a laugh and a cough. 'Yeah. That's what they said anyways. They're Celia's kids, right?'

'Yep. Can't you tell?' the songwriter scoffed. 'And I know what you're going to say. "They're posh!" Lynn said they were pretty snobbish to begin with last night.'

'What's snobbish?'

'Snooty,' her brother answered. 'You know... Up themselves.'

'Ha! Yeah. Everyone was until they got pissed, then we were all the same,' Madalena recounted.

Her observation was sound, the philanthropist acknowledged. Another piece of evidence that her natural intelligence was being wasted on the streets and in her bed. If only others saw the world in this simple way... His quest would be so much easier.

'True enough. People are all basically the same. It just depends how you wrap 'em up.'

The woman from Sydney's west laughed out loud, rocking on her chair. 'That's funny! Never thought about it like that, but you're right. 'Specially when they got no clothes on!'

Jeff emptied his coffee mug, muttering an affirmation and standing up. *You got it, lady.* Noticing Madalena's eyes following him, he realised she was staring at the tattoo on his naked chest.

'What's that?' she asked, pointing above his left nipple.

'It's a "J" and an "L" back-to-back,' he explained, tracing the letters with his fingers from top to bottom. 'It's supposed to look like the number one. Lynn's got one too, on her shoulder.'

'I know. I seen it yesterdy,' his sister nodded. 'It's nice. Better than a ring.'

The romantic man nodded. 'Yeah. I think so too. And cheaper!'

'Can you get me a tatt'?' she asked, puppy-dog eyes pleading.

'Sure. What'd you like?' Jeff answered, finding himself waiting for a "please", like a frustrated parent. 'We could do that after going to the MCG, if you want. The place we went was good. Should be open today.'

Her eyes lit up. 'Can we? That'd be amazing. Can you choose?'

Her brother nodded again. 'Sure. They've got hundreds to choose from. Maybe we'll go there first, so you can see the choices. Then you can think about it while we go round the "G" and go back when you've made up your mind. Breckie?'

Madalena was excited, jumping up and grabbing his arm. '¡Sí, sí! I wish all my customers looked like you,' she told him, pecking him on the cheek. 'You look hot! I'd fuck you if you weren't family.'

Jeff scowled, wiping his face after the *impromptu* kiss, and thanked her for the backhanded compliment. Diverting to the bedroom to put some clothes on, he felt mighty uncomfortable with being the object of his sister's proclivities. He thought back to Lynn's offer of free sex on his bucks' night and wondered whether he would take her up on it. A long time had passed since he had touched another woman, save for the suggestive choreography he and his dancers unleashed on stage, and he realised with some surprise that he didn't miss it at all. Yet now, faced with this full and final commitment, maybe a meaningless fling was warranted; for old time's sake, as his dream girl had proffered.

Back in the kitchen, Madalena had found a carton of eggs and was now searching in the cupboards for a frying pan. 'There's not much stuff in 'ere.'

The minimalist millionnaire smiled, recalling his teenaged beauty's innocent comment when she had first checked out the sparse kitchen in his old Richmond flat. 'Yeah. They cleaned us out while we were in the UK. Took everything.'

Madalena gaped in what was almost sympathy. 'That's shit! Bastards!'

'Only kidding!' he chuckled. 'It's all packed up, coming back from London.'

So his sister knew how to care after all, short-lived and shallow though it may have been. Retrieving an old skillet from behind another door, Jeff set about making breakfast. He melted a large chunk of butter, whistling a new melody that drifted into his mind. When it was piping hot and sizzling, the whole pack of bacon was emptied into the molten cholesterol, thinking he should make the most of this; his last chance to have a real man's breakfast for a while!

'What sort of a tatt' d'you think you'll get?' he asked, smelling smoke from yet another cigarette and full of gratitude at being on their own today for yet another unhealthy reason.

'Dunno. A bird maybe, or a snake,' Madalena mused. 'What d'ya reckon?'

'Something you're still going to like in ten or twenty years' time,' her brother advised, feeling old and prudish. 'Something tasteful, so you can still wear nice clothes and it doesn't look bad.'

'I don't wear nice clothes,' his sister cackled. 'Only for your weddin'.'

'But wouldn't you like to? Was the stuff Lynn bought you nice?'

'Yeah. Course. I chose 'em. She just paid for 'em.'

The musician shook his head, cracking four eggs into the pan. 'We could wrap you up differently. D'you know the story of "My Fair Lady"?'

The expression on the young woman's face turned vacant, telling her brother there was little point in pursuing this line of questioning any further. At least she knew what she liked, he rued, even though this particular street-girl would require a great deal of wrapping.

'Anyway...' he added, inserting two slices of bread into the toaster while scribbling a verse of lyrics onto a nearby notepad. 'Just don't put it where you'll have a big, red mark showing above your bridesmaid's dress, please.'

'No! I wan' it 'ere,' Madalena was pointing to her hip.

'*Bueno,*' Jeff laughed. 'What about working? Wouldn't that hurt while it heals? Not that I'm jumping to any conclusions about what you get up to...'

'Fuck off! You know what I get up to. How long does it 'urt for?' the ignorant woman whined, as if a light bulb had illuminated above her head.

'Not long. A week or so until it's properly healed, but only painful for a few days. I guess if you get one done today, you'd be fine for when you get home. Go for your life!'

The matching pair ate their breakfast outside, much to their visitor's delight. Madalena began to lose the pasty-faced guise with which she had woken up and was now more animated. Her host presented her with a small, rectangular card which he had picked up from the newsagent earlier.

'Have you still got that list of 'phone numbers?' he asked.

Madalena nodded. 'Yeah. It's in my wallet. What's this?'

'A phone-card. If you need to ring anyone, follow the instructions on it. Dial this number from any public 'phone, then you'll have to type in the code and the operator'll ask you which number you want to ring. Let's try it, shall we?'

Jeff made the flighty woman go through the motions of dialling Gerry's office, acting like a parent again, constantly having to refocus her attention. She panicked as soon as the call connected and she heard a woman's voice answer, thrusting the receiver in her teacher's face.

'Hey, Paula. It's Jeff,' he said, trying not to laugh at his sister's fright.

'Good morning, Jeff. How are you?' his manager's cheerful personal assistant replied. 'How can I help you?'

'Sorry to ring for no good reason, but I'm just trying out one of those phone-cards with my sister. It works, obviously!'

'Oh, OK! That's good, because Gerry's not here. No message then?'

'Great. No, thanks. But look, do you mind if we try it again?' he asked, anxious to make sure Madalena knew what she was doing. 'Hang up and we'll ring you again, if that's OK?'

'No worries,' Paula responded. 'I'll wait for your call.'

The twenty-six-year-old novice communicator stepped through the dialling process for a second time. She grinned when she heard the same voice at the other end, yet still transferred the receiver into her brother's hands.

'Hey, Paula. It's me again. Thanks for doing that.'

'Not a problem, Jeff. Have a good day,' the proficient secretary giggled. 'Oh, yes, and have a great wedding!'

'Cheers! We will. See you soon,' her firm's biggest and best-looking client signed off. '*Adiós.*'

Madalena sighed and slumped down into her chair, seeming exhausted by the last few minutes' activity. Her brother signalled for her to pick up her plate and mug, and they returned everything to the kitchen. Refilling both coffee mugs, he put them on the table while the sink filled with hot, soapy water.

'If you need to use this for real, you better say something when they answer,' the younger sibling teased, waving the card across her face. 'Otherwise, they'll hang up, and you'll still be stranded.'

While walking through the city towards the tattoo parlour, the famous tour guide pointed out various landmarks to his visitor, none appearing to meet with much recognition. Her universe was very small, and she didn't seem to want anything more. He got the sense that her trip to Melbourne would be a soon-forgotten disturbance to the regular routine of meeting men in bars, taking them to wherever they wanted to go and doing whatever they wanted to do. And this was only if she was freelance... Was there a middleman making a tidy mark-up on every sordid transaction?

What a life! Still, Lynn was right, the young man decided. In spite of all the pain and indignity she had endured, his sister looked reasonably stable and well-adjusted. Like him, she had learned to take care of herself. Perhaps he was overreacting again.

'D'you get checked out by a doctor regularly?' he asked, his serious question taking her by surprise.

'What? Oh, yeah. We have to,' Madalena replied. 'It's the law. Sean pays the bill too. Not like the old days.'

'The old days?' Jeff exclaimed. 'Like you're so old! Who's Sean?'

'My pimp. He's OK. They look after us, 'im and 'is mate.'

Inside the tattoo parlour, the brother watched their childish guest leaf through the myriad available designs, as if she were selecting the toy she wanted for Christmas. Turning corners over to mark her favourites, her finger wandered around the pages, and every now and again she would emit a whoop of delight. The tattooist who had created his and Lynn's matching design wasn't at work today, but the rock star's previous appointments were evidently significant milestones for the store, judging by the royal greeting he received.

After almost an hour of deliberation, Madalena was content to leave with a few photocopied options to help her with her choice, and they continued on their journey south-east and out of the CBD towards the MCG. Jeff pointed out the street where he used to live after first moving down from Sydney.

'I never thought you'd ever meet Lynn Dyson,' the skinny waif told her brother, once more in awe of the attention he attracted wherever they went. 'But now you're bloody marryin' 'er. Fuck, *chico!*'

Her guide smiled. 'Yeah. We do that too! Unbelievable, isn't it? I still have trouble believing it sometimes.'

'Wonder what Mamá'd think?' Madalena said, for the first time introspective.

'Hmm...' Jeff replied, his chest tightening. 'I often think about that. D'you reckon she even knew what was going on towards the end? Really?'

His sister made a coarse snorting noise. 'Na. Just kept on with drinkin' and the pills and needles. It was better that way. She told me.'

'Does that bother you?' her brother asked. 'I mean, does it kill you inside, what happened?'

'Na. Not now. I don't care. I was glad she died, after... You know... And nothing can change it. Oh, yeah... I forgot to tell you. Why did Lynn say do I 'ave nightmares?'

The former lost boy smiled. 'Did she? And do you?'

'No. Do you?' the young woman responded, nonplussed.

'Shit, yeah! Well, I used to. Every night. Not so much now though,' the superstar confessed, feeling the panic rising inside him.

'What about?' Madalena asked. 'Mamá dyin'?'

'*Sí*. And you with those arseholes,' her brother tested the waters, hoping neither of them would freak out. 'Hearing what they were doing to you.'

Tears were burning the rock star's eyes, unsure how far he could trust this stranger he had grown up with. Her face revealed no trace of empathy, nor did she seem to be affected by the subject in any other way. Could she really have escaped with no scars from those times? Hard to believe, but perhaps the girl had simply been too caught up in the horrific mess to acquire any sort of perspective on how wrong it was.

'I couldn't live with all those memories of how they treated you and Mamá,' he continued. 'And the fact that I couldn't do anything to stop it. It fucked me over big-time.'

Lifting her gaze, the Sydneysider saw her impressive little brother was crying and had no idea what to do. 'Fuck, *chico*! That was ages ago. I blame Dad,' she yelped, fixing her eyes on some distant landmark as they walked towards the giant structure. 'Everything was his fuckin' fault. You couldn't stop it. I know that, and I used to think you were an idiot tryin'. We were just kids back then.'

Embarrassed, the celebrity wiped his eyes, becoming aware of a headache pounding in his temples and keen to pull himself together in case any fans approached him at this awkward moment as they closed in on the crowded arena. It wouldn't do his image any good to be caught crying in public two days before his wedding. It was supposed to be the happiest day of his life, and it would be. He didn't relish the responsibility of providing the press with speculative ammunition.

'I know. Thanks,' he sniffed, 'but it doesn't make it go away. Lynn's made things so much better, but the guilt still kicks me in the guts every time I think about you back then. And you shouldn't be sleeping with men for a living. You should've got a good education and had a normal life.'

Madalena shoved his arm, smiling at his apparent recovery. 'Wha'? *Chico*, I got a normal life. You ain't. You can talk!'

The woman had a point. Laughing, The Australian Elvis put his arm around her, glad to have purged his system of the raw emotion. Just in time too, since a bunch of teenaged girls screamed and pointed to him. He waved, fully expecting them to rush him for autographs.

'Yeah. I guess so. But it's tough, Lena. I want to help you, to make up for all that crap. You know...'

His sister leaned into him for the first time. '*Gracias, chico*,' she said. '*Es bien.* Talk about somethin' else. Them girls're eyein' you up.'

The younger brother did as he was told, relieved they had at least opened a door between them. This wiry prostitute had come through their childhood better than he had, inexplicably. His excited fans had already guessed he was out with a relative, given the resemblance, and they passed a camera around until they had all captured themselves with the celebrity and his strikingly similar sister.

The Melbourne Cricket Ground loomed large in front of the *duo*. The celebrity took Madalena around to the museum entrance and bought two tickets. A guided tour was scheduled to leave in fifteen minutes' time, and the staff were thrilled to see none other than Jeff Diamond rock up. He urged them not to make a fuss, and his sister looked chuffed to be with such a popular drawcard, no longer so overawed by all the attention.

The guide's commentary largely went unheeded by the visitor, who had no interest in historic detail and was more intent on gazing around the stadium and taking in its enormity. By contrast, the avid sports fan had never made the time for this tour before and found every fact and figure fascinating, vowing to come back again without his familial distraction, so that he could take his time poring over the exhibits.

The dark-haired siblings grabbed some lunch in a laneway behind Collins Street, along with a swarm of tourists. The ambiance was extra-convivial leading up to New Year's Eve, with decorations hanging in most cafés, and again they were regularly interrupted for autographs and a steady flow of questions. Jeff made a point of introducing Madalena, since everyone had at least one comment about his upcoming nuptials. He decided it was best to join in with their happiness, and it further humanised the occasion to show off the sister who had flown down from Sydney for the wedding. His adoring fans lapped up every drop of information, begging for photographs with the tall, sultry-looking pair.

'You're such a big star!' Madalena stated the obvious, becoming agitated by all the adulation. 'People love you.'

'Ah, it's only because of the wedding,' the celebrity lied, calling over an equally star-struck waitress. 'It'll die down soon. Have you chosen what you want?'

Sitting with a cigarette and a bottle of beer in the cool summer air, having satisfied his public for the moment, the star acknowledged once again the great city that was Melbourne. He did feel at home here, and he knew Lynn was very happy they had returned. Two bowls of *pasta* arrived, steaming and laden with shaved *parmesan*. The skinny woman tucked into hers *con gusto*, as if she hadn't had a square meal in weeks.

'What the hell did you do with your breakfast?' Jeff cried out, amazed at her appetite. 'Didn't you eat anything last night?'

'I'm always hungry,' his sister replied, slurping a strand of *spaghetti* through pursed lips. 'This is good too. I like Melbourne heaps.'

'*Sí. Es muy buena,*' the city's adopted son agreed, recalling Lynn commenting on a similar voracity in his untamed years. 'You'll have to come down again sometime.'

Brother and sister clinked their beer bottles together and ate their food in the shade of a large umbrella. After a while, the lunchtime crowd thinned out, and the passing shoppers left them in peace while they ate.

'Are you guys gonna have kids?' Madalena asked out of the blue.

Jeff looked up and nodded. 'Yep. That's the plan.'

His companion shrieked, causing the people on neighbouring tables to look in their direction. 'Oh, my God! I'm going to be an auntie!'

The famous man chuckled and shook his head. 'Shhh! Not yet! Not so loud! People'll think we're only getting married because Lynn's pregnant. The year after next maybe.'

After their meal stop, Madalena followed the showman to his manager's office, entering via the front of the building rather than the back entrance he favoured for the sake of anonymity. The cavernous *foyer* of 333 Collins Street made the virgin tourist dizzy, and her brother laughed when she almost tripped over while looking up at the ceiling's intricate plasterwork. He wanted his wide-eyed charge to be able to find this building easily, and she assured him she would remember "Three-three-three". Striding through the bustling lobby to the bank of lifts, they ascended to Blake & Partners' headquarters on the eighth floor.

'Paula, hi!' Jeff greeted the woman on whom they had tested the telephone charge-card. 'Thanks for helping us out earlier. This is my sister, Madalena.'

The two young women acknowledged each other politely. The efficient assistant buzzed through to her boss, who burst out of his office, as ever full of the joys of spring.

'Thought I heard your dulcet tones,' Gerry joked, shaking Jeff's hand. 'Not long to go, mate. Still time to back out.'

Ignoring the selection of objecting expletives from his old friend, the accountant's eyes alighted on the scrawny, curly-headed woman who had flopped down into one of the sumptuous leather chesterfields in his reception area. Her slim, bare legs and her very short skirt grabbed his attention.

'This can't possibly be your sis',' he quipped, looking from one to the other.

Madalena scrambled to her feet and stood next to her brother, assuming the tall Irishman to be serious.

'How did you know?' Jeff laughed, putting an arm around her shoulder.

'Bloody hell, mate!' his manager exclaimed. 'I've known you how long? Twelve years or thereabouts? And today I meet your sister for the first time. Delighted, Miss Diamond.'

'Miss Moreno, actually,' his friend jumped in, before she could put Gerry in his place in her usual perfunctory fashion. 'Lena uses our mum's name. Madalena, this is the infamous Gerry Blake, my best man.'

The shy bridesmaid shook the suave executive's hand. 'Jack and Tammy's brother? Hi. Nice to meet you.'

'The very same, for my sins. You too,' Gerry replied, sneaking another gratuitous eyeful of her legs. 'Wow! I never realised you'd be so like Jeff. It's somewhat spooky.'

'Spooky?' the woman repeated, confused.

'Yeah. What *are* you talking about?' the musician added. 'Brothers and sisters often look alike, you idiot. What did you expect?'

'I don't know, really. Do I look that much like my sisters?'

'No. They're much better looking than you,' his client teased. 'In fact, they're entertaining Lena tonight while we're out on the town, remember? We'd better make sure we don't end up at the same joint. Anyway, we've got work to do.'

Jeff turned to Madalena and pointed towards the lifts. 'So you're going to be alright wandering around the shops for a while? Give us a ring if you can't find this place.'

'Yeah. All good,' the young woman replied, patting her skirt pocket into which Jeff had stuffed three hundred dollars, more money than she had ever seen at once. 'I'll see you back at your flat later.'

'Great. Have fun, *chica*,' Jeff told her. 'And no drugs, OK?'

Grumbling under her breath, the indignant woman turned on her heels and summoned the lift with confidence, leaving her brother somewhat bereft. Gerry showed his most lucrative investment into his office and extracted two beers from a refrigerator concealed under the window.

'Jesus, Jeff! She's a piece of work,' the lecherous man waxed lyrical. 'I don't know what I imagined, but she's exactly like you described her. Almost caricature proportions. How weird is that? And fuck! Those legs! They're as long as Lynn's.'

'Yeah, and not as bruised as yesterday,' the tired man bemoaned. 'But I'm not about to start telling my older sister what to wear. You know… This is the longest we've spent in each others' company since I was about eight. Actually, it's been good to spend time together.'

'Is she really a pro'?' Gerry asked, like a wide-eyed teenager. 'I mean, professional?'

Jeff laughed at his friend's innocent question. 'What other kind is there?'

'True,' his manager chuckled too. 'I guess not accepting money would kind of disqualify you from the institute.'

The rock star rolled his eyes. 'Piss off, mate! Leave her alone. It's all she knows.'

A Tiger, A Tango And A Tablet

Jeff returned to the apartment just after six o'clock. He had less than an hour to get back to Rosati's to meet his friends for the bucks' party. Gerry hadn't let on whether anything special had been arranged, but the well-liked celebrity felt sure something out of the ordinary would be sprung on him at some point during the night.

'Lena, are you here?' he called from the hallway.

The groom-to-be could hear shuffling from the spare bedroom, and the door was firmly shut. Receiving no reply, he jumped into the shower. Anticipation for the evening ahead was beginning to excite him, scarcely able to believe he was Chief Buck for this party. Never had he imagined himself the marrying kind. Yet now the stress of having his sister back in his life was dissipating, he was starting to enjoy the build-up to the main event which had occupied the forefront of everyone's mind for too long a time.

'Chico, look!' Madalena burst into the bedroom while her brother was dressing. 'Oh, shit! Should o' knocked.'

'Come in,' the half-naked man invited. 'Something tells me you're not going to see anything new.'

'Hey! Shut up, culo!' she replied, picking up a discarded towel from the floor and throwing it at him. 'Look at my tatt'.'

The tall woman was standing in her underwear, holding a drawing of a tiger next to her right hip, which was covered with a large, white dressing. 'Do you like it?'

Jeff's eyes squinted at the picture. 'Well, yeah... What I can see of it. It's better than a snake. Why a tiger?'

Madalena chortled. 'It's funny. They looked up nineteen-forty-nine in the Chinese calendar and said, "Year of the Ox", so I said, "What's an ox?" But I didn't want an ox 'cause it's a bit like a fuckin' cow, so I looked at the other years and went for a tiger.'

The musician raised his hands in despair, imagining Confucius spinning in his grave. 'Great! So it's a complete lie! What year's the tiger?'

'Nineteen-fifty,' Madalena answered. 'I'm only a year and a half older 'n you now!'

'Right... Did you see what animal nineteen-fifty-two was?' her brother asked out of curiosity.

'Yeah. Dragon,' his sister replied. 'You should get one.'

'Does it hurt? Ours did for a few days.'

'Yeah. A bit. Prob'ly when I'm dancin' tonight. Better not go 'ome with someone, eh?'

Dismissing the apposite comment with a flick of his hand, the buck finished dressing for his party. A charcoal grey suit he had had made on Savile Row, the palest blue, cotton shirt and a tastefully-striped tie which Lynn had given him for the occasion. He glanced from the mirror to the clock.

'Jesus! I need to get going. Where're you meeting the girls?'

'They're comin' 'ere. Soon,' his sister replied. 'I better get dressed too. You look smart as. Very cool.'

The good-looking party boy met Jacinta and Tamilla Blake in the lobby downstairs. They fussed around him as only they knew how. Breaking free of their wandering hands and smearing their lipstick off his cheeks, he buzzed up to Madalena, urging her not to forget the key. The sisters hugged him and wished him a good night.

Most of his guests were already standing at the long bar in Rosati's when Jeff arrived. A loud cheer went up as he entered, to which he gave a flamboyant bow, as much to psych' himself up than for any other reason. This was his night, and he had better play along. Gerry had adopted Pete Bourke, as his client had primed him earlier. They looked like longstanding work-mates on their first couple of beers after a hard day at the office.

Three of the star's band members were present, as was Junior Dyson, a few mates from his university basketball team and former colleagues from the engineering firm where he had worked for six months, back before he became one of Australia's richest men. Seeing these honest, nine-to-five employees again reminded him of when he had needed to watch for each pay-packet recharging his bank account. It was as if his whole adult life now stood in front of him in the one place, simultaneously surreal and validating.

'Get this down ya,' Pete shouted, thrusting a beer into the new arrival's hand.

'Cheers, guys!' Jeff responded, raising his drink to eye level, seeing the assembled throng raise their array of glasses and bottles in fine voice. 'Thanks for coming. So what's the plan, *maestro*?'

'Plan?' Gerry shrugged. 'Drink, drink and more drink. Is there meant to be a plan?'

'Not necessarily. Sounds good to me,' his old friend swallowed the last few mouthfuls of his first bottle in a matter of seconds. 'Set 'em up, mate.'

Junior Dyson appeared at the young man's shoulder, keen to buy the next round. 'Congratulations, bro',' the blond footballer yelled above the noise, slapping the musician on the back. 'Welcome home. I'm really happy for you two. Honoured to become your brother-in-law, Mister Diamond.'

'Cheers, Mister Dyson,' the celebrity echoed, hugging the big man in return. '*Ditto*. Have you met these reprobates yet?'

Jeff introduced everyone to everyone, but it didn't take long for the barriers to come down between who and whom. After an hour of meaningless banter and numerous rounds, a line of white *limousines* slinked along the kerb outside the bar, blocking the narrow laneway. Gerry instructed the all-male party to finish their drinks and climb into the *chauffeur*-driven cars, pulling the groom-to-be out by his jacket sleeve and shoving him into the first vehicle in line.

Already inside were Bart Dyson and Gerald Blake, Seniors both and in more ways than one. With three beers and a whisky sloshing around his empty stomach, the mystified songwriter took a second or two to come to grips with the situation, shaking their hands and taking a seat. He had most certainly not expected Lynn's father to attend his stag night!

Once all were aboard, the cars moved off in convoy towards the western end of the CBD, much to the amazement of the small crowd of early-evening drinkers who had spotted their idol in the well-known bar. A fresh bottle of beer was slotted into Jeff's waiting grip by none other than his future father-in-law.

'Where are we going, mate?' he asked his best man.

'Never you mind! Just sit back and enjoy the ride.'

Accepting his fate readily, the guest of honour turned to the elder statesmen. 'Thanks for coming, sirs. I can safely say I wasn't expecting to find either of you in here! You've met then... Goes without saying!'

'We have, Jeff,' Bart confirmed.

Big D looked relaxed and pleased to have been invited to share in the pretender's celebrations. Paradoxically, the two main men in Lynn's life had grown closer during their year apart, largely as a result of their women's insistence that they become friends. Now that his addled brain had dealt with the surprise, the groom was glad his former adversary was attending tonight's shindig. Another conspiracy cooked up by his *fiancée* and his manager behind his back, no doubt!

'I hope you youngsters can keep up with the real men tonight,' the enormous athlete joked, nudging Gerry's dad's elbow.

'Good to be here, Jeff,' Gerald added, 'but I'm not sure I can commit to anything like this pair's consumption rate. Not in their league, Bart, I'm afraid.'

The founding partner of the successful accountancy firm was the closest to a father figure Jeff was likely to find at his wedding. Truth be told, seeing his best mate's parents face off at the ceremony with Lynn's aristocratic family was ten times better than the real thing as far as he was concerned.

What on Earth would Paul Diamond have made of his son's current circle of friends, let alone riding in the back of a *limousine* with Bart Dyson? Or for that matter, of the whole wedding deal? *Enough*, the bitter man cursed. Who cared about that good-for-nothing arsehole? He had played absolutely no part in helping his son arrive at where he was today, except to serve as a lesson on who not to be.

The convoy attracted a large amount of attention on the city streets as it made a series of tricky right-angled turns on its way towards the western fringe, not far from where the swarthy superstar had made his life-changing concert *début*. He twisted round to peer through the distant rear window at the four or five matching stretch Holdens following theirs.

'Some spectacle, Gezza,' he slapped his mate on the knee. 'Thanks a lot.'

The cars stopped one-by-one in the circular driveway of the Grand Hotel and emptied like tubes of toothpaste squeezing out the last few suited gentlemen under the awning. Stretching back up to their full height, the *posse* regrouped and made their way into the *foyer*. Jeff made sure the two patriarchs were introduced to the others, all suitably awestruck at having both Dyson superheroes in their company for the night. For his part however, the humble world-changer was thankful the sportsmen were there to take the spotlight off him for a while.

Gerry had a flair for organising social events and was in his element tonight. More correctly, as he assured Pete Bourke, his staff excelled at organising them, leaving him with the onerous duty of participation. The select group of revellers were shown into a function room on the first floor, which had been decked out like a French *bordello* especially for the occasion.

'Tasteful,' the guest of honour leaned over to his best man, 'particularly after our conversation this afternoon…'

The businessman grinned. 'Don't worry. She's not here!'

'You fucking bastard,' Jeff hissed through gritted teeth.

Still processing his rapid intake of alcohol, he was seized by a strong urge to punch his best friend's lights out. A thunderous expression had covered his face, and anger coursed through him in a way he hardly recognised at first. Forcing himself to calm down, he made his point and determined to move on.

'That's absolutely not funny. OK.'

'Easy, buddy,' Gerry said, holding his hands up in apology. 'Jeez! I won't mention her again.'

The groom-to-be turned to Junior, who was seated on the opposite side of the table, anxious to rid himself of this violent reaction. 'So how's Julie? Things still going well with you two?'

'Going great guns, thanks, Jeff,' the blond footballer replied. 'Racking up the miles between us, driving back and forth from the city. She's thinking about moving in, but Narrandera's such a long way from anywhere. We're trying to work out how we split ourselves between there and here without spending so much time on the road. I may even pop the question too, once you and Lynn have surrendered the limelight.'

Jeff smiled and shook his future brother-in-law's hand over the assortment of beer bottles and glasses which now cluttered the table. 'Awesome news, mate,' he said, genuinely pleased. 'Lynn'll be stoked.'

The wine arrived in copious quantity, and orders were taken for food. The noise level generated by their various conversations was steadily increasing in volume, and the man of the moment surveyed the scene to ensure his bucks were all enjoying themselves. Catching his drummer's eye, he rose from his seat and went to share a joke with the band, hoping to jettison the legacy of Gerry's tactless comment along the way.

Annoyed with himself, the musician vowed to apologise for his overreaction later, but for now it would do them both good to let the good-time guy stew. He had done a wonderful job so far. The more Jeff gazed around the room, the more the *décor*'s finer detail told him a story very dear to his heart, and his conscience admitted that his nerves wouldn't have been half as raw last week concerning his sister.

The statuesque superstar returned to his seat while the *entrées* were served. One of the best things about the evening was that no-one was in the slightest bit interested in the fact that he was getting married. This was truly a feminine phenomenon, he concluded with relief, and an obsession fuelled by the press' desire to maximise sales.

To his left, Bart, Junior, Gerald and Pete were discussing the upcoming football season and which sponsorship contracts were the most expensive. To his right, Gerry and his former work colleagues swapped good and bad client entertainment venues and expanded on sordid tales from other events they had hosted. And at the far end of the table, whence he had returned to eat, his band-mates were simply content to tip as much amber liquid down their throats as possible. *All good*, he thought.

Piped music began to seep through wall-mounted speakers, carefully obscured behind false, curtained windows. Waiters bustled around, quietly refilling each glass and whipping cleared plates away. Looking around, the prime stag loosened his tie and undid the top button of his shirt. The music became gradually more intrusive, and the lights dimmed to create an air of relaxed anticipation which was soon satisfied when a line of brightly dressed can-can dancers trooped in wearing thigh-length, black boots. Their willing audience immediately began to clap and whistle appreciatively when the girls kicked their legs high and flounced their colourful, full skirts with white petticoats to reveal fishnet stockings and suspender belts and much, much more. The number of dancers matched the number of seats at his table, the seasoned performer noticed.

'Not a bad show from this boring old accountant...' Jeff slapped Gerry on his back, shouting over to his father. 'Very cool, mate. This is shaping up nicely.'

The affable executive shrugged and grinned, his confidence undented by the earlier brush with his old friend's ire. 'All in a day's work.'

The showgirls remained in strict formation, at first coming closer and then backing away from their admirers as the music continued. Halfway through the piece however, a brunette in the centre eagerly broke ranks and danced up to the special guest, holding her arms out towards him. Already falling victim to the evocative strains, he joined in readily, slipping both hands around the waistline of her *bustière*.

His red-blooded friends gave a rousing burst of applause, which sent the girls's kicks higher still.

'Who's paying for this?' Bart Dyson yelled, after the dance had finished and the troop had retreated through the door from which they had appeared.

'He is!' Gerry pointed to the man wiping a layer of perspiration from his brow and downing the last few mouthfuls of beer in one swallow. 'That's what happens when you appoint someone as signatory to your bank accounts.'

Pretending to reach for the suit jacket he had abandoned on the back of his chair, Jeff raised his hands and mimed a clapperboard cutting a final scene. 'OK. That's a wrap, folks. Show's over. Time to go home.'

Loud groans of disappointment rang from all around the table, and the members of the Jeff Diamond Band drummed up a familiar union rally cry.

'What do we want? Girls! When do we wan' 'em? Now!'

A set piece at post-gig drinking parties, pretty soon everyone else had joined in too. The older men sat back and laughed at each other, no longer accustomed to spending time in the midst of such youthful joviality.

'Fucking hell!' their leader scoffed, urging them to calm down. 'You guys are taking this very seriously. I'm impressed! Alright. We'll have a whip-round. Give generously, folks.'

Main courses were delivered to the table by amused waiters and waitresses, their work made all the more enjoyable by the vocal but good-natured diners. Conversation reverted to more staid topics while they ate, albeit with an undeniable buzz in the air. The food was delicious, and the wine continued to flow, courtesy of the songwriter's plentiful coffers. Joking with those closest to him, Jeff wondered what condition they would all be in for New Year's Eve, which was now only twenty-four hours away.

Expectations soon re-ignited for the next entertaining interlude once the men's meals were finished. Sure enough, the music struck up again, this time to loud hoots and whistles from the ignominious rockers down at one end. The same *burlesque* ladies streamed through into the function room, now with much shorter skirts and much more free-form in their dance moves for their second number.

Each man in the handsome celebrity's party was visited by two or three dancers at a time, venturing tantalisingly close, but never quite close enough. The choreography was cleverly arranged for the cultured crowd.

Rubbing his hands together as he watched two blondes making their way towards him and his best man, Jeff looped his tie over his head and prepared to put it to good use. 'This is pure gold, mate,' he shouted. 'Thanks so much. Sorry to snap your head off earlier. I was out of order. This is bloody fantastic.'

Gerry slapped his friend on the back. 'No worries. I thought you'd like it. The *Moulin Rouge* theme was originally Lynn's idea, I must admit, but I sort of embellished it a little.'

The *fiancé* smiled and shook his head. No wonder his beautiful best friend had made those suggestive remarks before leaving this morning. Her people and his people had been scheming all along.

'Remind me to marry that woman,' he grinned.

Bart had been eavesdropping. 'Did I hear you say Lynn's in on this?'

The musician nodded, his eyes fixed on a long pair of legs vanishing under a bright scarlet, satin mini-skirt. 'Apparently so. Did you know?'

'No. I most certainly did not. She didn't try and talk me out of coming either.'

The big man's son piped up from the other side of the table. 'You'd better be worried, Dad. She's after your life assurance,' he shouted, clutching at his heart.

Everyone laughed, including the veteran Olympian, who wagged a threatening finger. 'You just wait and see who's still standing at the end.'

Of course, the elder statesman received an even bigger laugh, more out of respect than for his comedic prowess. The dancers had continued to work their way around the table, causing chaos in their wakes. By this time, Jeff had been pulled up out of his seat to dance with them. The girls had assumed he would be up for strutting his stuff, most likely aware of the star's extreme fleetness of foot. He didn't disappoint them, fastening his tie loosely around the long, slender neck of one and tugging her in for a kiss while tracing his fingers up the other's tanned thigh until all was revealed. Jackets off and collars loosened all round, his antics left the other men nervously wondering when it would be their turn to enact control.

After three rousing songs, the leggy dozen exited stage-left again to vociferous applause. Yet more drinks arrived, along with dessert and a huge selection of cheeses. Gerry requested a tray of *liqueurs* for those who wanted to supplement their coffee with something extra.

'Did you know any of this was going to happen?' Pete asked his neighbour.

'Absolutely no effing clue,' Jeff replied. 'This bloke's always reliable when it comes to getting us into strife, so I should've suspected something. Lynn had her hens' night yesterday. They went to a *cabaret* club, but by all accounts it was pretty tame.'

'By all accounts...' Gerry scoffed with an affected wink. 'She's bound to tell you that, mate. You're getting gullible in your old age.'

The wise man shrugged, and the others laughed. 'All I know is there was a lot of this happening when she got home,' he said, bending his pinky finger in the air. 'And it wasn't directed at me.'

Another roar of laughter, and the handsome groom gave up trying to justify himself as bawdy comments abounded. Instead, he poured a generous slug of *Kahlúa* into his cup of coffee, topping it with cream and stirring it vigorously. Drinking the cupful down in one huge gulp, he waved to the waiter for a refill.

'This man could drink for his country!' Gerald Blake cajoled Big D. 'Sign him up!'

With the dessert plates cleared away, the music was turned up for the third time. The show was beginning in earnest, it appeared, given the military style drums and brass section that seized the audience's full attention. This time, skirts were pleasingly absent, boots had been abandoned for *stiletto* heels, and the dancers' lace-edged, boned corsets provided scaffolding rather than cover.

The bad-boys of the band, egged on by Jeff's former university friends, resumed their rowdy chanting, peppered with more whistles and uninhibited, lewd gestures. Pretty soon, the whole crowd was banging their fists, cups or empty glasses on the table. The best man made a run for the bathroom, and his old friend sprang to his feet to follow.

'Hey, Gez! Wait up. Before I get too pissed,' he insisted, 'I just want to say thanks again. You're an amazing man to have around, Mister Blake, sir.'

'That's OK, mate. You're welcome. Remember me in your will,' the businessman smirked.

The superstar laughed out loud. 'At this rate, there won't be anything left!'

The two friends embraced and shook hands again before passing through the doors to the lobby area and locating the toilets. Standing side-by-side at the urinals, as they had many a time before, they exchanged fantasies about the evening's Parisien courtesans and the delights they might have in store.

Gerry made the fatal mistake of returning to the table at the same time as his famous buddy. Two virtually nude dancers immediately pounced on the tall, good-looking pair, and they again found themselves swept up as part of the act. Jeff made sure his best man remained the centre of attention for as long as possible, and the clumsy Irishman worked hard to emulate his graceful friend. One thing this particular accountant did not lack was *bravado*. However, judging by the jeering from the table and the expressions on the girls' faces, he was scoring miserably in the talent department.

After a few minutes of highly fluid and provocative locomotion, the man regularly dubbed "Sex on Legs" made his excuses and sat down. His jacket long discarded, he rolled up his sleeves one at a time, feeling mellow but not at all drunk. The sight of his bare forearms taken as the signal for more action, the dancers took their cue to encircle the table and pick a guest, asking them to turn to face outwards as they twirled around the table in a bizarre game of strip musical chairs.

Timed with a change in the music, they all raised a knee and placed their right *stiletto* between each pair of legs, perfectly in unison, drawing breath from every man at the same time. The effect was magical, causing everyone to exhale at the same time too and applaud in bashful *camaraderie*.

Jeff clapped and whistled exuberantly, catching a few eyes and cocking his head in grateful acknowledgement of pleasures shared with his closest friends. The trick was soon repeated the next time the chorus came round, and the scantily-clad dancers progressively became more brazen with their chosen subjects. A few participants began shyly and with some reluctance, especially the conservative Gerald Blake, but others most definitely were ready for anything.

Bart Dyson, to his son's dismay, was not in the least uncomfortable. Junior prodded the guest of honour's arm and directed his eyes towards the senior Olympian engaged in a passionate embrace.

'Did you imagine you'd ever see that?' he chuckled.

The songwriter shook his head. 'Nope. I hope someone's got a camera. There's life in the old dog yet!'

Leaving the men on tenterhooks, the music came to an abrupt halt, and the *troupe* disappeared back-stage again. Everyone took their time to relax and recharge their glasses, any remaining barriers now well and truly broken down.

A few minutes later, when most figured the entertainment to be over, a lone dancer reappeared, elegantly dressed in Flamenco costume and carrying a deep crimson rose with a long, straight stem. The man of the moment instantly cottoned on to this latest segment, silently thanking his beautiful best friend.

The exotic, dark-eyed beauty with brilliant red lipstick sauntered wantonly up to the groom-to-be. He remained seated, simply pivoting on the back legs of his chair until she stood over him, holding the rose in front of his face.

'*Madre de Dios*,' the hot-blooded twenty-three-year-old muttered under his breath, his blood pressure already simmering just below boiling point.

To create the desired effect, the showman feigned exhaustion and scanned each face in the group, casually flicking the cap off his lighter and lighting a cigarette. His friends began a slow hand-clap, led by his irrepressible band members. Even though he could hardly wait to stand up and dance with this enticing woman, he milked the scene for as long as he could. He owed Lynn nothing less.

'Why me? Why not one of them?' he cried in vain, looping a long arm aloft.

'I need a Latin lover,' the girl crooned, in her best husky Spanish. '*Un hombre apasionado. Con fuego en el corazón.*'

'But I'm a Polish Jew!' Jeff exclaimed in a pronounced Yiddish accent, attracting another roar of laughter. 'Polish Jews can't dance *el Flamenco*. They dance the Hora.'

'Fucking know-all,' his bass player yelled from the other side of the table. 'Get up, you asshole. We want to see her taunt you, like on that TV show in LA. Butt-naked, both of you!'

Through the jet-lag and the added effort of having his sister to chaperone, the star had almost forgotten their recent festive performances. *That's right. Lynn had lit the fire in his heart, and it had been fun.* He wished she were here right now, exacting a metaphysical yank on their invisible elastic connection in the hope that she could pick up on his longing. A divine *frisson* slithered across his shoulders, and all became right with the world.

Wild, tempted eyes fixed on the woman in the red and black Spanish costume, and he let out a long sigh. 'Be gentle with me, *señorita*.'

The confident dancer nodded subtly, and their accompaniment faded up through the speakers. Jeff allowed her to place the rose between his teeth, leaning forward to steal a kiss before shaking his mane in defiance. A strumming guitar accelerated in the background. Game on!

'Now we definitely need a camera!' Junior stood up and clapped.

Most of the guys were also on their feet, some even stamping them in time with the beat. The dance was a tango; the young man's favourite. There could be no doubt that his dream girl had put them up to this, he smiled. She was the absolute best. She knew exactly how to excite him, and his loins were all set to give them the show they had foreseen.

The talented dancer grabbed his partner's side roughly, tugging her slim frame into his. Someone whooped behind him. The music had been started again, slowly and quietly, but soon its volume climbed in line with its *tempo*. He span the girl around, pouting his lips close to hers and then pulling them away with high drama. She responded to the hint and began to spice things up a bit too, her hands running up and down her graceful Latin lover's body.

The tango continued in the same format which Jeff Diamond had acted out a hundred times on stage, written up in many a rave concert review. The music became faster and faster and louder and louder while the performer wheeled his co-star in creative circles, in turn grabbing her and sending her away.

After a while, he spat out the rose, comically wiping the saliva away from his mouth. 'That's better!' he gasped, whisking his partner around as if as light as air. 'I can breathe now.'

He could almost make his heart believe this lithe woman were Lynn, but not quite enough to want to engage with her luscious lips. Both dancers were breathing heavily as the track came to an end. They finished with a flourish, and the striking stag hugged his pliable quarry close, kissing her on the forehead.

'Thanks very much. That was fantastic. What's your name?' he asked into her ear during a prolonged and steamy embrace.

'Julia,' the dancer answered. 'You too. You're the best partner I've ever had, by a long way. And I think it's great you're marrying Lynn. You really go well together.'

'Thanks. We think so too,' the happy man replied, treating her to a final extravagant move.

After having accepted verbal accolades galore from his friends and the entire staff, Jeff sat down and beckoned to Julia to sit on his knee. She obliged, putting an arm around his shoulder, and they relaxed into each other, still breathing hard. Different music played this time, and the *troupe* took their places for another choreographed set. The men were enthralled, and a rarefied atmosphere had descended on the room, the air perfumed with cigar smoke and *liqueur* spirits.

The handsome groom squeezed the young woman's ribcage. 'You deserve to sit this one out. Can I?'

On a natural high from the overdose of endorphins racing around her body, the giddy dancer kissed her famous partner directly on the lips. It felt wrong, almost to the point of depravity, yet he chose not to back off. With his nearby spies cheering him on, his confused mind wondered if this spontaneous decision was the result of peer pressure or whether he was truly intending to go through with it...

'Jesus, guys!' the songwriter exclaimed, giving in to the allure of someone else's vagina pressing against his balls. 'For Christ's sake! I'm still single.'

Lacking the inclination to look round and catch his *fiancée*'s father watching him too, he was sure Bart wouldn't miss a trick. But what the hell? It was his bucks' night after all, and Lynn and he were as safe as houses. Why should he care what Big D saw or which conclusion he might draw?

The dancers came back for two further *encores*, such was the rapturous reception. Julia reluctantly left the sexy superstar's arms and joined them for their formation curtain calls. Gerry was already on his feet and preparing to toast the ladies' good health, so Jeff stood up to join him, thanking each one in person. The girls couldn't wait to kiss him, delighted that the buck had played a significant part in their show. Reaching the end of the second row of beaming smiles, he comically took a deep breath and dived back into the front line for a second go-round. It was vintage *Vaudeville*, and his fellow patrons loved every minute.

Bart Dyson turned to Gerry's dad. 'He's got something special, hasn't he, this man? God knows where he came from?'

Gerald nodded, having long been of similar opinion. 'Yes, indeed. You've got to wonder, haven't you? His execution's perfect every time, and I've never met someone with such calculated but well-meaning powers of persuasion. It was quite uncanny to see him as a young teenager, let alone now.'

'I can imagine,' the statesman murmured. 'I had my suspicions, as you know.'

'Tough life though as a lad, to be sure. I was suspicious of him for a while too, always hanging around our house. Wondered if there was an ulterior motive, *et cetera*. But no. Something special's right enough.'

Now that the group's thoroughly engrossing dining experience was drawing to a close, calm fell on the makeshift cabaret joint. The best man tapped a spoon against the side of his brandy schooner and announced to the rest of the guests that Jeff Diamond's stag night would be continuing upstairs in the main club rooms.

'Gentlemen, these ladies are professional dancers and are sadly not here for our private entertainment,' he informed the others.

A chorus of groans expressed disappointment, certain men having already set their sights on seeing yet more of these women than had so far been revealed.

'But of course, ladies,' Gerry continued with a wicked smile, 'if any of you'd like to join us, you'd be very welcome.'

An excited *trio* rushed out to the band members, screaming at the tops of their voices and receiving a round of applause. The others disappeared after a final bow, including the Flaming *Flamenca*. Although he didn't dare show it, Jeff was glad to see Julia leave so discreetly.

Whatever tricks his *libido* might play on him tonight in the face of its last hours of connubial freedom, the star knew it would be regrettable if things were to end awkwardly for anyone. Plus, if he were about to take Lynn up on her offer, the deed mustn't be done with someone likeable who might get hurt in the process. His thoughts turned once more to his sister, and he dismissed them smartly. Julia was no prostitute, and this sacrifice his saviour had made in honour of a mercenary who stole both her virginity and her heart was far too precious to squander irrationally.

The millionnaire thanked his old friend yet again for such a memorable evening, as did everyone else. The party moved as an unruly and staggering bunch into a darkened room with low ceilings and lower lighting, met by an array of exotic dancers and a *chic* bar populated by businessmen and tourists. This exclusive, hideaway gentlemen's club which he and Gerry had visited several times before he had departed overseas was not busy during the festive season, since even affluent high-flyers who frequent girlie bars tended to go home for the holidays.

Bart Dyson tapped the buck on the shoulder. 'I'm heading off now, Jeff. A lot to do tomorrow.'

The empathetic intellectual shook the great man's hand, and they slapped each others' backs manfully. The statesman didn't care to watch the man who was about to marry his well-bred and highly-respected daughter cavorting with so-called escorts, however classy they might seem.

'OK, sir,' the young man nodded. 'Thanks for coming. I'll be good, I promise. Lynn's too important to me. I know how far I can go.'

Bart gave the impressive celebrity a friendly pat on the side of his arm. 'Good man. It's been a frighteningly good evening!'

The older accountant had also appeared at their shoulders. 'I'm leaving too, Jeff. I'm too old for these shenanigans. In fact, I think I always was too old.'

'Cheers, Gerald,' the musician replied with a wry smile. 'It's fantastic that you could come and that the two of you have met. Bart, are you staying at Admin tonight? How're you getting back?'

The sportsman stared at the two men, considering his options. 'I was thinking of walking. Warm night, I expect. Where are you staying, Gerald? The Sheraton? I'm going that way. We could grab a night cap at your hotel.'

'Lovely, darlings!' Jeff chided. 'That makes my previous comment all the more apt. Anyway, thanks a lot for coming, both of you. I'll give you and Celia a ring tomorrow, Gerald. We'll sort out tomorrow night's party in the morning.'

All three wilted at the thought of turning it all on again for New Year's Eve, but tomorrow was another day. The two stately gentlemen gave a cheerful wave to the rest of the drunken rabble and made their way out to the street, leaving the man of the hour to survey that which remained of his bucks' night.

Although the club's atmosphere was somewhere between seedy and select, as far as the new Jeff was concerned, it smacked of loneliness. He realised with joyful complacence that he didn't miss this side of life one *iota*. He thought again of the life Madalena described as normal… she who would have no conception of such a sophisticated house of ill repute… and then of the year in London which had turned him into the man he had always wanted to be. It was with no shred of regret that he now surveyed this scene with considerable contempt.

Still, the reflective superstar turned back to his remaining bucks, this was his party, he was about as replete with fine food and drink as he could be, and his best man wouldn't rest until they had all had a rip-roaring good time, so why the hell not? A final farewell to the tormented and twisted teenager was entirely appropriate.

***

Gerry had purchased a very expensive bottle of single malt and a handful of cigars. His client joined him at the bar to collect an ice bucket and some glasses, and the pair wandered over to a dark corner of the lounge. The musicians had wasted no time in forming their own *clique* and were enjoying the company of the ladies. Their leader took a seat with them, immediately pounced upon by the star-struck females.

After a few minutes, realising the guys were blind drunk and largely incoherent, Jeff re-joined Gerry, Junior and Pete, who had started on the whisky in earnest.

'This must be business-as-usual for you,' the rock star yelled at his neighbour above the music. 'Isn't this what life in Singapore's like every night?'

'Pretty much!' the businessman replied, laughing. 'The girls are a lot smaller though.'

The songwriter shot his friend a bemused gaze. This was an odd comment, but whatever! He liked the bloke a great deal, which evidently the others did too, and wished he had got to know him sooner. He sat forward on the comfortable couch to drop a few cubes of ice into a tumbler, which was speedily charged by his manager.

'What happened to my old man?' Gerry asked, toasting his attentive old friend. 'Did he go?'

Jeff nodded. 'Yep. He and Big D left together. It was quite romantic. The last I saw, they were walking hand-in-hand, heading for your dad's hotel.'

The accountant looked shocked. 'Fuck me! The Dyson clan's sucking us all in. Are you here to keep my most valuable client on the straight and narrow, Junior?'

'Absolutely not!' the footballer answered, raising his hands. 'I shouldn't be here either. What happens on tour stays on tour. Ain't that how it goes?'

His worldly would-be brother-in-law leaned across and shook Junior's hand. 'Shit, yeah! Too right, mate. We're just getting started.'

The foursome had scarcely settled back to let the mellow fluid flow through their systems when a complement of classy call-girls made their way over to the sofas as the final ingredient in Jeff Diamond's bucks' party mix. Attracting the hot-blooded men's attention with their elegantly sexy attire, hairstyles and subtly made-up faces, these young women gave the impression of being the cream of the crop; those who were reserved for VIPs, dignified, confident and more than a little intimidating.

Gerry welcomed their new companions into the fold, clearly expecting their arrival. They positioned themselves strategically among the men, as natural as can be, and assimilated into the conversation seamlessly. Quite a skill, the great communicator observed. The delicious scotch was beginning to cloud his thoughts now, and seeing Junior's strong resemblance to his father, felt scared it might also soon begin to impair his judgment.

Feeling himself being sandwiched between two sets of cosying hips, the erstwhile party animal supreme suddenly remembered there were two pills in his wallet, left over from a trip to the US almost a year ago. He had no idea why he had saved them for all this time, but what a godsend they would be right now! These were amphetamines, party drugs which he had bought and used in outrageous quantities in the early days of his meteoric rise to fame, with the ability to clear one's mind from the effects of alcohol while enlivening the night's great buzz. Furthermore, he recalled, they also lessened the severity of hangovers.

'Excuse me, folks. I'll be back soon.'

Smiling, Jeff took hold of the slim wrist connected to fingers that were stroking his thigh and stood up to visit the bathroom, urging the enquiring eyes of his newfound friend to continue chatting with the others for a few moments.

His best man was at his side, afraid that something was wrong. 'Are you OK?'

'Sure,' he responded, grabbing his mate's elbow. 'Walk this way, Blake-san.'

The two *amigos* disappeared into the gents' toilets, away from prying eyes. The musician checked there was no-one in either cubicle before opening his wallet and shaking the pair of tiny pills onto the black marble shelf above the wash basins.

'Fucking hell, Jeff!' Gerry exclaimed, hypnotised by the spinning white tablets. 'What the hell are they?'

His friend grinned at the clumsily camouflaged curiosity. 'Good time enhancers.'

The man from conservative, Irish Catholic stock had long been a regular pot-smoker but had never plucked up the courage to dabble in anything harder. The rock star watched him battle with his conscience for a split-second before greed settled on his face. He transformed into a mischievous schoolboy who had been shown a secret, stolen apple pie which had been stashed out of sight for a midnight feast.

Jeff nudged him out of his trance, almost causing him to fall sideways in surprise. 'Do you want one? We'll have to be quick.'

'What do they do?' the naïve twenty-six-year-old asked. 'Are they safe? Can I get arrested?'

The singer chuckled. 'Arrested? Not in here! Mate, it's perfectly safe. They're the end of a batch I bought ages ago. I didn't even realise I'd been saving them for such an occasion as this, but it's meant to be.'

Gerry was speechless, lost in drunken thoughts of letting go of himself and soaring to new heights with his sinful buddy. The younger man snapped one of the tablets into two and handed both halves to his loyal manager.

'Here's the deal, mate...'

The straight-laced executive accepted the magic, white semi-circles and stared into his palm as if they were about to explode into a bunch of flowers or a fluffy rabbit. The groom-to-be continued, breaking the second tablet in two for his own consumption.

'Let's take half now and save the other half for tomorrow night. We're going to be good for nothing by the time we turn up on Thursday morning at this rate. We'll pull up better in the morning too, so dual benefit. Ready?'

Without waiting for an answer, Jeff swallowed one of his pieces and slipped the other back inside his wallet. Turning on the tap, he slurped a mouthful of water from his hand and indicated to the hapless accountant to take his before anyone else arrived.

'OK. If you insist.'

Gerry popped his innocent-looking good time enhancer and stood nervously waiting for a change to come over him. At that very second, a cleaner barged into the restroom, armed with a fresh supply of paper towels, and took a cursory glance around. The dumbstruck occupants held their breath, and thankfully, the bored employee concluded there was nothing for him to do, swinging the door open again and leaving without batting an eyelid at the two tall men standing next to the mirror.

The boy from Canley Vale laughed at his childhood friend, usually so brazen and decisive, looking as if he had been caught smoking behind the bike sheds. 'Mate, lighten up! You'll have to wait longer than this before you feel anything. It won't hit you straightaway with only half a tab'. In fact, you'll hardly notice, I reckon.'

'What?' the comic yelped, turning to relieve himself. 'Until it's too late?'

The younger man slapped him on the back, sending a jet of urine splashing up the tiles. 'Yep. Something like that. Careful, mate.'

The *duo* stood at the stalls side-by-side, one wearing enough guilt on his ruddy face for two. Zipping themselves up and washing their hands without another word, they sauntered back out to find Pete Bourke and Junior Dyson languishing underneath their new lady-friends.

'Would you look at that?' Jeff's best man exclaimed. 'See what you made me miss out on? Ladies, move over for us, please. This man's not much of a lover, but humour him for now. He's got plenty of money.'

The two remaining escorts turned their attention from idle chit-chat to the handsome hunks who were pouring generous shots of whisky. After calling over a waiter to fetch cocktails for the women, Jeff filled four glasses of water and handed them round. He lowered himself down onto the leather cushion next to the pretty girls, wondering imperiously how they might decide who would pair up with whom.

However, with a subtle flick of her hand, the lighter-skinned woman turned her back on her colleague and focussed on Gerry, leaving the other beaming from ear to ear.

'Hi,' the exotic, dark-eyed celebrity said in a deep, sonorous voice. 'How're you going?'

'I'm Rachel and I'm very well, thank you,' she responded, inching her hips even closer to his. 'How've you enjoyed your bucks' night so far, Jeff?'

'Crazy, thanks. Getting better by the minute. Let's make the evening last, huh?'

Two Manhattans arrived and were dispensed to the courtly women. Feeling his heart-rate climb a little higher while Rachel's hand caressed his bare forearm, the songwriter drank a whole glass of scotch down at once and watched his best man do the same.

Putting a long arm around her shoulder and bringing his fingers to rest a millimetre or two below her right breast, Jeff and his companion for the night sank into the luxury leather and exchanged pleasantries between sips on her straw. She was a well-spoken, sleek young lady of about his age who, when asked why she was working at the club, was earning extra cash to pay her way through university. Her admission struck a chord with the former struggling student, and he leaned over and kissed her mouth out of pure empathy. *Some things never change*, he thought, as he felt the woman melt into his side.

They talked trivia, sometimes with the group and sometimes between the two of them. And mostly about the star himself, of course. Rachel was a huge fan and couldn't quite believe the hand she had been dealt tonight. She also asked about Lynn, although never in the context of their current circumstance. The Australian darling's *fiancé* chose not to mention the fact that he was little more than thirty-six hours away from becoming a married man either. Tactful oversight was Rachel's *modus operandi,* guessing where the boundaries were drawn for her statuesque partner.

Discerning a certain clarity in his head, Jeff reclined on the sofa, and Rachel climbed on top of him without being prompted. He didn't object as she unbuttoned his shirt right down to the waist, pulling its tails out with an exhilarating flash across his stirring genitals. The sensation of a pair of willing hands wandering around his bare chest and shoulders turned him on, and he returned the favour, her breasts small inside her scarlet push-up bra. His penis hardened in anticipation of where her fingers might travel next. The skirt of her satin dress had bunched up around her thighs, now and then tempting him to find out if she was wearing any panties.

The cloudy haze of a big evening's drinking had begun to lift, and the atmosphere the graceful pair had created was erotic and steamy. Despite his arousal, the songwriter's mind battled an overriding sense that he had become someone else entirely. Was this the new Jeff's way of justifying his behaviour? So was this how so many men could live with their own infidelity?

The buck sneaked a look at his friends, who had all adopted remarkably similar poses. At least Gerry wasn't suffering any ill-effects from his micro-drug, the superstar smiled, catching his manager's gaze and forming an OK sign with his right hand. The older man acknowledged him with a flash of his eyes and an impish nod, before his playmate pulled his chin round to focus on her again.

Laughing, the handsome rocker grasped Rachel's arms and leaned themselves over to reach their glasses from the table. He discarded the straw from her cocktail and began to tip the drink up and into her mouth, both giggling as the mixture of vermouth and bourbon spilled over the front of his suit pants. Squealing, Rachel used this as a convenient excuse to undo her partner's belt and then his fly, deftly slotting her hand inside and closing her grip around his erection. Her fingers were cold from holding the ice-filled glass, and he jumped, exhaling in shock.

While the celebrity and his eager and adept sex slave struggled humorously with a crumpled mess of trousers and underwear, Pete stood up abruptly and offered his lady a chivalrous arm. Quite unabashed, he announced their departure and reached into the various tangles to shake hands with the others. The girls cheerfully farewelled him and their associate.

'All in a day's work,' Jeff remarked to Rachel, who shifted her weight to allow him to stretch and grab the retiring man's hand.

'I won't say, "Don't get up,"' the chubby businessman laughed, as he spotted the almost identical situation each man was in. 'I don't normally do gang-bangs. Thanks for a fabulous night, Gerry, Jeff. See you when I'm next in town. Good luck for Thursday, mate!'

The men said their goodbyes from the comfort of the couches, and Pete left with his teetering blonde bombshell on his arm. She was taller than him by several centimetres, wearing very high heels, and he staggered to match her short strides until they were out of sight.

His neighbour's departure had done Jeff a favour, buying him time to draw breath and steady his rampant desire. With their hectic schedules unrelenting, he was accustomed to spending consecutive nights away from Lynn these days, yet his sister's presence in the apartment had somehow put the idea of masturbation out of bounds.

Rachel was keen to please her VIP client however, and he let her carry on doing so for another few minutes. Every time his hands went instinctively to caress the lips of her vagina or thought to loosen her bra and let his tongue and teeth play with her nipples, his maturing conscience sprang into action. Her touch was expert, and Jeff fought to delay the inevitable by keeping her in conversation. It was no good though. This was yet another side-effect of his tiny dose of ecstasy, of which his brain had omitted to remind him earlier.

'You know what?' the testosterone-charged rocker announced, precipitously sitting forward and catching his startled escort in his arms as she tipped backwards in surprise. 'I'm going to stop right here.'

As he fully expected, the woman's face dropped instantly. 'Why? What's wrong?'

'Nothing's wrong. You're fantastic,' the empath sought to pacify her, kissing her cheek and squeezing her body tightly. 'But as beautiful as you are, and as sexy as this is, I'm a one-woman man these days. And that's the way I like it.'

Rachel shuffled backwards and then twisted herself around to sit on the sofa, watching her customer zip up his pants and tuck his shirt back in. Her short skirt now covered the forbidden fruit which had abruptly lost its appeal in comparison to the treasures currently sleeping in an enormous farmhouse north of the airport.

'I'm sorry. I really am. You're gorgeous, and we would've had an amazing time. I finally get to say those immortal words, "It's not you. It's me." D'you understand?'

Both scrambled to their feet, and Rachel smiled broadly, reaching to finish buckling her handsome partner's belt. He reached into his pockets to straighten his swollen profile as best he could and caught Gerry's attention. By the expression on the Irishman's face and by his state of undress, the naughty schoolboy was making the absolute most of his stolen apple pie. Would the prime Collins Street accountant go all the way here on the couch, in full view of the club's long-suffering staff? *Hopefully not*, the superstar rued.

And Junior Dyson too… Where was his golden reputation destined tonight, at the mercy of someone who could sell her story to the newspapers? Oh, well… He was old enough to look after himself, Jeff could hear his dream girl reassuring him.

So was Jeff Diamond, who had been so reckless in his teens and early twenties, turning into the middle-classed prude his privileged Sydney Grammar mate should have been? Had he sold out, choosing to leave behind the thrill of chasing equally carefree females and running the risk of being caught *in flagrante*, preferring the comfort of his own bed and the girl of his dreams?

Yes, he had.

Did his transformation bother him?

A little now, the rock star confessed, yet fully confident it wouldn't bother him in the morning.

'Hey! I'm off, mate. Thanks again for everything. Awesome, awesome night! I'll ring you tomorrow.'

Gerry hurried to free a hand and waved it in the air, assuming the groom to be adjourning to a hotel room with Rachel like his new investment banker buddy, Pete. 'Good on ya. Let her have it, mate! I won't be far behind you.'

Jeff didn't have the heart to disappoint his fun-loving best man. Next, he lightly drummed his fingers on the back of Junior's head, wished him well and grabbed his jacket, inviting the nubile, young student to walk with him to the door. He saw the blond footballer lift his own companion onto the seat beside him too. The Pied Piper had started yet another trend, even though his night was set to end very differently.

The elegant pair paraded past the reception desk of the exclusive establishment, the superstar responding to a scatter of sycophantic greetings and some last-minute request for autographs. He put his arm around Rachel's shoulder, anxious for her work-mates to assume she was on the way to fulfilling her key performance indicators for the night. Filthy-rich celebrity and high-classed hooker walked to the lifts and descended to ground level, where they were to part company as equals.

On the steps outside the lobby, the songwriter watched as a bus-boy hailed a cab from the rank around the corner. 'Thanks, Rachel,' he said, kissing her on the forehead and pressing a roll of notes into her hand. 'Good luck with your degree.'

'Bye, Jeff,' she replied, wrapping her fingers around what she estimated was several hundred dollars. 'And thank you too. You're an extremely nice guy. Lynn's very lucky.'

The young man shook his head, thinking about how close they had come to Lynn being very unlucky. He stepped out into the warm night air and lifted his hand once more to wave the taxi on its way. Catching the valet's puzzled gaze, he smiled and shrugged. He had just paid someone not to have sex.

It was after two o'clock in the morning, and the sleazy King Street district was still lively. The singleton strolled eastwards down Lonsdale Street, with a two-kilometre walk ahead of him. He wondered if the three dancing sisters from Sydney were still out and about, where they had ended up and what trouble they might be getting themselves into.

And where was his beautiful best friend when he needed her? Tucked up in bed at Benloch, most likely. Christ Almighty! He was unbelievably horny… His encounter with Rachel had been way too close for comfort, but his prick of a conscience was perversely pleased with the restraint he had shown. The clear-headed buck upped the pace, keen to get home, rehearsing the songs the couple were singing during and after Thursday's ceremony and then later at the reception. As the cross-streets swept by, his *libido* began to surrender with reluctant resignation to its celibate fate.

Jeff unlocked the front door quietly and with his now familiar ease. Madalena's bedroom door was slightly ajar, so he pushed it open far enough that he could see whether she was home or not. She was. Or at least, a snoring lump topped with a mass of black, curly hair was in bed in his spare room. He was taken aback at how much he felt for his sister after only a few hours in her company. Successfully securing a positive identification via the new items of clothing he had seen her wearing earlier, now in a heap on the floor along with most of her other clothes, he wondered which sibling would have the sorer head tomorrow morning.

This morning, in fact. The exhausted stag hung his suit jacket and tie on a hanger and tossed the doused trousers behind the door, in a location nominated as the dry-cleaning pile until the lady of the house returned. He took a cooling shower before casting the remainder of his discarded clothing in a similar bundle on the chair beside the bed. He climbed under the sheet, still warm from marching through the city. What a show the ebullient Irishman had put on for him! The superstar hadn't spent much time envisaging how he would have liked his pre-marital shindig to unfold, but he certainly hadn't expected *les folies de Pigalle*. Memorable indeed.

Gerry and Junior would be satisfied, likely wending their respective ways home by now. Or perhaps they would stick together, like their fathers. The silly idea amused the drunken philosopher as he realised that all the different facets of his single life were slowly interweaving. It was a weird phenomenon, like finally knowing his place in the world order.

And poor Rachel. Jeff hoped he had let her down easily. He was a rat. He should never have started what he hadn't really intended to finish. That bloody pill, he cursed with a smile. Why had he sought clarity of mind over a last romp with a delectable stranger? His drunken self would most likely have stayed to the bitter end, totally negligent of the regret, shame and guilt which would have haunted his morning hangover.

Why hadn't he carried through with it? His erection had returned with a vengeance in the shower, having been brought fairly close to the point of no return in the club. The young man stroked and pumped away his pent-up frustration, with Lynn's beautiful image behind his closed eyes and as if she were treating him to a demonstration of her accomplished telephone sex skills. In his mind, she played with his pre-orgasmic senses, willing him to keep his desire at bay and then giving him the green light to come at the very moment when he was ready to give up and blow anyway. It was enlightening to be free of the tension, especially knowing he had done nothing wrong.

Gerry was bound to rib him about his gutless acquiescence to conformity, the multi-millionnaire thought, lying on his back and listening to the drumroll of his heartbeat pulsating his eardrums. It would be no different if the shoe were on the other foot, but who cared? What was the big deal? He could have sex once with a hundred women or a hundred times with the same woman. The physical act was the same. What made it special or otherwise was the depth each partner brought to the experience.

So the "Love 'em and Leave 'em Kid" was vanquished once and for all. For the man he was now, sex without love was no longer an option, and this was totally fine by him.

'Jeff Diamond,' the ambitious twenty-three-year-old spruiked into the humid air, 'you have grown up.'

Drifting closer to sleep, Jeff scanned the environs of his bedroom on his way back from closing the window and drawing the curtains. His exclusive penthouse *boudoir* looked exactly like any other soulless hotel room at this moment. Most of the couple's personal effects were still in transit and wouldn't arrive back in dock until after their honeymoon. No matter though. He had no particular attachment to this apartment anymore. Hell! He wasn't even that sorry he couldn't drive the Aston Martin either, although slightly disappointed that he wasn't able to show it off to his sister. Then again, clapping eyes on the luxury sports car would only give her greater cause to demand money.

Whatever was to be done about Madalena? Since making contact as adults, the scarred brother felt a growing obligation towards her. Yet as his wise and superbly beautiful best friend had intimated, taking her away from the only lifestyle she knew was not necessarily the right answer. She would never fit in to their Melbourne scene. He couldn't expect her to, and neither did he want her to. He and Lynn would be travelling so much in the first months of their marriage that it would be virtually impossible to help a newcomer settle in and develop a network of friends.

Sleep eventually overtook the contented world-changer. Any difficult decisions must wait until later. He had a New Year's Eve party to host tomorrow.

Alone.

For the very last time.

G'night, angel.

***

Not much later that same morning, New Year's Eve had arrived bathed in bright sunlight and stealthily entered Apartment Sixteen-Oh-Two without its owner noticing. Madalena had woken first, with a throbbing head and convinced she was about to vomit. She sat on the cold bathroom tiles next to the toilet, at first hovering over it and breathing heavily. After waiting for five minutes or so to no avail, the visitor from Sydney went to sit on the balcony with a cigarette, determined to add to the cocktail of poisons and force the issue one way or the other.

The dark-haired waif hadn't heard her brother come home. Perhaps he was still out partying? The taxi had dropped her off at the apartment shortly after midnight, all three girls were tired after their second consecutive night of dancing and having consumed a great deal of alcohol in quite a short stretch of time. Jacinta and Tamilla had entertained her well, introducing the seasoned drinker to champagne and vodka shots. Despite the fact they were still superior in their attitude towards her and had absolutely nothing in common, they had passed an enjoyable evening together.

Most people behaved in a similar way around the directionless prostitute, yet it had become increasingly irksome since her kid brother had announced his engagement to none other than Lynn Dyson. Madalena was happy being who she was, their single-mindedness a small price to pay for tapping into the family fortune.

The three hundred dollars which Jeff had given her for shopping and her tattoo had passed through the bridesmaid's fingers very easily. Sitting in the sun and swinging her feet like a six-year-old, she began to count up how much he would have spent on her during this trip: her return air fare; lunch yesterday; more money for shopping; money for last night's outing; attire for bridesmaiding; and probably a whole host of other things about which she had no clue. It was like having a sugar daddy, but without having to spread her legs.

The young woman's curiosity got the better of her, seldom left to occupy herself for long. She walked into the apartment, still nursing her sore head, and tentatively pushed Jeff's bedroom door open. A shaft of light streaked in through a gap in the curtains, illuminating an assortment of airborne particles above the bed and its occupant, who was fast asleep with the hint of a smile on his face. Madalena giggled when she saw the outline of his erect penis under the sheet. It was still weird to think of her little brother having sexy dreams.

'Ugh!' she squirmed, her eyes then alighting on a few screwed up tissues on the floor beside the bed.

So the buck *had* been a good boy last night after all! Although unsure why, this fact pleased the errant visitor. It seemed right. Startled by a lazy hand stirring and reaching towards his hips, she turned tail in case he woke up, not wishing to be snagged in his embarrassment.

The party girl decided to go in search of painkillers, finding them on the kitchen bench where they had been left after being dispensed the previous time. She filled the kettle from the tap, flicked its switch and made herself some tea. The nausea had subsided, with hunger taking its place. There were plenty of eggs in the refrigerator, but little else. She couldn't be bothered to descend to street level and locate a grocery shop, so settled down on the couch to wait until her brother surfaced.

The sound from the television slowly permeated Jeff's brain, and he awoke to canned laughter and a loud burst of applause. What time was it? Almost ten o'clock. Whoa! Putting two and two together to equal his sister in his lounge room, last night's stag opened his eyes and tested for pain. Nothing, so far... His right hand stroked his balls through the sheet, remembering fondly how the first half of this morning had ended. Lust burned red-hot for Lynn, and his thoughts turned to their wedding night, fantasising about how stunning she would look in her gown. And then out of it.

The shower afforded him sufficient privacy from Madalena to satisfy himself again, with the warm water flowing down his neck and over his body. As the last dregs of sleep washed down the plug-hole, Jeff felt positively healthy after his big night out. Dressing in a pair of old jeans which he found in the nether reaches of his wardrobe and a crisp, white T-shirt brought back from London, he combed his hair off his face and considered a shave for all of three seconds. The mirror reminded him of his need for a haircut, gladly putting off the inevitable fight with the razor until then. Bringing him up to bridegroom standard would be the barber's problem today, he smiled, imagining Lynn's scolding finger.

'Lena!' he announced *con brio*, entering the living room and reducing the television's volume with the remote control.

His sister's head turned, eyes round in surprise. 'Jesus Christ! You look normal,' she said, shocked. 'Don't you feel like shit?'

Jeff sat down on the other couch. 'Na! I feel good. I took half an ecstasy tablet at about midnight. Worked a treat. I forgot I had it.'

'Ecstasy? What's that?' Madalena asked, intrigued.

Damn, the musician cursed. Why had he opened his big mouth? He had assumed his sister would have heard of every new party drug in her line of work.

'Amphetamines. Not very strong. Just enough to give you a better time if you're already having a good time.'

'Wow! Can I 'ave one?' she asked, like a schoolgirl asking for a lolly.

'No. I haven't got any more,' her brother told a half-truth, imagining Miss Irony's glare. 'Gerry and I had the last ones.'

'So was it good, your bucks' night? You didn't get laid, but.'

'Yeah! No, I didn't,' Jeff gave her a puzzled look. 'How d'you know?'

Madalena cackled. ''Cause I went in your room and saw the tissues on the floor.'

The bad-boy sniffed, embarrassed at being sprung by his big sister again and amazed at how the years fell away at such moments. 'Aha! Excellent detective work, Agent Moreno. Quite right! I'm as randy as all fuck though. Can't wait for tomorrow night!'

'So why didn't you hook up with someone?' the twenty-six-year-old cried out, as if he had made the most illogical decision in the world. 'Wasn't there anyone you fancied?'

'Yeah. Sure there was. Plenty of opportunity, and I very nearly did... Had a woman sucking my cock and everything, but I piked out at the last minute. I don't need that shit anymore. I'll wait. At least, I hope I can wait...'

Madalena smiled, watching him shift uncomfortably. 'Yeah. Hope you're right! You can't walk down the aisle with a stiffy.'

With lightning reflexes, Jeff picked a magazine off the coffee table and flung it at the feisty woman. 'Fuck off! You'll be behind me, so you won't see anything. Change the subject, please!'

'I'm hungry,' the prostitute complained, laughing and rubbing her stomach. 'Can we get some breckie?'

'Sure. Are you buying?' the millionnaire was incensed by her demanding tone. 'What happened to the three hundred bucks? Have you got much left?'

'Yeah,' Madalena bleated. 'Course I have. About twenty-five.'

'Cents or dollars?'

His sister scoffed. 'Dollars, *culo*. Twenty-five bucks.'

'Cool. Then you can buy breakfast *and* lunch,' he instructed, flipping open his guest's packet of cigarettes and offering her one before helping himself to another.

'OK,' she answered, pouting. 'Bastard. I will. Where d'ya wanna go?'

Jeff paused for a moment, tossing up their options. 'Let's get the tram to St Kilda. I can show you the bay. That'd be a very Melbourne thing to do.'

His suggestion met with indifference, as usual. 'Yeah. I've heard of St Kilda. What's the bay?'

'What's the bay?' the songwriter rolled his eyes, blowing smoke into the air and fixing her with a sideways stare. 'You must know what a bay is! The seaside, but with no tide. You know…'

He drew a map of the south coast of Victoria with his finger in a layer of dust on the coffee table. 'Melbourne's at the top here, and all this part is called the bay. There's only about twenty kilometres from here to here…'

His sister mumbled. 'Like a circle?'

'Yep,' the teacher affirmed, pointing to the smears on the glass at the two towns of Queenscliff on the western point and Sorrento on the Mornington Peninsula on the eastern. 'Well, bays aren't usually so close to a complete circle, but basically, yeah. That's where the bay feeds into the ocean, or more specifically Bass Strait.'

'Oh, OK,' said Madalena, who remained unimpressed. 'I see. Sounds interesting'.'

Jeff laughed. 'Fine, *mentirosa mía*! Let's go then. I command you to find it interesting, or no lunch for you. Jesus! Who the fuck am I? Whatever…'

Brother and sister made their way on foot to Swanston Street. A baseball cap pulled down low and sporting sunglasses, the superstar bought two tickets from an open-mouthed newsagency assistant, along with a copy of The Age, and they waited for a tram outside the State Library. He started to explain the special place this building had in his heart, where he and Lynn had shared many an evening during the early months of their relationship, and finally raised a smile to the skinny woman's lips.

Within a minute an old, rattling tram arrived, coming from the direction of the university and packed with tourists. Jostling past more astonished faces and almost tripping over beach bags and boogie boards, The Australian Elvis and his mystery companion positioned themselves as inconspicuously as they could, standing against the window and looking out towards the east.

Undaunted and full of holiday energy, several of their fellow passengers tapped the rock star on the back and requested an autograph. Madalena was a hopeless bodyguard, he rued, while explaining for the umpteenth time that she was his sister, down from Sydney for the wedding. Roll on Friday, when he and his beautiful best friend would be on an aeroplane bound for their island paradise off the North-African coast.

Jeff pointed out the rolling lawns of the Botanic Gardens and the Shrine of Remembrance. At least the young woman knew the significance of ANZAC Day, even though she was unable to tell him the date on which it fell. Over on the other side of the road was the cop-shop, the comic advised her, causing a muted flutter of amusement from surrounding eavesdroppers. This predictably gave Madalena the shivers, as it did the lost boy inside the celebrity.

After rocking and rolling on the uneven tracks for another ten minutes, the tram climbed the hill at the intersection with Dandenong Road and turned right into Fitzroy Street, trundling down to the sea baths at the very top of the bay. The handsome musician directed his sister's attention towards the doors and pulled the cable to signal to the driver that they wished to get off at the next stop.

Madalena's mood brightened as soon as her feet had jumped onto solid ground again, and the pair wove their way through the side streets until they reached Acland Street and its array of busy boutiques and eateries. The weather was several degrees cooler than yesterday's, and they chose a café with tables in direct sunlight. Tomorrow's groom spread the newspaper out across the table and waited for their coffees to be delivered. With his sister content to gawp at the scenery, he lit another cigarette each and counted his blessings one more time.

'Excuse me? Aren't you Jeff Diamond?' a voice beside them asked.

Jeff looked up, expecting to have to dismiss yet another excited fan as politely as he could. Madalena was watching his reaction carefully, fascinated by how her famous brother dealt with being fair game for all and sundry, no matter where he went. Instead of the masked antagonism she had become used to however, a cheerful smile spread across his face.

'Suzie-Anna!' he exclaimed, jumping to his feet. 'How the hell are you? Steve, mate. Sit down.'

The obligatory air kisses and hand-shaking over, the couple were introduced to the star's breakfast companion. Poaching a couple of spare chairs from another table, they all prepared to eat together in the great outdoors.

'You're looking very *incognito*,' Suzanne said, flipping the underside of his peaked cap and dislodging it. 'I'm surprised you braved St Kilda in the holidays. Is Lynn up at the farm? You guys must be so excited.'

Quickly reassembling his disguise, their old friend chuckled. 'Yep. Impatient, more like... I wanted to show Lena St Kilda, but this was probably not the smartest move from an anonymity perspective.'

'We're starving,' his sister added. 'He said 'e'd show me the bay, but I 'aven't seen no water yet.'

'Shut up, you!' Jeff cut her off. 'All in good time. I need some strong coffee first. I'm sure Lynn's excited, secreted away safely in the middle of nowhere, but I'm bloody knackered.'

Steve laughed. 'Did you have a bucks' night? Is that what the sunnies are hiding?'

'Yeah, partly. Last night, you're right. Though I feel remarkably good.'

'He...'

Raising his left hand, the celebrity shot Madalena a stern glare to prevent her from going public about the little white pill, and mercifully she held her tongue.

'Remarkably good,' he repeated, reaching over and squeezing her pale forearm. 'It was a great night. Gerry did me proud, as always. I'll tell you all about it while we're eating.'

After breakfast, the foursome strolled along the promenade, passing most local landmarks in their lap of the fashionable, eclectic suburb. Madalena recognised the huge clown's mouth as the entrance to Luna Park, which had its twin on the Sydney harbour shoreline. Then the Palace Theatre, where Jeff and his riotous band had performed several times in the early days, before the legions of fans seeking concert tickets demanded a much bigger venue.

They talked about London and the many plans for the big day. Suzanne and Steve had been invited to the New Year's Eve charity gala dinner which Jeff was hosting on behalf of The Fellowship but had declined because she still felt awkward around the Blake family. The compassionate star tried once more to persuade them to attend, desisting after obtaining a half-hearted promise to think about it.

'Suze used to be Gerry's girlfriend,' he explained to his sister after the couples had parted company with another round of kisses, directing her back towards the tram stop. 'For years. That's why she's uncomfortable around Celia and his sisters. She was the third *amigo* who moved down here when we did. They won't come tonight.'

'Oh,' Madalena nodded, again not particularly interested in any backstory. 'This tatt' fuckin' 'urts.'

Her brother stopped and looked into her face, picking up on the plaintive tone. Despite the crudeness of her expression, he was racked with sympathy. She was indeed quite pale and had lost her previous boisterous vigour.

'D'you want to get a taxi?'

'Yeah. Can we? I feel like I'm gonna chuck up.'

Jeff flagged down a yellow cab, and the matching pair were soon heading back to the city. 'D'you think it's the alcohol or the tattoo? It will hurt for a few days,' he oozed an appropriate amount of sensitivity. 'Ours did too. Shouldn't think there'd be anything wrong with it, but we'll check it out.'

For the first time since she had arrived in Melbourne, Madalena Moreno looked vulnerable. Gripped in his own panic attack, fuelled by guilt-ridden childhood images, the songwriter concentrated on a flood of new lyrics in an attempt to control his breathing. Shit, he cursed. He thought he had said goodbye to his former self...

The taxi arrived back at the apartment fairly fast, the driver spurred on by the prospect of an unwell customer erupting all over his seats at the beginning of a long shift. Once upstairs and behind closed doors, Jeff instructed his sister to undress so that they could find the source of her pain. They laughed in embarrassment while he crouched down to examine the large red patch on her hip. It wasn't infected, as far as he could tell. God only knew the variety of substances Madalena might have in her blood to react with the ink, but she appeared in relatively rude health.

'It's fine,' he told her, raising back to his full height and staring anywhere but at her naked form. 'It's just healing. You're just going to have to live with it and keep taking the Panadol. It'll help keep your temperature down, which is probably what's making you feel sick.'

For the rest of the morning, the subdued guest was content to sit in front of a long series of dull, festive television programmes, giving her brother a welcome opportunity to escape. Filled with an overwhelming need to see his dream girl, a tug on their invisible elastic connection inspired him to call in at their South Melbourne recording studios, where he rehearsed the handful of solo numbers he had prepared for tomorrow. The time dragged, each song seeming to be shorter than the last, as the irritable rock star wished away the remaining hours until he could perform the songs for real.

Excitement, yes. Suzanne had been quite correct in her assessment, the young man acknowledged. The new Jeff Diamond was full of excitement for his future. But by Christ, this endless waiting was doing his head in!

Counting Down The Hours

Spirits were high at the Benloch homestead, with the sun blazing over endless paddocks, as far as the eye could see. Laughter and mayhem abounded on the first-floor landing. Behind the house, the annual funfair was under assembly, the air peppered with swearing workmen and the harsh noises of metal bars clanging together and large objects being dropped from trucks with earthquake-like thuds.

The traditional New Year's Day celebrations were due to go ahead despite the Dysons' absence, and with an extra reason to celebrate this year. The sporting family's usual sessions to analyse the previous twelve months' results and to set new goals had been postponed until after the Australian Open tennis tournament to make way for their special event.

Nine-year-old Anna was busy trying on her flower-girl's dress yet again, parading around proudly in front of everyone. With a smile and a shake of the head, her mother begged her to take it off carefully and hang it up before it became soiled with dirty fingermarks. Lynn was floating on Cloud Nine, having woken up on her last day as a single woman delighted with the way everything was progressing. Her happiness was impossible to hide, and the mood spread like wildfire through the active household.

The big sister had even found time for an early-morning gallop with her younger siblings, who lapped up the rare slice of attention. Neither child could believe she was about to be married. What a grown-up thing to do!

Bart had telephoned his wife that morning from their city apartment to relay details of their future son-in-law's bucks' night extravaganza. They were concerned that the man with the party-boy reputation would be disinclined to keep his promise when faced with the type of temptation on offer, hoping for the best for their daughter's sake.

Their daughter, in contrast, didn't seem at all perturbed. Indeed, as her father had been made aware last night, the raunchy theme had been largely her conspiracy. The true-blue parents hadn't heard from Junior either, thereby naming him as also complicit in the affair. The bride-to-be had urged them over breakfast not to worry, secretly curious about what had transpired after the sportsman had left the club at the top of the Grand Hotel.

Lynn too had been rehearsing her wedding and reception performances. Like her lonely man, she wanted everything to be perfect, meticulously working her way through the Order of Service to make sure the flow felt right. She had also telephoned the technicians that morning to arrange for a line of television screens to be set up on the street corner, outside the Dyson Administration building. She had heard a live radio interview earlier which suggested huge crowds would be gathered, waiting for the happy couple to make their vows and to catch a glimpse of the bridal party.

The sound crew had already rigged up a selection of speakers to broadcast the ceremony to those without invitations. This had been Jeff's idea, ever the people's advocate; a novel way to pay back the loyalty of the fans who had been all but unanimous with their best wishes. And now the consummate organiser had found a means to stream the cameras' footage out to those closest too, she felt sure her humble husband-to-be would be over-the-moon.

Up in her childhood bedroom, sitting at the electronic keyboard, the sun-drenched country's most eligible princess dreamily gazed out of the window towards Coldwater Creek, where she and her mystery man had first begun to get to know each other. She could hardly believe that was now nearly four years ago…

What a heady romance the popular schoolgirl had been treated to by her beautiful black stallion! In retrospect, far more than she could handle at the tender age of sixteen. Try as she might, she couldn't possibly picture life without him. Even though she hadn't known it at the time, nor really believed in it, greater maturity and a few subsequent comparators now left her utterly convinced that "love at first sight" was more than a sentimental notion.

A few of the young woman's friends were settling down too, and on the whole, their chosen partners were perfectly fine and worthy. Yet Jeff Diamond remained in a league of his own. She had never met anyone who made such an impression on people wherever he went, even more so than her own larger-than-life father.

Lynn still had no idea how or why, but the magician she was about to marry somehow had the ability to make the world's colours brighter and its music sweeter. He had singled her out, stolen her heart in a cyclone of love and passion and then pursued her relentlessly when most others would have thrown in the towel in the face of such stiff opposition. His boundless energy never ceased to amaze her, particularly given the brittle exhaustion he had endured alone in those early months.

Their year in London had provided the privileged star with a glimpse into their married future, where she had witnessed her man's adept negotiating tactics and powers of persuasion put to good use on a grand scale. Gone were the outlandish statements of a desperate man, and here to stay was a suite of deliberate strategies belonging to someone who truly wanted to change the world. And every one of those strategies involved her too, in some form or another. Jeff's enthusiasm for her participation was contagious, and the patience she had brought to the partnership had calmed his compulsive need for instant gratification into a good-natured acceptance that lasting change took time.

And although she remained committed to her own goals in life, especially the upcoming Olympic Games, Lynn found herself increasingly enamoured with the prospect of becoming a parent. Her mother and friends were advising her to wait for two or three years, so that she might enjoy her sporting and musical successes to the full, yet these priorities were fast fading in her mind in the face of creating new little beings who were half angel, half stallion. The idea had bewitched them both, and she felt totally ready.

'Please can I see your dress again?' Anna implored, bursting through her sister's door and bringing her daydream to an abrupt halt.

The bride obliged, swinging her legs out from under the keyboard and following the excited child to her wardrobes. She gasped too when unzipping the protective cover to reveal the shining waves of ivory silk and lace that she would soon be wearing to leave the family home. She had decided against a veil, using similar reasoning as for rejecting the *fiancé* labels. It scarcely seemed appropriate to shroud herself in intrigue for the lover with whom she had cohabited for over twelve months. This wedding was a commitment to each other as two equal and fully-fledged adults, and not some archaic transfer of a dependent, defenceless woman from one powerful man to another.

'It's so beautiful,' the flower-girl sighed, for the thirty-first time that morning. 'I can't wait 'til I get married.'

'Who will you marry, d'you think?' Lynn goaded. 'What do you think he'll be like?'

The nine-year-old threw her hands in the air with high drama. 'Oh, I don't know! Someone handsome and strong.'

'Good idea,' her big sister nodded, marvelling at how well females were programmed to select their mate, even from such an early age. 'What about clever?'

'Oh, yes. Must be clever,' Anna giggled. 'But mostly handsome. And tall.'

'Right! That's settled then. Can I zip up again now?'

'Lynn?'

'Yes?' the singer stopped in her tracks, seeing a concerned expression appear on the girl's face.

'Do you think you and Jeff will get divorced?'

'No! I certainly hope not,' she replied, shocked by such a direct question. 'I'm only just getting married. I don't want to think about getting divorced, thanks. What made you ask that?'

'Gina said she heard her mum talking about it on the 'phone,' Anna answered. 'She said that actors and singers always end up getting divorced.'

The worldly young woman smiled. 'Well, Gina's mum's wrong this time. Jeff and I aren't planning to get divorced. We love each other too much for that. Sometimes people rush to get married before they really know each other, and then they realise they picked the wrong person. We both know we've picked the right person, so we'll be fine.'

'Great!' the gymnast responded, clasping her hands around her sister's wrists and dragging her round in a circle. 'Then I'll tell Gina that. I'm going to make sure I pick the right man too.'

***

'I'm going to pick the right man too,' Kierney twisted around, hearing her father chuckle as the impersonation of Auntie Anna's childish resolution broke a prolonged silence in the dimly-lit study. 'I asked Mamá the same question, probably at about the same age.'

'I know,' Jeff smiled. 'She told me. She thought she gave you the same answer. It was like *déjà-vu* for her, she said.'

'Oh, that's spooky,' the teenager grimaced. 'That's made me go all shivery. Both sisters picked the right man, didn't they?'

The widower turned his attention away from the new portable computer which had been delivered in advance of his trip to Byron Bay. It was the perfect tool for putting the finishing touches to Gerry's own wedding plans. He had caught his daughter crying earlier, overwhelmed by the frantic, last-minute activities going on around her and unable to rationalise how the widower could throw himself into his best man duties without relapsing into grief.

'Apparently so,' he nodded, blowing her a kiss. 'And you will too. D'you think you'll get married?'

'I don't know yet,' Kierney answered. 'Mamá thought Jet would but I wouldn't, and I argued the other way round. Depends who I pick. He might not want to.'

'True enough, *pequeñita*. You'll know if you need to. Even Gerry needed to eventually, and I would've argued against that one.'

The young woman giggled. 'Hmm... Me too. Thanks for suggesting this, Papá. I feel much better now, re-reading all the gorgeous things you wrote about your wedding. I don't really know why I got so upset, because I know you're putting on a brave face for Gerry and Fiona. Can I do anything to help?'

'No. All sorted, thanks. That's good to hear. The diaries are still in that cupboard if you want to look at those too. She was a genius of understatement, your mamá.'

'Was she? What do you mean?'

Jeff's gaze went back to his new toy, purposely avoiding the seventeen-year-old's enquiring eyes. He didn't want her to see the effect Lynn's diaries still had on him. He had even planned to tuck the leather-bound volume for nineteen-seventy-six into his suitcase for his flight to northern New South Wales. The countdown to his manager's wedding date had educed similar erratic moods for him too, particularly when he had tried to write his best man's speech.

'I mean she had the knack of conveying powerful, emotional ideas using the fewest words,' he replied. 'Check out the third of January when you next need a harmless drug. I guarantee it'll make you smile. She almost says so much, whereas I would've poured my effing guts out.'

Unable to resist the invitation, Kierney sprang out of the chair and twisted the handle on the cabinet which now housed every piece of background research for her parents' autobiography. As usual, a dozen or so glossy magazines from the nineteen-nineties slithered off the second shelf and poured themselves onto the floor.

'Oh, for God's sake!' the young woman cried out in frustration. 'We have to get a box for these. This happens every time.'

'Yep. And every time you say the same thing. Get a god-damned box, *pequeñita*,' her dad teased. '*Kamikaze* mags are my speciality. Leave them on the desk, and I'll do it tomorrow morning, I promise. Chuck me 'seventy-five while you're there, please, baby?'

The teenager did as she was told, muttering under her breath in jest. Lynn's diaries for nineteen-seventy-five and nineteen-seventy-six were pulled out by their spines from the top shelf, where they had been lovingly filed after supplying a wealth of inspiration and motivation for the bereaved author over the past six months.

'Here's one I loved,' Jeff coughed, turning to the last few pages. 'It's from the night we did that Christmas special in LA, on our way home from London. We were interviewed beforehand by some TV show or other. Yeah, here... NBC, Mamá reliably informs us. The interviewer had been fascinated by the fact that Christmas is in summer in Australia...'

'But it's warm at Christmas in LA too,' his daughter interjected. 'Why was that so strange to her?'

The songwriter shrugged. 'True, but it's still winter. It's like here, when you see people wearing coats on the first of March even though the temperature's exactly the same as on the twenty-eighth of February, when they went to work in shirt-sleeves... Anyway, *tais-toi* and listen!'

"Tonight I loved Jeff a bit more because he told the NBC presenter that there was a sad irony in singing, 'The weather outside is frightful, but the fire is so delightful,' in Australia, when it's forty-six degrees in the shade and the news is showing yet another bushfire ripping through people's houses.

"Her face was a picture. She didn't know what to say, and neither did I. Then what did my magician say to finish his statement? 'And so they rebuild in the same spot, and a few years later the same thing happens again.'

"So perfect. I love this man so much."

'*Howzat* for a compliment, huh?'

Kierney smiled. 'Sweet as. What was that Oscar Wilde quote you used the other day with Gerry? This reminds me of that. About immoral books?'

'Ah, yeah,' her dad cocked his head. 'You're as bad as your mamá, feeding my ego. "The books that the world calls immoral are the books that show the world its own shame." What do you want?'

'Nothing,' the seventeen-year-old moaned, turning over a few pages in the following year's diary. 'I'm just grateful you guys cared enough to speak out, and then encouraged us to speak out too. Some of my friends look at me as if I'm walking into a lion's den when I threaten to say something contrary to a lecturer. They're happy to write their own views into assignments but never brave enough to talk about things in the open. Did you get that when you were a student too?'

Jeff cast his mind back to his university days, first as an undergraduate in Sydney and then in Melbourne, where he had been studying a subject about which even the academics knew very little at that point, and latterly in London with the revered John Francis, during which time he and his cohort had done nothing but argue with the lecturers.

'Not for my Bachelor's, no. But for logical reasons, *pequeñita.*'

'Which logical reasons?'

'Well, Computer Science isn't exactly a field that evokes a whole heap of passion! It's beginning to now, with companies stealing each others' ideas and making them better and getting rich in the process. But back then, it was all kind of dry and...'

'Nerdy?'

The widower whipped around in his swivel chair, dealing his daughter a thunderous stare. 'Technical, I was going to say.'

'My papá was a nerd! My papá was a nerd!' she chanted. 'How could Jeff Diamond have started out as a geek? My friends are always amazed by that too.'

'*Ta gueûle!* For Christ's sake. Heaps of musicians are also nerds. Some might say your brother's a nerd too. Would you sing that to him too?'

'Surely would,' Kierney feigned innocence. 'No hesitation. Oh, wow!'

The young woman's voice hitched, and she raised her left hand to her mouth, driven to tears again. While the playful pair had been trading insults, her eyes had fallen on the page devoted to events immediately preceding her parents' honeymoon voyage. By her reaction and an estimation of how close to the beginning the diary had been opened, Jeff knew precisely which paragraph she had reached.

'Conversation with Grandma?'

'It's beautiful. I don't remember this in the book. You can't leave this out.'

Behind the long, glossy blow-dried locks, his gipsy girl's rosy cheeks were glistening in the lamplight, yet the smile on her face showed a level of joy that had been missing earlier in the day. The father stood up and walked the two strides between their chairs until he was close enough to read over her left shoulder.

'Can I read it to you?' the teenager asked, tilting her head until she could see his upside-down visage nodding his approval. 'Gracias, Papá. I'm going to photocopy this page. *Alors, écoute...*

> "I had a conversation with mum today about my new husband. I can't believe I have a husband, but I have, and he's the best husband ever. She asked how his PTSD was these days, which was really nice of her. I told her how much better it was, without the dreadful nightmares every night, but that sometimes things were still tough for him.
>
> "I told her a story about how our life is now. How we'd go to a party, and he's animated and entertaining all night... His usual self, joking and loving the attention, *et cetera*. Then we'd get home to the flat (or sometimes even in the taxi on the way), and he'd say, 'Thank you for coming home with me,' and then dissolve into a tearful mess.
>
> "I hate that Jeff still finds it so hard to allow himself to be happy. Perhaps he always will... It's as if he's scared someone will take his happiness away if he talks about it too much."

'Oh, *Papá*. I can hear *Mamá*'s voice, can't you? Wasn't it great that she understood you so well? I hope my soul-mate and I understand each other this well. You should've written about this. Why didn't you?'

'Too close to the bone, I think,' the grieving man faltered, retreating to his chair and lighting a cigarette. 'Someone did take our happiness away in the end. We cheated that bastard, Gravity, for a long time, but he got me in the end. You OK? Want a coffee? Let's run Indie somewhere in the car. We could all do with a change of scene.'

A feathery, cream-coloured tail began to wag at Kierney's feet, thumping noisily on the floorboards. The rented Labrador retriever sprang to his feet and buried an affectionate muzzle into his master's outstretched hands before raising himself onto his hind legs and stretching his full length to apply licks of gratitude for what he hoped wasn't an idle offer.

243

'I know, boy. I love you too,' the emotional celebrity sniffed, grabbing the boisterous animal's two front paws and letting them drop to the floor. 'You don't want anyone to take your happiness away either, do you? I know exactly what you mean. *Vamanos.* Rabbits await!'

***

His special songs rehearsed until he could stand them no more, Jeff left the recording studios and headed into town to avail himself of a haircut and an overdue shave. He then went to Gerry's office for some last-minute speech coordination. His best manager already had the beers opened when the groom entered, and they toasted the year about to end, remarking on how much had changed in the intervening twelve months.

'Shit, yeah!' the rock star shook his head. 'This time last year, I'd just heard I was off the hook as far as Big D's detective work was concerned. And now I feel even more vulnerable than I did then.'

'Vulnerable? Why? I thought he'd dropped all that Mullarkey?'

'No. He has, mate. It's more as a result of some things my sister's been telling me,' the younger man explained. 'Things I'd probably be better off not knowing.'

The accountant frowned. He was responsible for his client's safety and security these days, not to mention those of his blushing bride. Another area of expertise which had unexpectedly been added to his *résumé* in recent years.

'OK. Do I want to know about this? Sydney gangland stuff, you mean? Your life is so bloody complicated. I take it these are real threats to your safety.'

'Yeah, potentially,' Jeff confirmed. 'We need to make some time to think more seriously about this crap once we come back from holidays. With Big D too, I reckon. Much as it pains me to accede to that.'

'Noted,' Gerry sniggered, tapping the desk. 'Now, I've got two Excellencies and an Honour. Are there any more pages in Burke's Peerage I need to brush up on?'

The groom smirked too, glad to veer off the previous disturbing path. 'What about Sir Brad Morrison? Does he count as a Lord? Can you believe it, mate? Fifty percent of your speech'll be spent getting through the effing protocolic introductions! It is somewhat humbling though, to think who's coming to this no-good Jewish *gringo*'s wedding, isn't it? To be honest, I'm trying not to think about it too much.'

His friend took a slurp from his half-empty stubbie, shaking his head. 'Oh, suck it up, princess. Get used to it. You made your bed, and all that... I'll check on the whole "Knight of the Realm" formalities. Good pick-up. Anyway, what can't I say about you in my speech? How long is that list?'

Smiling wryly and raising his eyebrows, the celebrity cleared his throat. 'Well, let me see... I'd rather you didn't mention that I had another woman's hands down my pants last night.'

Gerry pretended to scribble. 'Hands down pants. Yes. Check,' he mumbled officiously. 'You know full well I might confuse the two lists in my nervousness. His Excellency, Sir Maurice Bradson had his hands down my client's pants, Your Honour.'

'Right! Cheers, mate. I knew you were the man for the job,' the superstar jeered. 'You, nervous? I'd like to see that. It's only a couple of Governors General, the Prime Minister, Big D and your parents. What's there to be nervous about?'

'No, indeed. Your sympathy is gratefully received. Anything else?' his best man asked, shrugging and sipping out of his beer bottle.

'Yep,' the boy from Canley Vale's response was more measured. 'My dad being banged up should be off limits, and Madalena's line of work. And maybe the drugs.'

While his list of discredits were being rattled off, another two beers appeared. Pensive, the musician put the bottle to his lips and took a large mouthful. Between the various facts and fictions which had been smeared across all forms of news media about his on- and off-stage pursuits, there were very few he regretted. Excepting the aforementioned, he could safely expect to feel proud of anything his best man may say about him the following afternoon.

'Cheers, Gez. I can hardly censor you any further. I'll get my own back one day.'

'I doubt it, mate. But hey, that was a miracle, the little pill you slipped me,' the executive said with a grin. 'You were right about the hangover. I woke up fresh as a daisy this morning.'

Jeff nodded. 'We've got the other half for tonight too.'

'Good-oh! I had no idea where I was this morning though. I mean, I knew I was in some student digs, but I had no idea where, suburb-wise. I ended up somewhere in Parkville, at the back of the uni'.'

Both men chuckled, lighting cigarettes and staring out over Port Phillip Bay. Gerry Blake would never grow up. He was the mythical Peter Pan to the groom's Pied Piper. Whoever might have bet on this outcome, not even five years ago, would be banking significant profit come tomorrow.

'A far cry from Toorak,' his childhood friend agreed. 'Did they accept your currency up there? Why didn't you get a hotel room?'

'Should've. Well... Spill the beans. Where did you two pass the wee small hours? She was a cracker, yours...'

The stag winced, recalling Rachel's crestfallen expression when he had called a halt to their promising *liaison*. For all concerned, lying would be by far the most entertaining option for his response. However, the very fact that his escort's considerable guile and practised sleight of hand had not graced his memory until this moment was ample testament to his decision and to Lynn's place in his heart.

'I have to come clean.'

'Come clean?' Gerry looked up. 'Always a good idea. Come clean about what?'

His friend sighed. 'We parted company on the doorstep. I couldn't. Lynn even gave me her permission too, but I didn't want it enough.'

'Jesus, Mary and Joseph! What poor show,' the best man lamented. 'It was *your* bloody bucks' party, and you wimped out. I never in a million years thought that would happen! They were all piping hot. I interviewed six, I'll have you know. How the fuck did you do it?'

'Strength of character, mate,' Jeff replied in defiance. 'Something you'll never understand. Six interviews? Christ Almighty! What sort of interviews? Horizontal ones?'

'Fuck you, mate!' Gerry shot back, emphasising the word "mate" with mock vehemence. 'What else do you want me to steer clear of? Suddenly, I have great appetite for libel and slander.'

'Nothing,' the superstar smiled at the friendly threat. 'Everything else is public knowledge anyway. Go for it. Do your worst, Blake-san.'

Yawning as he stubbed out his cigarette, the younger man looked at his watch. 'Whoa. It's after five-thirty already. Drink up. We need to wander over to the hotel pretty soon. I have to go back home before dinner, to change and bring my wounded sparrow of a sister out with me in her bath-chair.'

The businessman looked puzzled. 'What are you talking about? What's happened to her?'

His old friend chuckled bitterly, again feeling like the parent of a delinquent teenager. 'Yesterday, when she left this office, she went to get a huge tatt' here,' he explained, pointing to the right of his groin area.

Lecherous Irish eyes widened predictably. 'Really? Can I see?'

'No, mate,' Jeff replied. 'You wouldn't want to, believe me. It's too sore! She got me to check it out. Now that's weird, staring at your sister's vagina, let me tell you!'

The accountant grimaced at this thought. 'Hmm... You're a better man than I, Gungadin. What tattoo did she get?'

'A tiger,' the despondent brother answered. 'She didn't like her own year in the Chinese calendar, so she picked the animal she liked best.'

Gerry roared with laughter, standing up and fetching a large bunch of keys from inside his briefcase. 'Jesus! That's a classic.'

'Yeah. Tell me about it. That's the kind of intellect we're dealing with, mate. Her idea of class is a line of dollar signs tattooed between her belly button and her...'

With an equivocal frown, the businessman slapped his client on the back, highly amused by the sorry tale. The pair cleared away the empties, turned the office lights out and set off to check in with the Blake family in advance of the New Year's Eve function Jeff had arranged at their luxury hotel.

'The end of another day,' the accountant chanted, feeling fatigued after the previous night's excesses, little white semi-circles notwithstanding. 'And the start of another party.'

The Cricketers Bar, which enjoyed prime position opposite Parliament House and the Victorian Treasury Building, was heaving with tourists intent on a swinging end to nineteen-seventy-five. Passing through without stopping, the celebrity and his manager found themselves on the ground floor of the Windsor Hotel. Jeff kept his baseball cap on as they walked up the wide staircase, but it was beginning to feel like ridiculously inappropriate attire for a five-star establishment.

'Oh, my God! Mum, that's Jeff!' he heard from the other side of the upper lobby.

The exuberant observation came from Sarah Markham, one of the cluster of his female conquests who had attended Lynn's hens' party. This evening's host had omitted to check the guest list prior to dropping in, clearly not in a fit state to be introduced to Melbourne's moneyed gentry. The young woman pointed him out to her parents, and thereby to everyone else who happened to be milling around. He sighed, acknowledging her with a raised hand and a smile. Anonymity comprehensively scuppered, he had masqueraded as nothing more than a dishevelled nobody walking through the smart hotel in jeans and a T-shirt until this point.

'Hey, Jeff! Come and say hello!'

'Sarah,' he answered, tapping Gerry on the shoulder to divert briefly to their right.

'You look such a mess!' his former lover informed him. 'These are my parents.'

The groom-to-be shook hands with Sarah's father and nodded politely to her mother. He had attended their elder daughter's wedding, before he and Lynn had got back together, and had ended up in bed with the chief bridesmaid. Not surprisingly, he hadn't been formally introduced on that occasion.

'Pleased to meet you, Mister and Missus Markham. Thanks, Sarah, for your honest opinion, as ever... Didn't they tell you it was a tramps' party?' the tired man joked, standing aside to introduce his manager too.

'Congratulations, Jeff,' her mother replied. 'I expect you could have done without this tonight.'

The young man smiled at the observant remark. 'Thanks very much. You're not wrong. Just too many parties this time of year, and someone we all know thought it'd be a good idea to add another one.'

Before he could successfully turn the conversation to his beautiful best friend, who was known to the Markhams since early childhood, the humble celebrity became aware of loud voices behind him. A small group of youths were walking towards them, speaking in what sounded like an Eastern European language. Occupational hazard, he rued.

'Here we go! Sorry about this, but I'd better move on. I'll see you later, at dinner.'

The off-duty star made a sharp left turn and continued to walk through the hotel lobby, flanked by his Armani-clad bodyguard. The vocal bunch of tourists also changed direction like a shoal of fish, pursuing him keenly. In only a few long strides, their front-runner caught up, reaching forwards and grabbing his shoulder. Gerry rounded on the offender and lifted his hand away forcefully, taking hold of the man's elbow and pushing him backwards.

'Come on, mate,' the musician turned to make eye contact with the eager fan, whose wiry frame and shorter stature were far less imposing than his loud voice. 'What d'you want?'

'To say I touched Jeff Diamond,' the young man retorted in a thick accent, securing the celebrity's full attention.

'OK. So you touched me. Now what?' the taller man asked, feeling the hackles rise on the back of his neck.

'That's all. Your father is Polish, yes? We are from Poland. An autograph?'

The rest of the rowdy group was by now bunched around the star and his manager, all trying to speak to him. A day's body odour clung to them, intensified by rather too much beer. Thinking back to the groom's earlier revelation, the executive found himself wondering what their strategy ought to be for warding off people intending to harm his VIP clients, especially given how poorly they were currently coping with genuine but aggressive fans.

Jeff relaxed and entertained the group by dragging out the very small number of useful Polish phrases he had in his vocabulary. He signed everything they put in front of them, all without coming to a standstill. By the time he had scrawled his name on the shoulder of the last person's yellow T-shirt, he could see the rest of the Blakes looking on in amusement from their ring-side seats in the bar.

'Good evening, boys!' Celia cried out, while they stood up to greet the terrible twins. 'You seemed to be having trouble shaking those people off. It must test your patience sometimes.'

Jeff hugged the ladies, relieved to be free from the minor *fracas*. 'Affirmative. How are you guys? Nice to see you.'

'Did you have a good time last night?' Jacinta asked, with a glint in her eye. 'Dad told us all about it. A French *bordello*! What a fantastic idea!'

'Yeah. It was amazing, thanks. Fantastic in every way,' the young man confirmed, winking at the older gentleman beside her. 'Everyone had a spankingly good time. Eh, Gerald? That is, those who didn't duck out early with the father of the bride.'

'So what happened after we left?' the senior partner enquired, sporting much the same expression as his daughter.

'Ha! That'd be telling,' the celebrity frowned. 'As Junior said at the time, what happens on tour stays on tour.'

Tamilla giggled as if she were in on the secret, which of course she wasn't. Like Sarah, she and her older sister also had a few elements of impropriety worth keeping from their parents when it came to previous indiscretions with this enigmatic, handsome man.

'Don't jump to conclusions, Tam,' the ineligible bachelor warned, seeing her about to add a lurid comment or two. 'Thanks for being so good to Lena, you two, by the way. It was really good of you to take her out. Hope she wasn't too hard to handle.'

'You're welcome,' the gregarious younger sister responded. 'She's a hoot, and quite a dancer. It must run in the family.'

Jeff shrugged. 'First I've heard of it, but maybe so. Anyway, I just wanted to come and say hello quickly. I have to go back to the apartment to change, and time's running out.'

'Oh, good!' interrupted Jacinta. 'I'm glad about that! I hoped you weren't coming to your own ball dressed like that. At least you've had a shave, which is more than Gerry's done.'

'Oh, yes!' Celia agreed, waving haughtily from one man to the other. 'It looks like you've got each others' clothes on, in fact.'

Everyone laughed. Her observation was accurate. After his trip to the barber, the rock star was in pristine condition above the neckline of his shapeless T-shirt, whereas Blake & Partners' Melbourne managing director had struggled to drag himself out of bed and into his designer suit before an early client meeting.

The celebrity took his leave from his guests and made for the first exit he could see. The self-sprung fire door turfed him out into a narrow laneway off Little Collins Street, and he needed a few moments to get his bearings after having been out of town for so long. The unexpected Soviet Bloc accents had fazed him somewhat, in his dilapidated physical state. Those fans were friendly enough, but the ambush had been too close for comfort nonetheless. However, as long as they were following him rather than Lynn or her family, he didn't feel so bad.

Reaching the apartment a little after six-thirty, Jeff slipped his key in the lock and entered through the front door, half expecting to be met by the old demons. Even if they had planned to scare him, their appearance was immediately diffused by a whirling dervish sprinting down the hallway. Madalena was evidently worried that she had been left behind, not knowing where tonight's party was taking place.

'Where the fuck've you been?' she shouted, almost in tears.

'Sorry, Lena. Really sorry,' Jeff apologised, grabbing her shoulders and kissing her forehead. 'I know I'm late. There's just too much to do. Are you ready? You look good. Is that what you bought yesterday?'

'Yeah. Like it?' the well-dressed woman twirled round in a circle, swapping her skittish emotions as easily as she exchanged clients.

'*Sí. Très chic.*'

'What's *traysheek* mean?'

'Cool,' the linguist changed his description. 'You look very cool. It's perfect for tonight. I need to grab a quick shower. I'll be ten minutes, and then we can hit the road. Can you ring for a taxi, please? There's a number on that sheet of paper I gave you.'

Madalena did as she was told, relieved that she hadn't been forgotten. Her brother soon emerged, dressed in a different suit from the previous evening, since last night's trousers had been marinated in bourbon, he remembered awkwardly. The same tie graced his neck though; the silk Christmas gift with its elegant diagonal stripes was fast becoming associated with missing Lynn, and he took heart from knowing that tonight was the last time he would need to wear it for quite a while. Finishing off the *ensemble* with a dark crimson shirt, he tugged at the cuffs to bring them down below the length of his jacket sleeves.

Australia's richest twenty-something checked himself out in the mirror. *One more night*, the reflection encouraged. His eye caught the shiny jet-stone ring on what looked like his left hand and did a double-take, at first thinking it was on his wedding finger. Whoa! He certainly was preoccupied, refocussing to check his wallet for cash and the all-important drug. This semi-circle of white powder would surely be his saviour tonight, since exhaustion was already beginning to engulf his senses, and he most definitely did not wish to be a mess for their big day.

'Ready?' he checked with his sister, holding out a chivalrous arm. 'We look good, *señorita!*'

He elongated the word "good", to give it the appropriate emphasis. Madalena was pleased to receive her brother's undivided attention.

'Yeah. We do!'

The taxi pulled up a couple of minutes after they reached the steps of the apartment building. Jeff opened the rear door for his guest, who shuffled across in a most unladylike fashion. It was all he could do to stop himself groaning in disgust as her skirt rode up as far as her knickers and revealed the lower edge of the dressing covering her tattoo. What a sight! He closed the door and climbed into the front passenger seat, the Australian way.

The driver recognised the famous singer. 'You're getting married tomorrow, aren't you? Can't wait to tell the missus that I picked you up the night before your wedding.'

Madalena cackled, and Jeff tried not to sigh, managing an appreciative smile. Fortunately, an answer came from the behind the driver's ear instead.

'Yes. And I'm 'is sister. I'm a bridesmaid.'

'Thanks, Lena,' the front seat passenger looked over his shoulder and grinned at her first public announcement. 'Nice one!'

The busy New Year's Eve traffic hampered their progress across the city. Frustrated at being trapped with this nosy man, the skilled communicator made idle conversation, keen to steer his endless questions away from the couple's private life. Parliament House loomed in front of them as they turned left at the end of Collins Street, allowing the driver to pull up at the side entrance of the Windsor Hotel, almost back to the exact spot where Jeff had emerged from the emergency exit just an hour ago.

Of course, as their name suggested, the building's emergency exits only worked for letting people out. The celebrity paid for the taxi and helped his high-heeled companion from the back. The car drove off, leaving them on the footpath to walk back to the main entrance after all. Minus his baseball cap and scrubbed up to befit his multi-million-dollar status, he and Madalena ran the gauntlet through a gathering of New Year's Eve partygoers.

Hearing his name being called left, right and centre, the musician marched straight through without making eye contact with anyone, as he had learned so well from his dream girl.

'Slow down,' his perturbed guest moaned. 'I can't keep up in these shoes.'

'Sorry. It's not much further. I don't want to talk to any more random people tonight. Let's just have a relaxing evening with friends and try our best to stay out of sight.'

'Oh, yeah. Easy!' Madalena teased, excited at the prospect of another, high-classed entertainment treat.

Her brother chuckled, decelerating slightly. 'Jesus! You sound like Lynn.'

The Blakes were waiting in the bar, as planned. Nearby were Bryan and Anthea Kingdom, longtime friends of the Dysons who had also jetted into town for tomorrow's proceedings. Bryan, Jeff reminded his manager, had been the *compère* at the hammed-up charity tennis exhibition for which his dream girl had given them tickets soon after the couple had met. Reminders of that fateful night still had the power to shake him up.

Realising he was likely to be unable to keep his promise of anonymity for long, The Fellowship's principal investor went to greet them. 'Bryan, how are you?' he said, shaking the older man's hand. 'And Anthea, nice to see you.'

The middle-aged woman stood up from the leather sofa, dripping with an ostentatious assortment of gold and jewels, and gripped his hand eagerly. 'Jeff Diamond! Lovely to see you too. Are you excited about tomorrow?'

The smart young man gave a polite sigh, unable to fake every single sentence. 'To be honest, I'll be bloody glad when it's over. It's as if we've already had six days of it. I'm never doing it again.'

'That's good news, dear,' the refined lady smiled. 'I expect Lynn would like to hear you say that.'

'Oh, she's heard it, I assure you. I've said it every day for the past three months!' Jeff laughed. 'Have you eaten yet? I'm with my best man's family over there. They're here from Sydney too. Why don't you join us?'

'No, we haven't eaten,' Bryan answered. 'Are you sure we won't be intruding?'

'Absolutely not. It'd be great. Come on over. I'll introduce you.'

As he knew they would, the Blakes welcomed the extra guests warmly. The Kingdoms and Madalena were presented to Gerry's clan, and a wine waiter was flagged down.

'Your sister's so like you,' Anthea gushed, scanning the others' faces for support.

The star leaned into his look-alike affectionately at the innocent comment, as if posing for a family happy snap. She seemed to be feeling better after her restful afternoon, the pain from her wounded tiger having subsided. She had little stomach for more posh talk however, adopting a sullen expression until a second glass of champagne arrived. Jeff did his best to involve her whenever the discussion came round to Sydney or any of the few topics likely to strike a chord.

'I'm like her actually,' her brother contradicted. 'Lena's older by nearly three years. Although plainly, that's not apparent. I really need a holiday.'

Realising instantly that any attempt to garner sympathy from the Blake sisters could only lead to trouble, it was too late for Jeff to withdraw his blatant tug at their heartstrings. Jacinta lived up to expectations and drew an imaginary bow across dumb violin strings, making Madalena howl in derision.

'Oh, poor baby!' the woman moaned. 'A year in London luxury and already he's cooked in Melbourne. Toughen up!'

For once, their childhood friend had been gifted a chance to kick Gerry's big sister in the shins and watch her struggle to ignore it, dealing an accurate blow just above the left ankle bone. She uttered a high-pitched squeal before ably composing herself, shooting daggers at the evil perpetrator, who shrugged minutely back. Who cared if he was supposed to be in charge tonight? He would grow up tomorrow.

The Diamond party moved through into the large function room, where the tables were decorated with elaborate centrepieces of balloons and streamers.

There must have been forty, the philanthropist estimated, with a temporary square of parquetry laid down near the stage, where the band was in the middle of setting up. Celia had requested that their host book a table of ten, unsure at that point whether any of her children might be bringing a partner. Only Raymond, Jacinta's new *fiancé*, augmented their number, which enabled them to accommodate their two extra guests without inconvenience.

'Do we get to dance again?' Madalena asked her sophisticated dinner date.

'Yeah. 'Xpect so. Are you up for it? How's the pain?'

'Not too bad,' she replied, almost as if she had only then been reminded of it. 'Will you dance with me?'

Jeff nodded. 'Sure. It'll be my honour, m'lady.'

The awestruck woman glowed with a mixture of pride and delight. She liked her little brother a whole lot more than she previously realised. Disco music played through the speakers while the guests found their tables, and her feet shuffled on the carpet as if warming up. A few couples and some giggling girls fuelled by pre-dinner cocktails were taking the opportunity to let off some early steam.

'Go easy on the alcohol, please,' the groom advised Lynn's bridesmaid as they made their way to the dance floor. 'Remember we've got to walk in a straight line tomorrow.'

Madalena tutted, unhappy about being told how to behave. 'OK. I will.'

Once he and his guests had found their places, The Fellowship's chief patron looked over at his manager, seated opposite him on the round table. They had to dodge the brightly-coloured balloons to see each other properly, but the view was clear enough to discern a certain shared *malaise*. Gerry had spent the early part of the morning in bed, making up for his *impromptu* landing in Parkville, but had then used up his remaining reserves during a busy afternoon. The generous star had also been on the go for most of the day. They exchanged sympathetic nods and raised a glass of red wine to each other.

'Where's Lynn tonight?' Bryan asked. 'At home with the folks?'

Jeff's heart skipped a beat at the mention of his favourite name. How about that? Someone actually remembered there were two human beings caught up in the machinery of this wedding. Even he had begun to forget that his *Regala* might be sharing the burden of this elongated festive interval.

'Yep. She's at Benloch. They're having a party out there too.'

'I expect she's looking forward to the ceremony. Lynn's always loved a good show!' Bart Dyson's buddy told the Blakes.

'Oh, my! We know someone like that too,' Gerry's younger sister interjected.

The host shrugged. 'And who might that be, Tammy?'

'I wonder, *Jeff*,' she jeered, making it quite clear whom she meant and receiving a subdued laugh from around the table.

253

Their food was served, dish after dish, by a human conveyor belt of drafted-in casual staff who had been given a crash course in silver service. The meals were nowhere near as tasty as last night's fare in the Grand Hotel's makeshift speakeasy. Neither was the entertainment. The off-duty performer sat back, content to let the others meander the conversation around in circles. Madalena did the same, rarely taking her eyes off the man of the moment.

'You OK?' Jeff asked after a while, catching her yawning as she refilled her glass. 'Don't forget to drink water. Look at you go! You didn't drink wine at all two days ago, and now you're tanking it down.'

His sister grinned. 'I know. I love it. I need a ciggie, but.'

Good idea, the young man agreed. He signalled around the table, and everyone bar Anthea lit up. The band was playing a selection of covers and standards, to which Gerry's sisters were adding their lusty *mezzo-soprano*s. The lead singer of the tight, local outfit was talented and had a strong voice, but their sound system was already creaking under the strain of having to fill such an enormous room. The professional on Table One caught the manager's attention, asking if extra speakers were available somewhere behind the scenes to stand them in better stead for the dramatic countdown.

Unlike their brother, Jacinta and Tamilla were full of energy, having returned to their hotel relatively early after their night out with Madalena and slept through until noon. They were desperate to get onto the dance floor and also for the pair of Diamonds to join them.

Keener on conserving his own energy though, Jeff urged his sister to go alone. 'I'd like to talk to Gerry for a while,' he told her, waving his hand at the girls. 'I'll be up there soon.'

The three slim, *stiletto*ed women swayed closer to the band, supplemented by Celia and Anthea as well. The menfolk shifted the chairs so that they could sit next to each other, drinking coffee and brandy and swapping notes about the football and cricket seasons. After fifteen minutes or so, best man pulled bridegroom to one side.

'I'm going to check out soon. I'm fucking spent after last night. I need a good night's sleep to be ready for some bastard's swanky wedding tomorrow.'

'I won't be far behind you,' his friend agreed. 'I have to keep an eye on the errant bridesmaid over there. She just can't say no to free booze.'

No words were necessary as his friend's father gave a brief chuckle. The best man shrugged innocently in response, reading this as a sign of recognition which both men deserved. While they were making a vain attempt at defending their dubious reputations, Jacinta strutted up to drag the young men back to the wooden floor.

'Come on, guys. We need you! Mum's orders.'

'You need *us*?' Gerry protested. 'Why the hell would she need *me* on the dance floor?'

The magnanimous *trio* obliged the ladies, begrudging the older generation's entitlement to hold the fort. The space next to the stage was proving too small for the number of people moving to the music, and Jeff was instantly mobbed by sparkling and resplendent revellers. He made a mental note to alert his organising committee to this lesson for subsequent functions before turning to field the same old questions. He agreed to answer them all in return for pledging donations to the night's worthy cause.

In the resulting *melée*, the young star lost sight of Madalena again. Surely she couldn't get up to too much mischief in the Windsor Hotel, and she wouldn't be game enough to leave without him. Would she? A fair few tracks later, he finally spotted her at their table, sinking another full glass of wine.

'Shit!' he hissed to Gerry. 'Look at Lena! Fuck! This is going to be a disaster.'

'Cool it, mate,' the best man chuckled. 'Don't stress. She'll be sober by the morning.'

Frustrated, Jeff ignored his friend's advice. 'It's not the drunkenness I care about,' he explained, becoming more anxious. 'It's more her ability to look like she's enjoying herself. I don't want Lynn's bridesmaid to be blind, scowling and hung over.'

A flash of comprehension spread across the older man's face. 'Oh, I get you. Good point. She's all yours, mate!'

The troublesome visitor was steered back to the dance floor, happy to find herself mixed up with a bunch of Richmond footballers, whose club chairman had donated a tidy some to The Fellowship. She wouldn't have known any of their names, being more familiar with rugby players north of the border. Nodding to the row of burly blokes looking very uncomfortable in their suits, the graceful musician grabbed her right hand and swung her in a flamboyant *pirouette*.

'*¿Quieres bailar, señorita?*'

'Prop'ly?' his sister replied, grinning.

'*Sí. Cierto* properly,' Jeff answered.

It occurred to him that he had been conversing in Spanish less and less with his sole relative. Perhaps this was another sign that he was leaving the past behind. Neither had any real reason to use their mother tongue anymore in their respective worlds, so why continue doing so with each other?

'*¿Hey, realizas que no hemos hablado el español una eternidad?*'

This observation was uninteresting to Madalena of course, so he whisked her off her feet to a tune with a strong beat. Being led so expertly in spirited and rhythmic motion took the young woman's breath away, and she completely forgot the throbbing pain from her tattoo. Her brother's aching heart enjoyed seeing the smile on her face too, since it seemed to transform her into someone sweeter and less hard-edged.

'This is great!' she gasped, righting herself after yet another spin. 'You're a fantastic dancer.'

'You're pretty good too.'

Soon there remained only a handful of this year's allocated minutes, and the atmosphere buzzed with anticipation. Jeff caught Celia's eye and shared a poignant moment of telepathy, a regular occurrence at this time of year for them in recent times. Having forsaken his early exit in favour of a cardiovascular workout on the dance floor, Gerry had predictably found a nubile, young playmate just at the right moment and was returning from the bar with two glasses of champagne, closely followed by Gerald and Tamilla with a whole trayful.

The groom picked up a pair of half-full flutes and passed one to his sister, who immediately started to empty it. 'I love champagne too!' the childish woman declared.

'Lena, take it easy,' the host scolded. 'Please. You've got to slow down. Tomorrow'll be really hectic, and you've got to feel like participating.'

'OK, OK, *culo,*' Madalena huffed, with only a modicum of good humour. 'Get off my back.'

Before her brother could reassert his authority, the band leader called everyone to attention, and the whole room began to count down from "Ten" to "Happy New Year." A resounding cheer went up as the last chime rang through the boosted public address system.

With kisses and hugs being exchanged all around, Gerry's mother whispered into her favourite celebrity's ear. 'Congratulations. Today is your day, darling.'

The handsome man nodded, biting back tears. 'Thanks. I believe it is, finally! Happy New Year, Celia. It's so great you guys are here.'

Turning to his dark-haired temptress of a sibling, he grabbed hold under her arms and lifted her high, eliciting screams of delight. '*¡Feliz Año Nuevo, Lena!*'

'*¡Feliz Año Nuevo, chico!*' his sister replied, and turned her cheek to receive a kiss too.

A serpent of uneven arcs soon formed on the dance floor as people joined hands and sang "Auld Lang Syne" in a typically tuneless tone, arms swinging back and forth with renewed energy. Again, Jeff felt tears prick behind his eyes as he recalled this time last year, when an infatuated couple due to make a break for distant shores had led a crowd of Gerry's valuable *clientèle* in a rendition of this traditional Scottish song.

A shiver ran down his spine as he sang. 'Have you still got that phone-card?' he yelled into Madalena's ear.

'Yeah. In my wallet, over there,' she pointed to their table.

The musician let go of Celia's hand, placing it carefully into the abandoned fingers of the stranger to his sister's right, and the dark-haired *duo* headed back to retrieve the card.

'You're going to ring Lynn, aren't ya?'

'Try, at least,' the romantic confirmed, taking the card from her outstretched hand. '*Gracias, chica.* See you soon. Go back and dance some more.'

The star made his way down the staircase and into the hotel lobby, searching for a public telephone. There were already fewer people milling around, many calling it a night and retrieving their cars from local car parks before the streets clogged up with drunken merrymakers. He located a booth near the *concièrge*'s desk; not in a very private location, but enough to serve its purpose. He hoped he could still remember the number for downstairs at Benloch, knowing full well that Lynn wouldn't be hiding out in her bedroom just after the New Year's chimes.

Standing between two wood-panelled partitions which came almost to his shoulders, Jeff couldn't make up his mind if they reminded him more of a urinal or a confessional. He propped himself against the left-hand wall and dialled the operator.

'Happy New Year!' he said to the jaded voice at the other end. 'Bummer to be working on New Year's, huh?'

'How can I help you, sir?' the monotone woman asked.

Smiling at her less-than-bright personality, Jeff read out the long serial code on the phone-card and gave the operator his best guess at the main number for the Dyson homestead. The line connected and rang four times before clicking through to an answering machine. He hung up. No doubt the whole family was celebrating together in the vast drawing room. He couldn't remember ever seeing or hearing a telephone in that cavernous *salon*.

The impatient groom dialled again. Before he had completed the number however, he realised these thoughts of urinals had set off a quite different sense of urgency. If he were lucky enough to get through to Lynn eventually, he might as well be comfortable while he spoke to her. He hung up again, slipped the phone-card into the breast pocket of his shirt and looked around for the restroom.

Of course, as always happened at such times, two attractive females had spotted their idol and were making right for him. The rock star didn't slow down, simply pointing to the symbol on the door. The girls laughed and shouted after him that they would wait. He half-expected them to follow him in. Jesus Christ! There were some things a man needed to do in private. Even an exhibitionist like him!

The songwriter turned a sharp right upon exiting the toilets and burst out through another emergency exit, stepping down onto the street. His evasive tactics would trigger an alarm one of these days, he smiled to himself. Luckily, tonight was not one of these days. He ran round the outside of the building until he reached the main entrance again, marched past a group of flabbergasted onlookers and soon found himself back at the courtesy telephone.

Dialling the same number for the third time, Jeff went through the tiresome process again. He couldn't be sure it was the same operator at the other end. They seemed to have been recruited for their robotic vocal qualities and lack of personality. The connection clicked into action, another four rings and the answering machine cut in again.

'Fuck,' he cursed under his breath.

One more attempt and then it would be time to give up, get blind drunk and swallow the pill. The new man could feel disillusionment burning inside, anticipating Gravity's arrival at any moment, roused by a mocking wail from Miss Irony. Right now, tomorrow morning's rehearsal seemed so far away. He knew it shouldn't, but it did.

His fingers set to work again, and this time, the operator broke protocol and asked if her caller was still trying to get through to his number.

'Yes, I am,' Jeff responded, relieved to find a compassionate automaton at last. 'Please could you try again?'

'It's a busy time of year.'

Miss Sparkle had hit her stride, to be sure, with this statement of the obvious. At the fourth go-round, the young man felt the vibration of the line connecting, heard the first ring and then a female voice.

'Hello?'

Halleluja! The rock star's head span, and all the air rushed from his lungs at once, leaving him gasping for breath and fast-forwarding to their wedding day after all.

'Angel! It's me.'

'Hey, wow! I knew it was you!' Lynn sounded so happy to hear from him. 'I heard the 'phone ring a couple of times and wondered if anyone would answer it. Then I heard it ring again. I just had a feeling it was you.'

Jeff's eyes were full of water, spilling over at the corners and running down his cheeks. Reaching into his pants pocket for a handkerchief, he leaned further into the booth so that no-one would see him.

'Jesus. I've missed you so much,' his voice croaked. 'How're you going?'

The cheerful chatter was more than welcome after the frenetics of the last few days. Temporarily, the superstar allowed himself to leave behind his delinquent sister and the vivacious screeching of Gerry's sisters, and he imagined himself once more at the dam with his dream girl; at the place where time stood still.

'I miss you too,' Lynn almost sung to him. 'Not long to go now. Are you excited?'

'Yeah, I know. Excited and exhausted. I just had to hear your voice.'

'Where are you? It sounds noisy.'

'In the lobby of the Windsor, outside The Cricketers'. I'm in a 'phone booth that makes me want to piss and at the same time give my last confession,' the charmer told her, sinking down onto the stool and crossing his long legs.

'Oh, no! That's funny. Do you have anything to confess?'

The lightness in his *fiancée*'s tone didn't quite hide the undercurrent of her question.

'No, angel,' Jeff allowed his pride to answer, supremely confident in his honesty. 'I don't.'

A viscous bubble of relief jammed the telephone line, leaving both stranded in the moment. He could tell from the long pause that his beautiful best friend's happiness had been raised at least one more notch on hearing these words.

'Thank you,' he heard her gulp. 'I can't wait to find out how the bucks' night went.'

'Baby, it was awesome,' the young man assured her, inordinately thankful that he had shown appropriate restraint.

What a sound decision the former playboy had made early this morning. One of the best of his life, he figured, judging by the warm stream of love that flowed out of the receiver and kissed the side of his face. Her big-hearted offer was no less of an offer for having been passed up, and he would make sure she knew it in good time. This woman was so, so worth it.

'Thanks for helping Gerry out,' the glowing soul added. 'He did a fantastic job at "MC-ing".'

'Excellent! Great news. I'm glad, and you're welcome. I'm pleased it was special. What's going on over there now?'

The host had almost forgotten about his guests, so content was he to be talking to the woman he loved. 'Ah, the usual. Drinking, smoking. Everyone's dancing. It's been a good night. We're tired, and I'm failing miserably at stopping Lena from getting tanked up. I just don't want her to turn up looking half-dead for you.'

'Don't worry,' the bride-to-be reassured him. 'I'm sure she'll be fine. She's not your responsibility anyway. She's old enough to earn her own reputation in the newspapers.'

Jeff laughed at the concept. 'Indeed! I'm glad you're cool with it. You shouldn't be, but it helps, so thanks.'

'I love you.'

'Angel, I love you too,' her boyfriend replied, inhaling as again he felt his heart melt, just when he had regained some semblance of control.

He stared at his black ring with the solitary stone in one corner, twisting it slowly round his warm, swollen finger. His lone-wolf period had not much longer to run. By the time the newlyweds returned from Tenerife, the heavy piece of jewellery he had taken so long to get used to would have been delivered complete with its second, shimmering diamond.

'Hey, are you coming back into town tomorrow?'

It was Lynn's turn to laugh; the sincere, sunny laugh which was reserved for appreciating the subtext of her lover's statements. 'Of course I am,' she answered. 'Why? Is there something going on?'

'Ah, you know...' he crooned. 'I thought we might have sex.'

'Sex?' his girlfriend repeated in a subdued voice, as if afraid of being overheard. 'Well, that's certainly worth coming back in for. Nothing else then?'

'No, angel. Nothing much.'

A lone teardrop escaped from the millionnaire's right eye, and he brushed it smartly away. It was fortunate that the hotel was large enough to have put some distance between his fans and the homing beacon that incessantly tracked his movements. With depression banished and Gravity summarily halted at the turnstiles, he moved on to more practical matters.

'What time are you getting there?'

'We should arrive about ten-ish,' Lynn replied. 'The hairdresser's booked for ten-thirty, and the musicians are turning up then too. I'm probably just as excited about the songs as I am about the rest of the ceremony.'

Her co-star sniffed. He felt the same way but hadn't been prepared to admit it. In fact, he still wouldn't, he decided. In case she was leading him... The subtle mind-games being transmitted over the telephone line turned him on violently. After the last couple of days of abstinence, his *libido* needed precious little encouragement.

'Will the rooms be open upstairs?'

His *fiancée* scoffed, having a fair idea what was taking place in the Windsor's confessional. 'Yes, some will. Why?'

'I know you know why,' the horny lover balked at her reserved reaction, hoping his ardour wouldn't be too long in subsiding after the call. 'Don't give me a harder time than I'm already having.'

'And you think I have a gap in my schedule for that?'

'Yeah. It's a priority, baby. You're good at prioritising. How about while you're having your hair done? You don't have to move your head.'

'Oh, shut up!' the refined young lady scolded his one-tracked mind. 'You're incorrigible. Get back to the party.'

'OK. As you wish,' Jeff laughed. 'Hey, wait! I forgot... Happy New Year, angel. Happy Our Year. Are you having a good time over there?'

'Happy Our Year to you too! Yes. Pretty laid-back. It's nice.'

'Ha! I'm very jealous,' her *fiancé* didn't want to let her go. 'Thanks for a wondrous nineteen-seventy-five, gorgeous. Let's make 'seventy-six even better.'

'It will be,' Lynn agreed. 'See you tomorrow. Thanks so much for ringing. It was great to talk to you, even though I can't tell mum. Everything's suddenly unlucky for her. She's injected some sort of superstition drug, I think. Sleep well. Can't wait to see you.'

'You too,' her appreciative audience chuckled. 'All of the above. Have fun, gorgeous.'

'Bye, Jeff.'

'*Adiós, Regala.*'

Rejuvenated by the five-minute cruise into peaceful, friendly waters, tomorrow's groom replaced the receiver and stood up from his confined hiding place, willing his erection to play nicely. He flipped open his packet of cigarettes. Only one left, and no lighter. Madalena had all but cleaned him out. Oh, well... At least there was one. He asked the *concièrge* for a loan of his matches and headed back outside to smoke in solitude. And to dream of his bikini-clad wife lounging beside him on a sandy beach a long, long way from their current locations.

The twenty-three-year-old smiled to himself when he remembered hearing the words "Not long to go" drifting from Lynn's enticing mouth. He was fairly sure she had meant not long to go until the ceremony commenced. As far as he was concerned however, his use of the expression was more directed to the point when the whole *fiesta* was finished and they were safely locked in their hotel room in this very building as a married couple, never to contemplate such a spectacle ever again!

To his utter astonishment, his tired mind next rocketed forward to a fantasy world where their own daughter was getting married. The young man shook his head. For Christ's sake! Where had this fanciful idea come from? Was his conscience hinting that he might one day need to do this all again? He dismissed the bizarre but altogether engaging vision and retraced his steps into the last hour of the charity fundraiser he had abandoned.

Jeff found the Blake men back at their table in the ballroom, having recently been delivered a fresh round of coffee. He helped himself, impatiently surveying the area. Where was his bloody sister?

His gaze alighted on a pair at close quarters in the middle of the dance floor. Great! Madalena had hooked up with someone. Now he had a different problem to deal with. Where would she be at the end of the night? Would he have to follow her and wait outside for hours in order to dispatch her to Dyson Administration by ten o'clock? For Christ's sake! This babysitting lark was no fun at all, but he couldn't afford to put his sister off-side and risk having a stroppy bridesmaid on their hands tomorrow.

Reluctantly, he re-joined the Blake ladies on the dance floor, causing a massive stir for which he had zero tolerance.

'Did you get in touch with Lynn?' Celia asked over the music, smiling at the attention her adopted son was receiving.

The young man nodded. 'Yeah. Eventually.'

'That's lovely, dear. You'll sleep well tonight then.'

Maybe not, the celebrity sighed inwardly. He grabbed hold of a delighted Jacinta and whisked her round in several circles towards Madalena and her attachment, who both looked up and grinned inanely at the sudden movement around them. She was away with the fairies, and her dancing partner appeared angry to see another man's gaze bearing down on them.

'What do you want?' the short, dishevelled man sneered.

'Nothing, mate,' the rock star responded, unable to stop himself smiling at the sight of the wretched pair, six sheets to the wind between them. 'She's my sister.'

Feeling less threatened, the guy relaxed a little, almost toppling over. 'Oh, OK. You're right.'

'Lena,' the weary child-minder ordered, much to Gerry's sister's apparent amusement. '*¿Qué haces? Tengo que dirigirme a tú. Ahora.*'

'*Chico*, leave us alone,' Madalena snapped.

'Now, Lena,' her brother insisted, taking hold of her arm. 'Excuse me, mate. She'll be right back.'

Abandoning Jacinta on the dance floor with the stunned drunkard, Jeff frogmarched his blustering sister to the side of the room. Fortunately, she was too relaxed to put up much resistance, merely bleating her objections as her feet trotted along beside him.

'What the fuck are you doing?' he demanded of her blurry eyes. 'You need to stay on the case. I'm fucking getting married tomorrow, and I don't want anything to spoil it. Don't do this, Lena. Please?'

'I'm not doin' nothin',' Madalena replied, an inkling of guilt penetrating her bewildered brain. 'I was just dancing.'

'With a view to what though?'

'What?'

'OK, listen,' tomorrow's groom grabbed her shoulders firmly but affectionately, realising he had confused matters further by the complex turn of phrase. 'If you're going to get off with this bloke, you gotta at least tell me where you're going. I need to be able to pick you up if you can't get back to the flat on your own. *¿Comprendes?*'

The woman nodded, but her brother wasn't so sure his message had been correctly interpreted. There was a vagueness in her expression which he trusted more than her passive acknowledgement. Remembering the little white semi-circle he had been saving for himself, he took a furtive look around in case they were being watched. Not as far as he could see. He reached his wallet out of his back pocket and opened it, shaking his head when he saw dollar signs spinning in his sister's slot-machine eyes.

'Take this,' the rock star suggested, waving the half-tablet in front of her face and lifting an abandoned glass of water from a nearby table. 'Swallow it and drink all this water. OK?'

The Sydneysider's eyes lit up. 'The ecstasy! Can I really 'ave it?'

'Yeah. It's yours, but take it easy. Real easy,' Jeff insisted, desperate for his words to sink in. 'And ring me at home if you need me to come and get you. D'you hear me, Lena?'

Madalena popped the pill into her mouth and swallowed down the glassful of water. 'Cheers, *chico*!'

Her anxious brother then took two twenty-dollar notes out of his wallet and sighed as he witnessed her lightning reflexes yet again. A survival instinct, he presumed, guilt once more intervening and forcing him to take the compassionate view.

'That's for a taxi,' he said, slapping the cash into her open palm. 'You know my address by now? Be good, please? Nine o'clock tomorrow morning. At the absolute latest. Or you'll miss the whole damned show.'

The Sydney prostitute groped inside her dress and shoved the cash into her bra, immediately on the lookout for the client who might have got away. 'Yeah. Thanks, *chico*. See ya.'

Jeff wandered back to the table to re-join the Blake menfolk, watching his sister reunite with her temporary boyfriend. Christ Almighty! He had been counting on that bloody pill to have its desired effect on him, and the thought of having surrendered his miracle sapped his few remaining drops of energy. At least the last half-hour's stress had removed all trace of his own drunkenness, and his hangover would be minimal if he were to stop drinking now. He found another glass of water and used it wisely.

'You're going to be in a fine state for your wedding night!' Gerald laughed as Jeff slumped into the chair beside him.

The host groaned and leaned forwards, clamping his head between his hands before sitting up again with a start. 'Jesus, sir! Please don't mention that fucking "W" word to me ever again,' he moaned, his left hand cutting a horizontal swathe through the air about ten centimetres above his scalp and slumping over again. 'I've had it to here with fucking weddings.'

His best man slapped him on the back, raising his eyebrows to Jacinta's *fiancé*. 'It'll all be over this time tomorrow, mate.'

'Cigarette?' Ray offered, passing one by the superstar's knees, where his eyes were focussed firmly on the floor.

Jeff sat up and accepted a light. 'Thanks, mate. Did the Kingdoms leave?'

'Yes. About half an hour ago. You weren't here,' Gerald answered. 'Nice couple.'

'Yeah. They are,' the musician agreed. 'Damn. That was rude of me. I should've been here to say goodbye. Any coffee left?'

The tired celebrity poured the dregs from the stout, ceramic vessel into a spare cup and added some cream and sugar. It was lukewarm, and he screwed up his face in disgust. A passing waiter noticed the well-respected idol's reaction and signalled that he would bring a fresh pot. Jeff gave him a thumbs-up.

'What's happened to your sis'?' Gerry asked.

His friend groaned again, dragging hard on his cigarette. 'Would you believe she's roped and tied some poor bugger out there who's just as pissed as she is?'

The accountant chuckled. 'So she really is your flesh and blood! Are you going to follow her?'

'No, I'm damned well not. I gave her some money for a taxi. I just hope to God she gets herself home or to a 'phone before ten o'clock tomorrow, or Lynn'll be one bridesmaid short.'

The others looked shocked.

'Are you going to let her disappear out of your sight?' the older man enquired, his tone laced with disapproval.

'Yep. She's her own woman, Gerald,' Jeff replied, sticking to his guns, as he had always done with his best mate's conservative father. 'I'm not going to treat her like a kid. As Gerry so kindly pointed out, I'd most likely be doing the same thing in her position.'

The hot, freshly-brewed coffee tasted very good. Looking at his watch, the groom-to-be saw that it was coming up for one-thirty. If he left now, he could be in bed by two o'clock. The prospect of being woken up to collect his sister sometime during the remaining hours of darkness was not filling him with glee. Without a car at his disposal, it would mean a taxi ride there and back, complete with more mindless discourse about his upcoming nuptials. He almost hoped Madalena would choose to stay out all night, in order that he might have a chance to catch up on some sleep.

'I'm off!' he announced, heaving his six-feet-four-inch frame to its feet.

Father and son both glanced upwards, startled by the celebrity's sudden decision. He was already making for the dance floor to say goodbye to the ladies and to have a final word with his sister. Tamilla grabbed his hand, assuming he was arriving for another session.

'No, thanks, Tam. I'm heading home,' the handsome man in the expensive suit told his former lover.

'Really? Why? Need to save yourself for tomorrow?'

Jeff scoffed. 'Yes, I bloody well do! That's exactly why I'm going. Where's Lena?'

The Blake ladies joined him in scouring the dance floor for the inebriated pair, finally spotting them sitting together at a table on the far side of the ballroom. The handsome star exchanged kisses for the last time with his throng of adoring groupies, and they wished each other goodnight.

Madalena looked up as she saw her brother approach. 'Hi, *chico!*'

'Hey!' he replied.

Praise the Lord for little white pills! What a difference he saw in the young woman's face. Her eyes were clear and focussed, and she looked in total control of whatever situation she was now in.

'Hi, Jeff!' she called out again, as he got closer. 'He's my brother. See? I told you Jeff Diamond was my brother. This is Tim.'

The star extended his hand to his sister's new friend. As expected, his condition had not improved. In fact, it had deteriorated to the point where he looked as if he were about to vomit. The musician smiled and retracted his hand.

'Mate, you don't look too flash. Should we get a taxi now?'

The *trio* progressed slowly to the vehicle lobby at the side of the hotel, and the *valet* hailed a cab from the rank around the corner. The celebrity turned his back to the road and stared into the frosted glass in front of him, praying not to be recognised at this stage. Before too long, a yellow Ford pulled up beside them, and the door was opened from the inside.

'Ask him where he lives, please, Lena,' Jeff requested, as the others clambered in. 'We'll drop him home.'

And please don't let it be Portsea or Dandenong... Or Sydney.

'Fitzroy?' Madalena relayed. 'Where's that?'

'Thank Christ!' the songwriter said out loud. '*Vamanos*, guys.'

The taxi sped away from the hotel and looped around the city streets, now covered in a swarming mass of vehicles and people all vying for the same stretches of road. Police on foot and on horseback were stationed at every corner, but for the most part the crowd was behaving well. His sister and her boyfriend were no longer locked together, their chaperone noticed. She had her quarry trapped, and the hapless gentleman had no idea what was in store for him. Yet another technique he would have employed himself in years gone by, he smiled in shame.

'Where in Fitzroy?' the new Jeff twisted round from the front seat to ask the little, green man in the back. 'Are you going to be OK?'

'Yeah,' came a weak reply.

Tim mumbled what must have been the name of his street, and the taxi driver put his indicator on and changed lanes, muttering under his breath about drunken party-goers.

'Come on, man,' the compassionate passenger cut him off. 'It's New Year's. He's entitled to live it up tonight. You OK, Lena?'

They continued on northwards through the centre of the city and out past Jeff's apartment. He pointed it out to his sister as they drove by.

She laughed, even with an element of sympathy. 'Sorry 'bout 'im, *chico.*'

Her brother shrugged. It could have been a whole lot worse.

'It's fine,' he replied. 'It's funny actually. At least you're OK.'

Once on Victoria Street, the traffic thinned out, enabling them to accelerate. The man in the back seat groaned when the car lurched round a sharp corner into Brunswick Street. Attempting to identify a landmark, he flung his hand out of the window and pointed to a right turn ahead, and the taxi swerved into the narrow, cobbled lane.

'I said he could come to the party tomorrow,' Madalena let on. 'Is that OK?'

Jeff marvelled at her audacity. 'Oh, did you? Great! The more the merrier.'

His sister had no experience of this type of event, nor any form of *étiquette* concerning inviting folk to other people's special occasions. He couldn't blame her for this. Unlike him, she hadn't latched onto an affluent family to learn how the other half lived. She had no catalogue of posh airs and graces into which she could dip whenever the circumstance demanded.

'Sure. Why not? You'll have to share your food though. Does he have a dress?'

The extra guest looked confused. 'Dress?' he muttered.

'It's my brother's wedding,' the young woman explained, obviously not having been this forthcoming earlier. 'He's marrying Lynn Dyson.'

'Lynn Dyson?' Tim blurted out through his haze. 'Then you *are* Jeff Diamond. I thought she was joking. Bloody hell! Where the hell am I?'

'It's all just a bad dream, mate,' the self-assured artist smiled. 'You won't remember a thing in the morning, trust me.'

The taxi pulled up in front of a relatively new apartment building, and Tim opened the door, almost falling onto the pavement. A number of passers-by moved out of the way, fearing a fight was about to ensue. Madalena shuffled along the seat and out to the footpath with him.

'See you tomorrow?' she yelled directly into the befuddled man's face. 'Where is it again?'

Her amused brother had heard the woman's question but waited until she knocked on the front passenger window and asked more civilly before he wound it down. If only he had a video camera to replay this odd spectacle at a later date! He wished Lynn were here to share it with him.

'Where is it, *chico*?' she yelled into the cab at the top of her voice.

Jeff scoffed, hearing the taxi driver laughing beside him. 'Lucky I'm here, isn't it? Dyson Administration Building on St Kilda Road, on the corner of Coventry Street. You won't be able to miss it, I reckon. There'll be one or two people outside. Don't come 'til after five though, when all the official stuff'll be over. Feel better, mate. *Adiós.*'

The superstar waved goodbye and closed the window again, sinking down into the seat and sighing deeply. Madalena slid back into the car and reached inside her top as they set off towards the edge of the city and their apartment. She pulled out a wad of cash and peeled off two twenty dollar notes.

Handing them to the churlish man in front, she cackled. 'Here... This is your money back.'

It was her brother's turn to look confused. 'Thanks. Where did all that come from?'

'Him!' the brazen flesh-trader laughed. 'That idiot there! He already paid me. I didn't even have to spread 'em.'

Momentarily frozen in horror, Jeff stole a glance across at the taxi driver, committing his face to memory and vowing never to travel with him again. He could only imagine the story the outwardly-unmoved Greek must have been itching to broadcast on his radio as soon as his cab was empty.

'What the fuck? That's extortion!' her brother barked.

Still the driver said nothing, and the songwriter relaxed a little. He quite possibly witnessed such transactions on a regular basis while working the night-shift. Trust his sister to have profited from the evening, over and above disencumbering him of his tiny lifesaver!

'What's extortion?' Madalena asked, annoyed at having scorn poured on her enterprising party-piece.

'You've got to give it back. D'you do that a lot?'

'Yeah. Sometimes,' the cagey professional admitted. 'Depends how pissed they are when I find 'em.'

'He won't turn up tomorrow,' the celebrity told her.

'No. So what?'

Well, Jeff thought, why should she care? She had her fee. *He* cared however, quite apart from the damage to his reputation if word were to spread. They knew roughly where Tim lived. Perhaps there was some way he could repay the unfortunate guy after the honeymoon. He may have been stupid enough to part with his money in the first place, but the world-changer's conscience was unable to ignore the fact that his sister had done wrong by accepting it. Even in his wildest days back on the Stones Road, the boy from Canley Vale would never have conned someone out of their hard-earned cash. Had he? He couldn't fully remember, if he were truthful. But then again, there were many things he couldn't remember about those years.

The taxi stopped again at the steps of the corner building on La Trobe and Spring Streets, and the dark-haired partygoers piled out. The relieved celebrity paid their fare, and the driver took off with a generous tip.

Once inside the apartment, the groom-to-be hugged his sister more to stop himself falling to his knees than for any other reason. 'You're quite a piece of work, Madalena Moreno,' he said with a smile. '*¿Qué tus abuelos dicen?*'

'So did you get to talk to Lynn?' the childish woman asked, conveniently ignoring his question.

'Yep. For a few minutes,' Jeff nodded, recalling the pleasant oasis in the otherwise irritating function. 'It was fantastic. Just what I needed.'

'That fuckin' pill was fantastic. Just what I needed too 'cause I don't feel steamed anymore,' the western suburbs night-owl replied. 'I'm off to bed. Can you wake me up?'

'Sure,' the tired man affirmed, taking hold of his sister's hand and pulling her into the kitchen. 'But first you tell me how much money Tim paid you and then you drink two more glasses of water. Right?'

'Eighty bucks,' Madalena answered, slapping the remainder down on the table. 'After your cut, pimp.'

She took the glass and drank it obediently, watching her brother do the same. She had spent the early part of the evening tracking his progress among the tables, schmoozing with the guests. Though not recognising any of them, she guessed they were all wealthy. He had smiled and laughed with them all while the women swooned around him and the men all shrank in his presence.

The great Jeff Diamond looked furious now, as if he meant business. Those eyes reminded the young woman of their father's, and they made her nervous all of a sudden.

'What are you going to do with it?'

'Take it with us tomorrow. If he turns up, you can choose whether to give him the money or the goods. If he doesn't come, I'll see if somehow I can get it back to him when we get home.'

Relieved, Madalena liked what she heard well enough. 'OK. Goodnight, *chico*.'

'*Buenas noches, Lena,*' he answered, kissing her on the cheek. 'Thanks for coming with me tonight. It was good to have you there.'

His sister turned and walked down the hallway, registering neither a positive nor a negative reaction to the charitable millionnaire's kind words. Swallowing down another glass of water and filling a third to take with him, he switched off the kitchen light and cursed the hollow pit in his stomach. Tomorrow's groom shut the bedroom door behind him, fighting back tears as the sanctuary within enveloped him. Less than five minutes later, he was in bed.

The enterprising gipsy's lack of feelings didn't surprise her brother, despite his lingering sadness. Rather, it had triggered memories of a very old conversation he had shared with his dream girl during their first visit to The Fellowship, when she had quizzed him about the highs and lows on his happiness chart. Madalena didn't know the joy she was missing, yet her minimal emotional spectrum had surely protected her well.

What a crazy night! Another crazy night! His last as a single man had been memorable enough, the songwriter chuckled to himself in the dark solitude. What did being single mean to him? Anything? What would he miss? Nothing whatsoever, he concluded. At least, nothing that a stressed-out mind weakened by a loop of endlessly repeating questions could think of. *Come on, man, there must be something?*

The ability to set his own agenda? No. Their relationship, not to mention their jet-setting lifestyle, afforded him copious quantities of freedom. His management team set his agenda these days anyway. If he sought to deviate from his schedule, it would be the frighteningly efficient Cathy Patterson rather than his new wife who was more likely to fold her arms and block his way!

Independence? No again. Same deal. Lynn knew how to balance their individual independence with his residual reliance on her.

Other women then? Absolutely not. The previous night had cemented this particular resolution once and for all.

His own space? Yes. Granted. The introvert was still apt to retreat into his own mind from time to time, whether for songwriting, his ambitious intellectual pursuits or simply to tune out and rest the other five hyperactive senses. The couple's hectic travel plans for the following months would provide them both with plenty of time on their own. Jeff spread his six-foot-four-inch frame out further in their queen-sized bed in a last ditch effort to hammer the point home!

Time with friends? Yes. Needed this too, in spite of his introversion. The challenge and stimulation supplied by the company of strangers served to force the philosopher out of himself, and although it exhausted him beyond measure, there was untold value in melding minds for the greater good. Again, his beautiful best friend never sought to curtail his socialising, and with kids as part of the equation, what better way to while away those long evenings at home but surrounded by friends sharing dinner and long conversations?

A gust of night breeze swirled through the open window, whipping the lead disc in the corner of the curtain's hem against the glass. It startled the drowsy resident, who scolded himself for still being awake. Turning to his left and tugging the sheet up to his shoulder, he smiled at Lynn's picture on his bedside table.

So what would be gained tomorrow through this legal union? In-laws! Once upon a time the rebel musician would have balked at this idea, fed up of Bart and Marianna Dyson insisting they knew best for their daughter. This thorny issue had largely been resolved, although now replaced with a nagging fear of the danger his family background might pose for Australia's sporting dynasty.

Becoming part of the establishment? This was closer to the mark. Lynn's good counsel, born from a lifetime in the public eye, had resigned him to the necessary evil of courting friends in high places. Who said establishment had to be all bad? He had often heard the maxim of change being easier to effect from the inside than by breaking and entering where one was not welcome. The celebrity newlyweds certainly had the establishment eating out of their hands right now, which would be an excellent topic to debate on the long flight to their tropical paradise.

Whoa! *Las Islas Canarias*, the traveller changed tack, slowing his breathing to encourage his brain to relax. Something to look forward to indeed... Several of their London contacts waxed lyrical about this cluster of Spanish-speaking islands, and the stars had been booked into a luxury resort in *Santa Cruz de Tenerife*, recommended by two separate but equally discerning couples. According to Cathy's envious description, a travel agent would be waiting at the airport to transport them to a motor yacht, wherein they would pass the first three days cruising around, doing and wearing not much of anything.

How good did that sound? *No*, Jeff sighed, spinning over to face the window. *Don't think about sex. Not now. Change the subject...*

The woman whose image the distracted man daren't picture had light-heartedly suggested they spend the entire holiday speaking only Spanish, to help her become sufficiently fluent to raise their children in their father's first language. He had been quite taken by the idea initially, but he was no longer so sure. Since being in Madalena's company after such a long break, he had come to realise that their Argentinean origins meant little to him. They were part of the old Jeff, as were his neglected Polish roots. All this baggage would end up stored away for posterity, saved for the obligatory autobiography his publishing company had been pressuring him to draft...

How could anyone justify writing an autobiography at twenty-three years old? How absurd! What might its title be? "Watch This Space" came to mind, causing his sleepy vocal chords to cough in amusement. The superstar's management company had amassed a great deal of material already for this exact purpose. Perhaps he should begin to stockpile personal memorabilia too, to speed up the process whenever the time seemed right. Of course, his wife-to-be was well down this path for her own documentary, but then she was super-organised, and he was not.

Jeff lifted his head off the pillow and peered at the dim figures on Lynn's alarm clock on the far side of the bed. He needed to be up in four hours' time. A compulsive urgency gripped him, hit by a panic attack that she might change her mind and not drive into town tomorrow morning. He almost gave in, willing his eyelids to block out the sight of the telephone.

For Christ's sake! Not even he could be that demanding... *Don't think about her*, his conscience urged his body. *Please don't think about her.*

Of course, it was too late. Whose side was he on? Why couldn't his brain have stayed in Tenerife and the not much of anything at all?

Never likely to fall asleep in such an extreme state of arousal, the hot-blooded singleton stroked his dogged erection rhythmically, pushing himself to come quickly with thoughts of Lynn stretched out on the yacht's deck in her bikini, red lips sipping a cocktail through a straw while he ran blocks of ice over her stomach and down to somewhere that was anything but cool. Wasn't that the same shade of red lipstick on his penis, her tongue licking the tip gently and teasing him to orgasm in her mouth?

Jeff arched his back as he came, letting the pleasurable release wash through him and purge any traces of a latent hangover. His sister had been funny this morning about the screwed-up tissues on the floor. She had made him feel like a fifteen-year-old again, so he dutifully got up this time to flush them down the toilet.

With sleep approaching at last, the old soul lay down on top of the sheet and glanced over at Lynn's side of the bed, imagining her there in her own post-coital bliss. Lynn Dyson and Jeff Diamond would put rings on each others' fingers later this very day in front of everyone important and legalise the commitment they had made long, long ago.

Jeff chuckled as he drew a parallel with the many Hollywood stars of stage and screen who married and divorced at the drop of a hat. How many times had he and Lynn been married before? And through how many more lifetimes would they go in search of each other all over again? Did the passage of time make it easier to find their new incarnations? Perhaps as souls got older, they learned to drop more hints to help in their next quest.

Or perhaps this was all ridiculous, romantic rubbish. *Go to sleep, get up in the morning, marry the most beautiful woman in the world, make babies, work hard, raise a family, change the world and live happily ever after.* What more did he want?

Hitched

'*¡Chico!*' Madalena was at his bedside. 'Get up. It's your wedding day!'

Jeff groaned and turned over, instinctively backing away from the grating exuberance. 'Already? Go away!'

'Y'ave to get up soon,' her next firm instruction assaulted his ears. 'Come on!'

What were yesterday's famous last words? *Praise the Lord for little white pills?* There was a song about that, the musician's groggy mind recalled: *Be careful what you pray for. You just might get it!* He turned onto his back again and opened his eyes to see a mop of dark-hair floating above him, framing a face bright with wonder.

'What time is it?' he coughed.

'Half-seven,' Madalena announced, clicking her fingers like a finicky governess. 'Time for bridesmaids and grooms to get up!'

Jeff marvelled at his sister's high spirits first thing in the morning and after so little sleep; another trait they didn't share. Moreover, he secretly rejoiced that her presence in his bedroom hadn't triggered a wild panic attack, given how closely she resembled their deceased mother. A year ago, this would surely have been a very different story.

'Ah, for Christ's sake, Lena!' he moaned, curling Lynn's pillow off the mattress and hitting his tormentor squarely on her tiger tattoo.

'*¡Ai!* Fuckin' 'ell. You did that on purpose! Get up, *culo!*'

The well-trained athlete pulled the woman's thin, gangly frame down onto the bed on top of him and flipped her over to land on the other side, which had lain undisturbed for a few days. A burst of additional expletives sprang forth between squeals and gasps as the twenty-six-year-old fought free of a very strong grip.

'Leave me alone!' Jeff shouted, tickling her ribs and hearing her laugh like a girl. 'Make some bloody coffee, and I'll shower. We can grab some breakfast on the way.'

'On the way to the church?' Madalena teased, laying still and starting to sing. 'For *Gawd*'s sake, get me to the church on time. I'm getting married in the morning. Ding, dong, the bells are gonna chime.'

Her brother released his grip and stared open-mouthed. 'What? Two days ago, you'd never even heard of "My Fair Lady", and now you're singing one of its most famous songs. Who put you up to that?'

The amateur turned bashful, realising she had been entertaining one of the biggest stars of the world's music scene. 'Jack and Tammy. They were singin' it the night of your bucks' party. They taught me it so I could sing it to you today.'

'OK! Very cool, actually. Thanks. Carry on,' the professional smiled, catching the embarrassed woman unaware and pushing her shoulders until she was flat on the mattress. 'Don't stop while I'm in the shower. I can still hear you. What else did they teach you?'

Now that he was properly awake, and the leprechauns of levity had chased the old troll back into his cave, Jeff had to admit to being giddy with excitement. This really was his wedding day! It was finally here, a very close second to knowing he would see Lynn again in little more than two hours' time. He vowed not to pressure her to have sex before the ceremony. That wouldn't be right. He was a mature, intellectual bohemian pre-autobiographer. He could damned well wait until the proper time.

The distracted groom inspected the contents of the suit carrier hanging on a wardrobe door knob: a jacket and a pair of pants that matched, he checked closely; a white dress shirt with the finest silver and gold threads woven in faint vertical stripes, hand-made on Savile Row; another tie selected by his fabulous and fashionable *fiancée*; and right at the bottom, two matching black shoes which he had polished yesterday morning in a rare fit of enthusiasm. One left and one right... Just checking!

Socks! Fine idea... He picked out two pairs of plain, dark socks and a spare pair of boxer shorts from his lingering London luggage. There had also been talk of a family run the following morning, so he reluctantly tossed in some sports gear too. Such torture was above and beyond the call of duty, in his opinion, but their fans would undoubtedly be ecstatic to see the whole clan out and about after such a high-profile event.

Rings. Jesus Christ! Would he call to ensure Gerry wouldn't forget them? *No, don't be such a control freak.*

Lyric sheets for their songs, just in case his memory failed him during their final run-through.

Peering at his chiselled, clean-shaven jawline in the mirror to check that his sideburns were even and that he hadn't missed any stray hairs, Jeff slapped on a lavish amount of after-shave, not wishing to risk the bottle leaking in his bag and having the wedding party overcome by fumes. He then checked his fingernails, declaring them pristine and short enough.

Fastening his watch and feeling the vibration of his own heartbeat fall in with its regular ticking, the handsome man dressed in his smartest jeans and another tastefully-fitted collared shirt for suitable rehearsal clothing. There was bound to be a jungle of journalists camped out in front of the Dyson Administration building already, necessitating at least semi-presentable rehearsal attire.

Noblesse oblige, his arrogant reflection scoffed. He was marrying Lynn Dyson after all. Lynn Dyson! This ragamuffin from the Stones Road was about to be legally wed to the poster girl who had adorned his bedroom walls. What was the probability of his evergreen teenaged dream coming true? *One*, he agreed with the man in the mirror, whose left hand was tracing the "JL" tattoo on his chest. Singular. There it was again!

'Lena, are you packed?'

His sister hadn't heard him. She was outside on the balcony smoking when Jeff found her. No. He wouldn't smoke this morning either. Well, maybe one or two to calm the nerves... Having made the first about-face decision of the morning, he returned to the master bedroom and quickly slotted his toothbrush and toothpaste into one of the suit carrier's zipped pockets, and then tossed in the after-shave after all, first tightening the top as hard as he could.

The millionnaire picked up the cup of coffee Madalena had placed next to his cigarettes and lighter. '*Gracias*,' he toasted her. 'Are you all packed?'

The young woman looked nervous now. 'Dunno. Can you check it for me? I don't want to forget nothin'.'

The kind man smiled. 'Not sure I'll be much help, but sure...'

It appeared the erstwhile fly-by-night was beginning to care a whole lot more, after only a couple of days in the company of normal people. This assessment was not terribly legitimate, coming from her tearaway brother, but he suspected it to be true regardless. Could he dare presume to be a role-model for caring these days, alongside his beautiful best friend? A sizeable portfolio of charitable causes laid testament to his altruism, but how much evidence existed for his personal contribution?

The rock star's arrogance withered in the time it took the pair to finish their cigarettes and coffee, suddenly thrown back to his childhood. He had always cared, he assured his waning self-confidence. Too much, in fact, and almost in inverse proportion to those around him. Lynn would have said he mustn't sell himself short. Taking a deep breath, he regrouped, leading his sister back into a bedroom so messy that the young man wondered at first if it had been ransacked by burglars while they had been on the balcony.

'Sorry 'bout the crap ev'rywhere,' the sheepish guest said. 'I wanted to make sure I didn't leave stuff behind.'

Jeff laughed. 'It's great. It's typical you, and I'd forgotten what typical you looked like. I'll take a photo' in a minute. What are you bringing with us?'

Madalena leaned over and hooked her fingers into the handles of a shopping bag from the Myer Emporium on Lonsdale Street. She peered inside, rifled her hand around and then held it out for inspection.

'Is that it? There's virtually nothing in there. Where's everything else?'

'Me dress and shoes are with Michelle. I'm wearing my undies,' his sister responded, mentally scanning herself from toe to head. 'Pantyhose is in, make-up's in, and I'm wearin' earrings. We're gettin' our hair put up, so that's all.'

The handsome musician hugged the dark-haired waif. 'It's so great to have you here this morning. And I love the fact that neither of us is hung over. There's a lot to be said for taking it easy with drink and drugs. Something it took me a long while to learn... Doesn't it make a difference, not feeling like you're made of lead?'

'Lead? I dunno,' Madalena replied with a shrug. 'I never done this kind o' thing before. So d'you think I've got ev'rything? I want some of them pills, but.'

Jeff nodded, laughing out loud. 'Yep, not a bad idea. They're pretty good, but Lynn's dad'd cancel the wedding if he found any on us. Sounds like this is everything, I guess. How should I know? I'm just a man. You seem to have it all under control. Wait there a sec'...'

The groom turned on his heels to fetch a camera from the main bedroom, then positioned the nervous bridesmaid among her belongings, strewn all over the bed, and took a photograph of a woman whose broad smile was still new to him. Leaving the inadequate plastic bag by the front door, the pair of Catholic Argentinean Polish Jews paused for a few more pictures on the balcony, trying out the nifty, new timer function Jeff had recently mastered.

'What's Admin?' his sister asked, as they climbed into the taxi.

'Just the name for the Dysons' office building, that's all,' her brother explained. 'There are apartments at the top where they live when they're in town.'

Madalena nodded. 'Like your penthouse.'

'Yeah. Just like it. My fucking penthouse, you mean?'

If the morning's taxi driver had been in Melbourne over the last week, he must either have been locked away from the rest of humanity or he was incredibly discreet, since he uttered not a single "W" word. The spruced-up superstar paid the fare, and they alighted in the circular driveway of Dyson Administration.

'Is this where the weddin' is?' the Sydneysider asked, unimpressed. 'It doesn't look very weddingy.'

'You wait!' her brother smiled. 'The ballroom's very weddingy, I think you'll find.'

The gate buzzed in response to Jeff's positive identification by the security guard inside, and he pushed it open to allow his sister to enter ahead of him. As they climbed the steps to the rear entrance, the sight of the performer's famous head sparked an excited reaction from the crowd on the wide St Kilda

Road promenade beyond the high wall which separated the public from the building's private courtyard.

Waving, the bemused man looked over and noticed that people had already taken up their positions, desperate to secure a bird's-eye view of the proceedings. A quick calculation confirmed five-and-a-half hours of waiting were still ahead of them, and he wondered how early they had begun to assemble. Such a display of commitment was a little overwhelming, but not surprising. The happy couple had received letters from so many well-wishers, filled with such intentions.

Jeff smiled enthusiastically, thinking they deserved so much more. 'Give me a chance to dump this stuff, and I'll come around.'

An even louder cheer went up, accompanied by clapping and spontaneous pledges of adoration. Again, the young man gave thanks for the absence of hangover. The new arrivals disappeared through the revolving doors and were greeted by Michael, the long-serving uniformed receptionist who, as the songwriter had discovered the previous year, also suffered from PTSD after two tours in Vietnam.

Shaking Jeff's hand and wishing them an enjoyable day, the former soldier ushered him and his obvious relative through into the lift lobby, chuckling in disbelief when the superstar needed to ask which floor the ballroom was on.

'Level One. You can't miss it!'

Jeff rolled his eyes at the sarcasm and pointed Madalena towards an open lift. Nearly four years had passed since he had made his low-key *début* in the same, imposing hall. His companion seemed nervous again, the tension in her jawline very familiar.

'You OK?'

Pomp and circumstance were second nature to the boy from Canley Vale these days, and he took pity on his sister. She had been relaxed and playful this morning, but he surmised this important occasion must seem pretty daunting to her now that her big moment was almost upon her. Her head nodded tentatively, having left half of her twenty-six years in the taxi.

'You don't have to come down and talk to them. If we go upstairs, you can just put the TV on for a while. I'm not sure what the plan is either. It'll be easy, Lena. They'll tell you exactly what to do.'

The sliding doors opened into a darkened *foyer* from which they could see into the main function area, every window-frame festooned with lemon-coloured balloons and white satin ribbons. It didn't feel as cavernous as he remembered from that first, spine-tingling performance for his dream girl. More than two years of packing out sixty-thousand seat stadia and every major concert hall around the world had downgraded this to quite an intimate venue. With a revised perspective on the space, he made a mental note to adjust some of the moves he had rehearsed.

'Wow!' Madalena murmured, spinning slowly around.

Watching her step falter while her eyes followed the ornate cornices along the edges of the ceiling rendered Jeff dizzy too. Christ! She wasn't the only one who was nervous, he realised. He signalled for her to put her bag down on one of the seats and follow him, and to his relief, her mood appeared to lighten a little.

'Fuck, *chico*! This *is* weddingy. Look at all the flowers and shit. It's beautiful! Where d'you stand?'

'Up the front by the stage, I'm guessing. We'll find out in about an hour. I've got about as much idea as you have about how it's all going to fit together. My plan is to stand wherever they tell me and not move.'

'Me too!' the positively pale woman agreed. 'Hope I remember ev'rythin'.'

'You and me both, baby!' her brother scoffed kindly, judging that the novice's minute tasks were easily commensurate with his mammoth starring role when juxtaposed against their relative levels of on-stage experience.

They dropped their baggage on the chairs in the back row. The performer steadied his heart rate by counting the rows in each bank of seats: fifteen rows, twelve seats in each, and with a wide aisle down the centre. There were far more chairs than the groom considered necessary, but what did he know?

His eyes were then drawn to a huge banner emblazoned with the same symbol as was inked into the lovers' bodies, strung high above the stage and also adorned with curled streamers and yellow, white and silver balloons.

Underneath, the polished floorboards were marked and partially arranged for the band, with sufficient space for a small chamber orchestra behind. Even a set of timpani had been installed. Ambitious, the star thought. What exactly was his beautiful best friend planning to do with that?

All in all, this imperial corner of old Melbourne had been transformed into a very tasteful and inviting ceremonial hall. Close enough to a church to give the day an appropriate *gravitas*, yet not at all stuffy or ecclesiastical. Forcing himself to take a few long, deep breaths, Jeff began to relax too.

'We're early. Let's get some breckie. You hungry, Lena?'

His sister frowned. 'Maybe.'

'We'll get takeaway, then you can eat it when you're ready,' he smiled, holding out his arm to the stunned young woman.

The dark-haired *duo* headed back to the lifts and descended to the lobby again. Obtaining the small amount of intelligence about the others' whereabouts as had been provided to the friendly security guard, they prepared to brave the outside world again.

'Can we bring you some breakfast, Michael?' the star enquired, as they passed through the turnstile.

The retired officer declined, letting them back through the barrier, and the noise level immediately rose as the siblings were spotted at the front of the building this time. They turned left onto the footpath, making for the river and the crowd which was patiently waiting behind a thick, red rope twisted around a series of chromed posts.

The well-respected celebrity shook as many hands and kissed as many cheeks as he could reach in the front rows. It was no surprise to find the throng predominately consisting of women, of all ages, screaming, crying and cheering like lunatics.

'Save your energy! You'll be asleep by the time the action starts,' the showman teased. 'Thanks heaps for coming out. We really appreciate it.'

Edging his way past the cordon, he posed for some photographs and introduced his overwhelmed sister to yet more of his ecstatic fans.

'Any second thoughts?' someone shouted out.

Jeff searched for the cynical female, eventually locating her standing on the wall at the back. 'Absolutely not! All good! We're going for breckie. See you soon.'

And with that, the handsome charmer marched his charge purposefully past the barracks, hailing another taxi and disappearing towards Flinders Street station. They alighted after only two minutes, ran into the first café they saw on Swanston Street and took their place at the counter.

Peace at last! Well, relatively speaking, the pair's eyes confirmed, since the tourists having breakfast soon got wind of who was queuing up to be served. Advising Madalena to make her choice quickly and putting in an initial order for two flat whites, the momentary calm was shattered when fingers started to point and an assortment of animated commentary floated over the tables.

'Yes. It's today,' the superstar confirmed for a flabbergasted English couple, having heard them asking around. 'Two o'clock. Clear out of town while you can!'

Jeff purchased a ridiculous selection of muffins, *croissants* and Danish pastries, requesting that the counter assistants cut them into quarters. Armed with their own breakfasts in separate bags, two double-layered paper cups of hot coffee and several large boxes of comestible goodies, he and his partner-in-crime raced through the swarm to the waiting taxi and back to the overpopulated Coventry Street corner.

'Here! Take these!' the happy man shouted, launching each box at intervals as they squeezed past. 'Don't say I never give you anything.'

The noisy gathering was grateful for the thoughtful groom's charity. A man's voice struck up a loud chorus of "Hip, hip!", and three cheers were duly issued, followed by a rousing rendition of "For He's A Jolly Good Fellow." Taking a bow, he thanked them for their support and took his leave, still with his sister in tow.

'They really love you!' the dumbfounded woman exclaimed once they were back in the ballroom. 'And you like it, don't ya? I can tell you like it, even though it's a pain in the arse all the time.'

Jeff cocked his arrogant head, swallowing a large mouthful of warm ham and cheese *croissant*. 'Yeah, I do. It's nice to be wanted.'

'I'm sorry Mamá was a bitch to you,' Madalena blurted out. 'I always 'ated it.'

'What? Shit, *chica*. Where the hell did that come from?'

The twenty-three-year-old was struck by a sudden pain in his chest which winded him for a few seconds. Jesus Christ, that hurt! His big sister's visit was full of surprises; this particular one unwelcome however, to say the least. If it were true that she had hated the way their mother treated him, it had certainly never been obvious at the time. Perhaps she wished she hadn't witnessed the incessant rounds of verbal and physical torture to which he had been subjected as a boy, but he didn't believe this spontaneous statement for a minute. He couldn't help thinking that history had been rewritten courtesy of the regular income she now received from the trust fund Gerry had established in her name.

'Don't talk about this today, please, Lena,' Jeff pleaded, gasping for breath and determined not to show his anger. 'Today's about the future, not the past. I can't handle it.'

'Yeah, OK,' the subdued woman said. 'I just wanted to say something.'

Her brother had tears in his eyes, shaken both by what she had claimed but also by the novelty of her apparent contrition. '*Gracias*,' he coughed. '*Te amo*. And I don't blame you. *Hablemos del algo más*. OK?'

'Sorry, *chico*.'

Seeing that Madalena looked as if she might cry too, Jeff stood up and hugged her close. 'I meant what I said back in the apartment,' he told her. 'It's been so good to see you for these last few days. I didn't really know what to expect, and it was hard to begin with, wasn't it?'

She nodded. 'Yeah. Bit weird.'

'But now I feel like I've got a sister again,' he continued. 'And I like you. We could have fun together, all three of us. You'll have to come down again. *¿Quizá en Pascua?*'

'But what about Lynn? Would she be OK with that?'

The millionnaire was discouraged that their guest would even think to ask this question, the rollercoaster of emotions adding to his frustration. His new wife would want what he wanted, of that he was sure.

'Yes. Of course she would. I told you... Lynn likes you heaps.'

A faint noise distracted the pair from any further discussion on the topic, both pairs of ears catching the distant excitement coming from outside in the open air. The celebrity looked at his watch: nine-forty-five. The Dysons had arrived, and his heart had leaped into his mouth. Things were about to get real.

'They're here,' he informed his sister, whose face also took on a paler hue. 'Don't stress! They're nice people. And everyone'll be nervous, so just be yourself. It doesn't matter what you say or do. You're here, you're smiling, and that's all we need.'

Jeff did his best to appear cool, calm and collected as he heard the hum of a lift rising. His blood pressure was rising along with it, and his head began to throb behind his eyes. No more cigarettes, he told himself, seeing Madalena light up and take a long drag of nicotine. Her startled expression reminded him of the first time Lynn had invited him to Benloch, when their relationship was only a matter of weeks old. They had both been stressed out about meeting her family as girlfriend and boyfriend, one's nerves feeding off the other's.

The lift didn't stop at the first floor after all. Its hum continued, and the doors remained firmly closed. The bridesmaid stood there bewildered, not understanding what had happened, and the groom breathed a sigh laced with both relief and disappointment. No doubt there would soon be another opportunity for a heart attack, hopefully with the payoff of seeing his dream girl.

'They've gone straight upstairs,' he surmised. 'Shit! Anti-climax or what? Panic over.'

Madalena exhaled and forced a laugh. 'Bastards!'

'Agreed,' her brother nodded, emptying his paper cup and tossing it into the box full of breakfast wrappings.

'Do I have to kiss everybody?' the young woman asked after a short pause.

He chuckled. 'No! You don't *have* to. But if someone kisses you, then you're pretty much committed. It's not polite to pull out!'

'I've been watching you,' she smirked. 'You kiss ev'ryone.'

'Do I? I don't even think about it. Not the blokes though,' the superstar coughed to confirm his manhood, making his sister giggle.

'No! Not blokes, *culo*. But posh girls always have to get kissed. I dunno why.'

'You're right,' her brother answered with a frown, trusting the under-socialised suburban lass would drop this line of enquiry once upstairs with the bridal party. 'I never thought about it. Good point! You're observant, Lena. Well, if you're not ambushed, just kiss the people you feel like kissing.'

While *les étrangers* debated whom to kiss and whom not to kiss, the lift had started to hum again. The pair stared at each other as fear struck anew. This time the cables stopped pulling, and the doors opened. Out stepped both posh girls at once.

'Jeff!' Lynn and Anna screamed at once.

The Dyson girls' grand entrance had clearly been practised. The flower-girl ran over to her future brother-in-law and gave him a huge hug. True to form, he lifted her high into the air, and she kicked her legs out behind her like a trapeze artist. Her graceful elder sister walked serenely towards him, dressed in skin-tight jeans and a white blouse, her hair loose in golden waves. She leaned into the man she adored, and they embraced passionately. So passionately that her kid sister thumped them both on the hips.

'See?' he called out to Madalena. 'You *are* right. I'd kiss anyone.'

Seeing the dark-haired woman giggling shyly and the bride-to-be decidedly puzzled, he laughed. 'Lena was just telling me that I kiss everyone.'

Lynn remained confused, her fingers pressing into the flesh above her man's belt.

'I'll explain later,' the handsome man shrugged. 'Never mind. You had to be there...'

His *fiancée* nodded in capitulation and diverted towards her second bridesmaid, who inched forward to kiss her like a pro'. The groom felt a *frisson* of pride at this slowly unfolding metamorphosis; the moth was turning into a butterfly. Or something like that.

'Hi, Lena,' Lynn said, also a little taken aback by the sudden warmth. 'This is my sister, Anna.'

'Hello,' Madalena responded, not choosing to kiss the nine-year-old. 'You're the gymnast, right?'

She grinned. 'Yes, I am. *Olá, Madalena.*'

Anna had been practising the pronunciation of this new sister-in-law's name.

'Very good,' the linguist congratulated her. '*¿Como estás, Anna?*'

'*Muy bien, Jeff. ¿Y tú?*' the little girl replied. 'Is that right?'

'Sure is!' the half-Argentinean confirmed with renewed exuberance. 'Nicely done. *¿Estás lista para que la diversión comience?*'

With no ready response to a phrase as complicated as this, Anna stared blankly at her sister. Madalena came to her rescue however, exactly as the Pied Piper had engineered. The master communicator at work, his girlfriend smiled.

'You have to say, *"Sí, chico."*'

'*¡Sí, chico!*' the youngster giggled. '*Chico*'s boy, isn't it?'

'*Sí, chica,*' Jeff replied, glancing at his beautiful best friend, who acknowledged the honest interaction taking place.

'*¿Estás listo, chico?*' Lynn asked, with a playful glint in her eye.

'You bet, baby!' he answered, squeezing her tight. 'What for?'

The dignified society girl smacked her renegade's arm, and they all laughed. Despite the smiles and happy banter, the atmosphere was strained.

His sex-drive had been kick-started by standing so close to the love of his life, and he sensed a certain impatience reciprocated between her carefully selected lines. It only served to turn him on further, so he loosened his grip and heard her sigh involuntarily.

'So!' the bride clapped her hands. 'Here's what's to do.'

'Oh-oh!' Jeff jumped to attention, engaging the nine-year-old instead and making her laugh again.

'Please!' Lynn scolded. 'One more piece of lip out of you and you're going home. You have been warned.'

Anna whooped at her sister's authoritative tone towards her future husband. Playing along, he raised his hands in apology and took a seat in the back row, amid their untidy stack of belongings.

'Yes, boss. Whatever you say, boss.'

The consummate organiser continued, refusing to smile at his antics and irresistible crooning baritone. 'The band'll be here any moment. Lena and I should go upstairs and get our hair and make-up done while you help the band set up and start rehearsing. Michelle's already up there.'

Jeff nodded vehemently before raising a finger and interrupting.

'Yes?'

'You forgot something,' he dared.

'What is it?'

Lynn had fallen for another joke, having replied before her brain had processed it. Figuring she was being toyed with again, she shot him an exasperated glare. His eyes apologised, hoping she wouldn't follow through on her threat to send him home.

Thankfully, the gorgeous creature continued along her original tack. 'And Anns, you can either stay here or come back up, whichever you want. After that, I'll come down and rehearse, either with you or while you're getting changed.'

'Changed? Am I getting changed? Jesus! I didn't know that.'

'Did you bring him, Lena?' his long-suffering girlfriend asked, feigning disgust. 'Why?'

Madalena laughed. 'I tried to leave 'im behind, but he was too fast.'

'Very good!' the tall blonde chuckled at her sister-in-law, who was so much easier to be around now than when she had first arrived.

'I'm sorry, angel,' Jeff said, kissing his beautiful best friend tenderly and running his finger across her left shoulder, tracing her tattoo. 'I'll be good from now on. See what happens when I don't see you for two days? I won't let you down. And I love that, up there.'

He pointed to their special emblem, strung high above the stage, pressing into her tanned skin at the same time. 'And most of all, I love *you*.'

His Regala nodded, her heart melting. 'Yeah. So do I. Great, isn't it? I love you too.'

Anna had sauntered off, fed up with the mushy language and romantic behaviour, now pretending to walk down the aisle with an imaginary *beau*. Madalena had followed her, as if rehearsing the same thing. Fleetingly, Lynn wondered if Jeff's sister thought she might one day get married.

'Are your menfolk here yet?' the groom asked, breaking her out of the daydream. 'Should I check in?'

'No. It's bad luck!' his *fiancée* answered.

'Now who's being facetious?' he scolded back.

'Anns,' Lynn called out. 'Please could you take Lena upstairs to meet Mum? I'll be right there.'

Straightaway, the older woman shot her brother a nervous glance. The youngster turned around eagerly and began to shepherd the thin, dark-haired woman towards the back of the room and the lifts.

'*Vaya, Lena,*' he reassured. 'You're doing great. Just go with the flow.'

In over her head, Madalena obediently returned to the last row of seating and picked up her single plastic bag without a word of protest. The two bridesmaids headed into the lift, and the doors closed to leave the happy couple on their own. At last where he wanted to be, Jeff wrapped the stunning blonde up in his embrace and pressed against her.

'You look fantastic,' he enthused. 'I was so over weddings last night, but today I'm really into it.'

Lynn smiled, her arms tightening around his ribcage. 'I can tell!'

'Sorry, angel. I'll tone it down. I'm keen to let Lena see that we're all a bit nervous and excited.'

'That's your excuse anyway,' his girlfriend teased. 'She doesn't seem hung over. She looks fine.'

The groom grinned. 'She *is* fine. I slipped her half an ecstasy tablet.'

His former private schoolgirl was shocked. 'You did what? Ecstasy? Where did you get that from?'

The ardent lover gave her an apologetic kiss. 'Don't panic. She took it last night. It's out of her system by now. I had two left over from years ago. Gerry and I shared one on my bucks' night because we were both knackered. We'd planned to share the other one last night for the same reason, but Lena was getting drunker and drunker, so I made her take my half.'

'Oh, my God! I'm constantly amazed by you!' Australia's darling exclaimed, not knowing whether to be grateful or angry. 'You're always so inventive. Well... As much as I ought to disapprove, it obviously worked well, so thanks!'

'Hasn't she changed too?'

'Oh, yes. I was going to say that next,' his *fiancée* affirmed. 'So much more open and interactive. You've done a good job.'

'Not just me,' Jeff refused to take full credit for the small triumph. 'It was you and Michelle too, and Jack and Tammy. We've all worked hard on Eliza Doolittle these last few days.'

Lynn nodded. 'I suppose so.'

'She hardly thinks about anything,' the philosopher added.

'Especially compared to her brother,' his muse giggled, 'but I know what you mean.'

'*Touché!* For example though... Christ, it's so good to be able to talk to you again. It's frightening how much I miss talking to you. Almost as much as I miss... Anyway, this morning, I commented that it was nice to wake up without feeling like crap after a night's drinking, and she wasn't even remotely interested in considering an answer. And then, completely out of the blue, she suddenly came out with how she'd always hated the way our mum treated me.'

'Wow,' the compassionate blonde exhaled. 'That must've been good to hear, in that case. What did you say?'

The appreciative performer kissed her lips, his heart feeling as though it were about to burst. 'It wasn't good, to tell you the truth, 'cause it's an out-and-out lie.'

'Oh! Do you really think so? Why did she say it then?'

'Don't rightly know, ma'am,' the comic cloaked his distress in humour yet again and was rewarded by the intimacy of his soul-mate's hand resting on his chest, pressing into the "JL" tattoo. 'I guess she might've believed it when she said it, but she certainly didn't give the impression she hated the way I was treated back in those days.'

Trailing her hand upwards and looping her fingers between his shirt collar and his neck, Lynn squeezed the tense muscles at the base of his skull. 'Let's hope she might think about it a bit more, now that you two've spent this time together.'

'Yeah. That's what I hope too, except if it drags back some of the other shit she'd do well to keep forgotten,' Jeff nodded, then suddenly smiling and fixing his dream girl with a quizzical gaze. 'And hey... D'you wanna hear something spooky?'

'Spooky?' the young woman replied, intrigued. 'Definitely.'

'We were talking about clothes and getting dressed up, and I asked her if she knew the story of "My Fair Lady." It drew a complete *nada*. Zero recognition. And then this morning, there she is singing, "I'm getting married in the morning", just like Stanley Holloway after hormone therapy.'

The singer chuckled and kissed the emotional man's smooth cheek. 'That's funny! You're so gorgeous.'

'Jesus, angel, so are you. And it's unbelievably good to be touching you again,' her boyfriend replied. 'Listen, Lynn... I just have to ask you something.'

'Ask me what?'

'Will you marry me?'

Disconcerted by his sudden change of tone, the young beauty's mouth broke into the widest smile. 'Sure. Why not?' she answered casually. 'Will here at two o'clock be convenient?'

Jeff looked at his watch. 'Could you make it two-ten? I've got to get rid of some other bird first, but then the coast'll be clear for us.'

The sportswoman punched her *fiancé* gently in the stomach, and he made another grab for her body. For a few breathless moments, they stood locked together and staring into each others' eyes before she wrangled herself out of his grip and attempted to thump him again.

'Hey, Mandy, lay off,' he complained, making reference to her character in "Reaching For The Stars", one of the first movies she had made during their time apart.

'I didn't know you'd seen that,' Lynn yelped, surprised but stoked that he made the connection. 'I didn't think it'd be your thing.'

Her Number One fan scowled, kissing her forehead and holding her at arms' length. 'Now come on... Gimme a break, my ray of gorgeousness,' he confessed. 'I may not have admitted it at the time, but too right, I saw it. I hated the plot but loved seeing you in it, even though it killed me to see you with a rev-head boyfriend.'

The star lowered her eyes, ashamed. 'I'm sorry. I did ask for him to be written in deliberately. To remind me of you.'

'Did you?' Jeff checked. 'Whoa. That makes me feel better. Why didn't you ask me to play him?'

This time, Lynn looked straight into her lover's big, brown eyes. 'I would have, believe me. I dreamed about it all the time.'

'What sort of dreams?'

'Those sort of dreams,' the seductress whispered, running her right hand down the front of his jeans.

The red-blooded musician pulled her close, this suggestive little gem quite sufficient to fire him up for what was to come. 'Get lost, angel. You'd better get upstairs before I rip your clothes off in full view of the band.'

'Did you want to come up?' she asked, remembering their early morning conversation.

Her simmering boyfriend exhaled and shook his head. 'No. Well, yes, I do, but it's not right,' he smiled. 'I want you to have the wedding you've been dreaming of, which I'm sure does not include a quick hump in your old bedroom while the others are having their hair done. Not that I'd take much convincing...'

He took hold of her hand and pressed it against his raging erection. 'Get my drift?'

Lynn moved her hand away smartly, also excited by how easily she turned him on. 'Thank you. I really appreciate that.'

Jeff kissed her. 'But go now, because I'll change my mind in less than five seconds.'

Grinning at his sudden urgency, the bride-to-be sprinted to the lift. 'See you for rehearsal!' she shouted back as the doors closed.

***

The mechanism echoed through the empty function room, spiriting the world's most beautiful woman to the top floor and leaving her *fiancé* to pace around for a few minutes in an attempt to calm himself down. The band would be here any minute, and his jeans were far too tight to hide such intense arousal. He walked along the aisle, climbed the six steep steps up onto the stage and sat down at the piano to play the reception's opening number. The lyric was completely appropriate for the way he was now feeling.

As soon as he had reached the first chorus, two lifts opened in quick succession, spilling out a selection of musicians and their instruments. The orchestra was almost assembled by the time he had finished the second song, and his rampant *libido* was successfully banished to the back of his mind.

Sir Bradley Morrison had been engaged as concertmaster and conductor for the occasion, naturally, and the services of several talented Melbourne Academy students past and present were also enlisted. Jeff Diamond greeted everyone in turn, playing the perfect diplomat and thanking them for sharing their special day. They began by rehearsing his solo for the ceremony, which he nailed first time due to his highly-charged emotional state.

'Cheers, guys! That was great. I only hope I can do it like that again when the time comes,' he joked with the session players, after a round of generous applause.

Next, the orchestra rehearsed the inbound and outbound music, which was all new to the rock star and particularly stirring. Perfect, he thought. Lynn knew how he loved a good statement! There was even a *trio* of trumpeters in the back row whose role was to announce the bride and her father's procession up the aisle, the vision of which moved the young man to tears.

And to think that at last night's party he had wished this all over with! No question about it, getting married had been a prodigious decision, and today was shaping up to be a very good day indeed.

Various camera crews were in the process of setting up too; five full-scale television cameras scattered around the ballroom, together with one more in the lobby downstairs to capture the bridal party's arrival. The couple had shared a laugh at the lack of authenticity of this particular stunt, since the family were already in the building, but agreed that a short circuit of the streets behind St Kilda Road would add custom-designed mystique to the memorable footage.

Soundchecks were soon signed off, apart from those for Lynn's vocals and the choir, as the star was reliably informed by Sir Brad. Choir? Were there going to be hymns? Backing singers, the veteran *impresario* corrected himself, to the younger man's great relief.

Lynn reappeared at midday, made up and complete with an exotically-sculpted hairstyle. Her boyfriend liked what he saw, whistling as she walked towards them, although the sophisticated look above the neck looked odd atop her jeans and thongs. The couple quickly ran through their duet for the ceremony and decided where each person should stand and how they would link one number to the next.

During this part of the rehearsal, lunch was served to everyone by uniformed catering staff. The groom found himself unexpectedly ravenous, high on adrenalin. His blushing bride-to-be, on the other hand, elected to steer clear of too much food, for even the woman who had spent her whole life in front of cameras had now become slightly anxious.

'How's Lena doing?' Jeff asked in a quiet moment. 'I can't go up, can I?'

'No, it's...' Lynn started to reply.

'I know,' he stopped her, kissing her tense cheek. 'It's bad luck. It's OK. I just don't want her to freak out and become a handful.'

'Michelle's up there. If there's any problem, Mum'll send Anna down with a code word.'

'A code word?' the amused man smiled. 'What? Like *culo*, or something?'

The gorgeous blonde nodded, grinning. 'Yes, or "bastards". She's already said that at least five times.'

Jeff grimaced. 'Jeez! Sorry about that. Hey, I didn't tell you about Tim.'

'Who's Tim?' the twenty-year-old asked, keen to catch up on the events of the last couple of days.

Memories of the unfortunate party guest were almost too hard to describe in the compressed amount of time available at this moment. The host of the New Year's Eve dinner was unable to stop himself from sniggering when he remembered the forlorn face of his sister's fleeced client lolling from side to side in the back of the taxi.

'Last night, while I was 'phoning you, Lena hooked up with this extremely pissed bloke. Then I gave her the tablet, and she straightened out after a while.

They'd planned on going back to his place, but by that time, he was sick as a dog. We ended up dropping him home in a taxi. Then, to add insult to injury for the poor loser, on the way back to the apartment, she starts pulling all this money out of her bra. She'd made sure she got her fee upfront.'

'Really? Oh, my God! What did you say?'

The cynic chuckled. 'I gave her a hard time. I said we'd have to give it back somehow.'

'But how?' the horrified woman was entranced.

Her partner looked sheepish. 'Yeah, well... This is the part you may not like...'

The bride looked slightly worried. 'Go on.'

'She invited him here,' he confessed with a half-smile. 'I said not 'til after five.'

Lynn's eyes widened in amazement. 'I see! Oh, well... I'd love to meet him, even if there's no place for him on the top table.'

'I doubt he'll turn up. He was off his face. He won't remember. And even if he remembers Lena, he won't know where to come.'

'But what about the money?'

'Oh, yeah,' the storyteller nodded. 'Well, if he doesn't turn up, I told her we'd have to drive back round to where we dropped him off and try to find out where he lives. Impossible, I know, but I wanted to hammer it home to her that she shouldn't fleece people like that. She's right though, I guess... He was dumb enough to pay in advance. Why should she give him his money back? They hardly signed a contract.'

'*Caveat emptor*!' the keen businesswoman laughed. 'My economics teacher would be proud of her.'

'Quite,' her handsome Doctor of Philosophy agreed. 'Good case study, huh?'

Lynn stole a glance at Jeff's watch. 'Yikes! Look at the time. You'd better get changed. Are you OK in the Gents or do you want to go upstairs?'

The young millionnaire burst out laughing, raising both hands in the air and distracting the musicians within earshot. 'There are so many angles I could approach that from.'

'What do you mean?' his *fiancée* asked, filled with joy at her man's obvious happiness.

'Well... First, you get the penthouse and I get the Gents behind the bar. That's very B-grade band, now isn't it?'

The stunning superstar looked shameful. 'Sorry. I see what you mean.'

'And then there's an invitation upstairs,' her court jester continued, 'when you got me in such a state last time and then just ran off, so now I have to go through that same agony all over again because there's not enough time.'

The refined young lady sighed. 'I'm sorry. It was selfish, I admit.'

'Nonsense, angel,' he kissed the back of her outstretched hand, dropping the act. 'It's perfect. It's just how I would've wanted us to be today. Ignore me. I'm just having a whinge to wind you up. And I'm about as randy as a man can get.'

The lift bell sounded as Jeff spoke, spilling little Anna out at a run. The pair froze, fearing the worst. Was this a code word on its way?

'Gerry's here!' the flower-girl announced to her future brother-in-law. 'He needs to get up from reception. Mum asked if you can go.'

The couple breathed a shared sigh of relief. 'Thanks, Anna. Sure. I'll go down right now.'

Lynn put her hand on Jeff's chest again, feeling his rapid heartbeat just under the surface. The gymnast turned tail, her message delivered, and ascended to the top floor again.

'Thank Christ for that,' the groom gasped. 'You have a habit of giving such accurate forecasts of what's going to happen that they almost become a premonition.'

'No dramas, thankfully. Relax!' his beautiful best friend grinned. 'Are you bringing the Blakes in here?'

'Yeah. I was going to,' he replied. 'Is that OK?'

His girlfriend nodded. 'Yes. Or they could come upstairs. Dad and the boys are up there, probably watching the cricket.'

'Can I come and watch the cricket too?'

'No.'

The sports fan frowned and shook his head, eyebrows raised in jest. 'Worth a try! They can have the choice then. Gerry needs to come here though, because we'll be walking through soon, I guess.'

To his very pleasant surprise, his pristine bride kissed him on the lips, albeit lightly due to her precision make-over. 'Perfect! I'll go up again then. I love you heaps and heaps and heaps.'

They both walked towards the lifts, selecting a button for each direction. Lynn's carriage arrived first, fittingly, and the lovesick actor made a big fuss of seeing his lover off. He caught the same lift on its way back down and descended to a lobby filled with Blakes, all smashingly smart in their wedding regalia.

Feeling emotional that his surrogate family were with him, Jeff opened his arms when he emerged from the lift to a row of excited smiles. The best man had assumed a supreme air, proud of his role in the proceedings, and was strutting about like King Rat. Michael let the group through, as courteous as ever, wishing them good luck for the happy occasion.

'Hey, guys! Welcome to the rest of my life.'

'Oh, look at that smile on your face!' Celia gushed, immediately moved to tears. 'And so relaxed.'

Jacinta agreed, embracing the groom at the first opportunity. 'Wow! You shouldn't be this chilled. You should be having kittens and practising your vows.'

Her brother's oldest friend shook his head. 'Kitten-free zone here, Jack. Come on up. Now, everyone except Gerry,' he explained, 'you can either go up-top to the apartments and join the Dysons for a drink or you can mill around down here and watch us finish rehearsing. Up to you...'

Celia and her daughters preferred not to see the run-through, lest it diminish the splendour of the real thing, so they chose the penthouse. Gerald decided it would be best to join them, a ready thirst most likely proving the stronger driver.

'And what is my fate, oh master?' their son enquired.

'You have to come to the Gents and watch me get changed.'

'Ooh!' shrieked the younger sister. 'You never gave us that option!'

'No. And for good reason, Tammy,' their mother scolded. 'Don't be silly, dears. Let's go up. The bridegroom's busy.'

Pulling a face behind the mother hen's back, Jeff pushed the buttons in the lift, and they started upwards. 'Lynn'll be up there waiting for you. She'll introduce you to the others.'

The doors opened into the function suite, treating the Blakes to a sneak preview of the venue. Groom and best man alighted and were left staring at each other while the rest travelled on up to the penthouse level.

'Well... This is it, mate,' Gerry said, slapping his buddy's shoulder. 'How does it feel?'

'Bloody fantastic! Everything's perfect. It's going to be great. How about you?'

'Mate! That little pill!' the star's manager exclaimed. 'I must procure a handy supply to keep in reserve. I was a smidge off-colour first thing, but now I'm firing on all cylinders.'

The suave Irishman's biggest client led him between the rows of seating and up to the stage, pointing to where he assumed they would be sitting and from where the vows would be spoken. 'We're going to rehearse in about fifteen minutes. Our bit's pretty simple. We just stand here and wait for the trumpets.'

Gerry guffawed in his usual bombastic style. 'Wait for the trumpets? Sounds more like a West Indies test match than a wedding. Or the entrance to the pearly gates...'

'Neither, mate,' his artistic companion corrected, laughing at the diametrically-opposed analogies. 'Not quite. William Walton's Crown Imperial March, if you're interested.'

'Right,' the older man pulled himself together. 'Apologies, vicar.'

The unusually pedantic songwriter lightened up. 'Then we say something, then we sing something, and at some point the judge dude'll ask you for the rings. Have you got the rings?'

Gerry tapped the breast pocket of his jacket.

'Good stuff,' the groom said, relieved. 'Then we say more lines, sing another song and walk out together. Married. End of story.'

'And then you fuck.'

Jeff gave the smutty executive another hard stare. 'Jesus! I wish!'

'A tad lion rampant after the other night, are we?' the accountant joked.

'Shit, yeah! I'd even go for you right at this moment,' the younger man admitted, lunging forward with open arms. 'They don't call it "Best Man" for nothing, you know.'

'Piss off!' Gerry scoffed, wheeling around. 'Is that why you told me I was to accompany you to the Gents?'

The musician chuckled, glancing down at his watch. 'Got it in one! Talking of which, I really do need to get ready. You can come with me or you can stay here. Either way, you're safe this time, mate. I need you fresh for my sister.'

His friend groaned before clapping his hands and heading in the direction of the restrooms. Feeling nervous again, the groom grabbed his suit carrier, and the two men adjourned to complete the transformation. Ten minutes later, they emerged both suited up and looking a million dollars, a handsome and striking pair. The Dyson-Diamond celebrity merger was surely a wedding photographer's dream, with such a photogenic bunch of people all lining up together.

'How's your sis' going?' the best man asked, admiring the groom's cufflinks. 'Did she pull up OK?'

'Yep. She's been pretty cool this morning,' Jeff answered. 'Bloody delightful, in fact. I swear she's a different person to the one we flew down with. I've got a funny story to tell you later too. Make your hair curl, as your mum would say…'

Gerry was interested to hear more but noticed that his friend's attention had already wandered elsewhere. Lynn had reappeared in the ballroom while they had been hidden away and was now rehearsing a brand new song. The two men stood behind the last row of chairs, mesmerised by the sound of her magnificent voice singing out over sweeping strings.

The groom felt himself becoming aroused for the third time in a very short space of time. Jesus! He was would soon be reduced to a gibbering wreck if this were to continue for much longer.

'I can't watch this,' he said, turning and walking away. 'Let's go outside and have a quick ciggie.'

Gerry approved wholeheartedly of this latest diversionary tactic, but it proved doomed before they had even made it to the exit. The downward-travelling lift that opened on their floor contained the whole upstairs contingent arriving to practise their parts in the ceremony, with all three bridesmaids in tow.

The two men shrugged at each other in resignation and joined the procession that was soon walking up the aisle in a strange form of mess drill. Lynn stopped singing when the *troupe* reached the stage, causing Sir Brad to crane his neck around to find the reason for her silence. With his baton signalling for the orchestra to cease playing, he declared a five-minute recess.

Madalena was calm and happy, chatting merrily with Michelle and Anna, her black hair sleek and stylish and made up almost imperceptibly. She beamed at her brother, clearly most pleased with the result of the last hour's efforts.

'*¿Te gusto?*'

Jeff whistled. '*Madalena Moreno, pareces absolumente hermosa. ¡Bellíssima, chica. Mucha' bellíssima!*'

He kissed the Hispanic beauty on the cheek and squeezed her hand. She really did look the part; classy, even. In place of the awkward, clueless overgrown adolescent he had brought with him this morning, he saw a grown woman who belonged in the gentrified set, her confidence also having increased in leaps and bounds. She held her head higher and her back straighter, and the expression on her face was nearly warm.

Lynn issued a knowing smile as she strolled arm-in-arm with her mother and the maid of honour. She knew how important this moment was to her humble, worried and totally gorgeous boyfriend. They had taken a considerable risk by including his sister in the ceremony, but everything was working out terrifically so far. Marianna had been disturbed at first by how unpolished Madalena was, especially in comparison with her younger brother's impeccable manners. However, with steady cajoling and a few sideways glances, they had all warmed to each other as a mutual understanding grew.

Anna was the only member of the bridal party who was already fully dressed. Jeff took her hand, a whistle complimenting her beauty too, and she walked proudly on the other side of her tall, good-looking brother-in-law elect.

'You look great, Anna,' he praised. 'How come no-one else but you and I managed to get changed in time?'

'It's a surprise!' the young girl whispered. 'They can't show you their dresses until they walk up the aisle.'

'Ah, I see,' her chaperone feigned ignorance. 'Is that right? Then Gerry and I should get changed again too. I'll put my jeans back on.'

'No,' Celia interrupted. 'You two look very smart. Don't they, Lynn?'

The smiling blonde released her arms and span around to check out the view. 'Definitely! Extremely handsome. My beautiful black stallion!'

'Thank you. You're very kind,' the accountant quipped. 'And who's he? Your broken-down, old nag?'

Everyone laughed, and the groom magnanimously accepted his fate. Arriving at the lectern, Bart introduced Jeff and Gerry to the gentleman who was to preside over the ceremony. Donald Rhodes-Boyson was another of the city's elder statesmen; a Supreme Court judge and before that, an outstanding barrister. All four men shook hands while the musicians shuffled back into their positions on the stage and began tuning up.

From the other end of the aisle, the bride scanned the scene. 'Where's Dad?'

She located her father and beckoned him back down so that the rehearsal could commence. Sir Brad instructed the orchestra to play from forty bars into the march, and the expansive melody filled the space. Above the sound, the family picked up a cheer from the crowd outside, triggering more happy laughter.

On cue, the three trumpeters did their thing, and the flamboyant conductor turned round to give the bride and her father a deliberate nod, before cutting the music dead and claiming success. The tension beginning to sap their energy, Jeff and Gerry sat down while the celebrant talked them all through the sequence of events. Lynn and Bart perched on the left-hand side about six rows back from the others, no doubt also sensing the electricity buzzing in the atmosphere.

Once they were all clear on their responsibilities and the procession's timing, Judge Rhodes-Boyson dismissed the ladies to go back upstairs and continue the beautification process.

The groom caught his sister's arm. 'You OK?'

'Yeah. I love it!' came the reply he was hoping for. 'I don't look like me no more.'

'Cool,' he replied. 'You do look like you. Stunning, Lena. Your picture's going to be in the 'papers tomorrow. ¿Sabes?'

Madalena drew a sharp breath and immediately walked taller still, chasing after Michelle in her high heels. Lynn had overheard the brother's encouragement, always intent on motivating people to give of their best. How she loved this man!

Jeff noticed the dreamy expression on the singer's face. He winked but said nothing, knowing she was deliberately keeping her distance. The anticipation was excruciating, serving a much more carnal purpose than merely assuaging her mother's superstition, and he wouldn't have had it any other way. He watched with a soaring heart as the close-knit group of attractive women returned on high. The next time he saw the girl of his dreams would be heralded by the Walton fanfare bona fide.

His head swimming, the musician had all but forgotten it was their wedding day during the frenetic production process, its format so similar to a sound check for any other big concert involving orchestral musicians and a choir. The grand purpose to all this fuss had become lost over the last half-hour. To his right, Gerry was busy conversing with Lynn's father and the judge, leaving the rock star to gather his own thoughts. Was there a jury going to issue a verdict for Bart Dyson's daughter's marriage too? He wondered if someone might utter an objection in the legally-prescribed hiatus. It was an unlikely prospect, but Gravity's lingering paranoia made him shudder regardless.

The seasoned performer stimulated a compensatory shot of adrenalin by bounding up onto the stage alone. From his elevated post, he stood looking towards the door through which Big D would shortly deliver his prize to the rest of their life singular. They had written this catchphrase, now so much part of their identity, into their vows. He breathed in and out slowly several times, making sure every last ounce of this special day sunk into the depths of his soul.

So the pauper was the prince today; Cinderella in reverse, but with no pumpkin or white mice. Just a poor boy ready to wear a crown at the swish of an angel's magic wand.

Feeling suddenly light-headed, Jeff crouched down at the front of the stage. It was familiar territory for him, and yet at that moment he felt extremely exposed. He didn't really understand why. He wasn't insecure; not for a minute doubting his own commitment or that he deserved what he was about to receive. The crown would fit him perfectly because he had played a part in its design. He had earned the right to marry Lynn Dyson, fair and square. This wasn't a lottery, nor had he won her hand in a duel. With her eyes wide open, she had agreed to walk through the fire with him, to have his children and to help him change the world.

Nothing should be different tomorrow but yet somehow, standing up here, the boy from Sydney's western suburbs succumbed to the strangest feeling that everything would be different. He looked at his watch again: one-thirty. Their guests must already be gathering downstairs in reception, drinking cocktails and eager to be given permission to ascend to Level One. He imagined the frantic scene up on the penthouse floor, with the girls zipping, buttoning and lacing themselves into their gowns, their painted lips no doubt sipping champagne with Celia, Jacinta and Tamilla. Not an ugly sister in sight!

The lost boy was glad that he had some sort of pseudo-parental representation at his wedding. Truth be told, he was so much more pleased to have the Blakes here than his own parents. He wondered what havoc might have been visited on the aristocratic family if Paul and Lucy Diamond had still been part of his life. Jesus Christ! It didn't bear thinking about! Madalena was a breeze compared to the litany of disastrous calamities they could have wreaked on Lynn's special day.

Jeff heard the double doors to the reception area swing open, convinced they were stealing his air. Sure enough, a slow tide of people began to file in, dressed in their finery and exchanging greetings this way and that. Picking out a number of well-known public faces and a few familiar private ones, he descended to floor level, not wishing to attract attention to himself. Again, he became aware of the noise of the crowd outside too and wondered what vision their devotees were being treated to on the screens Lynn had requested at the last minute. Only those close to the front would be able to see them, but doubtless any news would spread fast.

As more and more guests chose their spots and began to take their seats, the groom realised that his side of the hall was more densely populated than he had expected. Where were they all coming from? Rent-a-crowd? Rent-a-family, more like! Was this another secret his angelic project manager had kept from him?

The Sydneysider became yet more suspicious when he spotted an old gentleman bent over on a walking stick. It couldn't be... He looked more carefully, seeing there was a woman with him. It was Alberto Santos Fernandez and his daughter, Eva. Dumbfounded, the superstar jogged over to greet them, wondering how on Earth they had managed to sneak onto the guest list without his knowledge.

His former high school teacher was the next surprise; the one whose leather jacket had been stolen and then retrieved on the promise of Applied Mathematics. Yvonne Hawkins was sitting next to Suzanne and Steve, who waved him over. The string of coincidences began to blur his senses, he felt almost scared of overlooking someone important. He could murder a cigarette! John Francis and his wife were there, as planned, but so were three of Jeff's student mates from London. This scheming bride of his had a lot to answer for, as had Cathy and the others in the office, whom he suspected must have provided considerable assistance.

The elated groom found Gerry and thanked him for being his best man, which was really only an excuse for a manly embrace to steady the nerves. The two *amigos* took their seats in the first row, stage right, in front of the rest of the Blake family. Both old flames blew him lucky kisses. Assuring them that no luck was required, he accepted their affection with a sexy half-smile in full view of their parents.

The orchestra and band were soon in position, and following another brief tune-up, Sir Bradley's *baton* was poised for the start of the Walton Overture and March. Jeff threw his head back and let the sound of violins and *'celli* wash over him, breathing steadily in and out. He wasn't nervous after all; simply chock full of emotion. He felt Celia's maternal fingers press against his back, but there was no way he could turn to look at her without them both dissolving into tears.

***

A riverside cheer louder than any heard to this point was suddenly relayed across the speakers. The swollen crowd had gone wild at the sight of the beautiful bride and her father arriving at the steps of the building in a dignified carriage and pair, in perennial Melbourne tradition. Within a few minutes, a similar *brouhaha* erupted when the cameras showed them emerging from the lift and approaching the rear of the ballroom to begin their procession. The bridesmaids filed in behind, supervised by Michelle England, who lifted her best friend's train and spread its full length between them.

Animated chatter tapered off as more and more guests readied themselves for the bridal party's entrance, the atmosphere buzzing with electric excitement. All heads were turned, craning their necks to catch the romantic *vista* when the doors opened. All heads, that was, except those of the groom and his best man.

Trumpets will sound, as the saying goes.

'This is it,' Jeff whispered, struck by another electrifying moment of disbelief. 'She's here.'

Doctor Rhodes-Boyson gave the two close friends a sign to rise to their feet, and the guests gasped in unison at the sight of the tall, statuesque figure of Jeff Diamond standing with his best mate by his side. He shook Gerry's hand one last time as a single man. The Irishman patted his breast pocket, as if to say, "All set".

Eyes front, stomach in knots and heart pounding, the twenty-three-year-old visualised the glorious spectacle unfolding behind him, making its way towards him in time to the stately two-step. There was another gasp from the congregation, along with the sound of several camera shutters, presumably coinciding with the first close-up of the bride. He could hear whispers and oohs and ahhs rippling closer and closer, which could only mean that Lynn and Bart were on their way.

Christ, he hoped so. The old soul had never hoped for anything so hard in his life.

The former nobody from Canley Vale pictured his gangly sister trying to walk slowly and with adequate poise, along with Michelle and little Anna. Had any of the dignitaries found out what she did for a living yet? The lawyer, the prostitute and the gymnast, he chuckled to himself, drawing a strange look from his mate. How resplendent his big sister looked today, and how happy! A tear rolled down his left cheek at an impromptu memory of her distraught teenaged face at their mother's funeral. He quickly wiped it away, hoping no-one had noticed.

So where was his soul-mate now? Jeff could feel their invisible elastic connection slackening until she was right behind him. His heartbeat was mighty loud in his ears, and he took several more deep breaths in an attempt to temper its runaway pace. How would he find the composure to sing with all this energy coursing through him? Or even speak, for that matter!

The bride now stood at her groom's side, shoulder to shoulder. She was wearing a long, flowing, silk dress of a colour so close to white but without being white. From the briefest glimpse the sex-starved man permitted himself, it clung to every curve of her body and shimmered as she moved. No veil covered her face, and her eyes shone in declaration to the world. She was overjoyed to be standing next to the man who had chosen her.

Assuming all members of the bridal party were in their rightful places, the groom indulged in a longer look to his left. He feasted his eyes on the most exquisite sight he had ever seen: a woman at once dazzling and adorable. Her smile was more inviting than ever, greeting him with more delight and promise than he could handle. Here was his gift from heaven, and he was about to claim her forever.

Astounded that he had managed such minuscule muscle coordination, Jeff winked at his dream girl as if in total control of his faculties. Lynn's right hand brushed his left, and he instinctively wrapped them up together. He stole a glance down at the intertwined fingers, some with nail polish and some without, before looking back into those gorgeous, blue eyes.

The grey-haired celebrant cleared his throat and pushed his steel-rimmed spectacles up the bridge of his nose while surveying his subjects. Jeff sensed more than a touch of eccentricity under the man's businesslike carapace. Was he about to pronounce one of them guilty of a crime? He began to recite the script which had been finalised a few weeks previously, one rainy autumn day under a tree on Hampstead Heath. Both bride and groom knew the missive by heart, soon reaching the part when the judge asked who was to give this woman to this man. The old soul gripped his Regala's hand, then inhaled sharply as Gerry placed an unexpected hand on his right shoulder.

'I do,' came the resounding *timbre* of Bart Dyson's unmistakeable voice, clear and proud.

The rebel was sure he heard the tiniest sigh from his beautiful best friend and leaned sideways until their upper arms made contact. There had been a transfer from man to man after all, despite the progressive couple's attempts to reject the concept of betrothal and all such symbols of female subservience.

Lynn Dyson had been given and received, and by the grin on her face, was quite happy with the transaction. It had been her choice to be exchanged by her original owner, as their vows attested, much to the amusement of those gathered around them. Equally, it was now incumbent upon her new master to enable the fulfilment of her every dream.

As the stalwart stepped back, receiver's dark brown eyes fixed giver's grey-blue ones and nodded subtly. The gesture was returned. Lynn would tell Jeff afterwards that in their earlier rehearsal, when asked who was giving away the bride, her father had said, "That'd be me," and she had found it virtually impossible not to laugh this time, expecting him to say the same thing again in front of his old school-friend, Rhodes-Boyson.

Back in the moment however, the young woman thought she could hear her mother crying behind her, hypnotised by a magical force and content to hang on to her man's hand. The groom, in turn, sneaked a look over his shoulder to check on Madalena. Along with everyone else, she stood transfixed, half a head taller than Michelle. The adult bridesmaids' dresses were a pale apricot colour, and the pair held their chins high like ballerinas next to little Anna, who deserved full marks for cuteness, as per usual.

The celebrant was by now speaking directly to the bride and groom. Reaching the moment when they were to put their lifelong promises on public record, the tension instantly drained from Jeff's neck and shoulders. It was as if he had popped another ecstasy pill, which was exactly what had happened in the metaphorical world. From inside his surreal bubble, the former lost boy heard his dream girl's voice ring out next to him as clear as crystal.

'I, Victoria Lynn Shannon Dyson, take you, Jeffrey Moreno Diamond, to be my lawful husband...'

The rest of the bride's vow followed, flawlessly articulated yet a blur to her intended, captured for posterity and to be replayed properly more than a month later from a video tape. Their names had been spoken in the same sentence as the word "husband", and that would do, his brain told him. It had no need to hear more.

Jeff squeezed her hand, knowing that the judge was about to turn and ask the same of him.

'I, Jeffrey Moreno Diamond, take you, Victoria Lynn Shannon Dyson, to be my lawful wife and my only lover; to honour and cherish, to love and protect, throughout this life singular and forever.'

Jeff's sonorous, ever-confident vocal rendition was unequivocal, enunciating the words smoothly and without hesitation. Determined to taste every single syllable of this one-time commitment, he had no idea how he had managed to speak so fluently, but his statement had been made aloud and in perpetuity.

From outside along the promenade, not to mention in front of television sets all over the country, a tremendous roar of appreciation vibrated through the assembly. The official invitees clapped in a ripple of polite spontaneity, making Anna giggle behind the happy couple. The bride shot her man a loving glance, the first part of the deal duly done.

Judge Rhodes-Boyson then asked the guests to be seated, and the orchestra began to play Saint-Saëns' *Maestoso*. A robust man in black, who would usually be described as a roadie but who today was dressed more like an undertaker, handed microphones to the musical superstars in preparation for their first song as a partially-married couple.

The groom was under strict instructions not to kiss his bride even though he so dearly wanted to. They both cleared their throats before turning the volume up, giving each other a smile to mark the transition to their professional selves.

Transferring their attention to Sir Brad and his rhythm stick, The Australian Elvis was confident of making it through for the required duration, before the fuse burned out and he returned to his gibbering wreck self. But for now he had work to do...

The chart-topping couple sang their hearts out with no trace of nerves, backed by the small chorus which Lynn had arranged with her former musical director. They sang to each other, like they had done so many times before, turning to the audience of their loved and respected ones and repeating the specially-penned words over again. The groom again resisted an overwhelming temptation to break protocol and kiss those appetising, ruby lips, as he had threatened in rehearsals when the music faded, and they ended the song hand-in-hand, microphones raised to the roof.

The guests rose as one when the orchestra fell silent, clapping and uttering muted *encores* and *bravos*, befitting the occasion. Beyond the stout walls however, an infinitely more boisterous reception invaded the ballroom and set it buzzing with joyful chatter. The judge paused before continuing the ceremony for decorum to reign once again.

Jeff looked over towards the three bridesmaids, who had taken their seats to the side of the celebrant, in front of the Dyson clan. Madalena, Michelle and Anna were simmering with latent hysteria, holding each others' hands and scanning the colourful scene in anticipation. The flower-girl waved in response to a wink from the handsome star, causing a ripple of laughter through the congregation when the furtive exchange was relayed by the camera trained on them.

Scarcely having caught their breath and with the melody still ringing in their ears, the bride and groom were summoned back into position by Doctor Rhodes-Boyson for the ring ceremony. Michelle, already attentive at her friend's side, whimpered when Gerry was invited to be upstanding and present the shining bands of gold.

The rock star watched his best man carefully place the two rings onto a velvet cushion held by the maid of honour, never having seen him so sombre or deep in concentration. He then winked at his bride, who was following every minute movement, and she flashed him a heart-starting smile in return. He pressed the heel of his curled hand against his heart as an expression of emotional overload, hearing an involuntary gasp from Lynn's mother in the foreground and then several hundred more from other women at varying distances as his gesture was broadcast far and wide.

Indeed, to the couple's left, Marianna was dabbing her eyes. To their right, Celia was doing the same. As the faintest accompaniment of Beethoven's Pastoral Sonata began, the couple turned to face each other, and the judge continued with the official service. From the first row in the stalls to the piano playing in the bar, scarcely a whisper could be heard. The entire congregation was holding its breath.

First, the groom lifted the smaller ring from its resting place and twisted it onto his dream girl's long, slender finger. He toyed with everyone for a split second, conscious of the camera's lens only centimetres behind his shoulder, making the deliberate mistake of choosing the broader of the two. A collective gulp blew warm from the front rows, yet Jeff remained resolute. His bride's elegant left hand flexed its myriad tiny muscles once the band was in position, the brilliant stones in her engagement ring catching the light and illuminating the gold of her plain wedding band.

After savouring the moment and whispering her loving thanks, Lynn reached for the remaining eye-catching circle and wound it onto her lover's finger, squeezing his hand affectionately. In contrast to her very feminine hand movement a few seconds ago, the passionate powder-keg at her side clenched his fist before opening it out again and expelling a deep sigh of contentment.

The pair gazed into each others' eyes and spoke their second vow in unison. 'This ring is a symbol of my never-ending love for you. It's the circle of life. Just as we came from our parents, it signifies our chance to give life to the future. With it, I promise my unending commitment to your happiness and to the happiness of our children.'

The guests were spellbound, the silence broken only by a few nervous coughs and a rumble of satisfaction from the boulevard beyond. After giving everyone time for reflection, Judge Rhodes-Boyson broke the trance.

'Jeff Diamond and Lynn Dyson, I now pronounce you husband and wife.'

The commotion from fans lining St Kilda Road was louder than ever. Not to be outdone this time, those inside began to applaud and cheer as the long-awaited kiss took place. The boy from Canley Vale moulded his left hand round his new wife's bare shoulder and pulled her towards him, bending slightly until their mouths locked together for what felt like an eternity. Lynn could imagine her younger sister voicing her opinion of such revolting behaviour, and the corners of her mouth curled up against her man's determined lips.

'What are you smiling at?'

'Just wondering what Anna's thinking,' she whispered in return.

The groom kissed his gracious prize for a second time with even greater adoration. Their invited guests clapped for a second time, accompanying the couple's stately progress to the side of the stage, where a desk had been set up for signing the register. In a valiant effort to capture the happy couple in the act, a cameraman almost tripped over Doctor Rhodes-Boyson, who was waiting to offer a chair to the bride.

Hanging back until the bridesmaids had fussed around, reapplying lipstick to lips which were still tingling, Lynn Dyson's handsome husband surveyed the scene before them. It felt surreal to be looking over so many of the most important people in their life, with the faces of his bride's fellow musicians gathered around the piano. The singer had asked her three famous friends to perform JS Bach's "Sheep May Safely Graze", and the mellow tones of a great instrument in expert hands drew more audible admiration from the congregation.

Janice's trademarked *vibrato* had been pared down to a minimum for this simple choral piece, and a pure, angelic *soprano* voice swirled around the hall. For several seconds, the entire bridal party stood stock still in front of the certificates that would seal the deal on the marriage, Lynn's eyes shining full of tears as the celebrant handed her his fountain pen.

Jeff sat down beside his bride and put his arm around her. Every last detail had been considered, he realised, right down to his positioning at the table, in order that the right-hander might transfer the pen to the left-hander without the need for a change of camera angle. The gorgeous creature leaned into his body, letting out a stifled sob, and stared at the stage in appreciation of her longtime friends' talents.

'Take as long as you want, angel,' he whispered. 'This is your day. You are so beautiful.'

The young woman smiled. 'Thank you. This is perfect. I love you.'

With these most genuine of utterances, the star's familiar autograph flowed effortlessly onto the page. Memories came flooding back to the ambitious songwriter of the day his dream girl had signed his hairy chest in a pledge to jump on the runaway train which was propelling his life in the general direction of bigger and better things, and he exhaled sharply as she handed him the pen.

'I love you too. *Bienvenue à notre vie singulière, Señora Dyson Diamond. Tout ce qu'il faut pour te rendre heureuse, c'est à moi maintenant.*'

The choir made its entry for the final verse and broadened the piece out to its full four voices, together with two flutes and two *'celli*. The obligatory photographs in front of the register posed and taken, Jeff rose to his feet and rested his hand with the perfect amount of force on his wife's bare shoulder to prompt her to do the same.

Just as Lynn had come to expect from her chivalrous partner, as soon as her weight shifted forwards onto her feet, the chair slid away and she was free to stand and enjoy the music. They moved to one side to allow Gerry and Michelle to sign as their witnesses. A bolt of electricity shot through them both when her husband's right arm reached behind her, coming to rest on the point of her right hip.

The groom emitted a muffled whistle. 'Did you feel that too?'

'Yes. You're gorgeous. Look at Mum and Dad.'

Following her bright, blue eyes, the songwriter glanced across the floor of the ballroom. Bart had manœuvred his wife in front of his body, probably initially so that she could get a better view, and all four hands were clasped together. His lips appeared to be kissing the back of Marianna's head, and even from this distance, their happiness was transparent.

'Did sheep graze at their wedding too?' Jeff whispered. 'Is that why you picked it?'

'Partly,' the giggling daughter affirmed, 'but I love it anyway.'

Shortly before the song came to its peaceful conclusion, Richard Kerr's eyes lifted from the piano and caught those of his former school-mate. Lynn's furtive right hand acknowledged his smile, and a ripple of amusement ran round those close by. Conducting with his head, the accomplished pianist rounded out the final *rallentando*, which hung like a fine mist over their heads.

The bride and groom led the applause, back in concert mode again, before gracefully crossing the stage to thank their friends. A lingering echo set the mood perfectly for the rest of the proceedings, and the same smartly-dressed roadie presented the dark-haired superstar with another microphone. He let go of Lynn's hand one finger at a time and backed away, watching her being escorted from the stage by her school-friends.

The first solo of the evening was the eventual winner from an original selection of twelve short-listed songs, and the romantic poet had constructed it carefully to tell the right story to the assembly. The conductor's podium had been stealthily carried to one side, leaving two cameras trained directly onto Jeff. Sitting centre-stage at the piano and in full view of their guests, he took a gulp of water from a glass on a table hidden behind the gleaming black instrument and declared his intentions with a stirring introductory chord.

Lynn had taken a seat in front of her family to listen to the song she already knew very well yet couldn't wait to hear in this expansive auditorium. Her bridesmaids closed ranks, eager to see the new ring. She gazed out over the many friendly faces and issued radiance upon everyone with whom she made eye contact.

The rock star, who so rarely sat still at the piano on stage, sang and played with such emotive honesty that he had the audience in the palm of his hand by the middle of the first verse. All prior nerves banished, his gaze ranged from left to right and from front to back, all the while mindful of the loyal fans who had spent the whole day in the sun, hoping to share in the magic.

Singing the final chorus exactly as the musician had envisaged over the last few weeks, his beautiful best friend's eyes were filled with tears of joy. How he longed to reach out and touch her, making do with the piano keys against his hyper-sensitive fingertips instead. He remained seated until the last bass note faded to nothing before standing up and saluting his new bride with the noblest of subtle nods.

Those present were on their feet, clapping enthusiastically and enthralled by the depth of feeling expressed in the song, introducing a whole new dimension of talent to those normally on display at his live concerts. Jeff gave an understated bow and thanked them for their warm reception, gesturing to the camera with arms aloft in a similar message to those outside.

Running his fingers through his hair and catching the glint of his new ring out of the corner of his eye, the handsome singer strode to the front of the stage to transfer the show's spotlight elsewhere. It was Lynn's turn to woo their friends now, and his turn to take a seat and absorb the ambiance. He put on his best *compère's* voice and announced the song on his partner's behalf.

'Thank you. Whoa, that felt good! Now, you're going to love this next song. Lynn wrote it after she accepted my proposal, and I asked her to include it in today's ceremony. It's called "Two Fires, One Flame", and I love it. I'm sure you will too. Ladies and gentlemen, I give you Lynn ... Dyson ... Diamond.'

Jeff enunciated the revised string of names as slowly and as categorically as he possibly could, both to cement them into the audience's collective psyche and to convince himself that the transformation had actually taken place. This stunning woman was now his wife.

More cheering and applause greeted the angelic figure as she floated gracefully up the stairs, with Michelle and Madalena frantically straightening the train of her dress so that it didn't tangle on its way. The groom had moved to the top of the steps to pass over the microphone and lead her to centre-stage, where he was to accompany her on the piano. They kissed again quickly, twice for luck, and he took his place again. Never happier than at this moment, both performers awaited the conductor's cue.

Lynn began softly, singing directly into her man's eyes before turning to face the rows of seating. The volume of her soulful *contralto* voice slowly increased as the lyric's intensity built. Equally heartfelt, her composition was expressive and a fitting complement to the first, more sombre ballad.

When the rapturous reception had subsided from all quarters, Judge Rhodes-Boyson drew the ceremony to a close with final lines of gratitude to all-comers both inside and out. Lynn grinned, guessing that the judge's deft piece of ad-libbing had surely been influenced by her Pied Piper dreamboat. After having led his bride carefully back down the steps, the millionaire shook the distinguished gentleman's hand warmly, as did his zealous best man. Bart Dyson was soon on his feet to congratulate the newly-weds and also to thank his old friend for carrying out his duties with such aplomb.

Once descended to the main floor, the glorious couple could hardly move for well-wishers all waiting to pass on their congratulations. Jeff caught his sister's eye and beckoned for her to come over and join them. With his right arm around his dream girl, he tucked his left behind Madalena's waist and pulled her in close.

'Thanks, Lena,' he said, kissing her cheek. 'You were fantastic. I'm stoked you're here to be part of this.'

'Me too,' Lynn echoed. 'It's been great to share it with you.'

'And you, my gorgeous one...' the proud man turned to his sophisticated, blonde co-star, 'are the most exquisite thing I've ever laid eyes on. I have got to have you in that dress. I am the happiest and the horniest man alive.'

His sister chuckled under her breath, but his partner didn't hold back, slapping his chest hard. 'Shhh! Be quiet!'

'He was a good boy the other night,' their visitor interjected.

The hot-blooded man glared at her. 'Not here, please! But yep. I was a good boy.'

Lynn kissed him. 'Thanks.'

'Cheers, *chica*,' Jeff shook his head in frustration. 'You don't have to defend me. That's between Lynn and me. She has the choice whether to believe me or not, and I hope she does.'

The brand new wife placed a hand on his forearm. 'Leave it,' she whispered. 'It doesn't show much trust as a married couple if we start off not believing each other. Everything's fine, Lena. Don't listen to him.'

After a minute or two of idle discourse, the groom managed to extract his beautiful best friend from the clutches of her relations and drag her over to the Blakes, again causing havoc with the dress' long, trailing fabric. Everyone made a fuss of them, especially Celia, who had not yet stopped crying after the music.

'Oh, the ceremony was so romantic, darlings,' she said, clinging on to Lynn's arm. 'You're very special and look so happy together. When do we get a chance to take some photos?'

'Now, I think,' the young woman replied, looking around for someone to ask. 'The photographer's here. I've seen him. We're all supposed to go outside, into the garden.'

The born organiser broke away from the group, intending to search for the photographer, but the best man ran after her. 'Hey, Lynn. Go back. I'll find him.'

'Thanks, Gerry. That'd be great.'

The tall Irishman brushed her cheek with a sneaky kiss on his way past. 'No worries. You look ravishing, by the way. Jeff's the luckiest man. It's a shame your sister isn't just a wee bit older...'

'Excuse me?' the bride exclaimed, hoping no-one else had heard his typically crass *innuendo*. 'That's terrible!'

Her husband had already moved on to talk to other guests when Lynn returned to the Blakes, so she excused herself and mingled with some of her parents' invited dignitaries. Every now and again, his latent insecurities would stretch their invisible elastic connection a little tauter, leading him to seek her out through the sea of babbling bodies.

When the photographer had been rounded up, Gerry, Junior and Sandy did their best to herd the masses out into the courtyard. Following the flock, they all felt the sunshine instantly heat their faces, and it took a few seconds for their eyes to adjust to the brightness of the outside world.

Thinking that they had better not waste time arranging the various poses, since New Year's Day's vicious afternoon rays would waste no time in melting make-up and creating beads of sweat on red foreheads, the blushing bride collected her man from his London friends, whom she also knew very well, and they all filed over to have their pictures taken.

'We have to go out there soon,' Jeff told her, pointing over the wall to the crowd biding their time outside the Admin grounds. 'They can hear us. They've been waiting for ages.'

The gracious celebrity nodded. 'OK. Good idea. We'll sneak out after this with Anna. They'll love that. You bought them breakfast this morning, I heard.'

Her man of the people shrugged. 'Might've done... Lena can't keep her mouth shut, can she?'

Accustomed to having their picture taken from every possible angle, the Dysons and their newest family member twisted and weaved for the official and many more unofficial photographers, looking this way and that in response a barrage of conflicting instructions.

At one point, encouraged by a former RMIT basketball team-mate, Jeff swept his bride up into his arms and hoisted her face to his chin so that their mouths could connect. Shutters clicked madly all around, and their guests shouted with joy to see them so happy. People beyond the wall also responded to the frivolity, increasing the young man's guilt that their loyal fans had sound but no vision.

He broke ranks and ran to the gate that led onto the Coventry Street footpath, shouting through to the masses. 'Hang on, guys! We'll be out in a few minutes. There are fifty different cameras snapping away in here. Sorry it's taking so long.'

Armed with this new information, the crowd became more subdued. The groom jogged back to join the others, straightening his tie and making sure his jacket remained presentable in the wilting sun, pasting on his practised media smile for a few more moments. Eventually managing to steal the Dyson sisters away for a visit to their adoring public, it was the wedding guests this time who had to content themselves the distant commotion without being able to see its cause beyond the ivy-draped wall.

Due Recognition

To everyone's delight, the *trio* emerged through the gate, bride first, followed by the flower-girl and finally the groom. They had arranged for a waiter to stand by to let them back in again, in case the gate swang shut and left them stranded and absent without leave. Lynn laughed at her husband's cavalier attitude to blotting his copybook so early with her parents.

She drew both him and Anna in closer and whispered her instructions. 'We should answer every question with "After the Olympics."'

'After the Olympics? But why?' asked the nine-year-old, puzzled.

Jeff raised his eyebrows at his wife's devilish streak. 'Just do it, Anns. They'll love it. It'll be funny.'

The youngster shrugged and splayed her arms out in capitulation, smiling happily at her big sister and her new brother-in-law. Joining hands, they strode along the footpath, accepting their noisy fate. Starting at the end of the line closest to the gate, the celebrities shook hands with anyone they could reach and grabbed hold of *bouquets*, single flowers and presents, not to mention a slew of excited kisses. The littlest Dyson was charged with creating a pile of gifts off to one side once their arms became too full.

The stars posed for clamouring cameras all over again, and the athletic rocker repeated the elevation manœuvre he had performed for the official photographer for the public, complaining that Lynn had put on ten kilogrammes since he had last lifted her. Afterwards, the couple raised Anna horizontally across their bodies, to squeals of happiness at being part of the fun, her strong gymnast's body easily able to hold its position and writhe around in their arms to grin in each direction in turn.

Endless questions about the ceremony, their vows and where they were going on their honeymoon flew out of the throng in quick succession. Had they been nervous? Did everyone cry? Could they see the matching jewellery? What did it feel like to be married? And of course, after the prophetic lines spoken in unison during the exchange of rings, concerning their plans for children.

'After the Olympics,' was repeated over and over, soon being chanted by anyone within earshot.

A rare male voice yelled out a rather impolite question to Jeff about their wedding night. After gazing lasciviously at his new wife's sexy, contour-hugging attire, the star put on a forlorn expression and lamented.

'After the Olympics, mate.'

The comic's timing as impeccable as usual, the remark met with raucous laughter, except from Anna, who was just plain confused. The newlyweds remained steadfastly vague about their plans, not wishing to give away any more of their precious privacy than was necessary for sound public relations. The flower-girl was even asked if she was ready to be an auntie, but she didn't fully understand this connotation either.

It was high time to return to the confines of Dyson headquarters. By now, the ballroom would have been transformed from ceremonial gallery to banqueting hall, the rows of seating dismantled and replaced by twenty round tables of ten. Lynn and her parents had debated whether to put the top table on the stage but had changed their minds, since from this height it would feel too much like they were surveying their subjects.

The young woman had insisted that her *fiancé* would reject the idea, and therefore so had she. Thus, it was decided that the bridal party was to be seated on a long table on a slightly raised platform near the stage, and as a compromise to acknowledge tradition, they would sit in a row facing the rest of the guests.

'How long have we got?' a seductive voice whispered in the bride's ear while they listened to Bart telling a lame story from his daughter's childhood to the Governor of Victoria and his wife.

Hoping she wouldn't appear rude, the diplomat lifted her husband's right hand to read his watch. 'The breakfast's supposed to start in half an hour, but it probably won't.'

'*Carpe diem*, eh?'

Jeff's eyes were insistent, and Australia's darling was keen to make him happy. It had been an absolutely perfect day up until now, and a short interlude to satisfy her voracious lover wasn't too much to ask. They excused themselves from the jovial conversation for which she was only a prop' and walked casually towards the building's side entrance.

The groom caught his best man's eye and summoned him over. 'Mate, look after Lena, would you, please? We're going upstairs.'

Gerry looked a little astounded at first, assuming the meal was about to get underway. However, knowing his old friend's methods only too well, a wry, envious smile soon spread across his face. There was still some adolescent rebel in the man who had crossed the floor to the establishment after all…

'Just a quickie, I hope,' he said, checking the time.

His friend grimaced. 'What do you think, after all this hanging around?'

The best man winked at the bride. 'Treat him gently, Missus Diamond. He's about ready to blow.'

Lynn was embarrassed, afraid someone might overhear and jump to the correct conclusion. She grabbed Jeff's arm and kept walking.

'Sorry about that,' the groom frowned. 'Sometimes he just doesn't know when to keep quiet.'

The couple grinned and waved and nodded and excused their way indoors and across the lift lobby. It was impossible to guess if anyone suspected where they were bound or what they were planning to get up to when they reached their destination. The sliding doors closed on them, and the aroused groom took his quarry into his arms, leaning back against the mirrored wall. Although blood was pulsing through his every vein and artery, he was not about to revisit his reprobate tricks in the Admin building. Not today, with his dream girl so deliciously decked out and so indulgent of his wayward urges.

'I love you, Ms Diamond,' he told her. 'It sounds weird, doesn't it?'

Lynn smiled, picking up on his intentions. 'It sounds lovely to me. We'll need to tell Gerry it's not Missus. Oh, and I really loved the way you introduced me on stage, with both names. That was really classy.'

Jeff was chuffed indeed. The stars hadn't scripted the musical part of the proceedings. In fact, he couldn't even remember much about his *impromptu* introduction. The last couple of hours was but a sweet, blurred delirium of dreams coming true.

'Glad you liked it,' he kissed her cheek. 'You can share my name any time.'

The lift doors opened on the penthouse level. The newlyweds checked the opposite corridor for any signs of life before facing north and heading to where the sixteen-year-old tennis champion and her first and last lover used to hang out after school. He was the sole beneficiary of everything she had become in the intervening years, for which he gave a silent vote of thanks.

Apartment Six was unlocked, the boys' party having spilled out into the passageway earlier.

'It's been redecorated,' the bride informed her partner-in-crime. 'It's Sandy's room now, so we'll have to be careful.'

Lynn pushed on the handle, like in the dark days before the door demons departed. Jeff was spun back in time and had to catch his breath, with a chaotic cascade of sights and sounds rushing through his mind. His beautiful best friend saw the faraway look in his eyes and planted a kiss on his cheek, bringing him smartly into the here and now. He kissed her in return, chest rising and falling against her ivory silk dress, and allowed himself to be led over to the bed, where a quilt cover sporting a motorcycle design arrested the flashbacks abruptly.

The young woman giggled. 'We can ride a hog at the same time if you like.'

About as interested in Harley Davidsons as he was in door demons, the testosterone-charged rock star held his bride at arms' length and imbibed her from top to toe.

'You look unbelievable. Just like a real angel; pure white and glistening.'

'No wings though,' Lynn corrected him, her hands making haste to undo his tie and drag it out from underneath his collar. 'And not quite pure white either... I'm just me.'

'Just you?' Jeff echoed, running his fingers along the neckline of her dress and enlivening the soft skin of her breasts with his ravenous fingertips. 'No way am I going to go for that! Just you?'

He scoffed kindly as the vision of loveliness snared his torso and pulled his throbbing groin towards her. Under the outer serenity of his shining angel, this gown harboured a scalding temptress. They were both brim full of pent-up energy, and recognising each others' delicious pain only served to fuel their fire.

'Here's the rules,' she declared, gripping his erection through his suit pants and kneading it with the heel of her hand until he groaned.

'Rules? Don't I own you now?'

Australia's darling smiled sweetly, shifting her grip down a little further to squeeze his testicles. 'You wish, mate.'

With one hand cupped around her cheek and the other firmly on her behind, the handsome comic signalled his accession in the form of a long, deep kiss on her mouth. 'Sure thing, Brunhilde. Tell me what I'll agree to.'

The blonde beauty chuckled. 'Correct answer. You can't touch my hair or leave fingermarks on my dress. Otherwise, I'm all yours, husband.'

Her man didn't need to be asked twice. He reached down to the floor and lifted the heavy reams of fabric which formed the gown's skirt and began to stroke and caress every piece of bare skin he could find. Through his pounding head, he could hear her breath accelerate and felt her temperature rising in line with his own.

Jeff Diamond, you are one lucky bastard! He was about to fuck his wife in her wedding dress, finally enacting a fantasy that had kept him occupied in many a lonely hotel room since securing their fate in the tiny Edinburgh wine bar.

'I don't want to take this off,' he murmured, standing up and running his index finger across her impatient mouth. 'It looks so good on you. I want to remember this forever.'

Saying nothing, Lynn took hold of his belt and loosened the buckle, unfastened his fly and unbuttoned his shirt all the way down. Relishing the sensation of rough cotton skimming over his silk boxers, Jeff tugged the sleeve from each arm in turn and threw the shirt onto the floor. Slipping out of his shoes, he ripped off his socks and removed his trousers, tossing them all on the same pile.

'You looked very smart,' his dream girl said, enjoying the striptease. 'Completely dashing and delicious. Sorry I didn't say so earlier.'

'*Tais-toi*,' Jeff hissed, his tongue searching for hers again. 'Your eyes told me. I just want to love you.'

Under time pressure, both bride and groom were in a red-hot rush, but the gown refused to play along. He span her around to unlace her bodice, sensing the clock ticking on his staying power too. As soon as it was loose enough, she wriggled out of the dress, and it dropped stiffly to the floor. The athlete stepped to one side and stood up to reveal her tanned skin contrasted with the palest sky-blue *lingerie*, complete with their "JL" emblem embroidered in gold lettering.

The awestruck man stared, temporarily speechless, his hands poised in mid-air on their way to her silk-clad breasts. 'Jesus, Lynn! Where did these come from? You've been very busy behind my back with all these perfect touches. That's absolutely effing amazing, angel!'

'Something blue,' the happy celebrity kissed him. 'I wanted to make today as special as possible.'

'Well, you've succeeded,' Jeff croaked. 'No. Exceeded, I should say. Christ, I need to be inside you. I love you so much.'

The lovers fell onto the bed and connected with each other, eager to fulfil the dreams of their last few days and nights. Laughing at the awkward positions they were forced to adopt, still taking the utmost care to abide by the rules, both were overcome by tears of joy. They climaxed together within only a few minutes of wild abandon, in a tangle of long legs and *lingerie*.

After the orgasmic intensity began to die down, Jeff's hands wandered all over the lithe canvas before him and his eyes were transfixed by the symbolic replica stitched into her underwear. How appetising this bronzed body looked against the pale, lustrous material! In response to a short sigh, his gaze then moved to his angel's face, from which contentment shone despite the strain of not leaning too heavily on the bedcovers.

'You don't look very comfortable,' the sympathetic man chuckled. 'Let's get up. We can do all this again properly later.'

Between them, they righted the bulky gown from its heap on the floor and heaved it up until it covered her breasts. Lynn turned around so that her husband could fasten the hook and zip her back inside.

'Do you feel different?' she asked.

'No,' he rubbed his fingers and thumbs together and winked. 'I still use these…'

The comedian's long-suffering sidekick groaned at the pathetic, old joke, frustrated that she still fell for it every time. Squeezing the index finger of his left hand between the fabric and her bra and whispering *au revoir* to her body, the front-end of the "JL" pantomime horse dutifully tugged on the laces of her bodice before kissing the tattoo on her shoulder.

'Not really,' he answered with amused contrition. 'Do you?'

'No. Except for the ring,' Lynn replied, breathing in and adjusting the line of her dress until it fit her curves properly. 'How's yours?'

Tucking his shirt into his trousers and fastening the waistband, Jeff crouched down to retrieve one of his shoes, which had somehow slid under the bed. He slipped it on and stood up to consider her question.

The twenty-three-year-old stared at the bright, unblemished golden circle on his left hand. 'Can't even feel it. It must belong there.'

Lynn raised herself up on tiptoes to kiss him, her eyes instantly filling with tears. 'That's a lovely thing to say.'

Her groom shrugged modestly. He spoke as he found, as always. As far as he was concerned, it was one of the most obvious ways to a woman's heart, and fortunately, he found perfection wherever he looked at this stage of his extraordinary life.

Basking in a warm aura of post-marriage and now post-coital glory, Jeff Diamond stood behind Lynn Dyson; the multi-millionnaire re-knotting his tie in the mirror while his dream girl applied another fresh layer of lipstick and made sure her hair would not give their tawdry game away.

'How good do we look?' he admired the view, stroking her bare neck, newly exposed to the sun on its return from the London winter. 'And how good do I feel?'

Lynn smiled. They did indeed look sophisticated and *débonairs*. And flushed!

'How good *do* you feel?' she checked.

'The best. Thank you. And ready for the big breckie. Christ, you make me hungry, woman!'

Jeff caught hold of his wife's slender hand and held it up next to his, so that they could see both rings on their reflections' fingers at once.

'Look, angel. It's real. We're married.'

'Yeah,' the young star smiled, leaning back into his strong torso so that their tattoos were aligned. 'Fantastic, isn't it? And breakfast again! No eggs, I'm afraid. How long've we been away?'

'Twenty-five minutes, including *rassemblage*,' the songwriter looked at his watch. 'Mission accomplished, but I can't be too proud of that statistic, can I? Thanks for doing this. I needed you big-time.'

'I needed you too. You really turned me on when you were speaking our vows, and especially when you were singing. I was rapt when you suggested we come up here.'

Lynn watched the man in the mirror kiss the back of his blonde companion's neck. Both women reached up and touched their lovers' faces. She had been fairly certain, while stepping gleefully through the past few days' preparations, of the words she intended to use to describe this sexy intellectual in her bridal speech, now delighted that every word had retained its validity throughout the ceremony.

Yesterday, she had been set to marry an inspiring love-god. Today, she was this inspiring love-god's wife.

'Can you imagine what it'd be like getting married to someone you don't know?' the sportswoman asked in a dreamy tone, slipping on her *stiletto* heels and standing to her full height.

'What made you think of that?' Jeff smiled, winking in approval. 'Jeez, you've grown! But yeah, I much prefer it this way. I'd want to be certain I was marrying someone I could be friends with. How would you know?'

'That's exactly what I mean,' Lynn affirmed, sidling up to her man's shoulder as if measuring their relative stature. 'It's so great that we can sneak up here and be perfectly in tune with what each other wants, and then sneak back down again with our secret. It's magical. You just wouldn't be able to do that with someone you hardly know.'

Her rambling trailed off, noticing that the distracted groom now had an enquiring expression on his face. 'What is it?'

'Hey, can I try something before we go?'

'Try something? Try what?'

To her surprise, Jeff kneeled on the floor again and began to lift up the skirt of her dress.

'What are you doing?' the bride asked, giggling as his hands ran along the sensitive skin at back of her knee. 'We don't have time to do it all again. Hey? What are you do...'

Before she could finish her sentence, the headstrong man had taken hold of her lace garter, stretched it out and was tracing it down her leg. Confused, she lifted her foot so that he could loop it off.

'Sorry. I just need to see how this works.'

'How it works?' Lynn repeated, intrigued. 'My garter? What are you planning to do with it?'

'Aha!' her husband replied, tapping the side of his nose with his finger. 'Patience, my double-barrelled beauty!'

He stretched the elastic to its limit and shot the soft, red missile into the quilt like a catapult before providing his wife with his explanation. While he spoke, he fired it off a few more times, retrieving each attempt from the Harley Davidson on her brother's bed where he had been aiming at the headlight.

'I have it on good authority that someone close to you is about to pop a question, so I wanted to make sure I managed to shoot this in his general.'

The young woman's pouting, re-painted mouth fell open. 'Junior?'

'Yep. He told me the night before last that he might ask Julie tonight, after all our *rigmarole*'s done and dusted. I thought I'd give him a bit of a helping hand.'

Lunging towards her considerate partner, Lynn hugged him. 'Wow! I wondered if he might. You're so gorgeous.'

'I know,' Jeff smirked with mock arrogance. 'I do my best.'

He launched the garter a few more times, in various directions and with varying amounts of force until he had mastered the task at hand, before passing it back to its rightful owner. She threaded it up her long, toned right thigh, and the hot-blooded rocker whistled his appreciation as she did so.

The surreptitious pair straightened Sandy's bedclothes. He would never notice. He was a boy, after all. They closed the door on their secret *rendezvous*, slipped into the lift and descended quickly to the first floor where people were milling around the noticeboard to locate their names. All heads turned when they caught sight of the happy couple emerging with wide grins on their faces.

Desperate not to look too guilty, Lynn had no idea whether she was succeeding or not. Glancing at the handsome man beside her, she could see he plainly didn't give a damn. She wished she had his brazen, devil-may-care confidence. It made him totally irresistible and liable to get away with anything.

Walking into the ballroom, they wove their way through a labyrinth of round tables, all laid with an assortment of china, cutlery and crystal and decorated in the same colours as the bridal theme. Some guests had already taken their seats, either famished or keen to catch up with old friends' news. Others chatted at the bar, and the rest were lingering in the sunny courtyard.

The groom delivered his bride to her parents, who were enjoying a glass of champagne with their respective sisters and families. Bart reached a proud arm around his daughter, allowing the rock star to take his leave momentarily. He stopped to check the seating plan, to discover which table Alberto and Eva had been allocated. And Yvonne Hawkins too. He wanted to make sure he could point them out easily when it came to mentioning them in the speech he was in the process of revising.

Having obtained these pieces of information, the boy from Canley Vale went in search of the boxing club owner and his daughter. Halfway there however, changing his mind again, he diverted to collect Madalena on the way, conscious that he had deserted her for long enough. Their Chilean friends would want to see how beautiful she looked.

'There you are!' Jeff shouted, finally tracking his sister down in the garden with an upturned champagne flute swinging between her fingers.

She had been adopted by Michelle and was happily engaged in conversation with a number of Lynn's old school friends. The girls screamed when they clapped eyes on the smartly-dressed celebrity who had stolen their classmate's heart, rushing to hug him and clamouring to have their photograph taken while draped off his gorgeous frame. The self-confident ladies' man obliged, all too willing to lap up the attention of several attractive ladies at once, especially in front of his sister.

'Lena, can I drag you away?' he requested, once the women were satisfied. 'There are some people here who you'll remember, I think.'

After three glasses of bubbly, Madalena scarcely even feigned an interest, obeying her star-of-the-show brother without objection. 'Who is it?'

'Wait and see,' Jeff answered, holding her hand and pulling her along. 'Are you enjoying yourself?'

'Yeah, but I'm hungry. You enjoying yourself, but?'

On impulse, the groom hugged his skinny sibling. 'Yep,' he insisted, shaking her until she whined. 'You bet I am.'

'Are you still the horniest man alive?' the prostitute sniggered. 'Lynn didn't like you sayin' that.'

'No, I'm not,' her brother confessed in a whisper. 'I'm calm, relaxed and fully satisfied, thanks. Ready for anything.'

'How come? What 'appened?'

'What d'you think happened?' he turned her question around.

The woman's face was a picture. '*¡Culo!* Did you guys already do it? Where?'

Jeff laughed, putting his hand over her loud mouth. 'Shut up! Upstairs, in Lynn's old room. It was fantastic! I gave the bride one in her wedding dress. Well, nearly in her wedding dress. It was just too difficult in the end, so it had to come off. That thing can stand up on its own!'

His sister whacked the effusive showman hard on the arm, much to the alarm of Lynn's great-aunt and -uncle. Undeterred, he kept walking, eventually pulling up in front of a group of guests who were gathered at one of the rear tables.

Madalena's eyes fell on another young woman with dark curly hair, though shorter than hers. 'Eva?' she hesitated. 'That you? How come you're here? *¿Qué tal?*'

'*Olá, Lena,*' their fellow South American immigrant replied, giving her childhood friend a hug. '*Estás muy hermosa.* Bridesmaid, eh? *¡Muy bien!*'

'*¿Y Señor Santos, como están Ustéd?*' Jeff's sister's manners adjusted in deference to the elderly gentleman who had often caught her stealing from the local lolly shop, bending to let him kiss her cheek at his request.

'*La señorita Madalena,*' Alberto nodded in recognition. '*¿Qué dices a su hermano joven? ¿Estás orgullosa de él?*'

315

The young woman shot a glance at her brother, her Spanish too rusty. He was gripped by a spasm of disappointment to hear her revert to their mother tongue with these people, when she had refused to use it with him.

'*Señor Santos Fernandez* asked if you're proud of me,' he interpreted.

'Yeah, I know. We never believed 'im when 'e said 'e'd meet Lynn Dyson, but 'e did.'

Their conversation was cut short by a wave of waiters and waitresses requesting everyone to be seated. The groom shook Alberto's hand once again and told him he would return for longer as soon as he could. The dark-haired pair needed to traverse the whole length of the room. With a sense of magnificent dominion over the scene taking them to the top table, the upwardly-mobile metaphor was apt for an erstwhile tearaway about to embark on the next segment of this wondrous day's program.

'Come on, Lena,' Jeff urged, holding out his hand towards his sister. 'We have to go.'

***

The Sydney siblings were the last to arrive for breakfast. Jeff pulled his sister's chair out so that she could sit down, which she accomplished with surprising grace. He then pointed to her napkin, and Madalena copied him childishly by spreading it across her lap. The top table was now complete, and the waiters began to pour the wine and distribute bread rolls.

The bride and groom were in the middle of the line, overlooking the expanse of diners in front. On Jeff's left was his sister as the only member of his family present, then his best man and finally the mother of the bride. On Lynn's right was her father, with the maid of honour and Doctor Rhodes-Boyson at the far end. Little Anna had been excused further ceremonial duties and was sitting with her brothers and cousins at an adjacent table. Also at the top end sat the various dignitaries, due to be served first by the staff.

During the planning process, the former lost boy's compassionate *fiancée* had asked whether he would like Celia and Gerald Blake with them to balance out the table. He had declined after some deliberation, and now the meal was in full swing, he scanned port and starboard once more, feeling justified in having made this decision. The right people were present, and for the right reasons.

'You OK?' he asked his beautiful best friend, putting his arm around her.

'I'm great,' his dream girl replied with a broad smile. 'I'm having the most amazing day. Are you?'

Jeff kissed her left temple. 'Certainly am. I took Lena to see Alberto and Eva. Thanks for inviting them, sneaky though it was. I'll be interested to find out later how you did it.'

A general drone of easy, jocular conversation had settled over the function room in the Dyson Administration building. Judging from the absence of background noise, the crowd outside seemed to have dispersed, guessing the reception was underway and that they were unlikely to be treated to any further entertainment for quite a while. A few had indicated to the happy *trio* during their earlier dash through the gate that they had brought picnics to eat in the Botanic Gardens opposite, the thought of which added to the enchantment of the young couple's day.

The top table was second to be served their *entrées*, and the resulting lull presented a chance to take a short breather from the formalities. For Gerry, talking to Marianna Dyson was like talking to his own mother, relaxing and reassuring. Both women were sophisticated and worldly-wise while at the same time homely and proud of their respective families. The party king was weary after the recent few days of hard living and last-minute activity, and even men-about-town knew when they were running on empty. He was glad for some downtime when he didn't have to play the ringmaster's role and could talk about someone else's life for a change.

Mother and daughter could both overhear the self-made millionnaire instructing his uncultured family representative on which pieces of cutlery to pick up when and which glass to use for which purpose, encouraging her to follow his lead if in doubt. Fascinated by his forbearance, they also watched as he demonstrated how to push food onto her fork with her knife rather than scooping like a spoon. The dignified pair caught each others' eye and, realising they were eavesdropping, smiled and turned around to their respective neighbour to initiate a new conversation.

For her part, Madalena was growing ever more in awe of this little brother of hers, the adult version of whom she had only properly met a few days prior. She was amazed by the attention he commanded wherever he went. How had this lanky, bookish boy become a celebrity universally loved? She had followed his journey to fame with a distant curiosity, more through jealousy than pride, but only now fully understood how famous he was. And now that she sat on the same table as Lynn Dyson and her parents, there was no denying his star quality. There had been so much more to the incomprehensible hopes and dreams of this strange child she lived with than the fantasies of a teenager motivated by raging hormones.

Tipping his head over to whisper in the bride's ear, Jeff remarked that Doctor Donald Rhodes-Boyson was the most appropriate person to sit next to Michelle. Lynn agreed, reminding him that the fiery redhead was due to start the final year of her law degree in a few weeks' time and was eager to find a mentor who could further her career goals. It had not gone unnoticed by the determined wedding planner that the venerable judge had recently been appointed Chairman of an organisation aimed at promoting women into the legal profession, making their pairing no coincidence.

The guests at other tables looked on as the bride and groom ate and conversed with their fellow top-tablers as if it were an ordinary family Sunday lunch. Every now and again, someone would walk up and request a photograph with the bridal party, which was always granted with good nature and ready smiles. Celia was especially keen for a keepsake of this momentous day for which she had been praying on her pseudo-son's behalf for a few years.

Very soon, the main course was over, and it was time for the speeches. Staff clattered dessert bowls and jangled champagne glasses as they endeavoured to deliver them as fast as possible, necessitating the Master of Ceremonies to stand at the edge of the top table and bang a gong very close to Marianna's ear. As expected, the elegant lady barely flinched, smiling benignly at onlookers' sympathetic reactions.

'Thank you, Bernie. Your Excellencies, Your Honour, ladies and gentlemen, please could I have your attention? I hope you're all enjoying today's Wedding Breakfast to celebrate the marriage of our famous couple, Lynn and Jeff. Now, and to get the more traditional side of the proceedings underway, I'd like to call upon the bride's father, Mister Bart Dyson, to say a few words.'

Everyone clapped politely, and Junior whistled from the table next-door. 'Go Dad!'

Anna echoed another 'Go Dad!', much to everyone's amusement.

She received a light-hearted scolding from her mother, as old-fashioned as ever when it came to the type of behaviour expected of a young lady.

The six-time Olympian raised his huge frame to its full stature and removed a single card from his inside jacket pocket. One of the most physically-imposing men of his *époque*, Jeff studied the great man carefully as he took a couple of deep breaths and embarked upon his opening address.

'Thank you, and good afternoon, Your Excellencies, Your Honour, ladies and gentlemen. I'm not going to sing to you, so don't panic…'

The hushed audience tittered. Lynn looked at her partner, who drew his hand across his forehead dramatically. The gesture had not been missed by the speaker, who shot his new son-in-law a mock glare.

'That's enough from the cheap seats, please. I must say, this is the latest breakfast I've had for some time. And for those looking for dinner, you might try next Tuesday at ten AM.'

Another subdued ripple of laughter, and the experienced orator continued. 'Firstly, I'd like to thank everyone here for participating in this most joyous of events today. I'm sure I can speak for my wife, Marianna, too, when I say that it's been wonderful meeting you all; both those for the first time and our very good friends. Lynn is, as you know, the first of our children to get married, and boy, does it make us feel old! A whole generation has gone by since we were kitting Junior, down there, out in his first school uniform and taking Lynn to her first tennis or dance classes. And now look at them! In any case, we're very proud of all four of our children and are delighted to welcome everyone to this marriage celebration.'

The quieted guests clapped again. The young woman reached her hand under the table, finding her husband's waiting to take hold.

'Now let me tell you a little bit about my elder daughter... Born in September of nineteen-fifty-five, Lynn has always been a ray of sunshine in our lives. I can't count the number of times people used to come up to me and say, "That little girl... Your Lynn... She's such a happy child. She cheers us up." Lynn has always had the ability to look on the bright side of life, and very frequently on the funny side. I'll never forget the hilarity at one function, when she was about four years old, where we were holding a buffet lunch. Here in this building actually, for some sporting thing or other... Yes, you may well cringe, my girl!'

Beaming, father and daughter stared each other down while he took his opportunity to embarrass her. Jeff's arm tightened its grip around her shoulder, providing moral support and also conveying to anyone who dared doubt it that the transfer of property against which he had so adamantly rebelled had in actual fact taken place. *Let no man put asunder...*

Bart continued unabashed. 'She knows what I'm going to say! Arriving in the car from our house in Benloch, Marianna had mentioned that the lunch was a finger buffet, and you should have seen the expression on Lynn's face at this revelation! Well... After explaining what a finger buffet was, we were relieved to find that the matter appeared to have been laid to rest. It wasn't until the good lady wife of the guest of honour was introduced to the darling Lynn, here, that we realised the true peril of our brief education. The lady in question took Lynn's hand and perused the food selection. This one stared up at her with those huge, blue eyes of hers and said, "Which sort of fingers would you like?"'

Everyone chuckled and clapped again. The groom nudged his beautiful wife and wiggled the middle finger of his left hand under the table. Although her expression remained beguiling, her face reddened, and he instantly regretted his actions. Plus, to add to his shameful timing and stupid attempt at one-upmanship, Madalena had cottoned on and cackled, causing several others to look around.

'I'm sorry, angel,' Jeff hissed. 'That was unfair of me. I've hardly ever seen you blush before. It's very cute.'

Fortunately for the young woman, her father carried on regardless. 'On a more serious note, we are all aware of the successes Lynn has had in sport, acting and music. I don't think I need blow her trumpet on that score.'

The musicians in the audience groaned at the outrageous pun, only to be gazumped by Bart's next sentence.

'She has always conducted herself in a mature and sensible manner, and has grown up into a most elegant and intelligent diplomat for her family, her business and her country. This, perhaps more than any individual achievement, is what makes her the person she is today.'

The guests burst into a sincere round of applause, and the apologetic husband leaned over and placed a kiss on the gorgeous woman's cheek. He lifted his hands into the air above the table and joined in with their endorsement, even adding a loud wolf-whistle into the mix. Lynn's smile softened, and he knew he was forgiven. No two ways about it, he was the luckiest man alive. He didn't deserve forgiveness but would accept it gladly.

'Marianna and I were reminiscing only the other day about the first time Lynn brought a certain unknown student by the name of Diamond to our farm for the weekend,' the Dyson patriarch continued. 'She was just sixteen; much too young, as far as we were concerned, for a serious boyfriend. But to see the two of them together was the strangest feeling. It was as if they had known each other all their lives, right from the word "Go".

'I remember, we were looking out of our window, watching them load some gear into a ute, and they were talking incessantly. And that's a shared trait that quite a few people have remarked to me over the last few days: how much these two talk to each other. Marianna turned to me at the time and said, "There's something special happening there. I really think they'll stick together." How right she was, despite all our attempts to provide alternative distractions for Lynn.'

The big man paused, glancing over at his beautiful daughter, who continued to smile sweetly. Her protective *beau*'s hand had returned to her shoulder and was slowly stroking the soft skin along the top, from her neck to her upper arm and back again.

'I'll also never forget the day when I broke the news to Lynn that she would be leaving Melbourne for the United States for two years to pursue her UCLA studies, and that she would have to cease all contact with her boyfriend. I'm still convinced it hurt me almost as much as it hurt her, because, ever respectful, she simply stood and looked at me in disbelief. Her voice took on an ominous hush. "Isn't that a bit Victorian?" And then she gave me her agreement. I didn't offer any explanation for my decision at the time, and it wasn't until she had returned as an adult and immediately re-established her relationship with Jeff Diamond that we had a chance to clear the air.'

Bart fixed his new son-in-law with another firm but fatherly stare, which was duly reflected in the bold, no-nonsense way he had come to expect. No words were exchanged, so the speaker moved on promptly.

'Well, that's quite enough nostalgia from me... Now for the present day. Watch out for these guys! That's my prediction, folks. If you could buy shares in people, I'd advise you all to buy in now. When Marianna and I got married, it was our time to be "talk of the town", destined for greatness, *et cetera, et cetera*. But today, we are up here as proof of evolution. Our children are set to outclass us in ways we would never have imagined back then. Lynn and Jeff have plans the scope of which boggles my mind.

'Anyway... Without further ado, I'll get down to my traditional task for this point in the proceedings. Your Excellencies, Your Honour, ladies and gentlemen, there's no denying that the bride looks even more radiant than ever today...'

Lynn's father's toast was cut off mid-sentence by a spontaneous round of applause, chased by another piercing whistle emanating from over his left shoulder. Even Gerry was stunned at his old friend's flagrant hoodlum display, but piped down when it was augmented by yet louder applause and several other macho expressions of appreciation. For his part, Big D was obviously in too good a mood to raise any sort of objection to the exuberant response.

'But here on the top table, there are two other beautiful young women, and another one down there with her brothers, who've helped Lynn and Marianna to make today go smoothly and happily. I'd like to propose a toast to the bridesmaids: the lovely Michelle England, a very great friend of us all, who's been Lynn's best mate, *confidante* and fellow competitor for many years now; and Madalena Moreno, Jeff's sister, as beautiful as her brother is handsome, who's been plunged into this maelstrom of activity with no warning but joined in enthusiastically and has been a joy for us to finally meet. And lastly, but by no means leastly, our littlest, Anna, flower-girl *extraordinaire*! Your Excellencies, Your Honour, ladies and gentlemen, would you please be upstanding and join me in a toast to The Bridesmaids.'

Jeff looked at his sibling, who seemed nervous again. 'Smile,' he urged. 'That's you!'

With a scraping of chairs, the guests took to their feet and raised their glasses, drinking the young ladies' health in unison. After kissing his sister as camera shutters whirred, the generous groom stood up and shook his father-in-law firmly by the hand. The Olympian reciprocated with a manly hug before bending down and giving his daughter's school-friend a peck on the cheek.

The Master of Ceremonies, anxious to keep the show running to schedule, soon called everyone to order, requesting that the guests take their seats again. 'Thank you very much, sir. Mister Bart Dyson, ladies and gentlemen. And next! Now to respond on behalf of the bridesmaids and propose a toast to the bride and groom, it's my great pleasure to introduce you to the indomitable Mister Gerry Blake, truly the best man for the occasion. Gerry...'

Jeff shook his old friend by the hand too, as the suave executive pushed his chair back, flopped his napkin down onto the table and fastened his jacket button. The boy from Sydney's west grinned at his new wife. The apt adjective which had been attributed to the accountant by his dream girl during their first ever double-date had endured all the way to today. It was as if each minute detail of his life was in the process of shaping its whole, under the watchful eye of his master planner.

'Good luck, mate,' the groom murmured.

Gerald Blake Junior was in his prime, nervous but confident after a few drinks. He was ready to refer to a few well-placed crib sheets on the table and in his line of sight, shooting a proud glance at the bride, who had obviously worded up the MC concerning his special label.

'Thank you, Carl. Good afternoon, Your Excellencies, Your Honour, ladies and gentlemen. And you, me old mate.'

This crude sequestration drew a hoot of laughter, probably from one of the superstar's band members, and the musician gave a sarcastic wave of thanks to his best man for what was likely to be the first of many put-downs in the coming few minutes. He had confided in his beautiful best friend only a short while ago that he hoped he wouldn't be dragged into Gerry's speech too often. This was one of the few public opportunities these days that his friend had to represent himself, to step out of the oversized shadow cast by the Jeff Diamond brand.

'Well, thank you, everyone, for joining our happy throng today. I'll start as I mean to go on: fornication...'

A great many gasps and a few muted screams emanated from various tables, while ancient aunts reached for their concertina fans. Lynn's eyes shot across to her mother, who was doing her best to appear shocked, even though she had been forewarned. The singer could almost hear Celia bemoaning that her son could always be relied upon to lower the tone.

Gerry took another deep breath, his gaze scanning the whole space and his nerves completely dissipated. 'For'n occasion such as this...'

This time, the guests uttered a variety of groans, sighs of relief and hearty guffaws as the joke was executed. Jeff's expression remained unchanged, remaining tall in his chair and hanging on to his prize with grim determination.

'Snakes alive! Or some such expletive-free exclamation,' the best man laughed. 'I never in a million years expected to have to follow a Bart Dyson speech. Years of practice in public speaking, and I'm still a blithering idiot. How does it go? "Look, Ma! No hands"?'

The successful businessman put his arms out and swayed a little, giving the impression of gliding erratically through the air. Chuckling along, the young man's eyes fell on Celia, who remained rather cautious. He gave her a reassuring grin.

Gerry carried on. 'Equally, I never in a million years expected my best buddy from school days to marry Lynn Dyson! In fact, when Jeff first told me that he'd been on a date with Lynn, I refused to believe him. I should've done though... Since this man was about thirteen or fourteen years old, while we still lived in Sydney, he always insisted that one day he'd move to Melbourne and seek his fortune, and there he would meet the girl of his dreams and live happily ever after. Well, mate... *Now* I believe you!'

The groom raised his hand in acknowledgement, hugging his *Regala* still closer and kissing her temple. He was nearly ready to let himself believe it too.

'Best men's speeches are supposed to be full of embarrassing anecdotes that document the groom's adolescent immaturity. Well, I'm afraid here's where I reveal myself as a dismal failure. I've been almost constantly in Jeff's company for the last decade and can't think of anything embarrassing to relay to you. He's just not the sort of guy who gets himself into trouble. He's always one step ahead of everyone else.

'Of course, women have always been an important subject in Jeff's curriculum...'

Roars of laughter could be heard from various quarters of the room, and the best man picked out a number of offenders by name. Bart Dyson shook his head in disappointment, pretending to make a note on the reverse side of his speech card before bidding the speaker to continue. The confident executive obliged with a grin.

'Where was I? Oh, yes. Back to the beginning: women... Fascinating subject. This man here's three years younger than me but always had something new to teach me on this topic. No female was safe. Sorry, Lynn, but I know I'm not telling you anything you don't already know!'

This fact, which she used to find difficult to come to terms with, no longer bothered today's bride, and not merely because she had a ring on her finger. She made her *insouciance* plain to the attentive audience with a nod of resignation. Gerry was right. Flouting a surfeit of provocative sex appeal was so much part of Jeff's character that it deserved prominence in the best man's speech.

'There were teachers, work-mates and even my sisters, who are here today, over there... And then there was Donna Jade. Yes. There really was a Donna Jade, good people... But she soon got left behind too, didn't she, mate?'

The swarthy rock guitarist nodded his head vigorously, putting his hands over his partner's ears. A small number of people allowed themselves a tentative chuckle, but the former womaniser sensed an element of unease descending on the room. He hadn't wanted the gallant Irishman to go too far into his sexual back catalogue, both to save his new wife's family from hearing these unsavoury details but also because several of the aforementioned old flames were sitting here with their partners, listening to their own past being dredged up in the Jeff Diamond story.

The world-changer sighed as he read an echo of his own conscience in Lynn's mind. He believed in freedom of speech, didn't he? He had won his prize and therefore should be prepared to take the blame for every home truth that surfaced at the hand of his playboy co-conspirator.

Riding high, Gerry shuffled his crib sheets. 'Those who've known Jeff Diamond for as long as I have remember how he was always on the move. He broke as many hearts as the Dysons have broken world records; the original "Love 'em and Leave 'em Kid". Until, that is, he met the lady who today became his wife.'

A more confident round of applause acknowledged these words, along with a few whoops of joy from a table of Lynn's friends. Gerry cocked his head towards the father of the bride, who simply smiled approvingly in return.

'Jeff's always been one for springing surprises on us. I believe Lynn refers to it as making statements, which is appropriate indeed. As a schoolboy in a pretty rough area of Sydney, Jeff excelled at all academic subjects and sport too. With a little help from his grandmother, he taught himself to play the piano and the guitar, but these talents were hidden from his mates for a long time.

'He was just Jeff to me and my family. A great laugh, good sportsman and always fun to be with. I know my parents think of him as a second son, and both my sisters... Jacinta and Tamilla over there... just plain adore him in much more than a sisterly way!'

Madalena gaped at her irrepressible brother, and he kissed her cheek playfully.

'Don't believe a word he's saying,' he teased under his breath, well aware that many of these secrets had already been shared.

'So when I moved to Melbourne for work, Jeff decided he'd come down too, to study Computer Science at RMIT. More importantly though, he wanted to launch his long-awaited assault on an unassuming superstar-in-the-making by the name of Lynn Dyson. And from there, as the man himself would say, the rest is history.'

The room erupted with another vociferous round of applause. Gerry stood patiently waiting for it to die down, flipping the edges of his prompt cards and swallowing a mouthful of water while he had the chance.

'And in my capacity as his business manager, I can tell you the last three or so years have been an absolute whirlwind of publicity, contracts and sacks of money flowing in from all corners of the globe. But through this whole, surreal process of becoming who he is today, Jeff Diamond remains a bloody good bloke. Did you know, for example, that he gives fifty percent of everything he earns away? Fifty... Five, zero, the bloody fool!'

A large proportion of guests gasped, hoping this wasn't a stunt but nevertheless astonished at the extent of the star's philanthropy. By the look of surprise on Bart and Marianna Dysons' faces, this percentage was news to them too. Lynn looked lovingly at her new husband, whose turn it was to be embarrassed by the adulation. He merely shrugged, offering neither a confirmation nor a denial.

The businessman reached down and picked up another of his cards, pretending to read it word-for-word. 'He gave me some very strict parameters when we first started this incredible journey, and this was only one. After tax, in case there's anyone here from the tax office... I am an accountant after all, and don't much relish the idea of baring my auditable backside any more than I need to.'

'Gerry, please!' the top table heard a particularly shrill, disgruntled scolding from the orator's mother, evidently horrified to think that the Governor General's ears had been so brutally assaulted by accountancy humour.

'Yes, yes... Thank you for your contribution, madam. Anyway... Half of everything Jeff Diamond earns is invested in business ventures or given to charitable causes. This is who he is, ladies and gentlemen. He wants deserving people to benefit from his good fortune as much as possible. Although you're probably not much into sharing today's prize, are you, mate?'

Taken by surprise at the sudden twist, the groom's head shook most emphatically, smiling through gritted teeth as he tightened his grip on Lynn's hand under the table. 'No, mate. All mine, I hope.'

Gerry continued. 'Of course, fame has changed him. How could it not have? But only for the better, in my view. Lynn and Jeff are honestly so much in love and committed to their life's plans, and also such lively, generous people to have around. They'll do anything in their power to help you. I've known this man for more than half his life. When we met we had nothing in common, but we've been best mates ever since.

'I call Jeff the "learning leech". If he figures out there's something he doesn't know, he knuckles down and finds out who does know and sticks to them until he's sucked every last millilitre of information and experience. And you know what? He does it in such a nice way that you hardly know he's using you until it's way too late! And even once you work out his nefarious plan, there he is stroking your ego whilst picking your pockets. And at the end of it all, you shake his hand and thank him.'

Several loud roars of laughter burst through the hush, coming mainly from the couple's university friends who were all nodding in agreement.

The best man gestured towards them. 'It's a gift, I tell you! And I've done my share of learning from him as a result.'

Reclining in his chair and with his right arm determined not to let go of Lynn's shoulder, the humble multi-millionnaire sat fiddling with his fork and staring at his empty dinner plate. He was lost in thought, occasionally tuning in and smiling at the many flattering observations directed at him and his gorgeous bride. His mind was busy playing the tape of his life back and forth as he was reminded of events and people along the way.

The young woman kissed his cheek. 'Come back,' she whispered. 'We need you here. It's your turn next.'

After three years at the top of his profession, it no longer registered with the introverted musician that everyone was watching him. He snapped to attention on hearing the gentle request from his favourite lady.

'Sorry,' he answered, replacing his fork in line with his knife and re-focusing his mind on Gerry's speech. 'Thanks, angel. I'm here, and I'm so glad you're here.'

'It's a huge honour to stand here as Jeff Diamond's best man this afternoon and to thank Mister Dyson for his toast to the three little maids from school. Now comes my turn to propose a toast the happy couple,' Gerry began to wrap up. 'I've come to know and love, and yes, lust, after Lynn for these last few years. I understand exactly what they see in each other, and I wish them luck in their life together. Of course, we all know they won't need it. Your Excellencies, Your Honour, ladies and gentlemen, I'd like you to join me in wishing Lynn and Jeff continued success in their careers and eternal happiness in their very public private life. Good luck, Lynn Dyson and Jeff Diamond, husband and wife, the happiest couple.'

'Lynn Dyson and Jeff Diamond!' chanted the whole room, scrambling to their feet for a second time. 'The happiest couple.'

Everyone put their glasses down, clapping and cheering continuously for a lengthy spell, while the bride and groom kissed once more for the cameras. The Blake sisters were especially vocal, proud of the pompous accountant's performance on the big stage. The tall Irishman gave a theatrical bow and hugged his longtime friend, who was now upstanding to assume the speaker's mantel.

'Thanks, mate. Gerry Blake, that was just too kind. Cruel in parts, but too, too kind. The cheque's in the mail.'

Jeff caught the Master of Ceremonies' attention and asked whether he could use one of the roving microphones from the stage. Thinking on his feet, Bernie announced a small delay for glasses to be recharged and for tea and coffee to be served. Everyone took their seats again, welcoming the chance to discuss the last two speeches or to be able to take a comfort break without fear of missing anything.

A very capable audio-visual assistant helped the superstar attach a state-of-the-art battery pack to the waistband of his suit trousers. They tested the microphone with the sound engineer at the back of the room, who hadn't expected to be on duty quite so soon. Levels set quickly, thumbs and glasses were raised at both ends of the hall, providing the signal to resume. Jeff crouched down between Lynn and Madalena and explained that he was going walkabout.

'Great idea,' the bride agreed. 'Hope the technology works OK.'

'Doesn't matter,' the showman reassured her. 'If it stops working, I'll just come back here.'

'Or yell,' his fellow performer added.

Jeff smiled and kissed her. 'Yeah. Or yell. You OK, Lena?'

Madalena nodded, thoroughly overwhelmed. Her brother squeezed her shoulder affectionately. She had never attended such a fancy event before, and it was clear that she didn't know quite what to make of it all.

'Thanks,' he said to the young woman's pretty, smiling face. 'Won't be long. We can have a dance later.'

The Master of Ceremonies jumped up onto the stage, calling everyone to attention and threatening to bang the gong again if silence were not forthcoming. The groom wandered away from his chair, feeling all eyes on him. Suddenly hit by the significance of what he was about to do, a wave of emotion engulfed him too. He steadied himself by crouching down next to his loved ones and taking a few deep breaths.

Lynn tilted her head onto his. 'Go for it. They're going to love you. I love you,' she told him, feeling her mother's eyes drilling into her.

'*Gracias, Regala. Je t'adore aussi.*'

The groom kissed the top of her sculpted blonde hair as he straightened his legs, reaching round his belt to switch on the battery pack. Bernie checked with the showman if he was ready, and he nodded, tapping the microphone gently.

'Could I have your attention, please? Thank you again to Gerry Blake, the best of men,' the official coordinator recapped, initiating another round of applause from the expectant audience. 'Now to respond to all your good wishes, here's one half of the happy couple. On the move, so watch out! Your Excellencies, Your Honour, ladies and gentlemen, pray silence for that well-known shrinking violet, your bridegroom: Jeff Diamond!'

Absorbing another red-hot dose of hero-worship, the tall, dark and handsome stranger who had claimed the holy grail stood quietly while the excitement died down. With one hand in his trouser pocket and the other resting in the dip between his guardian angel's shoulder blades, he gazed down at the smaller of the two tattoos that had sealed their fate before leaving for London. All but the upper serifs of each letter were obscured by the top of her gown. The clapping and whistling eventually subsided, and the confident young man lifted the microphone to his mouth as if he were about to break into song.

'Thank you, distinguished guests, one and all. Whoa! To say this day was overwhelming would be a huge understatement. It's with a strange mix of pride and humility that I stand before you today and thank you for attending our wedding celebrations. Happy New Year, by the way! What a way to spend it, huh?'

An *impromptu* Mexican wave of toasting glasses roamed around the tables, as guests responded to the natural orator's best wishes. Jeff picked up his own wine glass and raised it, taking a small sip and placing it back onto the starched, white tablecloth.

'You know, I have to tell you that last night I caught myself thinking several times, "What kind of deranged idiot organises a wedding on New Year's Day?"'

He leaned over and placed a loving hand on the top of Lynn's blonde head, nodding suggestively in her direction. Everyone laughed, including the bride herself.

'And the answer is, "This one!" But it's been an amazing day so far, hasn't it?'

Yet again, the noisy gathering clapped and cheered, before submitting to a subtle gesture to quieten down.

'First, thank you very much, *messieurs* Dyson and Blake, for your kind words and for the embarrassing stories. When I hear such nice things said about us, it's hard sometimes to separate the truth from the hyperbole. And I'm sure I speak for Lynn too when I say that I wish this reception could last for ten more hours so we could to join each of you, just to catch up on what you've been doing and share a laugh or two.'

There was another ripple of applause, though quick to fizzle out in anticipation of further amusement. Bart and Marianna exchanged glances across the top table, admiring the Midas touch their daughter's chosen one possessed with his audiences. He was certainly blessed with the knack of appealing to people on the most basic, human level.

'Now I think too much, many will say, but often not enough about the simple things in life,' the groom continued. 'About the power of family and the value of strong friendships, for example. When we're all off slaying dragons from nine to five, the thing that sustains us is knowing where we belong and that we're loved. And this special occasion has reinforced the importance of these things to me, both the giving and the receiving thereof. So first, let me say, on behalf of my wife...'

Jacinta and Tamilla Blake screamed, which set off another spontaneous cheer from the rest.

'Thanks, ladies!' their childhood friend grinned. 'Lynn'll pass on her own thanks a bit later. As you can imagine, a small amount of planning went into organising this event. But I'd like to thank all of you again for being here and sharing this day with us. Many of you've travelled a great distance, and we're very grateful. I'm sorry if that sounds patronising, but I couldn't come up with anything better. It's great to see so many friends, colleagues and folks I don't recognise at all.'

Everybody laughed at the musician's characteristic frankness. Keeping the microphone away from his body to avoid sending squawks of feedback through the public address system, he walked to the end of the long table and made his way around to the nearest circular one, turning his attention back to the bridal party from his new vantage point.

'I'd especially like to thank Bart and Marianna Dyson for all their efforts in making today happen at relatively short notice, and also for allowing their beautiful daughter to fraternise with someone like me in the first place. There are so many people to thank.'

Receiving cheery acknowledgement from both parents-in-law, the former Sydneysider turned his eyes on his best man, who raised a wine glass in reply.

'Gerry, I'd like to thank you for remembering the hardware,' he said next, brandishing his new ring, 'and for accompanying me and the boys on last Tuesday's expedition into the unknown. That night was a blast!'

He then walked around the table where the rest of the Blake family were seated. 'But more seriously for a moment, there are some people here to whom I owe extra-special gratitude. Here's a family who's been there for me through thick and thin, introducing me to some interesting contacts, teaching me to dance properly and entertaining me through those two long, lonely, Lynnless years. In short, they treat me like one of their own. It's very much appreciated, and I'd like to take this opportunity to thank them for everything. I refer to my surrogate parents, Celia and Gerald Blake, their son Gerry and their daughters, Jacinta and Tamilla.'

Other guests craned around from wherever they were sitting to acknowledge the Blakes, during which the speaker roved a little further into the field of diners, this time to where the surprise visitors from his past were seated, along with some of his RMIT friends and Suzanne and Steve.

'OK! On this table, I was very surprised to find my maths teacher from first year high school, Miss Yvonne Hawkins. Ms Hawkins had to put up with me badgering her for weeks on end to get me some interesting work to do, and she came through. I owe this lady a lot for help she gave me to get the most out of the New South Wales education system.'

Jeff bent down and kissed the teacher's cheek. She was embarrassed to remember their last steamy encounter but was not letting on to anyone. He then made his way to the table where Alberto and Eva were sitting and introduced them to Melbourne's *glitterati* in whose midst the shy pair had been plunged. And then lastly to Professor John Francis, who was proud to be seated with the two governing Excellencies.

His perambulations complete, the showman loped back to the top table, the occasion's natural high stoking his inner fire. 'Now to the sole representative of my own family: my sister, Madalena Moreno. Doesn't she look fine? Hey! This technology works well, doesn't it?'

The relaxed performer bent down and kissed the sultry-looking prostitute's cheek, deliberately loudly into the microphone. She giggled, a little frightened that she was about to be asked to say something.

'I think I only really met my sister this week,' the star admitted, standing tall and sweeping the room with his own dark eyes. 'Madalena and I've led very separate lives for the last ten years, and having her here as one of Lynn's bridesmaids has been fantastic for me. It's like being confronted with yourself and being forced to look objectively at your own foibles and frailties. Quite disconcerting sometimes. So thanks, *chica. Que es realmente hermosa hoy.*'

Holding Madalena's hand, Jeff had come full circle to his original position, no longer harbouring any qualms and ready to put the finishing touches to his very public commitment.

'And so to Lynn,' he regrouped, reaching for the hand of his bride. 'More than anyone, I'd like to thank this amazing woman sitting beside me here today for sitting beside me here today.'

The beauty frowned in comic confusion, making the audience laugh again.

Her man continued. 'Victoria Lynn Shannon Dyson has been the object of my desires for a long, long time now. I still have the boxes of posters, newspaper cuttings and magazine articles that my sister so eloquently described a few days ago. How many of us men here today could say the same?'

The groom looked around, confident of seeing a bevy of bobbing heads, and heard several appreciative whistles into the bargain. 'Quite a few, I suspect! Yeah! But anyway, as Gerry's already mentioned, I wasn't content to stop there. My single-minded... one could say obsessive... intention was to lay my hands on the real thing; truly honourable intentions, as I tried to tell her father many a time...'

The understated salute Bart gave his son-in-law matched that which Jeff had issued twenty minutes earlier.

'OK! The ladies and gentlemen of the press, and probably a good many more people besides, have taken great pleasure in guessing how long Lynn and I'll last together, how much strain we'll be under and how I'm not good enough for Australia's finest, and so on. Well, I quite agree. I'm not good enough for this gorgeous woman. But then again, there's no man on Earth who is. Bart Dyson has already told us how Lynn always brings sunshine into people's lives. And let me tell you, from here, it's an absolute heatwave!'

Jacinta and Tamilla led another chorus of ecstatic screams, while the red-blooded groom bent down to kiss his bride's lips, waving his hand to fan the metaphorical flames. A number of people left their tables, jostling for position for the best photographs, and the couple humoured their guests by holding a static pose for longer than was comfortable.

Once they were sure that most had successfully snapped their souvenirs, Jeff stood tall again and carried on. 'Lynn was the one who provided me with the motivation to become who I am today, such as I am. Before she came along, I had no purpose to my life; no meaning. Well, that's not true. My purpose was to find her, so that I could find true meaning.

'And now everything's crystal clear. It took a while for us to figure ourselves out, but we're on track these days. I gave myself lock, stock and barrel to her endless charms, and she tamed a very wayward child. Just like there's a difference between hearing and listening, she took me on a one-way, if sometimes rocky journey from "give and take" to "giving and receiving". Yep. There's a whole heap of difference between "take" and "get". By this I mean instead of stealing what I needed from life, I learned to be patient until it came to me. And Holy Cow, did it come to me!'

The spellbound audience gasped as the orator's raw emotion washed over them.

'She also welcomed into this inner circle my wild but wonderful sister, Lena. So, before I hand you over to this gorgeous embodiment of perfection, let me do two things: first, to invite you back here in twenty-five years for our silver wedding anniversary party...'

More cheers went up. Lynn looked shocked at the unplanned suggestion, but very pleased nonetheless.

'And second, to ask Your Excellencies, Your Honour, ladies and gentlemen...'

The skilful artist paused for effect, eyeballing his best man.

'And Gerry...'

Those who were familiar with the friends' boisterous relationship whistled and jeered their reinforcements, and the accountant took another bow.

Jeff drew his speech to a close. '... to please stand and drink a toast to the world's most beautiful woman: my wife, Victoria Lynn Shannon Dyson *Diamond*.'

The groom's smooth baritone became louder and slower with each name he enunciated, lowering his right arm towards his dream girl. Then, joining in with the affectionate applause, he looked on in admiration as the stunning superstar rose gracefully to her feet and embraced him with no inhibition whatsoever in front of the important gathering.

Cameras flashed all around them. The striking entertainer sunk into his seat to leave the spotlight squarely on his bride, but Lynn requested him to stay standing next to her, gripping his hand.

'Thank you, Jeff. Thank you, Your Excellencies, Your Honour, ladies and gentlemen,' she opened, her voice as clear as a bell. 'I'd definitely like to echo Jeff's sentiments in thanking you all for being here to share our amazing day. And it has been the most amazing of days. It's a logistical miracle that it all happened without a hitch. My parents have been fantastic, dropping everything for us. Thanks, Dad, for giving me away. And Mum's been the linchpin in the team, so I'd like to present her with a token of our appreciation for all her hard work and perfectionism.'

A waitress arrived on cue with a huge *bouquet* and a small box which Jeff recognised as containing a piece of jewellery Lynn had bought during their final days in London. The bride carried on, her mother suitably overcome.

'I'd also like to thank Michelle, Madalena and Anna for helping me with all the "girlie" preparations, initially remotely before we returned from the UK, and over the last week or so here. I won't bore you with all the details, but we've had some great times together.'

The graceful woman in the ivory dress then turned to their best man, who immediately blew her a kiss.

'Gerry Blake. Well... What can one say about Gerry Blake that hasn't already been said?' she joked, grinning.

The Mosman family once again generated a large amount of noise. Celia caught the fabulous speaker's blue eyes and put her hands together in prayer, seeming astounded by the level of affection held by this beautiful, sophisticated young woman for her incorrigible middle child. Jeff witnessed the sincere and silent exchange, and it warmed his heart.

Lynn waved to the gregarious North Shore *duo* and the family's strong but shy patriarch, who sat with his head in his hands. 'Gerry comes with his own travelling cheer squad! Besides being Jeff's best mate and our superb business manager, he's spent tireless hours trying to track us down to make decisions on this, that and the other.'

She turned to her husband before adding, 'Decisions on the other are usually best left to Jeff.'

The guests sniggered, first checking to see how Bart and Marianna were going to react.

'Gerry's a man's man who likes to live the high life. I heard that when Jeff broke the news that we were getting married, he choked on his double brandy XO,' the worldly twenty-year-old quipped. 'But in all seriousness, Gerry, it's been excellent to have you on the organising committee of our life singular, and we look forward to many more years of successful partnership. You rose to the challenge of being Jeff's best man admirably, and it's always a delight to talk to you at three, four or five o'clock in the morning.'

The rambunctious accountant raised his glass to Lynn, and his famous mate gave him a thumbs-up. He knew from their practice runs that his beautiful best friend was about to sign off.

'I'd like to thank all my friends and family, coaches, and particularly Sir Bradley Morrison, for the support they've given me throughout my life so far. To Rich, Janice, John and the rest of the MAC crew for all the fun on the road, and to Michelle, Sonia and all the guys from the tennis squad, I hope you've enjoyed the day and continue to enjoy the evening's entertainment we have planned. As Jeff said, I hope we manage to get around to speaking to you all for at least a few minutes. As for the two of us... My husband and I, as I should say...'

The happy woman raised herself up onto her toes to give her new owner a brief kiss, which received another enthusiastic round of applause. He scanned the room as if searching for someone who fit the bill better than he did. Failing to locate a more suitable candidate, the comedian reached for her waist and kissed her again, much to the audience's delight.

'Our plans are simple,' the singer continued, shoving the eager body aside. 'I knew when I first met this man in February 'seventy-two that I was in for a wild ride. My instincts weren't wrong, and every day with him is a new adventure. I've never met anyone so loving, so driven to do good and so tolerant and broad-minded. He constantly challenges the way I think, and I love him to bits for that. I think it was PL Travers, who wrote the Mary Poppins books, who said that ideas pick on people, not the other way round. Jeff Diamond is a very good idea, and I couldn't be happier or more honoured to know that he picked me.'

Gasps of awe emanated from nearly all female mouths on hearing this most romantic endorsement. Lynn's eyes welled up with tears when she saw her new husband's do the same, expressing their telepathic thanks.

'We'd like to use our combined talent and influence to right a few of the world's wrongs, if we can. Through music but also through whatever other means are at our disposal. Jeff once wrote a song called "Believe Me, Believe In Me", and I hope I can live up to that belief for the years to come. I believed in him back in 'seventy-two and I believe in him even more now. I love Jeff Diamond with all my heart, body and soul, and I know he feels the same way about me. Together who knows what we can achieve?'

The assembly was on their collective feet once again, ready to chant a final toast. The nobleman who had started life as a pauper stood beside his princess. He hadn't expected her to speak so profoundly about their ambitions. Hearing their vision articulated so clearly by his principal partner-in-crime rendered him dizzy with expectation.

The Master of Ceremonies drew the speeches to a close by announcing that the cake would be cut after dessert. Waiters and waitresses were busy distributing bowls and plates as he spoke, and people began to settle down to stock up on sugar for a long night of dancing.

Finally with a few minutes to themselves, Jeff tapped his best mate on the shoulder. 'Smoke?'

Gerry's eyes widened, hoping this was code for "escape", which of course it was. Madalena sprang out of her seat at the same time, and the pair were happy to have her join them, collecting Jacinta and Tamilla on their way out.

Lynn watched the smart men walk out of the ballroom, followed by three furiously verbose sisters. Her mother slid across into Jeff's vacated chair, and the bride sat talking with her parents over dessert, discussing the four excellent speeches and the program for the rest of the evening.

When the others returned, the two friends insisted Marianna stay where she was and disappeared again to sit at the Blakes' table until it was time to cut the cake. As with every last detail, the three-layered cake was iced with the couple's life singular motif, matching the banner hoisted atop the stage, the embroidery on bridal *lingerie* and tattooed on the soul-mates' physical incarnations.

After the cake had been sliced and taken away for dissection and distribution, the Master of Ceremonies performed his penultimate duty, which was to announce a short break while the band set up for the entertainment.

'You're not changing, are you?' Jeff asked his bride, glad of a private moment to talk without anyone overhearing. 'Out of this dress, I mean.'

'No. Wasn't going to.'

'*Bueno,*' her lover responded. 'I want to see you like this for as long as possible. You look absolutely amazing, and I want an overdose of memories to feed on. Come and meet some people, angel.'

Two Of Diamonds

The groom proudly led his bride around the room to meet his various guests, looking like the cat with the cream. They had played these roles in reverse on the lawn earlier, while the photographer had been organising his shots, the numbers on Lynn's side far greater. Time passed quickly in bouts of blithe conversation, and it was soon time for the entertainers to prepare for their stage set.

Drafted roadies wired the couple up to their microphones and ear pieces, laughing at the ugly black plastic box now attached to the laces of the bridal corset. Before long, the stars were in full view of their guests, performing a quick soundcheck. The front section of tables had been pushed back to make room for dancing, and the Master of Ceremonies made his final official pronouncement that the bride and groom were to lead off.

Once more the centre of attention and with the orchestra and band in position, Jeff walked Lynn slowly onto the dance floor and kissed her with appropriate restraint while the introduction played. The atmosphere was unusually heavy around them, everyone hanging out for the entertainment to begin. This was going to be a show to remember.

The couple's first song was a duet, which they sang while gliding across the floor in a fluid waltz, every turn and pause timed to perfection with the lyric's phrasing. With three full-sized video cameras on wheels tracking different angles like drunken Daleks, the sound system sent the harmonies soaring around the ballroom, not to mention the accompanying deep breaths and soft kisses. They danced without haste and with a confidence missing from the majority of tentative bridal *débuts*.

Windows on one side of the function hall had been opened, letting in a cool, early evening breeze. Throwing his head back, Jeff took in a chestful of air while his stunning wife sang to him, their bodies barely touching yet inflamed with emotion. When the superstars' final note left them breathless, they acknowledged their guests' loving applause with a deep bow followed by a precarious embrace which took all their strength to sustain.

The second and third songs were female solos, leaving Jeff to find Marianna and then Michelle to dance with after escorting the blonde singer onto the stage with help from her adult bridesmaids. As decided during the planning, the bride's father then stepped in awkwardly with the maid of honour while Gerry and Lynn's mother revisited their vastly different dancing pasts. With the expert entertainer encouraging as many females as possible to take a spin, other couples drifted over to join the throng, the joyful scene boosting the singing celebrity's happiness yet further.

The next switch saw her husband's turn to have the stage to himself. Bart was dancing with his wife, so the best man swooped in for a long-awaited dance with the bride. Again on request, Junior Dyson left his girlfriend with some friends and asked Jeff's shy sister onto the floor. Madalena had forgotten this part of the plan but realised she didn't have much choice in the matter, awestruck to be shuffling face to chest with the famous athlete whose feet were much better suited to running than dancing.

'You look absolutely fabulous,' Gerry shouted to his partner above the music. 'Marriage really suits you. And him too.'

Lynn nodded in agreement, following his eyes up onto the stage. The rocking beat of the previous number had softened and transitioned into a ballad she had helped to write before they had left London. It made her cry again, and the affable accountant scoffed at the sentimentality.

After another lengthy set featuring both singers, the bride's fellow child-stars took over with a special arrangement of some of their more languid hits while the couple treated their guests to a seductively choreographed display of slow-dancing to a *bolero* that had been reduced to walking pace.

'Remember there are people watching,' Lynn hissed into her husband's ear, their hips pressed close together. 'Minors, even.'

'Why? They can choose to avert their eyes.'

The elegant woman kissed her mischievous associate's cheek, pulling away from his body but instantly feeling herself snapped back into position.

'We're no longer committing any sin,' the dancer's sensuous breathing reminded her, 'but we can still pretend. The passion doesn't die tonight, *Regala*.'

'Or ever,' his wife replied, resting her head on his shirt. 'I love you so much.'

Knowing the song would soon be over, Lynn and Jeff's mouths met for a long, drawn-out kiss, listening to Janice stretching the last few bars. By the time the orchestra played the final, dramatic chord, the dancers had climbed the steps back up onto the stage and were thanking their good friends for such a wonderful *finalé* to their musical interlude.

The night's cabaret sadly over, a disc jockey took over from Sir Brad and his raft of grown prodigies to play a varied selection of dance music. This latest lull in proceedings gave the bridal party time to gather their belongings from the upstairs rooms and to have them transferred to the luxurious suites which had been reserved for them at a hotel in the city.

Waiting for his bride to return, the reeling rock star enjoyed a few minutes off at the bar with a cigarette and the boys in the band, all the while caretaking Madalena from a distance. Official duties over, she was doing what came naturally: working the room, seeking out her prey and making her moves. The observation he had made during his speech about feeling confronted by the presence of his big sister was only too real. Her behaviour differed little from his own adolescent attention-seeking, except for the fact that the twenty-six-year-old was touting for money. He had described himself as a sexual mercenary to Lynn just after they had met. He had been paid too, many times, the young man admitted to himself. Just not in cold, hard cash...

Why did this matter to him now? He was more ashamed of his past than he was of Madalena's present. Having a ring on his finger didn't mean he had to deny his very existence, did it? Jeff spotted his former mathematics mistress, Yvonne Hawkins, and asked her for a dance. Just for the hell of it. For old time's sake. His beautiful best friend would understand, even if he didn't.

From the other side of the ballroom, the new bride could see her husband with an arm around his high school teacher. With just a hint of jealousy, she watched them flirt. Yvonne, a fairly short but attractive woman, was tightening her former pupil's tie after he had lowered it and undone the top button of his shirt once the speeches were over.

'Once a teacher, always a teacher!' the handsome man smirked. 'What are you doing, Ms Hawkins?'

The visitor from Sydney was embarrassed, having drunk a little too much. 'Sorry. You just look messy.'

'It's the end of a long day,' Jeff's voice rasped, loosening his tie again. 'I've earned the right to dress how I want, haven't I, Miss?'

Yvonne laughed, memories flooding back while his skilful lead helped her stay upright. 'Yes. I suppose so, you sexy beast. Have you enjoyed the day?'

'Jesus, yes! It's been fantastic, every minute. You? Didn't you get married?'

'Hmm...' his partner grimaced. 'I did, but it was doomed. I left him.'

The showman span his teacher round when the *tempo* changed, catching a brief glimpse of his beautiful best friend looking their way. He ought to feel guilty but he didn't. She knew him well enough not to think there was anything sinister in his dance for old times' sake, especially on their wedding day. She had invited all these extra people from his past, after all...

It's frivolous, Lynn could hear her former sexual mercenary's persuasive tone echoing in her head. *Superficial. Nothing.*

The sportswoman turned away, focussing on stacking their belongings onto a trolley. *Don't look back,* she told herself. He was fine. He was having fun, and she had had the best day ever. It was just Jeff being Jeff. Everyone loved Jeff Diamond, but he loved only her. Plus the attention, of course.

Frivolous, his insistence reinforced to the woman whom he had chosen to heal his troubled soul, his eloquence filling her mind. *It's meaningless beyond this moment, angel. From these women to you, it's like the difference between graffiti and a masterpiece; a radio jingle and a symphony. What we have is a priceless work of art to be treasured in perpetuity, not just a cartoon for our temporary amusement.*

The young woman laughed, distracted by Michelle and her mother struggling with their suitcases. She ran to help them, still listening to her man's telepathy winging its way through the airwaves.

It's like any sport, angel. You can do it for fun or you can do it with serious ambition.

Using or respecting, the bride smiled to herself. Out there on the dance floor at his own wedding, she knew her husband was only using his former teacher, just as he had always maintained. The new Jeff was repaying a debt owed by the old Jeff. No harm done.

'Whatever you need, baby,' Lynn mouthed, feeling butterflies in her stomach as she pictured his smiling, post-traumatic face anxious to reassure her.

She knew her beautiful black stallion meant every word he said, without a shadow of doubt. There was no longer any suspicion nagging within her that on some level she was being sold a line to suit his own purposes. How did her magic-man cross from Madalena's world into her world? Was it the search for significance? Their cartoon had most definitely turned into a masterpiece, through the competent allocation of respect.

'Sorry it didn't work out,' Jeff replied to his teacher's confession. 'Maybe next time? Today's everything I hoped it would be. And you and several others from the olden days being here without me knowing's made it even more special.'

'That's good,' Yvonne said, continuing to fiddle with the dancer's tie. 'Olden days? What an insult! Lynn really seems to care, doesn't she? You know... About real people.'

'You bet,' he replied, tugging on their invisible elastic connection and wondering when he would have a chance to introduce the two women. 'She's the best. An angel of the highest order. Tell you what...'

'What?'

'Once the "GG" and the "G Vic" are gone, you can have this tie as a souvenir,' the superstar offered, as if Yvonne were one of his groupies.

'Oh, I'd love that!' the teacher cried above the music. 'Really? Will you sign it? And could I get a picture with you two?'

'Yeah. Why not?' Jeff answered. 'It's just that I might still need to look a bit smart if anyone else needs to take photos of us before they go.'

Away from the dance floor, Madalena, Michelle and Lynn helped load each others' bags onto trolleys for the hotel staff to collect. The dark-haired bridesmaid had fetched her brother's suit carrier too and piled everything together.

'Can I ask you a question?' the new sister-in-law asked, as they walked back into the ballroom.

'Of course,' the bride replied. 'Is everything OK?'

'Yeah. I just wanted to thank you and Jeff for lettin' me be part of your wedding. What can I do to say thanks?'

Lynn hugged the bony frame. 'You don't have to do anything. It's been amazing to meet you, and I know Jeff's really loved having you here. Just go and dance with him. That's what he'd love.'

'Yeah?' Madalena cried, looking relieved. 'S'that all?'

She had developed a real liking for the elegant star, who was ready with another idea.

'Lena, I know a great song for you two to dance to. I asked the DJ to bring certain songs just in case, so we can request it. Do you know Peter Sarstedt's "Where Do You Go To, My Lovely"?'

The Sydneysider shook her head. 'No. Don't think so.'

'Well... Jeff always thinks of you when he hears that song. When we get back to the ballroom, I'll ask the DJ to play it, and you can ask him to dance. He'll love it.'

'OK,' Madalena nodded. 'That's easy enough.'

The celebrity was pleased to see how much more conciliatory and open the feisty woman had become. 'It's great to have you as my sister-in-law,' she repeated. 'Sounds weird, doesn't it? Sister-in-law.'

'Na. Not really,' the prostitute answered, to the bride's amazement. 'Nothing's weird about today anymore.'

When the blonde beauty and her bridesmaids arrived back in the function room, Lynn made straight for the disc jockey. After a couple of minutes, Madalena received an "OK" sign, which was to mean that he would play their song after the current track.

Her brother was in the midst of his London bohemian set, smoking a cigar and drinking brandy with Gerry, Professor Francis and their university cohort. He saw the tall gipsy walking towards him and held his hand out for her.

'Hey, sister of mine! *¿Qué tal?* Come and join us.'

Madalena took his hand, with no interest in sitting down. 'Will you dance with me?'

The young man looked pleasantly surprised by her request. 'Sure I will! It'd be an honour, Lena. Excuse me, gents.'

As the superstar followed his sister onto the busy floor, the strains of a familiar song started, and his heart constricted painfully. The lonely sound of a raw accordion riff was enough to transport him back to their disgusting Canley Vale excuse for a home and to the second-hand transistor radio the siblings had shared, batteries for which had always been up to him to buy.

'How did you know about this song?' he asked, taking her hand and placing it on his shoulder.

Madalena gave the faintest smile. 'Just dance, *chico.*'

Jeff Diamond did more than dance. He sang every word to the prostitute in his arms, regretting everything she never got the chance to be or do. The poignant words poured through the lost boy, purging his guilt into its wake, while the statuesque man of influence steered his sister gracefully around the dance floor. They negotiated past other couples, deep inside the romantic story told by the lyric he respected so much.

'Did Lynn tell you about this song?'

'Yeah. She said you think about me when you 'ear it. I wanted to say thanks for askin' me to your wedding.'

Tears welled up in Jeff's eyes, and he dipped her over backwards in an effort to hide them. The tipsy woman screamed in delight, scrambling to right herself.

'That's nice,' the star smiled. 'You're very welcome. And Lynn's right about the song. D'you know what it's about?'

Madalena shook her head.

'Listen,' Jeff told her, holding her shoulders at arms' length and staring into her eyes, begging her to pay attention. 'It's about a brother and sister. The sister's living the high life, and her brother's asking her if she still remembers where she came from.'

The errant bridesmaid made an effort to decipher the lyric, keen to please this Very Important Person. Foreign place names woven into the poetic language refused to resonate in her simple mind, music holding little meaning beyond an infectious beat for dancing or a chorus that was easy to memorise and sing along to with her friends.

Doing his best to ignore the vacant expression on her face, the musician continued. 'This is what I wish for you. That you can leave all the crap behind.'

'What crap, but?' Madalena whined. 'Why are you cryin'?'

'Shit. I don't know! I guess because it's been so great having you here and getting to know you properly. And also that Lynn was telling me some of the fucked-up things you have to do. With men, I mean. You know...'

The carefree hustler frowned, not having anticipated this sudden change of tack. 'Oh, yeah. They were shocked, her and Michelle. For me it's just work, but they thought it was gross.'

340

Jeff sighed, shaking his head and twirling his partner around in front of him in time with the evocative accordion music. 'It's worse than gross,' he moaned. 'Sex with strangers for money is fair enough, but subjecting yourself to disgusting, depraved... It's wrong, Lena. Perverted pricks! You shouldn't have to do that shit.'

'It's the way of the world, *chico*.'

'What? Who told you that?' the songwriter couldn't help but laugh. 'That's fucking priceless!'

Madalena chuckled at the look on her brother's face. It had been Michelle who had used this *cliché*, the afternoon when the *trio* had first tried on their dresses. However, she knew better than to dob on her fellow bridesmaid.

'Ah, no-one,' the young woman shrugged. 'Pimps. The other girls. It don't bother me. I just get high or tanked up, and it ain't so bad. At least I don't get hit much.'

The air rushed out of the old soul's lungs, horrific childhood memories flooding into his mind. By now, he also regretted having broached the subject on his special night. He gripped his partner's right hand and shifted up a gear. Focussing back into the moment, he realised she was enjoying being waltzed around the floor and acknowledged that dancing did indeed run in the family.

Desperate to suppress the old images, Jeff forced himself to admit that none of these distasteful acts appeared to be doing his sister any damage. If he tried hard enough, he could visualise their mother bopping around to the radio too, and maybe even their dad once or twice. Or was it some other man? He didn't know, opting to purge all such confusing data for now.

'Zoe 'ad 'eaps o' that violent shit for a while,' his sister continued, giggling. 'But Sean took care of it. And weird "lezzo" stuff we used to 'ave to do all the time... Not 'alf as bad for us as some girls.'

'OK,' the superstar gave in, suspicious that the hard-hearted woman may be exaggerating in response to his show of sympathy. 'We need to talk some more about this when Lynn and I get home. I just want you to be happy. Look how happy I am, even after all the crap we went through. I want you to be too.'

Madalena hugged the handsome groom, who switched direction amid high drama, making her laugh like a girl. As the words of the song drifted back into his consciousness, it suddenly hit him that Peter Sarstedt wasn't singing about his sister at all. Rather, it was his own story being told. He was the one who had made it against the odds, and he was the one who was obliged not to forget those who were left behind.

'*Chico*, I am happy,' the bridesmaid refuted. 'I've had a great time in Melbourne, and I'm going back 'ome tomorrow and I'll still be me. Then maybe in a few months, you can come and see me again, or I can come 'ere again?'

'Sure,' the emotional millionnaire replied. 'You've got a deal. I believe you. I just want to help, that's all.'

When the song reached the verse where the girl's name was mentioned, he sang into his sister's dark brown eyes.

> 'I remember the back streets of Naples,
> Two children begging in rags.
> Both touched with a burning ambition
> To shake off their lowly born tags.
> So look into my face, Marie-Claire,
> And remember just who you are.
> Then go and forget me forever,
> But I know you still bear the scar, deep inside.'

Jeff gulped as the lump in his throat prevented him from singing any more, and he fell silent for the rest of their dance. So what if they didn't want to live in each others' worlds? His sister had told him she was happy, and for Christ's sake, he was happy. So unbelievably happy.

Their requested song finally finished, the groom went to lead his partner off the floor. After a few steps however, seeking to brighten his mood, he changed his mind. The next track was much faster, and Madalena's eyes lit up.

'D'you wanna stay up here?'

'Yeah! That'd be good. I love this one!'

The matching gipsies strutted their Catholic Argentinean Polish Jewish stuff for three more dances, dispelling the gloom which their nasty conversation had visited upon them. Lynn and Michelle came to join them, along with the voluminous bridal train, much to the delight of other friends nearby.

The three women whooped with energetic joy, parading their wares in front of their favourite man and taking turns to weave around his willing frame, before the blonde noticed her mother signalling to them.

'Mum's looking for us,' she attracted her husband's attention.

Dutifully, the bride and groom left the others and walked over to where her parents were standing with the Governors and their wives.

'Their Excellencies are leaving,' Bart stated.

The distinguished Melbourne set said their goodbyes and expressed their gratitude to the honourable guests for attending. Since most of the bride's family and friends had gravitated toward the departing dignitaries, Lynn took the opportunity to thank everyone again for coming and to draw all the ladies together. Thinking ahead as always, she had dispatched Michelle to retrieve her *bouquet* of apricot- and cream-coloured roses from the top table, turning around and throwing it behind her, over her head as far as she could, into a jostling pondful of excited girls. The flying flowers were caught by one of her school-friends, resulting in an outbreak of high-pitched frivolity.

Not to be outdone, Jeff gathered all the eligible bachelors in a circle to prepare for the garter ceremony. Beckoning to his new wife provocatively, he enticed her closer, and the showman reeled her in like a hooked salmon. He winked and mouthed a quick thank-you, before reaching underneath the long skirt panels of her dress, egged on by whistles and chants from lecherous lads.

The Dyson parents and their extended family gazed on in amusement. Their elder daughter held out her slim, athletic leg and pointed her toe as the groom inched the elasticated lace down towards her ankle, uttering a long, low moan. As soon as it came free of her shoe, he whipped it up above his head triumphantly, shouting some unintelligible Spanish idiom.

Jeff checked his mark out of the corner of his eye, stretching the scarlet weapon in his left hand, and made sure he knew precisely where his brother-in-law was standing. Then he flexed the lacey item once or twice before spinning around to shoot it behind him. He scored a direct hit on Junior's chest, whose lightning reactions had no trouble in taking the catch.

'Yay, June!' Lynn cheered and clapped her hands, finding herself being corralled again by her exotic *matador* towards the footballer in a deliberate effort to bring the crowd's attention with them.

Embarrassed when he realised he had been specifically targetted, Junior nodded at the celebrities. The pressure was on. Never one to lack courage however, he walked the few paces to where his girlfriend stood and bent down on one knee. All eyes were on the blond sportsman, a turgid silence reigning supreme.

'Julie, I love you very much. Will you marry me?'

The spellbound audience gasped in surprise, none more so than the pretty brunette. Marianna put her hands to her mouth to stifle a sob. Her eldest child was holding out his sister's garter to the woman whom he had been dating for just over a year, who accepted it willingly, surrounded by squealing friends.

'Yes!' Julie replied, lurching forward into her boyfriend's broad wingspan. 'I will. Oh, I can't believe it! Yes, yes, yes!'

A huge cheer went up around them, while the second happy couple of the day embraced each other and indulged in a passionate kiss of their own, in front of everyone.

Lynn hugged her thoughtful man. 'You done a good thing,' she said, in gentle imitation of her sister-in-law.

Once the hysteria had died down, the newlyweds congratulated the will-be-weds. Primed by the hopeful world-changer, the bar staff served another round of champagne, rushing to dispense it as quickly as possible. Several people burst out laughing on hearing Bart Dyson's loud groan in the background.

'Oh, my God, Marianna! Do you mean we've got to go through this all over again?'

Jeff looked at his watch. It was only nine o'clock, but he was beginning to think the day had run its course. Nobody had thought to agree on the most appropriate time to draw the proceedings to a close, and he wondered if there were yet another protocol which ought to be followed. What the hell? It was their wedding.

'We should get going,' he suggested to his beautiful best friend in a quiet aside.

The young woman's eyes betrayed her inner thoughts, judging by what their reaction did to his insides. 'Yes, OK. No-one'll leave before we do, and they've been here for hours,' Lynn agreed. 'I'm tired. Are you?'

Her perfect stranger shrugged. 'To be honest, I don't know. I'm in emotional overload. There is one thing I have to do first though...'

The bride looked into his guilty face. 'Oh, yeah? What's that?'

'I promised Yvonne my tie as a *memento*,' the sheepish man confessed, knowing his beautiful best friend had picked it out for the occasion. 'D'you mind? Come and get a photo' with her.'

Shaking her head, Lynn was all smiles at her husband's inability to curtail his philandering. 'No, of course not. It's served its purpose, I s'pose.'

Jeff kissed her with all the warmth he could muster. 'You're fantastic, angel. Thanks. Will you marry me?'

'Thanks, but no, Mister Smooth,' the young woman pushed him away. 'I'm already spoken for. Let's go and play with your teacher.'

The couple abandoned their unwanted champagne and went in search of the mathematics mistress. The bride guessed Ms Hawkins would be in her thirties by now, appearing average in every way as they closed in on each other. She felt ashamed of her shallow reaction, yet it made her feel safer to consign the relatively plain face into the "using relationship" category with little room for doubt, further reinforced by the painful clamp of insecurity the star pupil maintained around his guardian angel's arm.

The two women shook hands politely, an initially stiff, cold introduction soon softening as both assumed their rightful places in the hierarchy of their shared lover's affections.

'I can finally say, "And this is my wife,"' the proud man grinned. 'Bet you never thought you'd hear me say that, Ms Hawkins.'

Yvonne received her gift with a shy subservience, as if she were accepting an award for delivering a numerate student to Australia's princess. Lynn's grace and sensitivity offset her husband's jovial teasing until the tie's recipient had relaxed enough to smile for the camera.

'It's been so good to see you again, Jeff. Please look me up next time you're in Sydney. And Lynn, of course.'

The groom chuckled. 'Of course! And did you know this is my wife? You did your bit to make me into me, for which I thank you again. But this angel here…' he squeezed the irresistible body to his hip and kissed her temple. 'She disassembled me, threw away some broken pieces, straightened a few bent ones out and then put me back together again in the right order. Awesome, huh? And she still wants to keep me after all that hard work!'

Superbly confident on the outside, the superstar pecked his former mentor on the cheek, and she blushed. A great deal of water had passed under the bridge since she had assisted this maligned boy who had been gifted in every way except by position in society. The way she saw things, any teacher worth her salt ought to help such motivated children to navigate the New South Wales school system, yet it was abundantly clear to all three adults that reciprocity had been at play all along.

'You're still the sexiest mathematician in town,' the successful student joked, buoyed by the sensation of loving fingernails scratching his spine through the fabric of his clothing.

Farewells were exchanged step by step, as bride and groom made their rounds through the remaining groups of guests. Now minus his tie and with the top two buttons of his shirt undone, Jeff sought out his sister and the elderly boxing club owner, Alberto, to ensure they knew how to get to their hotel rooms. After several emotional attempts to say goodnight, they all agreed to delay the inevitable and meet again for breakfast at nine o'clock the next morning.

The newlyweds were next swallowed up into the extended Dyson clan, bidding all three generations present a good night before bundling up Lynn's long train and heading for the lifts. Most followed them down and congregated on the lobby steps, where a pair of white horses and a black carriage decorated with apricot and white balloons were waiting to take the honeymooners less than a kilometre to the Windsor Hotel.

The romantic scene had been staged to typify Melbourne's glorious traditions, with the country's press and television stations beaming the picture-perfect showbusiness wedding all over the world. Neither celebrity minded too much, in reluctant acceptance of the positive energy the chintzy entertainment value added to their worthy causes.

Not unexpectedly, despite many hours having passed, a legion of die-hards had patiently waited outside for a glimpse of the famous pair. Guests official and unofficial cheered the couple off with revitalised enthusiasm, and Lynn and Jeff waved to everyone as the horses jerked the carriage forwards and clip-clopped around the corner onto St Kilda Road for their short journey into the city. Turning the final corner out of Collins Street, they found yet another, much larger cohort of fans ready to greet them outside the *grand foyer*, having somehow got wind of their imminent arrival.

No longer with their attentive bridal party to control Lynn's unruly train, Jeff and the porters did their best to spread it out on the steps of the well-lit hotel entrance. They graciously posed for more photographs and chatted to their excited followers after the carriage had departed, until a *concièrge* cleared a path for them to walk to the lift. He ceremonially handed the rock star a key to their suite, which was accompanied by a round of wolf-whistles and cheers from drinkers who had emerged from The Cricketers Arms on hearing the commotion.

As a final extravagant gesture to acknowledge everyone's loyalty, the gallant gentleman bent over and scooped the lady in the ivory dress to his chest and carried her up the first flight of stairs, presenting yet more priceless photo-opportunities. Reaching the landing, he set his smiling burden down onto the carpet, and they paused for a last, long, photogenic kiss before turning down the corridor and vanishing out of sight.

The sudden stillness was deafening. They found the first-floor lift lobby and ascended to their floor, where two members of the hotel's security staff were waiting with their luggage. Once locked inside their room, both bride and groom breathed a huge sigh of relief, leaning into each other in an exhausted embrace.

***

'Well... There ya have it, Lynn Diamond,' Jeff declared, tossing his suit jacket down onto the bed. 'Now do you feel different?'

The gorgeous twenty-year-old shrugged, glowing inside on hearing her new name again. 'I don't know. I feel like you said earlier: emotional overload. It's been a long day, but everything's been perfectly perfect.'

'You're perfectly perfect,' her husband told her, reaching lasciviously for her slim waist and becoming entangled in the angel costume again.

They kissed for a long time, feeling drained but completely elated. After a minute or so, the handsome groom broke away to fetch something from his suit carrier. The young woman smiled curiously as she saw a tape being loaded into the cassette player. She held out her arms to welcome him back, the sound of the ceremony's opening song, "Have And Hold", playing softly in the background.

Jeff lifted his wife's left hand in his right and kissed the two rings, then pressed it against his chest and began to dance. His other hand took its place in the small of her back, resting against the lattice, his thumb aimlessly strumming the laces.

'Now I can make love to you in your dress, and it won't matter if I mess up your hair.'

Eyes closed and tongues searching, they waltzed through the whole track, the singer singing along with his own recorded voice. Lynn let him lead her in slow, random arcs, confined by her dress, the furniture and their various pieces of luggage scattered around the room.

Her heart soared. How like this mysterious intellectual to want to seduce the one he now had and held on their wedding night! They belonged to each other under law, confirmed by signatures on a marriage certificate and with two new gold bands to prove it. One last statement, she sighed, to make sure their memorable day turned into a singularly exceptional night.

'This is beautiful. Thank you,' the bride murmured, her fingers tickling the hairy flesh inside his open shirt, as if tracing her hidden signature. 'I love you so much.'

Jeff's mouth closed around hers, his tongue running along the underside of her upper lip until he felt her body wilt ever so slightly. 'Mmm... You're right and you're welcome. Thank *you*. You know, I never dreamed I'd get married to a girl in a white dress with horses and a carriage, nor spend the night in a luxury honeymoon suite...'

The girl in the white dress closed her eyes, feeling happy tears brimming. This amazing day was all she had been thinking about for the last few months. For the last few years, if she were honest. Twelve months ago, she had not been expecting to marry her complex, bohemian love-god either, yet the wedding he had given her was beyond her wildest dreams.

The music in the background was fading out, and her husband's sincere voice made her shiver as he finished his sentence. 'But I always dreamed I'd be here with you.'

A muffled sob escaped Lynn's lips. She nestled her head into his chest and hugged him closer still. They continued to move in silence, the palm of Jeff's right hand now pressed tightly against her thigh as if he might never let go. Feeling her abdomen shift against his erection, he coaxed her chin upwards and kissed the corners of her tearful eyes.

'*Je t'aime, mon ami*,' she smiled. '*Para siempre*. You are so gorgeous. Shall we go to bed?'

Freed from her husband's grip at last, the bride instructed him on how to unhook the train from her dress, and they clumsily attempted to separate the two pieces.

'This is going to take some deconstruction,' the comic quipped.

'Oh, I'm sure you're up to the task. I've got no idea how my hair's been put together either.'

The sportswoman shuffled into the bathroom and began the laborious exercise of pulling out the collection of bobby pins and clips which the hairdresser had threaded into her hair. In the mirror, she watched her man follow her in, removing his suit trousers and white shirt until only his boxer shorts and a pair of black socks remained. What was underneath was familiar and irresistible, and she smiled appreciatively at his reflection.

'You look fantastic! Might as well see if there's something on TV though,' she lamented. 'This is going to take a while.'

Jeff sat down on the edge of the bath, shaking a resolute head while peeling off his socks. He folded them together into a ball and threw them gently at her back.

'Nope. I'm staying here. I don't want to let you out of my sight. I want to drink you in, from head to feet. Is that OK?'

'Is it OK?' Lynn echoed, giggling. 'What do you think?'

The groom helped the bride free her hair, section by section, and straightened each golden lock with care as it fell loose over her bare shoulders. During the evening, the heavy gown had gradually slipped low enough down her back to display the simple, delicate tattoo in its entirety, and he kissed it fondly.

Saying nothing, the expressive musician took hold of his co-star's waist and snatched her against his aching body. She groaned in pleasure at the power of her man's insistence and rubbed against him, feeling his hard penis pressing through the layers and into the crack between her buttocks. His hands moved upwards and caressed her breasts through the ivory satin, staring at their adults-only reflection in the mirror.

'You look stunning,' Jeff whispered against her neck. 'I love you so, so much. And I want you just as much.'

Lynn twisted around and started to remove his shorts, then pushed him backwards in the direction of the bed. 'I love you and want you too, just as much,' her huskiest voice replied, teasing his *libido* mercilessly. 'You remember how difficult it was to get it on in this dress?'

Jeff was breathing heavily, and his eyes drilled into hers. His dream girl was about to take control, in a statement of her own, and he was ready to let her do whatever she had in mind.

'Yes. How could I forget?'

'Well...' the sexy woman smiled. 'Your job is to look at me in my dress while I make sure you have a good time. Can you manage that?'

Without waiting for a response, Lynn knelt at her husband's feet and wrapped one hand around his testicles, drawing a cry of pleasure as they settled into its cool palm. Caressing his throbbing manhood with her best racquet grip, she guided it into her mouth. Again, he moaned in delight over and over, brought fast and often to the edge of restraint before being let down in a mixture of relief, frenzy and pure bliss.

'Angel, you're driving me crazy,' the ecstatic man told her, his hands unable to reach much of the dazzling dress which still covered the figure he worshipped. 'I like what this marriage thing's done to you.'

Their divine encounter continued for several more minutes before Jeff encouraged his lover to her feet. 'Stop. I want to come inside you on our wedding night. I want to be as close as we can be. I wanna make you scream like you've never screamed before.'

Lynn gathered up her skirt, stood and turned around for her man to undo her lattice, as he had done some seven hours earlier in her little brother's apartment. Her hands continued to play havoc with his self-control, knowing that needing to concentrate on unstringing the intricate web would counteract the rush.

When the long lace was pulled through the final pair of loops, the gown slithered over the bride's slim hips and fell stiffly to the floor, once again revealing the *lingerie* with their own unique motif. Even though this time its appearance was hardly a surprise, having thought about little else in the last hour, the heaven-sent items made the red-blooded *lothario* see stars when he finally set eyes on them.

'I have a special request for our wedding night,' his wife announced, her words punctuated by gasps of pleasure as strong hands and a hungry mouth worked their magic all over her body.

'Oh, yeah?' Jeff muttered, intrigued to discover what could possibly surpass the sensuous act currently engaging his every sense. 'Now would not be a good time to tell me you've re-joined that "no sex after marriage" cult you spoke of before.'

Lynn laughed out loud, sending shock-waves through the aroused man's chest. 'Oh, wow! That was ages ago! I can't believe you remember that,' she replied. 'No. That's not my special request.'

'Thank Christ for that,' her lover smiled, scanning upwards past her breasts and on into her beautiful blue eyes.

The young woman stroked his darkened cheek, and the eager philosopher wrapped his arms around her, pressing himself hard against her until the full length of their bodies touched. His soulful, smouldering eyes beckoned forth her words.

'Jeff, what I'd like is that every time we make love, we do it as if it's the last time we'll ever see each other, just in case one day it is.'

The romantic musician inhaled the whispered pledge into his soul, and her poignant suggestion hung in the air while the pair stood locked together.

'Whoa. That's some request,' the usurped poet answered, breathing out and hugging her still tighter. 'And I grant it unconditionally. I think we already do, but now I'll make sure I do.'

'Thanks. Me too,' Lynn agreed. 'Starting now.'

The world around the happy couple slipped into slow motion. Jeff laid his beautiful bride down onto the bed as if she weighed next to nothing and sank his full length into the welcoming warmth. They caressed each other with burning passion until it was all over in a bout of mutual, prolonged natural ecstasy.

'So *now* do you feel any different?' she asked, sitting astride her handsome groom to enjoy the smile of satisfaction on his face, while the tattoo on his chest rose and fell on their journey back to Earth.

The songwriter's eyes remained closed, and his shoulders pressed down into the pillow. After a short pause, two possessive hands reached for his lover's slender arms, urging her down onto the mattress beside him. She shrieked in delight when his mouth and hands began to devour her neck and breasts again, ending up in a passionate kiss.

'No,' the young man replied eventually. 'And that kind of disappoints me. Just think of all that money we spent and effort you went to just to feel the same...'

His beautiful best friend tilted her head backwards to allow her eyes to focus on his face, which was smiling broadly. 'Oh. Me too actually, but I wasn't going to say so. Maybe because we're tired of all the fuss.'

Jeff kissed her again. 'Yeah. 'Xpect so. You're still the most beautiful woman in the world, and you're here with me, so the uptick on the disappointment scale is negligible.'

Lynn chuckled. 'Good! Same for me. The way I look at it, we've been married since we got these...' she said, her fingers stroking the "JL" symbol through the hairs covering her man's left pectoral muscle. 'We always knew, didn't we? And now everybody else is in on the secret, so perhaps we'll only feel different when we're with other people. People'll treat us differently now, whereas we're used to us,'

The intellectual was content with this logical hypothesis, especially knowing they both felt the same way. He cast his mind back to the dangerous suggestion he had ventured about their souls being estranged from each other in a recent incarnation. Perhaps the fact they had found each other in this lifetime ought to be given greater significance...

Yet it had, he realised, in exactly the same way as his *Regala* had described. They had always been bound to each other. The rest of the world was only now catching up with the news.

The last few pink-tinged minutes of sunset lapped over the couple through their rooftop window, facing westwards from the city. Exhausted and deliriously peaceful, they lay still and nominated their individual highlights of the day.

Sensing the night becoming darker, Lynn turned to the clock beside the bed. 'Hey! It's still only ten-fifteen,' she marvelled. 'It's so early. It feels like two in the morning. Did you want a drink or anything?'

Jeff hugged her close. 'No, thanks. To tell you the truth, I don't even want a cigarette. Who cares what time it is? I've got you to myself at last, and that's the only thing that interests me right now.'

The blonde singer planted a kiss on his lips, thanking him for saying the right thing yet again. Then, taking a deep breath, she pushed herself up from his warm torso and sat next to him on the mattress, another question burning.

She looked deadly serious, and her lover couldn't help but smile. 'What now?'

'Can I make another request, please?'

'You're very demanding tonight, Missus Diamond,' the seasoned negotiator replied. 'But for you, anything.'

'Can we go home and sit on the balcony?'

Digesting this unexpected alteration to her meticulous itinerary, the groom leaned forward and kissed his bride. 'Oh, yeah,' he exhaled, much in favour of this idea. 'That'd be perfectly perfect too. Let's get out of here.'

Both globe-trotting millionnaires were more than happy to desert their sumptuous surroundings for the familiarity of their own home. They put on the clothes in which they had arrived for the morning's rehearsals, staring at each other and dissolving into a fit of laughter. It was as if the whole wedding *extravaganza* had been just another show, and now they were going home, back to their life singular. They would read the notices in tomorrow's papers while the rest of their guests slept in splendour.

'We still have these,' the pretty twenty-year-old said, pointing to her wedding ring, 'to prove it really happened.'

'Cool,' Jeff affirmed. 'And don't forget the undies. I'm assuming they're not set to self-destruct at midnight.'

Lynn giggled, slapping his forearm. 'No! You say the funniest things. I hope not. Especially not with me still in them!'

Leaving everything else undisturbed, the furtive pair closed the door, tiptoed down the corridor and let themselves quietly out of an unlocked fire door they discovered at the end. It led to an emergency stairwell, and the escapees ran down several flights and burst out at street level.

'I don't want today to've been a dream,' the husband confessed, putting his arm around his dream girl's shoulder as they walked the five short blocks home.

No longer disguised as bride and groom, the Diamonds strolled along Spring Street, past the Princess Theatre. At the corner of Little Lonsdale Street, Jeff suggested crossing the road and wandering through Carlton Gardens, where they had spent one of their first dates spinning on fairground rides. He had proclaimed his love for the sixteen-year-old starlet that evening, a memory she readily offered on their wedding night.

'I wonder what happened to that van?' Lynn mused. 'I wish we had a photo' of it. It wouldn't seem right to re-create it just for a souvenir.'

Reliving their teenaged romance, her husband gathered his giggling girlfriend up into his arms and stole them both into an alcove in the Royal Exhibition Building's cold stone wall. 'If I had a knife, we could carve our initials into this brick.'

'You wouldn't. That's vandalism! Jeff Diamond doesn't do vandalism.'

'Lucky I haven't got a knife, or I might prove you wrong tonight,' the young man countered, smothering her smiling mouth. 'Jeff Diamond didn't do a lot of things until he met Lynn Dyson.'

'Anyway,' the singer broke away, breathless, 'my initials haven't changed.'

'Yes, they have. You're double-D now. Sounds like a bra size.'

'Yikes! Double-D's too big for me. Can you imagine playing tennis with boobs that big?'

The reigning Wimbledon Ladies' Singles champion held her hands out in front of her, pushing her B-cup breasts up as far as they would go. Too good an opportunity to miss, her husband ducked his head until his lips made contact with the soft flesh, growling under his breath.

'Oh, I'm sure I could get used to them. But yeah. These are just fine the way they are. Shall we get back? I think I might need to claim my conjugal rights again before too long, what with all this talk of big tits an' all.'

Lynn slapped her grinning playboy lightly across the cheek, tutting like Celia Blake. He grabbed her hand and held onto it tightly while they completed the circle of the gardens. Not a dirty, white van in sight, the grounds contained a few scattered groups of people making the most of the warm evening, so the couple kept moving, not wishing to be recognised.

No-one would expect to see the celebrities out and about at this time of night anyway; not on their wedding night! They crossed the tramlines where Victoria Street turned into Victoria Parade and climbed the steps to the entrance of their apartment building. The penthouse key slipped into its dedicated slot and activated the lift, and within twenty seconds, they alighted on the sixteenth floor.

Jeff handed the key-ring to his beautiful best friend. 'Just in case.'

New Year's night was still warm on their tired faces when the man of the house slid open the glass doors to let some fresh air into the stuffy living room. Stretched out on sun-lounges and surveying the twinkling lights of the suburbs stretching to the north, they must have stayed talking on the balcony for almost two hours when he finally suggested retiring to bed. They were stone cold sober, he was relaxed, and his new wife looked radiantly happy.

'Lynn,' the humble world-changer began, as they reached for the sheet and pulled it over, 'thank you.'

'For what?'

'For being here. For being you. This has been the best day. Way beyond how I imagined it would be.'

'Oh, same for me,' the singer agreed. 'I'm glad you've enjoyed it so much.'

Jeff kissed her. 'And thanks for suggesting the Peter Sarstedt song to Lena. That was a fantastic idea, and it brought out something good in her.'

'You're welcome. It'll be weird not to have her around, won't it?' Lynn said, resting a comforting hand on his chest, sensing a melancholy mood descending.

'Yeah. It will,' the young man affirmed. 'But I'm also OK for her to go back. I've now put my mind at rest that she doesn't belong here, which is a relief. So now I have to have a good, hard think about what I do next for her. She's happy, as you say. I'm trying to change a life that doesn't want to be changed.'

The bride hugged her wise man. 'I'm glad to hear you say that. I agree, but I also think you've taught her a lot this trip. And perhaps you won't feel so guilty in the future, now you've seen she's happy?'

'Yeah, maybe... Hey! That Tim guy never turned up, I'm guessing. I didn't see him.'

Lynn smiled. 'Oh, yeah! I'd forgotten about him. Did Lena mention him?'

'Not once,' Jeff shook his head. 'Out of sight, out of mind. He paid already. Why should she think about him again?'

They both chuckled, settling down for the night.

'Anyway... That's enough about my sister,' the exhausted songwriter added. 'Time for sleep. I'm glad we're getting up early for a run tomorrow. I hated the idea this morning but I've changed my mind. It'll be like it's just another Friday.'

'*Excelente*,' Lynn yawned. 'Goodnight, husband. Sleep well. *Te amo.*'

Jeff wrapped his arms around his new wife. '*Buenas noches*, Lynn Dyson Diamond. *Je t'aime aussi.*'

Within minutes, the young woman's breathing had slowed right down, and she was out for the count. Her protective lover hoped she would dream about her wedding day all over again. He slipped his arm from underneath her torso and turned to face the other way.

So here he was... *Not bad, mate.* From good-for-nothing street kid to Lynn Dyson's husband in less than four years. From a nobody tormented by demons and insecurities but touched by a burning ambition to shake off his lowly-born tags, as the descriptive lyric went, to a towering colossus of self-assurance who had been granted the Midas touch by his perfectly perfect saviour.

Jeff Diamond was certain that when his parents had brought home their boy-child twenty-three-and-a-half years ago, along with an envelope of idiot-proof pamphlets on how to nurture their accidental new toy, the standard-issue, western suburbs template for his life would not have contained a section on thanking the Governor General for attending his marriage celebrations. Nor one on listening to the man's rather large wife bemoaning the uncomfortable four-poster guest bed at Melbourne's Government House, for that matter.

Lying in their own bed with less than a day to go before they flew out for three weeks in the sun, the multi-millionnaire philanthropist felt a rare but unassailable feeling of strength. Together, there was nothing the ambitious celebrities couldn't accomplish. All his debts had been repaid. In fact, he could even claim to be ahead these days.

He turned back and looked at Lynn sleeping peacefully beside him.

Yep, no doubt about it. Way ahead. Up yours, Gravity.

But with the invincibility, there also remained a large dose of humility. How did the saying go? Easy come, easy go, he was sure. Jeff vowed never to take anything for granted. Yet, not long shy of four years after meeting the girl of his dreams, here she was lying next to him as his wife. Who would have believed it?

***

By six o'clock on the second of January nineteen-seventy-six, both Lynn and Jeff were wide awake, refreshed and excited at the prospect of their honeymoon away from it all. They dressed for a run and packed their breakfast clothes before retracing their steps to the Windsor Hotel. Their room was waiting for them exactly as they had last seen it, courtesy of the "Do Not Disturb" sign looped over the door handle.

The enormous wedding dress hung draped over a chair, where it now sagged a little after a night left to its own devices. The pair gasped when they saw it, filled with wonderful memories.

'What are you going to do with this now?' the groom asked, running his fingers over the embroidered fabric. 'It's so big. It needs its own room.'

Lynn chuckled. 'I was thinking about auctioning it for Childlight, but not 'til next year. I want to be able to get it out and look at it every now and again.'

Jeff liked this idea. 'We'll find a good home for it until then,' he told her, giving his big-hearted partner a hug.

As the athletes ran over Princes' Bridge and turned left onto the path leading into Alexandra Gardens, they heard a conspicuous, booming voice shouting his daughter's name. They soon united with the rest of the family and hit the Botanic Gardens' gravel running track, the men breaking into a hard sprint and leaving mother and daughters to run at a talking pace around the three-and-a-half kilometre circuit.

'You two look well,' Marianna said to Lynn.

'Yes. We're fine, thanks. He's gorgeous, isn't he?' the dreamy young woman replied, watching her new husband keep up with Junior, Bart and Sandy. 'We didn't stay in the hotel after all last night, by the way. We walked home and spent the night in our own bed. It was brilliant. We sat on the balcony for ages, just talking.'

'That's nice,' her mother replied. 'It was a lovely day. I'm pleased you enjoyed it. Everyone seemed to. What time do you fly out?'

'Not 'til nine tonight. Plenty of time to pack, which is lucky because we haven't even started. And Jeff has to get his sister back to the airport.'

The elegant lady smiled. 'Hmm... It's hard to picture Jeff being like Madalena, presuming they used to be alike, isn't it?'

Lynn laughed, undecided on how to respond. 'There are heaps of similarities deep down,' she let on to her mother, who was unaware of much of what the young couple had been through over the last few years. 'But he's learned how to get the most out of life, whereas Lena seems content with much less. He was just saying last night that she's happy. Jeff always wanted to do something for her, to change her life, but now he's concluded she's happy enough being the way she is.'

The women changed the subject, involving Anna in the conversation by asking about her first experiences as a bridesmaid. Meanwhile, up ahead, the three men and the teenaged Sandy turned the corner to power up Anderson's Hill for the second time.

Jeff shouted breathlessly to his new in-laws. 'I suppose there's no point in offering the excuse that last night was my wedding night?'

'No way!' Junior scoffed, sprinting ahead of him. 'Absolutely none.'

The newest family member groaned and changed gear to follow the Dysons up the hill, tapping into his reserve tank. Mid-way through the third lap, he admitted defeat and slowed down to run with the women.

His wife laughed in sympathy when she saw him so out of breath. 'Working hard? What was that you said about us looking well, Mum?'

'I made the mistake of asking for pity because it was my wedding night,' Jeff panted.

Marianna and her elder daughter both grinned at the star's uncharacteristic *naïveté*. His long hair was extra-curly with sweat, and his T-shirt was drenched. Lynn wondered if her mother was enjoying the same naughty thoughts, although her face gave nothing away. This dark horse with smiling eyes was quite the most exquisite specimen of mankind she had ever seen. And he was all hers...

'Oh, I expect that excuse didn't wash with Bart,' his mother-in-law replied.

'You're not wrong! Zero compassion from any of them. In fact, they sped up.'

At the end of the third lap, the trailing party caught up to the leaders while they were stretching, and everyone jogged back to the hotel together. Other early birds were delighted to set eyes on the happy group of local heroes, seldom all in one place at the same time, calling out and waving cheerfully.

The only dark-haired one among them looked at ease and well-accepted in their company.

Lynn and Jeff arrived at the entrance of the dining room a few minutes after nine o'clock to find most of their guests already present. Elegant in high heels, last night's bride looked refined in a low-cut white blouse, with a fawn, swirling skirt which was short enough to show off her long legs as she walked but long enough to emphasise her grace and dignity. The outfit was finished off with a crimson belt around her waist. Her equally striking groom was unshaven, in yesterday's jeans and a black, collared shirt. They looked the picture of happiness.

Alberto and Eva sat at a table on their own, quite out of place in five-star luxury. The old man was wearing his suit and tie again and regularly reprimanded his daughter for being greedy with the buffet fare. Their faces lit up with pride when the happy couple joined them, placing their colourful plates of fruit on the table mats.

'Did you sleep well?' the budding stateswoman checked.

'Yes, thanks. Did you?' Eva asked back, with a glint in her eye.

The bride gave a gracious smile. 'Yes, thanks!'

'No sign of Lena then?' Jeff enquired. '*¿Estaba con Ustedes después de salir ayer por la noche?*'

Alberto nodded. '*Sí.* Was in the bar *aquí*. We went to bed earlier, *creo*. Don't know the room. *Perdóneme.*'

None the wiser, the rock star excused himself and went in search of a courtesy telephone to dial his sister's room and hurry her along. 'Lena, it's Jeff. Are you OK?' he said to a bleary voice at the other end.

'Aw, *chico*. What time is it? Where are you?'

'Downstairs at breakfast,' her brother answered. '*¿Bajas?* Eva and Alberto are already here. You can't miss your flight, so we don't have much time.'

'Shit!' the woman exclaimed, loud in her brother's ear.

She mustn't have seen the clock until that moment, judging by her change of tone, he figured, matching an appropriate facial expression to her language.

'OK. *Vengo, vengo.*'

Jeff heard the click of the telephone being hung up and stood staring at the receiver in amazement. '*¡Adiós, Lena!*'

Shaking his head, the groom turned on his heels and re-joined the others. They had teamed up with four of Lynn's friends, who were singing the praises of yesterday's glamour and romance. The popular singer-songwriter took his place again, ready for the next course. Before he could tempt the gleeful woman back to the *buffet* however, she turned away from the chatter to check on their missing bridesmaid.

'Is Lena alright?'

'Yeah. She's fine,' the hungry runner answered, scowling in mild frustration. 'Don't expect any sparkling conversation though. I think her head hurts. Was she on her own, Eva?'

'I dunno,' his diminutive schoolmate replied. 'You'll have to ask her.'

Jeff raised his left hand, complete with spoon, in apology. 'OK, OK! I know. She's a big girl. She can look after herself...'

With fewer ears to hear them and masked by the white noise of excited female voices, the former Sydneysider enquired into Alberto's brush with the law eighteen months prior. Away from his home turf, the old man was happy to talk. He was keeping his head down and no longer fraternising with Hassan and the Lebanese gangs.

'I run my club, that's all,' the frail Chilean told them. 'I teachin' more kids than blokes now. Keeps *esos hijos de puta* away. *Al menos tienen un poco de respeto para los niños.* When you give me those equipments, we get many more member. Is you to thank for this, *chico.*'

Eva thumped her father on the arm. 'Don't call 'im *chico*, Papá! He's a big star now.'

'I don't mind,' Jeff chuckled, stealing a sideways glance at his dream girl. 'In fact, I really like it. It's like nothing's changed.'

The empathetic do-gooder's Number One fan squeezed his thigh under the table and then began to shake it to direct his attention towards the restaurant entrance. 'Look who's here!' she exclaimed, jumping to her feet.

It was Gerry, and he had brought Heather and little Jenna to see his friends before they left the country again. Ever the diplomat, he waved to everyone he recognised while he steered the others between the tables, before making a hash of parking the baby's stroller next to an empty table nearby.

The best man shook his close friend's hand. 'Morning, mate! Nice night?'

Nodding nonchalantly, Jeff stood up to kiss the mother of his manager's child. Their baby girl was now eight months old and beginning to bear a definite resemblance to Heather. The father, as usual, paid no attention whatsoever to his child, preferring to work the room instead.

'Hey, little one. You're lucky you look like your mamá!' the handsome charmer told her, receiving a wide, toothless grin. 'How're you going, Heather?'

The amused doctor laughed. 'Good, thanks. I must agree! You guys look so happy.'

The young mother handed her daughter to her legal guardian, who cuddled the little mite enthusiastically, much to the delight of those around her. Lynn noticed Marianna's gaze dart straight across the room, intrigued to find out whose small, floral bundle this was.

'Sit down, guys,' yesterday's bride invited.

Jeff shunted the table next-door across to join theirs while Heather went to choose some food for herself and the baby. The blonde superstar sat with Jenna on her lap, bouncing her up and down while she finished her coffee, grinning at her husband. It looked like the most natural thing in the world, stirring peculiar emotions inside him that he didn't much wish to deal with this morning. He needed to get rid of his twenty-six-year-old baby before he could relax and consider his own future.

'You look gorgeous,' the handsome man told his new wife. 'Doesn't she?'

Alberto and Eva both nodded, doubtless acknowledging the difference between this impressive celebrity and the drugged-up tearaway they remembered from the tough years.

'After the Olympics,' Lynn shot back, confusing their guests altogether.

Jeff shrugged. 'Sure thing, angel.'

'Let's go and see my mum,' his beautiful best friend suggested to the new arrivals, after they had finished their first plate of food. 'She'd love to say hello to Jenna.'

The two former private schoolgirls took the baby over to Marianna, Bart and the younger Dysons, while Gerry and Jeff ate breakfast in peace. The boxing club owner and his daughter had returned to the buffet for second helpings, giving the men a chance to share a few personal words after their big day.

'So…' asked the best man with a smile, 'did you learn anything new about your wife?'

The songwriter laughed. 'No. Except that it's a bad idea to go running with her family the morning after,' he moaned. 'I'm absolutely fucked!'

Eva giggled, sitting back down and trying not to eavesdrop on the conversation.

'Yeah, well,' Gerry replied. 'You could've guessed that with half a brain. Could you keep up?'

'Keep up or keep it up?' the celebrity's eyes glinted.

His manager guffawed. 'Depends in which sequence these activities took place.'

'I kept up for two laps of the Tan, pretty much. That hill's a bloody killer, and you should see 'em go, mate. Jesus! It's as if I was the only one on a gradient. They were hardly even puffing when we got to the top, but it took me another "K" to recover.'

The accountant glanced over at the two Barts, senior and junior. They were role-models revered by every schoolboy in Australia, rugged men's men who exhibited sportsmanly conduct wherever they went. Even though his penchant was for rugby over Australian Rules football, the former New South Waler had grown up in awe of the Melbourne captain and his evergreen, record-breaking father. It was hard to believe his childhood mate had now married into the Dyson dynasty.

'Not bad for an old man.'

'Who? Me or him?' the songwriter scoffed. 'Listen, Gez. Thanks for bringing Jenna along. It'll go down well with my mum-in-law.'

The groom shut up, seeing a devilish look in his business manager's eyes.

'Hey, mate... I've got something to tell you. You'll never guess what happened after you left last night...'

'What's that?' Jeff was instantly intrigued and more than a little worried. 'Tell me you didn't end up in bed with my sister.'

Again, Gerry roared with laughter, as much at the shocked expression on his old friend's face as at the thought of such an unlikely pairing. 'No, I didn't, mate. Stand easy!'

'Fuck! Thank Christ for that,' the sibling-minder sighed. 'I didn't think she'd be your type but had to make sure. You know... Best men and bridesmaids, and all that.'

'Nor the lovely Michelle,' the best man added. 'But she *would* be more my type.'

Jeff nodded his approval. Their maid of honour had chosen not to stay at the hotel with the rest of the bridal party last night. He knew it upset Lynn that the law student seldom had a decent man in her life, and it was noticeable several times during the reception that she appeared lonely. Still, she was far too nice to be subjected to the treachery of Gerry Blake. Far too nice.

'I actually found some scintillating company after you guys called it quits,' the amiable rogue continued, 'courtesy of one of Lynn's old school friends. Karina Bloomfield. Do you know her?'

Another nod was given, to which the executive scowled. 'You haven't?'

'I haven't.'

'Good-oh,' Gerry wiped his forehead in relief. 'It's rare not to get your cast-offs, especially in this circle. Her father's one of my clients.'

The bridegroom shook his head, embarrassed to be having this conversation in front of Alberto, whose daughter could also be counted in this number. Cast-offs? He knew his longtime buddy was right, but it left a bad taste in his mouth nevertheless. One more piece of proof that loveless sex was merely a commodity to be traded to help people through the night. Jeff Diamond was done with notches on bedposts and damned proud of it.

'Never hurts to do a bit of customer relationship management on the side at these society parties,' the suave businessman added with a grin.

'Surprised you had the energy, mate.'

'Talking of which, that takes me neatly back to my original topic,' his best man laughed. 'Before I was so rudely interrupted.'

'Apologies. I'm a selfish pig, I know.'

'You are indeed. Takes one to know one,' Gerry slapped his friend on the back. 'Anyway... I was standing at the bar with Dad after you'd cantered off into the sunset, having one last brandy, when Big D came up to us and asked for my business card. He said it'd been great to meet us and that we were like-minded people and so forth, and then said, "In a gesture of goodwill for everything you've done for Jeff over the years, and the benefit it'll bring for my daughter, I'd like to explore transferring my business to your firm as soon as we can."'

'Hey! Way to go, mate!' the multi-millionnaire responded, pleased for his commercially-motivated friend. 'That's excellent. I assume you said yes.'

'Of course I bloody well did! I had my Chairman standing right next to me. I crawled appropriately, telling him it was a great honour and we'd be very proud to accept. Kissing of feet, licking of arses. You know my methods, Watson. Promised them both I'd make sure it's a very smooth transition and successful partnership... All that shit.'

'Fantastic,' Jeff acknowledged again.

'Cheers. It's like we've ended up in an old Indian movie,' the ebullient accountant went on, toasting the deal with his coffee cup and then emptying it down his throat. 'An arranged marriage. You know, a joining together of two families. A wee bit Mafia, in fact. I reminded Big D that the Blakes were just imposters where you were concerned and I thought my dad was going to kick me in the shins! Not an Argentinean Catholic Polish Jew in sight in our family, I said. Just a bit of Irish old school tie. But it works for him, so that's fucking that, old boy.'

Jeff shook his friend's hand. This was indeed a big *coup* for Blake & Partners. The Dyson empire would consume a large number of business services, and the Melbourne office would require yet more nubile female assistants to fawn over its boss, he surmised.

'That's great. Really great. We both need more floor space.'

Gerry was full of thanks, in a manly sort of way. 'I suppose I ought to give you some sort of finder's fee or something,' he joked, pulling a face.

'Definitely,' the superstar agreed. 'I expect no less. Not that I had anything to do with it. It'll be Lynn's finder's fee. He's her dad.'

Right on cue, the tennis champion returned with Heather and Jenna in tow, placing her hands on the young man's neck and kissing the top of his head. He leaned back into her body and closed his eyes.

'That's better,' the emotional man said, reaching to caress her fingers. 'I was missing you. The "IEC" was getting too tight.'

The doctor looked on enviously. 'The what? You two don't have to touch each other all the time, you know. You're married now. She's not going to run away.'

'I might!' the bride countered, giggling while simultaneously pressing down harder on Jeff's shoulders to reassure him that she was feeling the same way.

'See?' the comic whined to the friendly GP, gripping his wife's hand. 'Did you hear that? She said she might. I'm not risking it. No way, baby.'

As it happened, the young man realised, today they did need to touch each other all the time. It felt wrong to let go, even for the shortest separation. The supernatural force which had followed them around while Lynn was in California was pulling them ever closer together, and it had never felt better to be connected than right now.

The songwriter ran his index finger over his dream girl's wedding band and felt the second gold circle alongside the engagement ring they had bought in London. There... She had been right again. He did feel different in the company of others, and judging by her extremely sensual responses, so his gorgeous wife did too.

'That's going to make it pretty hard to go to the toilet,' Heather suggested, breaking the good-looking man's daydream.

Jeff gave her a puzzled look. 'True, I guess. You've been a mother too long already if basic bodily functions are all you can think about. I don't know though... Could be kind o' kinky.'

Lynn pulled a face. 'No. Fortunately, we're celebrities. Celebrities don't use the toilet. I read it in a magazine somewhere.'

'This conversation's going rapidly downhill,' Gerry rolled his eyes, joking to the immigrant Sydneysiders. 'Far too much romance in the air for my liking. It's putting me off my bacon and eggs.'

The rest of the Blake clan had made it down to breakfast, neither sister appearing in too energetic a mood. Celia rushed over to her little granddaughter, scooping her out of Heather's arms and covering her little face with sloppy kisses. Gerald Blakes Senior and Junior deviated at their earliest opportunity, ostensibly to speak to Bart, who had already called them over.

Lynn sat down next to her handsome man and sighed. 'This is all getting a bit too much, isn't it? I just want to be gone now.'

'Never a truer word spoken,' Jeff put his left arm around her and pulled her in tight to his side, kissing her temple. 'Can we escape, d'you think?'

'What about Lena?'

'Oh, shit. Yeah. Where the hell is she?'

Alberto and his daughter had booked to stay in Melbourne for the weekend and were keen to take a look around the city's sights. It was their first time in Victoria, and they had armed themselves with a map and a few suggestions of where to go. Their hosts stood up and thanked them again for coming down and sharing their special day. Jeff promised he would call in on the club the next time he flew to Sydney.

'Say 'bye to Madalena from us, *por favor,*' Eva instructed. 'Thanks for a great time. Hope you find her.'

The concerned superstar followed the tourists out into the lobby. '*Señor Santos*, stay safe. *¿Ustéd me oye?*' he begged the old man. 'Ring me if you guys have any problems, OK?'

The tall, handsome chart-topper stood watching the pair heading away from the hotel. It had been so good to see them so unexpectedly, yet a few short conversations had surfaced old fears with which he vowed to deal once he and Lynn were back from their honeymoon. Finishing his cigarette, he heard rapid, goat-like footsteps approaching from behind and swang around to see his sister trotting towards him.

'Hey, *chico*! What you doin' here? Are we leavin' now?'

'No. Hi! Soon though,' her brother answered. 'Alberto and Eva've just left for the CBD. They said to tell you *hasta la vista*.'

'Shit! I'm so late,' Madalena whined. 'I didn't get to my room 'til after four. Then I fell asleep.'

'Dare I ask whom you were with?'

Jeff shrugged, turning to lead the remarkably well turned-out woman back into the dining room. She was even wearing flatter shoes this morning, probably on account of her impaired balance, and it softened her whole demeanour. A quick scan around the room placed his dream girl at a table with some of her aunts and uncles, to whom he had been introduced yesterday. She slipped him a sly thumbs-up, setting his heart soaring.

'No-one from your wedding,' Madalena reassured him.

The celebrity was relieved. He couldn't stand having their worlds meet in that way. The less Lynn's family knew about his former life, the better off everyone would be, and this gaudy woman represented the last link in a very short chain. He ushered her to his table and summoned a waiter to bring a fresh round of coffee.

'*¡Bueno!*' he proclaimed, pulling a chair out for his sister to sit down. 'Where were you then?'

'Here. In the bar,' the sultry woman replied, shaking her hand to signify that her client had been hot.

'Business or pleasure?' Jeff nodded, annoyed at his own inquisitiveness.

'Both,' Madalena grinned, before becoming distracted by the cosy breakfast scene. 'Whose baby?'

'This is Jeff's sister,' Lynn informed the young mum, who was taken aback by such a direct question from a total stranger. 'Lena, this is Heather. And this is Jenna, who's Heather and Gerry's daughter.'

'Oh, right. Nice to meet you,' the dark-haired woman chanted, shaking the mother's hand before swinging back in her brother's direction. 'Jeez, I didn't think you could work that quick. Even you!'

The groom sniffed, slightly embarrassed, and his wife gave him a sympathetic look. Madalena was stirred up. It was a good thing she was going back to the airport soon. Lynn could imagine Jeff losing his temper with her if this exchange were to continue for much longer. Still, at least she hadn't dressed like a tart this morning, and her language was reasonably well under control; a vast improvement on her original arrival.

'Ah, the lovely Madalena!' cried Gerry, who had returned from schmoozing his newest client. 'I see you've met my daughter.'

'Yeah. She's cute,' the dark-haired woman nodded, letting the little one hold on to her index finger. 'She's very smiley.'

'At the moment!' Heather laughed.

'Angel, shall we get going?' Jeff asked, his eyes almost pleading.

'Yes, OK. Did you want to pinch a car from Admin to go to the airport? It'll be better than getting taxis there and back.'

The young man was grateful. 'Yeah. That'd be great, if you can. We're all paid up and checked out, so we just need to collect our stuff and we can *vamoose*. Gez, what are you guys doing now?'

His best man pointed to the rest of his family. 'We're taking them to South Melbourne Market apparently. Joy of joys! I just want to sit and read the 'paper, but someone had to have a wedding, with all the associated domestic aftermath that goes along with it.'

'Sorry, mate,' his friend replied, empathising closely. 'I'm over it all myself too. Sun, sea, sand and s… awaits, if you know what I mean?'

With the matching Stones Road siblings right behind her, Lynn said their goodbyes to the Blakes and the Dysons, promising to ring her parents when they arrived on Tenerife. Jeff had re-established physical contact with his wife and once more felt whole again. They walked hand-in-hand to the lift lobby, where they prepared to part again temporarily; one to collect the car and the other arranging to have their luggage brought down from their room.

'Lena, can you go upstairs and pack your stuff, please?' Jeff asked. 'Bring everything down here with Lynn, and I'll pick you guys up in fifteen minutes.'

He kissed his *Regala* tenderly, and she almost snatched at his hand. What had come over them? He concluded it was simply a deep longing for all the formalities to be over so that they could relax in each others' company. Not a moment too soon!

The *trio* reached the apartment just before eleven o'clock. Madalena's flight was in two hours; just enough time for her to pack her bags and say her goodbyes. They gathered at the foot of the couple's bed, upon which they had hastily piled the wedding dress and all its trappings.

'Thanks, Lena, for everything,' the bride said. 'I'm really glad we had this chance to get to know each other. Jeff told me you arranged something for Easter. Is that right?'

Although their visitor was sad to be leaving, she was determined not to show it. Typical of one who preferred to live in denial, she dismissed her sister-in-law's attempts to perpetuate their newfound friendship.

'Yeah, maybe,' she shrugged. 'Whatever works.'

Madalena reached down and took hold of the handle of her small suitcase. After all the shopping to which she had been treated, it had required some considerable effort to close and was now bulging at the seams. The suit carrier containing her bridesmaid's outfit was travelling back to Sydney with her too, along with all the memories which appeared to have been filed away.

Jeff gave both women a disappointed look, at which his beautiful best friend smiled back unworried.

'Hope we can arrange something. Have a safe flight.'

Lynn watched her handsome man and his skinny sister enter the lift, waving from the entrance hall. He blew her a kiss as the doors closed. It was with a fair amount of relief that she re-entered the apartment and began to sort out their room in peace.

Madalena was happy. Jeff was right to leave her in Sydney, but it was clear he still bore considerable guilt. That was fine. She would help him work things out. It was her duty now, and nothing would give her greater satisfaction.

An Abnormal Life

Lynn and Jeff's first months of married life flew by in a whirlwind once they returned from their honeymoon. Staying true to their promise not to respond to any calls or other imposts on their private time, they had immersed themselves in everything their equatorial paradise had to offer, scarcely letting one another out of their sight.

The energetic couple had hired an open-topped Jeep to drive around the island, getting caught frequently in brief but heavy downpours of warm, tropical rain. On another day, having tired of playing tennis, they had lounged by the hotel's swimming pool for hours, under swaying palm trees, writing songs and reading the large piles of books which had come on their journey. Their concentration was only broken for the odd cocktail or a swim in the inviting, blue water.

Most satisfying of all however, were the many languid, unconstrained and intensely meaningful conversations they shared about their future, peppered by equally relaxed but intense sexual interludes.

Gerry had trespassed on their peace at the beginning of the celebrities' third week, with Lynn's full support, and was spoiled rotten by his VIP clients. Their extra *amigo* took no time at all to decompress from all the stresses of work and family, easing into island time to offset Jeff's head-start on the local brews.

Trips to bars and nightclubs in town had resulted in some good-natured harassment, but the superstars had put up with it happily, unwilling to see the faithful manager come to their rescue while on holiday. Their public appearances only needed to last long enough for their guest to identify and snare a suitable female companion before the foursome could retire to their five-star resort for the rest of the night's entertainment.

Home in time to cheer her father to victory in his seventeenth men's singles final at the Australian Open tennis tournament, the newlyweds spent the following weekend at Benloch for the family's postponed annual planning day, focussing on the upcoming Montreal Olympics. Jeff was by now feeling very comfortable with his place on the outer fringe of the Dyson clan and was content to amuse himself while the sports assessments took place. There were always countless books to read, conflict resolutions to map out, movie scripts to write or review and songs to bring forth from his favourite vantage point up at Coldwater Creek.

His wife released a new album shortly afterwards, full of melodic new compositions to enhance her reputation as a mature songwriter and producer. Live performances were a different story however, where audiences cried out for the old hits with which many had grown up. Needless to say, the fans loved the complete package, and the sexy songstress concluded that it would take more than her new married status to shake off the "girl next-door" image.

Locked down in Australia while preparing for the Olympics, the athlete threw her intellectual energy into Childlight and developing The Good School program, liaising with fellow organisers all over the world to build strong foundations onto which the front-end of their fabled pantomime horse could mount his high-profile campaigns. She was never happier than when working behind the scenes and helping him to be successful. She didn't miss being part of the glory one *iota*, despite his frequent protestations that she was giving him too much credit.

The rock star had also been busy in the recording studio, launching his latest English language collection, the title track of which was inspired by sounds of New York City during a trip the couple took just after Easter to launch the movie made from his novel, "The Runner". The film was received with critical acclaim and huge box office success, elevating The Australian Elvis to a serious Hollywood player. He had released an *impromptu* single, with complex lyrics describing the weird juxtaposition of his own life with those of the characters in the film. This sophisticated pop song shot to the top of the charts in many countries, its driving rock beat making it an automatic addition to future live performances.

Throughout this seemingly unending success however, by far the most stubborn and hard to crack of the songwriter's Post-Traumatic Stress Disorder symptoms was the deep, dark depression. No matter how happy he felt at all other times, desperate to convince his damaged mind that there were no longer any grounds for him to feel disenchanted with life, the old troll staunchly refused to retire. Although innocuous in its silence and invisibility, after over a year under the same roof, Lynn had developed some considerable expertise in detecting the illness' level by the patterns of behaviour her gorgeous man tried his hardest not to exhibit.

'It really takes hold of you, doesn't it?' she remarked, first thing one autumn morning, seeing the predictable mood descend within a couple of minutes of regaining consciousness.

'Yeah,' Jeff gave an apologetic sigh. 'I wish you couldn't see it.'

His beautiful best friend leaned over and planted a kiss at the corner of his right eye. 'You follow a pattern when you wake up,' she continued. 'Whenever I wake you, I can see you fight with a few moments of confusion, then there's a wide smile that makes me feel so special and then the depression kidnaps your joy. From now on, I'll have to get you out of bed before that happens.'

'Good luck,' the downhearted man smiled.

Thereafter, whenever the two busy stars woke up in the same bed, the dedicated athlete would insist her husband come training with her, sometimes resorting to shoving him onto the floor and dressing him. For the most part, he was willing, as long as the rude awakening included the promise of sex and a hearty breakfast afterwards. Yet there were some days when he proved impossible to budge, and she would leave him in bed, only then able to rouse him upon her return from his reprehensible lack of effort by enticing him into the shower for some passionate lovemaking.

'Things'll be different when kids come along,' the lithe taskmaster warned.

'Yeah. I'm looking forward to it,' her husband nodded. 'They'll force me to be happy. You make it too easy for me to wallow in self-pity sometimes.'

The young woman laughed and waved a threatening hand. 'Oh, do I? That can change!'

'Oh, no, angel. All good. As you were…' Jeff answered, his smile belying the fear that she might one day be serious.

Their ridiculous travel schedules soon resuming, the Australian press hounded the couple incessantly, waiting for the slightest whiff of unfaithfulness. When they were spotted separately, whether on tour or for sporting events, barely a day went by without a collection of fabricated photographic evidence placing either one of them in compromising positions. In fact, it would have been very easy to succumb to transient pleasures of the flesh, protected by the fierce loyalty of their respective *entourages*. Offers of substantial bribes came thick and fast to many of their associates, with the *paparazzi* hungry for any hint of scandal.

For the handsome rock star, the paths to temptation were rendered yet more attractive by the constant adulation, losing count of the number of times he came perilously close to ending up in the wrong place at the wrong time with the wrong person, drunk on copious cocktails and with an overwhelming physical need to praise his inner narcissist after yet another triumphant stage appearance.

At first, he assumed his imagination was exaggerating the situation, but his band-mates soon corroborated that since his marriage women seemed to be drawn to him with still greater fervour due to the shiny, gold band on his left hand. It was as if "nice guy" had been appended to the list of qualities on his *résumé*, just below the line mentioning "sex-god"!

Boundaries were never breeched by either celebrity, and invariably the songwriter would bow out in front of a ring of pouting hopefuls, return to his hotel room and pour his unspent, testosterone-fuelled angst into new songs which also served as love letters to his beautiful best friend on the other side of the globe.

Telephone sex became their staple, often followed by the routine wake-up call that Lynn would make to set her demotivated lover on the right path and turn the ignition on his money-making machine again the next morning.

Jeff also nurtured a strong bond with his wife's younger brother during the early months of nineteen-seventy-six, while he continued to battle with adolescence in the high-pressured environment which his father built around him. The second Dyson son had turned sixteen in March and was becoming increasingly introverted and evasive.

'Angel,' the empathetic man had begun one night, after returning from another priceless and peaceful weekend at Benloch, 'have you spoken to Sandy about why he's so quiet these days?'

'Yes, I have. He doesn't want to talk about anything though,' his wife replied. 'I think he's really struggling, but how do we make him open up?'

'We can't force him, but can I try?' Jeff asked. 'I get the impression your dad doesn't want me to meddle, because whenever I bring it up, he changes the subject and behaves like I've just insulted his mother.'

Lynn stared intently at her husband, who was always so clued in to what people were feeling. 'You can try, but I agree you'll have to tread carefully. With Dad and with Sandy...'

'Do you think he'd come to The Fellowship one night with us? Then if he won't talk to me, maybe he'd talk to one of the others.'

'Do you really think he's depressed?' the young woman asked, concerned. 'I mean from some event or other in the past?'

'Who knows?' her amateur psychiatrist shrugged. 'It all depends on what he's not telling us. Perhaps he's been bullied and can't bring himself to say anything 'cause of how your dad'd judge him. You know what he'd say: "Stand up for yourself, man. You're a Dyson, and don't you forget it." I have a theory actually, but it's just a theory, and you may not agree with it.'

Lynn frowned, both at the startlingly accurate impression of her father and at the cynical overtones. 'Oh, yes? What sort of theory? And how long have you harboured this theory, oh wise one?'

Chuckling and leaning in for a kiss he knew he didn't deserve, Jeff knew he was on dangerous ground, never having shared the view he had formed since the very early days. It was unfair of him to spring his opinion of Richard Dyson's sexual orientation on the lad's sister after all this time without an apology.

'Baby, I had a suspicion about something right from when I first met Sandy. You know... Gut feel? But I never discussed it with you 'cause I had no clue if I was right or way off. No point in spreading vicious rumours without being pretty sure of myself.'

'What vicious rumours?' the sportswoman asked, perturbed by his aspersions.

Her compassionate lover took her hand across the dinner table. 'Sorry. "Vicious rumours" is just an expression,' he covered his tracks. 'I think Sandy's gay, that's all. But given how I imagine your dad'd react, I didn't want to say anything in case it coloured your view and somehow we forced either or both of them into a corner.'

Lynn relaxed a little. Jeff's motives were always so completely honourable, and it was just like him to have appended "that's all" to what was an extremely confronting concept to most men.

'Oh, wow. Sorry,' she said. 'You're right, as usual. I shouldn't get angry. Do you really think he's gay?'

'Jesus, I don't know! It's not information we should treat like *confetti*. I'm not sure, by any means,' the intellectual replied. 'But it's the best my powers of psychoanalysis can come up with, and you know how I trust my gut.'

'Hmm... So how do we get him to admit it?' his wife thought aloud. 'If he is, he must be going through such anguish. Or if he doesn't want to come out, or even if he hasn't put two and two together about himself yet, he should at least try to conquer how it's making him feel.'

'Yeah. *Exactement*, angel. What about Rich Kerr or John?'

Lynn's musical colleagues were both openly homosexual and leading highly satisfying lifestyles these days. They had also known Sandy reasonably well since their childhoods.

She nodded. 'Yeah. Great idea. I could ring them and ask them for tips on how to help. Those guys are in the right business to be gay though.'

Jeff's eyes widened. 'What are you insinuating? Are you stereotyping?'

'No!' his wife teased. 'Why? Do you have doubts about your own sexuality?'

Coughing, The Australian Elvis shifted in his chair. 'More wine?'

'No, thanks,' Lynn laughed again. 'But it is a good idea. I'll give John a ring later today. He'd be more like Sandy, personality-wise. Rich is so out there and gregarious, he probably wouldn't relate to keeping everything bottled up. I don't think his genie bottle even has a stopper!'

'*¡Excelente!* That's very funny,' the young man replied, kissing the compassionate woman on his way into the kitchen. 'That'll be a good start. Christ! I'm glad I've finally spoken to you about this. It's been crippling keeping it to myself for all this time.'

Before the couple left the US, Jeff had signed to make his second novel into a movie. "Sidewalk", the screenplay for which had been sketched out in London and then finessed on their honeymoon, had Madalena as its primary inspiration, and they were now grappling with the logistics of arranging for the cast to fly to Sydney and meet his sister and her circle in the coming months.

And during May, the newly-combined and even wealthier Dyson-Diamond legal entity invested a large amount of time and money into The Fellowship, giving a rousing speech at the opening of a new centre in Sydney's west. The raven-haired philanthropist had been quoted in the media using the Oscar Wilde quotation, "Every saint has a past, and every sinner has a future," which was immediately seized upon and over-exposed until the charity's adopted catchphrase caused such a heightened level of awareness and public sympathy that donations began rolling in faster than the management team could direct them.

The rehabilitated bad-boy regularly thanked his dream girl in front of the cameras for the support she had given him in overcoming the after-effects of his tough childhood, especially in dealing with the legacy of PTSD. The couple's adoring fan-base was treated to insights into how his ailing soul had been saved, as a foreword to his more serious message; that of making it his life's work to mentor others out of similarly hopeless situations.

Days and weeks passed quickly, both stars dashing from place to place, project to project. Lynn alternated between recording studio and sporting competition, and her husband jetted from continent to continent, wooing huge stadium crowds, television interviewers or corporate Boardrooms with his compelling ideologies. And whenever a deal was signed, control would switch from one end of the pantomime horse to the other; from charismatic front-man to the genius project manager who had the knack of making things happen.

'You'll get it done in half a day,' Jeff laughed, having telephoned first thing in the morning while on a stopover in Los Angeles.

'Half a day? That's a bit ambitious.'

'I bet you three million bucks you'll be done in a day,' her smiling lover insisted.

'Three million? I'm not taking that bet,' his wife chided. 'Your breath is undressing me.'

The songwriter chuckled. 'Clever. I'm more talented than I thought. And good call re' the bet, I guess.'

A stodgy silence clogged the line across the Pacific Ocean, rendered thicker as much by regret as by arousal. For a minute, the young woman had concluded that the pause was due to the sex-starved traveller's fantasies having distracted his brain. Her instincts soon told her otherwise however, and she changed her mind.

'Are you OK?' Are you still there?'

A sigh squeezed through the receiver. 'I remember when three hundred dollars was a lot of money.'

'Jeff!' the champion's voice was thunderous in reply. 'Don't castigate yourself. It was a joke. I'm naked. Make it worth my while, or I'm going to hang up.'

Lynn had learned her craft well, confident the pathos her black stallion would be fighting at the other end of the call needed to be chased away rather than laboured. His resilience was these days much improved, and he was genuinely grateful to be challenged once in a while. Sure enough, this time was no exception.

'Where are my hands?'

'One's wrapped around your gorgeous cock, and the other's finger is tracing a line backwards behind your balls,' the twenty-year-old's commentary picked up the pace. 'Where are *your* hands?'

'Jesus, angel. I love you. I'm licking my fingers, about to send two of them inside you while my thumb moves your clit' into hyper-drive. Feel that?'

His wife moaned. 'Yeah. Oh, yeah. That's fantastic. Keep going. I love it. I want you to make me come.'

'Sure thing. You can come any time,' Jeff whispered. 'Feel me inside you. Where's your mouth?'

'Biting the side of your neck.'

'Which side?'

'Does it matter?' the sportswoman couldn't help but laugh. 'Left side.'

Her long-distance lover growled, swapping the receiver to his other ear in order to relish the tingling in his skin as imaginary teeth took hold of the sensitive, stubbly flesh under his ear. 'You're the best, Lynn. Can't wait 'til I get home.'

***

Dinner over, Lynn and Jeff settled down in the cigar bar of their favourite Melbourne hideaway, a jazz venue on Bennett's Lane, on the northern fringe of the CBD. The band on the early shift had left the stage, and bluesy background music was playing before the main act. It was now June and the closest Saturday night to the songwriter's twenty-fourth birthday.

Another of the couple's commitments to their life singular was to respect the structure of the typical week, restricting their big nights out to Fridays and Saturdays. They had made this decision for two reasons: first, to pay their respects to ordinary people who worked a normal five-day working week; and second, to establish themselves a routine that would facilitate an easy transition to parenthood and fitting in with school calendars. No matter how hard they tried to ensure their private lifestyle observed these rules as closely as possible, their public obligations often fell foul of them.

Nearly horizontal on the comfortable leather sofa, Jeff motioned to his delicious, blonde dinner companion to lie alongside him while he smoked and they both finished their wine. He had been hypnotising her slowly since the band had vacated the stage for a short break between sets, recalling every minute detail about his latest trip to Paris. Responding to her quiet laughter and close body contact, he had gone on to describe the final, painstaking

371

touches made to an album of collaborations with French musicians. In their gloriously mellow state, the muse absorbed his rapturous enthusiasm for each song, the events or themes that had inspired it and how the artists had pieced it together.

Lynn also explained her idea for a combined schools project with the working title of "A Thousand Voices", designed to promote tolerance, understanding and solidarity through music. Her husband had fallen in love with the construct, which would begin with a single soloist and build until an enormous children's choir filled the Melbourne Town Hall.

'Hey,' she twisted round to look into the drowsy world-changer's eyes during a lull in the conversation. 'May I ask you something personal, please?'

'Personal?' he replied, wondering where she was planning to take him next. 'What sort of personal? You're my wife. You don't have to ask my permission to talk about something personal.'

'I know, but this is very personal. I've been thinking about the unfinished business with your dad.'

There was no point in beating about the bush. The twenty-year-old sought to broker peace between Jeff and his father, so that he might close those vexatious chapters of his life once and for all. She knew there were certain episodes in his complex past which continued to haunt him, particularly concerning the gangland threats he raised at almost every logistics meeting with their management team.

'Right,' he said, shifting uncomfortably behind her. 'Why?'

His patient partner stroked his thigh, as if it could soften the impact of a tough conversation. 'Because now things are better with Madalena and the flat situation is under control, I'm wondering what you think about contacting him and seeing if you can cancel out a few of the remaining bad memories. And maybe even find out if he'd be on your side if there's anything still happening.'

The former Stones Road tearaway took a long drag on his cigar. Too long, as it turned out, and it made him cough. Bouncing against his chest, the sportswoman giggled, leaning forward to give him some breathing room.

'Jeez! Sorry, angel,' he chuckled too, inviting her to relax backwards again. 'I'm not sure I'm ready to talk about this.'

'OK,' Lynn attempted to hide her disappointment. 'That's alright. It can wait.'

Jeff kissed the back of her wise, thoughtful head, cursing his ingrained resistance. He paused for several seconds, searching for a topic with which to change the subject seamlessly, but his efforts were futile. Of course, his brain was already racing. His sneaky saviour had foreshadowed this, hadn't she? From behind her elongated, nubile form, he grinned in reluctant acceptance that his muse frequently trumped him on matters of the mind lately.

'No, it can't,' the intellectual capitulated, the first, unstoppable rush of petulance subsiding. 'Not now you've brought it up, you wicked, bloody woman! My curiosity'll get the better of me. I need to know what you think I should do.'

The pair sat up and slid sideways on the couch until they faced off opposite each other. Lynn refilled their wine glasses, continuing happily.

'Great. Thanks for humouring me. I just thought... if you were allowed to, of course... that you might arrange to visit him. He must know something about who you've become. Surely he'd have some access to news, even if only from the staff or newcomers.'

'You can say wardens and prisoners,' Jeff whispered, smiling wryly at her euphemistic labels. 'I won't get offended.'

'Yeah, sorry,' Lynn scanned the room for potential eavesdroppers before being ambushed for a quick kiss. 'Or officers and inmates.'

'Indeed. Screws and cons.'

Sometimes the dark-haired philosopher was hard pressed to remember who between them was the peace-broker. He was about to say something sincere to let his wife know how much he loved her, when a waiter interrupted them to ask if they wished to see the dessert menu. They both declined.

Left on their own again, the romantic moment had passed them by, and by the lady's determined expression, neither was she for letting up any time soon. The battling superstar spoke somewhat tentatively, the extra few seconds helping him wrest the animosity from his tone.

'But what would I talk to him about? Hey, old man! I hear you killed two blokes. You gave me nightmares, you bastard, and I fear for the safety of my wife's family? He'd laugh in my face, I reckon.'

Lynn sat back, disheartened at the sadly plausible response. It had been a number of months since she was last subjected to the bitter and twisted side of her husband. Virtually no negative comments had passed his lips after their honeymoon, and he genuinely appeared to be enjoying life as much as she was.

'No, but that's where you need to get to,' the singer countered.

Jeff gulped down most of his Shiraz, annoyed with himself. 'Yeah. Sorry, angel, again. I'm not taking this seriously enough, am I? Maybe I'm too much under the influence and eager to carry on having a good time, rather than spoil our evening with this shit.'

'No, you're not,' his wife chastised him. 'That's just an excuse. You have to start with, "Hey, Dad. I'm a great success, despite you. You left me in the lurch." Then you have to tell him everything you've done. You know... exams, qualifications, rock star, the negotiations, the charities, films, rally driving, squash...'

'And you,' her lover added, cherishing the way his dream girl was brave enough to pull him into line. 'I'd effing well need to tell him about you, after he used to tease me stupid. He'd say, "What does a girl like that want with a moron like you?"'

Lynn put on a sad face, hoping its pity reminded him not to let himself slip too far down. 'Well, if he did say that, he's an idiot,' she contradicted, stroking the fabric of his silk shirt which veiled his "JL" tattoo. 'I love this moron. You can tell him that.'

Jeff sighed, taking the hint. 'Christ, angel. You're so god-damned right. I do need to do this.'

'Yes. You do.'

'But he fucked up my life, Lynn,' the lost boy's courage subsided as quickly as it had surged forth. 'I just don't know how I'd react, sitting across a table from him. I'd want to punch his fucking lights out.'

'Do you honestly think you would?' his dream girl asked. 'I mean, surely when you got there, you'd at least want to give him a chance to redeem himself?'

'Yeah. And then punch his fucking lights out. I like your style, baby! The other scary possibility is that it might freak me out all over again, and then you'll have to live with those consequences. What if it brings back the doors? Or even something else? Some new, previously undiscovered latent phobia for us to have endless fun with.'

Lynn shrugged. 'Hmm… That's a possibility. Do you think it might?'

'Jesus, I really hope not,' Jeff sighed. 'I kind o' like not taking ten minutes to get inside the apartment. I don't want to inflict that on our kids either. What if hearing what the bastard has to say makes all that worse again? The nightmares'd be brought closer to reality.'

'I didn't think your dad featured in your nightmares that often. Did he?'

'No. Not often, that's true,' the songwriter confessed. 'But those arseholes were only in the flat because they wanted payback from him. What if I find out the payback was justified? I don't know how I'd go with having to live with the fact that my mother and sister deserved to be raped.'

'What? No way! For God's sake!' Lynn exclaimed, taking offense at his statement. 'That's a terrible conclusion to come to. Maybe you *are* too drunk to be talking about this. There's no way anything could justify someone being raped, especially by association. You can't go there. Please?'

Jeff hugged the passionate woman and apologised for his extreme reaction. In their happiness, they had both forgotten just how fast he could slide down the snakes.

'Sure. That was a ridiculous thing to say. But something more reasonable is finding out they expect me… and by association, you and your family… to repay what they reckon's still outstanding. Maybe we should just leave well alone, angel. I know that sounds like a cop-out, but I'm not sure it's worth risking this perfect life of ours. Are we really likely to gain anything from speaking to him?'

'It's up to you,' his wife relented. 'You'd gain peace of mind that you've asked the questions you've always wanted to ask. And perhaps even gain some kind of relationship with your dad going forward? I'd like to meet him one day too. To show him how much I love this moron.'

Although the mental image of walking the incomparable Lynn Dyson in on his arm to face his dumbstruck father was almost too irresistible for words, the vulnerable man sagged under the pressure she was layering on him with each suggestion. He didn't want to give her this opportunity to manipulate his decision, but knew he ought to allow it. He was far worse on her when it came to playing the tyrant.

'Yep,' he nodded. 'They're good things to gain, I agree, but do I need them for us to be happy? And what might be lost in the process?'

His beautiful best friend sighed, smiling kindly. 'I can't answer any of those questions. I just think you'd be missing out on the chance to close things off. Will you think about it?'

'Doubtless.'

'Yeah. Sorry,' she giggled. 'I'm sure you will.'

***

Jeff thought long and hard about coming face-to-face with his father again. Only two days after the couple's very private conversation, the busy musician left home again for Geneva, Paris, Brussels, Barcelona and Madrid, where he was to promote the album which had been made for the continental European market while visiting the United Nations' Swiss headquarters for a round of high-powered talks with various non-government organisations.

From his hotel room near *Las Ramblas* in the northern Spanish city, having returned from an interesting evening practising his awkward *Catalán* and marvelling at the many ornate balconies and the narrowest streets he had ever seen, he picked up the telephone and dialled the number of his Melbourne penthouse.

The star heard the line connect and begin to ring, easily distracted by fantasies of short nightdresses, long legs and tanned skin. The owner of these alluring attributes wasn't at home, so he left a message on his own answering machine.

'Hey, angel. It's me. Hope you're OK. I'll call again later today but just wanted to tell you I've decided I do want to contact my dad. The reasons are similar to the ones you mentioned, I guess. Though mostly because I want our kids to know their grandfather for who he is now, and not who I remember him as. Does that make sense? Hope so. I love you. *Adiós.*'

The young athlete was overjoyed with the short message after returning from a tough training session, particularly the new angle he had described. It meant her beleaguered husband was able to project forward on behalf of their future family.

Over the next few days, Lynn made several telephone calls to the relevant New South Wales authorities in the prison service. Initially, her request for a meeting with Pavel Diament was refused on grounds of the severity of his crimes. Undeterred however, she then consulted two High Court judges recommended by her father's legal counsel, who posited that there ought to be no good reason why a person on a double life sentence should be denied a visit from a family member after having already served more than ten years, unless it was deemed harmful to the prisoner's mental wellbeing.

The young woman found it difficult to imagine what it might be like for Jeff's father not to have been contacted in all that time. She then wrote a letter to the governor of the prison where the convicted murderer was encarcerated, explaining the situation in necessarily scant detail. After an anxious week's wait, a reply came by telephone.

HM Prison Parklea's Governor James Whitfield agreed to have a member of the psychiatric team speak to Paul Diamond, as they knew him, and find out whether he was agreeable to a meeting. The master planner was pleased to receive a letter only a few days later from a wing warden, informing her that the prisoner was willing to spend an hour with his famous son.

Lynn gulped as she read the single, type-written page. So would the famous son still be willing to meet with the prisoner once he was back on home turf? Jeff was due to return in two days' time, and the excited celebrity decided to wait until he could see the letter for himself rather than risk a long-distance meltdown.

The tennis champion understood her man's reluctance to spoil the happy rhythm of their new life, and part of her shared his concerns. The obsessive, calculating impulses which directed the *yin* and *yang* of their relationship in the early days were now completely absent, and the two lovers existed in blissful, harmonious equity, looking after each others' every interest as true partners. She knew how much the peace and freedom of this situation meant to her handsome intellectual, forever guilty for the burden he had placed on her in days gone by.

Peace and freedom notwithstanding, having read the letter several times while sitting on the balcony of their apartment, the homecoming rock star eventually resolved to attend the meeting.

'You're right,' he told his nervous wife. 'It's another chapter to close properly. If I like him, I've gained a father, albeit inaccessible... And if I hate him? Well, that'd be it. Slam the door on the arsehole once and for all. *Sayonara, hombre.*'

Lynn climbed onto his lap to kiss him, squeezing his trembling arm. 'Sounds good. Either way, you'd know.'

'Yeah,' Jeff agreed, his cynical mind coming to its well-considered conclusion. 'It's not like he's earned the privilege of being a grandfather, is it? I mean, it'd be a shame for our kids not to know him, but what is there to know? They'd hardly be richer for the experience.'

***

Jeff's heart was beating fast as he sat in the stark interview room at Parklea Maximum Security Prison, forty kilometres to the west of Sydney. Horizontal rain lashed against the windows above his head like tiny ball bearings. For the last three nights, his mind had been rehearsing exactly what he would say to his father when he saw him for the first time in over a decade.

The millionnaire felt sick and dizzy, lighting his third cigarette in ten minutes, starving hungry after electing to forego breakfast. Save for a single door and two long, narrow windows just below ceiling level on the opposite wall, he was enclosed by four blue-grey panels of chipped plasterboard. Haphazard patches of white and cream paint masked all manner of stains, incisions and cavities, turning his stomach as he pictured the violent outbursts at their origin.

The Governor's letter had explained that the prisoner knew his son had become a major celebrity and that he had married Lynn Dyson. There had been no indication provided as to the lifer's state of mind or his opinions on meeting the child he had never taken the trouble to get to know. The young star had brought a handful of photographs of himself with his dream girl and of Madalena, but the longer he was kept waiting, the more nauseated he became at the prospect of turning this overdue confrontation into a type of quaint coffee morning.

The twenty-four-year-old was unable to second-guess his initial response, nor what to expect from his father. He was thankful Lynn hadn't come to the prison with him. This was no place for someone like her, even though she would have taken it all in her stride, as usual. For some unfathomable reason, he desperately wanted to dislike his father but feared he would not. How strange was that? Ought it not to have been the other way around?

Jeff was also undecided whether to let the murderer do the talking upfront, to force him to justify his actions to his son's face. Or should he mount his own offensive before seeking a response? He concluded that the sequence of events didn't much matter, as long as he managed to get everything out in the open. Would his father be open to being open? Had he taken advantage of any psychiatric services during his time in prison? He may well still be in complete denial, for all the young man knew.

The wall clock emitted a loud click behind the star's head when its minute hand jerked round to the three. Already fifteen minutes late, he cursed, flexing his ankles in an effort to stop his legs from jumping. Lynn had flown up to Sydney with him and would most likely be sweating it out in the hotel's gymnasium, almost as stressed as he was. Eternally grateful for her support, he recalled with fondness the kind but dogged persistence she had applied to steer him to this place today.

Before the multi-millionnaire had a chance to resist, the boy from Canley Vale reared up, feeling his grown-up self's willpower desert him. He wished his saviour was here in the room after all, to step in if it became all too much for him. They were such a great team. He summoned her radiant, smiling face to his mind's eye, which restored a modicum of self-assurance as he sat alone in the interview room.

Hearing footsteps in the corridor, Jeff braced his spine against the back of the chair. Sure enough, without a warning knock, the door opened inwards. All the air rushed out of his lungs, and the shock temporarily winded him. He stood up as he watched an older version of himself walk into the room behind a uniformed guard.

Ten years fell away in a split-second, and the superstar found himself staring into eyes he despised. His first instinct was to turn and leave. This man wasn't worth his time.

Adrenalin surged through the angry young renegade who sprang to life inside the mature world-changer, bursting with arrogant, reproachful bitterness. He felt the blood boiling in his veins as the two sides of his character merged together. Fighting to stay in the present, he extended his right hand towards his father, confident this was the better statement to make.

'G'day, Dad.'

The older man gripped his son's hand out of habit but then shook it half-heartedly, his face devoid of emotion. It was an automatic reaction by a man also in deep shock.

'G'day.'

Jeff exhaled, the initial exchange uttered at last. Jesus Christ! This was uncomfortable. He subdued his wild thoughts by convincing himself that the man across the table was by far the more nervous. Diamond Senior was not accustomed to performing in front of thousands of people or conducting conflict resolution talks between foreign government representatives and militant activists.

"G'day, son" might have been nice, the visitor cursed internally. Even "G'day, Jeff" would have done...

Forcing the slightest of smiles, the celebrity offered his father a cigarette, which was accepted with a curt word of thanks but no change of expression. The son flicked the lid on his chrome lighter, leaned forwards and lit one after the other. Sinking down into his seat, he took a long drag, exhaling towards the ceiling, more to release some of the tension in his neck than to avoid blowing smoke into the other man's face.

'Thanks for agreeing to see me,' the musician started, watching the older man slump into his chair like a disaffected teenager. 'This is fucking weird, isn't it?'

Paul nodded, scanning his son up and down. Jeff was wearing the leather jacket Lynn had given him for his twentieth birthday, with smartly-cut black trousers and a dark grey shirt with the faintest of crimson stripes.

'Yeah. Sure is. You look good,' his father responded in a brusque voice.

The younger man laughed somewhat bitterly. 'I look like you! So how're you going?'

'Good. You?'

'Yeah. Fine, thanks,' the star answered, maintaining a barely tolerable level of undeserved respect; just enough to retain the moral high ground.

'How's your sister?' the older man asked, with the first flicker of interest in his eyes.

The twenty-four-year-old saw red. *That'd be right! Don't show him you're pissed off,* he told himself. *Let it go.* Reluctantly, he gave his dad the benefit of the doubt. He might have cared more if they knew each other better.

'Lena's fine too. She lives in Fairfield. Shares a flat with another girl.'

Jeff reached into his inside jacket pocket and pulled out the photographs he had brought with him, hearing the guard shuffling his feet behind him. His rampant imagination wondered if the silent, hard-nosed man in the blue uniform was thinking he was about to shoot the wizen, old bastard. What a splendid idea!

'I've got some pictures.'

Sorting through the half-dozen happy snaps, the celebrity picked out two and laid them on the smooth surface in front of the prisoner. Staring intently into his face, he heard the older man inhale sharply as recognition triggered a rare show of emotion. The boy he used to be felt the knife in his chest turn a little further, but the man he had become refused to react. In fact, much to his annoyance, Jeff even felt a little sympathy for the tall, thin waster across the table from him, with deep furrows in his brow and bony, tobacco-stained fingers.

'That's Lena all dolled up at our wedding,' he said, remembering how beautiful his sister had looked that day. 'Remind you of someone?'

Paul turned his eyes away from his son's determined gaze, stubbing out his cigarette. Then, looking back to the photographs, his voice cracked a little.

'Yep.'

A revelation struck Jeff like a lightning bolt. Why on Earth had this not occurred to him before? Did the inmate even know the circumstances of his wife's death? He wouldn't know his teenaged son had found her, covered in blood and vomit, a needle sticking out of her ankle and already deceased.

'D'you even know what happened to Mamá?'

The young man needed his father to understand why he was here. Picturing his beautiful best friend spurring him on, his nerves steadied a little.

'She was a wretched, alcoholic drug addict, and your daughter's a whore,' he blurted out, his heart in his mouth. 'Yeah. That woman in the picture... She gets fucked by six different men every day. That's all she ever learned how to do. D'you know what you did to us, Dad?'

Meeting this hateful man eyeball-to-eyeball with the cold, hard truth was a risky tactic, Jeff understood, but he had to cut to the chase. He stole a glance at the guard, who remained motionless. He probably spent many such hours in this room, listening to equally distasteful conversations. Might he even have volunteered for this showdown, given the characters involved?

Dismissing the presumptuous notion, the musician halted his mind's evasive meandering. Yes, it was nice to swap photographs and speak pleasantly about family resemblance, but he had committed to return to Melbourne with unspoken opinions surfaced and residual issues on their way to being resolved.

Paul said nothing. Both men's body language was reserved but tense, and the prison officer surveyed the scene in silence, waiting apprehensively for their next move. It also crossed the intellectual's mind that his father must have been addressed with disdain countless times over the last ten years. He was most likely anaesthetised against raised voices and derogatory insinuations.

'Look, Dad... I need to get a few things off my chest and I want you to do the same. Can I go first?' the rock star brokered.

His father shrugged. 'OK. Fire away.'

'Cheers. Did you know all along what those bastards were doing to Mamá and Lena?'

The prisoner shrugged again, a blank expression settling on his face as if he had heard it all before.

'What the hell did you do to them that made them come into our home to fuck our women? And with Lena so young? Jesus! They hurt them so badly. Did you know any of that?'

The series of blunt questions elicited no reaction whatsoever. Jeff had no doubt he was being understood, furious not to receive anything back. Reining in his emotions once more, he raised his hands in front of his chest to suggest he would back off.

'No,' he reconsidered, gathering the photographs together and turning them over like playing cards at the end of a hand of poker.

Party over, old man.

'Why should I let you off the hook? You really fucked me up too, you know,' the young man let the sentences roll off his tongue, having dreamed of this moment for so long. 'You knew bloody well what they were doing, didn't you? Those arseholes in our flat, doing that disgusting stuff to Mamá and Lena, and I couldn't do anything to stop 'em. And then you'd come home and fuck me over into the bargain because I didn't stop it happening. The effects of all that shit were still living in me for years. Every fucking day.'

The prisoner dealt his son another blank stare, which the angry man wasn't sure if he should interpret as ignorance, disdain or simply a complete lack of connection. Watching him shuffle in his chair, Jeff sensed his dad gathering his thoughts. The visitor leaned back, almost goading him to go in hard.

'*Chico*, you never follered me,' Paul recounted, now with a sneer on his wrinkled face. 'I was on me own against them fuckers. There was only one o' me. *You* could o' stopped all that shit happenin' to the girls by helpin' me out.'

The scowling inmate pointed a finger towards his son, who thumped the table with enough force to shake it. Sneaking a quick look at the prison guard, the rock star sprang out of his chair.

'That's what I wanted to hear!' he shouted, without disengaging from the older man's indifferent gaze. 'You still think that way after all this time? That's fucking bullshit, Dad!'

Again his father scarcely moved, keeping a wary eye on the songwriter as he paced around the room. Why did this man from whom he was descended find it impossible to address him by name? A somewhat familial "*chico*" was a decent compromise under the circumstances, although it sounded more demeaning coming from him than from others. Despite the derisory glare which had accompanied it, this was a small step forward at least, he reluctantly admitted.

'Could we have some coffee, please?' the sophisticated celebrity asked the officer, who obediently pressed the intercom' button in the room and passed on the request.

Jeff sat down again. 'Let me get this straight,' he continued. 'You blame me for not wanting to be involved in your dodgy deals because it meant you couldn't compete against the others. Is that what drove you to do what you did to those blokes too? I didn't do what you wanted, so you took it out on everyone else?'

The young man knew better than to articulate the circumstances of this man's crime in front of Parklea staff. Another exasperating vacuous stare met his gaze, no doubt perfected after years of passive defiance.

'That's fucked, Dad. Alberto's sons weren't in on it, and no-one raped Eva. Those guys even came to my wedding. For Christ's sake!'

His father's eyebrows twitched involuntarily, hearing his son pronounce names from their past. 'Bloody Alby Santos,' he hissed. 'I always wondered what 'appened to that fuckin' grass.'

The charitable musician chose to ignore this latest snide remark. 'Come on,' he prompted. 'Don't dodge the question. Why did you do it? Why was it so important that I join you? Weren't you man enough to lead your own bloody life of crime?'

Paul let out a throaty smoker's cough, slotting an index finger inside his shirt collar and running it round his neck as if he were feeling the heat. Angrily, and probably for the first time in a while, he filled his lungs with a deep breath and straightened up, giving himself back the true height and stature which used to send shivers down the teenager's spine.

'I was man enough alright,' he sneered. 'You could never be. You were all bloody useless to me. I was trying to build a fuckin' business, and all you did was read books and play that bloody guitar.'

'Right,' the star nodded, balanced on the very fine ledge between latitude and contempt.

'All that talk about school and university,' his father continued. 'No son o' mine was goin' to no poncy university. You let me down, eh?'

'I let *you* down? So why didn't you cut me loose?' the younger man questioned, bile rising in his stomach at the underlying paternal rejection being verbalised for the first time. 'Why didn't you guys just give me away? Give us all away? Fuck off out of our lives altogether? Instead of taking your disappointment at my failure out on all of us? Yeah?'

The prisoner scoffed, apparently amused by the malicious impersonation with which his son had signed off his series of questions. He looked up at the guard over his right shoulder, as if he were about to demand removal from the room. The uniformed officer continued to stare straight ahead, to Jeff's relief. The songwriter wondered how many of these spiteful confrontations these blokes had to endure. They were bound to take their toll after a while, he guessed, deciding to ease up on both men.

'Me mates used to ask me if you were queer in the 'ead or somethin',' Paul took up the conversation, his mocking tone increasing in volume. 'Music and books and all that. You weren't like the other kids. Fucking cricket and rugby and tennis. Sucking up to people. It was fuckin' embarrassin'.'

Jeff shook his head, rapidly losing patience. 'So no-one in here likes cricket or rugby?' he chided, catching the guard's eye. 'Nothing much else to talk about, I would've thought. Or are you split down ethnic lines in here too? It's OK now to talk about music, obviously though. "Ride All Night" go down well in here? Or "Donna Jade"? I should do a gig in here one day. Would your mates like that?'

The star noticed their sentry stifle a smile. The prisoner didn't think to look over his shoulder anyway, allowing the man to relax for a few seconds. His eyes made contact with the impressive musician's, both still waiting for a response to his vitriolic humour.

'Fuck you,' Diamond Senior hissed.

'Just because someone likes what you don't like doesn't make them queer, Dad,' the young superstar insisted. 'Look at my life. I bet your mates'd trade places with me any day. Look at my bloody car…'

Jeff leafed through the small selection of photographs again and dealt one of him sitting in the driving seat of his sleek, black Aston Martin, with its personalised licence plate beneath the front grille. He could sense his father was impressed, and that was good enough for him. He was willing to bet that if he left this picture with his father today, it would soon find its way around the other inmates, regardless of the lack of kudos it might receive in his presence.

'What I like…' he continued, taking the photograph back. 'That poncy, queer stuff, as you call it, has brought me more success than you'd ever have. Think about it, man. Why the hell wouldn't I have wanted out of that life? What was there for someone like me to gain? None of those gangs had it easy, did they?'

His father sniffed. Jeff could tell the old man's patience was running thin too, but he had waited many years to talk to him like this.

'Sure they had money, flash cars and the rest… But those blokes had to watch their backs wherever they went, just like you.'

And just like me, come to think of it, Jeff conceded, though only to his own conscience. Hopefully, his dad didn't possess the intelligence to see through the gaping hole in this particular argument. A huge pang of longing broke free of his heart during this small epiphany, leaving him short of breath. The smartest arse-end of a pantomime horse in history, patiently waiting in their favourite Sydney hotel, would have pounced on such a careless flaw in an instant.

The superstar carried on, determined to make his point. 'No wonder you don't care about being in here,' he shrugged. 'Much safer than being on the Stones, isn't it? Much less to worry about; fighting for the next deal the whole time… What was it about that so-called life you wanted so badly?'

Paul Diamond raised his right hand to his forehead, spinning his finger around in a circle and mimicking the deranged grin of a madman. 'You're crazy, mate,' he jeered. 'What the fuck are you talkin' about? You always were so fucking weird. Wanting to know ev'rythin' and comin' on all 'igh and mighty, like you knew better than the rest of us.'

'Yeah. Maybe I am crazy,' his son nodded, refusing to be riled into raising his voice again. 'You made me this way. If not from birth, then certainly from the day you ended up in here.'

'Fuck you.'

'No, Dad,' the young man sighed, wondering how much longer he ought to prolong this discussion in order to complete the acquittal either to himself or to his gorgeous lover. 'Fuck you. What made you think I'd be into the gangland way of life? Your own dad wasn't.'

'Me own dad?' the prisoner echoed. 'What a useless piece of shit he was. No spine, no guts. At least I stood up to the bastards... How the 'ell would you know anyways? You were just a kid.'

'Yep. I was just a kid. And so was Lena. Exactly my point, but whatever... Your father didn't want you doing all that shit, but he left you alone, didn't he? All I wanted was for you to leave us alone too. I didn't care what you did with your life. Just don't drag innocent kids into that messed-up, sick world of yours. It wasn't fair, Dad. Look what it did to Mamá...'

Jeff waited for the faintest sign that his mother's life and death held some significance for the man on the other side of the table. He thought he saw a faint flicker of disturbance flash across the deeply-lined forehead. Did those sunken eyes blink infinitesimally more slowly for a few seconds?

Maybe not. It had been a very long time since this deadbeat had been required to feel anything, the philosopher supposed. Indeed, if their roles were reversed, and he himself were faced with spending the rest of his life in prison, he would be hard pressed to want to feel anything either.

'D'you know who paid for *Bubshka*'s funeral, Dad?' the twenty-four-year-old asked, leaning forward again and laying his hands flat on the Formica surface between them. 'And for Mamá's, for that matter?'

'Fairies at the bottom of the garden?' the old man snapped back, clearly very proud of himself for thinking of something so *drôle* to say to his jumped up, university-educated wuss of a son.

Jeff gritted his teeth, ready to lash out. Instead, he pointed an angry index finger back at his own chest.

'Me,' he spat. 'I paid for them. A teenaged kid, working in the butchers', hacking up dead animals into snags and chasing round after idiots who couldn't run their own lives.'

His father faltered, withering into his seat. 'Then I guess I should say thanks.'

The musician drew breath, momentarily floored by this unexpected expression of gratitude. His natural reaction was to disbelieve the prisoner's sincerity, yet his well-trained, conciliatory side opted to give him the benefit of the doubt again. Jeff Diamond could be very persuasive. People often told him so. It seemed that his persistence had paid off. Perhaps the pitiful sentimentality in his words had penetrated the old man's thick skull after all.

'Listen, Dad,' he continued, doing his best to smile. 'When your mum died, I was sixteen and I didn't even feel sad. I was totally fucked in the head. To me, hers was just another unhappy soul released from that shit-hole of a life while I was stuck there trying to make sense of it all. You know, I dragged Lena along to the funeral, and she cried! She hadn't seen *Bubshka* in two years and she still cried. Me, I just sat there and thought about girls.'

Jeff's father leaned forward, the previous malice gone from his eyes. 'Listen, you Countdown clown, I didn't even get to go to me mum's funeral,' he mocked. 'I'm the one banged up, eh? I didn't get to go to me wife's funeral neither. No-one told me 'til after it was over.'

It was strangely heartening to hear the old man fight back, even though there was no real venom in his tone this time. The musician reached his left hand across the table and squeezed his father's wrist, chuckling at the hurtful jibe.

'I know. I'm sorry about that too. Would you've wanted to go?'

If he were honest, Jeff doubted the hardened criminal would have attended his wife's funeral, had he been free to make the choice at the time, minus the facility of reflection during his years of incarceration.

Paul flicked his arm upwards, instantly belittling his son's peaceable gesture. No longer disturbed by the rejection however, the celebrity withdrew his hand and placed it on his thigh under the table. He recognised himself in his father's behaviour, or rather his former self, pre-Lynn; the self who would go to any lengths not to reveal his true feelings. This path to reconciliation was destined to be a slow process. Thinking he should draw the meeting to a close, his blood chilled with fear at having to go through this *fiasco* again.

What was it that they had started today? And where might it end?

The superstar sighed and cursed his naïve expectations. It was unlike Lynn not to have warned him of the need to take things slowly and that it would take time to break through. But no, Jeff smiled. The more likely scenario was that she had deliberately left him to come to this conclusion on his own, so as not to discourage him at the outset.

Christ Almighty! This woman was so absolutely perfect for him. There was no clear end in sight, nor even a real understanding as to the end he sought, yet the new husband had to own up to a definite catharsis taking place deep inside.

With a creak of its hinges, the door opened, and another guard delivered a tray with two cups of coffee and a plate of biscuits. Still lightheaded, Jeff eagerly helped himself to two biscuits and crunched them straight down, then scooping three spoonfuls of sugar into his drink.

'Those are good!' he laughed, gazing up at the officer and then at his dad. 'I haven't had a Monte Carlo in years.'

The older man lifted a chocolate-coated biscuit to his mouth too, revealing several missing teeth. 'You been livin' the 'igh life,' he smiled, slurping his coffee while chewing. 'This is all we get in 'ere.'

The young celebrity shrugged. 'Fair enough. Look, Dad... I know you don't give a shit about me and my life, and I can live with that. You blame me for not helping grow your pathetic criminal empire, and I blame you for all the nightmares and the fact I only got a handful of hours' sleep in eight years. But mostly, I blame you for wrecking the lives of two perfectly decent women.'

'What the fuck are you talkin' about?' his father sneered again. 'I did what I 'ad to do to survive. We all did.'

'Not from where I'm coming from,' the patient negotiator shook his head. 'But that's all gone now, and I can move on. I just want to hear what you've got to say and perhaps clear the air between us. And I want to hear what you've been through in here since I last saw you.'

The prisoner's expression softened a little, secretly impressed with his adult son. 'Oh, it's a fuckin' party in 'ere, mate,' he said, his tone friendlier. 'Dunno what you're after. They got me workin' in the sheds, mendin' furniture an' that. Piss-easy work; same every day. No surprises and nothin' to worry about. What else d'ya wanna know?'

'Ah, I don't know. Anything. That's all good for a start. How you feel after all this time, I guess. If you've got any regrets?'

Diamond Senior lifted his hands up to shoulder level and coughed in amusement, scanning his eyes round their salubrious surroundings. The sadistic streak the son remembered from his childhood was still intact, regardless of whether it was a *macho* act or if the attitude came naturally.

'Na! That's it, mate. There's nothin' else to tell. Every day's the bloody same, but I don't give a shit about that either. You said it, you rich, know-it-all bastard.'

Frustrated, Jeff sat taller in his chair and renewed his assault. He deserved more than indifference from the man who had brought him into this world and then left him to survive on his own.

'Alright, fair enough. So sitting here now then, who's the loser? You or me?' the rocker taunted. 'After this, I'm going back to a top-notch hotel to make love with a stunning, passionate woman who adores me. Then next week, I'm going to LA to make a movie. And where are you going, Dad? You're going back through that door.'

The twenty-four-year-old pointed with a strong left hand over his father's head. Again the guard stirred, expecting an equally angry retort from the double murderer, whose jawline hardened while his Adam's apple twitched imperceptibly.

'You didn't think of that back then, did you?' Jeff continued, the antipathy in his voice increasing as his blood reached boiling point. 'When you were lining your pockets with a measly few hundred bucks at a time at the expense of your family's safety and sanity. Was it worth it, Dad?'

'Fuck you, boy.'

His father was hurting at last. The empathetic man could see it in his narrowing eyes, which darted from the table to the ceiling and back again. He continued, more conciliatory this time.

'I knew it wouldn't be worth it, y'see, Dad. Even back then. That's why I refused to get involved. I didn't want that sort of life.'

'So you ended up marrying Lynn Dyson,' Paul assumed control of the conversation with a bitter laugh, quickly putting his roused emotions back to sleep and changing the subject. 'How the fuck did that 'appen?'

'I did,' his son chuckled. 'Damned if I know how it happened! I'm glad it did though.'

'You always said you would. What does she want with someone like you, but? You must've told her some good lies. The blokes in 'ere take the piss out of me all day long. They call me "Aussie Elvis" and sing your songs at me in the shower, all queer-like. I'm fuckin' famous in 'ere 'cause you're famous out there. Holy crap!'

Jeff smiled. 'Sorry about that. I wondered how much news you got in here.'

'Ah, I don't care,' his father quipped. 'It's cool, tell ya the truth. You turned out good. No thanks to me, but. I should o' never 'ad kids.'

'Yeah. You're right about that.'

Not even half joking, the younger man remarked to himself that he no longer smarted at the idea of never having existed. The thought pleased him. Another gold star his beautiful best friend could claim...

'A few years ago, I would've agreed with you, but now I'm glad I'm alive. In fact...' the accomplished communicator paused, making sure he had his adversary's full attention. 'In fact, thanks, Dad, for unwittingly giving me life. I want to be able to tell my kids who you are and what you mean to me. Not just based on the past. I want what I tell them to be based on now. Shit, Dad! Their other grandfather'll be Bart Dyson. You know how ironic that is, don't you? Does the term "chalk and cheese" come to mind?'

Paul pouted, completely missing his son's stinging observation. 'Quite a pedigree your kid'll have, mate. So is she pregnant then? Is she a good fuck, Lynn Dyson?'

Jeff shook his head, refusing to rise to the criminal's cruel jibes again after all these years. 'Cut that out, *mate,*' he snapped back. 'Show some respect. That's *your* daughter-in-law you're insulting. Didn't you ever look at what was on my walls?'

'No. Well, yeah. Maybe.'

'Christ, Dad!' the young man was fast losing patience. 'You had no fucking idea who I was back then. I'm amazed you even knew you had a son. Whatever... And didn't you just accuse me of being queer? Make up your fucking mind. No. Lynn's not pregnant yet. Later in the year, we hope. After the Olympic Games in Canada. Some people plan these things, you'll be surprised to learn.'

The final sentence in this latest tirade was uncalled for, admittedly, but the successful philanthropist enjoyed delivering such a sanctimonious message all the more for it. He had been waiting a very long time to speak these words to his father.

'You can thank your mum for that,' the older man replied, again utterly unmoved.

Jeff didn't bother to hide any of his disgust this time. It angered him to hear his father lay the blame solely at his mother's feet, but there was no point in moralising about this man's careless disregard for contraception at this late juncture. He could hardly make the same mistake in his current situation...

Instead, the mature, worldly and forward-thinking intellectual carried on articulating the purpose of his visit, and why his gorgeous soul-mate had pushed him into doing so. 'Dad, I have a responsibility to my future kids, to my wife and to myself to keep us safe and to tell them exactly how it is. You never took responsibility for anything, but I'm not going to be that kind of father because I know how bad it feels to be that kind of kid. Tell me what's going to happen to us, Dad, please. Do you talk to people out there, or in here? What do you know that I need to know?'

The older man shrugged. 'What *are* you talkin' about? You always did talk a load of crap. Why all the questions? Ya reckon anyone cares about comin' after you? You're off limits, mate. Imagine the noise that'd make in the 'papers?'

'Sure there'd be noise, but I don't believe you,' the streetwise young man countered. 'Do you honestly think people give a shit about the side-effects when they're planning a hit? You didn't.'

Paul Diamond let out a throaty laugh. 'I was stupid, *chico*,' came an admission his son never expected to hear. 'I got too cocky, didn't I? High on LSD and too fuckin' angry.'

'Christ!' Jeff leaned forwards, his chest tight with a sudden rush of mixed emotions. 'That I understand.'

Disregarding his son's compassionate comment, the prisoner's gaze alighted on the gold and black signet ring with its two diamonds, one a little brighter than the other. 'That's a cool ring. Your jacket an' all. You got a heap o' money now, eh?'

'Yep,' the star answered without any hint of swagger. 'And thanks. I've got way more than enough money. I give a lot of it away. We don't need much, Lynn and I.'

Ostentation wouldn't wash with the murderer, no matter how dearly the lost boy wished to prove himself. His head clearing after having spoken his mind, he took a moment to scrutinise this man whom he scarcely remembered. More distant childhood recollections were jogged by the faded, green-grey tattoos showing under the cuffs of his prison-issue shirt. Father and son had turned into strikingly similar adults. Different worlds called for different forms of adornment, that was all.

His dad would be younger than Gerald Blake and much the same age as Bart Dyson, the thoughtful songwriter estimated. He seemed much older than both of these men however; weaker, greyer and with definite curvature of the spine most likely accelerated by the rasping cough that followed almost every sentence uttered.

Perhaps faces aged prematurely when they only knew how to be mean, Jeff speculated. Lynn often told him he looked younger when he smiled. This bloke ought to give it a try once in a while…

'Do you need anything?' he found himself asking.

'That jacket,' his father snapped back in an instant.

'What? No way!' the star retorted, amazed at the man's gall. 'This was a birthday present from Lynn. You're not getting it. I meant smokes or magazines or whatever. Jesus Christ!'

The older man laughed out loud for the first time, the expression on his face almost friendly. His son still didn't like him though. Not one bit, and of that he was glad. From his side of the table, he slid over a car magazine which he had bought to read on the flight up from Tullamarine.

'Take this anyway. I've finished with it.'

Jeff had tucked a few photographs between the pages, unbeknown to his father; one of him leaning against his black sports car, and a couple of his sister during her trip to Melbourne. It didn't matter if the magazine were to be thrown away without the pictures being exposed to the stark lighting of a prison cell. The peacemaker had done enough for the time being.

Like an animal making a grab for an unexpected morsel of food, the inmate slid the glossy publication towards him without a word of thanks. By the shrewd sideways glance that was shot towards the burly guard, the celebrity wondered how long it would take before the gift was traded. And for which commodity would it be bartered in this god-forsaken place?

'You're welcome,' his son chuckled, heaving himself to a standing position. 'I'm going to call it quits, unless there's anything else you want to talk about.'

Paul Diamond rose to his feet also, and the two men eyed each other off at their full height for the first and probably only time. In the eleven years since the pair had last met, his adult son had outgrown him by ten centimetres and was decidedly broader and stronger.

Moving round to the other side of the table, the visitor placed his left hand on the lifer's shoulder and held his right out for a farewell handshake. To his surprise, he noticed tears in the old man's eyes.

Don't do this to me, Jeff said to himself, gritting his teeth. Managing to restrain any outward show of emotion in return, he refused to break eye contact. *Two can play at that game*, he thought.

'We're pretty alike,' the handsome celebrity conceded, 'aren't we? For better or worse.'

'Yep. Reckon so.'

Their short-lived reactions soon suppressed, Jeff shook his father's hand, and the courtesy was this time returned, full-blooded.

'Thanks, Dad. Stay safe.'

'You too, mate.'

The uniformed officer reached for the door handle, peering through the window before twisting it. Diamond the prisoner turned on his heels and vacated the room without hesitation. Diamond the free man stood watching the figure of his fallen nemesis disappear, suddenly thrown back to the desolate scene when Lynn had left his Richmond flat in the dead of night before their two-year separation.

Damn! He did feel something after all.

The expensive wristwatch the young man had received for his recent birthday informed him that the meeting had lasted just over an hour. What had he learned from it? Not too much. He had found out that the word "son" was too hard for his father to say. Or perhaps being reminded of his children meant little to him. Yet what had prompted those last-minute tears? The old man probably wouldn't give him another thought, and therefore neither was likely ever to understand.

***

Jeff was pleased to escape from the stuffy room and took a few deep breaths to wake himself up for the drive back into the city. He reached into the inside pocket of his jacket to retrieve his cigarettes and lighter, but before he had the chance to light one, the governor and another staff member had arrived to meet their celebrity guest outside the interview room door.

'No fireworks then?' the slimmer of the two asked, extending his hand. 'I'm Larry Shepherd, Mister Diamond. I'm the psych' in charge of your father's wing.'

'Hi. Jeff, please. Good to meet you, Larry,' the famous musician acknowledged the welcome greeting. 'No fireworks, no. It got close a couple of times. Thanks for arranging this, gents.'

Whitfield stepped forward and shook Jeff's hand too. 'I expect you've more questions than answers just now,' he said. 'How did you leave things with him?'

The governor was a Scotsman whose thick brogue had been contaminated with an *ocker* twang after twenty years in Sydney, almost a foot shorter than the statuesque celebrity.

The exhausted visitor exhaled through pursed lips, shaking his head. 'Who knows? I don't think I made him the happiest man in the world. Does he ever express himself?'

Larry confirmed Jeff's suspicions. 'Your dad's a hard nut to crack, that's for sure. I've never seen him show any remorse or compassion for anyone. He's pretty even-tempered most of the time these days. Gets annoyed when people mess with his things, but that's pretty normal. They don't have much to call their own in here.'

Alright! Here was some useful information, the intelligent young man smiled. He liked the middle-aged psychologist a lot after only a few short sentences and allowed himself to relax at last.

'Cheers. He never had much to call his own out there either. And what he did have he didn't treat very well. I'm glad to know at least it's not just me he reacts that way with. It's comforting, although I'm not really sure why. Would you do me a favour, please?'

Both men nodded.

'I live in Melbourne now and travel most of the time,' Jeff explained. 'And I don't want to come here again if I can help it. I can pay for some extra counselling or something, if that's allowed... God knows I hate the bastard for what he did, but it'd be good to get him to express what's inside.'

The Governor spoke up first. 'It's been tried before, sir. Your father won't talk to any of them. We can try to offer it to him again, but I doubt if he'll agree. We can force him to attend, but not to speak openly.'

'Sure. I understand. Thanks, James,' the superstar replied. 'Whatever you can do would be great. I know I kept everything bottled up inside for so long too, but the freedom I found when I finally let go of some secrets was indescribable. I know he's a con' and not exactly here on a Buddhist retreat, but it might do everyone some good in the long run.'

'You're a good man,' Larry added. 'You'd make a good counsellor, if you ever need a new career.'

The longtime student of the mind chuckled, not about to tell them how near this professional assessment was to the mark. 'Thanks! I might be glad of a reference one day. I'll look you up.'

The celebrity left the prison facility without ceremony, through heavy steel gates that clanged resolutely shut behind him. He ran to the car park where his rented Holden HX was waiting for him, breaking out in a cold sweat as a circle of heckling demons chased him over the pavement. The rain still fell in stair-rods, and he shook the droplets off his leather jacket before tossing it onto the passenger seat and jumping in.

To think his dad wanted to take the coat off his back! The former bad-boy laughed bitterly as he slammed the door and turned the key in the ignition. Lynn was going to love this light-hearted nugget. Here was a memory about his father worth keeping and even worth passing on to their children.

One thing was for sure, he sent to his dream girl through the telepathic airwaves... The importance of his impending fatherhood had never seemed so real nor so appealing as in this minute, fully confident that he would do the right thing by their children no matter what.

The nondescript sedan and its *incognito* occupant drove fast across the outer suburban sprawl, not even slowing down through his old stomping ground on this occasion. He considered dropping in and saying hello to Alberto, but changed his mind. He feared the temptation of mentioning where he had been. The boxing club proprietor mustn't be burdened by this information. He was a man rendered old before his time by life in the crime-ridden suburbs and was best left to exist in relative peace.

Turning his mind to his dream girl, who would be hard at work in their suite, the star pulled over at the first public telephone he saw. He obtained the hotel's number from the operator, and the switchboard patched him through to their room.

'Jeff, is that you?' he heard Lynn's mellow, endearing voice in his ear.

'Yeah. How're you going, angel?'

'Hi! Fine, thanks. Glad to hear your voice,' she told him. 'How did it go? Where are you now?'

The twenty-four-year-old couldn't help but laugh. 'Well... So far you've asked me more questions in under ten seconds than he did in over an hour.'

The sportswoman didn't know quite how to interpret her husband's opening statement. As usual, his quirky turn of phrase masked a less frivolous reality. Every silver lining had its cloud, she recalled with a rueful smile.

'Oh. Are you OK though?'

'Yeah, angel. I'm good. It was a great idea of yours, even though the full spectrum of emotions were unleashed,' her husband admitted to the woman he so needed to connect with, and as soon as possible. 'I just wanted to let you know I'm on my way back. Can I take you to lunch and tell you all about it?'

Satisfied that her haunted husband sounded fairly composed, Lynn relaxed too. 'Oh, yes. Thanks. That'd be lovely. How long will you be?'

'Less than an hour. Why? D'you need to get rid of someone? Did Celia ring about tonight?'

'No! And yes to the Blakes, and Madalena too,' she replied, giggling. 'We're all on for dinner somewhere. Celia said she'd think about where to go that wouldn't be too formal.'

'*¡Excelente!*' Jeff responded, feeling healthier with blood circulating to all the important parts again. 'Jeez, I want you so much, by the way. Cheers for sorting all that out. Now for Christ's sake, get off the bloody 'phone so I can get back and rip your clothes off.'

A sexy laugh egged his *libido* on still further. 'OK, sir! Drive carefully. You better make it worth my while, Don Juan.'

His dream girl hung up without saying goodbye, leaving the caller standing and staring at the receiver in disbelief. He had asked for that! His saviour had cast her spell yet again, for despite now being in even greater agony for the journey eastwards along the river, all vexing thoughts of Parklea Prison had been suitably re-prioritised in his mind.

The long drive into Sydney's CBD allowed the tired songwriter's mood to vacillate between relief that the visit was over and frustration that he hadn't accomplished more. He didn't want this to be the first of many visits, but perhaps this was now unavoidable. Meeting his father again had not spawned the same eagerness to remain in contact as he had felt with his sister. Good thing too, he reassured his self-doubt. Their father was a convicted double murderer, presumably as guilty as they came. The man was hardly the ideal father figure, so there was no need to reproach himself for his reluctance to rekindle their relationship.

The intellectual's agile brain cruised far and wide while the car drew nearer to the famous Harbour Bridge. Winding his window closed to reduce the chance of being recognised, he pitied the thousands of children who were alienated from their parents on much less serious pretexts. Perhaps Madalena, in her uneducated simplicity, was the smarter. She already knew her father wasn't worth keeping in touch with. As usual, her over-analytical brother was complicating matters again by leaving no stone unturned before deciding on a verdict. Regardless, now he had seen evidence of the man's cold, hard, unapologetic heart with his own eyes. He was callous to the core and seemed to have no regrets for the poor lot he had handed his family.

Could this high-profile millionnaire who considered himself somewhat wise dare to believe his father's vicious criminal connections posed no threat to the safety of those he loved? He wanted to, for everyone's sake. Yet accepting the word of someone who had been proven so utterly evil would be irresponsible in the extreme. He couldn't possibly trust him, given the fact that he had expressed no remorse at offering up the bodies of his own wife and daughter into the hands of his enemies.

Jeff had hurt his father today. A stab of penitence rose in his heart, in spite of his loathing for the man, when he recalled the involuntary moan that had escaped the prisoner's mouth when he had contrasted their current lifestyles. He had gone a bit too far, on reflection. Another shiver ran down his spine, suddenly envisaging his father taking his own life after their conversation. Jesus! Would this rollercoaster ride ever stop?

This eventuality was more than plausible. The ambitious world-changer was aware of his own powers of persuasion only too well. "A planter of seeds" was the label John Francis had pinned on him during their fruitful London association. What if he had planted some seeds in his father's brain today which grew into a vine of honesty that strangled him with pent-up grief and contrition?

Forced to brake suddenly when a vehicle turned right in front of him with very little room to spare, the troubled soul was jolted out of his daydream. *Don't be such an idiot*, he scolded himself. Who would care if Paul Diamond were to commit suicide? Apart from his son, of course, who cared about everything way too much. Madalena would say good riddance, as would their maternal grandparents. Swinging the Holden into the side street behind the hotel, his mouth stretched into a wide grin as he imagined their mother's ghost jumping for joy in her fiery home, while many of western Sydney's seedier pubs threw their doors open for the day.

Jeff parked the car underground at the Intercontinental and made his way up to their suite on the third floor. He let himself into the room with no sign of accompanying demons. So overjoyed was he at this fact that he shouted at the top of his voice, launching into a victory slide across the floorboards like a European soccer player.

'Welcome home!' Lynn cried out, rushing into his arms. 'What an entrance! I'm guessing you found it easy to get in.'

The happy woman hugged him tightly, and her husband immediately dissolved into a mess of tears and laughter. They flopped down on the bed, clawing at each others' clothing amid feverish kisses. Their exquisite sexual interlude was all too soon over, having thrilled both lovers exactly as the free man had described to the prisoner.

'He's a narcissist, I reckon,' the young man murmured, planting a soft, thoughtful kiss on his beautiful best friend's forehead.

'Your dad?'

'Mmm... Someone who preyed on the vulnerable to avenge his own misgivings.'

Lynn raised herself up onto one elbow, intrigued by this new and overly charitable theory. 'You're softening on him, which is good, I suppose. What happened to him to make him so evil? You've never ventured into this territory before.'

'No. I know, angel. And I don't know,' her husband frowned. 'How much of his narcissism was at the root of my early behaviour?'

Quite a bit, the twenty-year-old figured silently. 'You didn't pick me for my vulnerability, which suggests your higher intelligence at work again, even if you did inherit this behaviour somehow. You drummed it out of yourself.'

'With your help.'

'No. Not really. You were never narcissistic with me. You were with others, I think, but not with me.'

'Thank Christ, baby. I look just like the arsehole though,' Jeff whispered, post-coital warmth still overflowing with gratitude. 'I didn't think I'd be able to see the resemblance, but it was like staring into a mirror and seeing the year two thousand.'

'Wow! That's a scary thought. What did he sound like? Was he friendly at least?'

'Not at all,' the twenty-four-year-old answered, stroking her breasts and feeling her skin twitch under his fingertips. 'There were moments when I thought we might connect, but they were fleeting. I don't like him, angel.'

Lynn kissed his lips. 'That's OK. You don't have to like him.'

'I *love* you though,' Jeff reminded his beautiful wife. 'Hey! He said the other inmates sing my songs to him in the shower. How delightfully ironic is that? Revenge is "Ride All Night"!'

On The Wrong Side Of Town

The twenty-first Olympiad was to begin on the seventeenth of July nineteen-seventy-six with the Opening Ceremony at the new stadium on the banks of *La Fleuve Saint Laurent* in Montreal. The Dysons left for the athletes' village in the French-Canadian city's inner suburbs at the beginning of the month, intending to acclimatise to the opposite season at a nearby sports centre.

The entire family's preparation had progressed flawlessly. Bart had overseen their training programs, assisted by a number of highly-credentialled coaches, physiologists and psychologists. This orchestrated campaign was designed to put Australia on the map as a formidable sporting nation, and to prove to the sport-loving communities and political parties supporting the popular patriots that their investment in facilities and new coaching techniques would pay dividends on the world's stage.

Similar to Munich four years earlier, Junior and Lynn had been entered in a wide range of events, and were now set to spend many more hours with their younger brother and sister in tow, commuting between the various arenas, stadia and equestrian centres.

'Angel, d'you remember that crisis conversation we had ages ago about your dad saying you'd have to have an abortion if you got pregnant before Munich?' Jeff had reminded his new wife during a long telephone call from the other side of the globe.

'Yes,' the sportswoman replied. 'I'll certainly never forget that. You were as angry as I felt. You were great about it though. I loved how we dealt with it.'

'Well… Last night I was lying awake, trying not to think about how much I wanted to…'

A prim and proper voice tutted loudly into the telephone. 'Shhh!' she hissed. 'Don't remind me! What?'

Her husband chuckled. 'When it suddenly occurred to me...'

'Oh? What suddenly occurred to you?'

'When I asked you what would happen if you got pregnant after Munich, and you didn't have an answer. Remember?'

His wife frowned. 'Of course I remember,' she murmured. 'We talked about it before I left. I hated it.'

'We should have twigged right then and there that he planned to pull you out after the Olympics,' Jeff continued in an angry tone. 'You know... Split us up. It was so obvious with hindsight. I can't believe I was so blind at the time.'

Lynn sighed. 'Yeah. I suppose you're right. I try not to think about those horrible days. But I still regret not knowing what you were going through, so we could've found a way to stay together. I definitely expressed my opinion to Mum, but Dad would never've listened.'

'Sorry, angel. I shouldn't be making you think about it again now, should I?' the compassionate musician let up. 'From a distance, everything worked out for the best. That's actually what occurred to me last night; that I don't think we'd be as strong as we are if we hadn't had that time apart, painful though it was...'

The athlete gasped, unable to quite believe the words squeezing through the telephone line. She recognised her husband's voice alright, but was this really the same man who had forcibly removed her from a dance floor and confronted her about obeying her father too closely?

'Wow! Have you been completely brainwashed by the psychobabble?' she laughed, taking off her sports gear and preparing for a post-event shower, following the plan the lovers had schemed the day before.

'Probably,' Jeff agreed. 'What are you doing? You sound breathless.'

'Nothing. Be patient. You started this conversation. You've come a long way, Mister Diamond,' Lynn told him in her best motivational voice.

She thumbed her nose at an imaginary Big D standing in front of her, and it made her laugh. The combination of her beautiful black stallion's apparent adjustment to an episode which had once broken his spirit and the raw anger the same memories fired in her own belly was a powerful aphrodisiac, perfect fuel for their long-distance *rendezvous*.

'*Now* what are you doing?' he exclaimed, perplexed at what might be causing such merriment in her cramped digs in the Olympic village.

'Nothing,' his wife insisted, 'but I am naked and ready for your instructions.'

'You're still a kid sometimes,' the aroused Melburnian teased. 'I love it! I agree though. And I want to come further, in about ten minutes at this rate. Are you at least wearing your medals?'

'No! Would that really turn you on?'

Jeff's hand reached down to his aching genitalia and began to masturbate slowly, applying and releasing pressure in his best interpretation of his favourite handler's technique. His imagination was doing just fine without any kinky add-ons.

'Of course not,' he moaned. 'Stroke the sides of your boobs and underneath them for me, 'cause I miss them. Do you want me inside you?'

'Oh, yes. I want you inside me. Under the water?'

Her husband's contented sigh confirmed her good idea. 'And now direct the water at your clit'. My fingers don't reach, but you need to come. I'd love you to come. Loud, angel. Real loud, OK?'

The expressive sex-god paused for a few minutes, listening for her response. He was not disappointed.

Lynn groaned, her orgasm burst forth at her own hand. 'Oh, God, Jeff. That's fantastic! And can you see my lips around your cock and feel my tongue playing with the tip?'

'Jesus,' he murmured, moving his hand more quickly. 'You bet I can, angel. Do it again.'

'I am. Can't you tell?' his wife responded with a hint of playful sarcasm. 'I can't wait to do this for real again. You sound so sexy. I want to be with you, to feel you come inside me.'

'Oh, baby. You are so good to me. Keep that up, and I'll come in three seconds.'

Their telephonic liaison continued until Jeff had vicariously fondled every single part of the gorgeous body he craved, and they had both called out words of love when his climax overtook him. In the early days, his dream girl had only played this game for his benefit, but recently it appeared she had learned to enjoy getting her kicks as shamelessly as he did.

Jeff Diamond was but a plain and simple man after all, revelling in base, instinctive animal pleasures. He had met his match in Lynn Dyson, and by giving her his name, they had grown closer, day by perfect day. As the months passed, they made each other happy in whichever way worked, no matter where in the world they were.

While his beautiful best friend was in Montreal, racking up Australia's record medal tally with the rest of her family, the ambitious businessman and philanthropist took another quick trip to Sydney. Since making contact with his father, several serious forays into the underground scene of the western suburbs had been instigated using a former gang member who had turned informant for the New South Wales Police and two ex-soldiers who worked for the security firm engaged by the Diamonds while touring.

This team had garnered new intelligence, and between them all, including the star's indomitable business manager, they had scoped out an operation which would be safe enough for Jeff to meet with the sons of his father's murder victims. With Lynn and her family out of the country, the opportunity was too good to miss.

'Are you in search of retribution?' Gerry had asked, after his latest James Bond impression had fallen on bored ears. 'What are you expecting the outcome to be?'

The cautious celebrity shrugged. 'An assurance that the Jaworskis aren't going to come after Lynn, our kids or the Dysons,' he replied. 'That's what I'd like the outcome to be, but that's a whole different story to what I'm expecting.'

'But how can you possibly know if you can trust their word?' his manager counselled. 'I mean, these are not men of good character, me old chum.'

'Like us, you mean? I know. It's a risk, I agree, mate. I'm taking a risk just by stirring up the hornet's nest, but there's a certain honour among thieves, I think. That's what I'm hoping to appeal to. My dad almost said so.'

'But why now? So soon after you saw him?' Gerry asked. 'Isn't that asking for trouble? Why don't you keep watching for a year or two and then see how the land lies?'

Jeff shot an incredulous look at his smartly-dressed executive buddy, sitting there in his high-backed, leather chair with his vital organs protected by a huge mahogany desk. 'You haven't watched enough dubious TV shows,' he chided. 'These are not keen criminal masterminds we're dealing with here.'

The accountant shook his head. 'TV? That thing that sits in the corner of my lounge room, taking up space? I don't know if it even works! Masterminds they may not be, but they still kill people.'

'True enough. These blokes are driven by the seven deadly sins, mate. Impulses and short-term gratification. Animals sporting jewellery, basically. They might wear good clothes and drive flashy cars, but they're pretty low on the evolutionary scale. If they find out I'm back in touch with my dad, they'll jump to all the wrong conclusions. Gavin's guys say they'll want to move fast if they're going to move at all, and that's my gut feel too.'

Gerry exhaled, standing up and gazing out of his corner office window down to the wide, tree-lined thoroughfare below, where trams trundled by with monotonous regularity and stockbrokers darted from offices to boutique tailors to gentlemen's clubs, partaking in their own sins behind discreet doors. Unfamiliar with the unsavoury underworld his friend depicted, he was uncertain of his level of responsibility towards the man he was paid to safeguard. An Accountancy degree and being Captain of the school rugby team hardly qualified him in this new field of play.

'I see,' he turned back to face his client. 'What does Lynn think about this? And Big D?'

Jeff made a fist and thumped the desk in front of him. 'We have to leave the big man out of this for now, Gez, please. Not a bloody word. Let me deal with this on my own for the time being. I don't want to arouse any suspicion on his part until we know there's something worth getting suspicious about. He told me his daughter was my responsibility, so I'll deal with it. Is that OK with you?'

'Whatever you say, boss,' the businessman smiled. 'And Lynn?'

'Lynn understands the risks,' the celebrity rebuffed. 'She's concerned because she feeds off me. She's like you though: clueless about that world. She expects people to behave honourably, and I don't want to be the one to shatter that illusion either.'

'Thanks a lot, mate,' Gerry scoffed, 'on behalf of myself and your lovely wife. Clueless, indeed.'

'And long may it continue,' the lost boy snapped back. 'I'm not proud that I'm dragging you down into this shit. Not proud at all. Listen, mate... If these blokes are going to exact a revenge killing for their fathers, I'd rather they do it now. I don't want to leave Lynn high and dry to bring up our family on her own. That's the main reason I'm forcing the issue. Put up or shut up. *Capisce?*'

***

Diamond Junior's people had chosen a popular restaurant on Sydney's Circular Quay as the meeting place. Marek and Theo Jaworski, the men whom Diamond Senior had stabbed to death, had five sons between them. According to the best information Jeff could obtain, only three were actively involved in crime gangs. The fourth had died in a motorcycle accident. At least, that was how the official version read... And the last had emigrated to the USA and didn't appear to have any links with known gangland elements over there.

From the safety of several random and anonymous hotel rooms, the superstar and his associates had made a series of brief telephone calls to the new generation of Jaworskis. Only two cousins committed to a meeting initially, but the skilled arbitrator had managed to persuade them to bring the remaining brother. It was important to make eye contact with all three key players at once if he were to gauge their true intentions.

On the nominated date, the successful songwriter felt like a character in a Robert Ludlum thriller, being briefed by the police as to where their undercover personnel would be located and how to provide a subtle signal if any danger threatened. Gerry had offered to accompany his most important client in a fleeting act of *bravado*, in retrospect very grateful to have his attendance refused.

Also rejected was any bulletproof protective clothing. The negotiations had been proposed on the basis of full disclosure on both sides, so the young man opted for T-shirt and jeans even though the temperature on that August morning turned out to be chilly, with grey clouds gathering over the harbour. No-one would ever be granted the opportunity to call Jeff Diamond two-faced...

Bang on time, the rock star received word from a plain-clothed police officer stationed on Alfred Street, underneath Central Station, that four men had arrived in a black Holden Kingswood and were making their way to the quayside café. Four men? His heart jumped into his throat, and he swallowed down the last mouthful of coffee and lit a cigarette. Despite his nerves, the streetwise celebrity felt totally prepared and strangely at ease. He was in control for the moment. While he was on his own, that was!

The gang kingpins and their famous assignee identified each other in an instant, their eyes meeting across the outdoor seating area. They all bore a striking resemblance to their respective fathers, and by the dazed expressions on the men coming towards him, Jeff realised this had affected them all equally.

'Fuck! You look like your dad up close too,' Mark Jaworski announced, roughly seizing the musician's extended right hand and shaking it.

The tall, handsome rock star cocked his head and smiled slightly. 'Shit happens. You do too. Mark, Rob...'

Within a few seconds, an assortment of deleterious memories had started to stir. The boy from the Stones Road recognised two of these men from his nightmares, being regular visitors to his mother and sister back in those dark years. Mark and Robert were the brothers who had always done their father's bidding and had been rewarded with free access to the rival gang's spoils.

Jeff's stomach churned while he fought the urge to belt the living daylights out of these bastards. Instead, he gave his hand to the other two men. One was Joe, Theo Jaworski's middle son, who had been in Madalena's year in school and had been a trouble-maker through and through. The scowl on his face was ingrained, and he had lost his hair early, both contributing to the stereotypical physical traits of the thug he was through and through.

'Coats, gentlemen,' their host instructed, pointing to the café manager who was poised to collect them. 'That's what we agreed.'

Surprisingly, all four men complied, once they were assured their belongings would remain in plain view. Jeff's leather jacket already hung on a stand near the cash register.

'Joe, how're you going?' Jeff asked as politely as he could, before turning to the fourth man, a stranger. 'And who's this?'

'*Kolega*,' Robert answered from behind his cousin. 'He's with us.'

'I get that,' the star scoffed. 'Sit down, guys. Coffee?'

'Beer,' Mark contradicted, waving aggressively to a waitress.

Two jugs of lager from the tap arrived within minutes, and the men filled their glasses. The Jaworskis' associate introduced himself as "The Paddy", which didn't help the Melburnian much either. They spent the first ten minutes or so shooting the breeze about Jeff Diamond's rise to stardom, and he indulged them with answers to a barrage of inane questions. He didn't mind, since it helped them all to relax and measure each other up.

Honesty and transparency were more likely to follow if he gave them what they wanted, or so he hoped. If he had been asked while in London whether his studies in international relations and diplomacy would be much used upon his return to Australia, he might well have laughed in their faces. Today was no laughing matter however.

'So I guess you got plenty money,' Mark joked.

'Enough, yes. You?'

'Fuck!' Joe jeered. 'Not compared to you. Where'd you park your Ferrari?'

'Aston Martin,' Mark corrected his cousin, much better informed about Jeff's life in the public eye.

Without changing his expression, the celebrity answered the question anyway. 'Melbourne.'

'How long y'ere for?' the same man asked, obviously the leader. 'Didn't you move to London last year?'

'Yeah. That's right. I'm in Sydney today and tomorrow,' he replied as casually as his rapid heartbeat would allow.

Robert leaned forward and banged his empty glass down on the table. 'So you seen your dad again?' he hissed.

Jeff refilled everyone's glasses and then settled back into his chair. He wasn't about to let this vicious rapist intimidate him again. Their telephone calls over the previous couple of weeks had revealed that the local gangs had found out about the meeting at Parklea within days. He hadn't expected this information to stay under wraps for long, which was why he had initiated this convoluted exercise in the first place.

'No. Not since last month,' he answered. 'But that's why we're here. I need to know what me seeing him after all this time means to you guys.'

'Depends if you're going to make an 'abit of it,' Robert continued in the same tone, 'and what for.'

'Good,' the sophisticated peacemaker responded. 'That's good. I don't want to see him again. I shall though. I hate the god-damned bastard's guts, but he's my dad, and pretty soon he'll be my kids' granddad. That means something to you, doesn't it?'

'You 'avin' a kid?' Mark interjected. 'With Lynn Dyson?'

'Not yet, but we will,' Jeff nodded, as usual whenever reminded of this prospect, unable to keep the smile off his face.

'How the fuck d'you end up with her?' the Paddy yelped. 'She's bloody gorgeous.'

The boy from Canley Vale chuckled. 'Yeah. She is bloody gorgeous. You're not wrong, mate,' he affirmed, imitating the Irishman's strong accent. 'I need to know whether you're going to leave us alone. My kids have a right to know who their grandfather is, even if he is a murdering arsehole. And I'm sorry about what he did to your dads, guys. I really am.'

'Don't bring that up,' Joe butted in, the scowl deepening into the lines on his forehead. 'You got no right to talk about them.'

'Why not? You asked about mine. I was just a kid, mate. I had no fucking clue what was going on between the Jaworskis and my dad. I wanted no part in all that shit.'

'Did he tell you why he killed 'em?' Mark enquired, much to his cousin's disgust.

'Nope. No-one'd tell me anything, even after the trial. All I know is you guys took it out on the rest of us. Big-time.'

'Your dad never understood the law,' Robert blurted out.

'Whose law?' the educated songwriter scoffed.

'The law of the jungle,' the more mature brother laughed too. 'Robbo, shut the fuck up. It was every man for 'imself. Still is. So what's your link with the old gangs now, Diamond?'

'Jesus, mate! I haven't got time for any of that,' Jeff replied, deliberately keeping the conversation light. 'I never did, and you know that. I barely have time to undress my bloody gorgeous wife these days. And what d'you reckon I could possibly need from that life anyway? Come on...'

'So why d'ya go see him?' Joe asked.

'Because I wanted some answers,' the celebrity explained. 'I never got to talk to him back when it first happened. Like I said: no-one told me anything much. And I guess I grew up eventually too. I want to know why he knifed your dads, and also I wanted to tell him how much he fucked his own family up in the process. 'Cause he did, for sure. You all know what happened to my mother. You played a big part in those fun and games.'

'Bugger that! She fuckin' topped 'erself,' Robert snarled. 'Don't try and pin that on us.'

'Shut it, Rob,' Mark closed his brother down. 'Take it easy. It's his mum.'

'*She* was my mum,' the lost boy reinforced, his jaw locking tight with the stress of keeping his temper under control. 'Cheers, Mark. You blokes drove her to kill herself. No doubt about it. She never asked to be raped and beaten, and neither did my sister.'

'She hit the bottle though. She was a drunk, your mum,' Joe compounded the tortured man's anguish. 'And she loved the drugs. Desperate for it every time.'

'Fuck you,' Jeff raised his voice, pointing an angry finger at the youngest cousin. 'Ever heard of addiction? Of course she was bloody desperate for it. You lot and my fucking arsehole of a father fed her so much of that shit that she couldn't do without it.'

The seasoned negotiator saw shocked expressions spread across the faces around the table. They obviously hadn't expected him to react this strongly. He leaned back in his chair and drank a huge mouthful of beer.

'You married, Joe?'

'Yes,' the fearsome, bald man answered, looking ashamed in front of his older family members.

'He 'ad to. Got 'er up the duff, just like Marky here.'

'Lena's going OK though,' Mark changed the subject, embarrassed in the presence of this impressive adversary. 'She looked fine in your wedding pictures. She's livin' near me now. I see her around. You're buyin' 'er a place?'

Jeff sighed. 'Yeah. We're looking. She's OK. If you call being a prostitute OK. I hope you treat your daughters better.'

'We treat her OK,' Robert scoffed, rolling his eyes as his big brother shot him a glare.

'What d'you mean?' the millionnaire saw red. 'You're not still using her after all this time, are you?'

'She's an adult now, Jeff,' Mark answered for his uncivilised sibling. 'She knows what's best for her.'

Jeff jumped to his feet, ready to launch himself across the table at the classless scumbags, footage of the futile violence from his nightmares fast-forwarding in his mind again. He couldn't believe Madalena hadn't told him of her continuing connection with these thugs. Her little omission would now cost him dearly in leverage against the Jaworskis, and he suddenly felt sick with the disappointment of being betrayed by family yet again.

'Christ Almighty!' he shouted, forcing his backside back down onto the chair. 'Leave her alone. She never did anything wrong, God damn you. She was caught up in their racket, just like the rest of us. What right do you have to take your grudges out on her?'

Passers-by turned their heads at the raised voices, cast into a frenzy on seeing and hearing the great Jeff Diamond in full voice. Some rushed towards the low barrier next to the men's table, yelling his name and begging for autographs. The musician took advantage of the disturbance he had caused to simmer down, and also to refuel with the confidence-boosting adulation.

The superstar waved to the café manager to apologise for the *fracas* before turning back to the excitable crowd which had gathered on the promenade by the busy ferry terminal. 'Sorry, everyone,' he announced. 'We're having a private meeting here. I'd be really grateful if you could leave us to ourselves. Thanks heaps, guys.'

The authoritative celebrity turned away from his fans and took his seat, facing four dumbstruck villains from the western suburbs. More beer was ordered for the table, and the crowd dispersed about their business.

'Sorry about that,' Jeff told them, trying not to smile at the vacant stares on their faces. 'Hopefully, they'll think we're rehearsing for some film scene or other. Can we get back to what you're doing with Lena? Can't you let her go?'

'She's working for us now, but,' the ringleader responded. 'Her flatmate, Zoe... You've met her, 'aven't ya? She's Seany's sister. All happy families, mate.'

The Stones Road native became even more nauseated. This made perfect sense. Madalena had mentioned the name Sean, and her flatmate had spoken with a feint Irish accent. Why hadn't he made this connection before? As long as she was paying their family's debt, her brother was off the hook. He had been living in Nicetown for too long and had forgotten how to play by Boganville rules. "The law," as Robert had put it.

'Jesus, Mark,' the famous man let out a deep sigh. 'So what do I need to do to get you to leave her alone?' he found himself asking, almost pleading. 'Lena's not responsible for what happened to your dads. She's suffered enough. She was just a girl when you blokes started on her.'

Jeff was seething, and his mind whirled at full pelt. He had come to Sydney intent on securing the Dysons' immunity from persecution, not for one moment considering his airheaded sister to still be under the gang's influence. How would he free Madalena from the claws of these merciless beasts? There was no way on Earth he would entertain buying these sons of bitches out of the flesh-peddling business.

The twenty-four-year-old allowed himself a furtive smile, thinking how Gerry would balk at the idea of diversifying Paragon Holdings' interests to such an extent. And who was to say another pimp wouldn't treat his sister worse? At least she had some protection from the depravity of these men as long as Zoe was involved. Now he understood where "The Paddy" fitted in. What an unholy mess! Was he about to be forced to choose his wife and kids' safety over his sister's indebtedness? Bloody hell. That wasn't fair.

Cursing under his breath, Robert Jaworski got to his feet and disappeared to the restroom, quickly followed by cousin Joey. The visitor from Melbourne wondered whether their exit had been premeditated. His paranoiac insight had weakened to virtually comatose while living the bohemian life in London. It annoyed the intellectual greatly that his powers of lateral thinking weren't able to outsmart these numbskulls. He had kept himself out of trouble that way back in his teenaged years, yet thrust back into this bleak, cold world, he now felt somewhat impotent.

Jeff focussed back on Mark, concluding there was little he could do to keep tabs on the younger cousins while out of his sight. Now the head of the family, the well-built man in his early thirties had mellowed from the testosterone-charged, alpha bodybuilder whom the young Diamond remembered terrorising Alberto's boxing club.

Not dissimilar to the star's own journey from wild boy to mature adult in fact, now with less venom in his tone and none of the bloodthirsty rancour behind his eyes. With any luck, this change of heart heralded a new era for the Fairfield underworld. Perhaps there was some hope that in the hands of the second-generation Jaworski top dog, the scale of tyranny, violence and mistreatment of local businesses and rival gangs might lessen, since the sons weren't anywhere near as hard and hungry as their immigrant parents had been at the same age.

'So why d'ya think Lena wants to be left alone?' Mark turned the visitor's question around.

'Fair point,' the younger man nodded. 'She's happy enough, you're right. Mostly 'cause I feel responsible for her, given what she went through as a kid. When your fathers were taken away from you, whatever guilt my dad should've felt towards you guys and his own family is alive and well inside me, after what I saw and heard back then. Lena's paid the price a hundred times over, Mark. She didn't kill 'em, mate.'

The expression on the prosperous Pole's face turned sour, and his body language revealed a sudden discomfort which also appeared to put Sean on edge. 'Your dad was a piece of shit, Diamond. He had no loyalty. You do. I can see that good enough. And now you've even turned into some motherfuckin' cult hero, for fuck's sake!'

'Cheers, I guess,' Jeff shook his head, smiling at the embellished accolade. 'I try to make wrong things right, that's all. Like us here today, for example.'

The Paddy's eyes darted to the rear of the restaurant, to the door through which the others had disappeared, only to have his attention brought sharply back by Mark's rasping laugh.

'We never understood what you were all about: goin' to school, gettin' poxy part-time jobs an' all. Lena was one of us, but not you...'

'Yeah. That's what my dad said too. He reckons I was one o' them,' the quick-witted entertainer crooked his wrist in a camp Darlinghurst wave.

The oldest Jaworski shrugged. 'Yeah? We didn't even know what queer was back then.'

What was taking Joe and Robert all this time? The celebrity noticed a layer of perspiration glistening on Mark's forehead, shifting his gaze to his red-haired sidekick and seeing him tapping his fingers on the table. So were these two blokes worried he was strong enough to overpower them in the absence of their partners? Or had they jumped to the more dangerous conclusion that his supporting law enforcement personnel stationed behind the scenes had moved in on the younger cousins?

Either way, Jeff guessed, their fidgeting didn't bode well. It wouldn't serve him to mirror their unease.

'Who knows? But, mate, were your dads any better than mine?' he asked, offering his cigarettes around. 'I don't disagree with you, don't get me wrong... My old man *was* a piece of shit. He sold his own wife's body without a second thought. Her life, in fact. You can't get more of a piece of shit than that.'

Sean scowled, assuming his leader to be offended by the comparison. 'Watch it. These guys' fathers're gone, and your da's doin' time for that.'

The patient negotiator exhaled through his nostrils, making eye contact with Jaworski Junior, who appeared similarly annoyed by the interjection. 'But what makes your folks any better? My dad was an only child. He didn't understand family, or loyalty. He understood fuck all, pretty much.'

Mark chuckled, nodding in agreement. The absent men finally shuffled past the scattered tables, knocking a couple of chairs over in the process, their early dose of alcohol causing them to find something particularly funny. Their kingpin beckoned for them to sit down, which they did, sniggering like schoolboys planning a prank.

'Lena's OK,' the older brother said to them all. 'Isn't she, lads? She makes a good living. We don't hassle 'er, and she don't give us trouble.'

'Yeah, and she's a good fuck,' Robert laughed out loud.

Incensed, Jeff lifted his tall frame out of his seat and flung his left arm across the table, far enough to be able to grab the loudmouth by the neck. He relished the glint of fear in the other man's eyes, altering course and lowering his hand to pick up the cousins' empty beer glasses instead. The staff breathed a sigh of relief, realising at the last minute that this handsome prince was only toying with his unlikely guests in plain sight of the jostling midday crowd.

'Can't hold your drink, boys?' the celebrity teased. 'Why don't you take a harbour cruise while I talk to your boss?'

Humiliated, Joe cursed in Polish and lashed out towards the glasses, which were still hovering in mid-air, being held aloft by the showman while he made his point. Even though Jeff's reactions were quick in moving them out of the way, some beer splashed onto the table. As the youngest Jaworski swung his arm again, his T-shirt rode up enough to reveal a large switchblade tucked into the waistband of his jeans. Mark's eyes followed their host's, knowing they had been rumbled.

'We agreed no weapons here,' Jeff hissed through clenched teeth, pointing to the knife now only an impression through a layer of scruffy, blue fabric. 'This is Circular fucking Quay, guys. You *are* no better than my father, Joe Jaworski. How many times have you used that thing? And I don't mean your dick.'

The smarmy troublemaker slumped back down onto his chair, being given the silent treatment from his older associates. He mumbled another unintelligible phrase, stood up again and left the café, dragging the soles of his shoes along the ground as he walked.

The angry visitor wasn't going to let it end there. 'So what about you three?' he turned to the others. 'Are you carrying too? Fine line, isn't it? If I provoked you, would you hesitate? That'd make you no better than my dad either, Robbo. His problem was that he moved faster than they did.'

With a swift nod to his younger brother, Mark instructed Robert to follow his hooligan mate out of the restaurant. The skinny twenty-nine-year-old did as he was told, flicking a querulous finger at the superstar.

'Your dad got lucky,' the younger brother sneered. 'And then he got caught. He was a dumb-fuck, but.'

'Yeah, he was,' Jeff agreed. 'Still is, actually. Although he's a dumb-fuck in a safe place now, where he gets a warm shower and three meals a day. And he has to watch his back for different reasons.'

Mark burst out laughing this time, as did the Paddy. They certainly appreciated this impressive musician's dry turn of phrase, even if their bolshy partner didn't. The remaining *trio* watched the ejected pair making for the train station, clearly agitated and embarrassed.

Having reached the traffic lights, Robert wheeled round and began to run back to the restaurant at a pace. The songwriter was initially thrown off his guard, seeing the man hurtling back towards him, only to breathe a huge sigh of relief to realise the last in this particular line of dumb-fucks had left his coat behind.

'You're bloody funny,' the gang leader attracted his nemesis' attention again, grinning almost in deference. 'You always did have a smart mouth. So what's it like being famous? My wife thinks you're the bee's knees.'

'Oh, yeah? Sorry, mate,' Jeff chuckled, knowing full well that false humility would reel in another laugh. 'I have a good life. Can't complain, as they say. Better than living on the Stones, but that's not hard. Who did you marry? Anyone I know?'

'Don't think so,' the eldest Jaworski shook his head. 'She's from way up north. Almost bush.'

The global citizen gave a slight shrug, inwardly amused at how small this man's world was. Did he mean Alaska or Siberia, or maybe even as far as the Queensland border?

'Not that far north. Kids?'

'Yeah. Five.'

'Five?' Jeff exclaimed. 'Jesus! That's good going. Expensive though.'

'Piss off,' Mark scoffed, annoyed at the ease with which he had succumbed to the man's friendly banter.

This grown-up Jeff Diamond was so damned likeable. Even as a child, the gangland son remembered the young brainbox as somehow untouchable, set apart from the rest. It had infuriated him at the time, yet today he was less envious and more proud to have known him for so long.

The resentful redhead had disassociated himself from the discourse, busy scanning the promenade outside the café for their two cohorts. 'Jeff, good to meet you,' Sean declared, standing up to leave in response to a nod from the ringleader.

'Cheers, mate. You too,' the celebrity replied, unable to bring himself to return the compliment. 'Let Lena go, please? She's earned her freedom.'

'But what else would she do?' the Irishman sneered with a mean wink. 'She likes her work.'

Fuck you, Jeff's tortured mind cursed.

'Maybe,' was the alternate response his well-trained mouth chose to pronounce. 'It's all she ever learned how to do. It's bloody lucky she likes it. She didn't like it when you blokes were forcing your adult cocks into her thirteen-year-old...'

Mark raised his hand to stop the conversation. 'Yeah. OK,' he agreed. 'It is time, Sean. He's right. Lena'll have to move out of the flat, but. We'll need to get another girl in with Zoe.'

'Of course you will,' the songwriter taunted.

His conscience told him there ought not to be "another girl" who deserved to take Madalena's place with these thoughtless brutes. Yet this was his sister's future, and any new girl was a total stranger. Even though Jeff Diamond spent a good part of his life helping total strangers, it was right to help family first this time.

'Anyway...' the star inhaled and leaned forward, offering his packet of cigarettes round again. 'So tell me what I have to do for you to release Lena from our debt? What's left to be paid off after all this time?'

'Fuck, Diamond, I don't know,' Mark confessed. 'My mum says you're untouchable now 'cause of all the good stuff you're doing for Fairfield. You know... All them kids' events, and stuff in schools 'bout gettin' a good education and stayin' out of trouble. She says you turned out too good for the likes of us. She told us to drop the whole bad blood, revenge thing.'

'Well, I'm grateful for her support,' Jeff gave a wry smile, more than humbled by the widow's unusual admission of forgiveness. 'I'm pleased she can see me as disconnected from my father. That's more than I expected. What about Joe's side of the family? And what about Lena? Is she good or bad blood as far as your mum's concerned?'

'*Ciocia*'s cool. She's re-married now. Joey can't stand 'is stepdad. They moved over east somewhere, and we 'ardly ever see 'er anymore. Mum and our wives want you to put on a concert for 'em. Would you do that? With Lynn Dyson too? That'd be enough, eh?'

The best-selling artist was disgusted at the very idea, immediately reconsidering his opinion of old Missus Jaworski. He could just imagine the expression on the dignified better half of the Dyson-Diamond partnership's face when he conveyed this latest demand! Not to mention if Big D were ever to get wind of it. Jesus!

Strutting his stuff for the western Sydney underworld matriarchs was a huge mouthful of humble pie for the charitable superstar to swallow to gain their safety and security. But swallow it he must. He would prostitute himself out to the Jaworski women to appease the men who made dirty money by using people's sisters. Given what was at stake, debasing himself in this way was a simple trade, but he was damned if he would subject his beautiful best friend to such a chore.

'No way, mate. Don't drag Lynn into this mess. Who do you think she is? She's not a bloody circus animal, and neither am I, come to that. I'll come over and meet them. I could do something small. No band or anything flash. But there's no way in hell I'd put Lynn through that, *rozumiesz?*'

'Up to you, mate,' Mark let out a mean cackle. 'It was worth a try. Kaz said you'd say that.'

'Fucking bastard! Good. If I do that, will you leave Lena and my family alone? All of you and all of us?'

'Tonight?'

'If you want,' Jeff confirmed, vigorously shaking the gangland boss' hand.

'Cool. Where?'

The celebrity stood up and fished his wallet out of his back pocket, opened it and took out a business card. He had written the telephone number of his hotel on a batch of cards that had been printed in advance, in case he needed to be contacted by untrustworthy criminals. Flamboyant as ever, he turned the card over a couple of times in his fingers before presenting it to his gloating rival. He then pulled out another and placed it on the table between them.

'Write down the address of where you want me to meet you,' he requested, catching the waitress' attention for a pen and the bill. 'And the same rules apply as for here. No weapons, no associates. I don't want to be singing at my own funeral. Just leave me a message with what time, and I'll be there. Fair?'

Mark nodded, stubbing out his cigarette. He sat back and watched the millionaire pull out a gold credit card and slip it unceremoniously under the paper invoice which had been delivered on a regular china plate. He was in awe of this man's star quality, secretly relieved that the meeting was concluding without incident.

'You haven't answered my question,' the boy from the Stones Road persisted, with a slight smile. 'Is that the end of the *vendetta*, if I do this?'

'Yeah. Alright,' Mark held out his right hand again. 'I'll make it happen.'

The rock musician looked into the eyes of the bloke who had lost his father at the hands of his own, accepting the gesture of conciliation. He wanted to believe him. He had to believe him, otherwise what was the point of coming here at all? Honour among thieves? Who knew? If churning out a few lean ballads, posing for happy snaps and kissing other men's wives would assure the security of his loved ones, he had better believe it.

There! Lynn was going to laugh her head off at this latest update, he was sure. Jeff Diamond was still a sexual mercenary after all. Yet another bizarre chapter in a lifestory unfolding more and more singularly by the day!

***

Julie McLoughlin made the journey to Canada for the Olympic Games' closing ceremony with Marianna, her future mother-in-law. It was the first time all four Dyson children had accompanied their father to an Olympiad as competitors, and the two women were looking forward to celebrating a string of successes. By the time the last day of competition arrived, the family's list of triumphs had indeed turned out to be as long as anticipated.

Bart Senior had won the gold medal in the decathlon for the fifth successive Olympics, and Junior had come frighteningly close for silver. By Moscow, four years hence, the medal properties in each man's hand were expected to be reversed. Richard and Lynn had vied for first place in the showjumping, with Lynn pipping her little brother at the post with a two-second advantage. Bart had won the three-day eventing gold, with Sandy second and Anna third, putting Australia leagues ahead in the team competition.

Junior took out the eight-hundred and fifteen-hundred metre races in the athletics, posting record-breaking times, and had finished with a forty-metre lead over the nearest competitor in the five-thousand metres. The sweetness of his victories had been spoiled however, owing to the sparse field after twenty-eight African nations had boycotted the games as a protest against *Apartheid* in South Africa.

Lynn and Bart won both tennis singles golds, and while Lynn and Sandy took out the mixed doubles title, it was little Anna who stole the show. At still under ten years old, the tiny, blonde gymnast took the overall individual gold before backing up with three top spots in apparatus finals.

The Closing Ceremony was held on the first of August, a week before Anna's tenth birthday. With the highest medal tally of the team, Junior was chosen to carry the Australian flag into the stadium, and he made sure that his tiny sibling walked with him for the full lap, so proud was he of his family's achievements.

Bart and Marianna's eldest child and his *fiancée* were due to marry at the end of November, requiring the whole clan's focus as soon as they returned home; their second wedding in a year. Lynn and Jeff had written a few songs at Julie's request but were also anxious not to make the next Dyson family shindig a carbon copy of their own. The midfielder was a quiet man, as compared to the veritable Pied Piper whom his sister had introduced into the mix, so it was important that the event be tailored to the couple's personalities rather than to their fans' vociferous requirements.

On the flight back from Los Angeles, where Lynn had arranged for her younger brother to stop over for a few days, Jeff secured the subtle admission he had been expecting from the sixteen-year-old. The lad's generous big sister had spirited them all to Disneyland, where they had been joined not entirely coincidentally by John Betts.

The singer's childhood friend was patient and upbeat, easily able to provide the youngster with answers to the many questions he had bottled up for so long. She and her empathetic lover whiled the time away being accosted by eager holidaymakers in the queue for every ride and doing their best to ignore the queasiness in their stomachs as the rollercoasters shook, rattled and rolled them around the park.

The happy couple knew their stage-managed *tête-à-tête* had been worthwhile as soon as they clapped eyes on the two men walking towards their agreed meeting point. The teenager's face bore a grin from ear to ear, and it was plain to see that an enormous burden had been lifted off his shoulders. John flew back to New York that night after dinner, and no-one raised the topic again, sensing the youngster's need to ruminate on his new identity until he was ready to open up.

Lynn had fallen asleep on their flight back to Melbourne when Sandy took the plunge, deciding to spill the beans to the brother-in-law he had come to idolise. 'Jeff,' he started nervously, 'I need to ask you something.'

'What's that, mate?' the approachable genius replied, looking up from his book and seeing the lightness he had been hoping for in the lad's blue eyes.

Sandy faltered a little, looking sideways at his sister to make sure she wasn't listening. 'I want to ask your advice about speaking to Mum and Dad about something.'

'Sure. Anything,' the twenty-four-year-old nodded, folding the corner of his page and slotting the book into the seat pocket in front of him. 'What's on your mind?'

'How did you know, by the way?' the boy asked, half smiling. 'Was it that obvious?'

The musician shrugged, selecting his words carefully. 'I didn't know. I guessed,' he answered, seeing the youngster relax a little. 'Ages ago. Since I first met you at Benloch on Rob McLean's twenty-first birthday party weekend, I thought there was something you were struggling with. I could tell there was a barrier between you, your dad and your brother, but it wasn't age or ability. It was a logical conclusion, that's all. Am I right then?'

'When did you tell Lynn?' Sandy challenged, choosing not to answer the question directly.

'Only recently, mate. I wanted to be much surer than I had been at first, and I didn't want to screw things up for you by being the bearer of such significant news while I was *persona non grata*.'

The sixteen-year-old nodded, weighing up the nuggets of gentle wisdom. 'Hmm… Guess so,' he chuckled. 'Why were you *persona non grata* anyway? I never did get that.'

'Oh, right! I'll explain after, if you really want to know. But what you have to realise, mate, is that your sexuality is not your choice,' Jeff carried on. 'It's like being the only redhead in your family, or left-handed even… You don't wake up one day and say, "I'm going to write with my left hand." It's very awkward being left-handed, let me tell you. I wouldn't have chosen it. Like needing to wear glasses as a kid. It's a bugger, but we're stuck with who we are.'

Sandy smiled in agreement, rolling his eyes at the comedian's slick timing. 'Shut up! It's still tough.'

'Yeah. I know,' the compassionate man responded. 'But we southpaws are thankfully not lurking in the shadows anymore like you queer boys. At the end of the nineteenth century, schools made left-handed kids write with their right hands. Now that sucks, because it changes the whole way your body works, forcing you to rewire your brain. Shoe-horning homosexuals into a heterosexual world is the same, but magnified a thousand times. Whatever makes us different from the next guy, it's wrong to make everyone behave the same. Society's gradually learning, but it's taking a while 'cause people get so uptight about things they don't understand.'

'But how the hell am I going to tell Dad?' the teenager prompted, impatient with the parallels being drawn. 'I'm not stupid enough to think that admitting I'm gay would go down as smoothly as admitting I'm left-handed.'

This was a well-deserved put-down, the brother-in-law admitted. He of all people ought to know better than to make light of such deeply personal fears.

'Fair enough,' he acknowledged. 'And very funny too. Great delivery, mate. Sorry to patronise you. I didn't mean it to sound so trivial.'

'That's OK. It's very easy to talk to you. Thanks.'

'No worries. What d'you think your dad's objections'd be based on? Not religion, obviously. Conventionality?'

'Yes. I expect so. And *macchismo*.'

'Ah, *macchismo*. You got that from John, didn't you?' Jeff chuckled at the colourful word, glancing over at his dormant wife. 'I've heard him use that word heaps of times. Rich Kerr uses it too. It always sounds like a brand of coffee to me.'

Sandy shrugged, smiling at the imagery, suddenly at a loss as to how to continue.

His counsellor took the lead. 'Mate, you have to decide how open you want to be. There's no law that says you have to tell anyone at all. Many people live a completely double life, even getting married and having kids. But that's not being honest with yourself or getting the most out of your life. If you want to have a male partner and enjoy the type of relationship Lynn and I have, you'll likely have to come out. I remember the few months where Lynn and I were sneaking around because your dad had forbidden her to see me. It was bloody terrible. Quite a turn-on sometimes though, fucking someone you know you shouldn't.'

The awkward adolescent chuckled, picking up on his brother-in-law's enthusiasm for good, open dialogue without judgment or prejudice. 'God! That's actually scary as hell. I haven't thought that far ahead. I'm only just coming to terms with the fact that girls don't turn me on.'

'Don't stress about it,' the rock star insisted, lowering his voice as a nearby passenger knocked into the youngster's elbow as he shuffled down the narrow aisle. 'Everyone matures at a different rate. Plenty of straight men don't have real sex until they're eighteen or twenty. Some even older. It's not a race, you know, contrary to popular, hormonal belief. But getting back to your dad, he'll only need some education on the topic. Expand his mind a little, if you know what I mean.'

'Only?' Sandy looked incredulous. 'Care to reconsider that statement?'

'Yeah. OK,' Jeff took his words back readily. 'Point taken. I know it's not that simple, but it should be. His generation still thinks that sex should be between a man and a woman for the purpose of creating children, 'cause that's how his generation was taught that nature wants it. Anything else is unnatural. Perverted, even... But that's utter crap, mate! Marriage is a man-made construct to satisfy some misguided morality that someone imposed in their infinite wisdom, most likely a pope or a king, as a control mechanism. Many animal species are sex maniacs. You only have to look at S'malo, for example. He'll hump anything, given half a chance; animal, vegetable or mineral... No different to you or me, except we grow up with all these rules around us.'

'So could you have sex with a bloke?' the young sportsman asked, thinking he already knew the answer but excited to find out otherwise, reflecting on his idol's previous comments.

'Could I or would I?'

'OK. Would you?'

'No, mate,' the older man answered. 'Not me. I wasn't programmed to go both ways. But I guess I shouldn't knock it 'til I've tried it.'

Jeff heard a faint sound from Sleeping Beauty beside him in the window seat, assuming that she had woken up and was listening in on this long-awaited and intimate conference. He sneaked a look at her face and was reassured instantly that she had no intention of embarrassing her brother by regaining consciousness mid-way through his confession.

Fixing dark eyes on Sandy to provide a decoy, the new husband slid his left foot along the floor until it reached his wife's right, stroking it gently in the hope that she would cotton on that her contribution had been registered. It was such a good feeling to be so well attuned.

'Sandy, believe me,' the intellectual continued. 'Your dad can change his view. Look how he came around to Lynn and me being together. All his suspicions about my family were right on the money. I didn't clear my name. He accepted me for who I was, just by giving me a chance and letting me prove that not being like him or Junior wasn't necessarily wrong. It'll be the same for you, I'm sure. Just have the courage to be who you want to be. Lynn and I'll back you up. Just think, mate... If everyone was the same, we'd have a population explosion. The world needs people like you not to procreate, to make room for those who overdo it.'

Sandy couldn't stop himself laughing at the self-evident reasoning, before stifling the noise for fear of waking his sister. Lynn used this as her excuse to open her eyes, stretching and looking out of the window nonchalantly.

'Hey, baby!' her most favourite passenger whispered, leaning to his left and pulling her chin towards him for a kiss. 'Welcome back.'

'What time is it?' the innocent question came right on cue.

Overflowing with love for this sublime angel, the rock star looked at his watch. 'Six-fifteen. Three-and-a-half hours left to go.'

Standing up to visit the lavatory, Lynn pushed the blanket off and untangled it from around her feet, climbing across four long legs belonging to her husband and "little" brother. Jeff's lascivious gaze and wandering hands received vocal derision from their companion.

'Come on! Lighten up, mate. How could you not be turned on by that?' the star whined, his eyes hungrily following his wife's body down the gangway.

'She's my sister!' Sandy laughed. 'It's you who need to watch out. You're surrounded.'

The happy philosopher put his hands over his eyes. 'No, no, no,' he moaned. 'I can't cope with that. I can't even cope with more than one woman anymore. Jesus Christ! I'm getting old and conventional. Who'd have thought?'

'Yeah. I agree. Who'd have thought. Thanks, Jeff,' Sandy affirmed, slapping his neighbour's right thigh hard. 'I won't kiss you.'

'Cheers, mate,' the rock star summoned the most manly cough he could muster. 'Appreciate it.'

Satisfied, the contented songwriter winked at his dream girl when she returned to their row. She took this to mean he would speak to her later, and the subject was closed for the rest of the flight.

That night, safely back in their apartment, the matching pair of world-changers discussed Sandy's plight in great detail, both knowing that the next step needed to be his.

'You know, gorgeous,' husband shared with wife. 'Since going through the whole Olympics process with you, I've managed to figure out how to look at life more simply. To boil it down to discrete, manageable steps instead of one big, humungous puzzle to be solved in its entirety.'

The curious athlete looked at her wise man. 'What do you mean?'

Jeff sighed. 'Get with the program! You're always telling me I over-complicate things, aren't you?'

'Yes,' Lynn agreed, wondering where her mystery man was taking her next. 'So? Which program am I getting with this time?'

The philosopher chuckled, kissing two fingers of his left hand and smearing them down her flushed cheek. 'Sport's so different to music or anything else for that matter,' he enlightened his stunning muse. 'Having the ambition to win... to get the highest score or cross the line first, *par exemple, ma chérie...* is a very simple concept. When I'm on stage, I'm not thinking about putting on a better show than anyone else or getting through the set as fast as possible or louder than last night. I'm thinking about making everything work together. It's a good lesson, and I've finally learned it in these last few months. It's valuable for keeping things in perspective.

'Good,' the Olympian replied, hoping she would catch up at some stage. 'It's just a balance, I guess. Finding the right point on the scale. The skill is to notice and adjust. You've always been able to do that. My brain hurts. Can't we just have sex instead of talking for a change?'

A red rag to a bull, as the young woman had calculated, Jeff let out a loud roar and pounced on the slim frame sitting on the floor at his feet. Without further ado, he swept her up in his arms while she fought her hands inside his tracksuit trousers. Very soon, they were connected and writhing in ecstasy in an effort to reach simultaneous orgasm in Olympic-record time.

'Whoa! That was amazing,' the passionate songwriter proclaimed, the rush of sensation as keen on his lover's face as within himself. 'I love what you do to me.'

'That's good. I'll do it again.'

Flopping his whole weight down onto the rug, he kissed his saviour's swollen lips and sat up to drink in her naked beauty. *'J'suis complètement vide.* Purged. My brain is mush.'

'Really?' Lynn exclaimed, revelling in her lover's abundant happiness. 'I should take advantage of that.'

'Go right ahead. You can do that again any time. That was so unbelievably hot!'

'Now?' the playful singer suggested, climbing astride his hips and leaning down to kiss his sweat-drenched tattoo.

'Now? Jesus! Too much pressure.'

'But you know the answer now, oh, wise magician of mine. Forget the last manageable chunk of heaven and focus on the next one. I'm sure you'll rise to the occasion.'

Staring in disbelief as his own words were used against him in earnest, the spent force hoped he had the strength. 'Comin' right up!'

Lynn groaned, laughing softly and lowering herself down onto his chest. She was exhausted, her husband realised, having been hoodwinked again. His arrogant pride no longer cared if this sexy minx could still get the better of him.

'I can't believe you set me up,' he kissed her smiling mouth. 'Stop mocking my over-dramatisation.'

'Over-dramatisation?' a childlike voice echoed, sarcasm oozing from one elated body into the other. 'I don't know what you're talking about. Shall we go to bed?'

The sportswoman rolled sideways to allow her gallant gentleman to stand up. He offered his hand and pulled her to her feet, gathering her into his arms and holding her close.

'I thought I was going to get a "Fuck you,"' he grinned, yawning.

'You nearly did! I love you, you gorgeous hunk of brain and brawn. Tomorrow's going to be busy.'

The lovers made their way to the master bedroom, stopping to leave their empty dinner plates and glasses on the kitchen bench. Although neither said so, both used the few minutes' silence to give thanks for these short flashes of normality in their life singular. Tonight had felt like the old days, before they had become an international powerhouse couple with the world at their feet.

'So when are you taking your last pill?' Jeff changed the subject.

Taken completely by surprise yet again, his dream girl span around with wide eyes. 'After the US Open?'

'When's that?' the young man asked, grabbing her close and kissing her. 'End of September?'

'Yeah. Not long now.'

'*Excelente.* Don't tell me, OK?'

Lynn knew exactly what the old romantic meant. 'Of course not,' she promised with a kiss.

***

Lynn Dyson Diamond celebrated her twenty-first birthday at Benloch, surrounded by friends and family and with an uplifting speech from her father. With Olympic medals, wins at Wimbledon and the French Open, leaving only the US Open to go, the champion had fulfilled every goal she and her proud parents had set.

The celebrities hosted an after-party, as tradition demanded, in the huge indoor swimming pool, much to both brothers' delight. Junior was to be a guest for a change, and the sixteen-year-old Richard was presented with an official invitation to his first Dyson pool party.

Lynn thought back to her own induction, after a family friend's birthday party, and felt a shiver run down her spine. She and Jeff had only met a matter of weeks before this, as energetic and newly-awakened teenagers. Sandy still seemed so young to the doting big sister. Had she really been so wonderstruck and excited? Yes, she admitted. She certainly had!

Whereas Junior's twenty-first had seen him surrounded by school, university and sporting friends whom he had known from a very early age, his sister's cohort had dispersed much more widely around the globe. The eldest Dyson child's life had revolved around football, tennis and athletics since primary school, and therefore the majority of his mates had stayed in Australia and were gradually meeting and marrying other locals.

Music was by far the strongest link between Lynn's network of favourite party guests, sending many of them northwards to entertainment hubs in the United States, the United Kingdom or Germany. Jeff felt sorry for his new wife as she shared her disappointment that a large proportion of the people she now considered her closest friends were unable to attend her special birthday celebrations. It was unfair to expect them to travel down-under again, so soon after their wedding, and the couple had agreed with Bart and Marianna to keep the whole thing fairly low-key as a result.

With one notable exception however: the party animal *extraordinaire*, one Gerry Blake, had made sure he secured himself an invitation by rekindling his brief romance with Lynn's school-friend, Karina Bloomfield. It was the businessman's first trip out to the magnificent settlement, originally established in the late nineteen-twenties in the undulating central Victorian agricultural belt, and he was mightily impressed by the expanse of acreage and the modern, luxurious facilities it concealed in the middle of nowhere.

'For a city kid, why do you think your senses are so hungry for nature?' the country girl had asked her man on the morning of the eighteenth of September, two days before her birthday.

''Cause it's always changing? I don't know. Outside, the world's never still; always looking to be something better. I relate to it, I guess. Feel part of it.'

Lynn smiled. 'So do I, and probably for similar reasons. Just never really thought about it. Are you going to show Gerry Coldwater Creek?'

'No way!' the young man insisted. 'That's our spot and our spot alone.'

'That's good,' his wife replied. 'Thanks. I'm so glad you reacted that way. I want it to be something we keep secret, even from Gerry.'

'Ahead of you, angel.'

All the same, the extrovert accountant's talents were put to very good use over this particular weekend. Jeff had successfully infiltrated Junior's circle and found out that a good many of his close friends were available on the

Saturday night. Therefore, with his in-laws' permission, he issued separate invitations to the after-party and transformed it into a preliminary bucks' night for the older Dyson brother.

To Julie's great amusement, she watched a group of burly sportsmen manhandle her unsuspecting *fiancé* and throw him into the deep end of the swimming pool, fully clothed. Jeff and Gerry mixed cocktails behind the bar all night, and it was after four o'clock before the revellers crawled back up the stairs in the main house.

Lynn had written another album's worth of new songs to accompany her coming of age. She had been recording methodically over the Australian winter. Building on the success of her first self-produced record, this new offering showcased her growing maturity as creator, assembler and performer of her own brand of sophisticated popular music. Her voice was deepening and maturing into a soulful, classy *contralto*, most likely partly due to the smoke her husband continually introduced into their atmosphere.

More and more scientific evidence suggested that passive smoking may be as harmful as consuming cigarettes directly, and to his credit, Jeff took the emerging research as seriously as anyone. The couple committed to three-monthly check-ups to monitor their lungs for any damage, but neither of them felt compelled that the longtime smoker should quit.

'I know I should give up,' he told his mother-in-law at the twenty-first birthday party. 'I would if Lynn insisted, but she doesn't want me to either. I don't really understand why not, but we're OK with it all. It's a risk we've both accepted with full disclosure.'

Was the body's physical health somehow less important than its mental counterpart? It oughtn't to have been, with the prospect of a new and wholly-dependent generation in the offing, and especially with privileged access to the considerable weight of research sponsored by the Dyson movement and the newly-formed Australian Institute of Sport.

Why did they feel less necessity to heed the warning signs of lung disease than they did for the lasting effects of mental illness? Perhaps, the pair acknowledged, it was simply a matter of risk management. They couldn't eliminate the possibility of contracting cancer with any firmer guarantee than he could provide against the Jaworskis reactivating their dangerous *vendetta* on the celebrities' high-flying lives. Unlike the soul-mates commitment to saving each others' mental health from prior or future ill-effects, no amount of planning or insurance could guard against that which was beyond the influence of fame or fortune.

For the errant boy from the Stones Road, smoking and drinking now fell firmly into the domain of habit rather than addiction. He could cut them out altogether these days, now his needs were fully satisfied by much healthier compensations and with such a bright future ahead. He liked smoking and drinking, not to mention the odd joint now and then. And so did his dream girl.

Lynn had always found her perfect stranger incredibly sexy doing any of these things, and he used this to his advantage whenever he could. Yet certain other trappings of the rock star lifestyle were totally off the agenda, such as womanising or disappearing for days on end with the boys in the band, leaving the young wife confident that she had the best combination she could possibly hope for.

After The Olympics

Back in their city apartment, Jeff heard the front door opening from his seat in the study. He had just put down the telephone after a long conversation with John Francis, who had called him in the middle of the British night to impart some interesting but potentially disturbing news.

'Lynn!' he shouted. 'I'm in here.'

The preoccupied negotiator stood up and went to meet her in the hallway. They kissed. Was it his rampant sexual imagination or his heightened emotional state after John's call that gave him the impression that his wife seemed to hug him more urgently than usual? Very appealing regardless, he thought.

The couple had been apart for ten days, since the rock star had returned earlier that week after spending another worrying period in Sydney. He had been more than ready for some urgent skin-on-skin. Unfortunately however, his arrival in Melbourne had coincided spitefully with Lynn's departure for a television appearance and two concerts in Hong Kong.

'Whoa! It's great to have you back. You feel so good,' he told her, hungry for her touch. 'How was your trip?'

'Really good, thanks,' Lynn replied. 'What about you? You look a bit worried.'

Jeff loved the fact that she could see behind his eyes so easily. 'How can you tell?' he asked, following her into the bedroom. 'You're right. I've just been speaking to John. There's something new going on in Africa that we're going to work on together and it's pretty sensitive.'

The slender songstress was interested to hear more, and her lover happily replayed the whole conversation almost word for word, sitting on the edge of the bed while she unpacked. His new mission on the international negotiation stage would require regular flights back and forth to London and probably to Johannesburg too, but this didn't faze her much.

Even though their respective travel schedules were hectic, they had managed to find almost-nearly enough time to spend together during the first half of the year, between sporting commitments, making movies, recording albums, tours and these diplomatic consultancy trips which the peace-broker had been making since they returned from the UK.

'I've just come from the doctor's,' Lynn said, at last able to squeeze in a sentence while stripping off and preparing to take a shower after ten hours on an aeroplane.

Jeff looked up absentmindedly. 'Why were you at the doctor's? Are you OK?'

Clearly, his busy mind was elsewhere. The beautiful woman wrapped her bathrobe around her and walked over to the bed, where her man sat staring blindly at the wall.

'Earth to Jeff!' she giggled, tapping him on the shoulder. 'You don't seem too bothered about my doctor's appointment after all.'

'Yeah. Sorry, angel,' her husband shook himself back to reality. 'My mind's racing with all this new info'. Are you alright?'

Now distracted by something much closer to hand, the aroused man slipped his fingers inside her robe, stroking taut skin around the body he worshipped so much. Breathing sexily onto the delicate nerve-endings below her ear, his lips nipped at her neck.

'Are you coming to bed?'

'Jeff!' Lynn interrupted, taking a step backwards and out of his grasp. 'I'm trying to tell you my news.'

Dutifully, her irrepressible, red-blooded partner stopped in his tracks, gazing into her eyes. 'What news?'

At last, the young woman thought, she had his undivided attention. Preparing to speak, she found she could scarcely catch her breath as tears welled up in her eyes. Concern spread in an instant across her haunted man's face, and the caring therapist knew she must move quickly to prevent another death spiral.

'Jeff, I'm fine. You're going to be a father,' the twenty-one-year-old blurted out.

Inhaling sharply as panic surged and then subsided, the songwriter drew a long breath in and closed his eyes, attempting to absorb this latest bombshell. He hugged the woman he loved ever closer and kissed her lips again, this time more gently but with no less insistence. Two weeks of withholding information had weighed heavily on her heart, desperate for this afternoon's confirmation, and she dissolved into a flood of happy tears.

'Well! That's news,' her equally tearful husband gasped, kissing her face all over and savouring the salty taste. 'Bloody good news. Whoa! What am I saying? It's the best news I've heard since "I do". So that's why you were at the doctor's.'

'Err, yes!' Lynn reiterated. 'I was going to tell you over dinner, but I couldn't wait. Are you happy?'

Jeff pulled his hands away and gazed at his wife's partially shrouded body in wonder. 'Am I happy?' he repeated, pressing a warm palm against her abdomen. 'You bet! I'm over the moon. How about you?'

'Take me to bed, Jeff Diamond,' she teased. 'Of course I'm happy. We're going to be a family. That's really exciting.'

'Yeah. And really scary too,' her husband added, stroking her breasts while her hands roamed around inside his shirt. 'Am I going to hurt you?'

'No! I hope not. Why? What are you planning to do?'

'Well, I mean…' her lover mused, only half joking. 'That's my child in there. Our child. Our future medal-winning, vice-ridden child. Jesus, angel. Too right, it's bloody scary!'

That night, the dazed and delirious rocker hardly slept a wink. He lay in the bed beside his beautiful best friend, who as usual was out cold after a busy few days away from home. Fatherhood had become a reality, a mere eight months away. This was his chance to make good all the promises he had made to himself about giving back, about creating a legacy beyond that which money could buy. He and Lynn were going to make a person. No… They had already made a person, and now their job was to nurture it into the person it needed to be.

And they had made this person so easily! He hadn't even felt it happen. How weird! Almost an anti-climax even, to pardon the pun. Their child-to-be had obviously not inherited his propensity for making statements. Such a momentous event, yet it had taken place surreptitiously, without either interested party paying attention. Why was that? Why was a new human being's conception so far removed from consciousness? The potential reasons that sprang into his overactive mind were just too grotesque and cruel to contemplate, so he left this unanswered question behind.

And how on Earth would the thrilled loudmouth keep their good news to himself for two whole months, as Lynn had been advised by the doctor? They had spoken about it over dinner. What was the likelihood of something going wrong? They were both fit and healthy without any family history to worry about. It was the beginning of November, so strictly speaking, it would be January before they could go public.

An intolerably long time, the young man cursed. And practically, the sporting champion would need to wind down the level of training she undertook, which would automatically lead people to suspect something. The newlyweds had never kept secret their desire to have children. Lying still in the darkness, Jeff placed a bet with himself that their news would be public within the month, before slipping out of bed, into the lounge room, where he donned a set of headphones and took a seat at the electric piano.

The musician reminded himself first of "Roads of Stones", in which he had originally spelt out in song that he saw himself as a father. Before too long however, new themes demanded to be ousted. Who would this child growing in Lynn's body look like? Was it male or female? Did he want a boy or a girl? In all their conversations, neither had ever expressed a preference.

That was strange, Jeff decided, but also comforting. It proved that either gender would be equally loved. This fact was important to him, for some unknown reason. Jesus! Eight months was an absolute eternity in which to ask and answer so many unfathomable questions! It almost stretched further into the distance than their two-year separation.

What would their baby's first words be? Who would he or she take after? Or would their child be a perfect mix of both parents? Either way, their child would be happy, even if it meant giving up everything else. And this was only the first. Would they stick at two, as they had planned?

Lyrics came thick and fast, sung softly through heartfelt sobs. What a journey their family was destined to take! Despite their regular conversations about parenthood, this moment of discovery had filled him with more joy and awe than he could ever have imagined.

Lynn was even more excited the next morning. The couple made love in raptures, dreaming aloud about what life might be like once the third diamond had been inserted into Jeff's black jet-stone ring.

'Are you sure it's only one?' her husband asked. 'Can they tell yet?'

'Don't know,' the young woman frowned. 'I never thought to ask. I was so excited to find out yes or no that I never thought to ask how many. What if there are more than two?'

'Christ, no!' the showman threw up his hands in horror. 'A litter. That'd be just horrendous. It's put me right off. I'm never going to touch you again.'

It was true. The mood had altered, and the man of many statements collapsed onto the mattress beside his bemused lover, not knowing whether to cheer or groan.

'Now I know how you can't get pregnant if you're already pregnant,' Lynn laughed, seeing her husband's full erection instantly start to wither. 'No more sex until we've confirmed there's only one. Or two, max'.'

'Oh, no, you don't,' Jeff countered, recovered from the shock and ready to carry on where they had paused. 'You don't get off the hook that easily, woman. When can we confirm there's only one?'

'After the first scan, I suppose,' his wife answered, not having asked this question either. 'Sorry. I don't really know anything, do I?'

The handsome man smiled, kissing full lips and fingering her moist clitoris purposefully, allowing the sensuous movement beneath to spirit him away. What a sublime way to reunite after an absence. This life could not get any sweeter. Well, not for another eight months anyway...

'No. You're hopeless, as a matter of fact,' he agreed, spanking her bare behind as they shifted positions. 'I don't know why I even bother trying anymore. We should just fuck and forget about all this conversing lark. Isn't that what they say about pregnant women?'

'Don't ask me!' his pregnant woman answered indignantly. 'How soon you forget your own resolutions, Daddy.'

'Daddy?' Jeff cried out. 'Jeez! That's too close for comfort. Lucky we're not in a rush this morning.'

'Shut up! Can I tell Mum? And then swear her to secrecy?'

'Or kill her?' the comic laughed. 'None of us can keep this bloody secret. It's going to be pure agony but an excellent exercise in self-control.'

'OK. You're right,' the prospective mother agreed. 'We shouldn't tell anyone. After a few days, we'll even forget ourselves.'

'Will we?' her man smiled. 'I doubt it. Especially if you're throwing up every morning.'

'Oh, yuck,' Lynn responded, grimacing. 'Not so sure about that part.'

***

'What are you laughing about?' Jeff asked his daughter, tossing his mobile telephone onto the desk after checking a series of voicemail messages. 'Ryan says hi, by the way.'

Kierney swivelled round in her dad's office chair and grinned. He had sat up beside her from dusk until dawn while she pulled an all-nighter to complete the analysis of a problematic set of research questionnaires for her latest university assignment. She knew he was in the middle of describing her brother's arrival in lurid detail for the autobiography, requesting a sneak preview as reward for hard labour.

'The way you talk about Mamá being pregnant is funny,' she replied. 'All the "V" references: vessels, vaginas and vomitting! I'm surprised I ever came about, reading this…'

Her father shrugged. 'Ah, you know… She had a short memory, your mamá. She was soon ready to get back on that horse.'

'What?' the youngster leaped to her mother's defence. 'No, she did not have a short memory. You're lying. You weren't this heartless while she was waiting for Jetto to arrive, surely? Grandma told me you were lovely as an expectant father. Very loving.'

Jeff pouted. 'Did she? Whoa! It's good she told you that. We actually didn't see much of "G" and "G" during Jet's pregnancy 'cause we were both on the road so much. Most of these encouraging *stanzas* were coined over the 'phone. We missed being with each other for those special months, which is why we rushed into you so quickly.'

'Oh,' Kierney sighed. 'That's sad.'

'It wasn't really sad,' the widower countered. 'More frustrating that we couldn't share the various changes she was going through in person. Impatient to find a creative way to paint pictures.'

'Hence all the "V" words. I never got round to asking Mamá what carrying a child was like. She told me giving birth wasn't anywhere near as painful as she'd led herself to believe, but that was probably only so as not to put me off. What was it like, Papá?'

Jeff slumped down on the couch, flicking his shoes off and crossing his legs. 'Did you want breakfast?'

'Yes. Shortly,' his gorgeous gipsy girl chuckled. 'Are you going to answer me?'

'Coffee?' the comic persisted, whistling to annoy her further.

'Oh, for God's sake! I'll make coffee while you fix breckie. Come on…'

Father and daughter walked hand-in-hand across the dark hallway, the spring sun not yet risen in Burnley South. In truth, the doting dad had very little knowledge to impart on the subject, since Lynn had taken pregnancy very much in her stride. She had taken most things in her stride, he recalled, including vanishing from their life without notice one Friday morning in February.

'What can I tell you about carrying children?' he scoffed, keeping his tearful eyes fixed on the butter as it melted in the frying pan. 'She cooked you. I just put you in the oven and then helped take you out again when you were done. What d'you want to know?'

The young woman giggled. 'That's sweet! Why didn't you use that in the book instead of all the clinical alliterations?'

'Just trying to sound smarter than I am, I s'pose. Haven't got that far yet. I expect I'll pour my heart out all over the keyboard when I do. It was Lynn who used the term "vessel" first, and in fact, it wasn't even to do with pregnancy.'

'Oh, really? What was it referring to then? Mmm… That smells nice.'

Kierney lifted a full mug of coffee over to the stove, putting it down next to her father's left hand, which was deftly flipping half-cooked pieces of bacon over. She looked up into his eyes, hearing him sniff, and cuddled into his side. Another happy memory so painful yet so vital to remember together, she could almost hear him say.

'It was about smoking, *pequeñita*,' Jeff explained.

'Smoking?'

'Yeah. Smoking.'

'Smoking?' the young woman said again, louder this time.

It was her turn to play the comedian, willing the forty-four-year-old to hurl his usual insult. He was wise to her ploy however, so she gave it one more half-hearted try.

'I said, "Smoking?"'

Her dad leaned rightwards, almost toppling her over. 'I know you did. So did I. And your point is?'

'Argh! What about smoking?'

'What about smoking?' the storyteller appeased the frustrated student.

'Parrot face! I hate you, Papá! Why did you let me win? *Habla ahora.* Vessel, smoking and what?'

Jeff laughed, holding the spatula out for her to take over and heading to fetch some eggs from the refrigerator. 'I'm not five anymore, Papá,' he impersonated. 'You *are* too much like me for your own good. See?'

Kierney took the last four eggs out of the box, which was then tossed expertly into the open rubbish bin in celebration of another, long-perfected skill in the Diamond household. She cracked each egg into the pan and finished them off, hearing knives and forks being dumped on the table behind her. Feeling sorry for her grieving housemate, it was often these mundane routine tasks that caused him to miss their departed family member the most.

'We started talking about vessels when the first credible research came out about the dangers of smoking, because it coincided with me finding out that the first almost successful lung transplant was performed on a convicted murderer.'

'Wow! Really? I didn't know that. What does "almost successful" mean? Did he volunteer to be a guinea pig?'

'*¡Exactamente, pequeñita!* The smart-arse strikes again. I never found out. It was around the time of JFK's assassination, and I'd been digging around for information in the library when I came across a transcript. He received a pardon and died three weeks later, as far as I remember. Yet another triumph of human rights, but the unlucky bastard was on death row anyway. I guess, as long as he didn't suffer too much after the operation, it probably hastened his peace.'

The teenager grimaced, reminded once more of her beloved papá's quest for a similar fate. 'Shit! That's *macabre.* Change the subject,' she moaned, serving their breakfast onto large plates and ferrying them to the table. 'Trust you to dig that morbid piece of news up. Get to the point, professor, please.'

'Excuse me? Less of your lip, young lady! I asked Mamá's opinion as to whether smokers ought to be allowed to have lung transplants, once they'd figured out a way to stop rejection. I had offered to give up after we got married, and again when Ry was cooking, but she insisted she didn't want me to. She was always way too lenient on my vices.'

A happy expression on the bereaved husband's face belied the knot forming around his heart, and Kierney gave him a sympathetic smile. He scratched the skin over the "JL" tattoo through his shirt, only just avoiding a smear of tomato sauce being wiped off his raised fork.

'Thanks, angel. She said yes, depending on who else was on the list for available organs. Smoking was a black mark, sure... But, as she went on to say, what you do to the vessel you're occupying's kind of irrelevant. It's more about what you do while you're in the vessel.'

His daughter swallowed her mouthful, eager to make a comment. 'Oh, that's so great. I'm going to use that. May I, Mamá, please? If smoking was the only negative thing, and the person had a whole, long list of awesomely positive contributions, it makes sense that they should have the same chance as a non-smoker. Is that what you think too? As a smoker, I mean?'

'Yep. Pretty much,' Jeff nodded. 'You know me... I'm all for anything that poisons the system in the pursuit of a higher plain or two. Lynn was under pressure to change her views on a lot of things once she became a mum though.'

'Pressure from whom?'

'Friends, Grandma... Even Celia would stick her oar in every now and again. We both used to get the lecture about drinking in front of you guys, but your mamá bore the brunt of it. I guess they realised I'd give their over-protective rantings short shrift, as opposed to her tendency to sit and listen patiently before giving them long shrift.'

Kierney laughed. 'Long shrift! What is a shrift anyway? Do you want more coffee?'

'Yeah. Please. That'd be good. Shrift is sort of confession, strictly speaking, I think. Who knows where the term comes from, because a short confession doesn't make sense in context. Don't ask such ridiculous questions. Didn't you want to know about being pregnant?'

'Yes,' the intelligent seventeen-year-old replied. 'But it's been a fun journey getting there, and I thought you didn't have any useful information to share. Do Missus Diamond's diaries contain any pearls of wisdom?'

Jeff gathered their plates and cutlery together into a precarious pile and dropped them into a sink of hot bubbling water which his efficient daughter had prepared while a jug of percolated coffee spluttered away. 'Absolutely, pequeñita. Chock full of gory details, just waiting for you. Just don't be calling her Missus Diamond while you're talking to her about it. I can tell you that your brother caused her no problems initially but weighed her down towards the end, whereas you were trouble in the first three months and then couldn't wait to get out. That's about it for my summary.'

'I made Mamá sick?'

'Yeah, continually...'

430

'*Papá!* That's not fair,' the young woman objected. 'Do you remember at the trial, the coroner calling *Mamá* Missus Diamond? Graham Winton should've instructed him to use "Ms".'

Jeff chuckled, rubbing his chest again. 'Yeah, I should've said something, but it was such a minor detail at that point.'

'She hated "Missus". I think I would too.'

'Yeah, I know. That's your choice, baby. But neither Mister Bloaty nor Doctor Hanson knew she hated it. They never had the pleasure of finding out directly. She'd have given them short shrift on that one, wouldn't you, angel?'

***

Over the next few weeks, with no outward sign of their impending happy event, Lynn and Jeff gradually grew accustomed to keeping their secret. They talked long into the night, either in each others' arms where their invisible elastic connection hung slack and redundant, or on the telephone where it strained tight and cherished.

Boys' names, girls' names, decorating the bedroom, nannies, adapting travel rules, maternity hospitals... Sometimes one or the other would call a halt to their endless deliberations, feeling sure of boring themselves senseless with all this baby talk; from mundane, practical purchases to the most outrageous of parental fantasies.

'I'd like to put a decision forward to the Board?' the sportswoman propositioned at breakfast one rare weekend together in their penthouse apartment.

'Oh, yeah?' her husband's interest was piqued. 'Is your fellow Board member going to like it?'

She leaned over to kiss his stubbly cheek. 'I think he is.'

'Cool. Then it can go on the agenda. *Digame.*'

'Why don't we go public straight after Christmas?'

Jeff gazed in mock surprise at the woman who had been so determined to see out the first three months before giving the game away. 'What's brought this on?' he asked. 'Why the sudden need to tell the world?'

His wife shrugged. 'I don't know really. I just feel so healthy and normal. If something was going to go wrong, it would've already gone wrong. Don't you think?'

'Hope so. Sure. But d'you reckon there might just be a touch of wishful thinking in there too?' the father-to-be debated, loathe to quash his dream girl's positivity but also not keen to be overly *gung ho* about things either.

Lynn groaned. 'I know... Hope for the best but expect the worst. Damn you, Blackbeard! OK. Maybe you're right. I thought you were a great believer in gut feelings...'

Chuckling, the good-looking songwriter cursed his bluff having been called yet again. 'I am. Damn you in return! What about booking another ultrasound? Then we'll be able to get a better idea from the obstetrician. Just to be on the safe side. Logistically speaking, it'd be far less stressful not to deliberately put ourselves at risk of needing to backtrack on any media releases.'

Silence descended from the ceiling like a thick fog, and the young man felt like a rat for raining on his beautiful best friend's parade. Who was he to surrender their moment of magic to cold, scientific fact? And to think he used to be the impulsive one!

'Hey, I'm sorry,' he was quick to retract, cupping the gloomy face in his hands and kissing its lips. 'Ignore me. I'm sure everything's fine, and you should go with your gut feeling. Forget I even mentioned it.'

'No,' the twenty-year-old sighed. 'You're right. It would be horrible to have to deliver bad news after we'd announced something so fantastic. Why are you always right?'

The smile that greeted him from across the table was as adoring as it was wistful, such was the love inside this amazing woman. Jeff beckoned for her to sit on his lap at the kitchen table, and they sat gazing out at the uninterrupted view of the northern hills, sunrise washing them salmon pink.

'I'm no more always right than you are,' he assured her. 'Can you feel the baby move yet?'

Lynn snuggled against her husband's muscular chest, parting the edges of her robe and smoothing the fabric of her nightdress down her front, which currently showed no evidence of anything more than breakfast. 'I don't know. Sometimes I think I feel something, and then nothing happens for hours. Am I supposed to be able to feel it yet?'

Dark eyes drilled into hers as if they were willing her to come to a conclusion.

'Argh! Alright, yes! I'll book in for an ultrasound. It's such a bloody good idea, Jeff Diamond. I hate you for always having the best ideas.'

'Thank you, but I don't,' he replied, kissing her playfully on the cheek. 'And please don't swear in front of our baby.'

Receiving a resounding clonk on the head from an empty tea mug, the officious man turned serious again. 'When we have the scan, we could ask all these questions about what you should be able to feel when. And we could even find out the sex, if you want.'

'Do *you* want?'

'Yes and no,' the enchanted father-to-be shrugged. 'I only just suggested it to myself. I hadn't thought about it before now. Do you?'

Lynn's eyes fixed on a distant landmark beyond the inner suburbs. 'It would be the very sensible thing to do, wouldn't it? Then we'd know what sort of clothes to buy, what colour to paint the walls, *et cetera*.'

'Yes. But why do we need to be so dictatorial about blue versus pink anyway?' Jeff posed with a smirk. 'You're trying to impose gender bias onto our unborn child. Shame on you, Lynn Dyson Diamond. Call yourself a progressive mother?'

'Oh, shut up with your post-modernist pomposity, Dad,' his dream girl joked. 'Whatever that means... If we found out boy or girl, at least we could stop calling it "it" and start using its name.'

Evidently, this very modern idea didn't meet with approval, judging by the frown accompanying the songwriter's reply. 'What if the name we call him or her turns out not to sit right when we finally see it?'

'Maybe that's why people get called names like Jim-Bob or Mary-Ellen!' Lynn laughed, pointing with both hands to her expanding abdomen.

'Exactly! I'm serious though. Do you think we'll know Jim well enough to know he's really Ignacious?'

'Ignacious? Euch! No, thanks. Let's not find out then. You seem reluctant, and I'd still quite like the element of surprise. Otherwise, what will the nurse tell us? Congratulations, you've had a baby? Well, hello!'

Laughing hard, Jeff hugged his gorgeous wife so tightly that she had to squirm out of his grip.

'Hey! You're squashing us!'

'Sorry, Mary-Bob,' he replied in a broad, mid-western drawl, patting her stomach. 'You're getting a bit fatter, I think.'

'Am I?' the athlete challenged, anxiously looking down and tensing her Olympic-strength core muscles. 'I can't tell the difference.'

The songwriter raised his hands in front of his chin in self-defence. 'I'm going out on a limb here, but it must be because you're becoming a lazy slob and not running twenty "K" a day anymore,' he teased. 'It's just flab. I don't believe there's a baby in there at all.'

Lynn curled the corners of her mouth downwards. 'Don't say that,' she whispered, as if she were afraid the foetus might hear them. 'I hope there is.'

'Me too, angel. Of course there is. D'you want to go for a swim today? I really feel like some exercise and I'm not in the mood to leave you alone while I run. I missed you so much this week. Can't let you out of my sight, girl.'

'Yeah. That'd be perfect,' the happy young woman agreed, giggling at the gratuitous quote from her rock star's own recent Number One single. 'I need to stretch. My centre of gravity's changing, and I feel like I'm stooping all the time. Keep having to remember to stand up straight.'

'Weird. That sounds too technical for me. Well, while we're on the topic of ideas...' the philosopher changed the subject. 'I've seen your one and would now like to raise you two.'

Lynn slid off his lap and gathered up the cutlery and crockery which was all that remained of their breakfast. She dropped them into the sink, returning for a kiss, the butter and two jars of jam. Her flatmate sent her away empty-handed while he replaced the items in their rightful places.

'OK. One at a time, please,' she quipped, eager to hear more.

'*Alors. Número Uno,*' Jeff opened, 'is I'd like to discuss buying a block of land and building ourselves a house. Somewhere by the seaside, preferably.'

His wife wheeled round, sudsy hands dripping onto the tiled floor. 'Seaside? Wow! When did you come up with this idea?'

'A while ago. It's just been wandering around aimlessly until this week,' the millionaire answered, 'but I've done my homework over the past day or two and now have some pretty firm designs in my head that I'd love to share with you. See what you think...'

Lynn loved the first idea. She had never given much thought to where they would bring up their family, assuming the city apartment to be convenient enough for their non-stop lifestyle. Yet now however, recalling her husband's admission upon returning to London that he had outgrown the original attachment to his first home, why wouldn't they use some of their ridiculous fortune to create the Diamond family's equivalent of Benloch?

'Yes, yes! A house on the ocean? That sounds fantastic!' the dreamy woman smiled. 'It'd be great to have a hideaway beyond the city limits to escape to when we've got a few days free. So what's idea *Número Dos*?'

The couple met in the middle of the kitchen, hugging each other and pausing for a passionate kiss. Was it her imagination, but had Jeff's mood altered all of a sudden? He now appeared more than a little furtive. Even distressed, the young singer detected.

'What's wrong?'

'Nothing,' her evergreen enigma smiled. 'Well... This one's a bit more than just an idea, angel.'

'Oh, yes? Go on...' Lynn guessed that some outrageous plan had already been put in play on her behalf. 'What've you done?'

Sensing a need to reduce the pressure, the compassionate beauty returned to the sink, followed by her guilty schemer. He stood behind her, wrapping her attractive frame into his arms and kissing the back of her head while she dried the last of the plates.

'I was speaking to Pete Bourke while you were away,' he confessed, backing off and reaching for his cigarettes. 'He's selling up and moving to Singapore permanently.'

'Have you bought his flat?' the smart woman jumped to an obvious conclusion, a little overwhelmed by so many significant, life-changing events happening at once.

Her husband nodded. 'Yep. Well, put in an offer anyway. Subject to valuation, *et cetera*. *Whaddya* think?'

Lynn hesitated, leaning against the line of cupboards, her eyes alive with the possibilities. Jeff watched for more clues, eventually rewarded by seeing them flash her considered opinion only a few seconds later. In her excitement, she almost ran into him, overbalancing before raising up on tiptoes to kiss his inviting lips.

'Oh, my God! That's such an amazing idea!' she exclaimed, jumping up and down with joy. 'We'll have the whole top floor, with so much room for children and nannies. And even visitors too, like Madalena or people from London. Is Pete's the same size as yours?'

'Hey, careful! Pete's what?' Jeff laughed, catching her while feigning confusion. 'That's a very personal question for someone in your condition.'

The mum-to-be giggled. 'His apartment, you idiot! Will we have double the number of rooms?'

'Yep. I guess so. I've never been inside. Have you?'

Lynn shook her head. 'No. Of course I haven't! Oh, wow! *Número Dos es bueno* too. A house and a *pied-à-terre* in the city. How very grown up we are!'

The beautiful celebrity danced around the kitchen, holding out her hand for her partner to lead her in circles. He obliged, and they were soon in the depths of a scorching tango, shedding clothes with abandon and heading once more for the bedroom.

'You make me very happy, Jeff Diamond.'

'I'm glad,' the musician smiled, imbibing her good cheer. 'I wasn't sure if you'd prefer to move somewhere along St Kilda Road or even to South Yarra.'

Society's darling pulled a face. 'Ew, no! Far too snobbish and conservative. I'd much rather stay around here. And it's so handy for everything too. Does that mean we'll have four parking spaces too?'

'Yeah. I guess so again,' the young man chuckled. 'Details, details... How many cars do you want, for Christ's sake?'

'Three!' she chimed. 'Plus one spot spare for visitors.'

'Right,' he nodded. 'I'll see what I can do. Or rather what you can do. All that household management crap's soon to become an arse-end problem, lady.'

***

At Junior's wedding, held in the bayside suburb of Brighton on the last weekend in November, the groom's adult sister tried her best not to draw attention to the fact that she wasn't drinking. The stars had committed to provide the musical cabaret as requested, giving good reason to excuse herself several times from having her glass refilled, saying she wanted to keep a clear head for their performance.

Her bridesmaid's dress felt tight too, and from certain angles, she was convinced family and friends would notice her changing shape.

'I'm not going to get away with this,' she complained to her handsome co-star, as they prepared to take the stage after the ceremony.

'You'll be fine,' Jeff told her, hugging the gorgeous frame which was most definitely becoming rounder. 'It's only our secret for a few more weeks. You look amazing, Mamá.'

That night, entertainment duties discharged with their usual flair and having sent the second set of Dyson newlyweds on their way to a honeymoon touring through California and on down into Mexico, the chart-toppers paid homage to their own rookie marriage by catching the train back into Melbourne's CBD in their party clothes.

The romantic pair treated the late-night crowd to an *a capella* medley, complete with raunchy moves, while waiting at Flinders Street station for a tram to deliver them closer to their doorstep. They tumbled into bed as soon as they could, sleeping late into the morning after the celebrations.

'Jeff!' the young man heard Lynn call from the lounge room. 'Come quickly!'

The distracted husband's immediate reaction was negative, as usual. He jumped up from his desk and ran from the office to find his wife lying on the couch pointing to her bared stomach.

'Look! I saw something move.'

Jeff crouched down next to her expanding belly and waited for the something to move again. Neither spoke, lost in amazement for their potential person's next trick. Several minutes went by with their reverence going unrewarded.

'False alarm,' the songwriter sighed, stretching aching knees. 'Shame. Next time. Someone, not something, angel. You saw someone move.'

Swinging her legs off the couch and preparing to start her own day's work, the gentle correction caused Lynn to catch her breath. Tears had filled her eyes. The empathetic star bent down to kiss his beloved's mouth, resting his hand on her abdomen. The baby moved in response to the change in pressure through the loosely-woven fabric of her tracksuit trousers, causing Jeff to recoil in fright.

'Jeez! I felt that!' he cried out. 'Whoa! Do it again, will you, please, Jimmy-Sue?'

Concentration summarily suspended for the song he had been composing, the musician laid his hand back in what he hoped was the same spot and waited for further sign of life. Nothing happened this time either, and he shook his head at the baby's capricious lack of compliance.

'It doesn't like following instructions,' Lynn laughed. 'It's a baby who won't be pushed around; values its independence. Oh, my God! Who does that remind me of, I wonder? Another control freak in the making.'

However, just when Jeff was ready to give up and return to the study, their wish was granted. His hand felt a limb push the wall of her abdomen outwards, likely brought on by the high pitched sound from its mother. One sharp kick followed up by another softer nudge.

He caught his breath. '*Muchas gracias*, mate,' the dumbfounded man said, softly kissing his wife's stomach. 'I love you too.'

When he looked up again, he saw that Lynn had tears in her eyes at her magician's sweet words to their child. How he had changed, from a boy so disillusioned with life to a man positively enamoured with making more of it.

'That was lovely. You're so gorgeous. I love how you talk to the baby. You're going to be such a fantastic dad.'

Jeff smiled, not doubting her words for a moment. '*We're* going to be fantastic parents,' he countered. 'I love you too, angel. Now I've got a queue of songs I need to write down. You comin'?'

The initial plans for their house by the sea had been drawn up by neighbours who lived four floors below them, whom Jeff had met one day in the lobby and happily engaged in idle lift conversation. It had turned out that Don and Sue Jenner were both architects by profession, although Sue was currently on maternity leave with their first child. One loving the idea of getting to know Australia's most famous superstars, and the other craving the company of everyday folk, the two couples had developed a solid friendship. The young mother would soon also be a vital source of practical information for Lynn when the time came to impart their happy news.

The semi-Argentinean millionnaire's vivid imagination had conjured up a modest and tasteful *hacienda*-style design for their dream home. It featured an internal courtyard with a simple fountain, a range of uneven cobblestones set in a variety of patterns and huge, wooden, mediæval portals protecting its new residents from the outside world. His vision had been inspired by several trips to southern California and also from the Basque architecture of northern Spain. He had painted the picture in his lover's mind with such romantic accuracy that she had no reason to question its suitability as their country hideaway.

Everything fell into place remarkably smoothly. The Jenners commissioned a real estate broker to find a three-acre block of land on a cliff above the bay in Mount Eliza, complete with its own stretch of private beach. On the way to the Mornington Peninsula's holiday playgrounds, a few minutes' drive from the relatively unexciting Frankston, the preferred site was about fifty kilometres from Melbourne's CBD; not as far out of town as the

Benloch farmstead yet still enough of a distance to feel estranged from the "rat race".

There was an old house on the block, neglected but liveable at a pinch, vacated by a successful local businessman who was retiring to the Gold Coast. The young couple gladly opened this up to the team of builders as accommodation during the demolition and re-building phases, choosing not to relocate until their brand new home was finished, even if it meant their child spending the first year or so of its life in the city.

Don and Sue had been extremely excited with winning the contract to design Lynn Dyson and Jeff Diamond's country retreat, and their employer had taken full advantage of the publicity its new clients brought with them. Since the existing house was well away from the cliff and off to one side of the block, the foursome opted to keep it and turn it into living quarters for future nannies, drivers and so forth.

For their part, the Diamonds regularly acknowledged their good fortune in being able to build virtually any feature into the house that they desired: an outdoor, heated, twenty-five metre pool with separate *jacuzzi*; a large, airy gymnasium with views over the garden; a soundproofed recording studio; and a huge games room where Jeff was already planning a bar and a billiard table for blokes' nights. There would also be a covered *al fresco* entertainment area, with the obligatory barbecue and yet another bar.

The floor-plan itself was not huge by celebrity standards. However, compared to their apartment, the layout seemed enormous. Lynn had drawn the line at seven bedrooms on the second storey; less than half the number at Benloch and the same tally as Junior and Julie boasted at Narrandera. More bathrooms, though, they had all agreed. Gone were the days of forcing half-dressed guests to pass each other on the landing like bashful ships in the night, clutching towels and toiletry bags. The celebrities were intending to invite a constant stream of visitors to their private paradise, continuing their cherished London tradition of long, daring conversations over dinner, and the least they could do was to make their stay more comfortable.

At one progress meeting over a bottle of aged *Rioja*, Jeff rolled out the latest plans for review. He had scribbled a number of amendments, including two cartoon dogs sprawled in the hallway.

'Hey! Where did they come from?' his wife had laughed. 'I didn't know you could build dogs, Don.'

'Nor did I,' the architect replied. 'Hope they're not to scale.'

Jeff had feigned disappointment at the time, and later the happy couple discussed the possibility of adding pets to their dream home, along with their dream family. Both initially ruled owning animals an impossibility due to the amount of travel to which they had already committed, but her husband's doleful eyes convinced Lynn that this was a serious request.

'I think we could,' she concluded, yawning and nuzzling against his broad chest. 'What about if we made sure, when we enlist a driver, that he or she'd be interested in looking after a dog or dogs whenever we go away. Or they might even come with their own dog… That'd be better in a way. It'd save all that puppy training when we're so busy with other stuff. And anyway, once the baby comes, I won't be able to travel so much. I'd be able to pitch in with pet duties.'

The young man beamed. 'Yeah? You wouldn't mind? Thanks, angel. I'd love that. I've always wanted two dogs, for some reason. Even when I was a little kid, and it'd be great for our kids to learn how to look after something wholly dependent on them. Not yappy, whiny little dogs though. Biggish, like German Shepherds or a retriever like Monkey. He was such a great dog when he was younger.'

'Whose dog was on the back cover of "Ride All Night"?' Lynn asked, remembering a very appealing picture of the singer-songwriter on one of his early album covers, sitting on the ground and leaning against a graffiti-covered wall, with a lithe, young German Shepherd by his side.

'The sound engineer's, I think,' Jeff thought back. 'Can't remember. The photographer turned up late that day, and we'd had to hang around for ages. We were just wandering about, looking for run-down places that looked interesting as backdrops for the cover, and this dog started playing with me. He wouldn't leave me alone, actually. It's a good photo'.'

Towards the end of November, the contented rock star headed back to Los Angeles for another sell-out concert series at the Greek Theater. If anything, these latest shows were more successful than his last season in the same venue. His act was less rock'n'roll these days and more akin to a variety show, featuring dancing and guest appearances from other artists, though no less strident and sexy. The demographic of his audience had broadened considerably with the release of his more mellow albums, incorporating several intense and sophisticated new sounds.

During these shows, the consummate performer talked freely with spellbound audiences about his peacemaking work, the movies, the charitable foundation he and his beautiful best friend were running, and of course, said beautiful best friend herself. The rapport he developed always yielded the most excruciating temptation to divulge to his adoring fans that the Diamonds were about to become a family, but he managed to resist by the closest whisker each and every night.

If anything, and quite contrary to popular opinion, marrying Lynn Dyson had enhanced the handsome and outspoken showman's reputation as the sexiest man alive. His female devotees continued to scream at the top of their lungs, grabbing for his clothing and behaving provocatively whenever he came in sight. Yet somehow through the noise from these feverish crowds, he felt a greater respect from fans and the media alike. It was as if he had reached a new level of maturity not only as an artist but also as a man, marked by his ability to mix the raw emotions of a common Aussie lad with the refinement of a globally-recognised establishment figure.

Lynn, away on her own tour in Europe at the end of nineteen-seventy-six, felt so proud of her successful Prince of Peace. His transition was outwardly complete, and even their life behind the scenes was nowadays visited by very few remnants of the old troubles. He hadn't woken up shouting in a cold sweat from a nightmare for at least three months, and the previous fights with solid doors were consigned to the past. Only the occasional bout of anxiety reared its head whenever a hidden memory was triggered, but his compassionate wife knew to leap on it quickly, making sure they talked things through and applied sufficient, creative joy triggers until the afflicted soul was once more content.

The year's penultimate crowning glory for the truly great Jeff Diamond came in December, when he and Gerry were invited to drive in the Lombard RAC Rally, speeding through the wintry hills and dales of northern England and up into the southern highlands of Scotland. The amateur drivers had accepted with maximum enthusiasm but minimal expectation of success, jumping at the chance to squeeze in a blokes' holiday at the end of another busy year.

Maturity coming with new responsibilities and wealth on a gigantic scale, neither man regularly reverted to their boyhood antics, so this brief recreational burst in the British winter had been seen purely as a chance for them to behave like rev-heads again. They let off steam on the twisting, turning roads with the bleak landscape barely visible through the mud-splattered windows. The Ford Escort RS2000 which the pair had bought between them in nineteen-seventy-five proved itself eminently capable, and the two Australians were amazed to finish in first place at the end of five days of hard and sometimes quite dangerous driving.

The overgrown teenager was intoxicated with much more than beer when he telephoned home that evening, speaking to his dream girl in Melbourne's following morning. 'Angel, you're never going to believe this,' he shouted down the telephone, 'but we won!'

'You won? The whole thing? Wow! That's amazing!' she shared her husband's joy, listening to the elation in his deep, sexy voice. 'Congratulations! And to Gerry too. That's fantastic. Another string to add to Midas' bow.'

'Ha!' Jeff laughed out loud. 'You said it, baby! You know, it was a complete escape. No-one treats me like me, and we just covered ourselves in flameproof suits and walked around like the Unknown Spaceman for a week. I can highly recommend it for anonymity. We'll get one made that can hide your ever-increasingness.'

Lynn didn't need to be reminded of this plain fact. 'Thanks very much, darling. I'll think about it. Hey! I have to tell you something funny…'

'Oh, yeah? What sort of funny?'

'I was in the middle of an interview for Channel Nine, as a promotion for the Myer Music Bowl concert, and the interviewer asked the weirdest of questions.'

The rally champion's concentration was waning in favour of the simulated arousal his hand had encouraged to the sound of his woman's enticing voice. 'Yeah? Why weird?'

She giggled. 'She said, "Your husband's very sympathetic towards gay people. Do you ever think he might be gay?"'

Startled indeed, the red-blooded twenty-four-year-old snapped to attention, immediately feeling his ardour fade. 'Shit! What the hell kind of question is that?'

'I know. I did well, actually, I think. I said, "Well, I know he's straight!"'

'Thanks,' the front half of the pantomime horse chuckled. 'I'm relieved to hear that.'

'Shut up and listen for a minute! Then I said, "I've found out some very surprising things about my husband over the years, so I suppose I shouldn't rule anything out. But I know if I were to find out he's gay, it'd be from him and not from any other source." Was that OK?'

The unexpected angle of her response took the young man by surprise, almost prompting an involuntary ejaculation, such was the love that surged through his body.

'Whoa! Thank you.'

'You're welcome. I thought you'd like it.'

'It's amazing, angel. What did she say?'

'Nothing,' Lynn replied. 'She was floored. Changed the subject. She was distracted by her crew's gaping mouths! But could you ever commit a homosexual act, d'you think?'

'Could I or would I?' the intellectual challenged, summoning the patience to enter such a peculiar late-night conversation topic. 'Your brother got the same answer when he asked me.'

'Did he? Sorry to be so unoriginal!' the pregnant woman regretted turning serious too. 'Either, I s'pose.'

'I'm sure I could, if life depended on it, but I'm not sure I would otherwise. Is that OK?'

'Yes! I just don't think a woman could turn me on enough.'

'A finger's a finger, and a tongue's a tongue,' the traveller stated the obvious, his arousal reignited with various memories of rock-star debauchery. 'Depends on what's going on in your mind while these lesbian acts are going on with your body. All of a sudden I'm heaps more interested.'

'Yeah. But whose tongue?'

'Whose tongue? Anyone's! You've been married too long already! Let's not talk about this anymore. Blow me off instead, angel.'

Only too keen to oblige the lover she missed, the sportswoman wove a tantalising tale of physical manœuvres the couple would shortly be making for real, listening to his breathing becoming heavier and imagining his hand working on a turgid organ.

'You're amazing, Lynn,' he crooned. 'So amazing. Can't wait to be home. There's a quote from Fitzgerald's "Tender Is The Night" that this reminds me of. Dick Diver, I think the guy's name was. One of the main characters in the book was a psychiatrist who did what you did.'

'What did I do?' Australia's darling sounded surprised at yet another change in direction.

'Marry a lunatic.'

'Marry a lunatic? You're not a lunatic. What are you talking about? You're a rally driving champion, not a lunatic.'

'Yeah, well...,' Jeff continued, groaning as the effect of her supportive words pushed him ever closer to orgasm. 'The quote was something like, "I never did go in for making love to dry loins."'

Lynn yelped. 'Yuck! That's horrible. And that's supposed to illustrate your point how exactly?'

To her consternation, the young wife found herself listening to the story of the single and far less together celebrity's twenty-first birthday party, which had culminated in a sex romp with two women. Now carrying the child of this awesome, tamed bad-boy of hers, it was almost as if he were talking about a different person entirely.

'Do you want me to invite a friend over for when you get home?' she teased, once the whole sordid yarn had been spun.

'No,' he assured her. 'No. I don't, angel. That kind of thing's better left in our heads. Do you want *me* to?'

Again, his wife shouted in defiance. 'No way!'

'Good,' Jeff chuckled. 'I'm glad about that. Neither do I. And that's the truth, gorgeous.'

The couple fell silent, drowning in a river of love that deluged both ends of the telephone line. Lynn imagined her man's right hand stroking his long shaft slowly, trying to prolong the sublime sensation for as long as possible. She had no need to do the same. Her heart was bursting as it was.

'Not a bad choice, this whole marriage thing, was it?' the romantic whispered after a long pause.

'No. Did you think it would be?'

'No. Never thought it'd be this good though.'

'Oh... No. Well, yes,' the young woman felt tears rolling down her cheeks. 'Thank you. I love you so much, Jeff.'

'I love you too. How are you anyway?' her husband asked, belatedly remembering his grown-up priorities. 'Everything OK?'

'Yes, thanks. Everything's fine. I still feel pretty normal, although my clothes are definitely much tighter. I'm a bit tired too, but nothing to worry about. I went to the doctor yesterday, and everything's *hunky dory*. I'm just so tired of keeping this secret. Aren't you? Sometimes I see people staring at me and wonder if I've got "I'm pregnant" written across my forehead.'

Her empathetic lover smiled his best long-distance smile. 'That's beautiful, angel. You probably have, to those clever enough to see the invisible ink. I can't wait to get home. We're landing at six AM, so I'll see you around seven if you're home. Will you be?'

The chief administrator of their life singular thought carefully for a moment. 'I think so. My diary's in the office, but I'm fairly sure I haven't got an early start on Tuesday. I'm off to pretend to be "Lynn the Unpregnant" at the Sportsdrome again now. Dad's not going to be there, thank God, so I can take it a bit easy.'

Jeff signed off after another round of congratulations and their usual expressions of undying love, excited at the prospect of a passionate reunion to top off his triumphant week.

If anyone was clever enough to notice the metaphysical message on Lynn's forehead, they didn't let on during the weeks leading up to Christmas. The couple had signed up for the same crowded schedule as the previous year, performing in London and Frankfurt on consecutive nights before flying over Russia and China to stop briefly in Hong Kong, and finally appearing in both Sydney's and Melbourne's carol concerts.

This was the self-proclaimed atheist's first command performance in the Australian entertainment industry's traditional festive calendar. Even less religious than her husband, the child-star turned glamorous artist had been enlisted virtually every year since primary school, never once planning to let the viewing public down.

Having been allocated the melodic male solo in "Three Kings From Persian Lands Afar" by the show's director, none other than Sir Bradley Morrison, the irreverent rocker put his hypocritical pride to one side and vowed to give the lyric everything he had. Starting with a duet of "O Holy Night" with his wife, the audience lapped up the quality of the vocals, along with evocative images of their favourite young stars entering the stage from different sides and ending up in the centre together.

During the portentous carol's second chorus, Jeff touched his fingers lightly on his partner's naked shoulder, lost in the moment and mesmerised by the dazzling beauty in a sky-blue strapless evening gown. Both singers reeled momentarily as electricity shot in an arc between them. Lynn jumped out of her skin, but the ethereal sound of her voice never wavered.

When he reached the bridge line "Fall on your knees", the demonstrative singer enacted the scene right at his wife's feet, eliciting a gasp from the audience loud enough to be picked up by the television microphones, which then panned upwards to capture shining tears in the woman's eyes.

The *duo* finished the third verse in harmony, bringing the house down. While Australia's darling left the stage, waving to the crowd, her co-star prepared to cast yet another magic spell on the rows of eager people in the darkness. And also on those beyond the fence, sitting on the grass for their family picnics on a warm summer's evening.

Backed by a boys' choir and full orchestra, the smoky baritone better known for belting out rock songs or mega-ballads wrapped itself around the nativity scene, rising in falling in nuanced volume as the significance demanded.

Bit by bit, sometimes through contrived opportunities such as this and otherwise in observations during interviews and *impromptu* public appearances, the nobody from Canley Vale's reputation in the eyes of his countrymen ascended beyond cult hero status to an iconic, heavyweight social commentator.

Lynn threw herself onto the bed early on Christmas morning, another year's "Carols by Candlelight" masterfully executed by Melbourne's collegiate musical community, praising her novice festive season entertainer's *début*.

'I'm always amazed when I jump at your touch,' she gushed, his naked form looming above her, sporting a full erection as usual. 'You'd think my skin would be expecting it by now.'

'It's partly my fault,' Jeff murmured, sucking her nipple into his mouth. 'My generator gets charged high when it sees your tattoo on display, proving to the world that we're who we are. Just peeking over the edge of your dress.'

The ardent lover guided his quarry around so that his finger could trace their initials, drawing its singular symbol to remind them both again. 'My heart did a backflip, but you didn't miss a beat, you professional, you!'

His wife moaned as his full length slipped itself into her moist vagina. 'My arm's still tingling though,' she murmured. 'Did you hear the reception you got?'

'The reception *we* got,' the modest performer contradicted, holding her body tight into his as she came. 'They love seeing us together. Was that a "Fuck my parents" moment?'

Lynn laughed through the all-consuming sensation, pleased to recall one of her earliest acts of rebellion. 'Oh, God! Yeah. I think it was!'

'Do you think anyone's guessed?' Jeff ran his fingers across her writhing abdomen. 'This time next year'll be very different.'

'I know,' the young woman sighed.

'Can't wait.'

The pair spent the next few minutes in silence, immersed in their feelings both present and past. Spooning to alleviate the pressure on her belly, the star of the show sensed the sportswoman's energy fast running out. He smiled to himself as he sought to allow his muse one more glimpse of nirvana before pressing himself more urgently inside her.

'You know I want to make love to you every minute of the day.'

Lynn kissed his hand as it stroked lovingly upwards from her neck and across her lips. 'It's going to get harder and harder.'

'It's already getting harder and harder,' the comic sniggered, pushing his engorged penis yet further and feeling her frame twist with its fullness.

'Argh! You know what I mean,' she sighed.

Her sex-god climaxed, letting out a muted yell. 'And you know what *I* mean...'

When their combined heat subsided and sleep began to cloud their brains, the young woman returned from the bathroom to find her husband's face streaked with tears. He had fetched a photograph album from the lounge room while she was freshening up and cleaning her teeth, and he pointed to a set of pictures taken at the Blakes' the previous Christmas.

Lynn climbed into bed beside her *paramour* and was enveloped by a long, covetous wing. 'Did you imagine your life'd turn out like this?'

'When? Before we met?'

'When we first met,' he clarified.

The twenty-one-year-old paused for a second or two, formulating a statement of her own to mark the occasion. 'Well, I always wanted my life to turn out like this. Maybe not so soon, but this is exactly what I wanted from life. How about you?'

'Jesus! Yeah. One hundred percent. But never in a million years did I think I'd get it, or did I really believe it was what I wanted. Marriage and being a parent, that is...'

'I guessed that,' his wife sniffed, cuddling into his suddenly defensive side.

'I mean, why would I crave a family after the childhood I had?'

'Perhaps you secretly craved it *because* of the childhood you had. To prove it didn't have to be that way.'

Christmas was spent at Benloch this year after promising Celia that the couple and their firstborn heir would grace the North Shore in twelve months' time. Bart and Marianna Dyson made a special fuss of their augmenting family, particularly looking forward to seeing both sets of newly-weds reunited with their younger siblings again.

A day or two later, Jeff caught Lynn crying when Heather had asked Gerry to babysit Jenna one evening between Christmas and New Year. The job had been immediately outsourced to whoever failed to step back quickly enough. His formerly stoic wife was becoming increasingly emotional while the burden of their secret weighed more heavily than its physical incarnation.

'Hey! Stop that,' he ordered, kissing the top of her head and hiding her reaction from their insensitive friend. 'Don't let him see you.'

'Do you think he'd even notice?' the mum-to-be asked, wiping her eyes. 'He wouldn't put two and two together, would he?'

'No. He's only an accountant,' the star winked. 'He's not too good with numbers. It's lovely though, to see you like this. All pathetic and out of control. Just like me. It makes me want to smother you with good loving.'

With their first wedding anniversary fast approaching, the celebrity couple had planned to spend New Year in Scotland, to experience their first Hogmanay filled with whisky, wry humour and incomprehensible Rab Burns poetry. As soon as their last Australian festive obligation was acquitted, they boarded a Jumbo Jet and embarked on the day-long journey from their enormous island continent bathed in hot weather to the dot of rocks in the northern seas which was bracing for cold weather.

'I can't believe I can't drink over my first Scottish New Year,' Lynn groaned.

'No sweat, angel,' Jeff was quick to reassure her. 'I'll make up for it. I'll drink your share. *Nay bother, lassie, comme on dit.* No-one'll ever know.'

***

And so finally, on Wednesday the fifth of January nineteen-seventy-seven, Lynn Dyson Diamond woke up full of the joys of spring, announcing that today was the day. They had returned home from Scotland the previous evening and had spent the night sleeping and waking in fits and starts.

'OK,' her husband agreed, drawing a huge breath. 'I'm not sure I'm up for a big splash after all this time. It seems so long ago we found out. It'll be hard to sound spontaneous.'

'Who shall we tell first?' the young woman asked her growing bump. 'Grandma?'

'I'm sorry, but this is too weird for me,' Jeff chuckled, shaking his head. 'I'm going to make tea. Let me know when it's over.'

Lynn kissed her unusually shy husband and picked up the telephone to call her mother. 'Mum, it's me,' she said, hearing Marianna's voice.

'Oh, hello there. How are you?' the dignified lady asked. 'Are you in Melbourne?'

'Yes. We got back yesterday. Are you busy?'

'Busy? No. Not particularly. Why?'

'Because, Mum, I've been wanting to tell you this for so long,' her daughter could hardly contain her excitement. 'We're having a baby. I'm ten weeks pregnant!'

'Lynn! Really?' Marianna shrieked in as ladylike a fashion as due decorum allowed. 'How wonderful! Congratulations, darling. How do you feel?'

'Fantastic!' the sportswoman replied, tears streaming down her face. 'Especially now! It's been the hardest secret to keep. The three months isn't quite up yet, but we decided we'd tell everyone after Christmas.'

'Well, that's good news! What does Jeff think?'

Coincidentally, the man in question arrived at that very moment and was placing a mug of tea on Lynn's bedside table. She patted the bedclothes beside her, and he obediently sat down, clutching his own cup of coffee.

'What does Jeff think?' his wife repeated her mother's enquiry.

He leaned forward and kissed her lips as loudly as he could while making sure the receiver stayed close to their mouths.

'What was that?' Marianna asked about the strange, muffled sound.

Pushing his hulking frame away, the young woman giggled. 'He kissed me. I think that means he's happy.'

'What do I think?' Jeff shouted loud enough for his mother-in-law to overhear. 'Is it mine?'

Lynn hit him hard on the upper arm. 'Shut up, you bastard!'

Marianna chuckled in the background, pleased to hear the youngsters' friendly banter. The match she and her husband had done their best to scupper had borne out to be a relationship filled with affection and mutual respect. The swarthy and *avant-garde* Jeff Diamond had proven himself a most worthy suitor for their gilt-edged champion daughter after all.

'So when's the due date, dear?'

'Mid-July,' the twenty-one-year-old answered. 'We're already booked into the Mercy, and I've had an ultrasound scan. Everything looks perfect.'

'Do you plan to find out the sex in advance?' her mother asked, by now very excited for her daughter.

'No. We decided not to. We thought about it for ages.'

'You'll have to come to the farm this weekend so that we can all celebrate. Your father's out of town until Friday night, but I'll pass on the news when I speak to him. Unless you want to tell him yourself, of course. Have you told anyone else?'

Lynn smiled. 'No,' she answered, happy to have done the right thing by her mother. 'I wanted you to be the first. And you can tell Dad for us.'

'Oh, thank you, dear,' Marianna said. 'That's very thoughtful of you. Jeff'll be keen to tell his sister, I expect.'

'Are you keen to tell your sister?' her daughter asked the man sitting next to her, already confident of the answer.

'No. Not 'specially,' he answered with a wry smile. 'Not as keen as she will be to find out, at any rate.'

The very proper mother-in-law heard his response and huffed her objection. 'Typical man! Tell him to share in the excitement a bit, darling.'

Ashamed, Lynn scowled. 'Mum says you're to share in the excitement, darling.'

The songwriter kissed his dream girl's pouting lips, knowing full well that she harboured no misconceptions as to his level of excitement. From now until July, nothing could be more important to him than welcoming their new arrival into the world. He would simply prefer to do it with a minimum of fuss from those on the periphery of their life singular.

'OK,' he moaned with excessive melodrama for both women's benefit. 'I'll ring Madalena next, I promise.'

The Olympian terminated the call to her mother after swapping a few other items of news concerning the couple's working holiday in Scotland and receiving a quick update on how the rest of the family's annual assessments had gone. She had missed out this year due to their overseas engagements, and as it turned out, her father would be granted no recourse to exact his revenge. Mother and daughter both found this amusing, albeit just between the two of them.

The gorgeous blonde cut the line after saying goodbye and handed the receiver straight to her husband. 'Ring Lena now,' she instructed. 'You might as well. Then it's done.'

The comedian saluted, rolling his eyes at the dictator in their midst. 'I don't even know her bloody number.'

The star's very organised social secretary slid the drawer of her bedside table open and pulled out an address book. Madalena's number was listed, and she pointed to it. Taking a deep breath, the young man dialled the number.

'Hullo?' the brother's jet-lagged eardrums were jarred by the shrill voice, slicing through the air like the raw sound of tubular bells hit with too much force.

'Hi, Lena. *Es Jeff,*' he began. '*¿Qué tal?*'

'Good, *chico*. How're you goin'?' his sister replied in a friendly tone. 'And Lynn?'

'She's great, thanks. *Oyes... Hay notícias.* Lynn's pregnant.'

'*¡Ai!* Really? Shit!' Madalena Moreno shrieked in a far less ladylike fashion than had Marianna Dyson a few minutes earlier.

'*¡Sí!* Really! No shit, Lena! *Es verdad.*'

This excitement was infectious, he had to admit, feeling his heartbeat quickening and his head becoming dizzy. Lynn grinned at her very atypical man's refusal to join in the effusion. She didn't mind. Babies were necessarily a woman's thing, she supposed.

'Hey! *¿Quieres hablar con Lynn?*' he asked, passing the receiver to his wife regardless.

'Lena, hi!' the sportswoman greeted her sister-in-law. 'What do you think? Are you ready to become an auntie?'

'Yeah. Bloody oath, I am!' Madalena screamed again. 'Why'd it take ya so long?'

The patient young woman laughed, watching Jeff roll his eyes at having overheard his sister's question only too clearly.

'Ah, you know…' she joked. 'It took him a while to get it together.'

The Sydneysider howled with laughter, and her brother made a grab for his wife's expanding waist, wrestling her onto the mattress and snatching the receiver back from this untrustworthy woman.

'Fucking hell! Don't listen to a word she says, Lena,' the playful man snapped. 'She's delirious. She has no idea what she's talking about.'

'So why *did* it take so long, *culo*?' his sister turned the screws a little tighter.

'Christ Almighty!' the musician cursed, clearly outnumbered. 'Because we decided to wait until after the Olympics, and then the US Open tennis came along. And then we found out back in October, but the doctors advised us not to tell anyone for three months. S'that a good enough explanation for you? Jesus!'

'Ah, OK,' Madalena indicated, laughing heartily. 'I 'eard that bit before, about waiting three months, so you're not sick all the time in the morning or somethin'. When am I gonna be an auntie proper? With a real baby, I mean, but?'

'In July,' Jeff informed his naïve sister, who was at least taking his news seriously and appeared to be happy for them. 'You'll have to come down and meet him or her.'

The distant voice shrieked again. 'Yeah. I want to. Wow-wee! My kid brother's gonna be a dad. That's so cool.'

La Esperanza

'Nine months after the sixteenth of February is mid-November, Ry,' Kierney coaxed her brother, who was adamant in his avoidance of this creepy topic. 'It's close. You have to admit. Babies can come early, you know.'

'No. I don't have to admit.'

The human rights lawyer had arrived home to New York's Upper East Side from an overseas trip, impatient to revisit the paperwork for this year's student intake into The Good School. Sure enough, when she had recovered Freya Gunarwardene's application, her date of birth was unmistakeably recorded as the eighth of November nineteen-ninety-six.

'Come on, bro. Please! At least think about it,' Kierney urged. 'You make sci-fi movies, for God's sake! Take a leap of faith in this direction for once. She could be.'

'And so could every other kid born in the same month,' the thirty-eight-year-old father of two sneered. 'Or none of them could.'

'Jeez! You're being an absolute arsehole about this,' his sister cursed. 'We set up this scholarship expressly for this purpose, and now you're running away from it faster than a killer spider. What if she is, and we totally miss it?'

Ryan, his partner and their children were currently enjoying a well-earned break at home, where the Colorado wind had already turned bracing at their luxurious home's mountainside elevation. Both Diamond children had been actively involved in this year's selection process for the single fully-sponsored place at the *élite* leadership academy which had been their parents' brainchild.

The fun-loving intellectual had initially bought into the possibility that the timing was right for the two souls to manifest themselves again as adults. As the weeks had gone by however, he had become more and more disturbed by the dangers lurking behind this overly romantic concept. His daughter and her mother were on board with his persuasive sister, itching to discover if this pretty Sri Lankan painter might be the new Lynn Dyson Diamond.

'Reya and Sav are up for it,' Ryan confessed. 'But I think we're playing with fire. You have to admit there are so many ways it could backfire. A whole heap of things could get royally screwed up as a result of this one-in-agazillion chance that Mum's new incarnation was interested in applying for a year at MIT.'

Kierney laughed. 'No. I don't have to admit.'

'Fuck off,' the former cricketer groaned. 'Now I guess you want me to call you "parrot face". What does Arka think?'

'He thinks I'm nuts too. You men are hopeless. And you're going to be proved wrong, just wait and see. Freya had a copy of "ALS" in her bag. She says it's her Bible.'

'Jeez, Kizzo!' Ryan shouted into the telephone, so loud that his dog began to bark in the background. 'What about the word "best-seller" don't you understand? There's a copy of that bloody book in almost every household, particularly back in Oz.'

The clock on the microwave read after ten o'clock, and the United Nations executive needed to get some sleep before another busy day. It would be too late to ring the young woman's home in Brisbane now. She would most likely be already in bed. Still, if Kierney didn't attempt to solve this piece in her life's big mystery, what hope would there be in finding her beloved papá's soul again?

'Well, listen to this...' the young woman continued, determined not to give up on bringing Ryan along with her on this mission. 'Freya also thinks she might be.'

A long pause stretched from west to east while the successful movie-maker weighed up his response to this latest piece of information. 'Did she?' his voice sounded full of an uncharacteristic vulnerability. 'Without you planting a seed?'

'Of course I didn't plant a seed,' the humanitarian insisted. 'I don't want to jump to conclusions any more than you do. It'd be terrible to openly declare a position only to find someone else later, or to prove we're definitively wrong. I agree, Ry. We need to be careful, but I've got such a strong feeling about her. I found myself telling her all sorts of really personal stuff that I somehow felt compelled to tell her.'

'Shit! That must've been embarrassing. How did she react?'

His sister blanched, reliving the awkward eye contact the pair had shared after exchanging a photograph of her little boy. 'It was weird as hell. Oh, I don't know. It could be nothing, as you say, but what if it's not. Wouldn't you like to meet Mamá again?'

Monterey Diamond came running into her dad's office, chasing after the family's brand new golden retriever puppy. Screeching to a standstill, she buttoned her lip as soon as she realised a telephone call was in progress, lunging for the dog's collar and pulling him out from under the desk.

'Do you want to talk to Reya or Philo?' he asked his sister, beckoning to his daughter. The six-year-old gathered the squirming ball of fur into her arms and climbed up onto a chair next to her father, giggling as the pup attempted to nip his fingers.

'Yes. Sure,' Kierney affirmed. 'But you're avoiding the question. How long do you reckon it might take for a soul to enter its next body?'

'Kiz, I have no bloody idea,' the impatient man shrugged, raising his eyebrows to the young girl beside him and pressing a button on the telephone. 'Speakerphone's on, by the way, and Reya's here. Your auntie's gone bananas. And when does it enter? While the embryo's forming in the womb or when it's born?'

'Or is the gestation period the time when they're flitting back and forth in the process of helping those left behind to cope with their grief?' the lawyer added. 'See? You are interested, aren't you, you charlatan?'

The brilliant mind housed in the sportsman's muscular body admitted defeat. 'Yes. Of course I'm damned well interested. Tell you what?'

'Good. What?'

'If you can find us a bloke born around the end of September, beginning of October 'ninety-seven who thinks he was Jeff Diamond in a former life, and these two get it on like rabbits, I'll back you all the way. I'd love it to be true. Who wouldn't? But it's about the longest shot imaginable. Don't you think it's in the least bit far-fetched? Now, here's Reya for you. Change the subject, sis. See ya.'

***

Once the news of Lynn Dyson's pregnancy hit the press, the famous couple's world turned upside-down. Initially, both she and Jeff did their best to hide from the marauding crowds of journalists, photographers and television camera operators who seemed to pop up out of nowhere as soon as she left home, hoping to get a glimpse of the pregnant superstar. As the hype showed no sign of abating, the pair realised they had no choice but to go with the flow and use the *furore* to supplement their own excitement.

The tennis champion's schedule had been adjusted to the level of a mere fitness freak, as reported by her husband in an interview, with this spare time being quickly filled with invitations to produce other artists' records; a job she had grown to love. Her travel itinerary remained therefore almost as demanding, but this was very easy to manage since the most strenuous aspect of spending endless hours in the studio was migrating every morning and evening from her hotel.

The first few months of the new year passed in far too pedestrian a fashion, much to both millionnaires' annoyance. Instead of seeking to maximise their remaining time together as free agents, Jeff was surprised at how impatient they had become for July to roll round, and they found themselves constantly counting the days.

453

'Who designed humans to take nine months to produce their young?' the frustrated man asked, his finger tracing across the calendar in their office. 'I'm glad you're not an elephant.'

'Oh, please!' Lynn cried out. 'I'm glad you're glad I'm not an elephant too. I'm expecting to feel like one before long.'

March and April saw the two VIP directors of the Diamond Celebration Foundation make their first trip to South Africa and Zimbabwe together, to understand at close quarters the plight of indigenous farmers who were being driven off the land by agents of the new government. The black itinerant workers were housed in appalling conditions and being forced to work as not much more than slave labour.

Basking in his wife's admiring gaze, the determined philanthropist let loose with a bout of magnificent anger aimed at consular officials who had refused to accompany them into farm offices or community buildings, continually steering their famous visitors towards sanitised, pre-arranged events instead.

This eye-opening trip had been suggested to the Diamonds by an up-and-coming South African musician whom Jeff had met in London the previous year. They had written an enormous international hit entitled "Strong", the defiant theme for which had been kicking around in the rock star's head for many years. Originally a lyric describing his own childhood situation, it had been inspired by the time when Social Services and the school authorities had attempted to take him and Madalena into State care.

Yabo Mabuza and his band, along with their white collaborators, recorded the rousing anthem with a choir formed and coached in two days flat in the Soweto township. Subsequently released around the world using Lynn's newly-established, independent record label, the song and their stirring performance were an instant Number One all over the world, not to mention a source of considerable embarrassment to the South African and Australian governments. It was the latter's discomfort which had given Jeff the greater pleasure, since it drew timely attention to ongoing political two-facedness concerning the conflict discussions actuated by Professor Francis and his notoriously influential sidekick.

In early May, the couple flew to Sydney for the Entertainment Industry Awards ceremony, once more installing themselves in their old favourite, the Intercontinental Hotel.

'I'm so proud of Jeff,' Lynn told an excited studio audience in an interview before the show. 'He has so much passion for people and for combatting unfairness everywhere. I have no idea where he came from, my magic-man, but the world is a better place with him in it.'

The one black spot on their sun during this carefree time had been the moment when Lynn was confronted by her husband's philandering past quite unexpectedly at the Awards dinner. Donna Watts, with whom the old Jeff had briefly had a fiery affair and who had been credited with the inspiration for the monster hit "Donna Jade", had zeroed in on the pregnant superstar on the dance floor with old friends from the Australian music scene, taking advantage of the new Jeff's brief absence to hold court at the bar.

Now a middle-aged feature producer for Channel Seven, the former reporter had partaken of a few too many glasses of champagne, vexed and obnoxiously upset at seeing the perfect couple and their evident pending happy event.

Suddenly conscious of a twang on their invisible elastic connection while casually chatting with a bunch of record company executives, the likeable rock star spotted the two women in animated conversation out of the corner of his eye. Excusing himself with his heart in his mouth, he ran the whole width of the ballroom to where the altercation was unfolding.

'Hey, angel,' Jeff gasped, slipping a protective arm around Lynn's waist. 'You OK? Hello, Donna.'

His tired wife leaned into the warmth of her man's body, thankful for his overt show of concern. She had been at a loss as to how to avoid an awkward situation developing, especially surrounded by journalists and photographers. Even when technically off-duty, they would be quick to make a meal out of any scandalous behaviour.

'Yes,' the pretty twenty-one-year-old replied, disguising her relief. 'I'm fine, thanks. You?'

Donna pouted at her former lover. 'Hi, Jeff. So you got yourself what you always wanted then. I can't believe you'd fall for his charms, Lynn?'

The dignified musician forced a smile. 'Easily. He's irresistible. I know you already know that. It's nice to meet you finally.'

The embarrassed young man tried to walk away by subtly turning his steadfast partner around, worried that the minor New South Wales celebrity was unlikely to give up without a fight. She had caused him significant grief when he first released the hit single bearing her name, and he had taken his punishment both on the chin and *via* his wallet.

'Come on, angel. Let's go and get another drink,' he suggested.

'Too good to talk to me these days, are you?' the spurned blonde snapped. 'Now you've got her in the club?'

'In the club? That's a very quaint expression,' Jeff teased. 'Be quiet, Don, please. Leave it alone. We're very happy with everything the way it is, and there's nothing anyone can do to change that.'

'So is he still knocking off anything with a pulse?' Donna jeered, looking directly at Australia's virtuous princess.

The pretty superstar refused to answer, simply imagining what a red rag this comment must be to her prize beast. The controlled rage she envisaged building behind his smart, clean-shaven face was somehow even sexier than the wild-eyed fury he had demonstrated in Africa.

'Donna, you're pissed,' the frustrated man adopted a forthright air. 'You shouldn't be bitter about us anymore. It was never meant to last, and you know it. We never had anything going. And don't take it out on Lynn, please? This is between you and me.'

'But you wrote that song about me, and it made you millions of dollars,' Donna persisted. 'How do you feel about that, Lynn?'

Again, the Melbourne stalwart made no comment. Truth be told, the lingering possibility did still upset her whenever she heard the song on the radio. Her guilty man knew this too, but neither planned to give their current tormenter any extra ammunition.

'You're getting more than your fair share of those royalties,' Jeff hissed. 'Isn't that enough? You want more? We can talk about it tomorrow, if you need to say anything else.'

The handsome rocker grabbed hold of the older woman's arm and tried to walk her away from his wife, who had taken a seat nearby. Donna was reluctant to move however. It was the first time Lynn had seen the television personality up close, and she was without question a glamorous woman. She could understand how the old Jeff would have found her attractive. Now in her late thirties, the passage of time and many hundreds of cigarettes had not been kind to her skin, and tonight's chip was clearly weighing heavily on an unforgiving shoulder.

'Don, for the last time, that song was *not* written about you,' the chart-topper stated. 'We've talked this out countless times already. It just worked at the time. It's a good song, and you're getting much more than you deserve from it because of my mistake in giving it your name.'

The seasoned current affairs interviewer trembled, her anger passing. Fleetingly, Jeff wondered whether she might have the resources available to pry into his own seedy backstory. Should he treat her more carefully to prevent her exacting revenge by exposing the pact he had secured with the Jaworski family?

'Listen, Donna... I'm sorry about everything. We were a moment in time, both on our way to somewhere else. OK?'

'Oh, sure,' the crestfallen woman shrugged. 'So where is that? Where am I going, compared to you?'

The celebrity reached for his wife's hand. 'That's up to you. As you can see, this is where I was going. And where I want to stay, no matter what. Be happy for us, Donna, please, and I wish the same for you.'

Lynn looked at her man, on edge for all manner of complex reasons. She sympathised with him as he worked to pacify his former girlfriend. Regardless of how far he had come, somehow he was still paying for the past, and they both knew he deserved it this time. Donna eventually backed away on the verge of tears. Visibly comforted by this gesture, the tortured adolescent turned his *Regala* round, and they walked straight out of the ballroom for a convenient cigarette break.

'Are you going to frogmarch me into a function room again?' the patient songstress teased, keen to snap her husband out of the self-absorbing wrath. 'You're my knight in shining armour. I love you so much.'

Thrown back into his former world, the boy from Sydney's west had to struggle to see the funny side, dragging hard on his cigarette and blowing out a stream of angst-filled smoke. He relented, leading the bemused woman to a quiet corner of the lobby and wrapping her up in his arms, her extra girth still occasionally catching him by surprise.

'Frogmarch!' he chuckled, kissing her and breathing deeply to slow his heart rate. 'No. Not this time. That's such a good image though. I'm sorry you had to meet her that way, angel. I wasn't paying attention. I should've known she'd be here tonight, but it never even crossed my mind.'

'Jeff, it doesn't matter. It was bound to happen sooner or later, given she's still working in the media. Thanks for coming to my rescue. You were very gallant! And look...'

Lynn nudged her stressed out man and pointed both index fingers down towards her stomach. Jeff put his hand on the bump which had spent the evening elegantly clad in satin and sequins, biting back a rush of tears and comprehending her cryptic message perfectly.

'Gallant, huh? I like that, and I know,' he replied in a hushed voice, kissing her soft lips. 'We're the winners. I get it, angel. *Gracias.*'

The journey back to Melbourne from Sydney was to be Lynn's last flight before the baby arrived since she was now officially at the seventh month cut-off after which the airlines refused to take the risk of flying her and her precious cargo. Her husband was secretly pleased that Qantas had forced the issue of confinement, quite sure that the musical sportswoman would have continued her break-neck schedule right up until the due date.

Song after song burst through the father-to-be's consciousness, sometimes battling with each other to be paired with the next new tune. An expressive batch of poetry destined for Tex Fletcher's music was produced during Lynn's third trimestre, restless for their baby to arrive. It was an incredible, emotional journey for them both.

"Turn Away", which leaped from nowhere to Number One in a single day, was written for a campaign against domestic violence women that the songwriters launched together via the revitalised and fully-funded counselling service at The Fellowship. With it came further recognition for the work the celebrity couple was doing behind the scenes for disadvantaged people everywhere.

Jeff Diamond turned the corner from his quarter-century on an absolute high, reeling from the acclaim heaped upon him from all sides and wallowing in the loving arms of his pregnant dream girl. He felt supremely confident in his own power to succeed, for some reason unable to picture himself exhibiting any other attitude. His critical mind chastised him for his arrogance, only to be vociferously countered by his beautiful best friend. It was as if the young couple had boarded a train which did not plan on stopping, and neither was the slightest bit worried for where they were bound.

***

As the celebrity couple counted down to the beginning of July, they took stock of where their life singular had taken them in the last year. With the exception of some minor detours resulting from echoes of the past, the teenaged rebel from the Stones Road had completed his journey to his new self. With his dream girl beside him every step of the way, in some cases putting her own career aside, he had become a giant of a man, in every sense of the word.

Lynn too had transitioned to independence beyond any shadow of doubt, no longer under her parents' dominion and every bit her husband's equal. She encouraged the ambitious world-changer to believe there was no difference these days between him and her father in terms of world standing. He was reluctant to agree, but she made him promise not to dismiss the notion altogether.

Bridging the gap between the rock music fans who idolised the cool, bad-boy and the progressive *intelligentsia* who now welcomed him into their great debates, the self-effacing star was in high demand everywhere; from television chat shows to after-dinner speeches, and from gigs that perforated eardrums to rousing political rallies.

Jeff Diamond gained the respect of old and young alike, naturally able to talk the talk of the common man while simultaneously pricking affluent consciences in the most charming but incisive way. His eloquent, heartfelt opinions drew everyone in with disturbing realism. He allowed people to see what it was like to be him, and by consequence, they took strength from his empathy. It was a winning combination for the wild and willful pantomime horse's head.

And whichever ingredients went into making a heartthrob, this powerhouse of a man possessed them in truckloads. He remained a walking, talking set of contradictions, but Lynn Dyson wouldn't have had it any other way. The tormented and dangerous student with whom she had fallen in love had matured into a compelling and quite unstoppable force for social change.

Everyone who was introduced to the genial genius received attentive, low-key courtesy after a bone-cracking handshake. His conversation swerved from gritty to witty, yet his eyes still often betrayed traces of melancholy. As far as his wife was concerned, he was more devastatingly handsome than ever, with a hint of grey visible at his temples.

More softly spoken these days, the star's downplayed presence was offset by immensely confident body language. Lynn and he spent many of their precious quiet hours at home flicking through film footage of themselves, examining people's reactions to each subtle and not-so-subtle move.

Jeff Diamond's metamorphosis was nigh on complete, the couple resolved. They had made him into the kind of man who, try has he might, could not slip unnoticed into a crowded room. He stopped conversation wherever he went, using no more than a smile, a "G'day" and a wave of his hand.

At the end of June nineteen-seventy-seven, the rock musician turned peacemaker appeared on his third Michael Parkinson Show, this time without his beautiful but grounded best friend. Promoting another new movie, he sang to a respectful and hypnotised crowd, their reception announcing that the highly-charged sex symbol was worthy of his megastar status.

'There's something unusually special about Jeff,' Jessica Gough, the film's co-star and his fellow guest in the television studio told an excited audience. 'At the same time, there's both an instant familiarity and a mysterious distance. It's not hard to imagine being in love with this man. Sometimes you get on stage or screen with an actor and there's no way in hell you'd want to be with him in a million years. You can't say that about Jeff!'

And for his part, the good-looking intellectual took acting very seriously, more so even than his music. For this demanding, new role, he had spent over two months picking up tricks of the trade, interviewing the real-life characters who had inspired the script, refining a New England accent and learning how to sail on rough seas.

'Films are not only about entertaining,' he had told the BBC chat show host during another landmark interview. 'They're about informing, widening people's horizons and ridding them of their misconceptions. If we hadn't done this prep' work, I would've felt like I was cheating those we set out to help through this story.'

This gradual evolution was significant for many who followed the young man's career closely. From his public persona, already a multi-million-selling rock star at just twenty-five years old, outsiders might have been forgiven for assuming he was never bothered by how he was judged. His wife, his manager and the loyal staff at Stonebridge Music knew otherwise however.

Gone were the days of the party-going, hard-drinking Australian Elvis, with a raw talent for creating an illusion, for evoking emotions through songs about life and love and drifting from partner to partner as effortlessly as he progressed from stage to screen to negotiating table. He made the most of his charms for a whole new set of objectives, with fatherhood just around the corner. Lately, onlookers had reason to believe in his radical change.

His closest friends were quick to pass on to dogged media commentators that the Canley Vale export had ever been the grown-up; always thoughtful, considerate and serious-minded. All this despite the glitz and glamour of an entertainment world which couldn't get enough of him. Supported by Lynn's constant reinforcement, the young star learned to be content with his transformation, always ready to acknowledge its architect in front of the cameras.

'Lynn and I are private people living a very public life,' he told Michael Parkinson. 'Yes, we go to plenty of parties and enjoy ourselves with everyone else. But there's more to our partnership than the journalists were able to see up until quite recently. Acting's given me a chance to demonstrate this... as Lynn did a few years ago... and having a mass-reach platform for sharing ideas is important to us. I'm the world's greatest cynic but I've finally developed an optimistic streak. Well, most of the time anyway... I've experienced a great deal of success and happiness in a short time. I can't let this fact go unheralded, and movies are the best way I've found to shout about it without everything being about me.'

Candidly, Jeff blamed his apparent *volte-face* on two separate events. 'Doing my first film made me aware of the importance of what I say on a twenty-foot screen that millions are going to watch,' he said. 'There's a responsibility over and above what comes with performing with the band. I'm not saying I'm the good guy all the time now, but the fact that a film's not a one-off exposure that'll be forgotten in a day or two has made me wary of how easy it is to be characterised as something you're not, both on and off screen.'

Rumours and scandals about associations with nubile female company continued to hound the young man constantly. It went with the territory, he and his dream girl understood. Surprisingly though, it was his outspokenness on matters of conscience and humanitarianism which brought him yet more infamy and a great deal of *kudos* from showbusiness pundits and the general public alike.

As he explained to the packed auditorium, it was the fulfilment of a personal dream before his career had left the ground that had accelerated his change of focus. 'Being loved and being able to love someone so completely and unconditionally has made me wake up to what's really important in life,' he told his host. 'Money can buy us many things and take us all over the world, but the rewards to be gained from a rock solid relationship between two people who live for each other are second to none. For me with Lynn, the power of our relationship's heightened the importance of living life not for the stardom, nor for the benefit of earning megabucks, but for the sheer impact of making a difference. I tell you, Michael, it doesn't get any better.

'It's wonderful, everything that's happened, but I'm glad I've been able to deal with it sensibly. "Too much too soon" is all too easy in the entertainment world. I'm lucky I have a mental age of about forty-nine, although I realise I don't always behave that way...'

The mischievous celebrity turned to the studio audience for confirmation, which their keen feedback delivered. 'So essentially I can cope with anything. And the way Lynn and I've grown together's given me a real sense of who I am both here on Earth and spiritually. I got over counting the number of women I laid a long, long time ago.'

'Spoken like a man who's learned a lot and who still has a lot to give,' Michael Parkinson was as impressed as ever. 'The sky's limit may have already been reached, but I get the feeling that the real Jeff Diamond's life has only just begun. We wish you and the lovely Lynn all the best for the birth of your first baby in a few weeks' time. Ladies and Gentlemen, please join me in thanking our special guest tonight, Jeff Diamond.'

With a collection of music awards from Europe, the ink drying on another movie deal and promising in-roads made into conflict resolution talks in Africa, the veteran interviewer's prophecy was indeed coming true. Gerry oscillated between rubbing his hands with glee at the flood of cash into the Stonebridge Music coffers and tearing his hair out at the myriad commitments his VIP client scattered to all and sundry, while the newly-married Cathy Lane and her staff buckled under the fan-mail tonnage.

On the way back to Melbourne from London, Jeff telephoned his wife from Changi Airport in Singapore. 'Hi, angel. How're you going?'

'I'm well, thanks,' Lynn heard great excitement in her husband's voice. 'You sound happy! What's got you all fired up?'

'Yeah, I am. I just want to run something past you. I was thinking about it the whole flight.'

The young woman sat back on the couch, stretching out her encumbered body. 'Sure,' she laughed. 'What is it?'

The traveller took a deep breath. 'Baby, d'you remember when we went to Rome and climbed the Vittorio Emanuele memorial?'

'Yes,' she replied, curious as to where this was leading. 'The view was amazing.'

'Yeah. And do you remember the two bronze statues on top, one each side?'

'Unity and Liberty,' his dream girl successfully named them. 'What about them? What made you think of this?'

Lynn heard her husband inhale deeply, as if pleasantly shocked to find her on his wavelength from so far away. She felt the same way. There was a definite glow inside whenever their synchronicity crept up on them this way.

'Absolutely,' Jeff said, sniffing. 'I'm so glad it left an impression on you too.'

'Are you OK?'

'You bet. I had a parenthood attack on the plane and starting thinking about the enormity of it all, and I wondered about the themes of unity and liberty for our kids. I just think it's such a powerful corollary.'

'A message for them or for everyone else?' Lynn asked, unsure of how far he intended to go with this theme. 'Corollary or coronary?'

'Both, pregnant brain,' the poet teased with renewed enthusiasm. 'For all of us, to give them direction. Does that make sense?'

'Not really,' his patient lover giggled. 'I need more information. I didn't think about this all night actually. We'll have to talk about it more when you get home. Do you mean have the words as names?'

Jeff hesitated. 'Not sure. Sorry. No, not as names. Don't think so anyway. I think that'd be too much of an imposition on them. But I was thinking something along the line of some sort of dedication. Like instead of baptism, *et cetera*.'

'Hmm…' Lynn mused. 'Let's wait 'til you're home, and we can talk about it some more. I love you. Safe flying.'

'I love you too, angel. So much. Thanks for listening to my crazy rantings. And you're right. We need to be face-to-face to have this discussion. Not that I can get anywhere near your face anymore… I'll see you in a few hours. *Adiós a los dos*.'

Three Of Diamonds

'Michelle, are you awake?'

Lynn was sure the time had come. Knocking gently on the guest bedroom door, the young woman entered and walked over to the bed where her friend was sleeping. Her husband had been right to encourage her not to stay in the apartment alone.

'Mish, wake up,' she whispered, touching her lightly on the arm.

Michelle stirred and looked up to see Lynn standing over her. 'What is it? Are you OK? You scared me!'

'Sorry. Could you drive me to the hospital, please?' she asked, sounding agitated. 'I think it's happening. I'm sorry to wake you. You looked very peaceful.'

The athlete let out a sudden groan as a contraction took her by surprise. She sat down heavily on the bed, breathing through her mouth to ride out the pain.

'Oh, my God!' the redhead gasped. 'You're right. Are you in labour? Oh, my God! What do you want me to do?'

'Not panic, for a start!' Lynn replied, seeing her friend's sleepy consternation. 'We've probably got heaps of time, but I don't really know. I'm going to take a shower and get dressed. I wish Jeff were here. He wouldn't have a clue what to do either, but at least he'd take control.'

The lawyer chuckled, scrambling to her feet. She had grown very fond of her best friend's handsome lover and was jealous of the thoughtfulness he showed towards the pregnancy. Gathering some clothes together quickly, she listened carefully to her former schoolmate, who was endeavouring to sound as calm as she could.

'He'll never forgive himself if he misses the birth. I've already rung the Mercy. They're expecting us. Are you OK to drive? We could ring for a taxi.'

Truth be told, Lynn was more than a little frightened. She had been so well prepared by a complement of expert advisers, yet now the time was upon her, she felt more nervous than she had ever been in her life.

Michelle pulled on a pair of jeans and a shirt and tied her long, messy locks up into a ponytail. 'Shall I try and ring the airline while you're in the shower? I'm sure they can get messages to 'planes.'

'Oh, yes. Thanks. That'd be great,' her friend answered, breathless again. 'He's flying United. The flight number's written on the pad in the lounge. This is typical! Why couldn't it have happened tomorrow?'

Michelle gaped at the blonde Olympian in sympathy. 'Well, I'm glad it's not happening tomorrow 'cause then I would've missed it,' she countered, before qualifying her impetuous statement. 'Sorry. That was very selfish. Jeez! Look at you!'

The contractions were coming more frequently, and Lynn had beads of perspiration on her brow and cheeks, leaning on the bed and clutching her bulging abdomen. Her friend feared she was about to explode.

'Just think...' the visitor continued. 'Only a few hours ago, we were playing tennis. What do you want me to tell the airline staff?'

'Don't panic?' Lynn laughed, the contraction subsiding. 'Although, knowing Jeff, that won't make any difference. Maybe we shouldn't ring. He'll feel so helpless up there. Oh, decisions, decisions!'

The mother-to-be hesitated for a moment but then continued. 'No. I must tell him. He'd want me to. Just say that I've gone into the Mercy, and to meet me there. Does that sound OK?'

'That'll do, I suppose,' her best mate reassured her. 'Whatever you tell him, he'll draw his own conclusions anyway.'

'Yeah. That's true,' Lynn agreed. 'And then panic!'

The pair looked at each other and shrugged. They had grown up together, and so fast. The younger of the two was married and about to have her first child. For the elder, it seemed as if her life had marked time during her famous friend's adventures. She was still dating casually and avoiding the big commitment at all costs.

Simultaneously however, the two private schoolgirls appreciated their closeness. Lynn had invited Michelle to stay at the apartment while her husband was away overseas, both for company in her last weeks of confinement and just in case the baby decided to come early.

The sensible move had proved fortuitous. The baby was coming early.

'OK. Let's go,' they chanted in unison, as if plucking up courage to jump off the top diving board, before flopping back onto the bed in hysterics and grabbing for each others' hands.

'This is a big deal, Mish,' the superstar said, gripping hard when another spasm hit. 'I'm so glad you're here.'

As she climbed into the shower, Lynn could hear her friend on the telephone.

'Diamond. D, I, A... Yes. Mister Jeff Diamond. The singer... Yes, I know! I need to get a message to him, please.'

The water drowned out any further sound from the hallway, and the pregnant woman leaned back into the spray, feeling another contraction about to take hold. She pictured the airline staff flipping out in the office, knowing they were the first to break such exciting news. Within twenty minutes, both women were ready to go, overnight suitcase closed and apartment locked up like a fortress.

Michelle stopped her car in front of the main doors of the tall building to find Lynn waiting in the lobby, palms pressed against the window as she rode another contraction. The redhead ran around to the passenger side and helped the struggling celebrity, throwing her bags haphazardly onto the back seat. Within a couple of minutes, they had turned around, juddering over the double set of tram lines, and were heading along Victoria Parade. The hospital was less than a kilometre from their apartment.

'We should've walked,' the musician joked, finding the journey particularly uncomfortable in the little hatchback.

'Funny, funny,' her friend replied, the stress of responsibility weighing heavily.

The car radio was on in the background, emitting the type of bland music usually playlisted for five o'clock in the morning. The signposts were a little confusing, and the car circled the hospital until the pair worked out which door they required.

Pulling up outside the maternity wing, the Olympian squeezed her nervous mate's hand. 'Are you alright?'

Michelle nodded and got out of the car to help. 'Am I alright? I'm supposed to be asking you that,' she replied with a scared smile.

It appeared as though the entire nursing staff had assembled on the steps to greet their famous patient. Word had spread like wildfire, the friends marvelled. Lynn had dreaded this moment for several weeks, hoping no-one would take a photograph of her in this condition. Was she really that vain?

Taking a deep breath and smiling as broadly as she could manage, Australia's darling held her head high and marched purposefully into the building. Once inside, she relaxed a little, and a kindly, middle-aged staff nurse ushered her towards the lifts.

'Do you need a wheelchair, dear?' she asked, gasping as soon as she remembered whom she was addressing. 'I mean Missus Diamond. Sorry. I'm Maggie Thompson. I'm in charge of new arrivals.'

'That's OK! Thanks, Maggie. Please call me Lynn. No, thanks. I'm fine to walk.'

'She'll run if you give her half the chance,' Michelle piped up from behind. 'She was playing tennis this afternoon!'

'Shhh! It wasn't very strenuous,' the champion bleated in her own defence, scowling at her friend and lifting a finger to her lips to silence her.

Her unapologetic practice partner smiled back, knowing the athlete wasn't cross with her. The mum-to-be continued, shaking her head.

'My husband should be arriving after nine. He's flying home from Europe. I really hope it's not all over before he gets here.'

The nurse smiled at the beautiful woman, so well-mannered and graceful. The hospital staff had been informed during a meeting a couple of days ago that Australia's favourite daughter would soon be gracing them with her presence. Trying not to stare too closely, she noticed how little extra weight Lynn was carrying and that her wedding ring still fitted on the correct finger.

A huge fan of the Dyson family, Staff Nurse Thompson continually scoured the newspapers and magazines for gossip and pictures, and had prayed for an opportunity to meet the blonde superstar. Perhaps she would even manage to request an autographed picture before the celebrities returned home. She gulped at the prospect of having a personalised photograph of the baby who was starting a whole new Dyson generation.

And of course, there was Lynn's flamboyant and engaging husband. The conservative woman had initially disapproved of the match, as had many of her friends, fearful that the wild exhibitionist with all the hallmarks of a hedonist rocker destined to crash and burn after a few years in the limelight would soon leave the exquisite young celebrity high and dry.

However, in the eighteen intervening months since the couple's high-profile wedding, Maggie and her co-workers had begun to change their minds. The confident young man had revealed a sophisticated and altruistic side to his nature which had given the tight-knit nursing community cause to reconsider its position.

And now she would have the chance to see the couple together and judge for herself. How exciting! Plus, her daughters would be most affronted were she not to come away with at least one picture of the hunky Jeff Diamond!

Nodding and opening a door that led to the private delivery suites, the nurse gambled with a personal question. 'Is your husband looking forward to being a father, dear?'

Lynn smiled back a little tentatively. She had been told that certain newspapers had printed a story which had misquoted Jeff terribly when he had snapped a flippant reply to a reporter at the airport.

She breathed deeply and responded. 'Yes, thank you. We're both really looking forward to being parents. It's been a long nine months.'

A strong temptation crossed the dignified musician's mind to advise Nurse Thompson not to believe everything she read in the press, but the urge acceded to a sudden contraction. Not so naïve as to think such speculation would ever cease, the mum-in-waiting contented herself with the thought that their ordeal was nearly over.

The wealthy couple had spent many hours talking about the future with their children, sometimes deep into the night. There was absolutely no doubt in the young woman's mind that Jeff was looking forward to becoming a father. More even than for herself, she longed to provide him with the opportunity to give their offspring all the things his own childhood had lacked, whether materially or emotionally.

Theirs was going to be the happiest family in the world, discouraging insinuations notwithstanding!

Lynn managed a thin smile, the pain slowly retreating. 'Wow! That was a good one.'

'What do we do now?' Michelle asked, once they had made themselves comfortable in their new surroundings. 'Wait?'

The flushed woman nodded, shrugging and stretching her back against the angled mattress. Their small room was nicely decorated with flowers and paintings of peaceful landscapes and cherubic faces. It was a shame that no matter how much effort had gone into its homeliness, nothing could possibly disguise the stark, industrial furnishings and the odour of sterilisation fluid. There was a bank of buttons and lights at the head of the bed, which had creaked and rocked on its wheels as her tired body sunk down onto the springs.

The stunning celebrity looked over at her friend and giggled. 'Now I know it's time,' she whispered, shuffling again for effect. 'I haven't had that noise out of a bed for a few weeks.'

The solicitor looked shocked. 'Lynn, for God's sake! You shouldn't be thinking about sex at a time like this. I thought you were going to complain about how heavy it made you sound.'

'Good point,' the sportswoman laughed. 'That's what got me into this mess to begin with. Thanks for reminding me. Is there a radio in here? I wonder what's on TV at five-thirty in the morning.'

Lynn struggled off the edge of the bed again, only to be forced to sit down again by another painful spasm. She waved a dismissive hand to pacify her worried friend.

'These are starting to get annoying. I told Jeff we should have adopted,' the young star joked in an attempt to allay their fears.

'How can you be in such a good mood?'

Her ginger-haired lawyer shouldn't have been surprised at her resilience. She had seen the Olympic athlete in pain before, many times through their sporting careers, either in training or in competition. She knew how determined and stubborn Lynn could be when it came to giving in to adversity.

The older woman turned on the wall-mounted television and flicked through the channels. 'Nothing much.'

Another, much younger nurse knocked and entered with a tray of tea, instantly gaping at the sight of their famous patient. Michelle felt like telling her not to stare, her star-struck eyes ready to pop out of their sockets. Instead, the faithful companion stepped forward to take the tray from her hands.

'Where would you like me to put this?' the nurse asked the star upon whom she was hopelessly fixated.

'Thanks very much,' the defiant minder interjected. 'I'll take care of it.'

She took the tray from the young woman's outstretched arms and almost shooed her out. From the bed, Lynn was laughing.

'That was a bit heavy-handed. You know, that's exactly what Jeff does. Intimidates people until they turn round and walk in the opposite direction. Poor girl!'

Left to their own devices, having had the various call buttons and alarms explained, the two best friends settled down with a pile of outdated magazines, hoping the time would pass quickly. Michelle watched Lynn drift off to sleep at one point, only to be woken a few minutes later by another contraction.

***

Lynn awoke from another short doze and glanced over at the clock. She had become aware of excited voices in the corridor outside. Nine-twenty. Could it be? She hoped so. There couldn't be long to go now, judging by the frequency of the contractions and the increased hustle and bustle of the staff.

Michelle had also fallen asleep again, a magazine still open on her lap. Her school-friend smiled to herself, reminded of the many bus and aeroplane trips the pair had made growing up, attending tennis tournaments, athletics meets and netball carnivals with their team-mates. The flame-haired girl had always been a very heavy sleeper, and the others would often play cruel practical jokes on her. Many a time had she regained consciousness to find a lace of each shoe tied together or that a silly love note involving a random boy had been scrawled across a page in her exercise book.

The famous musician cringed as yet another sustained pain reverberated around her midriff, causing her to cry out. She concentrated on feeling grateful for such lovely friends and pictured herself in their midst and presenting her newborn for all to see.

She heard another loud shriek from outside the room, this time followed by a deep, throaty laugh which could only belong to one person. Sure enough, the door was flung open, and there stood the love of her life. Lynn's heart leaped into her mouth, and tears pricked at the corners of her eyes. His large frame filled the doorway, and his warm, smoker's voice resounded around the room in its inimitable fashion.

'Never fear, good woman. The cavalry is come!'

Jeff Diamond looked exhausted but clearly relieved to have arrived before it was too late and to see his wife faring relatively well. The young woman

468

knew his *bravado* was an act, since his eyes betrayed a familiar anxiety. She held her hands out to him, but withdrew them straightaway when a contraction seized her.

The twenty-five-year-old ran over to the bed, not sure what to do to help. 'Jesus, angel! Are you OK? That sounded painful.'

While the spasm gradually let up, Jeff bent over his dream girl and kissed her lips. The feeling of his stubble on her cheek and the smell of travel-weary after-shave unleashed a torrent of emotion. His concern was exactly the tonic she needed, and tears rolled down her cheeks. Saying nothing, her perfect stranger rested his forehead on hers and placed a huge, reassuring hand on her taut belly.

'It's been like this for hours,' Michelle said, from her chair in the corner of the room.

'Oh, hey, Mish,' Jeff grinned, slipping backwards from the side of the bed and walking over to give his wife's best friend a hug too. 'Sorry to ignore you. I'm a little preoccupied, in case you hadn't guessed. Thanks for taking care of Lynn so well.'

'That's OK,' the lawyer replied. 'I can understand. It's so good you got here in time for the birth. She was worried you wouldn't. I'll leave you guys alone now, shall I?'

Reluctantly, the young man noticed, the redhead returned her magazine to the pile and picked up her bag, beginning to make her way over to the bed to say goodbye.

'No! Where are you going?' Lynn asked, concerned. 'Don't go. Don't you want to stay to see it happen? Especially after all this time. Please stay, Misha. We'd love you to stay, wouldn't we, Jeff?'

'Absolutely,' he agreed without hesitation. 'You're on the team. Besides, you can pick me up off the floor when the time comes.'

The devoted husband had long been sensitive to the fact that his wife's closest female friend was essentially always just that: Lynn Dyson's closest female friend. Somehow, nothing exciting ever seemed to happen in her own life, and both celebrities guessed that she was secretly jealous of their success and happiness. Moreover, she had been there today when Lynn had needed her. He hadn't.

'Are you sure?' Michelle beamed. 'I'd love to, if you're sure you don't mind.'

'Sit down and shut up!' the bloated superstar joked before turning to look into her man's eyes. 'You've got a headache, haven't you? I can see it in your face.'

Jeff nodded, kissing her to stop her talking as another contraction rendered her breathless once more. 'The mother of all headaches, as a matter of fact, if you pardon the pun. It started about the same time I got your message. Funny that, huh? But now's not the time to be worrying about me. Let's concentrate on worrying about you.'

Making herself useful while the couple prepared for their intimate moment, their extra supporter handed round fresh glasses of water. The rock star had explained before that his headaches were like having a pair of invisible hands squeezing his temples and cheekbones almost until they caved in. His eyes had blackened rings around them, and his forehead was furrowed from the continual throbbing.

Lynn pursued her line of questioning, despite his futile attempts to distract her. 'Are you sure you're alright?' she asked. 'Do you need some food or anything? I'm seven centimetres dilated apparently, so you've got time. I'm sure the nurses have painkillers. This is a hospital after all…'

Michelle scoffed at her friend's statement of the obvious. 'Wow! You're so clever.'

'Really? Hospital? I told the taxi driver to take me to the nearest pub,' Jeff responded, grateful for the sympathy in her own hour of need. 'I'll get some Panadol in a while. I just want to make sure you're in good order first.'

Having spent such a long, long time in limbo, the jetsetter remembered how dumbstruck and helpless he had felt when the flight attendant gave him the airline's message. The remaining two hours of the journey had dragged on interminably, and he was never so pleased than when the wheels finally screeched onto the tarmac at Tullamarine Airport at eight-thirty-five.

To give them their due, he explained to the two women, the ground staff had been very efficient at accelerating his passage through immigration, informing him that his luggage would be sent directly to their apartment. There were occasionally advantages to being a "someone", they all agreed. A taxi had been booked to bring him to the hospital, but his paranoia convinced him that the rush-hour traffic was deliberately slowing their progress.

Seeing his wife and her faithful friend smiling and nodding along, the storyteller realised he was helping to reduce the tension in the room. He paused for a few minutes while another nurse entered and performed another round of routine checks on the celebrity patient. Lynn rolled her eyes when she saw him wink at the youngster's embarrassed smile, particularly when she then lifted the sheet to complete the latest internal examination. Nothing was private anymore, evidently!

Jeff shook his head at his wife's reaction, kissing her affectionately and wiping moisture from her face with a face flannel. He continued his recollection, saying that on arrival at the hospital, his first response had been exasperation at the number of people already milling around in front of the maternity unit. He guessed they were mainly well-meaning fans rather than journalists, all desperate to catch a glimpse of the new baby. Not a single person in Australia could have escaped the media's incessant fixation over the course of this pregnancy.

In the end, the driver had stopped as near to the doors as possible, allowing the respected father-to-be easy ingress through the surging shoal of well-wishers. Before he went inside, he had turned to wave at the crowd, promising to let them know.

And now he was staring into his wife's deep, blue eyes, wondering what lay before them. It was his turn to fail to contain his emotions, receiving a kind pat on the back from Michelle. How many hours would he need to listen to screams of pain and not be able to do anything about them?

When it came down to it, the father role seemed pretty useless so far. The proud sex-god's part in making this baby had been entirely pleasurable and comparatively short. Lynn's had been a protracted nine months, during which they had witnessed most of her clothes no longer fitting her body while she suffered the discomfort and indignity of her condition. All this time, although acutely in tune with what she was going through, his mates and business associates had encouraged his ego. How clever he had been to create half a person with the world's most beautiful woman!

Then to cap it all, his sweat-drenched but smiling saviour might easily have been going through the birth without him if his flight had landed any later. Although she might never admit it in so many words, Jeff knew she had not enjoyed being pregnant. She had lost out competitively of course, yet it was more the physical transformation which had been so hard to support.

This unexpected personality trait had vexed her husband. All her life, Lynn Dyson had been photographed as blonde, slim and beautiful. These last few months had seen her shying away from cameras, not wishing to be pictured as she grew larger, despite his special efforts to show her how attractive he still found her.

Jeff snapped out of his daze. 'Not long now before all this is gone,' he whispered, laying his hand on her bulge. 'I love you so much. I was so scared I was going to miss everything. I'm sorry I wasn't here when...'

'It doesn't matter,' his wife put her hand over his mouth. 'You're here now. And I love you too.'

Michelle returned to the room, holding out a handful of white tablets she had obtained from the desk. 'Here are some painkillers. How many do you want?'

Voicing his thanks, the king of vice helped himself to all four pills and downed them with a single gulp of water. The young nurse knocked and re-entered the room to check everything was OK. She gushed with great animation that *bouquets* of flowers were making their staffroom smell lovely. The *trio* thanked her politely before Jeff turned back to his wife.

'By the way, that's a nice dress,' he teased, running nervous fingers over the coarse fabric of her hospital gown. 'Haven't seen it before. Is it new?'

Everyone burst out laughing, including the junior nurse. Hooking her hand around his neck, Lynn pulled the comedian towards her and hugged him as hard as her body would allow.

'I wish this baby would hurry up and do its stuff,' she gasped, tracing her fingers down the side of his face. 'You look terrible. What a pair we are!'

Jeff scanned the room. 'Is there somewhere I can take a shower, please?' he asked the nurse. 'I'm wound up like a bloody spring here.'

'There's a shower in there, Mister Diamond,' she gestured towards the bathroom, 'but it's meant for patients.'

Without hesitation, Lynn hauled herself upright on the bed. 'That's alright. The patient's going too.'

Grateful amazement was written all over her husband's face as he helped her to her feet. 'Really? Are you sure you're up to it?'

Concerned that this effort was all for his benefit, he looked over at Michelle, who gave him a shrug of resignation. Once Lynn Dyson made up her mind, there was no stopping her. In fact, all three high-achievers were the same in this respect. The bathroom door clicked noisily, shutting the loving couple away from the rest of the world.

'Come here,' Jeff hissed, as he carefully put his arms around the struggling woman. 'Promise you'll tell me if you need anything?'

'Course I shall, you gorgeous mess,' Lynn smiled, kissing him. 'First off, I need you.'

This dark-haired Adonis truly was the perfect man. He had lost weight during his trip, she noticed, most likely worrying about leaving her at home alone. As their bodies pressed together, she found herself projecting forward to when the baby had arrived, making them a real family. Despite her discomfort, she took her time to admire his hairy, muscular body as he stripped off and prepared to climb under the shower.

'Is there room in there for someone the size of a bus?'

'Are you kidding?' the tired man grinned. 'Get in here!'

Between them, the ungainly pair untied the gown from around her throbbing frame and were soon both standing under a strong gush of water.

'Oh… This is heaven!' Lynn moaned in rapture, shifting her shoulders to take the full force of the welcome stream onto her back. 'Great idea.'

The lovers embraced and rode two contractions in quick succession. Somehow, now that they were on their own, Jeff felt completely calm and confident about the momentous task ahead. *No worries*, he thought. After taking turns at lathering each other up, it became patently obvious that a certain part of his anatomy was concentrating on a whole different activity. Lynn looked up as his erection brushed against her skin, and he smiled sheepishly, cursing such ridiculous arousal.

'Nervous tension?' she asked, giggling.

'Something like that,' the songwriter couldn't help but see the funny side. 'What a bastard I am, eh? There's your body going through nine levels of hell, trying to produce our baby, and all mine can think of is sex. That's men for ya. I'm sorry, angel.'

His voice stopped short, and adrenalin coursed through him. Purposeful, Olympian hands were already stroking his length firmly and regularly, as only they knew how. He cupped her face in his hands, crouching down on aching legs, and kissed her passionately. Her eyes indicated for him to stand up again, an order with which he fought not at all to comply.

'You don't have to do this,' he breathed, smirking, 'but you don't have to stop either.'

Lynn sank down onto the stool provided for patients, perching on its edge and trying to maintain her balance. She wondered how many women in labour indulged in such guilty pleasures in the maternity ward showers... Judging by how good it made her feel, she decided it should be included in the compulsory section of future pregnancy instruction manuals. The cold tiles were refreshing on her back, and her tongue found Jeff receptive and ready. Massaging her shoulders as her mouth swallowed his size and began to move on him, he tipped his head back against the wall and let the cool water run over his face, into his mouth and onto his chest.

'Angel, *je t'adore*. You are absolutely amazing.'

The wandering minstrel had never felt anything so erotic, and it wasn't long before he was on the verge of climax. The tension was draining out of his neck and shoulders, and the ache in his head had faded into insignificance. As the last vestige of self-control deserted him in a flood of raw energy and emotion, Lynn's body played its trump card, causing her to grip him so tightly that he cried out.

The clandestine couple collapsed onto the bathroom floor in a fit of suppressed laughter, both breathing heavily but for vastly different reasons. Jeff directed a channel of water into his wife's open mouth and pushed the hair back off her face. Not only did the mother of his forthcoming child look so beautiful, but she had miraculously relaxed him.

'Things are really starting to move now,' Lynn warned him, as they towelled each other dry. 'Looks like we sped the process up a bit. I don't remember reading anything about oral sex during labour in the birthing chapter, but maybe it's true. We'd better hurry. I wonder if they've guessed what we've been up to.'

'Who cares?'

The young man was ready for anything and anyone, scooping up his scattered clothing. To his surprise, his companion roared with laughter, and he looked over to find her propping herself up awkwardly on the toilet, her outstretched hand shaking with the strain.

'What's wrong with you now?' he scolded.

'I'm sorry. I can't help it. I've just seen what I did to you.'

Beckoning for him to come nearer, she pointed at the backs of his legs, just below his buttocks. Jeff tried to position himself so he could see the cause of such merriment, but the mirror in the bathroom was too high.

'What have you done?'

Lynn placed her hands back on the suspicious man's well-developed *gluteous maximi*, marking the exact spot where she had been hanging on a few minutes earlier. 'There's a matching set of four fingernail marks on each leg,' she chuckled, pressing into his skin. 'I must've really hurt you when that last contraction hit right at the wrong moment. I'm sorry. Didn't you feel anything?'

The patient continued to laugh, even though once more writhing in pain. Despite his concern, Jeff was keen to share in her happiness. Their lightness of heart would create an extra-special ambiance for their new human being to make its entrance.

'I'm glad my misfortune causes you such amusement, madam,' he replied with a heavy dose of sarcasm, fastening her sexy outfit with its three pairs of cords.

The couple giggled like naughty schoolchildren as they opened the bathroom door and ventured back into the main room. Fortunately, Michelle had fallen asleep in the chair again, and the two nurses were busy preparing piles of towels. Various monstrous pieces of equipment had been wheeled in and positioned next to the far side of the bed.

Lynn turned to her partner-in-crime and whispered mischievously, bundling her long, wet hair into a loose bun. 'I hope there aren't cameras in the bathrooms here.'

Her husband shrugged, kissing her damp neck and putting his hands on her shoulders to steer her back towards the bed. 'Make way for the amazing detonating woman!' he announced, making their snoozing friend jump out of her skin.

Maggie Thompson made her grand entrance a few minutes later, scrubbed up and issuing a barrage of instructions to all in turn. The next half-hour went by in a flurry of activity. Everyone shouted orders and words of encouragement to the pregnant woman, and the pregnant woman gave it all back in spades. Her two supporters proved to be towers of strength, alternating in their efforts to buttress against her gargantuan pushes.

'Resistance is useless,' Jeff countered, when she screamed her objections.

When at last the midwife told them that the crown was visible, the control freak couldn't resist the temptation of taking a look. Leaving his wife to her friend's care and attention, he paused for a second, wondering if this was something he really needed to see. *Yes*, he admonished himself. *You don't want to miss a thing, remember?*

'It's OK, angel. It looks like me.'

Staff, patient and other participants alike dissolved into peals of laughter, before the mother's body demanded attention again. Another fifteen minutes passed in the same vain until at last the miracle for which they had all been waiting rang out around the room like a fire alarm.

It was the sound of a pair of strong, healthy lungs uttering their first cry for help. While the attendant nurse bundled up the wriggling baby and readied it to meet its parents, the leading lady and her best supporting actors slumped back onto the pillows as one, all three heads resting against each other. None of them spoke. They were all too shattered, caught in a shared moment of incredulity.

'It's a boy,' the midwife proclaimed in the same matter-of-fact manner that she must have used on countless other occasions. 'Seven pounds exactly. Seven pounds on the seventh of the seventh. What a lucky number!'

The itinerant peacemaker looked at each woman in turn. Like him, both sported tear-streaked faces, and he kissed them one after the other, whispering his thanks. Once he had pulled himself together a little, Jeff congratulated everyone on a job well done, grabbing a towel and mopping his fevered brow.

Maggie, the middle-aged staff nurse, grinned from ear to ear as she handed the little white towelling bundle to its rightful owners. The new parents simply stared in awe at the silent, pink person lying there. His tiny face crumpled in a yawn, breaking the spell.

'You and me both, kid,' his father agreed, leaning forward and planting a soft kiss on the baby's head.

He then laid an equally gentle kiss on his wife's forehead, overcome with shock and happiness. The contrast between the hive of organised chaos ten minutes earlier and the surreal quiet of their union as a threesome left both stars a little bewildered.

'*Howzat?* We made him, angel.'

Michelle moved off the bed, telling the others that she was off to fetch her camera. The couple presumed she wished to leave them alone in their private peace, and the gesture was much appreciated this time. They were crying all over their brand new son, and Lynn brushed tear after tear off his face, watching his expression alter every time a drop landed on his skin.

'We did it,' she affirmed. 'We're parents.'

Jeff kissed his wife for the umpteenth time. In fact, he couldn't stop. His sister would be proud.

'You did most of it,' he corrected her. 'I can't believe this squirming thing was inside you all that time. It would've driven me crazy not to know who he was.'

The younger nurse brought her idols each a beaker of water and shyly stood by, glad to have witnessed the birth of the Diamonds' child. The new mum propped herself more upright and drank the entire contents straight down. Her husband poured half of his into her empty cup while the nurse disappeared for some more.

'Where's the beer?' Jeff joked, before turning back to address his wife and son. 'You realise that if you'd waited until you were supposed to, I would've been much better prepared.'

Lynn sniffed and smiled a knowing smile. 'Ah, but we've got something for you...'

She motioned to her handsome man to reach into the cupboard next to the bed, inside which he found the biggest cigar he had ever seen. It must have been all of twenty centimetres long and nearly three in diameter.

'Whoa! Cool, thanks!' he exclaimed, taking hold of the cellophane-wrapped Cuban. 'Where have you been hiding that? Now I see how you occupy yourself while I'm out of town. Quite an accurate replica, wouldn't you say?'

His wife was so deliriously drained that she was unable to laugh, nor even smile. In fact, she could only cry, leaning into her stoic husband's side. Catching Michelle's eye, he lowered one end of the cigar until it almost touched their baby's mouth, and the obedient photographer took a quick close-up.

'Pull yourself together, woman,' Jeff whispered, his own emotions running away with him too. 'Call yourself a Dyson?'

'Gorgeous, isn't he?' was all the young woman could say.

He planted another kiss on her flushed cheek and brushed the tears away from her eyes. 'You both are. Perfect.'

'Can I take a photo of you all now?' their friend hesitated.

'Why not?' the songwriter replied. 'The first for the family album. Might as well get us when we're at our most composed...'

The red-haired lawyer took several pictures of the new *trio* before Jeff took control of the camera and insisted she pose for some too. The staff delivered a tray of tea and biscuits, ravenously pounced upon between happy snaps.

'Would you like to hold him?' Lynn asked her husband.

'You bet!' he replied, scooping up the bundle of towel encasing their son.

Surprisingly, lifting their newborn for the first time felt like the most natural thing in the world. On the very rare occasion when he had handled anyone else's baby... and Gerry's Jenna was probably the only one, he realised... he had always been afraid of dropping or hurting her. Not this time; a fact that pleased him greatly.

Michelle carried on taking photographs of the father and son standing in the sunlight. Jeff looked authoritative and commanding with the tiny bundle in his arms, and his wife seemed relaxed, sleepy and incredibly serene.

A thought occurred to her. 'You made love in the shower, didn't you?' she accused them straight out, with a look of shock on her face.

Jeff feigned ignorance, and Lynn only smiled.

'No comment,' said the mother, without even opening her eyes.

'Might have,' her husband owned up, unable to dampen his male pride.

Their friend gasped. 'Oh, my God! You two are unbelievable!'

'I know,' the traveller laughed, only too aware of how selfish he had been. 'Any excuse, right?'

Still holding the baby, the front-end of the Diamond pantomime horse wandered over to the window and gazed down at the crowd still waiting patiently outside. Within seconds, someone had spotted movement; he had been positively identified. A cheer went up, and people began to chant their names. In places, the well-wishers sat five or six deep along the roadway, some even equipped with folding chairs, blankets and Thermos flasks to ward off the chilly winter weather. At least it wasn't raining, the humbled star thought. Would their fans have been that loyal? Yes, they undoubtedly would!

'There are heaps of people down there,' he reported back to the others. 'Shall I show them who we've made?'

'OK,' Lynn murmured, delighted to see that he was so happy.

Holding their son as far away from his loud voice as he could, Jeff forced the painted metal window-frame open and yelled down to the crowd below. The little mite didn't even flinch, to everyone's surprise.

'Hey, everybody! Look who I've found!'

Lynn laughed and cried at the same time at the sound of distant cheering and clapping. Eager fans issued their greetings while the enthusiastic celebrity held their child aloft for all to see. People began to shout at once, making it impossible to hear any specific question or comment, so the skilled crowd-pleaser made it up as he went along.

'He's a boy,' he shouted down to them. 'Seven pounds. Lynn's fine. Sorry she can't come to the 'phone, but she's late for tennis training. We'll see you later. Go home, please. It's cold.'

As the noise continued, Jeff waved goodbye and closed the window smartly, returning to sit on the side of the bed, where his wife was beginning to doze off. He placed the baby back into her arms, and she gathered him instinctively to her breast.

'So I'm playing tennis now, am I?' the young woman moaned. 'Thanks very much for your vote of sympathy.'

Her husband cocked his arrogant head to one side. 'Well, what would you have preferred me to say? "She looks like shit. Totally wasted. All sweaty and tired and completely exquisite."'

Lynn laughed weakly. 'OK. You're right, as always. I guess I got the better deal. Thanks, I suppose.'

The larrikin leaned forwards and kissed her lips, the baby becoming squashed between their chests. 'Sorry, mate,' he said. 'I'm going to have to get used to you being there. No freedom of movement anymore.'

His wife was too tired to do anything but smile. Prising the bundle out of her arms, Jeff handed their son to Michelle, who was grinning from ear to ear at having been included in her friends' most private celebrations. She knew it was only luck that had allowed her to be here. If this little baby whom she was now holding had arrived just a day later, his dad would have been on hand to take care of the whole situation, and she would have been one of the many people to receive a telephone call in the next day or two.

'Have you got a name for him yet?'

'Yes. But if we told you, we'd have to kill you,' her friend's husband chided.

The redhead laughed and put on a sad face. 'Oh, OK. I'll wait then.'

Lynn smiled but didn't open her eyes. They did indeed have a string of names for their son, but had decided that her parents would be the first to hear them. She wondered if her family had got wind of recent events via a sly newspaper tip-off. In her sleepy state, she tried to remember where each member of her clan was at the moment. Anna would be around town, most likely at the Sportsdrome. Junior was presumably local too, at football training as usual. She gave up at trying to guess her parents' whereabouts.

Michelle handed the baby back to his mother. 'Are you going to take me to lunch, Dad?'

'Lunch? Yeah, OK. Sure thing,' replied the new father, not having thought about his stomach in quite a while. 'Shit! I am a dad. It hadn't sunk in until you said that.'

Jeff looked over at his baby son, lying peacefully asleep on his wife's chest. His heart was full, but he didn't feel close to tears any longer. Reality was setting in at last.

'Whoa! Everything's changed now, angel. We have to be serious and sensible. It's frightening.'

Half buried in the deep, spongy pillow, Lynn's voice was faint but firm. 'Jeff Diamond, if you change, I'm leaving you and taking our baby with me.'

'Message received and understood,' he told her, leaning over the bed to give the lifeless dictator a long, lingering kiss. 'I love you so much. Get some sleep and ring me when you wake up. Congratulations, Mamá.'

The sports star's eyes were tired but full of love. 'OK. Thank you,' she sighed, hanging on to his hand. 'I love you. And so does he.'

As her husband left to take her former school-friend to lunch, once more reduced to tears at the thought of this little human already loving him, Lynn let her mind drift back to the early days of their incredible relationship. She smiled as she remembered his tiny, dreary apartment, near... but not that near… the river and the MCG. That first night they spent together, dreaming from his windowsill, was as fresh in her memory as if it were yesterday. *Cue for a song*, she thought.

'Jeff?' she asked in a soft voice.

He turned in the doorway. 'Yeah?'

'I mean it. Please don't change.'

'So do I, Lynn. I won't if you won't. *Je t'aime, mon amie.*'

No sooner had the door clicked shut than it was opened again by the senior nurse, who came to take the baby away. She explained to his mother that he would be bathed and put into a crib after they had checked him over. Lynn tried her hardest to pay attention and hoped she was lucid enough to have acknowledged the nurse's kind words. She allowed her baby to be carried out of the room and immediately drifted off to sleep. Her mind worried for a moment that something sinister might happen to her son if she let him go. She was becoming more and more like her soul-mate, she thought. Nothing would happen. Jeff would take care of everything. She was sure about that.

***

Before going to lunch, Jeff and Michelle stopped in at the penthouse apartment so that the traveller could change his clothes and make one important telephone call. He had promised Lynn that he would ring her parents, and for once it was a call he was dying to make.

'Marianna!'

The young man tried to sound wide awake and in control. However, he was failing miserably, the pressure of imparting their news to his wife's mother causing him to feel dizzy with emotion. He covered the mouthpiece with his hand and coughed to clear his throat.

'Jeff, is that you?' his mother-in-law asked. 'How's Lynn? Is everything alright?'

'Most definitely,' he answered, relaxing into the couch. 'She's had the baby. You're a grandmother.'

'Oh, darling! Really? Already? That's wonderful. When?'

The young man sighed, steadying his nerves so that he could recite the relevant facts and figures. 'About an hour ago, maybe an hour-and-a-half,' he thought back, checking his watch, which gave him no clues whatsoever. 'A boy. Seven pounds exactly.'

'Oh, my word! A little boy. Congratulations, dear,' Marianna chimed. 'That's marvellous news. Where are you now?'

'At home. Michelle was there too, and I've been told to make myself useful and take her out to lunch. You know... Stay out of my way, you no-good pain merchant.'

'Is Lynn asleep then?' asked the new grandmother, chuckling.

'Yep. I assume so,' Jeff replied. 'She looked very serene when we left. Jeez, he's so little...'

A fresh batch of tears started to roll down the new father's cheeks. He covered the telephone's mouthpiece again. Michelle had been sitting listening to the conversation, pretending to read a book she had found on the coffee table. She got up and put her hand on Jeff's shoulder.

'Thanks,' he mouthed, nudging her affectionately.

'That's lovely,' Marianna responded, picking up on the young man's highly-charged state and doubtless thinking back to her own children's births. 'I won't ring for a few hours in that case. When can we come and see you all?'

Jeff let out a heavy sigh. 'This evening, maybe? I don't know. We didn't get that far.'

'Bart's in town. At Admin,' his mother-in-law informed him. 'You should see if he's free for lunch too. He'd appreciate that.'

This was actually an excellent idea and one the proud man ought to have come up with himself. 'Cheers, Marianna,' he replied. 'I shall. Thanks for telling me.'

'I'll give you a ring later, darlings. Have a nice lunch. And thanks for ringing. Congratulations again. This is so exciting!'

They said their goodbyes, and the showman turned to his wife's school-friend, crumbling into a heap on the couch.

'Jesus, Mish!' he exclaimed. 'It's heavy going, being a dad.'

'You asked for it!' she laughed.

Jeff frowned and shook his head. 'That's exactly what Lynn would've said.'

He suddenly missed his beautiful best friend terribly, gripped by a rogue panic attack. They were supposed to be a family now. Why was he sitting here without her? *Get a grip*, he scolded himself.

'OK! ¡*Vamanos!*' the new dad announced, slapping his thighs and getting to his feet. 'We're going to take Big D out to lunch. You and me, Auntie Michelle.'

'Oh, are we? That's a good idea,' the lawyer agreed. 'Did Marianna suggest that?'

Jeff nodded, slumping down again and putting a hand to his head, feeling quite disoriented. 'D'you know?' he muttered. 'I can't remember the number for Admin. It's been so long since I've had to use it. Do you know it?'

Michelle looked in her bag for her address book. 'I don't. Not anymore, for the same reason. I should have it written down somewhere though. Hang on.'

Jeff punched in the digits that his wife's longtime friend read out from a dog-eared journal she had recovered from her handbag. He waited for the switchboard to answer, drumming his fingertips on his knee.

'Hello? Yes, thanks. Please could you put me through to Mister Dyson? It's Jeff Diamond.'

The superstar paused for the prescribed period which allowed the operator to get over the excitement of finding him on the line, and then waited some more for her to connect the call.

'Certainly, sir.'

The telephone was answered by Bart's personal assistant. 'Mister Dyson's office. Catherine speaking.'

'Hi, Catherine,' the caller opened. 'This is Jeff Diamond. Please could you put me through to Mister Dyson?'

Another intake of air could be heard from the other end. Without a word, the line clicked again.

'Jeff!' the statesman's booming voice rang out loud and clear. 'Good morning. What can I do for you?'

The younger man took a deep breath, coming straight to the point. 'Morning, sir. Can I buy you a beer, Granddad?'

A few seconds of silence followed. The celebrity had made a habit of delivering surprises to this man over the telephone, he realised, thinking back on the awkward post-proposal call he'd made from London. He shot Michelle a frightened look, enacting the great man in the process of having a heart attack, making her laugh aloud.

'A beer?' his father-in-law repeated. 'Good God! Has Lynn had the baby already?'

'Yes, indeed,' the songwriter chuckled. 'You have a healthy, seven-pound grandson. Congratulations, sir.'

'Grandson, eh? And many congratulations to you, Jeff! Excellent news. Everyone's fine, I assume?'

The young man thought he could hear a slight nasal tone in the stalwart's voice. Could it be that his boisterous, overbearing nemesis was falling foul of an emotional reaction for once?

'Thank you, sir,' the new dad replied. 'I didn't have that much to do with it, to be honest. Lynn's fine. Knackered, obviously. She's sleeping it off.'

'Name?' the Olympian had returned to his normal curt delivery.

'Yes, but not public knowledge yet,' his son-in-law stalled. 'We need to try it on for size first. I spoke to Marianna just a few minutes ago. She suggested you might be up for some lunch.'

The caller heard the sound of papers being shuffled on the big man's desk.

'Yes. Why not? That would be nice,' the sportsman seemed distracted. 'I have an appointment but I'll cancel it. This is much more important. It's not every day a bloke becomes an old fart.'

'You said it!' the millionnaire laughed. 'Michelle's coming with us too. We'll go to Chinatown somewhere, if that works.'

'Great! I'll ask Catherine to book for us. What time will you be here?'

Jeff looked at his watch again. 'Twelve-fifteen? About twenty minutes?'

'Okey dokey. See you in the *foyer* here then,' a modicum of excitement had even crept into the big man's response by now. 'Excellent. Thanks for the call, Jeff.'

'You're welcome. See you soon. *Adiós.*'

Drawing his hand across his brow, the songwriter gave Michelle an exasperated look.

'Let's go!' she said, grabbing his hand. 'Off to see Granddad, Daddy.'

The tired traveller smiled at her enthusiasm and once more wished it was Lynn he were lunching with and not her best friend. Once upon a time, he would have derived some perverted pleasure from the fact that he was heading out in public with another woman, ripe for the gossip columnists. But not today; not on the day he and his guardian angel had turned Bart Dyson into an old fart!

'Granddad, Grandpa or Pop, you reckon?' the redhead asked, on their way down Russell Street in a taxi.

'Who knows?' Jeff dismissed the difficult question, stifling a big yawn. 'Not Pop! Can't exactly see him going for that. Thank Christ! I expect Lynn and Marianna have already decided for him anyway.'

'Hey! I saw the drawings of your house,' the friendly woman changed the subject, sensing her companion was still a little overcome by the occasion.

'Yeah? Fantastic, aren't they?' he responded with more energy, thankful for a little light conversation to relax his confused synapses. 'D'you like the Spanish theme?'

'Yes. And the dogs!' Michelle laughed. 'In fact, 'specially the dogs.'

The taxi let them out in the circular driveway at the side of the Dyson Administration building. They ran up the steps and pushed their way through the revolving doors. Bart was ready and waiting, chatting with one the family's loyal security guards.

'Congratulations, Mister Diamond,' said Michael. 'Very good news. Please pass on my best wishes to Lynn.'

'Thanks, Michael. I definitely shall. I'm sure it won't be long before she brings the boy in to visit everyone. To scream your house down and all that...'

Father, grandfather and best-auntie made their way through the gardens where the couple's wedding photographs had been taken eighteen months ago, and through to the car park where a *chauffeur*ed Jaguar was waiting to drive them back into the city.

Unable to pass through the red-roofed gate into Chinatown in their vehicle, the passengers alighted on the corner of Elizabeth Street, exiting with James Bond stealth and ducking into the narrow laneway. Heads turned all around on the cool winter's day, and the threesome walked briskly through the Little Bourke Street Asian precinct and into a restaurant where the Olympic hero was greeted with appropriate deference by the staff.

'So!' Bart slapped the table with both hands, having soon dispatched the waiter with their drinks order. 'Details, please.'

Michelle leaned back in her chair to let her friend's husband have his moment of glory with the formidable father figure. She had known Bart Dyson a lot longer than she had known Jeff Diamond but hadn't had many opportunities to see how they interacted with each other. She was itching to see the two powerful men go head-to-head, given certain nuggets Lynn had offered about their former differences.

'Precious few details at the moment,' the new dad answered. 'Auntie Michelle knows more about when it all started.'

'In the middle of the night,' the lawyer took her cue, clearly chuffed with her label. 'Lynn woke me up about four-thirty-ish and said we had to go to the hospital. I was petrified of crashing the car, and she told me we just should've walked there.'

Both men laughed, easily able to imagine the sportswoman's straightforward approach to the matter.

'Then we were ushered into the building, and Lynn refused to use a wheelchair.'

Jeff shook his head. 'Stubborn, as usual.'

'That's my girl!' Bart contradicted.

Let battle commence, thought Michelle.

'By the time Jeff got there,' the young woman continued, 'her labour was pretty far gone. Contractions were so regular, and the staff were buzzing around like flies. Lynn was really calm though. Then Jeff turned up, just in the nick of time.'

'Hardly!' he interjected.

The storyteller pulled a face. 'Did you want me to talk about what happened in the shower?'

The guilty man coughed. 'Ahem. Moving on! I have no real idea what happened after that. All a bit of a blur, I'm afraid. I lost all track of time. The next thing I remember was hearing our son crying.'

Raising his beer bottle to his lips to hide the fact that he was close to tears again, Jeff looked down at the menu. Sympathetically, Michelle raised her glass to her friend's dad to buy the musician some time.

'Excellent,' Bart said. 'I remember that sound all too well. Pierces your ears, doesn't it?'

The younger man nodded. 'You're not wrong.'

'And then everyone cried a lot,' Michelle carried on with the commentary. 'We took some photos, and Jeff held the baby out of the window to the huge crowd downstairs, who all started cheering and clapping.'

'I did *not* hold him out of the window,' the celebrity objected, perturbed by the legal eagle's allegation in front of his father-in-law. 'I held him up to the window.'

'Where were you then earlier?' Big D enquired of his son-in-law.

'On a flight coming back from London. He's a week early.'

'Thought so. I spoke to Marianna after you rang. She's driving down this afternoon, so we'll drop into the hospital this evening if that's OK?'

'Sure thing,' the tired man agreed. 'Lynn'll be ready for anything by then. We should be able to introduce him to you by name by then too.'

'So what's the plan with official announcements?' Bart was full of questions. 'Have you got a statement ready to go?'

'Not that I know of,' Jeff answered, having given broader communication no thought whatsoever. 'I haven't spoken to Gerry yet, so he still doesn't know. Because he's early, it could be that even the Queen of Organisation hasn't prepared anything.'

Bart chuckled, dismissing the unthinkable observation. 'I doubt it. Let me know if you want any help.'

Michelle caught the young celebrity's eye, but he refused to react to the blunt barb. Their food arrived, and the conversation was allowed to divert onto other topics, such as plans for the Moscow Olympics and the year's Grand Slam tennis tournaments which were always high on the prickly man's agenda. After about half an hour, Lynn's father looked at his watch and announced his departure.

'Let me get this, Jeff,' he boomed, standing up and tossing his napkin onto the table.

'Thanks, sir. That's kind of you. We'll see you tonight at the Mercy.'

'You will,' Bart agreed. 'Michelle, will we see you this evening too?'

'Probably not. I've intruded too much already.'

'Rubbish,' came the quick retort, as Jeff reached for her hand. 'You can stick around as long as you want. It's great having you share all this.'

'Alright, if you insist. Thanks, Daddy,' the young woman replied, kissing the consummate gentleman on the cheek. 'I'm going to go now too. Are you going to see Gerry?'

Jeff nodded. 'I'll see if he's there. Yeah.'

'Say hi from me then,' the redhead requested. 'I should really go to work this afternoon, now all the excitement's over.'

Bart Dyson strode ahead, jumping into the sleek sedan which transported him back to Admin. The others walked through the grid-patterned streets and laneways criss-crossing the heart of the city, soon ending up on Exhibition Street. Before turning left onto Collins Street, Michelle stood on tiptoe and kissed Jeff's stubbly cheek again.

'Have fun, Daddy,' she said. 'Or get some sleep first. Then you'll be ready for happy families tonight.'

The young man groaned. 'Thanks heaps! Hope so. I keep trying to convince Lynn to move back to London. Life was much more peaceful there.'

'Ah! Don't be like that,' his wife's friend whined. 'We missed you. It won't be this frantic for long.'

'Sorry, Mish,' Jeff agreed, feeling guilty. 'I don't mean to sound ungrateful. Thanks so much for everything today. Thanks for being there when I wasn't.'

Michelle hugged him. 'Stop beating yourself up, you idiot. Go and see Gerry and then get some rest.'

The pair parted company after fending off a bunch of excited office workers clamouring for autographs. Jeff managed to slip into the rear entrance of 333 Collins Street and up in the lift to Blake & Partners without further assault.

'Jeff!' Paula chimed, her fingers diving into Gerry's diary, worried that she had missed something. 'Did you have an appointment?'

'No,' the company's most famous client responded. 'I was just passing. If he's busy, don't worry. I'll ring him later.'

Paula stood up and peered into the executive's luxurious office, only just tall enough to see over the stripe of frosted glass. 'There's clients in there but they've been in that meeting for ages. You can wait if you like.'

Jeff looked at his watch. He was feeling pretty tired and was keen to take Michelle's advice.

'No, thanks,' he told his mate's cute personal assistant. 'Can I just leave him a message, please?'

'Certainly,' Paula agreed, flirting a little and taking advantage of a moment with her most handsome visitor while her boss wasn't watching. 'Did you want to write it down? Is it a secret message?'

Jeff laughed. 'No. Not particularly. Not for long anyway.'

The young woman looked confused, so the compassionate man put her out of her misery. 'Lynn's had the baby. We have a son.'

His manager's leggy secretary fairly jumped out of her seat, shrieked and ran around the desk to give her boss' main meal ticket a giant, insubordinate hug.

'Wow! Your baby? Congratulations! That's huge news.'

Jeff broke out of her grasp just as Gerry's office door opened.

'What's going on?' the businessman was annoyed. 'Paula? Oh, hello, mate. Might've known it'd be you causing a disturbance among my female staff.'

'Sorry, Gerry,' Paula said, blushing and sitting down as sedately as she could.

'Yeah. Sorry, Gerry,' Jeff repeated and winked at the young woman. 'My fault. Are you still in your meeting?'

'Evidently not,' the impatient accountant snapped. 'What's up?'

'Paula, please would you pass on my message? I have to go now,' the star requested, turning on his heels to march towards the lifts.

'Yes. Lynn's had a baby boy,' the dizzy employee proudly relayed to her boss.

'What? Already? For Christ's sake! Wait a minute...'

Gerry ducked his head back into his office and excused himself from his clients, asking his assistant to apologise for the delay and to serve them some coffee. He ran after the fleeing newsmonger, darting into the next available lift.

'Mate!' the Irishman shouted at Jeff's back, loping across the ornate ground-floor lobby area.

His old friend was halfway to the main exit onto Collins Street by the time he had been spotted. He span around on hearing the familiar, classy yawp. The esteemed business manager was running towards him at a fair rate of knots. Pausing on the steps, the two men embraced warmly.

'You prick!' Gerry yelled in the musician's ear, grabbing his right hand. 'Congratulations, mate. When?'

'This morning,' Jeff informed him, tears welling up again. 'Amazing, isn't it?'

'Absolutely. Everything OK, I hope. A son, you lucky bastard. Have you wet the baby's head yet?'

'Yeah. Thanks. Very OK. Michelle and I took Big D to lunch just now. Look, I'm rooted, mate. I'm going to get some sleep before going back to the hospital this evening. Maybe tomorrow night?'

'You're on!' the busy executive slapped his client hard on the back. 'Give me a ring when you know your movements. Awesome, mate! Give Lynn a big kiss from me.'

'I'll do that with pleasure,' Jeff agreed, shaking Gerry's hand again. 'Cheers, mate. I'll talk to you tomorrow. You'd better get back to your meeting.'

The celebrity jumped into the first taxi at a nearby rank and made it back to the penthouse in no time. His baggage was waiting for him on the landing, having been abandoned in his rush to leave the airport. He checked the answering machine for any flashing light summoning him back to the hospital, but there was none. Climbing into bed, he was hit with another wave of blessed relief. He gazed across at Lynn's empty side of the bed and looked forward to it being occupied again.

So they had a son! The interminable wait was over, and they were a family. How about that! The image of the newborn's peaceful, scrunched-up facial features was already clearly etched into Jeff's memory. He soon drifted off to sleep, pondering life as the Three of Diamonds.

Jet-lag

The telephone rang by Jeff's ear, waking him with a start. He picked up the receiver without even opening his eyes, taking a second or two to remember why he was in bed in broad daylight.

'Hello?'

'Hey! It's me. Were you asleep? Sorry.'

'No. I *am* asleep,' the caller's semi-conscious husband corrected her. 'What d'you want, Mamá?'

Lynn hesitated. 'Mamá?' she repeated. 'That's lovely.'

'*Sí. Es muy preciosa.* It suits you, angel. How're you feeling?'

'Pretty good, thanks,' the young woman's bright voice sounded refreshed and happy. 'Tired and very sore in certain places.'

'No shit!' Jeff laughed, sitting up and wiping the sleep from his eyes. 'You won't be cycling for the next few days, I guess.'

The new mum groaned. 'Yuck! That's a ghastly thought. I feel sick just thinking about it.'

'Sorry, angel. Couldn't resist,' he teased. '*¿Com' está el pequeñito?*'

'Very small and very cute. He's listening, by the way, so don't be rude about him.'

Jeff imagined the tranquil scene in this morning's hospital room and wished he were with them. 'Can I join you over there?'

'I hope so. We have to see if he likes his names.'

The intellectual was already on his feet, stoked that Lynn hadn't started without him. Compared to the lengths to which they had gone in selecting names for a boy and a girl, they had spent no time at all on the process of unveiling them to their recipient.

'Great! I'm coming over now. See you in half an hour. Don't go anywhere.'

Buoyed by the humour in his wife's *au revoir*, Jeff dressed in tracksuit pants and a sweatshirt, grabbing his wallet and a single key. He was at ground level and out of the door in twenty seconds, ready to run the flat kilometre to the Mercy Hospital in record time. There were still plenty of people hanging around outside when he reached the maternity wing, all hungry for information.

'I don't know anything,' the casual superstar confessed. 'I've been at home while they slept it off. You might as well go home too. Thanks heaps for watching over them. We'll make an announcement soon.'

Lynn was standing up with their son in her arms, rocking him back and forth, when her husband entered the room. He paused in the doorway to feast his eyes on the glorious sight, hands folded across his chest and in complete admiration. After a while, the young woman turned around so that their son's face came into view, and he walked over to kiss them both.

'You look gorgeous, Mamá. "Slow Rockin'" just got a whole new lease of life.'

'Thanks,' the singer smiled at the reference to her recent hit. 'So do you. You look much better than earlier anyway. Very relaxed. Did you get some sleep?'

'Yeah. A bit. Until someone rang me,' Jeff teased. 'Michelle and I took your dad to lunch.'

'I know. Mum told me. That was a nice thing to do. Do you want to hold him?'

The young man nodded, raising a hand to stroke the baby's face. His narrow eyes blinked as his dad's finger came towards him, and a tiny hand pushed against the edge of his blanket. Instead of seeming fragile, as Jeff had imagined, the little tyke looked robust and ready for anything.

'Say hello to your dad.'

'*Buenos tardes, pequeñito. Te amo,* mate. *Gracias por estar con nosotros,*' the songwriter spoke softly, before coming clean to his wife. 'It wasn't my idea to take your dad to lunch. It was your mum's.'

'Oh, OK,' the new mother shrugged, guessing that her husband was annoyed with himself for not making the conciliatory gesture off his own bat. 'I don't care whose idea it was. It was still nice. Was he happy?'

'Yeah. I think so. In an obstreperous sort of way,' Jeff chuckled, joggling the lightweight up and down. 'So... Are we going to anoint him with his official identity? We can't leave him nameless. Doesn't seem right.'

Lynn nodded, perching on the side of the high hospital bed before deciding the position was too uncomfortable. Lounging back against the pillows, she held her hands out to receive their heir while the tall man took his place beside her.

'I'm nervous,' she confessed. 'It's a big thing to do, to name a person.'

The wise man couldn't agree more. 'Hmm... I was thinking about that while I ran over here.'

Wide-eyed, Lynn looked into her husband's smiling face, and they indulged in a long kiss. Whispered words of love made no impression on the dozing infant, lying peacefully while his parents prepared themselves.

'He won't remember this moment,' the father said, to steady their nerves. 'Not consciously anyway.'

The tennis champion took a deep breath in. 'He's a boy, so you should do it,' she chickened out.

'What? Where did that logic come from? You cooked him, so you should do it.'

His dream girl scoffed and kissed the baby's cheek. 'See? Arguing already. That's no good, is it?'

'OK!' Jeff proclaimed, his voice loud enough to elicit a reaction. 'Someone's got to take control here. And get used to this, *hijo nuestro*, because there are already two control freaks in this family. Join the queue.'

'Hey!' Lynn chimed in jest. 'I said that this morning. Great minds think alike.'

The father lifted the bundle that was their son and tilted him upright so that he could look both parents in the eyes. Nerves fluttered briefly in his stomach when he felt Lynn's breath on his cheek, but he reined them in, speaking slowly and with adequate solemnity for the occasion.

'Welcome to this crazy world, Ryan Jeffrey Blake Dyson Diamond. You've made us into a family,' his voice cracked a little. 'and you are truly loved. This is Mamá. She's the most beautiful woman in the world, and don't you ever forget it.'

The happy woman put her arm around the orator's shoulder, crying softly at the tender and poignant dedication that had been delivered to their son. 'And this is Dad, or Papá, *si hablamos en español*,' she added. 'He's the god of love and knows everything worth knowing. So that's something else for you to remember on your first day. We're going to call you "Jet", if that's alright with you?'

The famous firstborn proffered no objection to his names, nor to his induction into their family, save that Jeff felt his legs kicking against his thighs. He let the bottom of the wrapped bundle down gently on his wife's lap so that she could experience the weird sensation of him dancing away.

'Tripping the light fandango already? Please don't try and run away, Jetto,' she warned the little mite. 'Not yet anyway. It's dangerous out there. Your time will come.'

The lovestruck mother let out an involuntary sob, prompting the Master of Ceremonies to relinquish control of their new toy. They were in uncharted territory now, and time would tell how good they were at sharing.

'Hey,' he said, crying himself too. 'You should be happy, angel.'

Lynn leaned into him. 'Oh, I am. So completely happy. Are you?'

'Unimaginably. Couldn't be happier, Jet.'

As the light faded on the seventh of July, away from the winter chill outside, the couple told their third Diamond all the minute details about his new world. He learned about the joining together of their apartment with the one across the landing, the new house being designed for the Mount Eliza block, his dad's cool Aston Martin, his uncles and aunties, his grandparents on both sides, and their plans for two cartoon dogs to be shared around depending on who was travelling where.

'Look! We've bored him to sleep,' the young woman whispered, realising that the baby had nodded off in her arms.

On cue, Jeff produced some muted snoring noises next to her, genuinely open to joining his diminutive *compadre*. Lynn giggled like a girl when she saw his closed eyes and similar vacant expression.

'Wake up,' she nudged him. 'Mum and Dad'll be here soon.'

'Shit!' he moaned, opening his eyes in mock alarm. 'Sorry, I mean... I don't know what I mean. I have no substitute swearwords for the protection of delicate, under-aged ears.'

'Sugar? Why? What's wrong?'

'We haven't got anything to offer them. I was planning to bring in some champagne and some beers, but I was in too much of a hurry to get back to you guys and forgot.'

'Oh. That doesn't matter. Dad'll bring everything, I'm sure.'

'I know,' Jeff grunted. 'That's exactly why I wanted to do it.'

Lynn gave her husband a frustrated glare. 'Will you please stop competing with my father? They won't expect us to provide for them. You'll get your chance to one-up him soon enough.'

At that very moment, a host of inquisitive faces popped up at the window of their room. Marianna knocked politely before Maggie Thompson opened the door to make sure her star guests were ready to receive visitors. The staff nurse fluttered and fussed in and out of the room, extremely excited to be surrounded by almost a complete suit of Dysons.

'Hi, Mum! Come on in. Thanks, Maggie.'

Jeff rose to his feet and strode over to the *troupe* filing into the rather confined space. Anna followed her mother, then came Sandy and finally Bart. They all exchanged congratulatory greetings with the new dad, but he was soon forgotten when their collective gaze landed on Lynn and the newborn.

'This is Jet,' she announced in triumph.

The little bundle was raised high as if it were the Wimbledon Ladies Singles trophy, which had been claimed by Britain's Virginia Wade this year, a fitting tribute to Queen Elizabeth II's Silver Jubilee. Anna had reached the semi-finals, before being turfed out by the top seed, who was more than twice her age.

'Jet!' the family repeated.

'Hello, Jet!' the gymnast added for good measure.

The new dad stood aside with Sandy, both nonplussed by all the exuberance. He rolled his eyes at Lynn's younger brother and received a tacit smile in return. The little sister was very excited and couldn't wait to see her first nephew's face up close.

'Oh, wow! He's so tiny!' she exclaimed.

'Shhh!' Lynn requested. 'Don't shout, please. You'll scare him.'

'Sorry,' the ten-year-old whispered. 'He's so tiny.'

'I know. He can make a lot of noise though. You should've heard him cry earlier before I fed him.'

Bart stood back too, after having given his daughter a quick kiss and taken a cursory look at his grandson. 'Bearing up?' he asked his son-in-law.

'Yeah. I'm fine, thanks, sir,' Jeff replied. 'We're doing well. Keen to get out of here and into some semblance of normality.'

The old stager nodded. 'It takes a while, mate. Can I crack open a bottle?'

Mate? The only dark-haired person in the room had certainly not been expecting that! He glanced across at his beautiful best friend, but she hadn't been within earshot. Had his imposter status been repealed, if only temporarily for this special occasion?

'You can, sir,' the songwriter replied, dismissing his guilty competitive streak as well as he could. 'I'll see if I can find some glasses. Or plastic cups at least.'

Lynn watched the handsome man leave the room. Her family was firing a barrage of questions in her direction which she was doing her best to field. Was the baby feeding well? Had he smiled yet? When were they getting discharged? How tall was he? What was it like changing the first nappy? What was his full name?

'His full name is Ryan, the king, Jeffrey, after his dad, Blake, after Gerry, Dyson, after you lot, Diamond,' the proud mother recited, taking a deep breath both before and after. 'Ryan Jeffrey Blake Dyson Diamond. Wow! That's the first time I've said it out loud in full. Does it sound OK?'

Marianna clasped her hands together. 'It sounds perfect, darling. And "Jet" as a familiar name. Was that your idea?'

'Yes, but Jeff likes it,' she confirmed. 'And I think Jet does too.'

The rock star returned with a stack of white plastic cups. 'This is the best I could rustle up. Who wants some shampoo?'

Everyone raised a hand, including the new arrival, courtesy of Anna.

'Excuse me?' Lynn scolded her son. 'That's not a very good habit to get into so young. Only a sip.'

Laughter echoed off the bright, white, gloss-painted walls. They could all hear Marianna's best lecturing expressions coming back at them, and as one they turned to look at the matriarch.

'She's quite right,' the new grandmother shrugged, not prepared to be the butt of their joke. 'Mothers are always right.'

'Hear! Hear!' Jeff chanted, daring a sarcastic inflection along with his round of applause, while Bart popped the cork on one of the champagne bottles which the visitors had brought with them.

His son-in-law did the same with a second bottle, and they filled several more glasses than there were people in the room. Jeff and Sandy took the spares out to the staff and invited Maggie to share in their toast and to take some photographs. The mature woman clasped her hands together in abject delight, the invitation beyond her wildest dreams, and she dissolved into a giggling mess even before she had sipped from her cup.

The new grandfather took a deep breath and began to make a speech before hearing a surreptitious cough from his wife. 'Jeff, I'm so sorry,' he obediently deferred to the father of the moment.

'No,' the peacemaker declined. 'Go for it. The floor's yours.'

Big D shifted his feet, choosing his words carefully. 'Very kind. To Lynn, Jeff and little Jet... Thank you for allowing us to share your birthdate. Our first grandchild. That's something very special indeed, quite apart from the fact it makes us feel old.'

Everyone laughed. Lynn looked at her beautiful black stallion, wondering how old he was feeling today. She was dealt an impish wink as her answer, which she took as a very good sign.

'We welcome you, young Ryan, into our family,' Bart went on, 'and hope you'll spend many a weekend and holiday out at Benloch with the rest of us. Whatever your future holds, we wish you every success and happiness. You have two very loving and capable parents, and we're all ready and waiting to lend a hand. Let's drink to baby Jet, and to Lynn and Jeff.'

'To baby Jet, and Lynn and Jeff!' the family and invited midwife repeated, lifting their glasses aloft around the room before taking their first gulp.

Anna succumbed to a coughing fit at the unfamiliar feeling of bubbles up her nose, for which Sandy teased her as only brothers can. Jet was frightened by the sudden cacophony and began to cry.

'Sorry,' the girl said to the baby, who soon settled in the arms of her big sister. 'I didn't mean to scare you. Is he OK?'

Seizing his own moment under the bright fluorescent tubes, Jeff waved his hands to quieten the chatter. 'Thanks, Bart and all of you, for coming this evening,' he responded. 'On behalf of Lynn and our son... and I still can't say that without getting emotional... we're very happy to have Jet welcomed into our extended family. I suppose all that remains is to find out whether it's Granddad or Grandpa, and Grandma or Nana.'

Marianna looked at Bart, who demurred with good grace. 'Grandpa and Grandma, I think,' the elegant woman stated. 'Is that right, dear?'

The Olympian shrugged again. 'Either, either. Both make me feel equally ancient.'

'Alright!' Lynn took over. 'Grandma and Grandpa it is. Thanks! That's the most complicated part of this evening over. Drink up!'

Maggie took the next batch of souvenir pictures, with the whole clan closed in around the bed, thrilled to bits with her vital role in the proceedings. Following this, Jeff asked his shy brother-in-law to take one of the three Diamonds, remembering how good an eye the teenager had, before requesting the jolly midwife join them too.

Photographs, drinks and questions all done, Marianna called a halt, insisting that her daughter's family get some rest. Bart and Sandy shook the new father's hand, and the songwriter bit back tears when he realised how far he had now been accepted into the stalwart's favour. Everyone prepared to leave with kisses all round, and soon only an array of white plastic cups remained as evidence of their presence.

Once more with the room to themselves, Lynn breathed a long sigh of relief. 'Phew! That was exciting, wasn't it, Jet?' she said to her son, who was beginning to fidget.

'Did you want me to get out of here?' Jeff asked. 'To get some rest and do whatever you need to do with him?'

'No. Unless you want to shirk your fatherly duties?'

The twenty-five-year-old feigned innocence. 'Duties?' he enquired. 'I can't feed him. I don't have the equipment.'

'No, but you have hands that can change nappies,' his wife grinned, holding Jet out at arms' length.

'Hmm...' he mused, unable to engineer an escape clause fast enough. 'Rats! I guess you're right.'

The happy couple placed their son on the change table and began to unravel him. The tiny, pink body with its clamped umbilical cord took the young man by surprise, and he hooked the pair of writhing feet between his supple, guitar-playing fingers. The infant resisted his father's grip, remarkably strong for someone so defenceless.

'This is the first time I've seen more than his face and hands,' Jeff observed, blown away by how perfectly-formed Jet's small, wrinkly toes were. 'I never thought to check that he was complete.'

The young woman laughed. 'He's complete.'

'Of course,' her man changed his tune, boastfully pointing at the two of them. 'How could he be anything but perfect?'

Lynn slapped his arrogant arm. 'Mum told me Julie's pregnant too. They didn't want to steal our thunder, so they've been holding off telling anyone.'

'Cool! That's great,' the generous songwriter responded, kissing his wife on the lips. 'Jet, you're going to have a cousin soon. How about that? Instant playmate. We should ring them.'

'Yeah. We should. I need to feed him first.'

'Now this I have to see,' the comic smirked, fondling his wife's full breasts. 'Even though I may get very jealous.'

'Oh, for God's sake,' she frowned, pretending to be exasperated. 'Maybe you should go home.'

It felt completely natural for Jeff to see his dream girl lift their son towards her breast and rub his lips with her nipple. He was right. It did make him jealous, but it was also a beautiful sight. At first, Jet refused to show interest, so the instinctive father let some milk drop onto his finger and gently massaged the baby's mouth until the liquid came in contact with his tongue.

'You like that then? What are you waiting for, mate? Get stuck in.'

The patient couple repeated the process until their baby began to open his mouth before the milk touched it. It was a different story when Lynn tried to coax him onto her nipple the next time, when he was still not tempted to suckle.

'This is going to be painfully slow going, Pavlov, unless you get your act together,' the doting dad complained, kissing his wife's lips. 'I may have to take over and demonstrate how it's done. Let's try again, mate.'

Before long, Jet had cottoned on and was feeding happily from Lynn's breast. Jeff took a seat on the other side of the bed to watch the satisfying show and then to snooze. He could hear the sound of his lover's regular breathing and the occasional slurping noise when the baby's mouth became disengaged from its tap.

The traveller was soon fast asleep, with his head lolling at what looked like a very uncomfortable angle against the wall. Lynn swathed Jet in his blanket again and paced around the room, waiting for him to drop off too. Mission accomplished with comparative ease, she lay him in his crib and put herself back to bed. The television had been on since before her family had arrived, with the volume down very low. Lynn daren't turn it or the light off, for fear of disturbing her tired husband. He looked so contented that she allowed a few more tears of joy to escape in silence.

Sadly however, their rest was short-lived. A night-shift nurse burled through the swing door to check on mother and baby, causing them all to awaken rudely. Jeff shook his head and rubbed his crooked neck.

'What time is it?' he asked, before looking at his own watch.

It was just after eight o'clock, and pitch black outside. The couple telephoned Lynn's brother and his newly-pregnant wife to congratulate each other on their happy news, and to impart all the gory details as a sneak preview into the footballer's future.

When Maggie entered their room again a while later, more quietly than the previous attendant, to see if Lynn wanted some more painkillers for a good night's sleep, she found all three Diamonds out for the count, limbs entangled on the elevated, single bed. She picked up their camera and took a sly picture, as she had done for countless other couples before them. Despite her valiant attempt to exit undetected, the sound of the door clicking shut as she left woke both new parents.

'Jeez! It's so dark out there. Did you want me to get lost now?' Jeff asked, stretching and almost overbalancing off the side.

'No. Unless you want to. I'd love you to stay here if it's not too squashed.'

Her husband smiled. 'Perfect,' he replied. 'I didn't want to go home to an empty bed. I'll sleep in the chair. Or on the floor. Wherever.'

Jet slept soundly for the next few hours, giving the celebrity couple a chance to eat dinner. Both were famished, following their hospital meal with almost the entire box of chocolates left behind by the Dysons. After a final round of checks and tests, they settled down in their stark billet and switched off the light, leaving the television on while the news was showing.

The contented superstars were only half paying attention, even when coverage of the faithful crowd in front of the hospital building flashed into view. No doubt, they would see it all again, many times.

***

In the morning, the duty nurse found the famous mother sleeping comfortably in her bed, with her baby sleeping equally comfortably in his crib beside her. The new dad, on the other hand, was sleeping decidedly uncomfortably on the floor, his head crooked against the plastic seat cushion of a chair and with one foot wedged halfway up the side of the room's only cupboard.

With her *crêpe*-soled shoes squeaking on the linoleum and a tray sliding noisily across the surface of the cupboard's top, the woman's blundering entry made Jeff stir. Yet it was the sound of his own shoe hitting the tiles as his disturbed foot slipped down to the floor which actually woke him.

The nurse tittered. 'Oh, I'm so sorry. How long have you been there?'

The drowsy musician breathed deeply for a moment before responding, first checking on his wife, who was laughing from her raised vantage point. 'No worries,' he smiled and shook his head. 'I do a lot of sleeping on 'planes. I can sleep in pretty much any position.'

Lynn shot the prone man a fond flash of her big, blue eyes. Hang on a minute? Who was this man? The real Jeff Diamond or an imposter? Yes.

That's right. He was the new Jeff Diamond, husband, father and totally sane person. As if reading her mind, he shrugged and hauled himself to his feet. His neck was stiff and his back sore from sleeping at such a strange angle, but boy, did he feel pleased with himself!

'Good morning, angel,' he said, kissing his smiling wife. 'And good morning, Jet.'

'It is a good morning,' the new mother replied, sitting up in bed and wincing at the pain of moving for the first time in several hours. 'Ow! That's so sore! Lift him out, please. Is he awake?'

Jeff took hold of the tiny mite and whisked him up into the air. 'Yep. He's awake, but he's thinking. Like father, like son. Good man.'

'Thinking about sex probably, in that case.'

'*Mais bien sûr!*' her husband scoffed. 'What else is there to think about first thing in the morning?'

'You're amazing,' Lynn swooned. 'Can you believe how different you are? I love how happy and together you sound. And what's all this "I can sleep in any position" business all of a sudden?'

Before the songwriter could account for his uncharacteristically good mood, the junior nurse entered the room again to take the patient's blood pressure and to ask if she needed any more painkillers. She also informed them that a Mister Blake was on his way in to see them, and that he had rung earlier, while they had still been asleep.

'Gerry? Yikes! I'd better take a shower. I have to be presentable.'

'For Gerry?' Jeff cried out, encouraging their son to ridicule her panic. 'I don't think so, do you, mate? It's only Gerry, angel.'

But the superstar was already making a run for the bathroom, snatching a pair of pyjamas from her overnight bag to replace the hideous hospital gown. Her husband took full advantage of the empty bed, stretching out with the towelling bundle balanced along his shirt buttons. He heard the sound of water gushing and could scarcely resist the temptation to join her.

It was definitely too soon for a repeat performance, the young man smiled to himself, marvelling again at the miracle of childbirth and wondering why he wasn't more nervous at having been left in charge of their precious creation. Instead, he lay his head back onto the pillow and instantly fell asleep again.

Jeff exchanged places with his wife a few minutes later, both ready just in time. The suave businessman had taken a detour on his way to work. He breezed through the line of private rooms with a huge *bouquet* of flowers, and judging by the raucous laughter coming from the corridor, the couple had no doubt that he was up to his usual lecherous tricks.

'Ahoy there, me hearties! 'Tis me. These are for you, mate,' he joked, pretending to hand the floral arrangement to his client.

After first snatching the *bouquet* out of Jeff's open arms, to complete his premeditated stunt, the clown then noticed Lynn's hands were busy with a much more important object and handed the gift to his friend after all.

'How are you, you clever lady?' he asked, leaning over and leaving a sloppy kiss on her lips. 'You look well. And is this the heir to the Diamond fortune?'

The radiant celebrity smiled down at the wriggling form. 'Yes. This is Jet.'

Their bombastic manager awkwardly held out his hand to the baby. 'How do you do, Jet. I'm your evil Uncle Gerry. The handsome one.'

'Right!' Jeff scoffed behind them.

'Listen, guys,' the accountant whispered. 'Sorry I can't stop long, but I've got clients coming in at eight-thirty.'

'You can speak normally,' Lynn chuckled. 'He's awake. It's quite easy to tell. Open eyes kind of give it away.'

'Oh, OK,' Gerry feigned innocence, wagging a finger at the facetious woman. 'I still don't know how to do babies. You'd think I'd have caught on by now. Anyway, there's something in there for when you get home. Use it. You're paying for it.'

The young parents gave each other a confused look but thanked their friend profusely nevertheless. Bestowing another quick kiss and a handshake around the room, the executive turned and exited as quickly as he had appeared. The new parents burst out laughing as embarrassment lingered in the air along with their guest's strong after-shave.

'He didn't even look at the baby,' the sportswoman smiled, pulling a face on behalf of her son. 'He's so transparent, isn't he?'

'Sure is,' her man agreed. 'He has to be seen to be doing the right thing. Who cares if he really does it or not? D'you want tea? Breckie? Sex?'

Receiving the response he had anticipated, the twenty-five-year-old opened the envelope which Gerry had tucked among the flowers. Along with a card that had been signed by everyone in the office, it contained a glossy marketing brochure.

Jeff flicked through its pages. 'For fuck's sake!' he cursed, turning it round for Lynn to see. 'D'you know what he's given us?'

The young woman looked up. 'No. What is it? Can I see, please?'

The father skimmed the leaflet through the air carelessly, and it veered off and landed on the floor. Retrieving it from under the bed, he then dangled it in front of his wife's face while she breast-fed, stealing a kiss in the process.

'An at-home chef for two weeks?' she exclaimed. 'Does he think we can't cope? Bloody cheek!'

'*Exactamente,*' Jeff agreed, bending down and stroking her forehead with one hand while fondling both her breast and his son's face with the same finger of the other. 'Bloody cheek is right. I'm as good at collecting take-away as the next man.'

'Actually, it might be nice though,' Lynn mused. 'Lobster Thermidor for breakfast. Click our fingers, and there it is…'

The world-changer shook his head. 'Na. Not on my watch, lady. That's the stuff of holidays. Aren't we supposed to be living a normal life? At least for a few weeks, while Jet's new and we're both at home together, I want to be a normal family.'

His dream girl nodded, moved to tears by her millionnaire's simple request. 'Yes. I know. I'm looking forward to it too.'

'Good. You OK?' Jeff asked. 'Do you know when you're being released?'

'No,' she replied with a grin. 'Sometime today, I expect. Do you have anything planned for today?'

'Nope. Nothing. I thought I'd stay here for the next few days. Then when you've got it all figured out, you can send for me.'

From beneath his mother's frown of disapproval, Jet made a smacking sound with his lips, making them both laugh again.

'Hey! I quite agree,' Lynn told the little commentator. 'That's not on, Dad. You can brave the supermarket and get some supplies this morning, so we can cancel the Roux Brothers.'

Her husband shook his head in mock resignation. 'So far, this fatherhood lark's not quite what it's cracked up to be.'

The next hour-and-a-half passed over a leisurely hospital breakfast, improved by more light-hearted banter. The couple regularly found themselves staring for long, silent periods at their new arrival, who seemed very content to be the centre of attention. Michelle had telephoned to ask if she could visit during her lunch-break, and her friend optimistically advised her to call again before she left the office in case they had been discharged.

Sure enough, once Staff Nurse Thompson came back on duty at midday, their wish was granted. After a brief lecture on baby maintenance, the new family was free to go. Jeff checked out of the window to see if the coast was clear, trying to remember where his car was parked.

'You ran here,' his wife reminded him, much to Maggie's amusement.

'Oh, yeah! So I did! Well, we're running home then,' the handsome man quipped. 'You ready? You take the ten kilo' suitcase, and I'll take him.'

Lynn drew the little bundle into her chest. 'Very funny.'

'You're gorgeous,' the joker leaned down and kissed her forehead. 'I'll go now. Hopefully, no-one'll spot me and send the hordes back.'

The famous musician slipped out through a fire door on the hospital's ground floor, darting down a side road which ran perpendicular to Victoria Parade. Within minutes, he ended up on Albert Street and continued running towards the CBD, with his baseball cap pulled down low. He soon reached their apartment building and stopped in front of the entrance to the basement car park. Unfortunately, its keys were upstairs. Another piece of bad planning, he rued.

Still breathing heavily, the star in disguise met Sue Jenner in the lift.

'Jeff!' the architect cried out as the doors opened. 'Where have you been? Who are you running from?'

Chuckling, the penthouse resident leaned back against the mirrored wall and removed his cap. 'I've come to collect the car, but the keys are in the flat.'

'Oh,' Sue replied, nonplussed by the cryptic message. 'That was careless.'

'Lynn's had the baby,' Jeff blurted out. 'They're coming home now. You'll have to come up and say hello.'

The woman's mouth dropped open, and she jumped forward to kiss her attractive but sweaty neighbour. 'Wow! Congratulations! What have you got? Boy or girl? Oh, that's so great!'

'A boy. Jet.'

'Jet? As a nickname?'

'Yep,' the proud dad nodded. 'You know how the Dysons never call themselves by their real names. I don't understand it myself, but I like the connotation.'

'And it's enough like Jeff to be Junior,' Sue laughed. 'Is Lynn well?'

'Yeah. She's damned fine, thanks,' he answered, hit by another wave of emotion.

Why did his resolve always collapse as soon as Lynn's name was mentioned? *Get a grip! You're a father now. Be sensible.*

'She's beautiful and loving the whole mum thing.'

'Fantastic!' Sue exclaimed. 'I knew she would. We'll give you a ring when Don gets home. But you must tell us if it's not convenient.'

'Oh, it'll be convenient,' the superstar insisted. '*Mi casa es Sue's casa*, as I've said so many times before. Boring, isn't it? OK? *Adiós.*'

Their friendly architect stepped out of the lift at her floor, waving cheerfully. The doors slid closed, and the celebrity continued up to the top and closer to his car keys. A quick shower and a slice of toast later, the black sports car leaped into life and prowled into the hospital car park in no time, coming abruptly to a halt in a vacant space outside the front doors.

Good, the driver thought, looking around. No-one had rumbled him. The coast was clear.

Finding himself on an energetic high, Jeff bounded up the four flights of stairs and arrived back in the ward to the sound of familiar female laughter. Michelle spied him through the pane of glass in Lynn's door and pulled it open to let the new dad inside. Mother and baby were packed up and ready to go.

'You look like you've been evicted,' Jeff smiled, leaning over to kiss his wife. 'Homeless with two mouths to feed. Don't worry, love. I'll take you in off the streets. You look trustworthy.'

'Aw, thanks, guv,' Lynn put on her best Pygmalion accent. 'That's right kind o' ya.'

From the window, their friend informed the couple that a small, nosy group of staff and visitors had congregated around the Aston Martin. It was a safe conclusion to jump to, they all conceded. The car's famous owner gathered various bags and other items into his hands and stood back to allow the women to exit first.

'Do you want to take Jet?' the beaming mother asked him.

'No,' Jeff winked his thanks for her gracious gesture. 'You should be seen with him first. That's what they all want to see. I'm just an also-ran in this episode, and rightly so.'

Bidding their farewells to the ladies at the nurses' station, the foursome and all their paraphernalia descended, preparing to face the music. By the time they reached the front doors, there were at least a hundred well-wishers standing in a circle around the car. An excited cheer went up as soon as they were spotted making their way to the lobby.

A number of children were prompted to run forward by their parents, some clutching soft toys and flowers. Michelle took the unscripted role of present-bearer and scooped them all into the boot and slammed it down hard.

With his arm proudly around Lynn's shoulders, the striking father guided her and their newborn through the throng. Opening the passenger door for her, he took Jet out of her arms and held him aloft for everyone to see.

'This is our son, Jet,' he proclaimed, with a few opportunistic cameras being pointed at the happy scene. 'He's a baby, we're well, and Lynn's gorgeous. Nothing else to report, so we can all go home now.'

The good-humoured crowd clapped, watching their idol hand the bundle carefully in to his wife's waiting arms. The ginger-haired lawyer squeezed into the cramped space behind the driver's seat, and the new father waved once more before climbing in and shutting the door firmly.

'OK,' he said, turning the key in the ignition. 'Home, Jet.'

The throaty grumble from the powerful engine pushing air through the exhaust caused gasps of admiration as it passed by. The passengers flexed their wrists once more behind tinted glass, and the car pulled sedately away and turned onto Victoria Parade, heading back towards the city. Before the motor even had time to warm up, they found themselves pulling into their car park and waiting for the electric gates to open.

Once inside the apartment, Lynn handed Jet to a delighted Michelle, claiming she intended to put on a pot of coffee. Instead however, she followed her husband into the bedroom, where he was dumping their bags. Equally delighted with this unexpected turn of events, he span around at the sound of his name and smothered her into a bear-hug.

'I love you so much,' the twenty-one-year-old said. 'It's so good to be home with you. We're going to be so happy.'

'Christ, angel. I love you too,' Jeff replied, scared to hold on too tight, not only for fear of hurting her but also for his own self-control. 'Look at you! You're not bulbous anymore. You've deflated.'

Lynn chuckled, looking down between their bodies and seeing the floor for the first time in a few months. 'I still feel inflated. Not so much, but I still do.'

'I'm sure everything'll be back in its proper place in no time.'

In response to these encouraging words, her hip pushed against his growing erection and nudged up and down in a slow, tantalising rhythm. 'You feel as good as usual,' she whispered.

'Angel, I can't do this,' Jeff laughed, pushing her away. 'I'm way too wound up, and you should know better. You've just had a baby. Or did you forget already? D'you know how long Michelle's staying?'

Reluctantly, the tennis champion saw the error of her ways, leaving the aroused man to unpack her bag. She found her friend still rocking Jet from side to side, humming and strolling back and forth along the breadth of the lounge room windows and gazing out over the balcony.

'Are you OK?' Lynn asked. 'He's very peaceful with you.'

'Oh, he's a real sweetie,' Michelle gushed. 'He just keeps murmuring and staring up at me.'

The mother looked into her son's eyes, which seemed to recognise her immediately. 'I wonder what he makes of it all... I wonder whether this is what he expected.'

'What he expected?' the solicitor repeated, astonished. 'You're sounding way too like Jeff for your own good these days. He just needs feeding and changing and to be allowed to sleep in a comfy place.'

The rear-end of the Diamond pantomime horse decided to keep her mouth shut. How different her friend's attitude was to the parenting ideas she and her magic-man had cultivated over the last nine months. Either perspective could be construed as correct, but poles apart nonetheless.

'Who's for a beer?' Jeff shouted from the doorway between the lounge and the hallway. 'Or coffee?'

Both women opted for tea, so the obedient star swallowed a sly stubbie while the kettle boiled. He would be sensible tomorrow. He was also hanging out for a cigarette but vowed not to give in to temptation.

Their drinks finished, Michelle saw fit to return to work after her extended lunch break. With the front door closed on their new family situation, the couple breathed a sigh of contentment on finally being alone together. Jet had been fed and was snoozing in the cot next to his mother's side of the bed, and both parents stood mesmerised by the regular sighs and snuffles of the household's new addition.

'Are you coming to bed?' Lynn invited, holding her arms out.

'How?' Jeff enquired, surprised to be asked this question.

'How? How soon you forget!'

The young woman grabbed her lover's waist and began to undo his pants. He felt ashamed when a certain part of his anatomy needed no convincing, knowing he ought to desist. It was an acute turn-on to have his dream girl back, unencumbered and attentive. He cupped her plenteous breasts in his hands through her blouse, checking her eyes for any hint of pain. There was none.

'Are you sure you're ready for this?'

Lynn nodded, freeing his penis from his undies and kissing it tenderly, going back for more when she felt it jump in her hand at the delectable sensation. 'Yeah. As long as you treat me gently,' she smiled. 'I missed touching you.'

Jeff let out a long groan. 'Jesus! I missed you touching me too.'

Both with one ear open for noises from the cot, the pair caressed each others' skin all over, taking the sex-starved man to the edge and then pulling back again several times. He figured she wouldn't want him even to look at her body, having not allowed him to remove her clothes, still coming to terms with her new, formerly-pregnant state.

After a few minutes of passion, the aroused man became aware of a distinct downgrade in his wife's urgency. He took hold of her tiring hand and removed it from his shaft. 'I think you've bitten off more than you can chew, superwoman,' he whispered, stroking her forehead and pushing the hair off her face. 'Allow me.'

The boy from Sydney's west came by his own hand while staring into the soul of his son's mother, her fingers running riot over his most sensitive areas. It was the sweetest experience, and they lay locked together for many minutes at its end.

'I'm sorry,' Lynn sighed. 'I just ran out of steam all of a sudden.'

'Don't apologise. You shouldn't feel that way. Look what you've just done?'

'I didn't do it though,' his wife whined, looking down to where Jeff's hand had not yet moved.

'Not that!' he chuckled. 'You've just given life to a person. Our own little person. That's huge! Take a day or two off, Mamá.'

A tear escaped from the beautiful woman's eye and ran onto the pillow. Jeff leaned across and kissed it away, his own heart equally full.

'Why don't you get some sleep?' he suggested. 'You don't need to feed him for a while, do you? And I can do everything else. I'll wheel him out.'

Lynn nodded. 'OK. You're right. I shall. Thanks, Dad.'

The new parents freshened up quickly in the *en suite* before pulling the curtains across to shut out the early afternoon sun. Once his wife had made herself comfortable in bed, Jeff rolled the crib across the floor just as their son's eyes opened.

'Hello, Jet. Were you listening to all that? I don't think we should hide the fact that we love sex from him,' he said, hearing muffled laughter. 'I want our kids to know they came from pure heaven.'

Lynn was too tired to give this idea much critical thought. 'Hmm... Don't the text books tell you that it can mess with their minds? You're just an old hippy at heart.'

'Guilty,' the musician admitted. 'That theory's more about subjecting them to shouting and other violent experiences, I'd guess. We'll do some research. It'll give us something to do while you're resting.'

'Now? Where will you research that?' Lynn rolled over, laughing at his determination. 'Are you going to take him to the library on Day Two?'

'Why not?' the intellectual joked. 'He's a Commonwealth citizen. Well, he will be once he's registered. All those tight-lipped, sex-starved librarians'll just have to keep shushing us if he arcs up.'

'OK,' Lynn capitulated, anticipating a disaster but not game to argue. 'Whatever... Have fun, guys!'

***

Lynn remained in a deep sleep when her husband returned home, not two hours later, with a loose collection of blanket and son in one hand, a pile of books in the other and a set of keys dangling from his teeth. Jet had become a little fractious, which the new dad interpreted as hunger. The apartment warm after the wintry temperatures outside, he stripped the baby down to his nappy and laid the little squirmer into his cot. Attempting to pacify him, he played with the tiny hands and feet until Jet made it clear that the game was no substitute for food.

'Sorry, mate. I can't help you,' the father sympathised, picking him up. '*Tenemos que tu mamá despierta.*'

But Mamá was awake. 'Back already?' she asked, coming up behind them and stating the obvious. 'Was it a bad move?'

The fresh-faced beauty held out her arms for the newborn, who was transferred with some relief. Her eyes alighted on the collection of books which had been dumped on the coffee table, and her husband shrugged.

Accepting a loving kiss, she cuddled Jet into her shoulder and kissed his crying head.

'Hungry?' she asked the scrawny, mostly-nude form. 'We'll have to set Dad up better, won't we?'

Lowering herself cautiously down onto the leather cushion, Lynn prepared to meet the boy's demands. Leaving the connected pair in the lounge room, the ill-equipped parent disappeared for a few minutes, returning with two steaming mugs of tea. Jet was soon suckling calmly, watching his mother sipping her own drink.

'That was an interesting experience,' Jeff recounted. 'We didn't get much attention walking down La Trobe Street 'cause he's so small. No-one even knew he was there. I just tucked him inside my jacket like one of those rich bitches in Paris with their rat-like pooches.'

Lynn laughed at the image he had conjured up. 'Really? Don't stand for this treatment, Jet. Cruelty to babies.'

Her man continued, filled with love at the scene beside him. 'Then once we were installed in the library, I laid him down on the floor at my feet until I found a bunch of books. We drew quite a crowd at that point, but we made it plain that we were busy, so people backed off and ogled us from a distance.'

Lynn reached her hand over and squeezed the storyteller's knee. 'That's lovely. I can just picture it,' she smiled. 'I hope it was a clean floor. Was he quiet through all this?'

'Yeah. Totally,' Jeff affirmed, stroking the baby's head. 'Happy as anything. You're obviously going to be a keen student, mate. So then I went to one of those armchairs in the old section, balanced Jet out along my leg, wedged against the side of the chair, and browsed through the books to see which ones I wanted to borrow. That drew more of a crowd, admittedly, but he refused to sign autographs. He was quite rude, in fact. Gave 'em the silent treatment.'

'*Primadonna*,' Lynn teased her son.

'Anyway... That's enough about our first adventure. Are you feeling better? Are you hungry?'

'I am, actually. Are you going to dial a chef?' the young mum ventured with a grin. 'What shall we have? I have to say, it would be kind of good to have everyone over next week or at the weekend and have someone else cook a slap-up meal for us.'

'You'd better take back the "Bloody cheek" comment then,' her husband scoffed.

The next few days on their own with Jet were spent in endless happy experiments in parenting. He began to put on weight, and Lynn was pleased to find her normal body shape returning quite rapidly. Jeff took their son to watch his mum play tennis with Anna, and they had all messed around on the court with him.

'So if Jet'd been a girl, what were you going to call her?' the ten-year-old had asked.

'Not telling,' her sister answered. 'We might want to use those names later.'

'Are you going to have another baby? Already?'

The doting dad nodded, but his wife's head shook petulantly. 'No, thanks! And what do you mean by "already"?' she groaned. 'Jeff can have the next one.'

By the time another two weeks of domestic bliss had passed in Melbourne, the intellectual found himself itching for a change of scene. Not that he wanted to leave his family behind... far from it, in fact... but more because there were so many issues screaming for his attention around the world and precious little he could assist with from deep in the southern hemisphere. After all, as the couple discussed, he was the passionate, parasitic front-man.

Also during this first *exeat* from his period of compassionate leave, the couple's focus was brought sharply back to reality with the announcement that Elvis Presley had been found dead in his Graceland home. The traveller had paid the ailing man a visit only a few days earlier, recognising the trouble he was in only too well.

Lynn and Jeff talked and cried for a long time over the telephone, mourning the loss of someone they respected so highly and who epitomised the word "superstar" to them. The songwriter searched his soul for answers as to why he hadn't tried harder to arrest the artist's downfall, dissecting who had wanted what from whom and harkening back to his own dark and lonely years.

In a deliberate effort to pick up the pieces and rebuild their mental strength, his wife, stranded at home on the other side of the world with their child, summoned her musician friends together to work up her most ambitious album yet. It contained an eclectic mix of ballads, up-beat numbers and even a couple of jazz covers.

Lynn celebrated her twenty-second birthday in September by choosing her first car, an exercise her rev-head partner enjoyed being invited to manage. It was a long time since he had been car shopping for his sleek, black beast. Moreover, the privileged society girl remained suitably disinterested in anything more than the ability to ferry her son safely from "A" to "B". Extravagance was not in her nature, despite always having been surrounded by life's finery. With a nod of approval from Gerry, they decided on a silver-grey BMW 323i, a model which had been newly introduced that year, and the Bavarian machine looked *petite* and ladylike in its parking space next to its big, British brother.

Junior and Julie's own baby boy arrived three days before Christmas nineteen-seventy-seven, giving the growing family a whole host of reasons to celebrate at the end of the year. Bradley Alexander Thomas Dyson the Fourth was welcomed into a world of cheesy music and brightly decorated rooms, promptly allocated the nickname of "Sonny", as was traditional and to avoid confusion with his other two surviving namesakes.

Being photographed together for the occasion of his parents' second wedding anniversary, Jet was utterly nonplussed by the small creature making strange noises, not recognising his own very recent past in this little cousin. Jeff was particularly enamoured by another picture from the same shoot, which had been taken from behind Lynn while she was carrying their son. With smiling boyish looks developing under blond curls, his cute face was framed next to his mother's striking profile as she twisted round to look over her left shoulder, her "JL" tattoo prominent in the foreground.

Bart and Marianna had kindly agreed to look after both grandchildren while their elder children took their partners out for dinner on New Year's Day. Neither couple had the stamina to paint the town on their free night, all four deprived of sleep and satisfied with the simple pleasure of a few hours to themselves.

'Now we really have Jet-lag!' the songwriter joked to his brother- and sister-in-law. 'This teething thing would go so much better if we could feed him whisky in large quantities.'

'Lynn tells me you're already speaking to Jet in different languages,' Junior changed the subject, toasting the other couple with his own brandy glass.

'Yes,' his sister nodded. 'There's all this research we've been reading that says bi- or multi-lingual kids find it easier to grasp complex concepts. Plus, we'd like them to be able to travel around the world easily. The plan is to employ nannies from different countries, to help speed up the learning process.'

A sleepy Julie leaned into her husband's bulky frame, having difficulty staying awake. 'But how can they tell which language they're speaking? Do you speak one language on Tuesday, for example? French Tuesdays...'

'Nothing so scientific,' the rock star shook his head. 'It doesn't matter whether they know if they're talking French or Spanish. It's more forming associations with people and things.'

'And accents are so much easier to perfect when muscles are developing so fast,' Lynn added. 'What was that quote from Mick Mountain?'

The footballer caught his breath. 'Mick Mountain? Who the hell is he? Sounds more like a wrestler than a scholar.'

'*Michel de Montaigne,*' the philosopher chuckled. 'We're very disrespectful to our wise wrestlers, as you can see! *Monsieur de Montaigne* said, "I would that a boy should be sent abroad very young, and first, so as to kill two birds with one stone, into those neighbouring nations whose language is most differing from our own, and to which, if it be not formed betimes, the tongue will grow too stiff to bend." In other words, what she said!'

Affection burned in his wife's eyes, stoking the intellectual's own inner fire. Two years wed that day, and she had treated him to a scintillating floorshow before they had joined the Dysons for dinner. Married life was sublime, despite the Jet-lag, their master plan unfolding without a hitch.

'He should stick to wrestling,' the brunette across the table quipped. 'I didn't understand a word of that. Perhaps I've still got pregnancy brain. Can we talk about a nanny too, June?'

'You're kidding, aren't you?' Junior exclaimed. 'Our baby's a week and a half old. Not even my dad'd send you back to work yet!'

Julie grinned. 'Who says I want to go back to work? I just fancy the idea of leaving him with someone else, so I can have lunch with my friends, *et cetera.*'

The Diamonds watched on as their dinner companions sparred, with playful hands battling under the table and out of sight. Jeff checked his watch and allowed a yawn to escape, setting his gorgeous wife off too.

'Keeping you up?' her brother teased. 'Know how you feel. Let's get out of here, shall we? It's been fantastic catching up, but I'm cactus. Are you guys staying at Benloch tonight?'

Lynn confirmed that both couples would see each other again for breakfast, along with their two younger siblings. She paid for their lazy meal, which had now stretched into its third hour, and her husband hailed a passing taxi in Lancefield's almost deserted main street. It would only take ten minutes to reach the enormous homestead.

Once back in the bedroom that had been remodelled this year to accommodate their extra family member, the young woman gazed around the room and reconstituted a few childhood memories for their son. He had stirred when Marianna lifted him out of the bouncer where he had spent the evening entertaining his grandparents, but it didn't take long for him to doze off again on a full stomach.

The anniversary couple made love at a snail's pace, humidity contributing to the tropical atmosphere. The act was interrupted twice by new lyrics requiring to be given *sotto voce* while their baby slept. Attempting to stifle their wine-infused giggling when the keyboard stool suddenly gave way under their combined weight, they ended up on the carpet in a tangle of naked limbs.

Orgasming simultaneously in raptures, the exhausted pair stretched out, flat on their backs in the sticky summer air, listening to the wind whistling through the trees behind the house. Tomorrow was their last chance for a number of months to visit Coldwater Creek, planning an escape after breakfast.

Jeff launched himself backwards onto the mattress, having cleaned his teeth and snatched a cool shower before making the most of the remaining night hours. He rolled over to his right to kiss his beloved dream girl, full of triumph after sex and relishing the ecstasy beaming from her beautiful face.

'And for my next trick…'

'That was a trick?' Lynn chuckled.

'One of my finest, wouldn't you say?'

His wife paused for a couple of seconds. 'Not bad, Captain Marvellous. Does it work out the same every time, this trick?'

'No. I hope not. That's not my intention anyway. Always something up my sleeve.'

The amiable drunk tipped leftwards onto his back, moaning in pleasure as strong fingers traced lines through his chest hair.

'Go to sleep,' Lynn whispered.

'Yeah, I should. That's also my intention. I need to leave you alone.'

'Yes. You do, I'm afraid.'

***

Driving fast along the Autobahn in a rented Porsche, Jeff Diamond was in a real hurry to reach the hotel. Having been in Germany for two weeks to promote his newest album, he had opted to collect his wife from the airport rather than have her arrive by taxi. Frankfurt's city streets were well signposted, but they had already made two wrong turns in their haste.

'You look great, by the way,' the songwriter muttered, frowning because he had found himself in the leftmost lane at a set of traffic lights when he needed to turn right. 'But I mustn't think about it while I'm driving, or I'll crash the car.'

'So there really is such a thing as a one-tracked mind,' Lynn mused, staring out of the window and recognising the same landmarks passing for a second time. 'Over there, isn't it?'

'Cheers. Thanks, angel,' the driver whipped the steering wheel through his hands and accelerated to nip in front of a huge, lumbering Mercedes. 'Oh, yeah! One track's all I need. I so need to take you home right now.'

The singer, who was in town for her own string of concerts too, had spent the second leg of her journey eagerly anticipating being back in her man's arms. She had left Jet at home with their new *duo* of nannies, feeling far more nervous than she had expected. Her perfect stranger's soothing voice on the telephone the previous evening, when she had called him from Singapore, had brought her to tears.

'Home?'

'Well, no. Not home, obviously,' Jeff sighed. 'You turned me on so much last night. It's totally out of control, but I love it.'

His voice sounded hungry and insistent, which was the very message he wished to convey. This woman needed him, and being needed was the most important thing for the new father. It had taken Jet's arrival to hammer this idea into his head, yet it had strayed far away in the hour they had spent in the car.

'Not as out of control as you used to be,' Lynn hazarded, placing her hand on his thigh.

The handsome man smiled and winked, lifting his left hand off the steering wheel and pointing to his heart. 'It is in here.'

Through the hype and adulation surrounding the famous couple, the young mother was never happier than when she was ensconced in the office in the newly-combined penthouse apartment, with Jet playing on the floor or bouncing on her knee while she worked. She made endless telephone calls, wrote countless letters and planned every last stride and jump of their pantomime horse's adventures. Whenever Jeff was away, they would talk for at least an hour every day, discussing new projects that had been arranged and new opportunities for him to speak or launch a new campaign somewhere in the world.

Their partnership's reputation for driving real social change grew with each passing month. Africa remained one of their highest priorities, since the people there had the odds stacked against them: poverty, poor healthcare and few educational options. Apartheid and racism were ripping the soul out of the southern countries, while war and famine wreaked havoc in the north. The corruption and violence of the ruling tribes in the central, equatorial zones only added to the chaos in this massive and underdeveloped continent.

During the first half of nineteen-seventy-eight, Jeff used his few spare moments to write his first rock musical. Initially set to be a collaboration with his wife, the busy woman introduced him instead to a prodigious composer storming her way through Melbourne Academy's music program, an auburn-haired violinist by the name of Kiley Jones. The fifteen-year-old had been appointed as leader of the school's talented symphony orchestra two years earlier and had shown such promise that the Board of Governors for The Good School rushed to invite her into the first year's intake.

The story behind the *libretto* was vintage Jeff Diamond, set in New York but bearing a marked similarity to south-western Sydney. It told of people struggling with life in a big city. The lyrics written to Kiley's innovative melodies epitomised the intersection of simple pleasures and unrelenting hardship, and an initial single released to market the show soon garnered serious praise and grabbed the attention of music lovers all over the world.

Such controversial themes as prostitution, unplanned pregnancies, love across religions, clashing cultures and the loneliness of being surrounded by strangers led the critics to speculate that the Australians' musical would flop on Broadway and in London's West End; not to mention the dim view the entertainment press took of an innocent schoolgirl being exposed to these unsavoury, adult topics.

Since first coming to the public eye, the quietly-spoken *virtuosa*, whose father was a police marksman assigned to protect Victorian politicians and government officials, had been profiled as a devout Catholic. Yet Kiley's parents were quick to support the flamboyant songwriter's project, going on record to let people know that they were comfortable for the youngster to receive a broad education and hence make up her own mind about religious and moral beliefs.

Whereas the popular musicals written during the nineteen-fifties and -sixties had set the *genre*'s standard as light-hearted and chintzy, in the style of Rodgers and Hammerstein for example, the rock star reminded the press corps that there was no law against giving them a harder edge. Modern-day fairy tales, he suggested to one dubious interviewer. Fairy tales always had a message, and often those messages were sugar-coated. He considered an audience in the last quarter of the twentieth century deserved something a little more challenging than this, as long as some form of "happily ever after" prevailed.

Writing authentic songs like these kept the multi-millionnaires down-to-earth while enjoying their luxurious, contented life singular in Melbourne and mixing with other world figures and entertainment industry greats. As Lynn would privately attest, her beautiful black stallion still succumbed to the odd attack of vulnerability, when his insecurities would spring to the fore and remind him of how hard life used to be.

Fortunately, these episodes were few and far between and easily assuaged in the *milieu* of his loving family. The ambitious, versatile young man was adamant that he must never forget how it felt to be neglected and abused, in the absence of which he would cease to represent the people his life's work sought to protect.

***

Poring over the large, rolled-up sheet of stiff paper on which the latest plans for their new house were drawn, Jeff sat with his son on his knee and checked each tiny detail. Earlier, to keep the boy entertained, he had retrieved a model "JCB" from the toy box and played with it on the table, pretending to knock down the old house, along with the odd tree or two. The stunt had amused the father way more than the son, if he were honest.

'Gone!' he shouted, lifting the nine-month-old high in the air. '*Disparu! Obliteratum! Weg, weg, weg!*'

'*Weg!*' Jet echoed.

The baby's legs were growing much stronger, standing tall on his father's lap with little, bare feet digging their toes into the soft flesh at the top of his thighs. Thinking his wife would return within the hour, Jeff had given both nannies the afternoon off, and although the pair were happy in each others' company, a long list of urgent telephone calls needed his attention.

'Watch where you put your feet, mate,' the twenty-six-year-old laughed, kissing the boy's rosy cheek. 'Where's your darned mother? Do you miss her? Doesn't look like it.'

The child hit his dad on the nose with a poorly-aimed digger and proceeded to drive it all over his face.

'*Evidemment pas.* Are you trying to bulldoze me down too?'

Jet gave his human punchbag a toothy grin and bashed him once more on the side of his chin, receiving a loud roar and a vigorous cuddle in return. 'Ah, yeah. Beat me up all you like while you can get away with it. You don't care, do you? As long as you've got someone to bruise.'

By the middle of nineteen-seventy-eight, Lynn and Jeff had put the finishing touches to the design for their house in Mount Eliza. It would take over a year to build, but waiting was not a problem; in fact, it only added to the excitement. Regular visits to Benloch made apartment living more than bearable, especially now that they had so much space to play with. Their first pair of foreign nannies had moved into the other half of the conjoined dwellings, and after a short adjustment period, everyone found his or her place in the happy family unit.

The new parents had agonised over live-in child-minders for months, unsure whether to relinquish their privacy to such an extent. They threw in the towel when, even though she was at home, the young mum's commitments began to take up so much of her time that they decided it wasn't fair on Jet always to be left to play at their feet while Mum and Dad worked.

Jeff's ambition of having their children immersed in different languages from the youngest age was proceeding well, despite their son being barely old enough to utter a coherent sound. It was already clear that he understood both Spanish and English, so French and German were soon introduced into the mix as well.

The complicated overlay of four diaries worked perfectly for everybody, as it turned out. The parents were content that Jet was receiving plenty of stimulation when they weren't around to provide it, and the two nannies covered for each other so that they could pursue their individual education and travel aspirations. Sometimes the entire, extended family would fly together, and at other times the young Europeans would disappear on their own, leaving Lynn, Jeff or very occasionally both with the abnormal normality of looking after their child.

'We've got it right, angel, haven't we?' the peacemaker had said to his beautiful best friend, after returning to Melbourne from another trip to the US. 'It's all running very smoothly. Are you happy?'

'Am I happy?' Lynn had answered. 'I'm the absolute happiest. Remember you always said, "Hope for the best but expect the worst"?'

The comic nodded. 'Yep. I do remember overusing that line once or twice.'

'Well... My phrase is "Hope for the best and expect even better".'

'Really?'

'Yes. Really, really!' his wife echoed. 'There's absolutely nothing about our life I'd want to change. I'm so completely satisfied.'

The delighted man kissed her smiling lips with raw passion. 'And no fat cats?'

'Not one! What about you?'

'*Sí. Mismo*,' Jeff confirmed. 'I can hardly remember myself in the old days. Occasionally, I get thrown back by some random remark, or from seeing a film or looking at old photos. I have to force myself to recall what I was like though.'

His caring lover hugged him. 'I know that's not entirely true, but I know what you mean. You're now the man you always wanted to be: making change, resolving conflict, educating people about understanding difference... It's amazing to see our dream become a reality.'

'It *is* amazing,' the ambitious intellectual agreed. 'And the more amazing thing is how much there still is to do. I used to want to solve every problem straight-off, but now I've come to terms with the fact that fixing one problem only tends to lead us to the next one. We've still got so much scope to do good. It gets me down that we're still fighting uphill battles here and there, but somehow I'm confident we're doing nearly as much as we can.'

Whenever either superstar was interviewed about their family life, they were always at pains to stress that Jet would not be showered with expensive gifts and indulged with hobbies on a whim. Lynn had no issue with backing her husband's strict rationing of spoils, secure in the knowledge that her own privileged upbringing had not included these extravagances either.

'Jeff wants to give our kids what he didn't have,' she would tell endless snooping journalists from women's magazines. 'And that doesn't mean money or possessions so much. It means basic things a child should demand from its parents: love, respect, security and the opportunity to be who he or she wants to be.'

At Benloch over Easter, the young father found himself on his own with his mother-in-law and Jet while the tennis champion was training with her siblings. Marianna was overjoyed at her son-in-law's natural bond with the thriving youngster, seeing that nothing went unnoticed and unacknowledged with this eternally appreciative leader.

'You know, this parenting job is fascinating,' the multi-millionnaire had confessed to his son's doting grandmother. 'For instance, Lynn abandoned us all afternoon the other day, but I loved it. It's so interesting to watch this one make his own choices. It's hard to strike the right balance between helping him learn how to do things and leaving him to figure it out for himself. When he's tired, he asks for help more quickly, and then I feel like a real rat when I push him to work harder.'

The Australian Elvis and his management company signed a lucrative deal that April, booking the family for a UK visit the following month. He and Cathy had negotiated terms on an invitation from the Marquis and Marchioness of Tavistock to do a series of open-air concerts at Woburn Abbey, an English stately home in the heart of the Home Counties. The overture had originated from the Dysons' equestrian connections into the British aristocracy, and the socialist radical had resisted at first.

The commission presented the Sydneysider with a veritable crisis of conscience, to be selling out to the establishment in such a flagrant show of "someoneness". Yet, as Lynn was quick to remind him, what better way to mount his assault on wealthy insensibilities and alert them to the plight of those around them than from the inside? He could win their wallets and endorsements via their hearts, simply by applying his respected brand of friendly persuasion. The reception would be far more open for them this way, in comparison to the bitter contempt such people harboured for angry protesters marching with placards outside gold-leafed gates.

The boy from Canley Vale could see his esteemed wife's point of view, though it pained him to admit it. Their son was half blue-blood and half red-blood after all. If nothing else, baby Jet gave his father the right to be there. It was too good an opportunity to pass up purely out of stubborn, left-winged pride.

Moreover, the location was ideal for the type of show he wanted to put on these days: a typically quaint Anglo-Saxon version of the Greek Theater, where landscaped lawns sloped gradually into a basin perfect for a stage. The family had been given rooms in the main house, and the surreal experience of watching the arrival of more than ten thousand cars into the lush grounds each warm spring night from their tiny, lead-light window was not lost on the thoughtful entertainers.

The concert series was a spectacular triumph, reinforcing the songwriter and his band at the pinnacle of their career. With his wife and baby son by his side on stage, he and his faithful musicians accepted the tumult of cheers and applause from more than twenty thousand people per night, having provided them with an experience they would never forget.

For the star himself, as well as for many critics and hard-core concert-goers, the metamorphosis into Jeff Diamond the world leader was complete. His sophisticated set seemed so far removed from the open-air rock concerts he had headlined just a few years earlier, where young people fought among themselves, drugged to stupefaction, and often left in their wake a trail of damage and mayhem. The legitimacy he sought in this place of noble *largesse* was somehow lacking, using pure rock'n'roll credentials, yet he made up for this by launching a platform for his many good causes.

The whole audience stood from the first strains of the opening number, and Jeff made a joke at his hosts' expense, informing the rowdy populus that the prestigious outdoor venue had been used for the World Nudist Convention over twenty years prior.

Almost every British celebrity one could name was in attendance, including other members of the Royal Family. The performer gave the shows his all and was often caught on camera between songs breathing hard and throwing copious quantities of water down his throat. Female fans stormed the stage at one point on the second night, only to be chased away by overzealous security staff. One lucky woman managed to make it all the way through, and the hunky front-man capitalised on the moment by treating her to a kiss she would likely never wash out of her memory.

On the last night, both exhausted and elated at the recognition each performance gained from audience and reviews alike, Lynn Dyson's most significant other took her to bed in an intensely humble mood.

'Are you OK?' she asked. 'You've gone on a real slide in the last half-hour.'

'I know,' her husband agreed, rocking their son in his arms before laying him into his royal cradle. 'Sorry. I think I've hit some sort of wall. All this opulence and excess has all of a sudden kicked me in the teeth.'

'Why? Because the shows've been so successful?'

'Yeah. I think so,' he nodded. 'Too successful. It's like I'm someone who's been kidnapped by a god and granted this opportunity, and now I have to pay for it with my soul.'

Lynn stroked his face. 'No. Surely not. That doesn't sound right. No-one's asking you for anything.'

'Maybe,' Jeff let out a long sigh. 'Jeez, angel! You don't know how good it is to get these thoughts out into the open air. They came yesterday too, but I couldn't succumb to them because I had another show to do, so I just blocked them out.'

It was as if a lightbulb had lit up for the compassionate woman. 'With whisky and weed? I thought you went a bit over the top last night.'

'Yep. Sorry about that,' the sheepish musician replied. 'Angel, I could release a version of "Waltzing Matilda", and it'd be a storming hit. Any old crap'll do. Is my message getting lost in the hype that's me?'

Australia's darling understood this concept perfectly. From an early age, her parents and coaches had drummed humility into the up-and-coming Dyson generation, in order that their feet stay firmly on the ground. It had taken a number of years at the top of Jeff's game, but this diagnosis made perfect sense.

'Yes. Perhaps it is,' she hazarded, guessing this wasn't what her husband would want to hear but also that he already knew it to be true.

'Fuck!' came the brisk retort. 'You would have to agree with me, wouldn't you?'

Lynn kissed his irate mouth and began to stroke his penis, as if to force his mind into the here and now. The sensitive organ responded with a twitch, having built up a store of unspent passion as a result of his racy stage antics. He laughed at her expertise, embarrassed at how easily he could be distracted.

'You are fantastic,' Jeff moaned, writhing in pleasure and giving into the relaxing sensation. 'Just shut up and make love, will you?'

His partner giggled. 'There are no concerts for the next few months, and we've got Africa fever coming up fast, so this hype'll all die down as soon as we get home. Back to normal for a short while anyway.'

Jeff climbed on top of this adorable woman who had his measure in every possible way. He penetrated her, continuing the job his fingers had started, and the pair moved slowly together. Lynn orgasmed in a vociferous rush, no longer worried that their lovemaking would disturb the boy who had learned to sleep through anything.

'Can we start making our remaining Diamond tonight?' her lover asked out of the blue, pointing to the empty corner in his jet-stone ring. 'Please?'

His wife opened her eyes and suspended their rhythmic dance for a few seconds before carrying on with renewed intent. 'Of course. If that's what you want,' she agreed, kissing him hard on the mouth. 'That'd be a very normal thing to do for our life singular. A bit earlier than planned, but this is absolutely the right moment. I love you, Jeff.'

Pulling clear of her moist vagina, the breathless man removed the condom his angel had only recently rolled on, and they were soon ready to light the blue touch paper. Both had tears in their eyes on reconnecting, desperate to make this night special. They climaxed together not long afterwards, skin-on-skin, sending their separate, private wishes into the clear Bedfordshire night sky.

And, if only to prove beyond a shadow of doubt that the great Jeff Diamond could do no wrong, within two weeks Lynn began to tire early. A day or two later, she noticed a feeling of nausea at certain smells and a definite tenderness under her skin. All these little tell-tale signs could only mean one thing...

The young athlete rushed home from the doctor's surgery to find her inspiring world-changer rehearsing a speech he had written for an anti-Apartheid rally in San Francisco. Jet was being fed his lunch by Nadine, the French nanny, and a member of Gerry's legal team was checking a lengthy contract in their office.

'Hey, angel,' the intellectual smiled, prompting a whoop of delight from their little, curly-haired boy. '*Ça va? Tu sembles très heureuse.*'

Lynn bent over and kissed her son's cheek before sitting down and taking over the rest of the feed. '*Oui. Je suis très contente,*' she agreed, wiping his messy chops. '*Nous sommes enceints encore une fois.*'

Assuming he had heard correctly, Jeff looked up from his notes to see his own happiness reflected in his wife's eyes. 'Yeah? Hey! *C'est magnifique!*'

he exclaimed, standing up and swinging her around in a circle, much to their son's amusement. 'How pregnant are you?'

'Very! I think it really did happen that night at Woburn Abbey,' the young woman gushed. 'They gave me a due-date of mid-Feb', so that makes mid-May about right. This baby was really keen to be created; didn't waste any time allowing us to practise.'

Jeff grinned. 'I like that analogy. It knows how happy it'll be and how happy it'll make us too. Jesus, angel. Now we've got all that bloody waiting to do again.'

Lynn nodded, a little perturbed. She often forgot that a single piece of good news wasn't always enough to pull her healing soul-mate back above the line. His resistance to the depressive force had been under severe strain lately, faced with the seemingly insurmountable challenges of South Africa's peace talks. She was grateful that Nadine had disappeared back to her room, leaving the couple to speak freely.

'Yes. That's what I was thinking too. And Dad's not going to be too pleased either, because I'll have to withdraw from the remaining Grand Slams.'

'Big effing deal,' her husband teased, averting a sneer by a whisker.

'Don't be mean. It's a big deal for me too.'

The young man felt guilty. He knew how relieved Lynn was to be match-fit again after Jet's arrival and to have won back the Australian Open in January, only six months after giving birth.

'I'm sorry,' he muttered. 'That was mean. I apologise.'

'That's OK,' she placated him with a kiss, turning on her heels to change their son's nappy. 'We can celebrate properly next week, after the summit.'

Jeff refocussed onto his hard-hitting speech, finding it difficult to concentrate with this amazing news. His mind kept taking him back to the themes of unity and liberty. Now, more than ever before, these themes were the cornerstones of his mission. And now, along with its big brother, this new baby... their fourth Diamond... could fulfil its destiny as the defender of these two primal humanist concepts.

Don't be ridiculous! This was far too much pressure to place on an unborn child, the philosopher thought. He was doing what he had always despised: choosing his own child's destiny. But Grand Slams? Who cared? When did a Grand Slam ever change the world? Or a sell-out concert in the English countryside, for that matter? Innocent people were being persecuted in their millions, but it ought to be their children's choice whether to take a stand or not.

As the months went by, the rock star's guilt increased with every night he spent away from home. Lynn was much sicker during her second pregnancy, her body expanding faster this time compared to last. She was not enjoying being pregnant again. In his haste to complete their family, he knew he had forced her into this too soon. Never one to voice a complaint however, she decided that another year of relative obscurity was a small price to pay for her perfect stranger's happiness. The couple took the decision to invite the press into their apartment to record a documentary about life with the Dyson Diamonds and were interviewed shortly after their latest piece of domestic news was announced.

'I think we've confused our son,' Jeff told the cameras. 'He's been reading books about baby animals, and when we told him Mamá was going to have a baby, he asked if it'd be a puppy or a kitten…'

The blonde beauty, off to the left of camera, was heard to remark. 'Well, you have been away a lot.'

'No wonder the damned dog's looking so pleased with himself,' her husband shot back as quick as lightning.

The magic that Jeff Diamond wove was universally infectious, with the promise of a better world. Even Lynn became excited despite her discomfort. At least starting sooner would mean her child-bearing duties would be acquitted sooner. Their family would be complete, and their life singular would change to yet a higher gear.

Four Of Diamonds

Not a day went by that the old soul didn't give thanks for his rock solid life with Lynn, Jet and whoever was still to come. His dream girl made everything so easy, and all that was required of him in return was to make her happy. And therein lay some of his finest work; nothing ranked more highly on his priority list.

For the first time in a while, the ancient soul began to feel older than his age again. He was cramming so much into life and stacking the shelves of wisdom higher and higher inside his ever-hungry brain. Wherever he looked, there was more to learn and more to teach.

Compared to the exhaustion he had experienced as the old Jeff, paralysed by irrational fears and plagued by nightmares, this was a far healthier vintage. The new Jeff's mind remained sharp, unclouded and ready for more while his lithe, muscular body felt alive and never fitter, benefitting from regular workouts and long, fast-paced runs with a brutal trainer enlisted by his Chief Punishment Officer.

The nineteen-seventy-eight variety of old age was purely a mental maturity, and not the energy-sapping physical old age which had given him concrete shoulders, cramping legs, lock-jaw and endless headaches. This new veteran possessed the refinement of expensive red wine: full-bodied and not in the least acerbic. Jeff Diamond had become the master of all he surveyed, and this status sat well with him.

'It's important that we don't know everything,' the perennial student explained to a hall filled with Melbourne Academy students. 'If we did, we wouldn't keep coming back and trying again to make things better.'

Accepting a place on the prestigious private school's Board of Governors for the nineteen-seventy-nine school year had been both an honour and a crossroads for the twenty-six-year-old superstar. Bart Dyson had retired as Chairman at the end of the previous term after having served almost two decades in various roles. This had paved the way for a changing of the guard, and the unlikely candidate who had married into Australian aristocracy assumed the mantle in advance of his own children's attendance.

Lynn had dissolved into tears when her husband presented her with the confirmation letter he had received from the bursar, never expecting him to accept. He assured her he hadn't compromised his principles in the process, merely paving the way for modernisation which would result in an even better and much broader curriculum base.

'Whoa!' Jeff laughed, jumping back as a loud spit of electricity leaped between them as his wife's elegant hand made contact with his forearm. 'If we keep doing that, they'll have to plug us into the grid. We could save thousands.'

'Is it electricity?' his wide-eyed muse asked, rubbing her fingertips together. 'It can't be.'

Fresh out of the shower after a sexual interlude on their balcony under the stars, the pair spread out on the mattress in the sultry January heat. The intellectual couldn't believe how contented he felt, his eyelids becoming heavier, and his mind relaxed by the bottle of Shiraz they had shared, one part to five, before turning in.

'Damned straight, it is,' he countered. 'If it's not electricity... attraction, I mean... what is it?'

Lynn screwed up her tanned face, stretched out on her back so that only their shoulders touched, with her distended belly covered by the sheet. 'I don't know. It can't be chemistry because wouldn't you have to mix things together to get a reaction?'

Her amused lover leaned over, his lips searching for hers. When they connected, another jolt of excitement coursed through both bodies as their tongues tasted each others' lingering passion. After he had made his point, Jeff lowered his head back onto the pillow, feeling chuffed.

'Feel that? Chemistry in action, gorgeous,' he sniffed. 'Wouldn't you say?'

'OK, know-all,' the flushed woman scowled. 'Organic, obviously. But how can humans generate electricity?'

The handsome man looked peaceful, with his eyes closed and his mouth moulded into a lazy half-smile. Lynn propped herself up onto her elbow and ran a finger down his cheek and over his lips, which puckered up each time its tip passed by.

'Anything that has power can generate electricity. Our nervous system needs it to function properly,' Jeff explained in a slow, almost bored tone. 'We don't generate much normally. Just enough to control our muscle movements. We conduct it way better.'

'Professor Diamond, you are exhibiting *ennui encore une fois*,' Lynn accused. 'That all makes sense though. You don't want to talk about this, do you?'

'Yes, I do.'

A fuller smile spread over his rugged face, bronzed after an afternoon making music on their balcony, his eyes crinkling at the corners. The young mum's heart melted, realising how tired her generous rock star must be after such a busy week and being so much in demand. Since having their little one to look after, she had forgotten what it was like to crash after a long day with only the prospect of the same tomorrow.

'But you're not a willing contributor.'

'True,' the peacemaker agreed. 'But I like hearing how your mind works. It's beautiful listening to your innermost thoughts while they're forming on the fly. It makes me feel like you're trying to work things out in a new way.'

'Are you patronising me after I called you "professor"? What do you mean?'

'No,' his voice was not in the least bit defensive. 'It was meant to be a compliment. Sorry you didn't hear it that way. I mean you're trying to work out the things I can't work out. So you can enlighten us both. Teamwork. Two heads are better than one, and all that jazz. That's how the world changes, angel. And we're damned well going to change it, so keep talking.'

Lynn sighed. 'Oh, that's nice. Sorry. It's just that I sound so *naïve* in my head.'

Jeff's heavy left arm raised itself up from the far side of the bed and winged its way over towards the contrite woman, curling his torso round with it until his hand alighted on her stomach. Strong fingers stroked the sensitive skin underneath her nipples, spreading a tingling sensation through her whole body.

'Don't be sorry,' the same sultry tone continued. 'It's not *naïvetée*. It's trying to find the simplicity. Life's too complicated, baby. We have to distill the simplicity out of it. The rest is superfluous noise. And now we have to have sex again, unless you really want me to take it out on you for calling me "professor".'

***

'Jeff, can you help me, please?' Lynn asked, levering herself up from the sun-lounger.

The tall, handsome man looked over, hearing some urgency in his wife's voice. He had been floating Jet on his back in the outdoor pool for the last half-hour, relishing the sun's rays beating down on his face. It was Saturday the tenth of February nineteen-seventy-nine, and the young family had been enjoying some "R and R" at Benloch after another hectic holiday season.

He watched his heavily pregnant wife struggle to stand up. 'Hold on,' Jeff shouted, wading towards the steps with his bleating son slung casually over one arm. 'What's up?'

'We have to go,' she smiled, breathless. 'We're in business.'

Jeff's eyes widened. 'Really? Whoa! We better had then.'

Unable to overhear the couple's exchange, Marianna looked up from her book. 'Lynn, are you alright?'

'The baby's on its way,' her daughter reported, grimacing as a contraction caught her unawares.

The European nannies had taken advantage of their bosses' kind offer of a long weekend in Queensland. Nadine and Ursula weren't due to return until late on Monday night since medical opinion advised that the new Diamond baby would not arrive for at least another week.

The concerned grandmother rushed to help, surprised by the sudden onset of labour. Keen not to upset the toddler, Lynn tickled his neck while his father wrapped him up in a towel and began to dry himself off.

'Please can we leave Jet with you?' she asked her mother. 'We have to go to the hospital. This feels like it's going to happen right now.'

'Of course,' Marianna said, agitated. 'He'll be fine here. You've got plenty of clothes with you, haven't you?'

The tennis champion nodded, leaning heavily on Jeff's arm. After the contraction had subsided, she stood up straight and held her arms out to carry her son. He wasn't interested in being carried however, much preferring to walk these days. Laughing at his determined stare, they all started back into the house to prepare for their unscripted plot diversion.

'Told you we should've bought that chopper,' the frequent traveller joked.

Once upstairs and in their room, Jet began to cry, not sure what had triggered this sudden flurry of activity. Mum and Dad's toys were being packed away, but his were not. It was rare to see them both leave at once. Why couldn't he go wherever they were going?

'Hey. It's alright, mate. Mamá's going to bring your little brother or sister back with us. It's very exciting! Only I'm allowed to cry.'

It was true! Jeff's emotions were coming to the boil, stewing in his overflowing heart. They had been enjoying a wonderfully relaxing weekend, with Marianna much more successful than he was at convincing Lynn to take things easy. And now, to cap it all, he was about to ferry his gorgeous wife to hospital to deliver their second child. This life singular they had been granted was so utterly perfect.

'Thanks for asking your mum to look after *Número Uno*,' the twenty-six-year-old said, as he bounced the youngster on his knee. 'It'll be good, just the two of us to welcome him or her into the world.'

The threesome decamped to the bathroom together while the young woman showered before leaving. Her face was flushed, but her manner was serene.

'This is all old hat to you now, isn't it?' her husband quipped.

'Not quite,' she responded, rolling her eyes and flicking some soap suds at the boisterous pair. 'And exactly how would you know?'

'Hey! Go easy on me, woman,' Jeff laughed. 'I missed this bit last time, remember? This fills in some blanks for me. It's very special to be driving you back into the city to have our baby. For you, I nearly missed the whole thing, didn't I, mate?'

Their son was smiling once again, his fears cast aside for a game of his choosing, which largely involved throwing a variety of bath toys at his Dad's head from close range. Luckily, he was still a poor aim. The gallant *chauffeur* insisted on carrying both bags and their weighty firstborn down to the ground floor of the enormous mansion, leaving Lynn with only her handbag and the keys to the Aston Martin.

Marianna met them at the foot of the stairs. Handing Jet to her, the beaming father departed to bring the car round to the front of the house. Her daughter was excited too, stroking the little one's face and tickling his bare feet.

'Papá's very happy, isn't he?' she said, mostly to her mother. 'Fatherhood suits him so well.'

'It certainly does,' the older woman agreed. 'He's very kind to you too. It's lovely to see.'

'*Avanti, avanti,* people!' Jeff waved from the doorway. 'No time to lose. I knew there was a reason I bought such a fast car.'

'Drive safely, dear,' Marianna warned, smiling at her impetuous son-in-law.

'I shall,' he assured her, watching his wife dispensing parting kisses to mother and child. 'Precious cargo. I get it. Thanks very much for looking after Jetto.'

Standing with one foot inside the driver's door, the proud man shouted from the car. 'Mate, you better look after the farm. We'll be back with the new baby tomorrow or the next day, and we'll ring you before bedtime. *Adiós.* Have fun with Grandma.'

The swift, black vehicle kicked up two plumes of red dust as it sped down the driveway. Jeff turned the music up, and the *duo* sang at the tops of their voices. This was indeed a special moment, and they were both ecstatic to be together and alone to enjoy it without the distraction of looking after their son.

'This feels like that first time we drove back from here,' Lynn said. 'When we were first dating, after Rob's party. We made up that song, do you remember? In the rain, with the syncopated rhythm from the wipers.'

'Yeah. Of course I remember,' the romantic replied. 'I remember everything, angel. Are you feeling OK? Are you going to give me another blowjob? Or do you have something even more mind-blowing in store for me this time?'

Mid-way through her third contraction in fifteen minutes, the woman made her true feelings known via a tired grunt. 'The way I feel now, you'll be lucky to get any action ever again.'

Jeff nodded, feigning alarm. 'Fair enough. Forget I ever mentioned it.'

In just over an hour, they were pulling into the car park of the same hospital they had attended only seventeen months ago. The celebrity parked the ostentatious vehicle in a free space close to the door and ran round to help his wife extract her encumbered self from the low-slung passenger seat. The staff swarmed around them, leading other visitors to investigate the fuss being made of the new arrivals. To a chorus of shouting and cheering, they and their white-coated *entourage* walked briskly through the building and into the lift, bound for the familiar delivery suites.

Lynn's contractions were almost running into each other, excruciating in their relentlessness. 'This kid's very anxious to escape,' she laughed.

'*Excelente,*' her husband acknowledged, grimacing along with her. 'Can you really tell or are you just making that up?'

'Who knows?' she shrugged. 'I just remember things being so slow last time. Compared to that, it's all happening on fast-forward.'

'I'm glad,' Jeff whispered into her ear, kissing her sweating forehead as she sank down onto the mattress. 'If it'd been like this for Jet's birth, I'd definitely have missed it. You're so amazing. I love you, angel.'

Lynn leaned over and rested her head on his shoulder, gasping as another spasm gripped her. 'It is good actually, 'cause at this rate it might all be over in a few hours. We don't need to spend ages waiting, trying to amuse ourselves when neither of us can concentrate on anything else. When Michelle was here, I was willing Jet to take his time. She got a bit bored, poor thing. So perhaps I'm subconsciously trying to speed it up this time because you're already here.'

The door to their room swung open, and in walked the same senior nurse who had attended Lynn when Jet was born. Was it coincidence that Maggie Thompson was on shift, or had her colleagues been on notice to telephone her the moment the Diamonds reappeared?

'Lynn, Jeff! It's lovely to see you again,' the lifetime fan demurred, shaking their hands politely. 'How's the little boy these days? Jet, isn't it?'

'He's fine. Thanks, Maggie,' the blonde singer replied. 'He's with my mum. Getting spoiled rotten, I expect.'

'Good news. We have to get you into bed now,' the midwife instructed her famous patient. 'By the regularity of your contractions, you're fairly advanced already. Baby Number Two is in more of a hurry to arrive than its brother.'

Lynn smiled at Jeff, who nodded back. He and Maggie helped her out of her clothes and tied her into her sexy hospital attire while three other nurses entered the room with a trolley laden with equipment and machines which beeped and flashed their lights tirelessly. Very soon, activities of labour became their sole focus.

In a quiet moment and in front of a full house, the playful father winked at his wife after another very painful contraction had made her cry out. He cocked his head towards the bathroom, eyebrows raised.

'No! We bloody well can't!' she exclaimed, trying to laugh through the pain. 'No way, José!'

'Worth a try,' the larrikin laughed, kissing her forehead and gripping her shoulders as she put all her energy into riding another almighty spasm. 'We have to ring Jet though, before he goes to bed. I promised.'

Lynn's eyes widened as if to question his sanity. Clearly, he was serious. Jeff lifted the telephone off the bedside cabinet and dialled Benloch. The lady of the house answered after a few rings.

'Hi, Marianna. It's Jeff and some woman who keeps screaming,' he yelled.

'Jeff? Pardon? Is everything alright?' the grandmother sounded confused, not knowing whether he was being facetious or not.

'Yes!' Lynn shouted. 'Hi, Mum! I'm OK. Just a bit busy right now.'

'That monster was your daughter, in case you didn't recognise her,' her husband continued the joke. 'Her body's been taken over by aliens, but other than that, we're fine. Is it possible to talk to Jet for a second before he goes to bed, please?'

The elegant woman chuckled. 'Certainly. I'll bring him over. He's all fed, bathed and clothed, so you're just in time.'

Lynn groaned loudly as she felt the baby slip further down the birth canal, pain ripping through her body. Jeff looked on helplessly, cursing his own stupidity. He could hear his son's soothing, childlike breath at the other end of the telephone.

'Jet, hello. It's Papá,' he said, putting the receiver close to Lynn's ear and leaning in to wipe the perspiration off her forehead.

The mother smiled. 'Hello, darling. Can you hear us?'

Some animated but unintelligible noises were transmitted from the big house north of the city, followed by laughter from the boy's babysitter, who was urging him to say hello to his parents.

'Bedtime, Papá,' Jet informed his father. 'Grandma take me.'

'Great, son. Are you tired?'

'Yes. Mamá baby?'

'Not yet,' Lynn interjected. 'Very soon though.'

'When you wake up in the morning, you'll have a new brother or sister,' Jeff assured him. 'Go to sleep now, and we'll see you tomorrow. *Ser un buen' chico para la abuela, por favor*, mate.'

'Goodnight, gorgeous,' his mother wished, gritting her teeth and preparing for another huge effort. 'Sleep well, little man.'

'Night, night,' Jet replied. 'Night, night.'

'G'night, mate. *Te amos mucho*. Thank you, Marianna. Gotta go,' his dad rushed to terminate the call and focus back on the job at hand. 'OK, team. You can let her go now.'

After only ten more fevered minutes, the nurse announced that the baby's head was on its way out. Jeff felt suddenly dizzy with the excitement and overwhelmed with love. Their second child. Their family was about to be complete, and he could hardly wait. A final few pushes and a strangled sob signalled the expulsion of a long, slithering body which seemed to reach out to Maggie's waiting hands.

The tearful woman cleared the baby's airway, and a pair of lungs spluttered themselves into full voice. The plaintive but healthy din relieved the atmosphere of its tension, Lynn and Jeff both straining to catch a glimpse of their new addition.

The midwife was smiling when she stood up and stepped closer to the head of the bed. 'She's a little girl. A perfect little girl to go with your perfect little boy. Congratulations, dears.'

The couple let out a combined sigh, both instantly moved to tears. A girl. Perfect, indeed. From Lynn's right, the opposite side from the array of machines, a huge hand reached around his wife's neck and drew their faces closer together. He kissed her lips so passionately that it took what little breath she had left clean away.

'You are awesome, angel. *Tenemos una niña.*'

Lynn looked into the shining eyes of the man she loved so much, unable to think of anything clever to say in reply. One thing was certain though… She had never seen such joy on his face.

'Now we're completely complete,' the deep baritone whispered against her moist cheek. 'Our family is perfect. Christ, we are so unbelievably lucky. *Gracias, Regala.*'

A junior nurse brought their brand new daughter to the head of the bed to meet her parents. She was wrapped in a *crêpe* blanket and looked tiny, with a shock of dark hair and an untroubled, clear-eyed expression. History had repeated itself with one small variation.

'Hey, little one,' Lynn said, eliciting a startled gaze into nowhere from lively eyes, and issued an instruction destined more for her porter than for the baby herself. 'Go to your papá first. He's waiting for you.'

Smiling broadly, Jeff took the little towelling parcel in his arms and sat down beside his wife on the bed, lifting the head of dark hair towards its mother's lips. Lynn placed a gentle kiss on the baby's face.

'Look at you two,' he crooned, tears rolling down his cheeks. 'I've got two angels now. Can you believe that? You're both so gorgeous.'

'Look at her eyes,' the tired woman added. 'She's staring at us so attentively. She's definitely your child. Look at that determined expression. This one's not going to let us off easily.'

His wife was right. There was an intensity in the new arrival's stare which hadn't been present in their son's. The superstar sniffed back his tears, causing the baby to startle again.

'Sorry, angel,' he whispered, stroking her tiny forehead.

Exhausted by the significance of the past few hours, the young couple and their extra friend gazed at each other in turn, mesmerised by the magic of bringing yet another soul into the world. As rare as it was between them, words seemed superfluous.

'Would you like a photo' of the three of you?' Staff Nurse Thompson broke the silence, pointing at her trusty instant camera.

Lynn nodded. 'Oh, yes, please. That'd be lovely. Thanks, Maggie.'

Jeff pushed several strands of wet, golden hair away from the patient's stunning facial features, and they positioned their daughter in the direction of the lens, doing their best to look awake and lively. The amateur photographer gave a rapid countdown, and the shutter clicked three times in quick succession.

'You OK?' the young man asked, slumping back against the pillow and letting out a long, contented moan. 'I love you so much.'

'I'm very OK,' Lynn affirmed, smiling. 'Are you going to wave her out the window this time?'

'Is there anyone there?' Jeff answered with typical rhetoric, handing the tiny bundle over and crossing the room to see if a crowd had gathered outside. 'Jesus! There must be a hundred people out there already. Who the hell spreads the news around here?'

And sure enough, a keen-eyed fan spotted their idol as soon as his face appeared at the window, marshalling a cheer within seconds, loud even through the glass.

Australia's darling chuckled, seeing a row of astonished nurses. 'Here we go, little one,' she said to her daughter. 'This is your life. I apologise for all the fuss.'

Her husband pushed the handle, having to lean on it to budge the painted-in frame, and waved down to the people below. 'Good news travels fast, eh? We've got a full set now. It's a girl, and she's as beautiful as her mamá.'

Lynn heard the screams and clapping and lay back onto the pillow. The labour had been so quick-fire that she hardly even felt sleepy. Elated and very tender, but not sleepy. It energised her to see her man so lively, and the vision of their complete family filled her with an odd sense of achievement too. Tears began to roll down her cheeks.

'Hey, gorgeous,' Jeff said, concerned. 'I hope they're happy tears.'

She grinned, holding out her hands. 'Course they are. You're right. This is just perfect, isn't it? A brother and sister.'

'Sure is,' the philosopher agreed, walking back around to perch on the edge of the bed. 'I suppose this means no more sex.'

Maggie gave a subdued laugh in the background.

'I think so,' his wife replied. 'Right now, I quite like that idea.'

Jeff reached down and scooped his daughter up into his arms again. 'Did you hear that? We'll have to figure out a way to change Mamá's mind, won't we? Let me know when you've come up with the solution, *pequeñita*.'

The younger nurse who had first handed the baby to the superstar returned to the room to collect her again. 'We need to run a few checks. Weigh and measure her. I'll bring her back in a minute.'

Reluctantly, the enamoured dad passed the little mite over and followed them until they disappeared into the corridor. Maggie took her leave at the same time, giving the couple some time alone. Lynn reached out for her beautiful black stallion, who went to her side, hugging her close and crying pent-up tears. Jeff kissed the corners of her eyes, tasting the salt, each soaking in the love they felt for the other.

Suddenly drowsy, she murmured, '*Je t'aime, mon ami.*'

'*Merci. Je t'aime aussi.* So much. Do you still think the names are appropriate, now you've met her?'

The new mum frowned, as if running them through her mind for the first time. 'Nothing tells me they aren't. What do you think?'

'They're still perfect. We could see what she thinks when she gets back. Did you notice the depth in her eyes?'

'Yes,' his dream girl chuckled. 'We've produced another version of you. I get the impression she's going to be one of life's true critics. She looks so aware already. Maybe she's been paying attention for the last few months. Jet didn't have any family vibes to give him a flavour of his future. Just a lot of rushing around and endless interviews and meetings. I don't know if that'd make any difference.'

Jeff nodded. 'Yep. I think it might. We've got Action Man and a mini, female Plato. What a combo! I love it. It'll be fascinating to see how we're all going to fit together. I hope she liked the vibes she was picking up. That's why she was in so much of a hurry, maybe.'

Lynn stretched her arms up into the air. 'You know... I don't even feel tired.'

'You're kidding!' her husband scoffed. 'I wouldn't say that too loud, if I were you. I have the power to use it against you later. Can we go home now then? You can make dinner.'

The hard-working woman let out a groan. 'No! Yes, that was a very stupid thing to say. I regret it already!'

The pair were laughing as Maggie re-entered the room with their daughter, excusing herself for interrupting a private moment. 'This little girl's heavier than her brother. Seven pounds and three ounces. Everything's normal, and she's a placid little tot.'

'Oh, well,' Lynn smirked. 'That's where the similarity ends then. We were just saying how like Jeff she was, but you could never use the word "placid" to describe him.'

The erstwhile enigma shrugged. '*Whaddya* mean?' he enquired. 'I can be placid, if only in very short bursts.'

Not willing to be drawn into this debate, Maggie handed the baby to her mother. 'There you go, Lynn. Thank you again for allowing me to be present at both your children's births. It's a real privilege. I'm going off duty now, but do you mind if I drop in before you leave tomorrow?'

'No. Of course not,' the diplomat answered. 'You're welcome, and thank *you*. You could come and visit us next week, if you like. Then you can see Jet at the same time. He's not exactly placid these days either.'

Jeff sniffed. 'And I suppose I'm going to get the blame for that too.'

'Oh, shut up,' the young woman joked. 'Go and phone people. Make yourself useful, Papá.'

The songwriter saluted his wife before placing gentle kisses on each angel's forehead. He left with Maggie, who showed him into a private room with a telephone, and he did the right thing by dialling Benloch first. Marianna's voice was breathless with anticipation as he heard her lift the receiver and discover who was calling.

'Jeff! What news?'

'Hi! News is you have a granddaughter. Seven pounds, three. And she's absolutely perfect.'

An initial silence was followed by an emotional sigh. While he waited for the dignified lady's response, the father recalled the concentration on his daughter's face, almost as if she recognised him. Was that possible? There he went again with his wild fantasies of eternal souls!

'Oh, how lovely! That's wonderful, dear. I'm so pleased for you both. Lynn was hoping for a little girl, I think.'

'Yeah. We both were, secretly,' her son-in-law affirmed. 'She's fine too. All very quick, in fact. Lynn just admitted that she wasn't even tired, but I advised her to keep *stumm* about that.'

Marianna laughed. 'That sounds like Lynn. Please give her my love. Are you still at the hospital? I'll try and get hold of Bart to give him the good news. He'll probably ring later anyway. Congratulations, Jeff. You must be very happy.'

Tears stung behind his eyes, still unable to picture anything except Jet's little sibling. What would the noisy tyke think of the squirming, pink thing with tiny fingers and staring eyes? She may not quite be the puppy or kitten he was expecting…

And how on Earth had the bad-boy from New South Wales ended up so well regarded by the Dysons? It wasn't so long ago that Lynn's mother had warned him to keep away from her daughter, and now she was congratulating him for his part in creating her third grandchild.

'Thanks. I am. Couldn't find anyone happier.'

'May we come by tomorrow?' Marianna enquired. 'Bart gets back into Melbourne first thing, so I'd love to bring Jet into town to see his baby sister.'

'Definitely,' Jeff agreed. 'I don't know what time they'll chuck the girls out, but I'm sure we can string it out until lunchtime. And we'll only be in the apartment if you're any later than that.'

'Thank you. I'll give you a ring at home later. Leave a message.'

'Sure. No worries. How's the boy? Is he asleep?'

The tired man heard the patient grandmother chuckle. 'Yes. Finally.'

'Why? Did he give you a hard time?'

'Ah, no. Not really. I've just forgotten all the games one has to play, that's all. He was as good as gold, Jeff. Ate a huge dinner and wouldn't stop repeating the word "baby" over and over again.'

The millionnaire chuckled. 'Well, what do you expect? He has songwriters for parents. There's a lot of versatility in the word "baby".'

'Oh, I suppose so! I never thought of that,' Marianna laughed. 'Have you chosen a name?'

'Yes. But we haven't introduced her to it yet, so I'll wait in case we get a bad reaction. Don't know what we'd do if we did, but bear with us, please.'

They finished their call, and the proud dad walked down the corridor to the nurse's station to request a cup of coffee before going downstairs to the staff car park to grab a cigarette, hopefully undiscovered. While he was smoking, he paced up and down the bays, lost in a daydream about his new daughter. He still couldn't get the image of the peaceful little mystery out of his mind's eye, and it unnerved him how deeply those dark eyes had bored into him.

He had seen traces of his mother and sister on her face, and some of Lynn too. He knew they had been manufactured by his own imagination, since this little, zero-hour-old baby couldn't possibly yet resemble anyone so closely. He was convinced she had been telling him who she was, where she had come from and that she understood who he was. And perhaps he had subliminally done the same for her. Time would tell…

Young Ryan was more than fifty percent Dyson, both in looks and personality, but this little girl was way more than fifty percent Catholic Argentinean Polish Jew. Their family had counterbalanced perfectly. What a journey they were now on! Having allowed this thought to take flight, a new song leaped straight into the musician's brain: the Diamond train was rolling on, having picked up its latest passenger.

Jeff stared at the black jet-stone ring on the middle finger of his right hand, with the three out of four diamonds in place. The one which had been added after Jet's birth, now nearly a year-and-a-half ago, was at first so brilliant that it had made the others look dull. Its lustre had since faded, and already all three looked the same. So at last it was time to fill the space in the remaining corner, thereby signifying that his whacky plan of producing their little gems between two Olympics had come to fruition.

He kissed the ring and whispered a quiet prayer to his curious new child. *'Bienvenido, pequeñita.* We need you to make our family complete. We're going on such a ride, you know. Your feet won't touch the ground.'

When the songwriter crept back into the room, Lynn was sleeping with the new baby's head resting against her face. He rummaged in her overnight bag and pulled out their camera. He took a couple of photographs, hoping the noise of the shutter wouldn't wake them. It didn't. He sat in the chair next to the bed and scribbled down his lyric idea before it had the chance to drift away, periodically looking up at his new daughter, peaceful on her mother's pillow. Her left hand was visible in the fold of the blanket. It was amazing to see such delicate features again.

Jeff must have dozed off a few minutes later because the next think he knew, the change in air pressure and vibration of a swinging door woke him from a deep slumber. The latest nursing staff member hadn't bothered to knock. Lynn stirred and opened her eyes to find out what the noise was.

'Sorry, Missus Diamond,' the young attendant said. 'I didn't know you were asleep.'

She's just had a baby, Mister Diamond muttered to himself. *Chances are she'd be asleep...* There was no point in making a scene, but really!

'Hey, angel,' he greeted the bleary-eyed beauty, standing up and stretching his fingertips to the ceiling. 'You two look so gorgeous there, side-by-side. I took some good pictures. Hope they come out without the flash.'

'Thanks. How are you? Did you get hold of Mum?'

'Yep. She sends her congratulations and love. I told her you were ready for anything. They're bringing Jet here in the morning.'

'Oh, great,' Lynn smiled. 'It'll be fantastic to see how he reacts to his baby sister. I wonder if she'll know him the way she seems to know us.'

'Jesus! You noticed that too? I can't get it out of my head,' the young man marvelled.

Wincing, the Olympian sat up against the thick pillow, flicked her long hair over her shoulder and picked the baby up. 'Are you awake, little one? Oh, yes. You are. Hello! Can we see if you like your names?'

Jeff grabbed the camera again and snapped a few more pictures of the cherub with her mother, to see if he could attract her attention with the activity. It worked. Heavy eyelids opened to reveal dark brown eyes just like her dad's, and he stared back into them while he took his place on the bed.

'Welcome to our happy family, Kierney,' his wife began, jiggling the small bundle. 'That's you. You are Kierney Lynn Freedom Diamond. Is that OK?'

The emotional father lay a gentle kiss on Lynn's head and wrapped his huge fingers round his daughter's hand. 'It's beautiful. We love you so much, Kierney. We're going to have heaps of fun. Your brother's coming tomorrow to meet you. He's a bit of a boisterous pain in the bum sometimes, but he'll love you too. He's called Jet, by the way. Or Ryan for special occasions.'

Little Kierney blinked, and her mouth twitched at the sound of her parents' voices. Both hands tried to reach in front of her, and her dad held his index finger still, waiting for her tiny digits to close around it.

'She likes it,' he said, choking back tears. 'That's a handshake. Done deal, Kiz.'

The new mother leaned into her husband. 'Thank you, Kierney. She's full of questions, isn't she? Look at her gaze darting about, chasing every noise. We'll answer as many of your questions as we can decipher, Kizzy, to make sure you keep asking. I'm your mamá, which you've probably already worked out, and this is your very handsome papá.'

The naming ceremony over, Jeff took his leave so that both ladies could partake of their evening meal. He wove through the hustle and bustle of the maternity ward, headed down in the lift and back to his car. And to a small crowd of waiting fans, of course. He fought his way through the vociferous bunch and provided them with a brief update on mother and baby. After a few minutes of cooing and stolen kisses, they graciously permitted him to drive away.

When he reached his parking space, the superstar found a golden teddy bear pinned under one of the windscreen wipers. As ever, he felt humbled by the kindness shown to his family by their fellow Melburnians. A soft toy under the wiper was so much better than the jealous scratch of a key across the Aston's paintwork. He drove the single kilometre to their apartment, parked up and ascended to the top floor.

Once inside, the lone Diamond in residence was blindsided by a panic attack. Where were his beautiful best friend, their rambunctious toddler and this exquisite, new baby girl? Shaking his head, he cursed the remnants of his tortured mind. Gravity the troll was still capable of persecution, even when technically in retirement.

No, you haven't been abandoned, you idiot. You left the hospital voluntarily, and they'll welcome you back with smiles and open arms tomorrow morning.

Nevertheless, Jeff knew he needed to find some company. He couldn't bear to spend the night alone in the apartment. It had been a good ninety days since he had slept on his own in their bed, with Lynn unable to travel during her final trimestre. Where would he go at almost eight o'clock on Saturday evening?

The lost boy sat down and dialled his manager's number. Answering machine. He left a message and then tried the office, just in case the executive was making up from some hours lost through his very social brand of business development. This call diverted to a voicemail system too. Perhaps the perennial bachelor had gone to the footy? He was most likely in a bar somewhere, holding court with girls who followed football for the express purpose of getting laid by rich men.

Next he tried his sister, also unsuccessfully. The despondent dad spoke to her flatmate, leaving a message for Madalena to ring back on Gerry's number if she didn't find him at home. Whom else did he need to contact? Michelle. Again, no-one was home.

Where was everyone? Served him right for having a baby on a Saturday night, Jeff surmised. He then dialled the Blakes on Sydney's north shore and was rewarded for his persistence by the sound of a woman's cheerful voice at the other end.

'Celia, it's Jeff.'

'Oh, hello, dear. How are you?'

The young man put his hand over the mouthpiece as a huge swell of relief engulfed him.

'Are you there, Jeff?' Celia asked.

The caller coughed. 'Yes. Sorry. I came over all emotional for a minute there. It's so nice to hear a real person. I've just hit a whole series of answering machines in quick succession and I'm anxious to share my good news with a voice that'll have a conversation with me.'

'News?' the well-spoken Mosman native sounded interested. 'How's Lynn? Has she had the baby?'

'Yeah. She has. Just this afternoon,' he told his friend's mother, 'and we've got a little girl. Can you believe it?'

'Oh, that's lovely, darling. I'm so happy for you,' Celia's response was typically effervescent.

Jeff clenched his jaw, feeling sentimentality overtaking him again. 'Yeah. It's perfect. Lynn's fine, and we're calling her Kierney. I forgot how tiny they are when they're brand new.'

'Yes, they are. Thank God, as I'm sure Lynn would agree. What does Jet think? Keely, did you say?'

'Kierney,' he elongated the syllables more clearly. 'The Irish name, you know, but spelled differently. It means "She knows," and she absolutely does. Jet doesn't know yet though. He's at the farm with Lynn's parents.'

'Oh, I see. Kierney, with an "N"? That's nice,' Gerry's mum chuckled. 'Jet's in for a surprise tomorrow then!'

'Yeah. Too right! They both are. We were up there and had to leave in a hurry, so Marianna's looking after him. They'll bring him down to the hospital tomorrow morning. It's going to be amazing to see the pair meet for the first time.'

Celia recognised how significant a moment this was for her favourite pseudo-son. 'It will be magical,' she agreed. 'Don't expect too much though. He might not be too impressed at having to share the limelight.'

'No. I know,' the father acknowledged. 'We've talked about that. It's bad enough having to share the limelight with me, huh?'

The middle-aged woman laughed. 'You make sure you take a video film, so we can see it next time we're down.'

'To be sure,' Jeff mocked. 'We shall. Anyway... What's new with you guys? Your family all fighting fit?'

'Yes. Thank you for asking, darling. We're looking after the twins tonight while Jacinta and Raymond go to a party. We're all surrounded by babies, aren't we?'

'Sounds like it. I hope Tammy's doing her fair share of babysitting.'

'She does, on occasion,' the grandmother sighed. 'She's far too busy living it up, like her brother.'

'Well, I'd better go. Enjoy yourselves,' Jeff signed off. 'We'll send you some pictures over the next few days. Talk soon, Celia.'

'Goodbye, darling. Give my best wishes to Lynn, and the children a big hug. And congrats again.'

'Thanks. I will. *Adiós.*'

The musician replaced the receiver and went into the bedroom to change into something smarter, in anticipation of hitting the town with his old friend later. While he was in the process of dressing, the telephone sprang to life, and he answered it with one leg stuck halfway down a pair of pants.

It was Madalena, suitably ebullient. '*¡Olá, chico!* Am I an auntie again?'

'Yes. You are!' Jeff shouted back. 'A girl this time. She's gorgeous and so bloody *pequeña.*'

The Sydneysider screamed. 'What's her name?'

'Kierney.'

'What?' the insensitive woman crowed.

'Kierney,' her brother enunciated more slowly, not bothering to spell the name out because he knew his sister wouldn't write it down.

Predictably, Madalena was nonplussed by a name she didn't recognise. 'OK. Not a Spanish name then. Thought you'd name 'er somethin' Spanish.'

'No. We thought about it but decided not to. We chose to keep the Irish theme going. To go with Ryan.'

The caller showed no concern for the deliberations which had gone into her niece's naming. She was obviously excited however, which pleased the man in Melbourne. For all her faults and lack of empathy, the former prostitute had repaid his generosity with more than a passing interest in his children.

'When can I come down?'

'Whenever,' he answered more cheerfully. 'Just book it with Cath. You're welcome any time.'

'Does she look like Jet?'

'No. She looks like you and me,' the songwriter replied, instantly feeling a lump in his throat again. 'Even more of a mongrel because she's got some Dutch Aussie in her too. *Es muy hermosa, Lena. Bella, bella.*'

'Oh, ace! Can't wait to see 'er.'

'Cheers. Gotta go,' her brother's voice cracked. 'Ring me when you know when you're coming, and we'll send a car to the airport.'

'OK,' she replied, without a word of thanks. 'See ya.'

After terminating the call, Jeff finished dressing and splashed on some after-shave. He figured Lynn would contact Michelle to give her the news, so began to rack his brains for anyone else who might have an evening's entertainment he could gatecrash. With the exception of his drummer, his band-mates were all overseas pursuing their independent musical ambitions between albums.

The detour into the office to locate Marty's number proved unnecessary since Gerry returned his friend's call a few minutes later. Relief surged through the star's veins anew. Over the worst of the anxiety, his priority had switched to breaking out and having a few drinks.

'Hey, mate. What's up?' the accountant was his usual vibrant self, and his client could almost smell the alcohol fumes through the telephone. 'I thought you were down on the farm.'

'Yeah. We were, but we had to make a dash into town. I've got more kids than you now.'

'Oh, shit! Have you? Lynn, I hope.'

The celebrity coughed, his mate's response only bordering on funny. 'Ah, yes. Hilarious you are, Yoda.'

'Fantastic news, me old buddy!' the Irishman chuckled. 'Good news indeed. Boy or girl?'

'Boy or girl?' Jeff parrotted. 'Whoa! I'm impressed by such a relevant question from the Party-Animal-in-Chief. A girl, and she looks like me.'

Gerry laughed. 'Bugger! My commiserations. Poor thing. Lucky you can afford the cosmetic surgery she's going to need.'

'Your humour knows no bounds tonight,' his client groaned. 'Listen… Are you at home?'

'Yeah. Just got in. Where are you?'

'At home. D'you fancy a beer or two more?'

The older man took no convincing. '*Bonzer* idea, mate. Any excuse. Are you coming over here?'

'Yep. I'll get a taxi, and we can grab some dinner,' Jeff suggested. 'Sounds like you need something to soak up what you've already drunk.'

'True enough,' Gerry agreed. 'Good idea. What about a curry? I could murder a curry.'

'Done! I'll be there in fifteen to twenty. *Adiós*, mate.'

***

Jeff woke with a start when the alarm on the digital watch he had been given for Christmas began to beep loudly. It was the first time he had tried to set it, and the bloody thing worked well. Much too well for people with hangovers! Gerry's couch was not made for six-feet-four-inch drunks to sleep on, but sleep on it he had. His head was thumping, and there were stale layers of beer, whisky and cigars plastered onto his teeth and tongue.

The beeping tone became progressively louder during the several seconds it took for his sluggish mind to remember which button cancelled the alarm. Fortunately, his manager was a heavy sleeper, and the high-pitched noise was highly unlikely to penetrate through his usual weekend haze, let alone his bedroom door at the other end of the spacious South Yarra apartment.

'Fuck!' Jeff swore at this offensive, new gadget, hoping he had managed to turn the infernal noise off permanently.

Seven o'clock beeped to spite him, signalling that it was about time the King of Diamonds hauled himself back to his own *pied-à-terre* to prepare it for occupation by his queen and baby princess. His stomach felt decidedly queasy as he screwed his shoes onto swollen feet and stood up, and the room swung round in circles while his head adjusted to the rarefied atmosphere at its normal altitude.

Quite apart from the effects of sleeping through a warm, airless night during which the temperature hadn't dropped below thirty degrees Celsius, it had been a long time since the family man had been on such a bender. His tolerance had evidently plunged to disappointingly humiliating depths.

'Gez,' Jeff said, knocking on his friend's bedroom door. 'Hey, mate? I'm leaving now.'

Only the sound of loud snores emanated from the narrow opening, and the unpleasant odour of an abused and overused male body greeted the guest's heightened sense of smell as he pushed the door further open. He decided against rousing the monster and thereby bringing forward the inevitable Sunday morning suffering.

The millionnaire wrote a note on the pad by the telephone, called for a taxi and let himself out of the apartment. Downstairs on the quiet, tree-lined street, he walked towards Toorak Road and loitered for a few minutes on the corner. This turned out to be a bad idea since he immediately attracted significant attention from a fashionable set of young joggers who had settled in for their morning coffee at the café opposite.

Not knowing how long it would take for his taxi to appear, the star took a deep breath and mingled with his adoring public. Much excitement ensued as he ordered *un espresso doppio* and sat down at a table among the trendy upwardly-mobiles, stirring in three spoonfuls of sugar and gulping the lethal shot down.

'Have you guys had your new baby yet?' asked one Lycra-clad woman. 'Isn't Lynn almost due?'

'Yeah,' Jeff replied, trying his hardest to smile without splitting his head in two at the temples. 'She arrived yesterday. Nine days early.'

A whoop went up in the café, causing some of the older regulars to tut loudly at the disturbance.

'A girl?' another svelte runner asked. 'Ahh! That's so good! What are you calling her?'

The new father chuckled. 'I can't tell you, on pain of death from my marketing manager. It has to go out in a press release first, can you believe? Sworn to secrecy, I'm sorry.'

'Is she named after one of your songs?' someone else hazarded.

'No. There's no point trying to guess. You'll never get it in a million years.'

A collective sigh ran around the small establishment, followed smartly by another when a yellow taxi pulled up on the other side of the street. Jeff swallowed down his final mouthful of coffee and said goodbye to the friendly group.

Back inside his apartment, the twenty-six-year-old cleaned his teeth vigorously and jumped into the shower, beginning to feel human at long last. He wolfed down a heaped bowl of cereal to set him up for the day. Lynn's smiling face filled his mind, pleased by infinitely more responsible behaviour than he had exhibited the night before.

For some unknown reason, the two *amigos* had found a very rough hotel in Richmond where they were showing a one-day international match live from the Sydney Cricket Ground. The pair had been welcomed into the *melée*, mainly because the hardcore drinkers were incapable of recognising them.

Even if they had, Jeff recalled with a smile, they had definitely been too far gone to string a question together.

The young father opened the door to Jet's room, which had lain empty since before the weekend. Soon there would be two little occupants in this bedroom. He and Lynn had decided that their children should learn to share everything, including each others' space. The cot in which their little girl would be sleeping was ready to be moved into the master bedroom for the first few nervous days, and Jeff stared at it in wonder. It seemed like only yesterday that their baby son had been lying in it, but he had long since graduated to a much larger cage.

So what sort of personality would Kierney have? Jet had been an in-your-face child from the very beginning; loud and gregarious, and unfailingly happy. The idea coalescing in her dad's mind of this exquisite daughter was of a more serious and thoughtful being; someone who would spend more time listening than making noise. He ought to be careful though... Was she telling him who she was, or was this his own prescription for who he wanted her to be?

Regardless, one thing was absolutely certain: the philosopher couldn't wait to find out. The Dysons would be bringing Jet into the city to meet his new sister; probably already on the open road from Benloch. He picked up his wallet and car keys and shut the front door behind him.

Stopping at the florist in the ground floor of the hospital's reception area, Jeff bought three separate gifts: a *bouquet* for his mother-in-law to thank her for looking after their son; a dozen blood-red roses for his beautiful best friend and the mother of his children; and another, single white rose for the discerning new lady in his life.

Lynn was dressed for homecoming when her husband was ushered into the room, laden with flowers and the teddy bear which had been left under the windscreen wiper of his car the previous evening.

'Hey!' she called out, running to give the handsome man a hug. 'Wow! You're so gorgeous. I'm so glad to see you.'

Jeff kissed his dream girl wantonly, attempting to wrap her up in his gift-bearing embrace. 'Christ! Me too,' he replied, placing the colourful and highly-scented arrangement down on the table and handing the dozen roses to his wife. 'Those are for your mum. These are for you.'

'Oh, they're beautiful. Thanks, Papá. I love you,' Lynn said, breathing in their fresh, strong scent. 'Mum'll be stoked that you thought of her.'

'*Y esta,*' the visitor continued, turning to the crib, '*señorita, es para ti.*'

Kierney Lynn Freedom Diamond lay on top of her blanket, gazing calmly up at her surroundings. Her eyes blinked on hearing the deep voice which had suddenly come closer. Jeff placed the rose across the baby's stomach, wondering if she too would pick up the scent. She displayed no reaction, but he left the flower where it was so that he could grab their camera and take a snap at the start of Day Two.

'How did you go last night?' he asked. 'Did you both get some sleep?'

'Yes, thanks. A few hours here and there. She's very quiet. Doesn't seem nearly as demanding as Jet was, unless she's working up to it.'

The introvert chuckled. 'Perhaps she's doing what I did when I first met you: on her best behaviour until you get to know her better, and then she's going to unleash a torrent of demandingness.'

'Oh, well,' the young woman sighed, smiling at the memory. 'If she does, at least I know what I'm in for. I wheeled her into the shower earlier, and she just lay there kicking her feet at the sound of the water. Not in the least bit bothered.'

'Can I pick her up?' Jeff asked, longing for a cuddle.

'Go for your life!' Lynn exclaimed. 'She's your baby too, you know.'

'Are you sure?' her husband gave a sly wink.

'Look at her! Who else's could she possibly be?'

The dark-haired man sensed this was true, although unable to see the striking resemblance as clearly as his wife could. To help prove her point, she asked him to hold Kierney's head next to his and took a photograph. They both laughed when their little one jumped at the shutter's clicks and whirrs, more out of curiosity than fear.

The doting dad cuddled his daughter into his chest. 'Whoa, *pequeñita*. You're alert to everything, aren't you?'

'You'll probably be able to tell better from these,' Lynn told him, snapping another close-up of both faces. 'Did you speak to people last night?'

'In the pub? Yeah. Heaps of people. Can't remember a thing though.'

'Serves you right!' the athlete scolded, rolling her eyes. 'Where did you go?'

'I have no idea,' the comic lied, making his night out to sound even more debauched than it was. 'Richmond. We went to some place where the cricket was on TV. Gerry was already shit-faced from the afternoon session, so we grabbed a curry and then carried on where he left off.'

'Ugh! So how do you feel now?' his wife asked, putting her hand to her own head in advance of his answer.

'Fine, to be honest. Almost, anyway. I only drank beer, except for two whiskies back at Gerry's place before I crashed on his couch. Jesus, I was bloody sore when I woke up though! I'm getting too old to play up, you'll be glad to hear.'

The new mum chuckled, having a pretty good idea why the former night-owl hadn't taken advantage of his friend's spare room. 'I *am* glad to hear! So did you speak to anyone who wasn't at the pub?'

Jeff twisted the bundle around until he could see the little girl's face, a picture of contentment lying in his arms. 'Oops, Kizzo! Why didn't you remind me I hadn't answered Mamá's question? What sort of partner-in-crime are you?'

Lynn smiled, sitting on the bed and finishing the pot of tea that had been delivered by a friendly Philippino orderly just before her handsome *chauffeur* had arrived. She loved to watch her husband interact with their youngsters, deliberately drawing them into every aspect of their life.

'I was really pissed off when I got home,' the songwriter continued. 'All prepared to impart our happy news, and all I got was a series of bloody answering machines. Celia was the only one at home.'

'Oh, no! Poor you. Was she happy?'

'To be sure, to be sure!' he replied, putting on his best cultured Irish accent. 'She sends you her love, of course. Then Lena rang back and screamed at me. She told me off for not giving Kierney a Spanish name. Like she cares anyway...'

'Really?' his wife said in surprise. 'I wouldn't have thought she would expect it. She never mentioned that about Jet's name.'

'No. But maybe she thinks Jet's like Jeff Junior.'

Lynn nodded. 'OK. Yeah. That's logical. So does she want to come down?'

'Yep. Brazen as ever. Did you talk to Michelle?'

The young woman shook her head. 'Just left a message.'

'I didn't ring her because I thought you would. Maybe she's away?'

'No. Don't think so. Maybe there's a new man on the scene. It was Saturday night after all. I watched all the rubbish television programmes that we never usually see because we're out. I even did some work for an hour or so.'

The drowsy rocker sat down on the bed with his wife and daughter. Kierney barely made a sound. He would have forgotten she was in the blanket if she hadn't occasionally twitched an arm or leg. After a while, the little one drifted off to sleep, only to be woken shortly afterwards by a cacophony outside their door.

Lynn and Jeff looked at each other and grinned, realising their peace was about to be shattered by the lovable peace-shatterer *extraordinair*. Maggie Thompson had turned up right on time, her dignitary radar working to perfection. She was followed into the room by Marianna and Bart, who was carrying Jet, presumably because it was the only way they could control his hyperactivity. A bemused Sandy filed in last, slinking in and leaning against the wall in true teenaged fashion.

'Mamá! Dad!' the little boy shouted at the top of his voice.

'Shhh!' his parents hissed as one, before laughing at the futility of such a request.

The Dysons both leaned in to kiss their daughter and to check out the latest addition to their dynasty, who was resting in her father's arms. Jeff stood up and handed the little one to her grandmother.

'This is Kierney Lynn Freedom Diamond,' he announced proudly. 'Your granddaughter.'

'Kierney?' Bart repeated, turning to his daughter for confirmation. 'That's unusual. How long have you had that one in mind?'

'Ages. It goes with Ryan and it just stuck the moment we came up with it, didn't it?'

Her husband nodded. 'Yep. And it works for her too.'

Shaking the sportsman's hand, Jeff stepped aside to watch the new family members acquaint themselves with the new arrival. Thrusting their video camera into Lynn's brother's hands, he asked him to play cameraman and capture Jet's introduction to his sister.

Sandy was more than happy to be given such a responsible job. Playfully, Jeff wrestled for his son's attention and made him rehearse some words to say to the baby. He kissed the attentive child on the forehead and fixed his eyes with a businesslike stare.

'Now Jet... Listen a sec', please. You say, "Hello, Kierney. My name's Jet. I'm your big brother and I love you." She won't talk to you. She's too little, but she might blink or move her hands or something. That means she heard you. "Hello, Kierney. My name's Jet. I'm your big brother and I love you." OK, mate?'

The boy nodded, keen to make his dad happy. Lifted up onto the mattress, he began to bounce up and down on the bed, which allowed Sandy to train the camera on his subject while waiting for a cue from his sister.

Shuffling along the bed towards his mum, Jet plonked his bottom down on the sheet and took a deep breath. Smiling sweetly, he recited his lines like a professional; word perfect. Hearing another different voice, the baby blinked and opened her mouth, somehow prompting the little charmer to lean forward and kiss her. The new parents marvelled at the learned habit which had been instilled in him since he was tiny. He was merely carrying on the family tradition.

'Hey. That's priceless, mate,' Jeff praised, sniffing back tears and ruffling his son's hair. 'Good job. *Gracias.*'

Even the crusty statesman had a tear in his eye after the cute siblings' introduction, putting his arm around Marianna, who was in floods.

'Oh, Jet, darling,' she wailed. 'That was such a lovely thing to do. And so gentle. What a good boy!'

Jet beamed, at first loving the limelight and knowing he had done something very much appreciated, before coming over all shy. Cuddling into his mother's side, next to the fascinating bundle called Kierney, he listened intently as Lynn asked him to describe each person to his sister.

The confident child's eyes whipped around the room to select his first subject. 'That's Grandpa,' he pointed at Bart. 'Hard work.'

The Olympian nodded gratefully at the well-chosen words.

'Grandma, big dinner,' Jet said about Marianna, causing everyone to laugh, wondering why he had selected that particular description.

'He was very full last night when we finished our meal,' the elegant woman confessed. 'It must've stuck in his mind.'

The toddler's gaze swept round to his father, who was leaning against the cupboard beside the bed and wiping tears of joy from his eyes. 'That's my dad. He's our hero, Mamá.'

Taken aback, Jeff's lungs took in a deep breath, and his heart leaped into his mouth. He shrugged comically at the others, who were equally stunned at the directness of Jet's comment.

His wife broke the spell, reaching her spare hand up to her handsome magician. 'We always call him our hero, don't we?' she said to Jet. 'When he's away helping someone or working with poor, unlucky people. He's Kierney's dad too, isn't he?'

'Superman?' Marianna offered to her grandson, who dismissed the suggestion out of court the way that only toddlers can, vigorously shaking his head.

Lynn came to the lad's rescue. 'Only cartoon superheroes wear their knickers outside their trousers, don't they? Not real ones like Papá.'

Her effort at saving her mother's embarrassment fell on deaf ears however since Jet had already moved on.

'Mamá sexy,' he guffawed, as if he had said something naughty.

Eyeing his father out of the corner of his eye in a particularly grown-up way, the larrikin drew a curvy figure in the air with both hands. Sandy almost dropped the camera as the whole room dissolved into hysterics.

Jeff coughed and copied his son's gesture. 'You're right, mate! Very sexy. That's what got me into this trouble in the first place.'

'Oh, thank you! Two sex maniacs in the family,' his dream girl sighed, listening to everyone's reaction. 'I don't look like that now though, I'm sure.'

'And Sandy, drive very fast,' Jet shouted over the noise, waving an arm dramatically towards the cameraman, before mimicking a racing driver on an extremely winding road.

Lynn smiled at her brother, who had recovered his composure and was wandering around the room to make sure he covered every angle. Their father was mellowing as his parenting responsibilities were on the wane. He would never have agreed to sit in the passenger seat with her at the wheel!

'Dad let me drive here, and I was speeding a bit,' the teenager admitted from behind the camera.

'Well, that's on tape forever now, as your confession,' Bart mocked his second son.

'And one more,' the lad was still playing to the crowd. 'This Kierney, scrunchy face!'

It was true. The baby's features were twisting into a strained expression, her complexion turning a definite shade of puce.

'Alright! This is all too much for her delicate constitution,' Jeff declared, feeling for his tiny daughter. '*Déjame te han, pequeñita.*'

Seeing his wife struggling to the edge of the bed, the embarrassed man waved a hand for her to stay where she was. He whisked the towelling bundle up through the air, both disappearing into the bathroom, leaving the others to congratulate Jet on his excellent introductions.

'What did he say to her?' Marianna asked.

'He calls her *pequeñita*,' Lynn repeated. 'It means "little one" in Spanish. I'm not quite sure what the other phrase was.'

'So! Well done, young Jet,' the boy's grandfather clapped his hands, fixing his daughter with enquiring eyes. 'What's the plan now, everyone?'

'We're going home,' she answered. 'That's all I know. What are you all doing?'

Marianna spoke. 'Your father and Sandy are going to the Sportsdrome, and I'm going to catch up on some charity correspondence and then meet up with Anna this afternoon.'

Jeff re-emerged with Kierney dressed in a smart all-in-one outfit, spruced up and ready for her very short journey home. She looked so tiny, and her little face remained ever tranquil.

'Come to dinner this evening,' the proud dad suggested. 'I'll cook. I'd like to. It'll be the first time I'll have been useful in nine months...'

His partner nodded. 'That's about right!'

Jeff leaned his wriggling missile over the bed and swooped her down towards his wife's beautiful face. 'Thump her, Kizzy,' he instructed, knocking a little fist onto Lynn's head before depositing their daughter into her mother's lap. 'Nothing fancy. Just peasant food, 'cause that's all I can do! I'll get Gerry and Michelle to come too. How does that sound?'

Considering the invitation unanimously a grand idea, the three visitors took their cue to leave.

'Thank Grandma and Grandpa for looking after you, Jet, please,' Lynn requested, receiving a parting kiss from each parent. 'See you later on. Come any time. We'll be in.'

The world-changer picked up their firstborn and hugged him, ecstatic that his family of four Diamonds now found itself alone. 'You were fantastic, mate,' he told the beaming toddler. 'So unbelievably fantastic! What d'you think of your little sister then? Isn't she beautiful?'

To the parents' surprise, their son burst into tears. Laying Kierney into her cot, Lynn stood up and went to give him some undivided attention. She stroked his back as he was rocked from side to side in his father's cradling arms.

'What's the matter, gorgeous?' she crooned.

Jet cried softly for a minute or so before starting to smile again, every now and again letting out a small sniff. The celebrities looked at each other and shrugged. It had been an emotional half-hour for them all, and even bombastic toddlers had the right to be overcome occasionally.

The caring mother took the nineteen-month-old outside to the nurses' station to say goodbye to Maggie and her crew while Jeff loaded Kierney into her bassinet and scrambled their belongings together roughly. He stared around the room for the last time, realising that this particular chapter was about to close. The master plan for their life singular involved no more maternity wards, and there would be no more cute introductions. Their family was complete: two males and two females. How perfectly balanced!

Australia's favourite couple posed for last-minute photographs with all the staff, whose numbers seemed to have been boosted way beyond the normal Sunday morning skeleton coverage. The cluster then descended *en masse* to see their guests off. Thankfully, there was no shortage of helpers to carry their disorganised set of bags. Jeff walked with Jet to the Aston Martin, which was surrounded by well-wishers once again. How on Earth did people always find out when they were on the move?

In a repeat of the last time they left this very building, the crowd surged forward to catch sight of the new arrival. Taking the baby from Lynn as she dropped into the car seat, the millionnaire held Kierney up like a trophy.

'Isn't this wonderful?' he yelled. 'And so much fun to make...'

Their fans laughed at the star's cheeky comment. His stunning co-star frowned and shook her patient head, reaching out to take their daughter on her lap. Holding Jet briefly aloft to ensure he wasn't left out, Jeff bent over and strapped him safely into his seat in the tiny rear compartment and waved before jumping in and speeding away.

'*Adiós*, Mercy. Shall we go to a hotel instead?' he joked. 'They can make their own dinner.'

The blonde singer giggled. 'Hmm... I dare you.'

Within ten minutes, the happy family was inside the apartment. Jeff distributed the various bags to their most appropriate rooms and went into the kitchen to put a pot of coffee on. He was starving after his big night out, so set about preparing a makeshift luncheon for whomever wanted it.

Finally free to run riot again, Jet sprinted down the hallway towards his bedroom, shouting at the top of his voice. 'Kierney, here sleep.'

Lynn followed him at a more sedate pace to allow the baby time to survey her new home. 'Kierney won't be sleeping with you for a few days, Jetto. She's too little at the moment, so she'll sleep in with Papá and me.'

'Oh, why?' the boy whined. 'I sleep you?'

'No,' his mum replied firmly. 'You slept in our room when you were first born too, and then you came in here when you were four days old. That's what we'll do with your baby sister too.'

Jet nodded reluctantly, his eyes distracted by a gift-wrapped parcel on the floor beside his bed. 'OK.'

Watching their son tear into the brightly-coloured package and extract a robust model earthmover from its box, Lynn leaned on the doorframe and rocked Kierney in her arms. She was grateful for her husband's forethought. He who rarely descended to detail could certainly pull out all the stops when required.

'Who's hungry?' Jeff asked, taking hold of the tennis champion's shoulders and encouraging her to lean back against his chest.

'What's on offer?'

The red-blooded man looked into her eyes with a broad grin on his face. 'What's on offer? Oh, don't tempt me, woman!'

'Shame,' her pouting reply was swallowed into a deep kiss. 'We'll have some toasties, please, won't we, Jetto? What did you have at Grandma and Grandpa's?'

'Weetbix,' Jet replied. 'And "OJ".'

'"OJ"?' his dad chuckled. 'That's very grown-up, mate. Next you'll be asking for a gin and tonic.'

'Yeah! Yeah! Yeah!' the boy shouted, showing off. 'Gin and tonic, please.'

'Calm down,' Lynn warned, stroking the top of their son's head. 'It's all very exciting having Kierney home, I know. Now we just have to settle down and do what we normally do. Nothing special, alright? Go and help Papá with the lunch, please.'

The happy mother laid the baby into the cot beside their queen-sized bed and stood mesmerised by her facial contortions. This brand new person was quite the most calm and contemplative thing she had clapped eyes on. Had her husband been this calm at first, in the months before his precarious domestic environment started to cave in? She smiled to herself, unable to believe Madalena ever being placid. Yet, knowing her perfect stranger as she knew him now, she could well imagine the same serious, cogitative type of baby who was content simply to watch, listen and learn.

After their first meal together as a foursome, Lynn retired to bed for a few hours. Jeff sat at the piano while Jet played with his cars. A song had been running around inside his head since he had woken up and took shape quickly once his hands constructed a suitable chord sequence. Then, after an hour or so of playing, his son also began to show signs of irritability.

Initially full of objections and worried about missing out on more fun, the youngster refused to lie down on the couch. The determined father took him into his bedroom and read him a couple of stories before telling him to get some shut-eye so that he was refreshed for when Grandpa and Grandma arrived for dinner.

'*Mamá y Kierney se despierta cuando te levantas, no te preocupes, hijo mío,*' the songwriter told his overtired offspring, gently stroking his hair until he fell asleep.

Wandering back into the lounge room alone again, as he had been that morning, Jeff became overwhelmed by his fortuitous circumstance. The three people he cared more about than life itself were home, safe and sound. He felt incredibly protective towards them, unable to stop himself creeping into the main bedroom to check on his dream girls. He stood watching them both sleeping, with tears rolling down his face and his new song churning around in his mind.

The lost boy who had succeeded beyond his wildest dreams could hardly wait to instal his loved ones into their custom-made, secret bolt-hole, where they planned to shut themselves away to enjoy being the Four of Diamonds once the house was finally finished. The vision of their *hacienda* was almost a reality, with only the furnishings and other finer touches remaining, soon to be brought to practical completion by a small army of contractors. The cottages where their drivers and nannies would be accommodated had fallen behind schedule by a few weeks, but the end was well and truly in sight.

Another batch of random words formed into a poem as Jeff stood there, not atypically in French. Not so many years ago, the tearaway from Sydney's south-west could never have seen himself owning even one home, let alone two. And now he had a wife and kids too.

Marvelling at how much he had changed, the humble bard allowed the poetry to percolate for a few seconds. It spoke of his old plan; the one that had been formulated during the couple's year in London, even before he had proposed to her. He wrote out the opening line on a scrap of paper and left it on his wife's bedside table, tucking the edge silently under her glass.

'Lynn, t**u** *m'as rendu la vie complète entre Montréal et Moscou. Je t'aime, mon amie.* Jx'

Yet another of his audacious plans had worked. Had his old soul driven his current life to where it needed to go, or was it merely a passenger in this modern-day fairy tale?

***

'So where did that sweet, little boy go?' Kierney asked, accepting a mug of coffee from her father. 'Thanks. Are you alright, Papá?'

'Ha! Christ knows, *pequeñita*,' Jeff chuckled. 'He had an innate skill, your brother... Even from a young age, he always turned it on for the cameras.'

'Did I?'

'Not to the same extent. Your demeanour never did such an obvious one-eighty as his did. A bit like your mamá, I suppose. She would disguise her true feelings from the public way more than I ever could. And you were somewhere in the middle, I think. D'you agree?'

The seventeen-year-old shrugged. 'I don't know. I don't ever think about it. I try to be myself all the time. Are you sure you're OK? You look scared or something. Nervous...'

'Well spotted,' the widower sat down in the office chair, vacated by his steadfast proofreader. 'I'm preparing to document something that now feels like a premonition. Something else we never acted upon at the time.'

'What was that? Something you've already told us?'

'No. I doubt it. Unless your mamá told you...' Jeff twisted the chair around to face Kierney, who had made herself comfortable on the couch, with her legs curled up underneath her and the mug pressed against expectant lips. 'I had the worst nightmare in three years on the night we brought you home.'

'Did you? Oh, no! Mamá never told me about that. *¿Qué ha pasado?*'

The author forced himself to articulate the disparate memories which had been vying for position in his mind while he had been waiting for the coffee to brew. 'I'm not sure if it was because that was the first night our whole family was under the same roof, or whether it'd been influenced by spending the previous night on my own at Gerry's.'

Lighting a cigarette and offering another to the remaining girl of his dreams, the forty-four-year-old was hit by a flash of clarity. 'No. Shit! It wasn't either of those things. Jesus, Kiz! *Gracias por tu ayuda.*'

The young woman sat up, amazed at this sudden change of heart. 'What? What did I do?'

'It was thinking about moving to Escondido,' her father explained, jotting a few words down onto his notepad. 'So far out of town. Secluded, you know... Like I was tempting providence. Making it easier for someone to do us harm without being detected or apprehended.'

'Right. Did you want me to get Ry? He should hear this too, I guess.'

Ryan Diamond had not yet emerged from his bedroom that morning, having been on a reckless night out with some mates after returning from Cambridge at the end of term. The threesome had had dinner together the evening before, over which the children teased every last detail about their early childhoods out of the autobiographer.

Before Jeff had a chance to answer, Kierney was on her feet. He turned to the computer, transcribing the hastily scribbled notes under a new chapter heading. Within a few minutes, the friendly pair burst back into the room, his son red-faced and dressed only in boxer shorts and an old T-shirt.

'I can wait,' the older man smiled. 'What time did you get in?'

'No, Papá,' his daughter insisted. 'He showered before he went to bed. Let's go!'

The chief Diamond looked bewildered. 'How do you know he showered before he went to bed? Did you rig up some sort of clean-squad camera?'

'I told her,' the nineteen-year-old jeered. 'She wanted to know if I stank or not. Is there any more coffee? Anyone want a top-up?'

While the cricketer was away on his caffeine quest, his sister leafed through another diary which had been left on the arm of the sofa. Jeff watched her out of the corner of his eye. Both kids were doing well, so much more level-headed than he had been at the same stage of life. They knew how to enjoy themselves within the bounds of legality, seldom damaging their iconic brands by exhibiting unsuitable role-model behaviour.

'*Vamos!*' Ryan cheered, collapsing his enormous frame onto the floorboards, cool in the absence of the direct sunlight which had been streaming into the kitchen.

'You can summarise, *pequeñita*,' their father requested, 'while I gather my thoughts.'

Kierney recounted the few sentences which had been imparted before she had paused the writer mid- epiphany. 'So I'm not sure why this realisation came as such a shock. Why did it matter that you had such a bad nightmare?'

'I was punishing myself... then and now, I think... about accusing that bloody imaginary troll of sabotaging my happiness at having Lynn and both of you in my life. I'd gone to bed blissfully happy with our life singular, and also pretty damned arrogant that I had made it happen quite systematically. I always blamed this audacious self-congratulation for Gravity's evil attack, bringing the arsehole demons back to haunt me after so long.'

'Record this,' his daughter suggested, pointing to the Dictaphone device on the bookshelf. 'If you get on a roll, you won't need to worry about missing something when you do it again. Capture the spontaneous, didn't you say the other week? Like Sandy did when I was born.'

'Yeah. Go on then. Turn it on,' the nervous man muttered, thinking of the contrast between his mood on that splendid February Sunday and the way he felt at the present time. 'Good idea, gorgeous. Cheers.'

His son reached a long bowler's arm behind his sister's head and slipped the voice recorder off the shelf with one finger until it fell into his expert fielding grasp. After flicking the button and waiting for the light to change from blinking to solid, he blew into it. The sound level on both channels surged momentarily into the red zone, and with a flash of his approving eyebrows, the nineteen-year-old sat the machine onto the desk beside his father's left elbow.

'Ready to go, boss.'

'No shit!' his dad laughed. 'It's probably broken now. Anyway, we're in bed. You, Kizzy, are in the crib right next to us. We've zonked out, dead to the world, after we had a houseful for dinner. Apparently, I let out a bloodcurdling scream and sat bolt upright, my hands making straight for Lynn's head.'

'To strangle her?' Ryan yelped.

'No, not her neck. Her head, mate. I scared her big-time. She whipped her arms out from under the sheet and blocked her face, so she told me, wondering if she were about to be belted. She assumed I'd mistaken her for one of the gangland brutes invading my old flat.'

Jeff shuddered as he remembered waking up to his wife's terrified eyes, his hands falling like dead weights onto his thighs. 'Christ! I didn't usually regain consciousness so quickly. I think it was because you were in the room, *pequeñita*. You didn't cry though. You were awake but you didn't cry. I wanted you to, in case the shock festered inside you.'

'Well, it didn't,' Kierney smiled. 'Perhaps I was sleeping too soundly? Carry on. What were you dreaming about?'

'I dreamed your mamá was pushed down the stairs. I was completely frantic, desperate to speak but my jaws were clenched shut. Her skull was crushed against the tiles. Blood everywhere…'

The gruesome scene brought the billionnaire to tears, too similar to the sight he had witnessed seventeen years later. 'But the guardian angel in my bed lifted one of my trembling hands and placed it on her intact, blood-free head, keen to reassure me that it was just a dream. At first, it didn't do any good. My eyes were thunderous, I think she says in the diary.'

His daughter knelt on the cushion of the couch and reached down the volume for nineteen-seventy-nine. She knew its exact position in the pile since she had only been reading it the day before. Skipping over the first month's pages, her fingers slowed down until she arrived at the eleventh of February.

'Here…

'"Did she fall or was she pushed? Jeff dreamed last night that he found me dead at the bottom of the stairs in the new house. That's what he said he was thinking as he ran down the stairs to see me."

'Oh, my God. That must've been horrible. But awesome to find out it was a nightmare, I'd imagine.'

'Yep. Eventually,' her father answered. 'Lynn was unnerved by it too. It wasn't like the other nightmares. You know... In the old flat and with *Abuela* and Lena being abused by my dad's enemies. This was in the house we'd designed as our sanctuary, and before we'd ever even lived there. It freaked us both out.'

'Weird,' the blond student mused. 'And you never dreamed that again?'

'Nope. Mum reckoned it was all the talk about the design of the house over dinner, and discussing the materials, *et cetera*.' Jeff continued, feeling better after purging the emotion from his old soul. 'She asked me if I recognised where we were, and I told her I didn't know. I didn't remember anything I'd dreamed before that point, but I was adamant it was the new house. White marble tiles and a long, curved balustrade. Exactly what we'd put in the plans. "OK, scratch those," Lynn said, trying to pull me out of the doldrums.'

Kierney giggled. 'Yes. It's here...

'"Shag-pile carpet and rubber railings it is," I told him, to which he replied, 'No way!'"'

'I did. Jesus! She always wanted to make me feel better. She said we had to strike a balance between safety and prison. That was scary too because it was precisely what'd been going through my head as she spoke. Like *aussi-vu* rather than *déjà-vu*.'

Ryan burst out laughing. 'But that's OK. You are an Aussie. That's the only type of *vu* you can have, old man.'

'Bro! That was the worst attempt at a pun I've ever heard!' his sister whacked the conceited sportsman's knee with the leather-bound diary. 'You're forbidden to open your mouth again for the rest of the day. Get on with the story, Papá, please.'

Jeff shook his head, chuckling at his children's antics. 'That's probably about it really. It was rational and irrational fears conspiring together again, we concluded. Your mamá was right about that, even though I disputed it at the time. I said that to fear for her safety wasn't irrational. She said it damned well was. "Inside the house? How likely is it that someone could get all the way up the stairs in the new house, with all the gates, doors and alarms we specked out yesterday?" She was right.'

'She could've fallen,' the dark-haired teenager muttered, immediately wishing she hadn't voiced this thought.

'Yeah. She could've. And so could either of you.'

'Or you,' Ryan dared, receiving another, more subdued slap from his contrite sister.

'Falling was pretty unlikely, and a person... well, an adult or older kid... can normally stop him- or herself relatively quickly after a fall, before they can be too badly injured. Rather than being pushed, where there's all that momentum on top of the element of surprise.'

'OK. I s'pose so,' the young woman frowned. 'So what did you do?'

'We agreed to get more security,' Jeff replied. 'Whereupon your genius of a mother unveiled her secret weapon...'

'What secret weapon? Does this have something to do with sex?' his son perked up.

'No! Not straight after I was born, surely! Not another blowjob?'

'No!' her father remonstrated in almost as high-pitched a tone as his flabbergasted gipsy girl. 'Nothing whatsoever to do with sex! You two have filthy minds. I have no idea where you get that trait from. It's disgusting. She told me Big D wanted us to get more security too.'

'Oh-oh,' the burly sportsman smirked. 'Now it all makes sense! She asked you to talk to him.'

'Indeed. Clever minx. She was sure a left-field reference to her dad's opinion on the matter would be sufficient to buck my mood up again. It worked a treat. I said, "No, thanks. He told me you were my responsibility," at which she accused me of being pig-headed.'

'Oh, really?' Ryan's voice was perfectly poised between innocence and sarcasm. 'Can't think why?'

Jeff waved a threatening finger. 'Easy, Captain Marvellous. You're already on a yellow card. She said he'd used security firms for years, and that he could advise us or hook us up with someone. I said, "I don't need his advice," and stormed off into the *en suite*.'

'Mama writes about that too,' Kierney piped up. 'Listen to this... It's funny and lovely at the same time.

> '"When Jeff came back from the bathroom, with his hair partially towelled dry and his body smelling fresh and scented, I cuddled into him. His demeanour was much calmer, much more like his daughter's, and he welcomed my touch warmly, planting a kiss on my apprehensive lips. He was admitting defeat without admitting defeat; the Jeff Diamond way."

'Ahh! That's even a bit poetic.'

'Yep. Denuded yet again,' the grieving husband let out a deep sigh. 'She said we could always stay in the apartment, but I didn't want you guys holed up above sea-level your whole childhood.'

'Because you were?' his daughter asked.

'Partly,' he nodded, 'but I wanted our kids to have space, fresh air, adventures. Normal kid things.'

'Because you didn't?' Kierney cocked her head.

The great man chuckled. 'That's exactly what Mamá said. She was always determined to get to the root cause of my angst. She taught you well, *pequeñita*. It turned into an argument in the end. I said not to make it about me trying to atone for the past because it only encouraged the paranoia locked up inside me. This did the trick.'

'Yes,' the spellbound law student whispered. 'There's a line in here:

> '"Perhaps we should be paranoid about our own security. I'm glad Jeff has a sixth sense."

'What did she say to you about it?'

'Ah, you know... I apologised for getting riled, but she said I wasn't as screwed up as I might think. She was right, and you should remember this too... It's normal to want to protect your family.'

'Hey?'

The widower looked around at his daughter, perturbed that his poignant lesson had been cut short. 'What?'

'I always forget to ask you,' the young woman smiled.

'Ask me what?'

'Did that Tim guy ever get his money back after your wedding?'

Her father sniffed, surprised by this strange memory. 'No. I decided to let it go. Lena never asked me either.'

'*N'aucune surprise, n'est-ce pas?*' Ryan sniggered, his deep voice impersonating the wise man in their midst.

Escondido

Over the ensuing weeks, little Kierney grew stronger and livelier day-by-day. Her parents were sure she was deep in communication with the rest of her family, her eyes darting from one side of the room to the other to keep track of everyone's contribution. Several different but most distinct noises regularly emerged from her tiny mouth, leading the couple to chastise each other for reading too much into them.

When the time came for Jeff to head back to London for more talks on the South African crisis, he had never felt more of a pull towards home. It reminded him of the panic which used to engulf him whenever his former self said goodbye to his sixteen-year-old schoolgirl, forever taunted by the spiteful troll that he would never see her again. The difference now, after this intense period of happiness and healing, was that he no longer had the uncontrollable compulsion to throw everything else away for a single moment of connectedness.

Regardless, the peacemaker missed Lynn and the children terribly while he was overseas, spending ages on the telephone talking nonsense with his son and at his daughter, and reciting endless, ever stronger *stanzas* of devotion with his gorgeous soul-mate.

Kierney was four months old and beginning to sit up unaided when the Diamond family readied itself to move into its beautiful house, perched high on the cliff above a surf beach in Mount Eliza. Jet hadn't found his sister at all interesting once the novelty of having a crying machine in his bedroom had worn off. However, as soon as she was old enough to be plonked on the floor, the baby served a useful purpose as a centrepiece for his imaginative games.

Not to be outdone by his son for cool toys, Jeff took delivery of a charcoal grey Holden WB Caprice, brand spanking new off the production line. He had found Lynn's little BMW never quite made the grade when travelling back and forth between the city, Benloch and the airport, and with regular commuting to the Mornington Peninsula on the cards as well, it was time to "invest" in a luxury family car.

This latest model Statesman variant, built in South Australia and re-badged in the USA by Chevrolet as the *de Ville*, was equipped with a thirsty five-litre engine manufactured only a few kilometres from their city apartment. He had seriously considered the newly-launched models of both the Daimler Sovereign Series III and the Mercedes SEL W126, and briefly even an equivalent Cadillac or Lincoln, but couldn't stomach the political and social leap into upper-middle-classed conservatism, not to mention the boat-like suspension in comparison to the Aston Martin's road-hugging ride.

Therefore, much to his mate's disgust and his father-in-law's amazement, Australia's best known global citizen went local. Lynn wholeheartedly approved of her husband's choice, bringing back fond memories of speeding along in his old, blue Ford Fairlane, but with none of the worrying rattles and no constant threat of overheating.

Moreover, the statement the rock star's decision made about their partnership was important to her too, given its ever-accelerating social justice agenda. The promise the couple had given each other while in London to reserve one day every month when no money changed hands had never seemed more significant than now, eager to set a good example as parents by appreciating the value of money and its relative unimportance to the more fundamental needs of life.

The celebrities were also determined to remain in touch with their fans and the media middlemen who treated them with unprecedented respect. After many heart-to-heart conversations about the pros and cons of living in the public eye, Lynn and Jeff opened their new house to a television crew to document everyday life with their growing youngsters. They battled with the narcissistic image it might portray, eventually resolving that if the cameras were to pay witness to "warts and all" events, this fear would be dispelled by refusing any cutting room censorship.

Thus, monthly visits by a film crew commenced where no corner was out of bounds. The first programme followed the journey from acquiring their property, through knocking down the old structures and then building the new one. Regular splices, including awkward guest appearances by their architect neighbours, had been shot as their home took shape and were strung together as part of the series opener.

'Now no-one'll bother us if they see us out in the big, wide world,' Jeff laughed with Don Jenner during the first interview, while the family conducted a tour of the spacious ground floor, ''cause they're sick of the bloody sight of us. Anonymity through saturation, eh, mate?'

'Our kids are going to have cameras and microphones thrust in their faces wherever they go anyway, just like I had,' Lynn explained further. 'So why not train them to accept it? Then they'll learn to behave naturally.'

The next episode brought Jet's second birthday into the Australian television viewing community's lounge rooms. To the audience's delight, it included a visit from Bart and Marianna Dyson and a trip inside their city apartment.

A divine piece of family history was caught in the third, when Jeff was playing on the couch with the two children, teaching them how to communicate different emotions by pulling faces. He had asked Jet to create a scary expression for his sister, and the little boy's attempt at the grotesque had been so successful that Kierney screamed and burst into tears.

'Oh, Kizzo,' the empathetic dad gasped, wrapping her up in his arms. 'I'm sorry, baby. It's only Jet. He's not really that scary. ¿Estás OK?'

The cameras tracked the older brother's efforts to make amends, also upset at having frightened his baby sister. Despite the father's best endeavours, it had been a good few minutes before Kierney would let him come anywhere near her.

'She's scarred for life now,' Jeff turned to the camera with tears in his own eyes. 'What a stupid game that was.'

The response to these documentaries was overwhelming. The Diamonds had captured a moment in time when Australia's population yearned for some happy news with which they could easily identify, especially after the political turmoil the country had been through during the closing decade. The accessibility of their favourite local family made the dawn of the nineteen-eighties somehow more palatable.

And as the weather warmed up towards the end of the year, the cameras followed the Diamonds outside. One particular episode saw Jet running around naked as the crew accompanied their handsome and hunky host out to their outdoor pool, ad-libbing with an impish smile.

'Lynn, I'd thank you not to let our son appear in public in that state,' the comic scolded, before turning to the lens with a theatrical aside. 'Though how deliciously embarrassing it will be for him later in life...'

Right on cue, the young boy had run up to his father, presenting the perfect opportunity to continue the joke. 'What's happened to your knickers, mate? He doesn't take after his dad, by the way.'

Walking into view, dressed in a translucent sarong over her bikini, his wife's voice was incisive in its retort. 'He's lying,' she intimated to the television audience, waving her pinky finger in the air.

By the time the holiday season *finalé* fell due, the family had become well-practised at moving around the house without getting in the way of the cameras and sound engineers, and *vice versa*. The couple included footage of stopovers by several of their long-term songwriting partners, including Tex Fletcher and Greg Marlow, and students from Melbourne Academy were bussed down to Mount Eliza for a "Carols by Candlelight" rehearsal during the week before Christmas.

It was early in the New Year of nineteen-eighty that the celebrity parents discovered yet another genetic similarity between father and daughter: Kierney was showing signs of being a southpaw. To the thrilled songwriter, this represented the crowning glory for the pair's special bond, because the other dark-haired Diamonds had all been right-handers.

After a six-year incubation, Lynn and Jeff officially launched The Good School on Australia Day. The program was to be run from a new, state-of-the-art building attached to Melbourne Academy, with an initial intake of twenty divided into two streams: one for recent graduates and the other for students in their final year of high school.

The smallest Diamond celebrated her first birthday on the tenth of February as the family's next milestone, only a few days before her father flew out on a tour of the USA. She had been tottering around since the New Year celebrations at Benloch and was already fairly sturdy on her feet by her birthday. However, it was her fluent speech which continued to delight and astonish all who met her. Frequently articulating complete sentences, she showed a prodigious ability to memorise every word she heard and then regurgitate it in its proper context.

There seemed to be no assuaging the public's appetite for either artist's music. Jeff had made three hit albums since Jet had come into the world, the latest of which had been released in January, and it was with this material that he was armed for the new tour.

By contrast, Lynn's touring schedule was deliberately on hold while she focussed on their children. This gave her ample freedom to produce other artists' records. Travelling for more than a couple of days at a time was impossible without a major upheaval to the whole family, which incorporated two full-time nannies and talk of a third. She had no regrets whatsoever, content to live the performer's life vicariously through her husband.

Just when the Diamonds' life singular appeared to settle into blissful perfection however, in March that year, disaster and despair were precipitously visited on them out of the blue, in the middle of a sell-out concert in Chicago. The audience down on the floor of the packed stadium had been up on their feet dancing right from the opening number. Noticing that those nearest to the stage were having a fantastic time relating to the dynamic singer-songwriter directly, more and more ticket-holders abandoned their seats and pushed towards the front.

Extra security personnel were soon drafted in to prevent the fans in the first few rows from becoming squashed against the fence, and a number of young women had to be pulled up and over the barrier to safety. At one point, Jeff had even asked the band to stop playing while he instructed people to take several steps back, which they had obediently done at the time. Unfortunately, it wasn't too long before the same thing happened again.

A group of three females to the right of the platform had caught the superstar's eye, hearing their screams turn from cries of adulation to pleas for help. He had summoned over another uniformed guard and shouted out for everyone to move back, turning round and demonstrating just how easy it was to walk in reverse.

The struggling *trio* were lifted out by fellow audience members and security staff, two appearing to have lost consciousness. From his position at the front of the stage, Jeff was unable to see clearly but feared the neck of one woman was crooked at an unnatural angle. The sight was horrific in the extreme. For a third time, he stopped the music and begged those who had abandoned their seats in the stands to return and continue dancing there, assuring them that he would turn up the volume if they did their bit to free up some space.

'Look, guys... You can't see what I can see from here,' the angry man yelled into the microphone. 'I'm not going to carry on unless you move back and stay back. There are people being dragged out of here unconscious. This is bloody serious. OK?'

Persistent to the end, the crowd gradually began to take the superstar at his word. The band struck up where they had left off once everyone had created more room around them, and their distressed lead singer did his best to put the gruesome images out of his mind and revive the high-octane performance. Mostly unaware of what had taken place, the audience burst into song and danced along with the energetic, driving beat.

Jeff Diamond came off stage for the final time about thirty minutes later, having rocked on through two enthusiastic *encores*. He was informed by a nervous venue official that three young female fans had been taken to a local emergency department.

'Did you see them?' he asked his tour manager. 'One of them looked like her neck was broken.'

No-one could give him any answers, so the celebrity told the band to go on ahead of him to the press reception. He jumped into a waiting car, bound for the nearby hospital. Once inside, feeling unhinged, he peppered the registrar with questions about the people who had come in from his concert. The staff tried their hardest to source the information he was after, swiftly directing him to a resident doctor.

'Mister Diamond,' the young man addressed him, gingerly shaking his hand. 'I'm a huge fan of yours. My name's Doctor Jacob Freiberg. Jay.'

'Hi, Jay. Thanks. I'm looking for the women who were brought here after being crushed at my gig. Can you tell me what happened to them, please?'

The medic was nervous. He showed his idol into a consulting room and invited him to sit down. The demeanour of the man in the white coat told Jeff to expect bad news.

'Mister Diamond...' Doctor Freiberg began again, wringing his hands like an elderly woman.

'Jeff, Jay, please.'

'Sure. Jeff... There were five people brought in, I believe, from the stadium.'

'Five?' the musician echoed. 'Jesus! I only heard about three.'

LORRAINE PESTELL

'No. There were five, sir,' the medic corrected him. 'Two are doing fine; just a little shocked and suffering from a few bruises, heat exhaustion and dehydration. They'll be released in the next hour, as soon as their family or friends can pick them up.'

'That's good. And the others?'

'Yes. With the others, we have a more serious situation, I'm afraid.'

'Yeah,' Jeff exhaled, his head starting to swim and his heart-rate increasing. 'That's what I thought.'

'Would you like a glass of water?' Jay asked, seeing the superstar's genuine reaction to the news.

'In a minute, thanks. Please tell me they're going to be OK.'

'Well, I wish I could,' the wide-eyed young man continued. 'One lady died at the scene, sir, and another we were unable to save when she was admitted into the "ER".'

'Christ Almighty,' Jeff muttered, wind rushing out of his lungs. 'Two dead? And the fifth?'

The resident's expression lightened slightly. 'The remaining patient of the five is in actual fact the sister of one of the deceased. She's basically OK. A couple of broken ribs, but you'll understand she's in shock at her sister's passing.'

The celebrity put his head in his hands and stared at the floor. He said nothing while his thoughts raced at a million miles an hour around his ancient mind. 'May I talk to the survivors, please?' he asked, briefly lifting his eyes. 'Where are they?'

'I don't know, sir,' the doctor replied. 'I'd have to check with the families. The parents are on their way. I can certainly let you meet the couple who've been discharged, but I can't allow you...'

'No,' Jeff stopped him, resting his hand on Jay's arm, sensing he was becoming distressed too. 'I'd like to meet the ones who are going home, please. And then I'll wait 'til the families get here.'

The man in the white coat stood up and gathered his wits, impressed by the decisive calm shown by his hero at this time of crisis. 'Of course, sir. I'll go check and get back to you. I'll ask someone to bring you coffee, if you'd like.'

'Yeah. That'd be great. Thank you.'

The young doctor left the room. Jeff slumped against the sofa and slammed his head hard on the wall behind in frustration. How could something so terrible have happened so quickly? Two people who had shelled out for tickets to his concert were not going home. Not tonight, and not ever. Surely he was dreaming again...

'Jesus, Lynn,' he whispered, tugging on their invisible elastic connection. 'How could I have let this happen? What else could I have done?'

560

The lost boy once more found himself alone in a strange place, preparing to take the blame for another tragedy. He cursed his oversight at not having asked his tour manager or one of the boys in the band to accompany him to the hospital. Why did he always end up shouldering these situations on his own? Tears welled up in his eyes as his thoughts turned to his own children. How would these families be feeling right now? He couldn't bear the prospect of being told that Jet or Kierney had died.

Jay Freiberg re-entered the room with a steaming Styrofoam cup of black coffee and two sachets of sugar. Jeff took them with a nod of thanks, wasting no time in stirring all the sugar into the drink.

'We've located the couple who've been treated. They're waiting to be picked up,' he reported. 'They're still in the "ER". Are you sure you're up to meeting them? You don't look too good yourself. Can I call someone to join you while you're here?'

'No, thanks,' the negotiator politely waved his hand. 'Don't worry about me. Would you take me to these guys, please? What are their names?'

Jeff Diamond was introduced to Candace and Peter Birch, a married couple from the outer Chicago area who had been keen to see him perform live after being fans since the beginning of his career. It was a painful experience for the successful artist to listen to the pair singing the concert's praises up until the time when they had been hoisted above their fellow revellers, only to end up in a downtown emergency room.

'Well, I'm truly glad you're alright,' the empath told them, having the good sense not to reveal the other tragic news to which he was party. 'I hope you get home safely.'

With a dumbstruck Doctor Freiberg standing alongside during this strange conversation, Jeff obliged with an autograph on the couple's discharge notices and graciously wished them a good night. Their friends had come to collect them, all heading straight back to the parking lot at the venue to pick up their car and go home. What composure the rock star was showing by not loading these lucky victims with the information that others had not been so lucky, the doctor thought. No doubt, they would find out soon enough on the television news.

The resident steered the tall, striking celebrity past gaping onlookers, back to the consultation room and to a decidedly lukewarm cup of coffee. 'Now,' the exhausted musician opened, resigning himself to his next obligations, 'please could you give me an update on the situation with the others?'

Jay explained that the three girls were all students at the same college, and the two sets of parents had been given the news just ten minutes earlier. Both men agreed that it was too soon to impose on their grief and shock.

'Is there a 'phone I could use that can dial international?' Jeff asked. 'May I call my wife, please?'

A vision of Lynn Dyson flooded the younger man's mind, having overlooked until this point the connection between his two favourite recording artists. 'Of course, sir,' he nodded. 'I'm sure you could use our room out back. Let me go find out.'

Behind closed doors in the residents' office, the tormented soul dialled his home number. Then changing his mind abruptly, he terminated the call before it rang. What time would it be in Melbourne? He checked his watch and calculated that it would be four-thirty tomorrow afternoon. If ever there had been a good case for time travel, this was it. He punched the series of numbers again.

'Hello?' Lynn's voice was like a bolt of lightening on a very, very dark night.

'Hey. It's me.'

'Jeff, hi!' the cheerful voice replied. 'How did the gig go? What time is it? I didn't think you'd be finished yet?'

The temptation to keep talking about the pleasant aspects of life was overwhelming. The treadmill of post-concert parties normally numbed the performer's senses, trotting out harmless anecdotes to fans who had won radio station contests and signing endless copies of overpriced memorabilia, yet the one he was missing tonight looked so welcoming in his mind just at this moment.

'Angel, wait. I'm in a hospital in Chicago,' he began to explain.

'Hospital? Why? Are you OK?' Lynn's tone immediately switched to one of concern. 'What's happened?'

'Jesus!' he cursed aloud, the tears flowing from his eyes again. 'You cannot believe what's happened.'

'What? What's wrong? *Digame.*'

'Two girls are dead,' Jeff blurted out, 'and another one's injured. A sister of one of the dead girls.'

'What?' his wife asked. 'Which girls? At the concert? Oh, my God. Fans, you mean? How?'

'Fuck, baby. Yeah. Fans. It was gruesome,' the musician answered, over the worst of his emotional rush and now keen to reassure his beautiful best friend, who sounded extremely distressed. 'People flooded the floor area. From all over, I think. The crowd just pushed further and further forwards and crammed the aisles. Security had to lift people over the top. People were screaming, and I had to stop the show twice to yell at them to move back.'

'Crushed?'

'Yeah. Crushed,' her husband sobbed. 'Two twenty-year-old friends and one of them's sister. The families have just arrived at the hospital. I haven't spoken to them yet, but I will, as soon as they'll see me. If they want to see me, that is...'

'Oh, God, Jeff. That's so awful. It was an accident. You know that, don't you? Are you alright? Is there anyone there with you?'

'Yeah. There's a doctor,' he affirmed, although he knew this wouldn't satisfy his caring wife. 'A resident in the "ER". He looks about twelve, but he's been very helpful.'

'No. I mean one of your guys,' Lynn stressed, giggling softly at the irresistible image of a schoolboy in a white coat with a stethoscope around his neck. 'Where's Brian Hardcastle? You can't do this all alone again. Do you want me to fly over?'

'No,' the twenty-seven-year-old insisted. 'Thanks, but no. You can't leave the kids, and I'll be fine. I love you. Christ, angel, I love you so much. I kept thinking about how bloody terrible it'd be to lose one of our kids.'

Jeff put his hand over the receiver as another wave of emotion washed through him. He could have sworn he could feel his dream girl's love forcing its way through the telephone line and into his bloodstream.

'Oh, no,' the young woman exhaled. 'You mustn't torture yourself. Are you still there? Are you sure you're OK?'

Her perfect stranger sighed. 'Yeah. I'll be OK. It's just a shit thing to have to do, but I haven't lost a child or nearly lost two. Is everything alright over there? Can you give them a big hug from me?'

'Of course I shall. What are you going to do? Come home?'

'Baby, I don't know yet. Let me talk to these poor folks and see what I can do. I suspect nothing much, but I want to help if I can. Then I need to go back and talk to the band, and we'll decide whether to cancel tomorrow night or whatever.'

'Jeff, please don't take all this on yourself again,' his wife urged. 'It was an accident. It wasn't your fault. Please believe that.'

'Angel, I do believe it. I have to do this though. You understand, don't you?'

Lynn was crying now; not for herself or for the children, but for the potential of this tragic event to undo the healing they had managed to effect over the last few years. 'Yes. I do understand,' she confirmed. 'You are such a good man, Mister Diamond. *Such* a good man. You understand that too, don't you?'

'Yes. Thanks, gorgeous. I've got to go,' the relieved husband lowered his voice, seeing the top of what looked like Doctor Freiberg's head at the window. 'I'll talk to you in a few hours. *Te amo, Regala.*'

'*Te amo* too, Jeff. Hope it goes OK. Good luck, and talk later.'

Hanging up, the world-changer stood tall. 'Jay, thanks for letting me use the 'phone. What's going on?'

The young man took a deep breath, delivering rehearsed lines. 'I've spoken to the relatives of the deceased. They're very distressed, obviously. They're in shock and don't really know what to think right now. They all know each other pretty well, which is good. And the injured sister's doing much better. They're with her now.'

'Could I talk to them, please?' Jeff requested. 'What are the girls' names?'

'Yes. They know you're here at the hospital and would like to talk to you,' Jay nodded. 'The first deceased is Amanda Fallon and her sister is Joanne. Or Joanna. I'm not sure.'

The celebrity frowned, committing the names to memory.

'And the other deceased's name is Mary-Anne Pearce.'

The young man walked out of the room, followed by the instantly recognisable figure of Jeff Diamond. Refusing to make eye contact with a row of stunned passers-by on each side of the corridor, his heart was in his mouth while his brain recited the three names over and over.

The lonely man's head felt progressively dizzier with every step they took. What was he going to say to these bereaved families? Sorry I killed your daughters? It was an accident? Thoughts jumbled around as he attempted to come up with something that he would want said to him. Steeling his resolve, he passed through a door which was being held open for him, breathing deeply.

Inside, there were six people spread across a number of armchairs and sofas, sitting down and looking bewildered. The lonely star searched for the sister who had survived the ordeal. A short girl with light brown, shoulder-length hair revealed an unseemly thrill, even eyeing him up and down before smiling through tear-stained eyes.

'Joanna?'

'Yes,' the young woman replied, standing up with difficulty and clutching her side. 'Hello. It's nice to meet you.'

Jeff's eyes welled up at her simple, friendly and wholly uncalled-for greeting. 'Sit down, please,' he smiled back. 'Are you OK?'

The injured woman steadied herself by holding onto his outstretched hand, then sinking down into a chair. 'Yes. These are my parents, Pat and Audrey.'

Jeff leaned forward to the closest mother and embraced her warmly before looking across at her husband. 'Mister and Missus Fallon?'

'Yes,' they both replied, also awestruck.

'I'm Jeff Diamond. I am so sorry,' he told her, fighting his emotions. 'Your daughter. It's just terrible. I'm so, so sorry for what happened; that you've lost your daughter.'

The curly-haired woman said nothing, simply sobbing into a white handkerchief. She clung to the statuesque Australian for a good few seconds. Both hearts were beating at a similar rate. He leaned back and shook the man's hand.

'You too, sir. I'm so sorry this happened. So sorry.'

'Thank you, Mister Diamond,' Patrick Fallon replied. 'It's good of you to come talk to us.'

Jay Freiberg interrupted, eager to introduce Mary-Anne's parents. The fifth person present was an uncle who had driven the Pearces to hospital. Jeff repeated the same unworthy gestures and words for a second time, unable to think of any other way to express his sorrow at their loss. Missus Pearce's brother beckoned for him to take a seat in the circle of chairs, and everyone else returned to their seats.

'Can you tell us what happened?' Mary-Anne's mother stuttered.

'I don't know the whole story myself,' Jeff answered. 'I'm going to find out though, for all our peace of mind.'

Shaking his head, the performer's quandary was only too real. He knew his most prudent option in this most litigious of countries was to keep his mouth firmly shut. He also felt morally bound to tell them everything he knew.

'The audience was pushing forwards. More and more of them. Up on stage, we were all doing our best to get everyone to move back, but they just kept coming. People at the front... your daughters, among others... had nowhere to go.'

The parents listened intently with blank expressions on their faces before Joanna confirmed the star's recollection. 'It was hell. I couldn't breathe and I saw Mary-Anne get pushed to the ground. That's when everyone started screaming, and Jeff stopped the show.'

The celebrity exhaled deeply. 'Folks, I'm truly sorry,' he repeated. 'I couldn't believe I was seeing people being dragged unconscious out of there. Is there anything I can do for you?'

'No, sir,' replied Mister Fallon. 'I can't think of anything right now. It's all too much of a shock.'

Picturing his dream girl and their precious babies back in Melbourne, Jeff assumed control of the dreadful situation. It was the role he was best placed to fill, after all. He retrieved a slim wad of business cards from his wallet and wrote his home telephone number on the reverse side of two. Then he searched for the card belonging to his US agent, which he found after flicking through his diverse set of contacts, and transcribed her name and number under his own.

'Please take these,' he requested of both mothers. 'I'm not sure what my plans are yet either, but here are the details for my management company back in Australia and my right-hand woman in New York, Beth Dixon. The other number is my home. Please ring any of those numbers whenever, and I'll contact you as soon as I get the message. Do you feel comfortable giving me your numbers?'

Bill Pearce pulled out his own business card and gave it to the sincere celebrity. Audrey Fallon read theirs out for him to write down.

'Thank you,' the musician sighed, a lump forming in his throat again. 'Are you sure there's nothing you need now? Apart from your daughters back?'

The whole room fell silent, soaking up the sympathy emanating from what ran the risk of being construed as a flippant comment. All assembled knew it hadn't been intended thus. Joanna stood up and hugged the star she had always worshipped from afar, thanking him for taking the time to see them. Preparing to leave, Jeff embraced each parent in turn and shook the steadfast uncle's hand.

'Please don't hesitate to call,' he reiterated, turning round to locate Jay Freiberg.

The doctor appeared washed out. Entering the original consulting room once more, the sullen man came face-to-face with his US tour manager who had recently arrived at the hospital with Mark, the band's longtime bass player.

'Jeez. Am I glad to see you! Thanks for coming.'

The newcomers sat for a few minutes in the privacy of the small office, giving their leader a chance to replay events. Now with a clearer mind, Jeff wondered why they had yet to encounter a police presence, crediting the families for this measured response to the tragedy. They concluded between them that there was little point in sticking around, so the star thanked Doctor Freiberg for his help and left with the others for their hotel.

'Man, what a night! What do you want to do?' Brian asked in the taxi. 'Cancel?'

'Tomorrow? Yep. Absolutely,' Jeff confirmed. 'Out of respect, more than anything. Jesus Christ! We need to sleep on it, or at least lie awake on it.'

New to the Diamond tour crew, the burly American was growing accustomed to the impressive songwriter's quirky, self-deprecating humour. 'Good idea, mate.'

***

The other band members were still in the hotel bar when the threesome returned. The atmosphere was relaxed but sombre, unusually devoid of groupies and other hangers-on. Martyn Bailey stood up and vacated his stool for the songwriter before ducking across the darkened room to retrieve a few more.

'Whisky, Jeff?' invited Brian, attracting the barman's attention.

The star's shoulders drooped under a gentle slap on the shoulder from his supportive drummer. 'Please.'

'So... What's the story?' asked Phil, a keyboardist who had joined the band at the start of this tour.

'Oh, this ain't no story,' his boss snapped back. 'It's fucking real, mate. Two girls are dead.'

'Dead?' came a chorus of stunned voices.

'Yep. Two med' students. And another one's injured but not too badly, thankfully, except that she's also the sister of one of the dead women. It's very bad.'

'Bloody hell,' the piano player murmured. 'That's dreadful. What does that mean for the rest of the tour?'

'Not sure yet,' Jeff replied. 'I want to cancel at least the next few dates, while we make sure the families are alright, *et cetera*. It'll depend how we all adjust to it too. I saw everything. Did any of you see it happen too?'

'I did,' Mark responded. 'I saw them pull out the girl with the broken neck. It was horrendous. I'm with you, Jeff. I couldn't play tomorrow.'

'No,' the singer sighed. 'We'll talk more about it in the morning. I'm fucked, I've gotta tell ya. Don't know how long it'll take until we can perform normally with this hanging over us? I know damned well I won't do a good job.'

'Shit,' Brian cursed. 'That's going to be a nightmare. That's seven nights' worth of tickets.'

'I don't give a flying fuck about that,' the celebrity scowled at his agent. 'It's only an admin' hassle to process refunds or reschedule, that's all. You didn't look into the eyes of those parents who'd just lost their daughter. There's no way we can go on stage before the funerals, at the very soonest.'

'Will you go to the funerals?' the tour manager asked.

'If I'm welcome, no question,' Jeff affirmed, 'and so will you.'

Marty agreed. 'He's right. We have to show some respect for the families. It'd look pretty bad if we just carried on while they bury their loved ones.'

'Too true. And I don't know if I could be convincing anyway, so what's the point giving people a mediocre performance? Are we all OK with that?'

Their leader had spoken, and none was game to vote against him even if they had wished to. They swallowed their drinks down and arranged to reconvene in the morning, after he and Brian had discussed the matter with Gerry back in Melbourne. The newly-appointed tour manager was a Chicago native and had been looking forward to taking the star and his *entourage* out to the best night spots on the Magnificent Mile.

Instead, on only the second night of the northern US string of dates, they were dialling long-distance to apprise Stonebridge Music's management of the awful situation. At almost one-thirty US Central time, it would already be the end of the following business day on the other side of the international date-line.

'Blake and Partners. Good evening,' came the receptionist's voice.

567

'Evening, Kim. You're working late. It's Jeff Diamond. Is Gerry there, please?'

'Yes, he is, Mister Diamond,' the young woman replied. 'How are you? Are you still in America?'

'Yeah. I'm in Chicago,' the firm's biggest client answered. 'Could you put me through, please? Oh, and could you do me favour and ask Cath to join us on the call, if she's still there?'

Kim apologised, realising she was getting carried away. 'Oh, yes. Certainly. Hold on, please.'

As the line clicked and began to ring, Brian glanced sideways at the superstar. The habitually hyperactive and mischievous rocker seemed to have aged by several decades since taking the stage that evening, nervous hands fidgeting with his lighter. With one cigarette butt already extinguished into a twisted stub in the room's ashtray, another was well on the way.

'Blake,' the familiar sonic boom informed them.

The formality in his old friend's telephone manner made the anxious man laugh. 'Diamond,' he did his best to replicate the intensity.

'Shit! G'day, mate!' Gerry relaxed. 'We've been tick-tacking with brokers on a public offering this evening. Can't get used to all these "big business" niceties. How's it going over there?'

'Funny you should mention it, but shit actually,' Jeff replied. 'Brian's on the line too, by the way. We're on the loudspeaker thingo.'

'Oh, right. Hello there, Agent Hardcastle. What the hell are you talking about? Nothing ever goes shit for you. You're Midas, remember?'

'Yeah. Well... Not today,' the lost boy lamented. 'There's been a disaster out of all proportion.'

For the fourth time, he found himself stepping through the haunting sequence of events, and then for a fifth time when Cathy Lane rushed into the room. Restless, their downhearted boss scraped his chair across the carpet and began to pace around the table.

'Guys, how the fuck could something like this happen? Two people are dead because of me. We kept telling 'em to move back, but by the time they got the message it was too late.'

The pair pieced together the torrid sequence for the benefit of their Australian management. Jeff felt the blood draining from his face as his stomach churned, fearful that he were about to throw up. Shocked to the core, the Irishman dropped his usual comedic routine and made sure of transcribing the name of the hospital and the doctor's contact details correctly, along with the names of the deceased and that of the injured sister. Lastly, he did the same for the Birch couple, mainly for their insurance records, in case any claim were forthcoming after the fact.

Pacified by the knowledge that he had done everything he could, the multi-millionnaire dismissed any talk of refunds or rescheduled dates until the grief had taken its course. They then discussed wording for a press release offering his condolences and promising that Stonebridge Music would fund a full investigation into the cause of the tragedy. The diligent administrator signed off, promising to leave a note for her public relations staff to fax the statement to all the news outlets for immediate publication the following morning.

Brian sat back in his chair, listening to the impressive negotiator fire off remarkably clear instructions to each of them, bemused by a passing comment from Gerry about murders and murderers that had appeared to trouble the celebrity greatly. The subject was cast aside, so he didn't press for details.

'Mate, we'll let you go,' Jeff terminated the onerous call. 'Anything special going on over there?'

'Oh, not much. More of the same. Good luck, guys. We'll get onto this announcement first thing tomorrow.'

'Cheers, both of you,' the musician sighed. 'If either of us has been left any messages you need to be aware of, we'll ring back.'

'Sure,' Brian agreed. 'Gerry, good to talk to you.'

'You too,' the executive acknowledged. 'And mate...'

'Yep.'

'Take it easy,' his old friend urged. 'Rid your mind of those dastardly thoughts, will you? It was an accident. We'll deal with it. Get some sleep.'

'Yeah. Will do. I hear you. Could you give Lynn a ring in the morning, please? Make sure she's OK? I'm going to talk to her now, but I'd appreciate it if you could check on them first thing. Thanks and *adiós*, mate.'

Jeff hung up and sprang out of the chair. He helped himself to two beers from his tour manager's mini-bar and offered one across the table. Both men stood staring out of the hotel window over the illuminated cityscape.

'Cheers, Brian. I'm sorry you have to go through all this. You didn't sign up for such shit, did you?'

'No sweat, mate,' he replied, the typically Aussie term of endearment sounding odd when delivered in an American accent. 'But tell me what was all that about murder? That got me intrigued.'

Jeff stood facing the window, hands in his pockets, and fixed his eyes on the city lights with the dark ribbon of the Chicago River in the foreground. 'Yeah,' he answered. 'I guess some news doesn't travel this far. You may as well know that my father's serving life for killing two men. It's hard for me to take the moral high ground when something like this happens. Two people are dead because of him, and now two people are dead 'cause of me. You can't deny the similarity.'

The tour manager shook his head. 'I see. Wow. I had no idea.'

'No,' Jeff nodded, smiling. 'Obviously not. It's not something I go shouting from the hills. Anyway... Let's get some rest. Tomorrow is another day. Shall we meet at nine-thirty for breakfast? We'll need to bring Beth up to speed. Jesus effing Christ!'

'Sure thing,' Brian shook the tired star's hand, slapping his upper arm like a familiar sparring partner.

Jeff departed in silence, thankful for a deserted corridor. By the time he reached his room, his whole body was shaking violently as delayed shock set in. He lay on the bed for a while, staring at the ceiling and wondering how long this latest side-effect would last. It was gratifying at least that he had remained in control of his faculties while it mattered.

After fifteen minutes or so, frayed nerves gave way to a deep-seated sorrow. The old soul leaned over and dialled his home number, hoping that his compassionate and very beautiful best friend would be there.

'Hello?' Lynn answered.

'Hey. It's me. Tell me something good.'

'Hi,' his wife sounded relieved and delighted to hear from him. 'I love you, and the kids love you.'

Jeff smiled, his eyes stinging. 'Thanks, angel. That's definitely something good. Very good. And I love you guys too.'

'Oh, and Jet figured out how to jump off the diving board.'

'OK!' the proud dad gasped. 'Is that a good idea? Did he get it to bounce him upwards?'

'Yes!' Lynn laughed. 'He was a bit disoriented by the force at first, but loved the result.'

The exhausted traveller relaxed, pressing his head into the pillow. 'What about the little, dark one?' he asked. 'What's she been up to?'

'Oh, not much. She expended a lot of effort telling me about a short story that Nadine read her. Over and over. I probably didn't say the right thing at the right time, so she thought I didn't get it.'

'I can relate to that,' Jeff sniffed. 'That's exactly what she's doing. I wonder what she wasn't able to express.'

'Or I wasn't able to understand,' the young mother countered.

'No. I doubt it's that way round. She's only a year old, angel. Give yourself a break.'

Lynn laughed at the adoration oozing through the telephone. 'You're too kind. So how are you?'

'Ah, you know...' her husband answered. 'Do we have to talk about me?'

'Yes. How are you? That's the price you pay for being loved. Spit it out, mate.'

Feeling very loved and grateful for it, the twenty-seven-year-old capitulated. 'I've had better days and worse days. Brian and I just got off the 'phone with Gerry and Cath. She's going to issue a press release of condolences in the morning. I hope I've got all their names right.'

'I'm sure you would've. That's a good idea,' the rear-end of the pantomime horse assured. 'What did you decide about the remaining gigs?'

Jeff took a deep breath. 'We're cancelling at least until after the funerals. I'm going to ask Brian to go with me, but I'll leave it optional for the boys. Most of them didn't see it happen, thank Christ. They were too far back.'

'And then? Do you think you'll be ready to carry on?'

'No,' he sighed deeply, her empathy pushing tears out of his eyes. 'I don't. You should've seen me when I left Brian's room... I went into some sort of shock as soon as the pressure was off.'

'Oh. Are you OK now?'

'Yeah. More or less. It was the first time I'd allowed myself to relax, and the physical backlash was extreme and immediate. I just lay here on the bed and vibrated for what seemed like ages. Then it just gradually faded away.'

'Well... I'm proud of you,' Lynn said. 'It's fantastic that you know not to put your sanity in danger again. People'll understand. When do you expect to hear about the funerals?'

'Thanks, gorgeous. Don't know,' the musician answered, lighting a cigarette and waiting for the nicotine to flood his bloodstream. 'I've offered to pay for them, and we all exchanged numbers, so it's up to them whether they take me up on it. I'll also ask Beth to follow up once, in case they find it difficult to make the call. I've asked them to let me know when and where the funerals are. Jesus, I'm not looking forward to that one bit. Can you imagine what they'll be like? My being there'll make them into a fucking circus too. That's my biggest fear, angel.'

'Can't be helped, under the circumstances. I'm sure you'll be as invisible as you possibly can. Were they OK when you met them?'

'Yeah. Of course,' he recounted. 'As polite as Americans always are. The sister who was injured was quick to tell them that I'd stopped the music when things got bad, but who knows what they really think?'

Lynn was silent for a moment before forcing an admission. 'And what do *you* really think?' she asked the man who was suffering so far away. 'Now that it's been a few hours?'

'That I wish you were here,' Jeff sobbed, instantly hit by an honesty high. 'Jesus, angel. I love you so much for what you do to me. Or that I could turn back time, I guess. No. Both. That I won't sleep tonight because the vision of those families looking at me for answers will keep flashing into my head, and the image of the girl with the broken neck being carried off...'

'My God. That sounds like a cocktail of horribility. I'm really sorry, Jeff,' Lynn said, sniffing back her own tears. 'I wish I were there too. I want to be touching you now, to help stop all the shaking. Are you sure you don't want me to come to the funerals?'

Her husband sighed. 'Yes. Sure, I want you here by my side. Goes without saying, baby. But this is for me to deal with, and you need to stay with the kids. There's no good reason for you to come over.'

'Why do we all of a sudden need a good reason to support each other?'

'Yeah. I know. It just doesn't feel right that you should jump on a 'plane and fly halfway across the globe because of something I caused,' the rock star hesitated, hearing his dream girl inhale and guessing what she was about to say.

'Jeff,' his *Regala*'s voice was firm but kind. 'You didn't *cause* those women to die. You didn't. I'm sure no-one in that audience thinks that.'

He laughed, less bitterly than he wanted to. 'You're right, angel. I hear you. Gerry was saying the same thing. But I can't absolve myself of all the blame, can I? I could've stopped sooner. I could've asked security to start moving people out earlier. There are things I could've done that I didn't do.'

Eager to come up with useful parallels, Lynn was desperate for her tormented soul-mate to believe the night's awful outcome had not been his fault. 'So if you recommended a restaurant to someone, and they got food poisoning when they ate there, would you blame yourself?' she asked, almost teasing her husband.

'Yeah. Most likely,' Jeff chuckled, seeing through her valiant ploy. 'And if I lent someone my car, and they ran over someone in it, I'd blame myself. Lynn, you can throw all the scenaria you can think of at me, and I'm always going to give you the same answer. It's who I am, baby. I *am* the blame consultant. It's my lot in life.'

'Alright,' his *confidante* resigned. 'I understand. But if you change your mind and want me to come over, please tell me. The kids'll be fine with Nadine and Ursula, and I can ask Mum to check on them regularly. Everything'd run smoothly for a few days. It wouldn't be a big deal.'

'But wouldn't it look like we're chasing free publicity?' the philosopher asked, painting a picture with words like only he knew how. 'I can see the tabloid headlines already... Look at those showbiz posers! They're making a gaudy show of solidarity because they still have each other while these families are suffering because of their loss. Doesn't that sound wrong to you?'

The young wife couldn't deny some validity in this acute angle. 'Yes. When you put it that way, I do see what you mean,' she admitted. 'I won't come. But I'll be thinking of you all the time and can't wait to find out when you'll be home.'

'Jesus! I'm a fucking idiot sometimes,' Jeff scoffed. 'There's nothing I'd like more than for you to fly over. Why did I shoot myself in the foot?'

'You can change your mind. Neither of us can win this way, can we? Just tell me what you want me to do.'

The caller sighed. 'Stay there.'

'Then you are a fucking idiot,' the twenty-two-year-old giggled. 'And I love you even more for it.'

'Thanks, angel. That's what I need to hear. S'pose I'd better get off the 'phone. I don't know when the story's going to break, so I'd better try and steal some sleep before the fun starts.'

'OK. Hope you can,' Lynn replied. 'Ring again if you need to. Keep strong, and I'll talk to you soon.'

'I shall. I love you. *Adiós*.'

The superstar heard the line cut off and replaced the receiver, all alone with an enormous bed and a full mini-bar in one of the busiest cities in the world. He scarcely remembered playing to a capacity crowd at the stadium that evening. The longer he lay there, the more anger and frustration grew inside him. He knew he wouldn't sleep, and even if he did, the likelihood of his mind messing with the tragic event and inserting new pages into his nightmare's storybook was virtually guaranteed.

Jeff got up and dressed for running until sunrise. He had promised Lynn long ago that pounding city streets at night was a thing of the past, but today's alternatives would have far, far worse repercussions. In fact, the alternative currently plaguing his depraved psyche was almost as wrong as its ultimate and irrevocable stablemate; using an anonymous, innocent woman to gain relief for his lonely body and restless mind paled into insignificance when he contemplated being unfaithful to the other innocent ones whom he loved so intensely.

Christ Almighty, the young man cursed aloud. How quickly he had regressed to his haunted past! It wouldn't take much to derail this transformation train spectacularly. Recovery? What recovery? The compulsion to bring the final curtain down was exasperatingly familiar.

Spending the next few days holed up in their hotel accommodation in Chicago, Jeff, Brian and three band members who had chosen to attend the funerals of Mary-Anne and Amanda passed the time as productively as they could by writing and arranging new material and organising future tour dates. When they discovered the autopsies would delay the funerals for the best part of a week, the megastar allowed himself a sightseeing trip or two.

Jeff also took the opportunity to trek north to Toronto. Professor Sarah Friedman receive him gladly, keen to provide a progress report on the research project funded by his charitable foundation. It had been an awkward meeting at first, with their mutual carnal knowledge brought front-of-mind for Jeff in his heightened state of stress and loneliness. Ever the professional, Sarah had respected his need to keep things on a platonic level, arranging seminars to talk with patients and doctors, swapping notes and learning which of their techniques were effective and which required refinement.

The brief stopover in Canada served as a welcome vaccination against the worst of the celebrity's return to The Windy City. He felt ready to face the bereaved families again, confident that his resources were being put to good use. Working towards changing other people's futures for the better helped in a small way to counteract the grief for the futures cleaved at his concert. His soul would recover from this setback, as Lynn had promised, because he continued to fight for the things that mattered.

The Pearce family were the first to approach Jeff Diamond and his darkly-dressed associates as they approached the doors of a large Catholic church in a leafy suburb. They thanked the entertainers for attending their daughter's funeral the previous day and invited the whole party to join the family rather than sit apart from the rest of the congregation.

Initially, Jeff had insisted they oughtn't to intrude, given the circumstances, but the Pearces remained insistent. Joanna Fallon had recovered well from her physical injuries and waved furtively to her idol when she saw him step inside the church. Reluctantly, he raised a hand to acknowledge her friendliness but looked away as soon as was politic.

After the service, the girls' parents even insisted the superstar come back to their house, where Amanda's wake was being held. It was a formal invitation that the celebrity knew would be rude to turn down, no matter how inappropriate he considered it to be. He had been forced to take Joanna aside and counsel her that it might not be good form to appear excited when introducing him to their friends, concerned that he would find himself the centre of attention for all the wrong reasons.

The crestfallen young woman insisted the families bore him no malice, making him feel even guiltier for not playing along. Why shouldn't he use his circus performer credentials to cheer up the grieving sister and her friends? Yet another bizarre circumstance to add to the old soul's crowded chronicle!

Jeff feared that once the novelty of having a famous person in their midst had worn off, a more normal grief cycle would commence, and he would no longer be held in such fond regard. He ended up agreeing to put in a brief appearance at the house and promised to return in a few months' time to see how they were all doing. There might even be a possibility of bringing Lynn and the children, although he stopped short of a promise. This tempting offer was more than a good compromise, and the family were appreciative of his humility.

That night, nearing the end of an unpleasant but necessary detour in their life singular, his guardian angel's tender, soothing words lifted more than Jeff's spirits to a higher plain. He had been accepted as a friend by those he had wronged, albeit unintentionally. The heartache lingered however, assuaged in no minor part by the love of two small saviours who sang to him through the telephone, obediently responding their mother's animated baton. The remote sexual encounter which followed eased the tension in his shoulders and took him to a paradise he suspected he didn't deserve.

***

By the time Jeff and his loyal bass player returned to Australia after reuniting with their band-mates to play the tour's remaining five gigs, media attention on the story had died down. Cathy had organised a press conference to be broadcast from the airport, during which he spoke of his intention to ensure the deceased fans' parents received all the help they needed and were fully informed of the results of the investigation.

In a speech concocted over the Pacific Ocean, the country's hottest export expressed his sorrow at the loss of two beautiful and intelligent young women, both to their families and friends and to the meaningful careers for which they had been destined, and finished by telling his fans and critics alike how the event had given him a renewed appreciation for making each life count.

All this was true enough, not that he really needed reminding. The multi-millionnaire could sense his own loved ones but a security cordon away, never more anxious to be barrelled into by the boisterous jumping bean. Endless, repetitive questions frustrated him, but he answered to the best of his knowledge and with unfailing courtesy.

'Never let your kids doubt how much you love them,' he told the flashing cameras and array of microphones. 'You never know what's going to happen next or what it may do to those left behind. My parents never cared if I existed... never even pretended they did... and that's hell to live with. You don't realise it at the time, but it hurts deep inside and can turn everyday people into monsters. So go home and tell 'em today. OK?'

Once the reporters and their crews had dispersed, Gerry led his wrecked but inspirational client away, through the sliding doors into the arrivals hall. A large number of supporters had gathered to welcome the well-respected superstar back to Melbourne, yet his eyes were only interested in three among them. Television cameras captured him dazzled by thousands of flashing lights as the doors opened, and the homecoming celebrity waved and smiled generously.

Lynn allowed Jet to run forward under the barrier, and he was soon swept up into strong arms, with kisses and tears all round. Carrying his son on his hip, waving like a true professional, Jeff walked slowly over to the blonde beauty bearing his tiny mirror image, and their lips locked together without inhibition. Tumultuous clapping and screaming accompanied the transcendent photogenic kiss, leaving their trusty business manager gazing around in amazement, feeling very spare indeed.

The couple hardly spoke two words to each other while they battled through the crowds to reach Gerry's waiting car. Once on the road, they were able to relax and have a good laugh at the hysteria.

'Who the hell have I become?' the superstar sighed, looking round at his best mate and then at his wife from the front passenger seat of the capacious BMW sedan. 'Two people die, and I'm greeted like royalty. It's totally nuts.'

'People love you,' Lynn told him, having rehearsed just such a pep talk in preparation for his return. 'You didn't run away from it. People respect you for taking responsibility. They admire you and they're showing their support, that's all. Accept it for what it is, and not for what you're scared it might be.'

The couple's business manager chuckled. 'It is out of control though, I have to admit. You should see the mountains of mail piling up in the office. We're going to need an army of temps just to open it, never mind replying to them all.'

'Jeez. That makes me feel sick,' the traveller moaned. 'What are they writing about? Does this mean we'll be living this tragedy over and over for weeks to come? I hope not.'

'Probably,' the tennis champion affirmed. 'Let's not talk about it now. Jet, tell Dad what you did yesterday in the pool.'

The driver cringed. 'Yuck! I hope it's not of a bodily discharge nature.'

'Gerry!' Lynn exclaimed. 'Our children don't do things like that. What an insult!'

'Yeah, mate,' her husband added. 'Why d'you think we waited 'til now to get a pool? Jetto, *digame*.'

'Dad, I did a head-first dive,' his son announced, attempting an arrow pose within the restraint of his seatbelt.

'Great! That's fantastic, mate,' Jeff shouted, turning round and tapping the youngster playfully on the knee. 'You'll have to show me when we get home.'

Pleased with himself, Jet looked to his mother for permission.

Lynn nodded. 'Yes, OK. If it's not too cold when we get back. Once we're unpacked and settled.'

The rock star grinned at the lively kid, recalling a promise his wife had made to adjust their schedules and squeeze in a quick break in far north Queensland after his ordeal. Had he dreamed it? Hopefully, he would soon be re-packing his suitcase for a much more pleasurable journey.

'So when do we go to Port Douglas? I've been fantasising about sandy beaches and lapping waves for too long. I just need to be there.'

She smiled. 'Even with another 'plane ride?'

'Yeah, well... Necessary evil.'

'Tomorrow afternoon,' Lynn confirmed. 'We're meeting the Jenners at two at Check-in.'

'You haven't told anyone, have you?' Gerry enquired, grinning. 'The average Joe and Jane can't afford all these sickies to keep up their welcoming committee obligations.'

'Very funny, mate,' Jeff moaned.

The executive's grin only became wider, clearly with a point to make. 'And, might I ask, what's wrong with this picture?'

'Sorry, Gerry,' the kind woman crooned. 'You're welcome to come with us.'

'No,' her husband's old friend shook his head. 'That's not what I meant, but thanks for the offer! I mean you've just constructed this spectacular house beside the seaside, and what's the first holiday you go on?'

Jeff laughed. 'Yeah. Decadent, eh? Have a dog and bark yourself.'

'Dad, please explain to your son how dogs and Queensland beaches go together, will you?' Lynn suggested, seeing a quizzical expression on little Jet's face.

'Ah, yeah. Sorry, Jetto. We can't take Merak to Queensland with us 'cause it's too far and the seatbelt won't fit him.'

The boy let out a wild cackle at the image of the family's gangly German Shepherd pup strapped into an aircraft cabin before breaking into a series of canine impersonations. The unexpected noise woke Kierney from a snooze, and she leaned sideways out of her car-seat and grabbed hold of her mum's long hair.

'Hello, darling. He's funny, your brother, isn't he? It'll be so much warmer up there though. It's going to be wonderful.'

Once back at Escondido, Jeff opened bottles of beer for himself and his manager. They sat on the patio in front of the pool, waiting patiently in the autumn sunshine for the child to demonstrate his new skills. Lynn had been a sight for sore eyes at the airport, and both men waxed lyrical about the delectability of her lithe post-baby body.

'Whoa! It's good to be home. What a fuckin' 'orrible month,' the star sighed. 'Can't believe I feel so normal. I expected to be completely out of whack when I saw the kids, but I'm not. Maybe that's what it means to have a home to go to.'

'Home is where the heart is, mate,' Gerry shrugged. 'That's what my dear, old mum always says.'

'She's damned right then,' Jeff agreed. 'Nothing like an old wife with a tale. Or a young one, as long as she's as hot as mine.'

'Rub it in, why don't you?' the Irishman laughed. 'You're a lucky fuck, and don't you forget it. You've come out of this latest *débacle* squeakier clean than I thought possible, and I just can't get over how everyone wants a piece of you.'

Jeff raised his half-empty bottle to his friend. 'You're so right, mate,' he frowned, taking a large gulp of cool liquid gold. 'It constantly blows me away. I still can't control how my mind works though. We just work around it these days.'

Their manly conversation was cut short by an ear-splitting yell. Jet thundered through the kitchen door, his bare feet slapping noisily on the flagstones. He was waving two pairs of board-shorts above his head like semaphore flags, landing one on his father's lap and tossing the other to Uncle Gerry.

'Put these on,' he commanded. 'They're Dad's but they'll fit.'

The visitor held the colourful swimwear up against his chest, stretching the elastic waist to its limit. 'No. They won't, old mate. My arse is nowhere near as big as your dad's.'

Jet breathed in sharply to stifle a laugh, not knowing if this statement was supposed to be a joke or not.

'Get out!' the musician sneered. 'Don't listen to him, Jetto. We'll get changed. Thanks.'

The outdoor pool was cool and refreshing, tempting the two grown men towards it while they watched the youngster practising his diving. Once he had completed his demonstration, even attempting a somersault off the springboard as his *pièce de résistance*, competitive spirits and grain-based alcohol teamed up to provide a dubious exhibition of adult boys' acrobatic prowess.

'Can I see you jump off the springboard again?' Jeff asked his son, shielding his eyes from the sinking sun. 'Mum told me you learned how to make it bounce you upwards.'

Jet put on a frightened face and laughed hesitantly. 'It's not very good. Only sometimes.'

'Try it. It doesn't matter if it takes a few goes.'

The cocky *trio* larked about in the pool, showing off with handstands and various other tricks. Lamenting their beers warming up on the table, the two giants caved in to the toddler's cries to throw him up into the air like a beach ball and let him splash down into the water. This was the second most perfect way to take Jeff's mind off the previous few weeks' misfortune, doing little to rid it of the first most perfect way. An evening of quiet anticipation was a very attractive proposition, if rather hard to disguise...

The red-blooded star compelled himself to be grateful that Lynn was not wearing a bikini when she brought Kierney down to join the fun. The fearless girl jumped into her papá's outstretched arms, happy for him to paddle about lazily on his back while she balanced on his stomach.

'Not swimming?' Gerry asked the athlete, decidedly disgruntled. 'It's the only reason I'm still here.'

His old friend scowled. 'You never give up, do you?'

'Would you? I seem to remember the good sport you were not around my girlfriends not so many years ago.'

The young woman put her finger to her mouth, her eyes directed to Jet, who was already showing a certain curiosity towards the birds and the bees. 'Be quiet, you two. Ears are flapping.'

Jeff lifted his daughter onto a *lilo* and speed-boated her through the water to the poolside, the front edge aquaplaning on the bow wave. Sitting the squealing baby safely on dry land next to their guest and entrusting him with both kids' wellbeing, he jumped out to fetch another round of drinks.

Lynn followed her husband into the kitchen, and they kissed for a long time while he dripped all over the tiled floor. 'Are you OK?'

'Yep. This is just fantastic,' he nodded, resting his forehead on hers. 'Just normal family stuff. Simple and absolutely spot-on for what I need.'

'That's good. I'll make dinner in a few minutes. Any requests?'

The glistening, half-naked swimmer eyed his wife's body and opened his mouth as if he were about to respond, only to turn away with two bottles. Sighing, he shook his head and headed for the door.

His wife giggled. 'You are so gorgeous.'

'Don't say that,' he almost pleaded, 'or I'll make a request.'

Having delivered one of the beers to his mate, Jeff returned to the kitchen to fix drinks for Lynn and the children. She had disappeared, leaving him filled with regret and relief in equal parts. Placing a glass and two plastic cups on the counter with their cutlery, he scribbled a note and pinned it to the refrigerator door with a magnet.

'You're the best, I love you and I can wait... maybe! Jx'.

The blonde tennis champion smiled when she saw the message a few minutes later. As usual, she and her perfect stranger were on exactly the same wavelength. She had avoided dressing provocatively because she knew her man would be desperate to prove that he didn't need to slip back into his old, compulsive ways of dealing with extended absences. Previously, they would have raced straight into the bedroom and collapsed on the bed in a frenzy of urgent lovemaking in order to satisfy his persecuted mind that he was still wanted.

Lynn knew the last few days had been very tough for her healing soul-mate. She fervently hoped it hadn't set his recovery back too far. She had been worried when he arranged to see the good Doctor Friedman; not only for her own fears that he wouldn't be able to resist an old flame, but also because he had placed unnecessary temptation in his path at a time of renewed vulnerability. Yet there was no doubt that Jeff was committed to conquering the obsessive, rollercoaster responses that rushed into his mind during such pressured times, and the patient woman chose to afford him every opportunity to behave like a happy, well-adjusted family man.

With dinner underway, the long-legged blonde slipped onto one of the poolside lounges and watched her brood and their longtime friend playing in the water without a care in the world. Her thoughts turned to Gerry, the perennial party animal who was never short of company but who was somehow always alone. Was he beginning to tire of being unattached? Occasionally, he seemed jealous of the Diamonds' comfortable togetherness, and at times like these, she wondered if he might be looking to assimilate into his mate's environment; trying it on for size, as she had written in her diary before.

Jeff gave his beautiful best friend a wink when she caught his eye, and a *frisson* of teenaged excitement shimmered through her. The latest magic moment was interrupted by Kierney calling to be lifted out of the water, so her mother walked to the side of the pool to retrieve her. While she was there, she knelt down and kissed her man tenderly.

'Thanks for the note,' she whispered. '*Ditto.*'

The grateful serf stroked his princess' face with a chilly, wet hand before kicking himself off the wall and swimming away, bound for Jet and Gerry. Lynn wrapped a towel around her daughter, and they both sat on the lounge chair to wait for the little girl's hair to dry in the late afternoon sun.

'I'm hungry,' the boy shouted across to his mother.

'Me too!' his fellow swimmers chimed in echo.

Their uninhibited laughter skimmed across the surface and rebounded off the *stucco* walls of the luxurious *hacienda*. Jeff had dunked his indomitable business partner, holding his head under the water for several seconds. Not wishing to give the youngster ideas, the beauty shot her husband a disapproving glare.

'Thank you. Good,' she shouted back, when their guest's face burst out into the air. 'Dinner's soon. You'd better dry off in a few minutes. *Chilli con carne.*'

Jeff and his refined henchman bounded out of the water, intent on sinking another beer each before dinner. Climbing up onto the diving board again, Jet wheeled round to find himself on his own.

'Hey! Come back!' he yelled, to no avail.

Gerry seemed oblivious of the boy's calls, drying himself with his back to the pool. He would never have thought to acknowledge him, and the Diamonds wondered if his ears were even tuned in to young people's voices.

'Hello! Goodbye! How are you?' his mate's son tried desperately to attract his attention. 'Why won't anyone play with me?'

'Hey! What's that racket?' Lynn slid the screen door open from the kitchen. 'Dad's coming straight back, Jetto. Get out and come and get changed, please.'

Unbeknown to the others, the songwriter had frozen in front of the refrigerator, unable to turn around and confront his wife. Left without a playmate, his son's cries had triggered a flashback which sliced his reconditioned heart in two. Memories of his cruel father calling him over, a little boy eager to spend time with his idol, only to have the door slammed in his face on purpose.

Leave me alone, you bastard, Jeff inhaled oxygen into his disquieted brain.

His mind tried valiantly to change the scene as he jogged through the kitchen and back out onto the deck. The sound of arrogant laughter on the landing outside the Stones Road flat had subsided, replaced by a similarly mean roar of triumph. This time, it was food being snatched from the boy's plate moments after his mother had put his meal down in front of him.

'Jesus Christ!' the world-changer muttered under his breath, chasing the cheeky villain across the lawn and swooping him up in the air, towel and all. 'Hey, champ! Come on. Let's dry you off. You are so clever with that diving!'

No child of his was ever going to feel unloved. Such cruelty was abhorrent, and not only because he had experienced it first-hand.

***

Later that night, after their casual dinner on the patio was over, two drooping children had been put to bed and Gerry had insisted on driving home with rather too much wine inside him, the repatriated wanderer took his lover's hand silently and danced her up the sweeping staircase, Fred Astaire and Ginger Rogers style, continuing all the way past their bed and out onto the balcony.

A gentle northerly wind blew warm air, whistling through the shutters and rustling the top-most branches of the gums and pines which marked Escondido's cliff-side boundary. The soul-mates stood contemplating the sea's dark majesty, Lynn wrapped up in her hero's embrace.

'Thanks for being so wonderful today, angel,' Jeff whispered against her cheek, pent-up passions finally being allowed to bubble to the surface. 'You've made everything feel so right. Special, normal and comfortable all in one. You know me so well, don't you?'

'I hope so,' his lover replied, leaning back into his body and relishing his grip tightening around her. 'You're doing better than I expected, and as well as I hoped.'

The poet kissed the sweet-smelling, blonde hair, flattered that she thought to reel off his worn-out phrase on such a momentous night. 'I'm OK,' he told her. 'Better than I expected too. May I rip your clothes off now?'

'You may,' Lynn smiled.

Jeff poured every last skerrick of overwrought energy into pleasing his wife that night, so sweet was the feeling of togetherness after so long in the waiting. While they made up for lost time with choreographed zeal, she forced him to describe in detail how the poor victims were stretchered out of the auditorium, both to slow him down and to mix the good experiences with the bad. He recalled how difficult it was to carry on performing to a crowd who had no idea what was going on, after having watched Amanda being carried out with her neck so badly broken that her head was at a ninety-degree angle to her shoulders.

In return, to prevent the struggling musician from retreating entirely into his own misfortune, the young mother explained how hard it was for her to be stuck at home, unable to help him, and then how inconceivable a prospect it was that his time with Sarah Friedman might damage this perfect moment.

'That part of me's completely gone,' he affirmed, kissing his dream girl's tattooed shoulder blade as they lay staring out of the window over the glassy, moonlit calm of the bay. 'I thought I'd be at least tempted, given how long it had been since we'd last done this, but when I got there, the thought repulsed me. Only we can be like this.'

'I'm so happy you feel that way. I didn't want you not to touch her because you didn't want to hurt me, 'cause that'd mean you still wanted her on some level.'

'Exactly,' the handsome enigma replied. 'I hate myself for putting you through all that before. I don't know how I could ever have justified my actions. Nor why you ever let me.'

Lynn chuckled, tilting her face downwards to kiss his forearm. 'Neither do I! You were worth it, I suppose. I didn't want to lose what we had, so it was a risk I took. And it paid off, didn't it? We're here, and nothing and no-one's ever going to break us apart.'

Jeff rolled onto his back and groaned. 'Do you know how good it is to hear you say that?'

'Of course! It's the truth. It's no different for me.'

'Thanks, angel. Back then, when I was hanging on by a thread and fighting to convince myself that you even liked me, there's no way on Earth I would've dared believe you didn't want to lose me,' the boy from Canley Vale confessed. 'Blokes were queuing up to go out with you. I was expecting at any minute you'd just give me up for some better offer. Then now you tell me you were actually scared of losing me.'

The athlete turned onto her side and propped herself up on one arm. 'You bet I was,' she confirmed, stroking his tired face. 'And I still am. Jeff, I'm serious. I know I probably came across as confident and at ease, but I didn't always feel that way inside. I so desperately wanted to be the woman you'd want to go out with. Usually went out with, I suppose I mean.'

'Oh, Jesus! That's not fair! How can a man keep it together when you say something like that? But why?'

'Because you were so exciting, so grown-up. Opinionated and independent. And I was just a schoolgirl who'd never done anything daring in my life. I thought I'd hold you back.'

The pair collapsed onto the mattress, the walls of Lynn's vagina pulsating in pre-orgasmic tension, where her husband's erect penis had withdrawn in a hurry. She was holding him back now, and he was making the statement to prove it. Screaming in frustration, she lunged for his dark red, throbbing tip with lightning reflexes, giving him no choice but to fall into line.

'But your school uniform was so sexy,' her love-god teased, receiving a poke in the ribs for his trouble.

'I thought you'd lose patience with all the limitations that came with me,' she gasped, flicking her tongue along his shaft and applying extra pressure when riding over the bulbous tip.

Jeff moaned, scarcely able to maintain his cool. Guiding the supple body round so that he could sink deep into her and finish what they had started, he shook his head emphatically.

'Never, angel. Never, ever. Sure, it was minorly annoying to have to work around all your commitments, but I didn't want anything you weren't. Still don't. But you're one hundred and fifty percent woman now! The innocent schoolgirl's long gone.'

The mother of two smiled, immediately smothered in a deep, passionate kiss. Assuming there were unspoken words still to come, the empath backed off to let his beautiful best friend finish.

'No. Hear me out, please. I don't know why I've never told you this before, but tonight is actually the perfect time for it to come out.'

Her husband was entranced. What sort of secret had she been withholding all this time?

'What haven't you told me? Are you bi-sexual?'

'No! You always jump to the kinkiest conclusions! That'd make you happy too, wouldn't it?' she laughed out loud. 'Shut up a minute... Even in those early weeks, I couldn't bear to think of us not being together. Sometimes, if a guy asked me out, I'd feel physically sick at the thought of not being held by you ever again. And you had a queue of hot girls dying to go out with you back then too, remember? I wasn't so conceited not to think it might be too hard for you to go out with me. You know... Being only sixteen, under Daddy's thumb and always away. And then, when I was in the US and going out with other people, it didn't take me long to figure out that what we had was in a whole different league. No-one's touch felt like yours. Nowhere near.'

'Christ, angel. I know what that feels like,' the lost boy sighed, prompted with some memories of his own. 'I know you don't want to hear this, but believe me, when I was having sex with a meaningless woman and fantasising that she was you, I'd wait for your hand to travel up my back and grasp my neck when I was coming. But it never happened, and it was so bloody hard not to show how much it hurt that she wasn't you.'

Lynn shook her head, frowning. 'You're right. I don't want to hear it. But I do, at the same time. I'm glad none of those people we slept with can hear us. Can I make you come now?'

Needing no encouragement to reach his long-awaited nirvana, Jeff whipped his nubile bedfellow's body over until he could pin her to the bed with ferocious determination. Using his own special brand of dexterity, his fingers set to work as he plunged through her warm folds, bringing her quickly to the brink of climax and then letting it ebb a little.

With a cry emanating from deep within, his dream girl's hips rose in perfect harmony with his own thrusting movements until they were both poised on the edge of paradise. She couldn't and wouldn't let him down this time. Her right hand drifted from its place on his hip, across the small of his back and traced along his spine, the sensation seesawing between luscious and ravaging. At the very last possible second, the traveller came home again with the sublime gift of her fingers wrapping around the base of his skull.

Elated and blissfully satisfied, both lovers hugged each other and kissed until they floated down from heaven. Twice would not be enough tonight, Jeff thought, knowing his tanks were by no means empty after such a stressful month. There was always tomorrow though, as his dream girl had been at pains to reassure him earlier that evening.

'What a pair we are!' the intellectual scoffed. 'There I was thinking there was nothing hidden between us anymore, and yet there still is. I guess that's human nature. Don't show your hand completely, just in case it gives the other person too good an opportunity to do you over. Survival instinct or something.'

'Guess so,' his wife agreed. 'Anyway... We're here today, so whatever we did worked. We're stuck with each other whether we like it or not.'

'Ha! Is that what you think?' the superstar shouted, rolling over and grabbing her relaxed oblique muscles under the ribcage. 'Just stay together because of the children. Isn't that how it goes?'

Lynn wriggled out of his grip and headed into the bathroom. 'Yeah. That's it. It's too expensive for us to get divorced, so I'll stick with you. I'll put up with you hanging around every now and again 'cause I like the house too much to leave.'

Jeff threw his hands in the air in mock disgust, watching the girl of his dreams disappear behind a closed door. It had never felt so good to be safely tucked away with his gorgeous soul-mate and their miraculous, little soul-babies, Unity and Liberty. Whatever happened henceforth in this life singular, theirs was the real deal. Of all the opportunities and experiences that came his way, whether amazing or terrifying, being home was the most valuable of all.

***

Lynn returned from the *en suite* to find her husband sitting up in bed scrolling through the pages of his diary. He had written a list of dates on a sheet of paper which he tore off with aplomb, folded in half and placed on his bedside table, underneath his watch.

'What are you doing?' his wife asked. 'Where are you going now?'

Smiling broadly, the hard-working millionnaire beckoned for her to sit beside him. 'Nowhere. You know that recovery holiday we're having next week?'

'Yes. I can just about remember this afternoon.'

Jeff kissed his fingertip and pressed it on the bridge of her nose as if affixing a postage stamp. 'Sarcasm will get you nowhere, baby. I've made a decision.'

'OK. What's that?' the young woman recognised the serious look on his face. 'Are you alright?'

'Yeah. I'm applying to Cath for a leave of absence. Long service leave. I'm not going to do any more live performances for a while.'

'Really?' Lynn asked. 'Not anywhere? Because of the girls?'

'Mainly, yep. But also because of you and the kids. It's a sabbatical. My place is here with you, not strutting around on a stage like a madman in front of thousands of people. That's just not important anymore. I want to spend as much time as I can with you guys.'

'But still carrying on with all the other projects?'

'Oh, yeah. Absolutely,' her husband confirmed. 'They're important too. I'm going to concentrate on building the businesses for the next six months, with only the occasional trip overseas. And I want to keep you all safe from the Sydney crowd.'

A shiver ran down the singer's spine at this surprise tangent. 'Oh. Why? Have you heard from them?'

'Yeah. Right again. Gerry's security people reported some activity last week. They don't think it's anything to worry about, so let's not panic.'

'No?' Lynn chuckled. 'Let's not. Just take a sabbatical instead of a year's worth of your career! Do you want to move away again?'

The old soul shook his head. 'Gimme a break, oh conscience of mine. No.'

'Because I'm happy here?' his wife leaned into his shoulder and kissed his cheek.

'In part,' Jeff shrugged. 'But more because I don't want them to win.'

'I will, if you want to move...'

'No, angel. We belong here for now. Maybe in years to come, when the kids no longer need us. Then I'd like us to go north.'

The sportswoman yawned. 'OK. Depends where they end up, I suppose. But I'd like that too. Plenty of time to consider our options, you old forward-thinking dreamer!'

The tired man laughed under his breath, knowing he was becoming aroused again at full speed. He tried to suppress his desires at first, not wanting to appear so demanding of his ever-obliging lover. Instead, he began to tell her about how much he looked forward to getting back into French literature and that he planned to adapt one of his favourite novels into another musical.

'Can we get it on again?' Jeff gave in after exhausting his stock of distractions, pulling the heavenly body over on top of him and kissing her lips with a subtle insistence that oozed as much affection as sexual need. 'I've missed you to the power of infinity. We have a lot to catch up on.'

Lynn kissed her plaintiff and stroked his full erection. 'Looks like it! I think that's a wonderful recovery plan for your soul, by the way.'

'This, or taking time out from performing?' the traveller asked, rolling themselves over again until her back came to rest on the mattress and sending his fingers in hot pursuit of her arousal.

'Both,' she smirked.

'You won't get sick of me hanging around the house?' he grinned and watched her eyes close in sensuous rapture.

'Probably,' his wife giggled, 'but I'll deal with it.'

'Cheers,' he said. 'This feels so good. You are the most gorgeous woman ever to walk on this Earth. Past, present or future.'

'Thanks to you too,' Lynn replied, kissing the tattoo on his chest. 'Welcome home, Don Quixote.'

The happy couple drifted into peaceful slumber in each others' arms, only partially waking to put some distance between their flesh in the still, late-March shadows. They had not been asleep for long however, when the shrill ring of the telephone broke through the silence.

'Shit!' he groaned, sitting up and snatching the receiver before the noise woke the children.

The call was announced by an operator, coming through on the secure line which Gerry had arranged. While waiting for one of his South African negotiator colleagues to be connected, the dazed twenty-seven-year-old's mind drifted back to the childhood memories stirred up by his son's loud lament the previous day. Had he been miraculously spared an accompanying nightmare, or had this telephone call interrupted its coalescence?

Gulping down a glassful of water, the peacemaker listened to the man's detailed message, interjecting a comment here and there. It appeared a breakthrough had been made in talks between the African National Congress and the ruling government, meaning their summit could be brought forward. So much for staying at home for a while, the young man rued...

While he was on the telephone, Lynn slipped out of bed to check on the children. A couple of minutes later, she returned, depositing the one-year-old onto her father's lap. Cuddling the drowsy, little body to his stomach, he curled his chin down and kissed the top of her head.

'She heard you talking,' his beautiful best friend whispered. 'She'll settle.'

Sure enough, daddy's girl stretched out, warm and comfortable, and fell back to sleep within seconds. Her mother retrieved a camera from the chest of drawers and took a picture, doubtful of sufficient light.

The call came to an end soon afterwards, and Jeff lifted Kierney clear of his sweat-drenched skin and set her down onto the mattress beside his wife. He disappeared into the *en suite* before settling back down next to his two favourite females, his mood sombre and his heart heavy.

'What's up?' Lynn asked. 'I wish you didn't sink down so fast. What can I do?'

'Me too,' the intellectual frowned. 'Nothing. We'll talk about it in the morning. Sorry, angel. I must look so bloody ungrateful after everything you did for me yesterday.'

'No. I know you're not ungrateful.'

'Do the kids?'

'Think you're ungrateful?' his wife checked, following him while he deposited the sleeping baby back into her cot. 'I doubt it.'

'There's nothing I can do about it,' Jeff sighed.

Lynn kissed his sad mouth. 'I hope it doesn't always happen.'

'Me too. I hope it doesn't wear you down.'

'It won't wear me down. It'll never wear me down. *¿Comprendes?* Think of something funny that happened during yesterday's press conference.'

'Something funny?' the exhausted songwriter repeated, bailed out again by a joy trigger courtesy of his *Regala*.

'Yes. There must've been at least one question you answered with a vitriolic comment they didn't know how to take.'

Jeff felt lightness inch into his aching neck, gradually penetrating his head. 'Actually there was... I was asked by a journo how we managed to get time, with two young kids, to rehearse so many song and dance numbers.'

'Oh, yeah? And what did you say?'

'I said, "We live together. We can rehearse in the bedroom, in the kitchen, in the back-yard. And we do."'

'*¡Excelente!*' his collaborator-in-chief applauded softly. 'And we always will. Now go to sleep.'

Unexpected Retribution

'D'you want me to get up?' Jeff asked his wife, admiring the way the light streamed through her short, silk teddy when she emerged from the bathroom, letting his imagination feast on those long, slender legs and the heavenly hidden treasure further up.

The celebrity had returned from the airport in the dead of night after a fortnight in Cape Town and Pretoria, spent in virtual lockdown with government officials, academics and tribal leaders. Security was necessarily much tighter these days, with the talks covering their quest to free some of the country's political prisoners now reaching a critical stage.

Lynn had cried when she heard the front door open and then smiled at the master of the house's vain efforts to quieten an excited dog intent on welcoming him home. One shoe and then the other dropped onto the tiled floor, followed by footsteps jogging up the staircase. They had made love without a word, the respite of being together again expressed in so many other ways, all under the covers of darkness.

'Up to you,' the beauty smiled, kneeling on the bed and bending to kiss him, far enough that the neckline of her *negligée* billowed to reveal her bountiful cleavage. 'Breakfast is on its way.'

'So do you want me to get up?' the mischievous man asked again, reaching for her breasts.

His dream girl placed her hand on the sheet and squeezed his growing penis. She felt it harden in her grip and moved closer to help it along a little further. Stretching his back and tucking one hand behind his arrogant head, Jeff flashed his gipsy eyes at the woman who loved to spoil him.

'Don't do it,' he moaned, urging her down beside him and kissing her mouth.

'You're right. I shouldn't. You have to come to breakfast,' Lynn teased, as she let the turgid organ flop against his belly and watched his smile fade to shattered disbelief.

'Don't do it,' he said again, insanely turned-on at her flaunting his agony.

Unable to stop herself from laughing, the Olympian's hand returned to its rightful place, alternating between slow, purposeful strokes and fevered pumping, while her other hand fondled his testicles, elongating him steadily, and then stopping yet again.

'I should go.'

'Christ! This is a torturous game,' Jeff's voice rasped, only half joking. 'I thought you were pleased to see me home.'

With a flirtatious flick of her hair, Lynn masturbated her willing victim some more, and this time even faster, causing him to breathe in sharply as he drew closer to the point of no return.

'OK!' she declared, springing off the bed. 'Breakfast time. Are you joining us?'

The stunned songwriter's eyes nearly popped out of their sockets as he watched his beautiful concubine exit the bedroom at a trot, leaving his genitals hammering in painful ecstasy. They both knew that following her was not an option, given the happy sound of kids and nannies making breakfast echoing up from the kitchen.

'Fuck!' he whispered, reaching his own hand down to stroke himself.

It was no good. He daren't touch the hair trigger that the temptress had left in his custody, too close to the edge even to enter a solo holding pattern. Turning onto his side, he pulled the sheet up over his shoulder and focussed his mind on the day to come. Was she coming back? The wait was excruciating.

Not many minutes later, his tormentor returned with two glasses of orange juice. She casually offered one to her husband and sipped from the other. Issuing a sardonic thank-you, Jeff dared to disguise a grab for her leg. She was too quick, though only running to shut the door.

'Jesus Christ, woman! D'you know what state you left me in?'

She grinned, stretching the top of her G-string and letting it fall to the floor. 'I had a pretty good idea.'

'You bitch! Come here,' her sex maniac lifted the satin and lace shroud and spread both hands around her slim waist.

'I love you,' Lynn murmured, squirming as he entered her with such urgency. 'You're so hot.'

Jeff kissed his lover's mouth hard, their temperatures rising as they moved together, a carbon copy of the silent, horizontal tango they had danced just a few hours earlier. No wonder he no longer gave into temptation on the road, the rock star thought aloud while they lay together afterwards, listening to the clatter of plates and cutlery being laid out on the kitchen table. It was a secret to no-one that a multitude of corporal lures were cast into his path wherever he went, yet this amazing creature he had married made sex so exciting, so tantalisingly delicious, that the promise of more on each and every homecoming easily prevented him from straying.

Interrupting the couple's post-orgasmic calm, there was a tentative knock on their bedroom door.

'Mamá and Papá coming to breckie?' a hushed voice asked.

'Come in, Kizzy,' her father invited, straightening out the sheets. '*Abrir la puerta, gorgeousita.*'

Lynn and Jeff watched the door handle turn on its own. They imagined the toddler standing on tiptoe and struggling to open the door. After a couple of false starts, it swang into the room with the messenger still attached.

'Well done!' Jeff shouted, putting his arms out as the little girl ran to his side of the bed. 'You've grown since I went away.'

'I knew you were back,' Kierney said triumphantly. 'I heard in the nighttime but I didn't get up.'

'Good girl,' the jetsetter kissed her forehead.

While the dark-haired pair cuddled, the young mother climbed out of bed, smoothing her nightdress to cover her tingling body, and slipped into the shower. She liked to give the twin gipsies plenty of special time alone, knowing how much it helped her man's healing process.

'*¿Que la mamá está bellissima, sí?*' Jeff crooned, watching Lynn slink away.

'*¡Sí! ¡Muy bellissima!* Hungry, Papá?'

'*Sí, pero preguntasme en español porque no te comprendo,*' he complained, shrugging.

'*¡Papá!*' the indignant toddler cried out. '*Comprendesme bien. ¿Tienes hambre?*'

'Huh? *Quoi? Tu veux dire, «Est-ce que j'ai faim?»*'

'*Oui!*' Kierney giggled, squirming out of his embrace and turning to face the source of her frustration.

'*Bien sûr,*' he answered, grabbing his pouting daughter under the arms, lifting her over his torso and dropping her gently onto Lynn's side of the bed.

'Under the covers?'

'No, baby,' Jeff shook his head. 'Stay here. I have to go in the shower in a minute anyway. You need to make sure Mamá gets dressed right for breakfast.'

The little girl laughed, standing up and looking at herself in the dressing table mirror. 'OK. Like me?'

'Yeah. As beautiful as you, *pequeñita.*'

Father and daughter exchanged vital pieces of child-friendly news, swapping languages in short, clipped sentences. Through the bathroom door, Lynn listened in amusement to their stilted conversation, knowing the account he would soon receive from their son would be totally different. When she emerged from the *en suite*, towelling her hair dry, Kierney immediately jumped up and began to bounce on the mattress.

'Mamá! Papá's turn!' she ordered, rocking him backwards and forwards.

Jeff pretended to be asleep, with his face turned to the left, from where his half-open eyes could ogle his wife's naked form while she put on a matching set of lace-trimmed *lingerie*. His daughter applied more energy to her efforts, but her father only coughed and turned over to face the other way, drawing the quilt over his head.

'Papá, wake up!'

'*¿Qué?*' murmured the large snoring lump under the covers.

'*¡Papá, levantate* now!'

'*¿Levantate* now?' the polyglot exclaimed, snatching the giggling bundle of flailing limbs into his arms and tickling her. 'What sort of a mixed-up kid are you?'

Jet came running into the room, fearing he was missing out on all the fun. 'Dad! What's going on? Let me up there.'

With his usual ham-fisted bluster, the three-year-old pushed his sister to one side and started kneading his father's flesh with all his strength. Fending off the blows with his right hand, Jeff extended his left to make sure Kierney didn't fall off the edge of the bed.

'Hey, mate!' he warned, slipping a sly grimace at his dream girl, letting her know how painful the boy's attack was. '*Que estás muy fuerto.* Watch your sister, please.'

The young mum called a halt to their frivolity. 'Come on, guys,' she said, her tone firm but with a wide smile on her face. 'Leave Papá in peace to take a shower. Let's help Nadine and Ursula get breakfast served, and then we can all plan what we're doing today.'

The children slid down to the floor and ran out of the room at their mother's behest. She blew her husband a kiss before following in their footsteps. As soon as the door clicked shut, he sprang out of bed and into the shower, unable to envision a sweeter life.

Once the extended family's noisy meal was over, Lynn checked her watch. 'Nine-thirty. Kids, please will you give the girls a hand with clearing breakfast away, 'cause I have to talk to Papá about something.'

Jeff looked up from the newspaper. 'Oh, yeah? What?'

Searching her expression for clues, he got the distinct impression that the attentive mother didn't wish to answer this question in front of the others. 'Jet, grab these, please?' he asked, handing the boy a bunch of dirty knives and forks. 'Go on. Let me have a quick chat to Mamá, and then we can go out.'

'Ducks?' Kierney tugged at her dad's trouser leg. 'Can we, please? *Creo que tienen hambre.*'

The songwriter chuckled, bending down and hugging. '*¿Verdad? Excelente, pequeñita. Te gustas, Jetto?*'

'Yeah! Yeah! Yeah! Please may I ride my bike?' the boy jumped up and down, the large handful of cutlery slithering through his fingers and almost cascading to the floor.

Catching her husband's eye, Lynn smiled at the reality of their youngsters already dictating their life's direction. 'Careful! Well caught! Yes, darling. Of course you may. You want to go to Albert Park to feed the ducks? That's actually a good idea.'

With the nannies supervising their two hard-working helpers, the celebrities sloped off into the office and shut the door. Jeff stole a kiss before his beautiful best friend could divulge her news, becoming suspicious of her secretive actions.

'What's up? Why so serious?'

The business-end of the Diamond pantomime horse handed her front-man an envelope. The words "HM Prison Parklea" were franked in red ink in the top left-hand corner.

'This has been sitting here taunting me for nearly a week,' she reported. 'I was going to wait for a day or two before giving it to you, but it's burning my soul.'

Anxiety instantly constricted the young man's chest, and he exhaled to dispel it as he read the red franking. A typed label had been stuck onto the front, addressing it to the couple's city apartment. He leaned his full weight against the filing cabinet and turned the envelope over, where another stamp had printed "New South Wales Department of Corrective Services" above a return address.

Predictably, the lost boy's first response was to send the letter back unopened, and the luckless piece of mail found its way back to the desk. If his *Regala* hadn't been standing right in front of him, it might even have been tossed directly into the waste bin.

'Thanks,' he whispered. 'What the fuck is that about?'

Lynn moved closer to the downhearted world-changer, and they put their arms around each other. She could feel his heart pounding against her collarbone, and his eyes had taken on a familiar craze. Stepping back, he began to wring his hands as if desperate for a cigarette.

'You don't have to open it now,' she suggested. 'I just needed you to know it was here.'

Jeff kissed her. 'I don't want to open it at all.'

His sympathetic companion chuckled. 'I thought not, but you will, won't you?'

'No. Let's just pretend it got lost.'

'They'll only send another one after a few weeks. It's obviously something important. They wouldn't be writing otherwise.'

Her husband nodded, ceremoniously lifting the envelope with two hands like an Asian businessman offering his card. 'Yeah. S'pose so. You open it.'

Smiling, Lynn shook her head. 'No, you coward! It doesn't matter which of us opens it. The contents are for you.'

'Aw! You're so mean!' the intellectual scoffed, putting on his best Madalena Moreno whine. 'You never 'elp me no more. You used to be so nice to me.'

'Oh, just open it!'

'OK, OK!' the comic agreed, shrinking from his organiser's authoritative command and ripping straight into the top of the envelope.

It contained three sheets of paper folded twice to fit into standard stationery. The second and third pages were stapled together, and a metal clip attached them to the first, which had been typed on prison letterhead and addressed to Mister Jeffrey Diamond.

'Well, that's me,' Jeff assented, breathing heavily. 'Whoa. How fast and furious all these old symptoms come back, huh?'

Lynn felt sorry for her complex partner. It had been a long time since she had witnessed panic take hold so instantaneously. She watched him read the letter's three short paragraphs and then flick over to the following page, handwritten in two very different styles, one in black ink and the other in blue.

'He's got cancer,' the recipient broke her concentration. 'Lung cancer.'

The skilled therapist's expression didn't change, softening the blow in her usual, expert way. The grateful negotiator reverted to the first page to show her, tears brimming on his lower eyelids. His jawline became tense, and she could feel his stance wilt a little.

'Are you OK?'

'The second page is a letter from him,' Jeff said, kissing her cheek. 'Thanks. Looks like he's got a guilty conscience after all.'

The initial attack had begun to subside. The murderer's son handed his wife the envelope's contents and paced around the office, trying to absorb this unexpected news. She read the cover letter first. It was from a prison doctor who described his patient as being in the advanced stages of lung cancer.

Apparently, there was the potential of a transplant, but this would require his next of kin to agree to pay for the surgery and post-operative treatment in a private hospital. How harsh the world could be sometimes, the privileged woman rued. And what a tough decision the neglected son now needed to make... Should he save the life of someone who had taken two and caused such harm to several others?

The Olympian slotted the letter underneath the other sheets, clamped in her right hand, and scanned the scrawl on the next page. It appeared to be written by Paul himself, but had been corrected and supplemented by another person's handwriting; possibly a warder or a counsellor. She decided not to read beyond the introductory line, knowing his words ought to remain private. She would wait for her husband to take her through it in his own time.

Folding the stapled pages over to the last, Lynn found a single-sided medical report. She was shocked at how little detail was provided when informing relatives that a prisoner had contracted a terminal illness. How impersonal! Surely there were some prisoners serving life sentences whose nearest were still their dearest... She imagined being the wife of such an offender and hoped a different process existed for those not estranged from their incarcerated family members.

'Did you read it?' Jeff asked, seeing her look up.

'His letter? No. Only the first couple of sentences. It's for you. The form says three to six months. Did you read that?'

The washed-out man nodded, slumping down onto leather cushions and resting the back of his head against the window.

'It's for you to read first,' Lynn reiterated. 'What are you thinking?'

Her husband invited her to sit with him on the couch, with the morning sun streaming in through the glass above their heads. 'I'd like you to read it, please. I can't read it objectively. You'll be able to judge his sincerity better than I can.'

The young woman nodded, being kissed by nervous lips. 'OK. Sorry to spoil your day. Do you wish I'd waited?'

'No. Not really. There's no good time for something like this. It'd feel the same whenever you showed it to me. At least we have something to distract us when we try and stop the kids drowning in the lake.'

The superstar put an arm behind his saviour's back and drew her in close. Resting her head on his shoulder, she laughed at yet another bizarrely terrifying image.

'Did you get as far as the medical report?' she asked. 'It says he can have a transplant.'

Jeff took the papers back from his wife and flipped to the form on the third sheet, then re-reading the accompanying letter. Curious, she noticed him hurriedly skipping over the middle page as if it contained something too frightening to risk seeing again.

'Mmm...' he mused. 'Even if a donor could be found, does he deserve it?'

Lynn shrugged, once more saying nothing. The prisoner's son needed to come to his own conclusion on this topic.

'I mean, over and above some poor, unfortunate law-abiding, tax-paying citizen who's nice to his family?'

'I know,' his wife countered. 'He's your dad though.'

'Really? Could've fooled me.'

'You don't have to decide today. Think about it for a while.'

Jeff stood up. 'Would I deserve one?'

Australia's poster child for pure, clean living stared straight ahead, incredulous. 'What do you mean? A transplant? Are you asking me if I'd save your life?'

'Yep,' he replied, an ominous shadow cast across his face. 'I've been a life-long smoker. Do I deserve a replacement set of lungs if I ruined these ones myself? Just because we can afford to pay for it?'

Lynn got up and held her arms out to her husband. 'Enough, Mister Morbid. As your wife, I'd do everything I could to prolong your life, if that's what you wanted. You know that, Jeff. For the kids, for me and for you, but mostly for all the good you still have left to do for this world.'

'Yeah,' the grateful superstar kissed his partner, still distracted. 'But if you only had one pair of lungs available and were the person looking down the list of transplant candidates, which one would you choose? The one with a tick in the "Smoker" column?'

'Am I allowed to say "Yes and no"?' his dream girl threw back her complex conundrum's well-worn philosophical in-joke. 'If the choice were mine... not as your soul-mate, of course... I wouldn't only look at one column. I'd try to decide based on who would contribute more to the world after being given a chance to finish his or her life.'

'Hmm...' the young man's eyes lit up. 'Fantastic, angel. Thanks! In that case, my dad should go straight to the bottom of the pile. Locked up or not, he wouldn't contribute anything positive to the world.'

'Yes, maybe. But even if you weren't such an important public figure, it doesn't mean people who love you wouldn't try their hardest to make a case for you. And that's what you need to do for your dad. You have to decide whether you feel enough for him to fight his case.'

Jeff turned away and stared out of the window, across to the tennis court and pool. 'Guess so,' he muttered. 'The voice of reason speaks. *Gracias*, angel.'

'You don't sound very convinced by my reasoning,' Lynn chuckled.

'No. I'm not,' the philosopher forced a smile. 'Let's go out now. Let me ruminate a while, and we can talk it through a bit more tonight, once the elves are in bed.'

'OK. That's good,' his wife agreed, holding her hand out for the three sheets of paper, folding them up and slipping them into a drawer in their secure filing cabinet.

The *duo* of diminutive dynamos with their delightfully different perspectives on life were a welcome distraction as they piled into the Caprice and headed off to Albert Park. Ursula and Nadine left the apartment at the same time, bound for a shopping spree in their free hours. Armed with several bags of stale bread, Jet and Kierney were excited to be going out with Mamá and Papá together.

With Melbourne's nine-to-five working population locked in their places of servitude, the pantomime horse on a break from its own schedule exercised their two gambolling foals in relative privacy, with only one or two inquisitive tourists impinging on their path. Lynn was keen to gauge her pensive husband's mood, with Jet's superfluous training wheels skidding along the track ahead of them and Kierney being pushed in the stroller. Taking him by surprise, an elegant index finger reached up and stroked the side of his face.

'Are things OK in there?'

'Oh, yeah!' Jeff replied with more enthusiasm than she expected. 'I've got you holding my hand and I can see our kids happy and healthy and changing every day, so why shouldn't I be OK?'

'You know what I mean,' the caring woman chided. 'Stop avoiding the issue. I bet your mind's still rolling over and over.'

'Yes. Alright. Not too bad though,' he reassured her, thinking twice before dismissing the typical questioning look and laughing at having been exposed for a fraud yet again. 'Seriously... It's just brewing away. Not like before, where I'd have to fight with the obsession. You've done a good job on me, angel. I'm pretty normal these days.'

Lynn laughed, prising his right hand off the stroller's handle and shaking it. 'Thanks. And congratulations! Congratulations on becoming normal, Jeff Diamond. You're just that run-of-the-mill kind o' guy who blends into the crowd.'

The world-changer flicked his worthy co-star across the top of the head and ran on in front, to where his son was beginning to feed some rather large swans. Kierney screamed with joy when she saw her beloved papá lift her brother into the air and threaten to dunk him in the murky water.

***

Later that evening, once the Diamonds had the lounge room to themselves, Jeff turned off the main light and sat back down next to his own private *cabaret* artist at the piano. She had been testing various melody ideas on him for their developing musical, but they had exhausted their creativity for the time being.

'Would you read my dad's letter with me, please?' her audience asked out of the blue.

'Yes. Of course. Go and get it. Did you want a whisky?'

His eyebrows answering in the affirmative, the apprehensive man detoured to the office. Enthusiasm waning on the way there and back, he returned to find a tumbler already filled on the coffee table.

'Thanks,' he said, raising his glass. '*Saludos*. Aren't you having anything?'

'No, thanks. Don't feel like it this late.'

'Are you pregnant again?'

'No!' Lynn objected. 'Definitely not.'

'Shame.'

His wife was surprised. 'Really? Do you want another child?'

'No. But it's a nice thought,' the romantic smiled. 'You know, all that wondering and anticipation. Two's right though. We're fine the way we are.'

The busy woman nodded. 'Yeah. I know what you mean. But then I think about all the nappies and midnight feeds and toilet training, and that soon puts me off. I think there's still a fair amount of wonder and anticipation ahead of us with these two.'

'OK! You've convinced me,' her husband smirked, beckoning the delectable creature closer and opening Parklea's correspondence out to the second page. 'Come and tell me what you think of this.'

Obediently, the slender, long-legged frame of Lynn Dyson, mother *extraordinaire*, tennis star and all-round musical genius, seated herself next to her perfect stranger on the sofa. Jeff coughed to clear his throat and read out the sentences his father had written, first as his initial version and then repeating them with the corrections. The contrast between before and after was stark but comedic, lightening the mood a little.

'It's pathetic, isn't it? Both his ability to write and what he's trying to say.'

'At least he sent it,' Lynn replied, not wishing to cast her vote too far on Diamond Senior's side. 'Do you think he wrote it solely because he's dying, or do you think the doctors encouraged him to send it so it might make you more likely to agree to the transplant?'

'Jesus! You're more of a cynic than I am! I hadn't even reached that conclusion myself yet, so your suspicious mind's working quicklier even than mine. Would they want to prolong his life?'

'Morally, I guess they would,' the singer posited. 'It's the right thing to do.'

Her husband shook his head, frowning. 'D'you reckon? It'd only mean he'd take up a cell for longer. I'm sure the statisticians don't analyse the reasons behind how many mouths taxpayers are feeding. Do they get funded per prisoner? Who knows?'

'When's his parole up for review?'

''Eighty-five,' Jeff replied, wise to the change of tack.

Lynn smiled. 'Would he get it?'

'Lena doesn't think so, but the Jawo boys aren't so feral about it anymore. Not sure he'd take it anyway…'

The compassionate woman was pleased at how relaxed her man seemed in discussing this delicate topic nowadays. There was no hint of angry reprisals, nor his prior readiness to grab for an easy solution to rid himself of the pain.

'Sorry. That was unfair,' she regretted expressing such a harsh opinion. 'I shouldn't say negative things about your family.'

'No. It's all good,' the negotiator insisted. 'I need you to speak your mind because I want to tackle this from all perspectives. I don't want to make a judgment based only on my bitter and twisted recollections.'

'So you want *my* bitter and twisted opinion too then?' Lynn nudged his shoulder.

'Absolutely!' the handsome musician kissed her. 'You're so fantastic. I love you so much.'

Paul Diamond's letter spoke of how he often thought about the visit Jeff had made to the prison five years ago, although he hadn't gone as far as to refer to him as his son. He also complimented his choice of vehicle and thanked him for the photographs tucked into the car magazine. It told that he was aware that the two stars had married, with his congratulations on the births of their children added in the second handwriting style. Neither child was referenced by name either, their mother remarked.

'He didn't write this himself,' the disconsolate man sighed, leaning his head back on the couch and closing his eyes. 'Don't you reckon? It's way too contrived.'

'Maybe,' his wife agreed. 'Perhaps he had some sort of therapy session and opened up a bit, so the counsellor gave him some words to write. I wonder how long it's been since he's had to write a letter.'

'Yeah. If ever. You're right. You're a good defence attorney.'

Lynn nuzzled into his chest, raising her bare, tanned legs off the floor until they came to rest across his thighs. 'Is that OK though? I don't mean to take his side, but he deserves the benefit of the doubt.'

'It's fine,' the peacemaker repeated. 'It's exactly what I want you to do. Give me the dispassionate view.'

'You're pretty dispassionate yourself. Compared to when you met him. Don't you think?'

Jeff paused before continuing, considering her observation. 'I know, but that's my passive-aggressive response, I guess. I could get all bent out of shape about how I hate the bastard, but I'm trying to keep out of that old, unhelpful trap. The malice is more in what I don't say; the stubborn resistance to it all.'

Mulling over the positives and negatives of this explanation, Lynn prepared to read the remaining paragraphs of the letter aloud. 'But you're not happy with that either, by the sounds of it. Listen to this…

'"I regret not sharing my feelings with you during your visit and that you left without knowing my side of the story. I am ready to talk now, if you are still willing to listen. I am proud of you, even though you don't believe me."

'Do you believe him?'

Jeff scoffed at the last sentence. 'That he's proud of me? Well, *howzat*, eh? That makes everything OK. Bloody hell!'

'He doesn't mention anything about your mother,' the reader pushed on. 'I wonder if he wanted to but didn't know what to say?'

'Hmm... Who knows? Lena cracks a mention though, as usual.'

'I know,' his wife nodded. 'Do you think she'd want to see him? Maybe it'd be better if you both went together to hear his side of the story, if he's really offering to tell all? You'd be able to support each other. Better than if you went alone again, I think.'

'Yeah. Absolutely. But she wouldn't go,' the Sydneysider said, emptying the tumbler down his gullet, smacking his lips and refilling it from the almost empty bottle of Johnny Walker Black Label. 'This is a good vintage, angel. Is there any more? She'd vote against the transplant, without question.'

Lynn nodded. 'In the pantry. Do you think she got this letter too, or are you the only one the prison contacts?'

'More good questions,' Jeff sniffed. 'Probably not. I didn't get stuff before I went to see him. She didn't even know which jail he's in.'

'Nevertheless, you should talk to Lena about this. She has a right to know, even if she mightn't agree with the action you want to take afterwards. At least then you wouldn't be making the decision completely on your own.'

'But I'm not making it on my own now, am I?' her husband countered. 'I hope. But you make yet another excellent point, my learned colleague. She's old enough to help out with this.'

'*¡Excelente!*' the sexy adviser slapped her man's chest, a mischievous smile on her face. 'You know... That's the first time you've given her any real responsibility. That's a big change from before too.'

The twenty-nine-year-old was caught off-guard. 'Yeah. S'pose you're right. I am the little brother after all.'

'Coffee?' Lynn asked, getting to her feet. 'You can ring Madalena tomorrow. It's too late now.'

'I doubt she'll be sleeping. Can you imagine? *Olá, chico.* Can't talk now...'

The performer reclined suggestively across the couch, making panting noises to simulate his sister's responses punctuated by a variety of moans and groans, before miming mopping up, slamming a door and counting out notes from a wad of cash. Lynn laughed, happy that their discussion hadn't reduced her entertainer to a ranting mess.

After a couple of minutes alone with his cogitation, Jeff followed his wife into the kitchen, wrapping his arms around her waist while they waited for the coffee to brew. 'Angel…'

'Yes,' she said with a cautious tone. 'Sounds ominous…'

'I'm going to pre-empt the idea I know you've already got going on in there,' he said, tapping her forehead.

'Which idea?' the Olympian put on a vacant expression, turning round to face him. 'There ain't no ideas in 'ere, mate.'

'Oh, really?' her stooge smiled, kissing her lips hard. 'That's not what I've heard.'

'*Digame… ¿Cual es tu idea?*'

'Let's see if we can engineer another visit. This time with you and the kids,' the intellectual chanced his arm.

Lynn's expression morphed into one of utter delight. 'Are you serious?'

'That's what you said when I asked you to marry me,' Jeff flashed a smile. 'Don't know. I'm a hell of a lot less sure about this! But it's the right thing to do, as you said before.'

'Don't do it because you think I want you to do it,' Lynn urged. 'Is that why you're suggesting it?'

'Suggesting what? Getting married? Why would I do something that stupid? Are you sure you're not pregnant?'

'No. I'm not!' the sportswoman shook her head, slapping him harder this time. 'Don't keep distracting us!'

Her husband rallied after his lapse in concentration. 'In truth, I don't know why I think we should do it, angel. You're very perceptive. It's just that your ideas are usually the ones we need to do, and I tend to resist them for far too long. This time, I decided to get on the front foot.'

'Well… Think about it. I do think it's a fantastic idea, but you've got to be comfortable with it for your own reasons. And you can invite your sister along too. She might come if the rest of us are there.'

Lynn pulled away from her troubled soul's cloying grasp and poured the coffee, stirring sugar into one of the mugs. Helping himself to a packet of TimTams from the refrigerator, the chivalrous gentleman stood back to allow her to leave the kitchen in front of him. She handed him his drink, and they walked back into the lounge room together.

'Did you want me to arrange it? Like last time?'

'No. I'll do it,' Jeff replied. 'It's got to come from me. I have to make a decision about the transplant quickly, if he's only got months to live.'

'Oh, yes. That's true. Would he want one?' the young woman mused. 'Do you think he's happy being in prison for the rest of his life? Maybe he wrote those conciliatory words because he wants to make peace with you before he dies. He might be looking for a way out.'

'Jesus, angel,' her lover gulped, his eyes filling with tears. 'You are the echo in my mind. That's exactly what I was thinking.'

Sitting down in the same places as before, Australia's darling was determined to keep her forlorn man from spiralling downwards before bedtime. 'Do you think he's religious?' she asked. 'Do you know if he believes in God or the after-life, or whatever he grew up being taught?'

Jeff shrugged, smearing moisture off his cheeks. 'No idea. I don't remember him ever talking about religion, apart from criticising either his mum or my mum's mum for their simplistic beliefs. He would probably have had some induction into the Jewish faith, but I never spoke to him about it.'

'I wonder if he had a *bar mitzvah* like yours?'

'Ha! Perhaps,' the rejected son managed a smile. 'I guess he must've been a sweet kid at some point.'

'Just like you?'

Jeff put his hands out in defiance. '*Whaddya* mean? I *was* a sweet kid.'

'I'm sure!' Lynn chided.

'Ah, you'll pay for that when we get to bed, woman... I was sweet for one or two days in my life, at least,' he contended. 'But seriously... That's even more reason to meet again before I make this decision. I need to know what he wants. He's the main man in this equation, despite what he did. Shit! It's hard work being reasonable, baby, isn't it?'

***

A month later, every last detail had been checked and double-checked for the Diamond family's flight to Sydney to visit the man who had been born in nineteen-thirty-three as Pavel Diament in Queens, New York. His son had arranged everything himself and had been doing his best to convince Madalena to join them. At Lynn's suggestion, he had requested a meeting in a family room, in the hope that their surroundings would not be too austere and alien for the children. After a couple of telephone calls back and forth, Parklea's governor had agreed.

James Whitfield, the former boss whom Jeff had met during his previous visit, had been promoted to a desk job, now heading up a correctional policy division in the Department. The new governor was a long-serving member of the Prison Service and had taken quite some convincing to grant a social call to the unremorseful perpetrator of such a serious crime, finally relenting on compassionate grounds due to his illness.

Tom Maloney, his disposition shouting exalted status at every opportunity, met the famous family in the reception area and personally accompanied them to the room that had been allocated for the next two hours.

'Thanks, Tom,' Jeff said, shaking the man's hand. 'We really appreciate you allowing this to happen.'

Governor Maloney showed no emotion, puzzling the youngsters and causing them to retreat behind their parents' legs. 'You're welcome, sir, madam. I hope you get what you want from the meeting.'

Left alone in the large room with bright artificial lights and the tiniest of windows, the tense couple watched how Jet and Kierney reacted to the environment. They had arranged to stay at the Blakes' house on Sydney's North Shore for the weekend, and the kids had been promised a visit from Jacinta's twin girls after meeting their granddad for the first time.

The family had also paused for a quick stop at a playground on the way through Pennant Hills, to give the excited pair the chance to run wild before being cooped up for the rest of the morning. Over an ice-cream, their father had explained the purpose of their visit and warned them that their grandfather might appear a little frightening because he wasn't very well.

The children had asked only a few, very tentative questions as they prepared to enter the grey, foreboding institution. They were so young to be in this situation, Jeff rued, gazing into their innocent eyes as he imparted sanitised stories about how their dad's dad had come to be locked up for such a long time.

Since finding out about their upcoming trip, Jet had been fascinated with the prospect of visiting a real jail and had been enacting prison games all week with his best friend, Dawson Jenner. Kierney on the other hand, ever her father's daughter, had been full of morbid curiosity as to why her grandfather had killed people and whether he was sorry.

'You can ask him yourself,' Jeff promised. 'He might not tell you, but I'll help you ask him. I want to know these answers too, Kizzy.'

Running into the brightly-lit room and away from the strict, humourless man in uniform, the youngsters spied a toy-box in the corner of the room. Digging their hands in to select something to play with, they calmed down, no longer appearing to need reassurance.

Their dad hugged his steadfast *confidante*, to steady his own nerves more than anything. 'D'you think we've done the right thing in bringing them here?' he asked, knowing she would take his question as rhetorical. 'Look at them. They're so little.'

Lynn kissed her strung-out husband. 'They'll be fine. We're here to stop anything bad happening. It's you I'm worried about.'

Jeff was extremely nervous, that much was beyond doubt. Every few seconds, his eyes fixed on the small, square window in the door, waiting to see the wizen face he remembered from five years ago; the older and thinner version of himself who had stared him down and refused to acknowledge their relationship.

Time had softened the younger man's attitude towards that meeting and, especially after receiving the news of his father's advanced cancer, vowed to make a final, desperate effort to part on better terms today.

Both celebrities had tried to persuade Madalena to come with them, but she had remained resolutely resistant. In a last-ditch attempt, they had left the youngsters with Celia the previous day and sat in an open-air café with Jeff's sister for a few hours, trying to convince her to settle a score before the man passed away. Her bitterness prevailed in a never-ending shower of expletives, causing Jeff to drop his case and leave her with the details of the time and location of the meeting, a hundred dollars for taxi fares left as his parting inducement.

Ten minutes after the scheduled start time, the door into the family room was opened by a stout, kind-faced woman in a dark blue uniform. 'Good morning,' she said to the two stars, walking towards the couch where they had been sitting, hand in sweating hand. 'Mister Diamond, I'm Chris Williams, the prisoner's mental health counsellor.'

Jeff shook Chris' hand and introduced the two women. 'Thanks. It's nice to meet you. This is my wife, Lynn.'

'And these are your gorgeous little ones!' the middle-aged officer gushed, looking over to where Jet and Kierney were happily playing, oblivious of someone else having entered the room.

'Yes,' the proud mum replied. 'Guys, come here, please.'

At the sound of their mother's request, both children looked up and realised they were being summoned for introductions. Such duties were second nature to them, having spent their whole life in the public eye, regularly having to behave nicely for total strangers when all they wanted to do was play with their toys. However, as well schooled as their mother had been at the same age, they showed no antagonism at having their games interrupted and smiled politely as their tiny shoulders were cuddled by the motherly psychologist.

'It's so lovely to meet the Diamond family,' Chris cooed. 'Under better circumstances would have been preferable.'

Jeff nodded. 'Yes. Obviously. Thank you. How's he doing?'

Lynn bent down to distract Jet and Kierney, intent on shielding them from as much adult discussion as she could. The older woman motioned to the handsome superstar to sit down on the couch, and she sat opposite on another two-seater which was presumably where the prisoner would be sitting in a short while. The children returned to the toy-box, leaving their mother free to join the others.

'Your father's getting very poorly,' Chris explained. 'He's lost a lot of weight recently, over the last couple of weeks, and is receiving regular pain medication. He's been told to stop smoking, but finds it difficult after so many years.'

'I can imagine,' the younger man nodded, a mixture of bitterness and empathy swirling around his stomach. 'I'm a smoker myself, for my sins.'

The professional passed no opinion, continuing with her report. 'This meeting was his idea, just so that you know, Mister Diamond.'

'Jeff, please. OK. Thanks. That answers one question. In response to what though?'

'Many things,' the psychologist replied. 'I believe you requested for him to receive some counselling when you saw him a few years ago, and initially he wouldn't do it. Then he began to get sick and was diagnosed with cancer, which must have caused him to reflect on his life. It often happens.'

Lynn was watching the relaxed counsellor talk to the amateur empathiser and sensed they were exchanging much more than the spoken words during this discussion. She could tell Jeff felt a *rapport* with this woman and was pleased he had found a trustworthy ally. It was important that he speak to someone after this session, to work through whatever decision he would eventually make about his father's fate.

'I've only been seeing the prisoner on a fortnightly basis,' Chris went on, 'and he gradually broke out of the crabby silence he was giving me for quite a while.'

The rock star grinned at his dream girl. 'Does that sound familiar?'

She nodded. 'Oh, yes. Two angry men! Too proud to talk.'

'Indeed, Lynn,' the older woman agreed. 'Some of them carry everything all the way to their grave, and others can't wait to spill their guts. You can never tell.'

'So what can we expect today?' the Olympian asked, sensing her husband needed some time to process this information.

'Well...' Chris considered for a moment. 'He's ready for the meeting. I think, although he's never actually said so, he's looking forward to seeing the littlies. You'll know he wishes to see his daughter too.'

The musician stiffened. 'Yep. She's always been his favourite.'

His patient wife put a hand on his knee, both out of sympathy and to prevent him from saying something he might regret. The star winked to confirm he understood.

'We've told the kids to expect him not to look well,' Lynn continued. 'How does he look?'

'Oh, he's OK. Not at all scary. Just like an old man. He hasn't had a tracheotomy or anything, so his voice is still normal, softer than before and croaky. His breathing is noisy sometimes, and he's thin and stoops quite a bit.'

Jeff watched their children's attentive expressions, shuddering at the thought of his precious Unity and Liberty sitting on this abhorrent criminal's knee. He wondered whether Kierney would be brave enough to ask all her questions.

'So,' the son said, snapping himself out of his daydream and slapping his knees in the most forthright manner he could muster. 'Shall we get the show on the road?'

'Yes. Let's,' Chris agreed. 'If you're comfortable and don't have any more concerns.'

'No,' he shook his head. 'We'll just take him as we find him. Thanks very much, Chris.'

The counsellor went over to the play area again and knelt down with Jet and Kierney. 'Hello again. Are you looking forward to seeing your granddad?'

Jet looked straight into the kindly eyes. 'Yes, I am. Even though he's done something bad, it's very sad that he's dying.'

Lynn gripped Jeff's hand tightly. 'Oh, that's so sweet! His heart's in the right place,' she whispered, watching her emotional wreck blink back tears.

'You bet,' his voice wavered.

Chris stood up, her knees cracking much to the children's amusement, and left the room. Crouching down with his little ones, the young dad kissed both their heads.

'Relax, kids,' he said, more to himself. 'You don't have to say or do anything. If you want to ask Granddad questions, just do it. But don't be upset if he doesn't want to answer. Some things are hard for him to talk about. No harm in giving it a try. We'll help you.'

Their mother stood behind them, listening to the pep talk. 'Yes, we shall. And tell Granddad all about you. What you like to do: your toys; your friends. Anything. It'll be good for him to know about you.'

While the parents set the scene, the door creaked open at the other end of the room. Two men entered, both in uniform. One was a prison officer. The other was Paul Diamond.

The adult visitors got to their feet, and Lynn put a steadying hand on her husband's shoulder as she imagined the tension consuming his muscles. The tall pair faced off in the middle of the room, both with tears in their eyes.

'G'day, Dad,' said the younger, holding out his right hand. 'How're you going?'

'G'day, Jeff,' replied the older, gripping his son's hand in a weak handshake. 'Not so bad. How're you?'

Jeff's insides flipped over, amazed at the difference from their previous meeting, when he had been met with hostility and insolence. This was a man who had come to make peace, as Lynn had ventured. His father had even used his name. It wasn't quite "son", yet it was music to the young man's ears nonetheless.

The elegant blonde stood a couple of metres behind her partner, guiding each child by the shoulder. Verging on smug, he turned and extended his arm to the woman walking in their direction.

'And you know who this is, Dad. This is the mother of your grandchildren and the reason we're here.'

'Lynn Dyson,' Paul said. 'Pleased to meet you.'

'Lynn Dyson *Diamond*,' his son corrected him, enunciating each syllable and imbued with an audacious pride.

The songwriter saw his father scan the stunning figure up and down in appreciation and stifled his possessive objections for once. His gorgeous wife had dressed strategically for him, as he knew she would, choosing faded blue jeans which emphasised the length of her legs, with a white blouse open to reveal a low-cut top. Her long, blond hair was clipped back off her face, and she offered her most brilliant of smiles as she greeted her father-in-law.

'Mister Diamond, hello,' the practised crowd-pleaser said, shaking his hand. 'It's nice to meet you too, finally. I'm so sorry to hear you're not well.'

Transferred from their mother while she was being introduced, the children were each holding on to one of their father's legs, gaping at this stranger who seemed to growl instead of speak. Jeff wondered if they saw the resemblance. Did kids think that way? Probably not. At any rate, the older man was now fragile and haggard. He appeared to have shrunk considerably since the last meeting, with deep lines on his face and significantly more white hair than before.

Standing tall, the multi-millionnaire walked his offspring forward, their small feet balancing on his insteps, making Kierney giggle.

'Papá!' she yelped, almost falling over.

The prisoner was smiling, Lynn noticed.

'This is Jet,' her husband announced, ruffling his son's thick, curly, blond hair.

'Hello, Granddad,' the boy said clearly, just as they had rehearsed while driving from the airport, and offered his right hand to the old man.

Coughing, the prisoner bent over and took the youngster's hand. 'Hello, Jet,' he responded, seeming to battle with his emotions. 'How old are you?'

'I'm four,' he answered, looking up at his dad for reassurance and receiving a wink in return. 'And this is my sister, Kierney. She's two-and-a-half.'

'Two-and-a-half?' Paul echoed. 'Hello. Can I shake your hand too?'

The little girl was less forthcoming, still hanging on to her papá's trousers. Lynn had moved forward to rub their son's back while her gentle husband coaxed their daughter into action.

'It's OK, *pequeñita*,' Jeff cajoled, playfully bending his left knee. 'Please shake Granddad's hand.'

Hesitant, Kierney held out her hand and had it clutched by the stranger who was nearly as tall as her papá.

'Hi, Granddad. Are you really my Papá's papá?'

'So they tell me,' the older man quipped, unsettled by the dark-haired child standing in front of him.

It wasn't hard to guess his thoughts. Kierney was dressed in a long, flowing dress, with her black, wavy hair pulled back into a clip behind her head, just like her mother. As she grew out of her babyish phase, she was acquiring more and more Moreno features. And therefore, to her grandfather, she must have seemed like the spitting image of his late wife or his estranged daughter.

'Let's sit down,' Lynn piped up. 'We've got some photos to show you, and we need to find out how you are.'

Realising his *Regala* had assumed control, the younger man watched her usher the children towards the toy-box. He led his father to the couches on the other side, so stressed that his brain appeared to have switched into autopilot mode. So far, so good, he mused. And largely not to his credit!

'So,' Jeff opened, while the sexy woman poured three cups of coffee. 'Thanks for writing that letter, Dad. It was good to read you'd been thinking about things. And I'm very sorry you're so sick. Seriously.'

Paul shrugged. Lynn was struck by the similarity in the two men's mannerisms. It was startling, in fact. Even though the older man's face had weathered and his cheeks were hollow, she acknowledged that he too must have been a good-looking man in his younger days. She also noticed how little he smiled, remembering the broad grin with which her nineteen-year-old enigmatic stranger had hypnotised her on those first few dates.

'I'm OK,' the prisoner replied. 'To be honest, I don't give a shit. Makes no difference to me in 'ere if I'm sick or not.'

Jeff wasn't sure how to take this comment, so chose to move on. 'Madalena's well,' he offered. 'We tried to get her to come, but she wouldn't. She's still very bitter about things, Dad.'

'Sure. I reckoned as much. I've been talking to counsellors, you know.'

'Yeah. I know. Chris Williams told us.'

Diamond Senior seemed surprised. 'You know 'er?'

Feeling comfortable that the men's conversation was going reasonably well, Lynn excused herself and went to play with the children.

'Not before today, but yeah,' the intellectual answered, stretching his arm to its full extent in an effort to hang on to her hand for as long as possible. 'She came in just now. Seems nice enough. What d'you talk about with her?'

'Ah, not much,' his father inhaled. 'Just about dying and clearing my conscience. All that "It's good to talk" crap.'

Jeff sniggered, watching the old man draw quotation marks in the air. 'It *is* good to talk, Dad.'

'Depends what you got to talk about, eh? So you're a dad now...' the older man stated. 'Cute kids. The girl's gotta be yours.'

'Thanks heaps,' the young man smiled at his father's benign but spiteful insult. 'They're both mine. They're a lot of fun and never stop surprising me. You missed out on all that, but what d'you think of being a granddad?'

'Good,' came a monosyllabic response that warmed the star's heart.

'Yeah?' he said, before he could catch himself. 'Fuck! That surprises me too.'

'I'll bet!' Paul laughed, clutching on to his coffee cup as he coughed hard.

'You OK?' Jeff asked. 'D'you want some water or something?'

His father shook his head, a strange sneering noise his only means of communication. The long bout of guttural hacking caused both kids to suspend their games and look back towards the couch, each face a study in concern. Their mum bade them not to worry, and they continued to play with only the occasional stolen glance.

Keen to capitalise on the prisoner's conciliatory remark, Jeff called over to the others. 'Bring some toys over here, guys, please. Let's talk together for a while.'

'She's good-looking,' Paul leered at Lynn while she moved around, helping the children to select a couple of toys to carry with them.

'Of course she is,' his son agreed. 'She's bloody perfect. Better than perfect. Can you believe I'm married to her? I can't, even now! Do they still sing to you in the shower?'

The lifer chuckled, only to gag and cough up a mouthful of phlegm and spit it out unceremoniously into his coffee cup. 'Na. Not so much. I've been moved since I got sick. Don't see much o' them idiots no more. You're more famous in 'ere for all the political soapbox crap now. You're some kind o' cult hero, you bastard.'

The dignified woman approaching flinched at the bad language, seeing her husband scowl too. He was willing to tolerate the dreadful cacophony of bodily expulsions as side-effects of the illness, but foul language was within anyone's control.

'Hey, Dad. Watch the swearing, please.'

'Yep. Sorry,' he scoffed. 'I never was much good around children.'

'Excuse me, Granddad?' Jet asked, waiting for a chance to interrupt.

The old man's eyes moved from the youngster to his dad, once more unsure of himself. Distracted by the mysterious gaze of the little girl hanging on to Jeff's knees, he noted his son's dark eyes insisting on a reply.

'Yes, mate,' the old man responded with as much enthusiasm as he could.

'Do you like it in here?'

'In this room or being banged up?'

The grandson was confused for a second, looking around the room they were in. The origin of her husband's dry sense of humour was becoming clear to Lynn, although her father-in-law's was baser and less forgiving.

'In jail,' the boy clarified.

'It's OK. Boring a lot of the time. But there's TV, and the food's alright.'

Jet was satisfied with this answer, no doubt filing it away for new games with Dawson. The young mother's eyes flashed to attract Jeff's attention to their daughter, who was staring at her grandfather and rolling some silent words around her tongue as if she were preparing a speech.

Her papá ran his index finger across the little girl's cheek. 'What are you saying, Kizzo? Something for Granddad?'

'Yes. Granddad, do you wish you could come to our house?' Kierney asked, innocent eyes lifting upwards.

'To your house?' the prisoner echoed, not prepared for such a direct question.

'Yes. It's lovely. All new, and I've got my own room,' the girl added, feeling more adventurous. 'But you have to go on a 'plane to see it.'

'I don't like 'planes,' the gruff prisoner answered.

Like you'd know... Jeff's temper flared, turning to give his daughter a supportive smile and a wink. 'We do, don't we, kids?'

Both children were nodding eagerly, unconcerned by their newfound family member's opinion on air travel. Lynn took over, sensing the musician's disappointment.

'We brought some photos of our dog and of the kids' rooms, in case you'd like to see them.'

Paul nodded, with the hint of a smile. 'That'd be nice.'

Glad of this shift in topic to gather his thoughts, the younger man caught the eye of the prison guard who was standing to attention by the door. What did he make of this odd encounter? It was difficult to imagine his father being a threat to anyone, given his poor health, but the man's presence was reassuring regardless. Exhaling to slow his angry heart, he saw his beautiful best friend hand their little girl a small pile of photographs.

'Jet, please help Kizzy explain what all of these are,' she instructed.

Full of loving pride, the father watched the two tiny, innocent souls take responsibility for developing their own relationships with their grandfather. He squeezed Lynn's shoulder and eased her back to lean against him, putting an arm over around her to make a point. As her face turned to look at him, he stole a kiss.

The display of affection did not go unnoticed by the older man, which of course was wholly the intention. It felt strangely illicit to fool around with one's own wife in front of a parent; something he guessed he would have experienced in his teens if he had been from a normal family, rather than when heading for his thirties.

Drink deeply, pilgrim, Jeff gloated in silence. *You have no idea how good my life is now, despite what you put us through.*

Only too happy to prove her husband's point, Lynn leaned down to help their son re-assemble a toy which had fallen apart, fully expecting his father's eyes to be tracking her. Yes, it was demeaning, but no less so than the peculiar exhibition her perfect stranger had staged for the Jaworski family and their dubious friends.

Face To Face

Little by little, Jet and Kierney relaxed into their play, allowing the adults to discuss the prisoner's failing health over their heads. The family bonded for fifteen or twenty minutes under the watchful eye of the prison guard until a knock at the door startled them. They all looked up to see the door open for a few seconds and then close again, after which the guard called the rock star over.

'Jesus Christ!' he muttered under his breath.

Peering through the small clear section of the otherwise frosted glass, Jeff's eyes met Madalena's in the hallway. He quickly looked around to check that Lynn had noticed he was stepping out before grabbing the handle. The door swung towards him, and he went to meet his sister.

'You came!' he almost shouted, hugging her. 'This is great, Lena. *¡Muchas gracias!*'

'Is 'e in there?' she asked, avoiding looking through the window.

Jeff could tell the new arrival was super-agitated. 'Yeah. He's in there. He's pretty friendly at the moment. Much different to last time.'

Madalena nodded, shifting from one foot to the other. The celebrity was pleased to see her taste in clothes had improved with the healthy monthly allowance now coming her way. A strong smell of cigarette smoke floated around her, and not many left in the packet, judging by the hollow, tapping sound it made in nervous hands.

'It's amazing what staring death in the face must do to you,' her brother joked, trying to put her at ease.

'Fuck, *chico*!' the young woman gasped. 'I can't go in there. I don't know why I come now. I felt bad.'

'Then come in. It's fine. He wants to see you. He was disappointed when we told him you didn't want to come with us.'

The prostitute weighed up her brother's comments. 'Will you do all the talkin'? If he asks me a shit question, like?'

Jeff laughed. 'What sort of shit question?'

'Oh, I dunno. Stuff about whether I 'ate his guts or about Mamá.'

The peacemaker placed his hands on his sister's shoulders. 'Just be honest with him,' he suggested. 'He's as nervous as we are. Probably more. This isn't easy for any of us. Just come in and have a coffee with him. You only have to stay for ten minutes, but it'll mean the world to him. He's pretty sick. Coughing his bloody guts up, he is. It sounds revolting, and the kids are gob-smacked by it. They'd love to see you too.'

Madalena steeled herself. 'Fuck! OK then.'

'Great. Thanks, *chica*,' the young man said, kissing her cheek. 'I'm so glad you're here.'

Checking there were sufficient cigarettes left in his own packet to tide them over, Jeff rapped on the door to attract the guard's attention. He manœuvred his sister round before she could change her mind. As soon as the door opened, he shoved her through first, ignoring her squeals of objection.

'Hey, guys! Look who's here,' the showman called across the room.

'Auntie Lena!' Jet cried out, immediately jumping up and running over to the skinny woman, closely followed by his little sister.

The chorus of innocent and impetuous joy served well to break the tension, and Lynn took her place by her man's side as his father struggled awkwardly to his feet. They could see he was fighting back tears. For her part however, Madalena was doing her best not to make eye contact with anyone except the children.

Jeff coughed. 'Lena,' he barked, as if instructing one of the youngsters to display their best manners.

The seasoned campaigner smiled to his wife, finding himself in charge of this latest conflict resolution mission, this time right on his own doorstep. The tennis champion steered the children away from the others, tempting them back to the play area.

The dark-haired woman continued to look in every direction except towards her father. The sick man now had tears rolling down his cheeks, which made her brother feel sick too, seething with childish jealousy. Dismissing the reaction to the best of his ability, he followed through with the task at hand.

'Dad, Lena... Come and sit down.'

Taking his sister by the arm, Jeff sat on the couch next to their father, and pointed to the armchair at right-angles. Reluctantly, Madalena sat down, still craning her neck to see what Lynn and the children were doing.

'Kiz looks lovely,' she shouted over to her sister-in-law, who nodded her thanks.

'She looks like Lena, doesn't she, Dad?' the negotiator pounced on this opportunity.

'Yep,' croaked the old man. 'So how are you, Lena?'

'Good. You?'

'Come on,' her brother's stern voice said. 'You came all this way, and doubtless you're going to spring me for lunch, so the least you could do is look Dad in the eye.'

'Who's side are you on, *culo*?' the bitter young woman snapped. 'How come you're now all best buddies with 'im?'

Jeff looked from one to the other, smiling slightly. 'We're not best buddies. We're here because Dad's sick and we want to sort a few things out. We already spoke about this, didn't we?'

Lynn trained one ear on the conversation behind her and the other on keeping the children occupied. She listened to the master at work, feeling very glad they had come. Her healing husband would draw a great deal of strength from this meeting. She had been struck by the dull greyness emanating from her father-in-law, and it occurred to her for the first time that Jeff had exhibited the same aura in the early days of their relationship, back when he was deprived of sleep and haunted by demons and phobia.

Today, seeing father and son side-by-side, the influential star's authoritative body language, his bright, dancing eyes and animated gestures were the antithesis of Paul's washed-out, monochrome bearing. The sophisticated celebrity felt sorry for the older man, without question, but moreover so very happy for the role she had played in restoring the colour and vibrancy in her beautiful black stallion's world.

True, Jeff had never seemed quite as apathetic and disinterested in life, but then again, the adoring wife felt sure she had never seen him at the lowest point of his depression. This presumably final meeting had reinforced in her mind exactly how much effort her boyfriend must have needed to make himself attractive to her. No wonder he had always been so fatigued and craving artificial stimulants. How things had changed!

'Mamá?' Jet's voice broke into her trip down Memory Lane. 'Is Auntie Lena angry at Granddad?'

'Yes, darling,' Lynn confirmed. 'Very angry. He didn't look after her or Dad when they were little. They had a very sad life together. I'm sure he'll tell you about it when you're older.'

Kierney stood up and leaned her head on her mother's thigh. 'It's not fair, is it?' she said, beginning to cry. 'Papá's trying to make things better, and Auntie Lena's being horrid to Granddad.'

'Yes. She is being a bit horrid,' the kind woman stroked her daughter's hair. 'It's because she remembers all the horrid things Granddad did to her, and to Papá and their mamá too. Sometimes it's hard to be nice to people like that.'

'How can Dad be nice then?' her son asked.

'Because he always tries to see both sides,' Lynn told her son, not really knowing whether he would understand. 'Papá used to be very angry too, just like Auntie Lena. He just learned how to control it better. Like when Mairi threw your train over the balcony, and you thought it was broken... Remember that? I had to ask you to stop being angry at Mairi.'

Jet nodded, hanging his head. 'Yes.'

'It was good that you managed to,' the born teacher continued, 'because when we went downstairs to find the train, it was OK. Remember?'

As it happened, their papá wasn't controlling his anger too well at this precise moment. He was suddenly torn between sympathy for his sister's point of view and the objective of reuniting the threesome as some sort of family. Madalena was right in this instance. They had never been a family. What was he trying to manufacture at this very late stage?

'Lena,' the prisoner spluttered. 'I'm sorry you feel like that. Thanks for comin'. I know how you're angry. I'm fuckin' angry too.'

'You are? What are you angry about?' Jeff asked, offering round his cigarettes and readying his lighter.

'Being in his fuckin' place,' their father blurted out, 'and getting caught. Lettin' things get as far as they got, and for bein' a crap 'usband and father.'

The songwriter could hardly believe his own ears. He glanced over to Lynn, who had heard every word. She gave him a subtle nod and then turned back towards the children. He battled to compose a suitable response to these gratifying admissions.

'That's all good, but you pissed your life away,' he told his adversary straight. 'Didn't you?'

'*¡Ai, chico!*' Madalena laughed, shocked at the diplomat's uncharacteristic frankness.

Paul chuckled too before starting to cough like a chimney-sweep. Jeff put an arm around the old man's frail frame and felt his chest heaving desperately. He remembered this feeling so well...

'*¡Chico!*' his father panted. 'Haven't 'eard that in a fuckin' long time.'

'Just "a long time", Dad,' the feisty woman pulled him up. 'Jeff doesn't like people swearin' in front of 'is kids.'

Eureka! The ice was broken; daughter had addressed father directly. Job well done, the negotiator congratulated his sullen delegates for their small step forward.

'Nice one, Lena. Thanks for that. Come and sit here, will you?'

His sister shot him a glare but swapped seats with him nonetheless. Their father stared at his daughter's face, and his eyes filled with tears again. Once more bristling with envy, Jeff felt some strange, curative power taking hold. He couldn't change their family's story. He could only bring it to a better conclusion.

'I hated you for years,' Madalena admitted. 'Did you do it? Kill those Jaworski bastards?'

'Whoa, Lena!' Jeff whistled, convinced Lynn was tugging hard on their invisible elastic connection. 'Your turn! Go straight for the jugular, why don't you?'

The boy from Canley Vale dare not look at his wife and kids, simply picturing them sitting in a bewildered silence, open-mouthed and frozen in time. He had become too soft in the high-minded world he gatecrashed a decade ago. This was how people spoke in his old world. His mind transported him back into their messy, run-down flat on the Stones Road, recalling other such basic conversations, where people spoke their mind regardless of whose feelings might be hurt.

'Oh, I killed 'em alright,' the murderer confessed again, a hint of pride simmering under the surface. 'One after the other. One o' the bastards knifed me as well, y'know...'

Untucking the shirt tail from his belt on one side, he displayed the rough remnants of a stab wound underneath his ribcage. Madalena leaned in and stared at the scar, then at her brother and then back at Paul. The younger man realised that for some bizarre reason his sister was impressed. The hero they had worshipped as misguided youngsters was once more sitting among them.

Jeff wasn't impressed however. His sister was oblivious to the similar marks on his own body. Hopefully, they would remain undetected, so he would never be required to tell how they had got there.

'Why did you kill them?' he asked, not permitting his father to avert his gaze.

The prisoner shifted uneasily in his chair. It would have been many years since he had been subjected to this level of questioning. But his son's eyes were insistent, unlikely to give up without some straight answers this time.

'They were screwing my deals,' Paul hissed, hatred still boiling inside. 'Ev'ry bloody time. Bribin' me snoops to give me bum intel'. They 'ad heaps more men in their gang, and I didn't 'ave nobody.'

'So was I the only one you could've found to join you? How come you couldn't recruit some of the blokes who went with them?'

'It's about blood, mate,' the criminal sneered. 'You was all I 'ad. They 'ad brothers and sons and nephews and school-friends of sons... You know 'ow it is.'

'No. Thank Christ. I don't know how it is,' the star's response was eerily calm. 'So as soon as I turned you down, you were screwed. Is that what you've been blaming me for all these years?'

'Pretty much,' his father nodded, coughing hard. 'You let me down.'

'*I* let you down,' Jeff repeated, raising his voice again. 'Is that right? I can see how you think that, and I'm sorry. But none of us can force people to be like us. It wasn't my fault you didn't have brothers or nephews. I could only help you with the son *quota*. I tried it for a while, Dad. D'you remember? I did a few jobs for you, and I got a juvie record for my trouble.'

Paul Diamond scoffed, refusing to show any emotion.

'The Jaworskis were already your enemies before that. They dobbed me in, and you know it,' the lost boy carried on. 'You would never've protected me, even as blood, as you say. Why would I want to get involved when I knew I'd be shafted by all of you whenever it suited? I got out because I wanted to do more with my life than collect a string of offences against my name. And let's face it, Dad, not much else to show for it.'

'Compared to now, ya mean?' his sister added, impressed by her brother in full flight. 'Look what 'e's got now, Dad. You should see 'is car. It makes a real mean noise and goes like the friggin' wind. They've got an amazin' 'ouse too, and 'is apartment's gigantic. Even the Jawos didn'ave that kind o' money. Never would of, would they, *chico*?'

By now, Jeff was on his feet, pacing around and feeling light-headed. The blame game had begun to eat away at him. He thought he had left this petty acrimony behind but obviously not. There was something in his father's hopelessness that struck an intense chord of guilt.

'I could've been a good Godfather,' the statuesque celebrity chuckled, strutting back to the couch and standing over the prisoner. 'Instead of putting all this energy into things I believe in, for the greater good, I could've run the western suburbs' Mafia. You would've ended up working for me, Dad. Both of you, perhaps!'

'Fuck you, mate,' the murderer swore. 'You're too much of a bloody big-shot for your own good.'

'Yeah. Maybe so. You might've ended up killing me instead?'

'*¡Chico!*' Madalena shrieked.

'No, Lena. Wait a minute,' Jeff cut her off, trying to block out the sound of his daughter crying in the background. 'We've waited a long time to have this conversation. For Christ's sake, Dad... You killed your own wife.'

His sister screamed, aghast. This well-mannered do-gooder who had earlier accused her of going for the jugular now had his hands around their father's neck, metaphorically speaking, slowly squeezing the air out of a sick man's lungs.

'I 'ad no choice,' the prisoner said, knowing he was beaten by a finer mind.

'You did so have a choice,' the young man retreated a little and sat down. 'You could've got out and found a real job. You could've moved to another town. You could've gone into partnership with someone else, or even the Jaworskis. You could've divided the turf between you. You could've languished on the dole or in the pub, with all Lena's friends.'

'*¡Ai!* Don't bring me into this!' the prostitute shouted. 'What friends anyway?'

'And hey!' the musician added, raising his hand in the air as if he had been struck by a bright idea. 'You could've been Lena's pimp. Keep it in the family! That's what you wanted, didn't you? Instead of me, you could've gone into business with her... Equal opportunity!'

Madalena looked at her wretched father, suddenly finding herself wondering whose side she was on after all.

'Yeah, big man Jeff fucking Diamond. Maybe I should o',' Paul jeered. 'Where's *your* fucking respect, Mister High 'n' Mighty?'

Jeff raised both hands in front of his face, stealing a sideways glance towards his children. 'Fair point,' he capitulated, breathing deeply. 'I'm sorry, Dad. It just pisses me off so much that you never thought of any of this back then. We could've had a reasonable life. There are so many other ways to live than being a murderer or a thief. Or even a stand-over man...'

'I didn't kill your mum,' their father rasped, bending double as another coughing fit hit him. 'She bloody well killed 'erself, but.'

Scared for what her brother might do next, Madalena jumped in before he had a chance to fly at this dangerously flippant remark. 'No way! It was 'cause o' you she died. That's what Jeff's sayin'. She was sick of bein' a poor pro' druggie, and she 'ated what you let them bastards do to 'er and me.'

'So tell Dad exactly what they did to you, Lena,' the twenty-nine-year-old encouraged, concerned that his children would hear too much of this conversation but now in too deep to curtail it.

'He knows fuckin' well what they did to us,' Madalena sneered. 'The Jawos. And the others: Akim's mob; Cafici; all them bastards. They came to 'elp 'emselves to whatever they wanted from Mamá and me. Just a little kid, I was.'

The young woman burst into tears, and so did the old man. As disconcerting as his indifference to his dad's knife-wound, numbness gripped the superstar on hearing his sister call the reprobate to account. Lynn wandered over to sit on the couch beside him, and he willingly leaned into her. His beautiful best friend had dissolved his hatred and replaced it with more love than he could handle. Those heart-wrenching times no longer meant much to him, and now it was his sister's turn to get them out of her system.

'I'm sorry, Lena,' their father hissed, staring down at the floor between his legs. 'I'm sorry to both of you.'

'And to Mamá,' Jeff added, feeling sympathy welling up inside him. 'Don't forget her in all this *mea culpa* drama. She was your wife, Dad, and you let them rape her and fill her with God knows what drugs.'

Surreptitiously, Paul Diamond watched the elegant blonde put her arm behind his son's back and hug him as tears rolled down his cheeks. If the affection made him jealous, it was nothing compared with the hollow pit that formed in his stomach when Jet and Kierney ran over, eager to find out why everyone was crying.

'¿*Papá, por que todos llorando?*' Kierney asked, close to tears herself.

'*No se preocupan,* guys. *Es nada,*' Jeff smiled, hoisting his little daughter onto his lap and signalling for Jet to do climb up with his mother. '*Somos* alright. We just need to talk about some upsetting stuff from the olden days, that's all.'

'Shit!' Paul coughed, saliva catching his breath again. 'Your kids speak Spanish as well?'

'Yeah, Dad,' Madalena sniped. 'Jeff wants his kids to grow up knowing shit. Stuff, sorry. Not like me. You made me into a dumb-ass.'

The young boy couldn't help but laugh at his auntie's bad language before letting his eyes wander between his mother and father.

'It's OK. Funny, isn't it?' Lynn cuddled the four-year-old. 'Everyone's swearing. Let's talk about something else, shall we? Auntie Lena, we've got some more pictures of our house.'

'No, angel,' Jeff interrupted his astute, well-meaning wife. 'Sorry, but can we change the plan a little?'

'Sure,' the compassionate woman smiled.

'Please could you take the kids for a walk somewhere, so that we can talk freely?' Jeff asked, holding her hand. 'I'm concerned about them hearing any more of this conversation.'

Lynn nodded with considerable relief, standing up and accepting the car keys from her husband. 'Definitely. Good idea. Come on, kids. Grab your coats, please, and come outside for a while.'

The guard, who probably watched over family spats like this on a regular basis, let Lynn and the children out of the room, fulfilling his politely impassive duty. Jeff breathed easier to see his pristine, unspoiled treasures leave with their mother. Hopefully, the family's pre-emptive discussion this morning had immunised them sufficiently against any ill-effects from the last fifteen minutes' onslaught.

'Fucking hell!' he hissed, leaning back on the couch. 'That's better.'

Madalena burst out laughing. 'Did you see Jet's face? He thought it was real funny. Now 'e'll start saying shit like that at school.'

'Don't worry about it,' the celebrity frowned. 'He knows what he can and can't get away with. Now... We have to talk seriously for a while, guys.'

Their father had gone quiet. It was as if the young ones had stolen his spirit, bringing him back down to Earth with a thud.

'You OK, Dad?'

'You're a good man, son,' Paul blurted out. 'A bloody good man.'

Jeff inhaled through his nose and gritted his teeth. Now would not be a good time to go to pieces, having sent his guardian angel on walkabout.

'Thanks, Dad,' he replied, hanging on to his composure by the skin of his teeth. 'That's the first time you've called me "son" for a long time. Probably ever, eh?'

'Yeah. I know and I'm sorry 'bout that an' all. In you, I see what I was s'posed to be like. For fuck's sake. I was never a dad to you. Either o' you.'

'No, you weren't,' the world-changer answered. 'You did your best, I guess. And so did Mamá.'

His sister was less charitable, scoffing and thumping the couch's cushions. 'What? What the 'ell did ya think you were doin'? All that time, just stealin' shit and gettin' up people's noses?'

'I dunno, *chica*,' their father confessed. 'I never grew up, I reckon. That's what the counsellor says anyways... I never got past that teenage anger at the world, they said. Me mum an' dad 'ated that I was such a bogan fucker, so I went an' 'ooked up with other blokes like me. And when you didn't wanna get involved, mate, I couldn't take it. It's the only thing I knew for a bloke to do. I couldn't get it that you wanted to be someone famous and marry fuckin' Lynn Dyson.'

'My wife is not "fuckin' Lynn Dyson",' Jeff riled. 'Have some respect, Dad, please. I didn't want to be someone famous back then. I just wanted a decent education, a job and a normal life. All the big ambitions came later, well after you'd been put away.'

The older man stared at his mirror image and nodded. 'I apologise.'

'Good,' Madalena said. '*Chico*, what did you wanna talk about?'

The songwriter gave the thirty-one-year-old an appreciative smile. She was actually helping for a change, rather than sitting back and letting all around her take responsibility. He felt proud of her, thrown back to the bridesmaids' procession at the wedding. That amazing day had been a turning point for her too.

'Cheers, Lena. Yeah. We need to talk about your future, Dad.'

'My future?' Paul gaped. 'What about me future?'

'You're sick, ain't ya?' Madalena gave him an unwanted reminder, her brother wondering if it had been done on purpose, to turn the screws a little tighter.

'No shit!' the prisoner snapped, phlegm rising in his throat right on cue. 'Tell someone who cares.'

'Tell someone who cares?' Jeff echoed back at him. 'That's fucking ridiculous. We care, Dad. It's why we're here. Are you still smoking, for example?'

'Yep,' came the response he expected, their father raising his right hand to acknowledge his oversight. 'They've tried to get me to quit, but what's the point?'

'Good,' the younger man said, smiling and reaching into the inside pocket of his leather jacket.

'That the same coat you wore last time you was 'ere?'

'Yeah. The one you wanted off my back.'

'You got millions o' dollars and only one coat?' Paul teased, wheezing until he almost choked.

Jeff let out a caustic laugh, handing round his packet of cigarettes again. 'Yeah. Something like that.'

He flicked his lighter and lit all three cigarettes before getting up from the couch and fetching an ashtray from a nearby table. Madalena switched couches as quick as lightning.

'Hey!' the musician whined, nudging her sideways until they both sat facing their father. 'Listen, Dad... I got a letter a while ago from the medical people here. It told me you've got lung cancer and not many months left to live.'

'Yeah. That's about the size of it. I prob'ly 'ad it a few years by now. Just didn't know. They told me they were going to see if you'd OK a transplant.'

'They did,' Jeff confirmed, encouraging his sister to participate in this part of the conversation.

Unsurprisingly, the narrow-minded woman had nothing to add.

'So, Dad... D'you want a transplant? If a donor came up?'

'Nope. Not really,' the lifer's response was genuine. 'As I said before, what's the point? I'm either stuck in 'ere for the rest of me life, or stuck in 'ell. And 'ell might be better, for all I know.'

Madalena laughed aloud. 'That'd be right. Hell'd be full o' your old mates!'

'Lena,' the negotiator scolded. 'Ease up. This is Dad's life we're talking about.'

Their father breathed in slowly. 'Fuck me, Jeff Diamond. You are one powerful bloke. It's really true all this peacemakin' stuff they write about you, ain't it? You know what you're doing.'

'Oh, I know what I'm doing alright,' his son sighed. 'I'm just not used to doing it with my own family.'

The young man paused for a moment, experiencing an intense, overpowering sense of gratitude at having finally received praise from the old bastard after so many barren years; an element of sweet vindication for persevering through his dark, lonely and desperate youth. Miss Irony was alive and well however, he chided inwardly. He had finally become someone whom his father could be proud of, just when the bugger was on his last legs.

'Jesus, Dad,' he groaned, wiping a tear from his eye. 'D'you know how long it's taken for you to say something like that? Shit! It was all I ever wanted in those days: to do something to impress you.'

The prisoner's face contorted, torn between sadness and derision. 'I liked your guitar playin',' he offered a puny olive branch. 'That was pretty good back then.'

'Well, you never fucking told me! Anyway... This isn't about me today. We need to decide what treatment you want. You need to tell us whether you want a transplant, if one becomes available, or if you'd like chemotherapy to slow down the cancer's progress, or morphine for the pain.'

'Or fuck all,' the frail man appended to the list.

'Yep. Or fuck all,' the boy with the deathwish readily agreed. 'Is that what you want? Fuck all?'

'Maybe,' the old man replied, looking his son straight in the eye. 'I'm not worth more 'n 'at, am I?'

'It's not a question of what you're worth, Dad. Is it, Lena?'

Again, Madalena struggled to think of anything to say, and her brother realised he had put her in a difficult position by inviting her to answer this question. She plainly felt sorry for their father on some level, although equally obvious that she wasn't enjoying the experience. It was hard for either of them to be sympathetic towards the man who had wronged them so comprehensively.

'No,' she agreed. 'Jeff's right about ev'rythin'. I never seen it 'til today. It's about what you want, Dad.'

The millionnaire gave his offsider an approving nod. It was the perfect *rejoindre*, under trying circumstances.

'Dad,' he began again, reaching for his father's hand with his left and his sister's with his right. 'I spent my whole bloody childhood, and a good few years of adulthood as well, begging not to wake up the next morning. For Christ's sake. I know what it's like to want to die.'

Madalena gasped. She had never heard her brother speak this way. His dad nodded, relaxing into the strong grip.

Jeff continued. 'But you never know how your life's going to turn around. Look at Lynn and the kids... They're so fantastic. They're my world. She saved my life, Dad, like I always knew she could. She saved my fucking life and helped me shake all the nightmares and shit that you so kindly visited on me.'

His normally impervious sister had been reduced to tears. 'You never told me all this, *chico*.'

'Don't cry, Lena,' he squeezed her hand. 'All that's a long time ago now. I'm just trying to say that you shouldn't make the choice to give up on your life if you still want something out of it. Does that make sense?'

'I don't want nothin', but,' his father announced outright. 'What can I have in 'ere? More 'ot chips at dinner time? Big fuckin' deal.'

The intellectual nodded. 'I understand. Really, I do. And from where I sit, I'm inclined to agree with you. But it's your choice, isn't it, Lena?'

'We've talked about this already, Dad,' he went on, seeing his sister nodding sagely. 'I'm happy to pay for anything you want in terms of treatment. Put you up in a comfortable hospital, you know... Whatever you need. But only if it's what you want, and what you can reconcile with yourself.'

'What the fuck does that mean, you bloody pooftah?' the prisoner suddenly turned on him, boxed into a corner. 'Reconcile with yerself?'

'It means what you think you deserve,' Jeff tried not to sound patronising. 'And you know very well what it means. You're no idiot, Dad.'

'You're no idiot either,' Madalena swooned. 'I wish I knew all them fancy words, like you do. I'm sick of being so dumb.'

'Then go back to school,' her brother smiled. 'Why not?'

The woman's mind immediately went exactly where her brother expected it to. 'Will you pay for me?'

'Yeah. If you stick to it.'

'See?' the prostitute sneered. 'Your son believes in people; gives 'em a chance. Even me! I wouldn't give *you* a fuckin' chance.'

'Shhh,' Jeff warned her. 'Don't bang on about all that. And Dad, you don't have to make a decision today. But you can't leave it long either. I don't know for sure, but in order to survive the transplant operation you've got to be pretty resilient. Strong and healthy... Otherwise your body'll reject the new organs. If you leave it too long, you won't die of the disease. You'll die of the cure.'

This time his sister cackled. 'That's bloody funny, *chico*! Either way, it's the same.'

'Yeah,' their dad agreed. 'She's right.'

'OK then. Whatever,' his son called a halt to the sick humour. 'You two talk together for a while. I'm going to fetch the family I sent wandering in the wilderness.'

The superstar nodded to the steadfast officer, who stood so stock still that he could almost have been deep in a meditative trance. 'Thanks, mate,' he said, seeing him snap to attention. 'We won't be much longer.'

Stretching his spine as he walked out into the reception area, the famous man scanned up and down the corridor to see where Lynn and the children had decamped. He found them outdoors, his dream girl sitting on a bench by a small garden while she put her mini-athletes through their paces.

'Dad!' Jet shouted, diverting across the wet concrete to meet him. 'You were ages.'

'Yeah. Sorry. Look where you're going, mate. This is a car park. Everything OK?'

The tall blonde beauty drew herself up from the bench as he approached, taking a good look in her husband's eyes. They looked tired but content, she concluded.

'Everything's cool with us,' she replied, kissing him fondly. 'We've just been having a good chat about grandparents and parents and children. Haven't we, guys?'

Kierney climbed up onto the bench and sat between her parents. '*Te amo, Papá.* You're like our big tree.'

'Thanks, *pequeñita*,' her dad encouraged the little girl onto her feet to bring her face close enough to kiss her lips. 'I love you too. All of you. What sort of tree am I?'

The pair clung on to each other for a few seconds before turning round to see where the big brother had got to. Finding him examining a motorcycle a few metres away, Kierney called his name and crooked her tiny index finger, urging him to join them. As if rehearsed, the boy tore over and leaped onto the wooden slats to his father's left, and the pair grabbed an arm each and raised themselves towards the sky.

'Papá's our big tree,' the toddler chimed.

'The trunk,' Jet corrected his sister, standing as tall as he could. 'You're the trunk.'

His arms still aloft, Jeff kept a straight face, seeing that his wife was trying to do the same. 'An elephant's trunk or a tree trunk?' he teased.

'You know!' his son bleated. 'A tree trunk, because you're strong and stay standing in the wind and rain.'

'That's Mamá too though,' the proud man smiled. 'So are you guys the leaves or the branches?'

'We're the leaves when we're kids, and we turn into branches when we grow up,' Jet continued to explain. 'And Grandma and Grandpa and Granddad are the roots.'

Lynn chuckled. 'That bit we weren't sure about, were we?'

Getting her suggestive drift, Jeff raised his eyebrows. 'No, but we all need each other for something, even roots. If we didn't have roots, Mamá and I'd fall down and then there'd be heaps of leaves to sweep up.'

Giggling hard, Kierney enacted patterns of swirling leaves with her fingers. Her mother did the same before springing up off the bench to grab her daughter's waist and twist her around in an elaborate dance. The songwriter cheered and clapped his hands, ably assisted by the boy who was already far too grown up to be seen dancing in the open air.

'Shall we go back in?' Lynn asked, dispatching the children for a last race across the grass. 'What's happening in there?'

'I left Dad and Lena talking. He's going to think about what treatment he wants. I told him he had to decide quickly in order to get the best outcome. And Madalena says she wants to go back to school.'

First to finish as always, Jet looked up at his dad. 'School? Auntie Lena's too big to go to school,' he cried at the top of his voice, dumbfounded. 'She has to go to work.'

Lynn took the boy's hand as they all walked back into the building, Kierney now safely back in her papá's arms. 'Adults can go back to school. Only not the sort of school you go to. A school 'specially for adults. I think it's a great idea.'

'So do I, except she's already decided who's paying, of course,' her husband scoffed.

Lynn put her spare arm around his waist. 'Well, at least your auntie wouldn't be a dumb-ass anymore, kids.'

'Mum!' the four-year-old shrieked. 'You can't say that!'

'Sorry, Jetto,' the mother agreed. 'No, I shouldn't, but it was funny.'

The family stopped to say hello to the staff working in the prison's administration centre, who were delighted to have the chance to meet their famous visitors. Opening the door into the family room, the guard smiled at Lynn and the youngsters as they filed in. It transpired that the uniformed man had broken protocol and taken a seat at the table, more coffee having been delivered.

'Hey, guys... Look!' Jeff exclaimed. 'These are the bickies I was telling you about. We used to have these when we were kids, didn't we, Lena?'

His sister stood up and joined the family at the table. 'Oh, yeah! I forgot.'

Lynn gave the plate of biscuits to Jet and asked him to offer them to Granddad. Kierney followed him, keen to watch the sullen, clattery old man eat something.

'Thanks, mate,' Paul said, taking two biscuits and biting into one with a sparse mouthful of teeth. 'Sit down 'ere, kids. Tell me about your 'ouse. Is it flash? A McMansion, like?'

'It's bigger than our apartment, with lots of grass for cricket and footy, and a pool,' Jet boasted. 'And we've got a dog we share with Greg.'

Jeff looked at his wife. This was an easy, innocent conversation where the boy wouldn't pick up on any of his grandfather's bitter undertones, and the grandfather would have no concept of how big the house was nor who the heck Greg might be!

'Coffee?' Lynn asked, pouring anyway. 'Mister Diamond, why did you and your parents move to Australia?'

The songwriter looked up from a book that Kierney had brought over from the toy-box, first at his beautiful best friend and then at the prisoner. This was a good question, and one he should really have asked himself while he still had the opportunity.

'From New York?' the grandfather asked in return, as surprised as his son.

His classy daughter-in-law nodded, handing him a cup and saucer, which he took with shaky hands. The children were worried their granddad was about to spill the contents all over the table, just like they had each done several times in their young lives. Fortunately, despite a few rattles, the coffee stayed in the cup until it came to rest on the shiny surface.

'I was only 'is age,' the old man responded, looking at his wide-eyed grandson. 'Dunno really. Somethin' to do with jobs, I 'xpect. Not a Jewish thing, like them leaving Warsaw. Wasn't my idea.'

Jeff exhaled, amused. The old man had no knowledge of his own history. Furthermore, he couldn't care less. Migrating hadn't been his idea. Not his responsibility, the son smiled. No change there then! There was little value in pursuing this line of enquiry. The Diaments' migration was fortunate for him however, or else his soul would have needed to travel even further to reach its mate.

'It was Mamá and Papá's idea,' offered a soft, high-pitched voice from between the two men.

The romantic man gasped, entranced by Kierney's unexpected fantasy. Where had she heard about eternal souls? He racked his brain, unable to recall them having spoken about such things as a family. Was this his *Regala*'s doing as well, or had the little girl conjured up the notion all on her own?

'Yes, Kizzy. I think so too,' Lynn agreed wholeheartedly with their daughter's *impromptu* fairy tale. 'That's a lovely thing to say, darling.'

The two-year-old grinned, shyly leaning on her dad's arm and receiving a long, heartfelt kiss through her hair. Husband and wife shared a telepathic message of affinity, while neither Madalena nor her father batted an eyelid. Not to worry. It wasn't important that they appreciate their daughter's fanciful explanation.

Since the sickly prisoner evidently had no more to tell on the original topic, Lynn kicked off another innocent conversation. 'Jet, please ask Auntie Lena what she wants to do at school?'

'Hey!' Madalena objected. 'You talk too much, *chico*.'

'Answer him, Lena, por favor? We all want to know.'

The tennis champion sat down on the couch next to Kierney and her granddad, who were leafing through the photographs again. She listened while the toddler described where everything was in all sorts of confusing ways that would leave the old man totally bamboozled.

'Sometimes I get lost,' the little girl giggled, ''cause I haven't learned where everything is yet.'

Her grandfather chuckled and then coughed again, lining his throat with hot, sweet coffee.

'And when she's in our apartment, she thinks her bedroom's disappeared!' Jet interjected, teasing his sister. 'May I have another biscuit, please, Dad?'

'Yeah. Sure you can. Offer them to everybody, please.'

After marshalling the group for a short session taking every combination of family portrait, even enlisting the custody officer's help, Lynn noticed her father-in-law had begun to look very tired, coughing more and more regularly.

'We should go and leave you in peace, Mister Diamond,' she suggested. 'Come on, kids. Let's get ready to go.'

Jeff winked at his wife and mouthed his thanks, as much for forcing the meeting to a close as for showing regard for his ailing father. They all got to their feet and stood facing each other. Paul was drained of all energy, needing to lean on the table to stay upright. His multi-million-dollar son embraced him as warmly as he could, worried that the withered frame might snap if he were to grip any more tightly.

'Thanks for this, Dad,' he said, shaking the man's right hand. 'Let us know what you decide. Get them to ring me, OK?'

'Sure, Jeff,' the reply contained little enthusiasm.

Madalena took a couple of steps forward and gave her dad a hug too. It was awkward for them both, their skinny skeletons in close proximity; the sound of bones clacking together saved only by their clothes, as was the comedic image painted by her descriptive brother on their way back into the city.

'See ya, Dad,' she said. 'Hope you're OK. Do what your son says.'

'Yeah. I will,' Paul nodded. 'Nice to see you after all this time. You're OK, Lena.'

Jeff's eyes switched nervously from his father to his wife and back again. Would they ever see him again? If this meeting were their last, given the circumstances, would its result be positive overall? He owned up to a modicum of sadness, yet this was more due to the fact that his children were only just beginning to warm to their grandfather.

As far as the songwriter was concerned, he felt no impending loss. 'Well,' he said, putting his left arm around Lynn's shoulders and his free hand on Jet's head. 'Look at your grandkids, Dad. Look at our family. Your family.'

He pointed to his wife, himself, Jet and Kierney in sequence, as the older man rested back onto the table. 'We are strength, compassion, unity and freedom.'

And then, at Madalena, 'and dumb-ass!'

Waiting for the laughter to subside, Jeff pulled a typed manuscript out of the inside pocket of his leather jacket, folded in half lengthwise and with a stout bulldog clip holding the sheets together. 'Your family, Dad... Our purpose is to think of what the world needs and make it happen. Take this and learn about us, so that when you're reincarnated, you can make up for all the bad things.'

Surprisingly obsequious, his father reached for the document, giving the front page so cursory a glance that he couldn't possibly have read the three lines of text written on the cover. He tucked it under his arm as Lynn stepped forward to give him a hug.

As the diverse group finished saying their goodbyes, the multi-millionnaire began to swivel his black jet-stone ring with the four diamonds; the one the prisoner had admired during his last visit. He wound it off his finger and held it out.

'Dad, keep this for a while. Leave it to me in your will,' he offered, fighting to hold back the tears.

Diamond Senior burst into tears too, overcome with his son's generous gesture. His eyes scanning around the room, he took the ring and peered at it.

'It only 'ad two diamonds in it before,' he recalled, wiping a rough hand across his mouth and noisily clearing his nasal passages.

'Yep. That's right. Because at that stage, there were only the two of us,' Jeff sniffed too, cuddling his children. 'Now all four of us are here. That's what Lynn designed it for.'

The young woman leaned heavily on her lost boy's arm. She hadn't expected him to give away the ring she had designed for him but understood why he had done it. She hoped Jeff's judgment of the prisoner's change of heart was sound, and that they would see it again before too long.

She needn't have worried however. The prison guard stepped in, under strict instructions to prevent any items of value being passed from visitors to inmates.

'Fuckin' bastard,' Paul muttered under his breath, before removing it from his finger and handing it back. 'Cheers anyway, son.'

'Say goodbye to Granddad, please,' Lynn requested of the children.

Kierney was the first to step forward this time. ''Bye, Granddad,' she said brightly.

Jeff swooped both children up so that they could stand on the table, better able to hug the old man, who put his arms round both of them and gave them a friendly squeeze.

'You're good kids.'

Jet jumped down, falling forward into his father's waiting arms with the unswerving trust of a happy child. The handsome celebrity delivered him in a wide arc to the floor and hoisted his little girl onto his hip, and they all walked towards the door. Stopping to make sure nothing had been forgotten, he put his other arm around the lifer's shoulders.

'Who goes first?' he asked the officer.

As if he had forgotten why he was there, the prison guard jumped to attention and instructed the prisoner to follow him. Lynn, Madalena and the children slipped through the half-opened door and began to walk along the corridor, turning to wait for Jeff while he said a private farewell.

'There's another kid, y'know.'

Spinning around to face the two men in uniform, the songwriter's brain froze. 'What did you say?'

'Another kid,' his father repeated.

The younger man covered the short distance in a single stride, fury boiling at this startling revelation so casually cast into the air. The old man stood firm, clearly expecting an adverse reaction.

'Another kid?' Jeff echoed, feeling the hairs on the back of his neck prickling against his shirt collar. 'After me, you mean? Lena and I have a brother or sister?'

'Yep,' Paul Diamond confirmed. 'Yer mum 'ad three abortions after you come along, mate. I wasn't gonna tell ya, but s'pose I should.'

A low growl escaped from the celebrity's mouth, suddenly gripped by an urge to flatten this spiteful, hard-hearted arsehole. If it hadn't been for the burly warder, the old Jeff Diamond would have wrung the prisoner's scrawny neck.

Instead, the new Jeff Diamond calmly requested more information. 'What happened to the baby?'

'She was too far gone,' his father shrugged. 'Too fucked-up to even know she was pregnant 'til it was obvious. It was a boy. I gave it to Theo for 'is cousin.'

'You what?' the celebrity's head span, his shoulder thudding against the wall. 'Jesus fucking Christ, Dad. You handed our brother over to those bastards? Was it yours?'

'Dunno. Didn't give a fuck.'

Jeff felt nausea rising in his stomach. 'Why the hell did you do that, full- or half-brother? For Christ's sake! And I thought I had it bad!'

The guard placed a steadying hand on the prisoner's shoulder when he saw him lurch forward. Was he about to fall? Or run? The evil in this man knew no bounds. Not only had he allowed his under-aged daughter to be used as a sex toy and subjected his son to a multitude of abuses, now he was confessing to giving a third child away to the underworld kingpin whom he eventually stabbed to death.

Whoa! The tortured soul battled to remain conscious, such was the adrenalin building up in his system. Presumably, this baby had neither identity nor memory to link him to his birth family. Who was he now? On the one hand, he had missed out on the neglect and suffering which would undoubtedly have come his way on the Stones Road, but on the other... Shit! It didn't bear thinking about.

'Jack wanted a son,' the old man sneered. 'Theo said he 'ad three girls and was willing to pay for a boy. I needed the money, mate. I just wanted you to know. Before I drop off the perch, y'know...'

I could hasten that outcome, the musician cursed in his head. His propensity toward dramatic statement was inherited too...

'Yeah. OK,' the musician groaned. 'Fuck, Dad. If it's true, that's the confession to end all confessions. Bloody hell. I should say thanks, I guess. But I'm not sure why. What's this guy's name? D'you know what happened to him?

'Na. Dunno.'

'Not interested?'

Of course the murderer wasn't interested. Why would he be? The loot had changed hands, Jack Jaworski had a son to induct into their sorry gangland operation, and Luciana had been in no fit state to mount a coherent objection. The world-changer watched the sickly figure shuffle slowly past the line of doors and windows and on out of sight, never once turning his head.

'Good luck, Dad,' Jeff called after him.

***

The visitors escaped from Parklea's dour visitors' centre as quickly as possible, after having signed out and received a brief exit interview by Governor Maloney. The fresh air in the car park was welcome, despite the cold. Kissing his gorgeous gipsy girl, Jeff put the soles of her black patent shoes down onto the bitumen, and she and Jet ran to the family's hired car.

'Do you mind if Lena and I grab a quick ciggie?' Jeff asked his wife. 'There's something I need to tell her. And you, angel, but I'll update you later.'

'Oh, OK. Go ahead,' Lynn said. 'I think we're all looking forward to something a little stronger than a ciggie.'

Madalena laughed. 'She's so good to you, *chico*.'

'You're not wrong. She's the best. I'll have one of yours this time,' the songwriter smirked, pointing to his sister's handbag, where he was sure she would be hiding another packet of cigarettes.

'Bastard!' the woman cursed, rummaging until she located it and then offering them around. 'What were them papers you gave 'im?'

Jeff held his lighter in front of the naïve street-girl's face, and she sucked in the smoke greedily. He was now debating whether their father's last-minute news item ought to remain a secret to this hapless nobody. After successfully freeing her from the next generation of Jaworski brothers, would introducing her to an extra sibling see her swallowed back into their prostitution racket?

'It's the beginnings of a book about right and wrong,' he explained, keen to ingest the nicotine into his bloodstream too. 'It's rough as guts at the moment, but enough to give him something to think about while he makes his decision. Listen, Lena…'

His sister had been distracted by a heavily-built man walking across the car park. 'I know 'im. He's a cop. Booked me once, the pig! What'd'ya say?'

The millionnaire frowned. 'Yeah? He was just doing his job. Anyway, if I said Dad told me something significant after you guys left, would you want me to tell you?'

'What kind o' significant?'

'Important. About our family.'

Madalena pouted. 'I dunno. Will it change my life?'

'It could,' her brother answered, 'if you wanted it to.'

'Na. Nothing he told me would be good, so no. I've had a gutful of me dad, 'aven't you? Time to get 'im out o' my brain.'

The sound of languid heels on the concrete footpath played havoc with her husband's sex-drive as Lynn walked towards the dark-haired *duo*, free to join them after installing the children into their car-seats. She hesitated to come within earshot, in case her husband wasn't ready for her to hear the information he needed to pass on.

Hearing the lanky woman's disinterest, Jeff decided to keep their younger brother to himself for the time being. He and his exquisite partner would discuss it tonight. She would help him figure out what to do with this new character in their complex lifestory.

'I didn't know you were going to give him a copy of your manuscript,' Lynn said, being gathered into a loving embrace. 'Do you think he'll read it?'

'Yeah,' Madalena said. 'He said you were a bloody impressive man. He'll read it.'

The sportswoman laced her arm around Jeff's waist, slotting her thumb into his waistband and hearing him sigh in contentment. He hovered his cigarette in front of her face, and she helped herself to a distinguished dose while pressing her backside into his libidinous loins.

'What do you think he'll decide?' she asked.

'He won't go for a transplant,' her man guessed. 'He'd be mad to.'

His sister wasn't so sure. 'Not even to give us the shits?'

Jeff shrugged, laughing. 'Nope. Doubt it. And I bet you didn't know I was going to give him my ring either,' he said to his blonde bombshell, somewhat ashamed.

'No. I did not!' Lynn almost shouted. 'I appreciate why you did it, but I wondered whether we'd ever see it again.'

'Yeah. Me too,' the young man admitted, kissing her indignant lips. 'I gave him the benefit of the doubt and hoped you wouldn't be too angry with me.'

'You gave me the benefit of the doubt too then,' the singer smiled. 'But the prison system didn't.'

Madalena's expression was one of confusion, once more shut outside the couple's private discourse. Meanwhile, Jet had managed to roll down the car window to sound the alarm. Tolerance limits for waiting were about to be breached.

'OK, Jetto! We'll be there in a minute, mate,' his dad yelled back, before turning back to the women. 'I should've thought about it for longer. Of course he couldn't keep it. Someone might've mugged him for it, or he'd use it as a weapon or trade it. Who knows? It was a stupid thing to do, in hindsight.'

'No, it was a lovely thing to do,' his wife countered. 'Just a bit risky. Are you coming back with us, Lena?'

'Where're ya goin'?'

'Well... We can either drop you home,' Jeff offered, 'or you can come back with us to Celia's, and I'll take you home later. Or tomorrow morning, before we fly back.'

'Would you like Auntie Lena to have lunch with us, kids?' Lynn asked, turning to the tired youngsters in the back seat and eliciting two loud cheers.

'Right on!' Madalena seemed stoked by the children's enthusiasm. 'I'll come back with you. I'm supposed to be busy tonight, but too bad.'

'Busy tonight?' her brother repeated with a sly smile, thinking of the questions their other passengers were likely to ask as to the pleasures their auntie might be foregoing this evening. 'Thanks for that.'

The car turned onto the road and drove back towards Sydney at high speed, with their extra occupant squeezed in between the two child-seats. Within five minutes of monotonous highway thrumming through the tyres, Jet and Kierney had both fallen asleep, leaving the adults free to conduct a *post mortem* of their morning.

'So did you like him?' Lynn asked the pair of Catholic Argentinean Polish Jews.

The ambitious rock star stared straight ahead for a few moments, deep in thought.

'I did,' Madalena piped up from behind. 'I didn't at first, but then it was like before. Just don't take any shit from him.'

'Shhh!' Jeff requested, before offering a response. 'No, angel. Can't say I liked him, but I respected the attitude he came in with. And I feel sorry for him. Extremely sorry for him, actually.'

'I could tell,' his wife acknowledged. 'But then that's you all over, isn't it? He was OK with the kids, considering he probably hasn't seen any for such a long time.'

'Yeah. That's true. Lena, you could get away with not taking any flak from him. I'd have copped a kicking if I'd said the things you said today.'

'Yeah,' his sister acknowledged. 'You would of.'

No-one was home when the family reached the Blakes' expansive residence in Mosman. They had driven for over an hour through busy lunchtime traffic, singing along to the radio and chatting about their plans. After picking up a takeaway meal on the Pacific Highway and being mobbed by North Sydney's entire population of fast-food consumers, the car's tyres crackled and crunched as the driver swung it off the road and onto the hooped driveway.

Madalena looked around in amazement as the car drew closer to the front doors. 'Wow! This place is amazing!'

Jeff handed the keys to his wife, still feeling rather shell-shocked and disturbed by the final few minutes at Her Majesty's Prison Parklea. He was disappointed in himself that they hadn't achieved more, and Lynn knew it. She kissed him and squeezed his arm, saying nothing.

'Who's for a game of tennis?' the athlete suggested, by way of re-establishing some element of normalcy for the day.

The young, active bodies, replete with burgers and French fries, jumped up and down with excitement. The adults had descended into a sugar stupour however, with the Olympian the only one game to entertain those with the opposite affliction. She took them upstairs to change their clothes.

'That's a winner,' her husband smiled, giving his sister a short tour of the ground floor. 'You OK after all that? Are you glad you went?'

'Dunno,' Madalena replied, shrugging. 'It's weird to see him after so long, and weird that he was still the same but older.'

'I agree. That's what I thought last time. It was as if the other meeting never happened. Like we'd gone back to the time when he and I just prowled round each other in the same house and didn't have anything in common.'

'Today it was like you were the dad and he was the kid,' the prostitute grinned, removing her shoes and accepting a glass of cold water, complete with ice from a dispenser in the refrigerator door.

'Really?' Jeff exclaimed, surprised by this insight. 'Fuck! That's not how it felt for me. He still scares the shit out of me!'

Madalena screamed. 'No way! You scared him today.'

'It's just an act, Lena,' the millionnaire shook his head. 'I look like I'm in control but I'm really not. He was always nice to you, remember? He always hated me, and I despised him for it. As soon as I'm in the room with him, all my courage goes out the window.'

'Well, it didn't show,' his proud sister contradicted. 'You were awesome. Tellin' 'im like it is, and all that stuff about deservin' a transplant.'

Jeff sighed. '*Gracias.* It went better than I expected today. I just hope he goes back and talks to that Chris woman again, so she can steer him towards the right choice. You didn't see her. She seemed like a good counsellor.'

The serious conversation was cut short by two deafening whirlwinds dressed in sports gear running headlong into their father's legs, their shoes squeaking on the polished floorboards. Lynn followed them at a more sedate pace, looking as sensational as ever in very short shorts and a cropped top. She kissed the man with a lecherous grin on his face who was pulling closer with every breath.

'Come on!' Jet shouted, thumping the tops of his dad's thighs with all his strength. 'You have to get changed. Hurry up!'

Auntie Lena burst out laughing. 'You don't want 'im to get any taller!'

Wrestling the day's stress away with his son, Jeff beamed. 'You're bloody right! I've copped a few good ones already, don't you worry. You guys go on out. I'll join you in a minute. I just need to make a couple of 'phone calls.'

Lynn ushered everyone out of the French windows which led to the swimming pool, and then on behind the house to the tennis court. The woman from the wild, wild west walked open-mouthed, following the children.

'Do you like tennis, Auntie Lena?' Kierney asked.

'Dunno,' she replied. 'I never played before.'

'We'll show you,' her sister-in-law suggested, more to encourage the kids than for Madalena's benefit. 'Can you run in those shoes?'

'Run? I don't even know how to run.'

Kierney looked at the tall, skinny woman in amazement. 'Running's easy!'

'Yeah. Just walk fast,' Jet quipped, demonstrating how to walk faster and faster until he broke into a run.

'Like father, like son!' the young mother shook her head. 'At least he doesn't append the word "stupid" on the end of his sentence. Sorry about that.'

The bemused aunt didn't care. There was no place for niceties in her world. And besides, she was feeling very relaxed with the family after their intense bonding experience, enjoying the bonus time with her lively niece and nephew.

Lynn and Kierney took up positions on the far side of the net and Jet stood next to Madalena. He demonstrated how to bounce a ball so that it could be hit from waist-height over the net. The foursome exchanged gentle lobs, spending more time chasing stray balls than producing successful rallies.

Madalena was soon out of breath, years of minimal exercise and plenty of cigarettes having reduced her lung capacity. Lynn thought of her father-in-law's disease and couldn't help wondering if the same fate lay in store for his daughter in the next few decades. The older woman's solution to the problem, however, was to take a cigarette break.

After about half an hour, Jeff jogged down to join them. His sister whistled as she saw how fit and tanned her brother looked, his well-toned legs and bulging biceps on display in his running attire. The afternoon had warmed up more than ten degrees from a particularly chilly morning, and the court's grass covering was already yellowing off.

'Who's winning?' he asked, picking Kierney up from her spot next to the net and folding his huge hands over hers on the half-sized racquet. 'Can I play with you, please, Kizzy?'

Gaining a much better view from the baseline than from ground level, the toddler giggled and screamed as she was bounced up and down while her dad lunged for imaginary shots. Her legs swang from side to side and her feet scraped the ground occasionally.

'Do that with me, please, Dad!' Jet cried out.

Obligingly, Jeff put his daughter down and scissored his long legs over the net to where they boy stood expectantly. He groaned under his son's heavier weight, valiantly returning a few gentle balls hit by the reigning Wimbledon Ladies' Singles title-holder.

'You guys have so much fun,' moaned Madalena. 'I wish you lived 'ere.'

'Come in the 'plane to our new house, Auntie Lena,' chimed Kierney. 'I can show you my room.'

Handing the racquet back to his son, the songwriter attracted his wife's attention. 'Angel, can we go for a run, please? I really need to burn some fast energy.'

Lynn made contact with the soul behind his pleading eyes and took pity on it, as she invariably did, straightaway turning to the others. 'Kids, why don't you teach Auntie Lena how to play squennis?'

'Squennis?' their extra player echoed in confusion. 'What the f... What's that?'

'Tennis up against the wall,' the four-year-old know-all informed his auntie.

'Oh.'

'It's a cross between squash and tennis,' the boy's mum explained. 'You'll get used to us. We make up new words for everything.'

'Yeah,' Jeff whispered into his sister's ear, winking mischievously. 'It's tennis masturbation.'

Seeing Lynn roll her eyes, Madalena looked shocked. 'Eh?'

'You heard!' he shouted, feigning innocence. 'You can play it by yourself.'

Ignoring the *innuendo*, Lynn turned to their children with a serious face. 'OK, guys. Please stay here, won't you? No wandering off anywhere and making Auntie Lena worried. Are you OK to watch them for a while, Lena, please?'

'Sure! We won't go nowhere. This is fun.'

The celebrities waved and left the tennis court at a steady pace, heading down to the rear exit of the Blakes' inner-suburban home. Madalena felt very envious of the family's healthy togetherness. She turned back and watched both children diligently hitting tennis ball after tennis ball against the bricks at the back of the court, taking it in turn to pick a row at which to aim.

She picked up a racquet and joined in, every so often hitting one or other of the kids on the backside accidentally-on-purpose. The youngsters circled through a selection of their regular games, such as hitting the ball hard against the wall and running full pelt to gather it up before it reached the net. Madalena sat down on the hard surface of the court and happily listened them amusing themselves in the sunshine.

It was almost an hour before the parents returned, receiving a rousing cheer as they sprinted back towards the wire mesh gate. Lynn crashed through it about five metres in front of her husband, and they both immediately flopped down onto the court, breathing heavily, each with a child on top of them.

Their babysitter was dancing around too, very glad they were back.

'Auntie Lena's got jumping jocks,' Jet whispered into his father's ear.

'Oh, has she?' the handsome man chuckled, sitting up and watching his sister rock back and forth in apparent discomfort. 'You in a bit of strife, Lena?'

'You said I couldn't leave 'em,' his sister whined.

'Thanks,' Jeff said, feeling guilty that she had taken them so seriously. 'Kiz, show Auntie Lena where the toilet is, please.'

'Good for her pelvic floor,' Lynn laughed, watching the children run off with their auntie in tow.

'Hey! That's mean, coming from you.'

The couple hauled themselves up off the ground and began collecting the tennis equipment, their temporary peace disturbed by a greeting spoken in the unmistakeable North Shore accent. Celia had returned while they had been running and was now calling them in from the pool fence.

'Hi, Celia!' her son's best friend called back. 'We're on our way up.'

The couple greeted the elegant lady with kisses, warning her that they had brought an additional person home with them. As they imparted this news, the children reappeared, dragging their relieved co-conspirator up the steps. They were evidently sharing a joke that revolved around coloured knickers. All three stopped in their tracks when confronted with their augmented welcoming committee.

'Hello, Madalena. Nice to see you again. Hello, Jet and Kierney.'

'Hi!' the overgrown teenager replied. 'You too.'

Celia hugged the children, who were out of breath after their little detour. 'Did you see your Granddad today?'

'Yes,' Kierney answered, shooting her father an uncertain glance and receiving permission to say whatever she wanted to say. 'He coughed all the time, and there was shouting and crying sometimes.'

'Oh, dear,' the older woman commiserated. 'Was everything alright in the end though?'

Jeff chuckled. 'Depends from whose perspective.'

Celia nodded and then turned to the ever-opinionated boy-child. 'And what did you think of Granddad, Jet? Was he like you expected he would be?'

The boisterous blond took a few moments to consider his answer. 'Yes,' he replied. 'He was like Dad but very old, and his voice was croaky like a frog.'

'Ribbit, ribbit,' his father teased. 'A bit like that?'

Madalena laughed. 'No. More like effin' ribbit, effin' ribbit.'

Everyone except the innocent Kierney turned and stared at their foul-mouthed guest, before laughing anyway.

'You are terrible,' Celia chastened. 'You'll teach them bad habits.'

Jet bounced around the room, fortunately omitting the expletive from his frog call. Kierney joined him, and Celia returned inside to make a pot of tea, always the best remedy for any household irregularity.

Lynn followed her in. 'Sorry, Celia,' she sighed. 'Madalena's still pretty unpredictable. The kids love her to bits for it though, mainly because she's not much more than a child herself. I found out today that she'd never played tennis before.'

'Is that right, dear? Did she join in?'

'Oh, yes. She was fine. Perfectly willing to join in, except she had to be taught from scratch. Jet was in his element, coaching her and pulling her up when she forgot one of his instructions. He's getting very bossy these days.'

Celia laughed. 'They all go through that at some stage. It's nice that he has so much confidence, Lynn. Sit down for a minute, if you don't mind.'

At the middle-aged woman's insistence, Australia's darling took a seat at the kitchen table while their host fussed around preparing afternoon tea for them all. She had bought some very rich and expensive-looking cakes from a local *patisserie*, which led the sports star immediately to anticipate Madalena's wide-eyed reaction.

'They look delicious,' she waxed lyrical.

'Thank you, dear. So how did it go? Was it traumatic?'

'Not really. Except at the end, I suppose,' the compassionate wife reported. 'Jeff's pleased enough with how it went. You know what he's like... He really wanted a miracle but was ecstatic just to hear his dad call him by name. We didn't expect Lena to appear though. We were already in a family room, all together, and the guard called Jeff over to say she'd arrived.'

'Was it awkward with Jeff's father and the children?'

Lynn nodded. 'A little bit. No, actually... A lot! It must be years since he's seen a child. Jet was brave to begin with, but Kizzy ended up being the more friendly. He became quite emotional when he set eyes on her because she must've reminded him so much of his wife and daughter. The older she gets, the more like them she looks.'

'Kierney certainly is turning into an adorable little lady,' Celia affirmed. 'Does your father-in-law seem as unwell as their letter suggested?'

The twenty-four-year-old considered her response. 'Oh, yes. He's really thin and coughs all the time; making horrible noises, clearing his throat, *et cetera*. Thankfully there wasn't much spitting. I shudder to think what Jet's going to do with that new skill. He looked exhausted by the time we were leaving. But then, we all were... You'll need to ask Jeff really, because this was the first time I'd met him.'

'Oh, naturally, dear,' Missus Blake apologised. 'I forgot it was only Jeff who met him last time.'

'The kids and I went out for a walk when the conversation turned morbid,' Lynn went on. 'We'd overheard some pretty angry exchanges, so Jeff suggested we take a break.'

'Probably a good thing. You never know what the children might take in.'

'Exactly. Beforehand, Jeff had wanted them to hear everything, and then we'd discuss it with them afterwards. I was very glad when he asked us to leave them to it.'

The younger woman picked up the tray of colourful cakes and followed Celia out to the pool. Warmth was fading from the afternoon, but the family was still hot-blooded after all their exercise. As predicted, Madalena swooned at the sight of the sophisticated fare.

'¡Ai!' she screamed. 'What's that?'

'Cakes!' Kierney replied, excitedly clapping her hands. 'Yummy cakes!'

'Do you like yummy cakes, darling?' the sophisticated grandmother smiled at the little girl who indeed closely resembled the gangly urchin sitting among them.

'Mmm...' the toddler answered, rubbing her hungry stomach. 'Yes, I do. Please may I have that one, Auntie Celia?'

Kierney was pointing to a piece of strawberry *gâteau*, which their host halved and placed deftly onto a plate. 'You certainly may, since you asked so nicely, darling.'

'Eat it with your fork, please,' Lynn requested.

The rest of the family was soon served, and everyone gorged themselves after their long day. The sugar-high gave Madalena an unbearable nicotine craving, but she resisted lighting up until everyone had finished.

'Please can we go for a swim, Auntie Celia?' Jet put on his most polite voice.

Taking her cue from the boy's parents, the older woman shook her head. 'I'm sorry, children. The pool hasn't been cleaned for a long while. It's been so cold. It wouldn't be a good idea.'

The corner of Jet's mouth turned downwards until his eyes met his mother's. 'That's OK,' he said, cheering up on demand, and ran off onto the lawn to find another game to play.

'Do you want a football or something, Jeff?' Celia asked.

The absentminded larrikin gave his host a confused stare. 'Why would I want a football, Auntie Celia?'

'For Jet, you horrible boy!'

Madalena howled. '¡Si! ¡Para Jet, chico horible!'

'Would *you* like a football, Lena?' her brother taunted, remembering what a tom-boy she had been during primary school. 'You can go and entertain him.'

'OK. I will. I 'aven't played for yonks.'

Lynn called to the youngster, who came running at full pelt. 'Jetto, do you remember where the Blakes keep the soccer ball?'

The four-year-old drew a blank and shook his head. Celia pointed round the far side of the swimming pool, where there was a cupboard full of sports equipment.

'Try in the shed behind there, darling. They might need pumping up, but there are a few different balls in there.'

Madalena lit a cigarette and went to help her little nephew.

'Go on!' laughed Lynn, seeing how envious her husband was at having the combination of a kick-about and a cigarette present itself.

'D'you mind? Are you coming, Kizzo?'

Kierney shook her head. 'Too full with cake.'

'OK. Wise move,' Jeff replied, kissing the top of his daughter's head. 'You stay there then, with the other pretty ladies, and we'll find another game for you and me to play later.'

'So...' the young mother said to her happy little girl. 'Are we going to take Auntie Celia and Uncle Gerald out to dinner tonight?'

'Yes!'

'Oh, you don't have to do that, dears,' Celia protested. 'We've got plenty of food here. It's so nice to see you. We don't have to go out.'

'We'll put it to the vote when Gerald gets home. Jeff wants to go out, and especially now we've sprung Madalena on you too.'

'Whatever you'd like,' the Irishwoman capitulated. 'Kierney, darling, did you like your Granddad after you got to know him a bit?'

The dark-haired girl paused, this time less enthusiastic. 'Yes. But he made Papá cry.'

'Oh, did he? That's a shame. Not for long, I hope.'

'It doesn't take much to make Papá cry though, does it?' Lynn smiled at her daughter.

Kierney shook her head and smiled. 'No. Big softy!'

'That's right!' her mother agreed. 'Lovely, big softy.'

'You can see how much he's enjoying these little ones, can't you?' Celia observed. 'It's nice to see. You must make each other very happy.'

The singer nodded. 'Yes. We do. Thanks, Celia. That's exactly what my mum says too! Jeff loves being a dad. Every minute of it. He's away a lot, so that makes a difference. We're always so glad to be back together after he's been away. It's true what they say about absence making the heart grow fonder.'

'He should have a word with my son,' the grandmother moaned. 'Did you hear Heather's pregnant again?'

'Yes,' Lynn replied, uncertain whether the businessman's parents would be happy with this news or not. 'Have you met her husband?'

'We haven't. Jim, isn't it? Gerry's not too keen on him, but he should make more of an effort because this man's been kind enough to take Jenna on as his own.'

'Exactly,' the Melburnian smiled. 'Jim's tried hard, we hear, but Gerry's been very standoffish. We only hear this second-hand of course, since neither of us know Heather all that well. She's actually a friend of a friend of mine, so I hear most of the gossip once removed. The town's a bit too small like that.'

Score Settled, Door Closed

A huge shout went up from the lawn, to the side of the house, rousing the lazy ladies from their afternoon naps. A goal had been scored by someone. Kierney slipped down off the couch and trotted over to the bay window, barely tall enough for her eyes to peep over the windowsill.

'It'll be good to see Robyn and Megan, won't it?' Celia removed her spectacles and began to clean them with a tissue, embarrassed to have fallen asleep.

The girl span around and nodded. She had been reminded that Jacinta's twin three-year-olds were coming over the next day and ran back to her mother's chair to check that she also remembered.

'Tomorrow, Mamá. *¿Sí?*'

'*Sí. Cierto,*' Lynn confirmed, stroking her face. 'Come and sit up here for a cuddle. Actually, Celia, I might see if they'll sleep for a couple of hours before dinner. Is that alright?'

'That's a good idea. Would you like that, Kierney?'

The little girl's head moved up and down against the tennis champion's chest, tempting her to kiss the smooth forehead. Such moments of togetherness were too rare these days, with a full diary of appointments and frequent nights away from home. Lynn felt privileged to have been granted this short interlude.

'I'll go and call a halt to their game,' their host offered, standing up.

The Diamonds' pseudo-grand-auntie walked down the steps to the lawn and stood for a few minutes to watch a fiercely-contested football match. The players had removed their shoes and socks, and all six legs were scrambling around the ball and tripping their opponents up, aided by flailing hands that pushed each other in the back. Every now and again, one of the adults would make a break for the other end, eagerly chased by little Jet. He was game to take either on, the spectator observed.

It warmed Celia's heart to see her extra son happily engrossed in such an innocent pastime, totally relaxed and carefree. How wonderful that his life had turned out just as he had planned... He and Lynn were clearly still so much in love and appeared in tune with each other on all aspects of parenting.

Their two precious gems were a joy too; loving, full of spark and a credit to the firm but fair attention they received. In fact, Gerry's parents paid more visits to Escondido than they did to his own salubrious Toorak abode, especially since Jeff had called a temporary halt to touring and was spending more time at home.

'Do you want to play?' the tearaway cried out, panting hard. 'Swap you. I'll wash the dishes if you take on these two bandits.'

'No, thank you, dear,' the elegant lady laughed. 'You're much too rough for me. Lynn wants the children to have a couple of hours' sleep.'

'Oh, no!' Jet whined, stopping in his tracks and ramming his hands onto his hips in disgust. 'Why?'

'That's enough, mate,' his father pounced. 'D'you want to be bored and cranky at the dinner table?'

'No. Do you?' Madalena snapped, catching the lad's eye and giving him a naughty wink.

'And you're not helping,' the disciplinarian scolded, pushing her so hard that she fell sideways into a hydrangea bush.

'¡Ai!'

The rock star held a hand out for his sister to grab onto and focussed back on his indignant son. 'Do you, Jetto?'

'No.'

The four-year-old ran to retrieve the ball from the flower-bed and handed it to Celia to be put away. He sucked in air manfully, in an effort not to cry with disappointment at the final whistle having been blown on their game. His playmates also adjourned inside, and the empathetic father hugged him close before Lynn took both children up to their bedroom.

'Your good lady wife mentioned you'd prefer to go out for dinner this evening,' their host checked when the multi-millionnaire returned to the kitchen. 'I told her it was no problem to eat here.'

Nodding, he picked up a trayful of crockery and left-over cakes, asking his sister to do the same. 'Yeah. I thought it'd be nice to be in an environment where we didn't spend the whole time talking about death,' he reasoned. 'If we eat here, I think we'll end up getting all morose about Dad. Don't you, Lena?'

His sister shrugged. 'What's morose? Talking about death?'

Jeff nodded. 'Yeah. Talking about people getting cancer and making ourselves depressed. Celia and Gerald don't want to talk about that all night.'

'No. You're right, dear,' their host agreed. 'We had enough of that with Gerald's mother last year. You're very considerate, darling.'

'Pick somewhere kid-friendly,' the celebrity proposed, 'and not too far to drive.'

'Would you like to stay here tonight, Madalena?' Celia asked.

'Is that OK?' Jeff asked, embarrassed that he had forgotten to ask either of them if this were possible. 'Sorry. I didn't mean to take your hospitality for granted.'

'Oh, don't be silly. That's perfectly fine. We can lend you something to change into as nightwear, and there's a couple of spare toothbrushes upstairs. It's no trouble.'

The flushed woman gladly accepted the offer of a night in this luxurious house, having already written off lost income. Lynn re-joined the kitchen hands, who were about to complete their duties.

'Nice timing,' her husband accused, flicking the tea towel at her legs.

His dream girl had taken a shower and changed out of her sports clothes, again wearing the leg-extending jeans which the testosterone-charged star found so irresistible. He grabbed for her slim hips covetously.

Madalena groaned. 'For God's sake, *chico*. Leave it out.'

'Yeah, *chico*,' the pretty blonde echoed. 'Leave it out!'

Jeff yanked his hands away and backed off comically. 'Right!' he stated. 'If that's what you want. Anything you say, ladies. I'm going to have a shower. On my own.'

Lynn looked downhearted. 'Sorry. I didn't mean it, Dad,' she impersonated their son.

'Too late,' the man laughed, shrugging. 'You made your choice.'

The spurned lover wheeled round on his heels amid high drama and left to clean himself up after the day's activities. The beauty grinned at the other women. After digesting the news her husband had imparted during their run, she was quite sure his spirits weren't anywhere near as high as they appeared.

'Good! That's got rid of 'im,' Madalena joked. 'You really look fantastic in them jeans.'

'Thanks!' her sister-in-law replied, surprised to receive such a gratuitous compliment. 'Did you want to borrow a top for tonight?'

'Yeah. That'd be great. An' a shower too?'

The well-mannered socialite made eye contact with Celia, knowing she was waiting for a "please" or a "thank you". Realising no such well-mannered response would be forthcoming, the affluent housewife gave a perfunctory nod, and the two women adjourned upstairs to Tamilla's bedroom.

***

Not long afterwards, a spruced-up and clean-shaven gentleman sauntered around the corner, leather jacket over his arm and checking the contents of his wallet, almost bumping into the world's most beautiful woman on the landing of his best mate's parents' house. His mind was instantly thrown back to yesteryear.

'Good evening, miss,' he announced his presence, creeping up on her as she closed Madalena's bedroom door. 'I'm Jeff. Do you live here too?'

Lynn smiled at his formality, spinning round and being swallowed into a bear-hug. They kissed passionately.

'I am a guest at this residence, sir, yes,' she responded. 'Can I help you with anything?'

'Yes. You can,' he replied, taking hold of her hand and placing it on his crotch. 'You can help me with this.'

'But I don't understand, sir,' the young woman complained, with a worried face. 'What assistance do you require? You gave me the impression you were self-sufficient in that regard.'

Jeff caught his breath. 'Ha! That's classic!'

Unable to pass up the opportunity to share some bottled-up passion on the first-floor landing, the couple exchanged whispered words of love between kisses and amorous groping. At his compliant hostage's breathless insistence, the aroused visitor dragged her into the Blakes' guest suite and threw her down onto the mattress.

'Jeff, careful!' Lynn raised her voice, thrusting his chest away with both hands. 'Please calm down a bit. You're all hyper.'

'Christ! Sorry, angel,' her tormented husband exhaled suddenly, sitting down on the edge of the bed. 'You're right. Do you want to wait 'til later?'

'No. You obviously need to wind down, but that doesn't mean I'm happy for you to push me around. I'm not your jagged-edged sister, remember?'

The songwriter shook his head, reaching up to stroke his wife's beautiful, patient face while she unzipped her jeans and began to remove them. 'Jesus, Lynn,' he hissed. 'That's the last thing I want to do. I'm really sorry. I got carried away with all the weirdness. Forgive me?'

The blonde reached out a long, elegant arm and hooked her hand round the apologetic man's neck. The rough and tumble of the soccer pitch had fired cylinders which had been shut down by the old Jeff on leaving Parklea. They simply required a quick tune-up to perform within the new Jeff's boundaries.

'Of course I forgive you, you sexy idiot,' his wife purred. 'Let's get naked. But hurry, or else Celia'll send out a search party, and we'll get caught.'

The lovers combined in a hurricane of intense abandon, rendered more acute when Lynn reminded her black stallion that his sister would shortly be roaming free in close proximity to the unsuspecting housewife. And adding insult to injury, no sooner had they collapsed in ecstasy onto the mattress, still breathing heavily, than they heard a familiar smoker's cough outside their room.

'Christ Almighty!' the musician hissed, both leaping for their clothes. 'Sprung by my sister at twenty-nine! That's not pretty.'

'*Chico*, you in 'ere?' Madalena's dissonant tones blared like an air-raid claxon.

Pulling on a pair of boxer shorts in record time, Jeff bolted for the door as the handle began to turn, giving his embarrassed bedfellow enough time to slip out of bed and into the bathroom, both trying not to make a sound.

'Lena!' her brother yelled. 'For Christ's sake, don't just walk in on people.'

The woman's face was a picture, winded by the shock of being bawled out at close range. 'Shit!' she screeched. 'I didn't know you were fuckin'.'

The handsome man laughed, showing his sister in while zipping up his jeans and gathering Lynn's clothes from the floor. No doubt the tell-tale signs of a recent orgasm were easily detected by a professional, regardless of the steps one took to disguise them. He opened the door to the *en suite* and passed the crumpled items in to his partner.

'We shouldn't need to give you our itinerary,' he jeered.

'What?'

'Nothing,' her brother smiled, deeming an explanation of little comedic value after the fact.

The tennis star emerged a few minutes later from the bathroom, hair and make-up perfectly in place and looking blithe and unsullied to the amateur's eye. 'Oh, my God! This is hilarious. It's like one of those 'sixties English farces. Hi, Lena!'

'What are you talking about?' the other woman moaned, becoming increasingly frustrated. 'Did you guys smoke something?'

'Sorry,' Jeff put a friendly hand on his sister's shoulder. 'No. We're only having a bit of fun. We haven't smoked anything, although it's an awesome idea. We're cutting loose after a weird day, that's all.'

'The kids are asleep,' his wife added, 'so we took advantage of our freedom. Let's go downstairs and pretend to be mature again.'

The joker grinned, feeling sorry for his flummoxed sister. 'Nice shirt. Lynn's got one just the same,' he remarked, receiving a sharp slap on the arm.

By this time, Gerald Blake had returned from work and was sitting at the breakfast bar with his nightly homecoming gin and tonic, listening to a detailed account of the day's news from Celia. He stood up and held his arms out towards their guests. Or more precisely, towards Lynn.

'Hello, all.'

'Hi, sir,' the younger man responded, offering his hand to his manager's father. 'How're you going?'

'Well, Jeff. Thank you,' the shy executive replied. 'And you? You look relaxed after today's ordeal. And Madalena, my dear. How are you?'

The rock star nodded, giving his sister a friendly push towards the master of the house. 'We're a whole lot more relaxed than earlier,' he told him, winking at the two women whom he had escorted down the staircase.

'Hello, Gerald,' the attractive blonde greeted the accountant, diverting the man's attention and receiving an enthusiastic hug.

Madalena gingerly stepped forward and allowed Gerry's father to peck her on the cheek. She hadn't seen him since the wedding, forgetting he was the posh woman's husband. Predictably and not before time, the next move was to fill everyone's hand with a glass.

The younger man requested a beer, conscious that it would help his sister to feel comfortable to ask for the same. Lynn joined the Blakes in a refreshing gin and tonic, complete with ice, a slice and a swizzle-stick, much to the Fairfield native's amusement.

'We've thought of a nice Italian family restaurant in Manly, if you're still insisting on going out,' Celia told the couple.

'Great,' Jeff agreed. 'Sounds perfect. Shall we book?'

'Already done,' Gerald confessed. 'It gets pretty busy on Fridays, so we took a chance.'

Lynn placed her drink on a coaster and elevated her tall frame off the couch. 'I'll go up and rouse the babes. What time did you want to leave?'

'Seven-ish'll be fine,' Gerry's mother said. 'There's no rush, dear.'

'So!' the ageing businessman looked from one dark-haired gipsy to the other. 'How was your dad?'

'Sick,' the musician answered, 'angry and even a little bit repentant.'

'Oh, really? That's the *craic*, is it not?'

Jeff nodded, seeing his elder sibling's eyes glaze over again. 'We had one hell of a shouting match for a while, didn't we, Lena?'

His sister stared straight ahead, annoyed at being subjected to an inquisition by a relative stranger. She had always harboured an aversion to ties, particularly when they came with superior accents. Not on point for this topic, Lynn disappeared upstairs, leaving the antagonistic pair to field the questions.

'We all needed to get a few things off our chests,' the young man continued. 'He met Lynn and the kids, which was fabulous. And a phenomenal ego trip for me after all the darkness. Finally a chance to prove I hadn't been bullshitting.'

'To be sure! And how long was it since you'd seen your father, Madalena?'

'When 'e got put away,' a gruff voice responded. 'He looked heaps older but still the same. Don't know why I bothered, honestly. I forgot 'im for all that time.'

Celia, who had gone to prepare some fruit juice for the children, shouted over from the refrigerator. 'Will your dad be able to keep the photographs in his room?' she asked, placing two bright red plastic cups on the counter.

'I guess so,' Jeff nodded, amused by the genteel shroud. 'His cell, you mean... Don't know how much they'll mean to him though.'

'We're not going to see 'im again,' Madalena blurted out.

Her brother's head whipped around, taken aback by the anguish in her tone. 'No. Don't expect we will. D'you mean because you don't want to see him or because he's too sick?'

'Both. It's unfair to let 'im meet 'is family and then the bastard just 'as to forget us again. What was the bloody point?'

The refined Mosman couple looked at each other, pondering the meaning of this outburst from the unfortunate product of Sydney's underworld. Celia felt some sympathy for her; Madalena was clearly unaccustomed to reflecting on serious issues and was perhaps beginning to find her conscience.

'It does seem a bit rough on him, especially if he's so ill. But he is a convicted criminal, dear. He's serving a sentence, regardless of his health.'

Jeff listened and watched with interest to see where his sister would go with this rather right-winged opinion. He had no idea as to his sister's political views. In her own tiny, suburban world, she was as much the selfish capitalist as the Blakes were in their middle-sized, metropolitan world. As one who had become accustomed to dealing political hands on a global scale, he was again reminded how easy it was for one's perspective to change depending on one's field of vision.

Madalena nodded. 'Yeah. I know. And I 'ate 'is guts. But 'e needs to be in 'ospital, not banged up.'

'He won't be able to smoke in hospital,' her brother added spice to the argument. 'Is that fair?'

Gerald whistled, guessing the playful intellectual's game. 'That's a bit rich, mate. Don't complicate the issue. If he wants to get better, he'll give up smoking.'

'Would you?' came his wife's retort, a reformed smoker herself. 'You'd find it hard, I expect.'

'Yes, love. I know,' the Irishman stuck his polite tongue out. 'But faced with certain death, I'm sure I'd have enough motivation to stop.'

Seizing his moment before the party trooped off to the restaurant, Jeff set out to canvas some more opinions for the decision he and his sister needed to make on behalf of their murderous parent. He and Lynn had promised that the indelicate topic should not dominate their dinner table conversation, particularly with their inquisitive children absorbing every word.

'OK, then... Hypothetical: if you were in a maximum security prison with the very real prospect of dying before the end of your sentence, would you want to prolong your life?'

Another shrill blast of air burst through the businessman's pursed lips. 'Well... Depends on how long I'd survive after a transplant, compared with how long before I'm likely to be released.'

'He'll never get released,' Madalena snapped. 'My grandparents won't go for it.'

Jeff leaned into her arm kindly. 'I'm not sure their opinion'd hold enough weight these days, to be honest. Would you agree to it? Now you've seen him again?'

'Jesus, *chico*. I dunno. He couldn't kill anyone now, could 'e?'

'I doubt it,' the intellectual chuckled. 'And where the hell would he go? He'd have to live with you or me. Not sure any of us wants that. I certainly don't want him hanging around Lynn and the kids while I'm travelling. But anyway... Even though it's unlikely, does he deserve his freedom and a chance of a healthier future? The Jaworski parents... if they're still alive... they don't get their sons back if Dad gets released. Their kids don't get their fathers back.'

'Good point,' Gerald nodded. 'That's a sensible way to look at it. It's not as if some magic gets woven to make everything alright again just because a convicted man's done his time at Her Majesty's.'

'Yeah. But isn't that exactly what justice is supposed to amount to?' the philosopher contradicted. 'Isn't that the idea of a sentence in the first place? Let the punishment fit the crime? By the time you get out, everything'll be back to normal.'

'I don't think so,' Celia shook her head. 'Not when we're talking about murder. I'd prefer life to mean life.'

Jeff nodded. 'Yeah. I'm with you, Missus B, if they're like Dad and not genuinely rehabilitated. A lot of people don't think that way though. One murderer's not necessarily like the next murderer.'

The Blakes laughed, ending up precisely where they had started, which was often the case in the company of this philosophical acrobat. Madalena had become completely lost by now, idly playing with her empty beer glass and kicking her feet, staring around the room as if she were waiting to be excused from detention.

'Whatever...' her brother continued. 'It's not likely to happen in Dad's case, so we don't have to solve that conundrum today. His counsellor told us he was going downhill pretty fast. I need to find out what they reckon his life expectancy would be if he had a transplant, but personally, I don't think he's strong enough.'

'And 'e doesn't want one,' the bored woman interjected.

Celia was surprised. 'Oh. Is that what he told you today?'

'Yep. Pretty much,' the celebrity confirmed. 'He needs some time to sleep on it. I've asked him to let me know what he wants. At the end of the day, it's his choice, but I just want to hear as many different opinions as I can, in case he abdicates the responsibility to us.'

'Well... If it helps,' the distinguished lady offered, having lost her own father to cancer many years ago, 'I would take whatever options were open to me because you never know what scientific developments might be discovered and suddenly become available.'

Gerald scoffed at his wife. 'Darling, we're talking a matter of months! With the best will in the world, there won't be any new discoveries by then.'

'No. Maybe not. Thanks anyway, Celia,' the empath smiled. 'It's the principle though. It's good to know what other people might want.'

'Sorry, dear,' the accountant said, feeling guilty for poo-pooing his wife's comment. 'As for me, I'd tend towards the pain relief option, in your father's position. In my own position, of course I'd go for the transplant, the chemo' and the pain relief, because hopefully my family wouldn't want me to give up.'

'Are you sure about that?' the quick-witted star quipped, winking at Celia. 'They might be glad to see the back of you.'

This dangerous jibe broke Madalena out of her apathy. 'You guys are funny! D'you care if Dad lives or dies, *chico*?'

Her brother exhaled. Reaching for his lighter, he turned it over a few times in his left hand while gathering his thoughts, the habitual storm clouds converging overhead. He offered his packet of cigarettes around. Gerald lit his own and their discourteous guest's, leaving the impressive leader to light up and reflect on his response.

'Whoa!' he answered after a long pause, nodding to his sister. 'I require notice of such questions, Lena. Do I care if he lives or dies?'

'You don't have to answer in front of us, dear,' Celia suggested, seeing the young man's disquiet.

'No. That's not what's making me hesitate. My answer's no, Lena. I don't care. In my opinion, it depends on who it affects... His constituency, as Lynn's sick of hearing me harp on about. I don't care for myself, or for you, Lena, really.'

He saw his sister's bottom lip curl, wishing he could read the rogue thought rattling around her empty head. 'And not for our mum. She doesn't give a damn from where she is. Maybe a little for our kids because they won't know much about their granddad. But then again, they weren't going to ever really know him.'

Madalena nodded, the convoluted opinion gradually making sense. 'Yeah. Same. I don't need 'im in my life.'

The songwriter groaned, missing his dream girl's steadying hand. 'Wrong, isn't it? Don't you think? We should want our parents around forever. Isn't that the moral thing to want?'

'Under normal circumstances,' the supportive grandfather agreed. 'But not necessarily. You said yourself, everyone's circumstances are different. You're trying to do the best you can to make his last days comfortable. That may be more than he deserves after the life he gave you.'

The street-girl's eyes lit up, and she slapped her bare thighs where her skirt had ridden up in the couch's pliable cushions. '*Ezzackly!* What did 'e ever do for us?'

Jeff shook his head. He was getting slightly more than he bargained for in this conversation; all excellent material for his forthcoming introspection with Lynn on the flight back to Melbourne, and doubtless a few songs for their musical into the bargain.

'How old is your father?' Celia asked the matching pair.

Paul Diamond's offspring both shrugged, then laughed at each others' identical responses. The superstar felt ashamed that neither had this basic information memorised, attempting the calculation from known statistics.

'So you're thirty-two next birthday, Lena, which means they were married in 'forty-eight. And he would've been eighteen or nineteen then?'

'Nineteen, I reckon,' the clueless sibling guessed.

'OK. Let's say nineteen. So that'd make him fifty-two.'

'Younger than us,' Gerald observed to his wife.

'Yes, dear. Most people are these days.'

Madalena laughed in response to her brother's nudge. 'You look much better than 'e did,' she complimented her hosts. 'So it's not all 'cause o' the ciggies!'

All four shared a wry chuckle at this conclusion, turning their heads towards noises from the hallway. Rapid footsteps clattered down the stairs, with a triumphant whoop followed by a heavy thud to signify that a small boy had launched himself from the sixth step and survived to tell the tale.

'Fifty-two's not old, is it, dear?' Celia reinforced.

'Depends on your perspective,' Jeff teased his friend's mother, grabbing hold of his re-energised son and hoisting him high in the air. 'Does fifty-two sound old to you, Jet-star?'

'Fifty-two!' the human comet yelled at the top of his voice, as if it were the biggest number he had ever heard. 'Who's fifty-two?'

'Granddad?' his mum assumed, seeing the lad turn to his little sister for moral support.

'Wow! That's very, very old. Older than you even,' the child shouted at his dad.

'This is true. Older than me even,' Jeff admitted, kissing his wife and ruffling their daughter's freshly-combed hair. 'It'd be hard to have a dad younger than me, now wouldn't it, genius boy?'

'Is that how old your dad is?' Lynn asked. 'Only fifty-two?'

'How old's your father, Lynn?' Gerald chipped in.

'He was born in 'thirty-two. Both my parents were. Fifty next year. Wow! We'd better start planning for a party. Thanks for the heads-up!'

'Not even fifty yet,' the middle-aged lady groaned. 'Well, that definitely makes us the oldest people in the world, doesn't it, Jet?'

'You're not the oldest person in the world, Auntie Celia,' the boy insisted, putting on the sweetest smile and receiving a cuff round the ear from his father, who would have done the same if he hadn't been so old.

'The second oldest,' the rock star mocked. 'Who do you think is older, mate?'

'My form teacher. She's ancient!'

'Ancient?' his mother repeated. 'Where did you hear that word? This woman must be forty, tops!'

'She's had a hard life then,' Jeff joked. 'Like Dad.'

'Shit!' Madalena exclaimed, before clapping an apologetic hand to her mouth. 'How can you say 'e's 'ad an 'ard life? He's been in that bloody hostel all 'is life.'

Everyone stared in silence, paralysed by the uncouth verbal shower, before one-by-one deciding to laugh politely for the sake of the youngsters. Kierney hurried to put her hands over her ears to block the naughty words that had escaped from her auntie's mouth.

'Never a dull moment when you're here, Lena!' Jeff told her. 'Cool it around the kids, will you, please?'

'Sorry,' she said, shocked at the attention her comment had received.

Celia lifted the little girl up and planted a kiss on her tiny nose. 'Right then! Are we ready to eat? Your hair's still a bit wet, darling. Did you have a good sleep?'

'Yes, thank you. Now I'm hungry for *pasta*.'

'Are you indeed? So am I. Good girl,' Gerald praised, getting to his feet to say hello to the pretty toddler. 'You look lovely in that dress.'

Lynn and Jeff leaned into each other, wondering if they were both struck by the same thought: it was nice to be among caring, loving people who said what they meant and meant what they said. Was Madalena thinking the same thing? Or was she simply focussed on where her next drink might come from?

'Thanks, Uncle Gerald,' Lynn replied on her daughter's behalf. 'It's actually the same dress she wore to see Granddad, but we won't tell anyone.'

Kierney put a finger to her lips, shushing everyone. Her papá went to retrieve the future sporting champion, who was balancing on the arm of the couch to check out the impressive cabinet full of golfing and rugby trophies Gerald and his son had collected over the years.

'Let's get this show on the road,' Jeff called them all to attention. 'Who's going with the Blakes, and who's coming with us?'

'You go with Celia and Gerald,' his wife suggested. 'And take one of the kids with you. Then we'll follow you.'

'OK. Sounds good,' their leader answered, whisking his daughter into his arms. 'Thanks, angel. Woohoo! I get to have the hangover tomorrow, Kizzo!'

The loving child spread the palms of her hands over her daddy's forehead in advance of his pain and kissed it too for good measure. Her big brother, accepting his mother's hand, thought only to chant the word "hangover" in a menacing tone, over and over again while they left the house.

'Thanks, gorgeous,' Jeff said, touched by Kierney's compassionate act. 'I'll make sure my head remembers that kiss in the morning.'

The group filed out and loaded into the two cars. Gerald swang his black BMW round in the driveway, and Lynn turned onto the street behind it in their anonymous, rented Holden.

'Is that car the same as Uncle Gerry's?' Jet asked his mother, smearing his pointing finger across the side window.

'Yes. I think so. It looks powerful, doesn't it?'

'Yeah!' the boy approved. 'Please can we swap on the way home?'

'I expect that'd be fine, if you're not already asleep. Then you won't notice which car you're in.'

'I will,' Jet insisted. 'I'll dream faster.'

Madalena chortled at her nephew's quirky reply. 'You *are* like your dad! They're not drivin' very fast, eh?'

'I know! Dad'll be saying, "Come on, come on,"' the boy laughed, swerving round imaginary corners and pretending to lean on the horn.

'Are you hungry, Lena?' Lynn asked her passenger. 'I'm still recovering from all that sugar.'

'I'm always hungry. What d'ya reckon Granddad's having for dinner, Jet?'

The driver smiled, looking in the rear-view mirror to watch her son's reaction.

'Granddad? *Pasta* with meatballs.'

'No. That's what *you're* going to have,' the born teacher rejected his reply. 'What do you think the cook in the prison will make for all those men?'

Her son took a moment to consider the image of eating meals in the inhospitable, reverberating building. 'Chips!' he offered. 'Granddad said he wanted hot chips.'

'That's right. 'E did,' his auntie confirmed. 'And rubbery steak.'

'Rubbery?' Jet scoffed, confused as to why a piece of beef might be described in such a way. 'That sounds disgusting.'

'Yeah. It prob'ly will be disgustin',' Madalena agreed. 'Cooked for too long. D'ya reckon they 'ave food fights in jail?'

Lynn glanced sideways at her sister-in-law, hoping she didn't intend putting too many evil thoughts into the lad's sponge-like brain. Given recent form, he was bound to choose a lull in the conversation to try them out on Celia and Gerald, and perhaps one or two of their well-to-do neighbours too.

'What are you going to tell your friends at school about your granddad?' the young mum changed the subject.

Jet stared out of the window while he thought. 'I'll tell them that my granddad looks like my dad but much more wrinkly, and that he's not very well and coughs all the time,' he paused to provide a demonstration, finishing off with repulsive choking and spitting sounds. 'And that the man looking after him wouldn't let him keep Dad's ring.'

'Good boy, Jetto. A bit too much reality, but that's a pretty good summary.'

Having eschewed the morbid conversation to everyone's satisfaction, dinner was relaxed and entertaining. The children were in high spirits, and the staff curried favour with their famous guests by offering them a tour of the kitchens and a free bottle of champagne. With the latter declined and the former obligatory, the wine began to flow while they tucked into the delicious authentic dishes.

'Look at me!' Madalena smoothed the borrowed blouse over her bulging stomach. 'I'm so stuffed, I look pregnant.'

'Oh, sweet Jesus!' her brother moaned, tossing his napkin in the air. 'Not again, please.'

Gerald chuckled. 'That response only usually comes from the husband,' he slurred his words.

'I want a Diamond cousin,' Jet declared.

'I'd *like* a Diamond cousin,' Lynn corrected him, rocking a drowsy Kierney on her knee. 'You've already got two cousins, greedy-guts. Dyson cousins. Auntie Lena doesn't want another devil like you to look after.'

'I'm not a devil!'

'No, you're not. That's true. You just behave like one from time to time. Sorry, darling. But it's hard work looking after children.'

'Remember you're going back to school, Lena,' Jeff reminded his sister. 'We made a deal.'

She grimaced. 'Oh, yeah. That was a bloody stupid thing to say yes to, weren' it?'

'No, it's not,' the kind man countered. 'What's stupid about it?'

Madalena shrugged. 'Nothin'. I forgot everything from school, but. It'd be like startin' again.'

'You can come with me, Auntie Lena,' the two-year-old suggested from the warmth of her mum's lap. 'I'm going to school soon.'

'You are,' Celia crooned. 'That'll be exciting, won't it, darling? Just like your clever big brother.'

Jet's chest puffed out at the compliment. 'She won't be in my class.'

His father looked up from the credit card docket he was signing. 'Who won't?' he pulled the boy up on his poor manners.

'Kierney won't be in my class. She's too little.'

'That's right. Good boy. Your sister will be in a different class to yours,' the grandmother nodded. 'You enjoy yourself a bit longer before you have to go to school, Kierney, darling.'

Lynn sighed. 'That's good advice, Auntie Celia. Thank you. Funny, isn't it? Before they reach school age, all they want to do is go to school. And when they're at school, they want to stay at home and play instead.'

'Bit like marriage,' the quiet accountant remarked from the other end of the table, puffing on a cigar.

The Diamonds smiled at each other in mild shock, and then at the dignified housewife, who shrugged dismissively as if she had heard it all a thousand times before. Now they knew where Gerry got his indomitability from!

'Right! Sorry to hear that,' the world's happiest husband smirked. 'Evidently, I must go to a very good school.'

'Are you going back to school too, Dad?' Jet stared at his father. 'Why?'

'No, mate. Just a joke. D'you want some of Kizzy's *pasta*?'

His dream girl smiled, squeezing the attentive dad's hand under the table. In fact, their Good School concept had come to fruition, and they were looking forward to pitching an overseas expansion to potential investors and funding bodies in the coming weeks.

'Thanks,' she nudged him. 'I think I should put my fees up then.'

'How *élitiste* of you,' Jeff teased. 'I didn't realise I went to such a snooty school.'

'Times've changed, haven't they, Lynn?' Gerald backed her up, ever the sucker for a stunning, long-legged blonde. 'You can't keep on letting any old riff-raff in.'

The adults laughed; all except Madalena, unable to relate to the highbrowed discourse around her. The two youngsters began to droop into their dessert bowls, leading the famous couple to pass on coffee. The multi-millionnaire recovered his credit card from the awestruck cashier, and everyone piled out of the restaurant and into the cool evening air.

Jeff and Lynn carried the small, limp bodies up to bed as soon as they reached the house, neither child waking while their shoes and clothes were peeled off. Madalena was invited for a nightcap but decided she would turn in as well. Following a rather unsubtle hint from her brother, she thanked her hosts for accommodating her and wished them a good night. The remaining four adults talked trivia over coffee before they too called it a night.

'Sleep well, dears,' their host said. 'We'll see you for breakfast in the morning. No rush.'

'Thanks, Celia,' the young mum replied. 'You too. What time are Jacinta and company arriving?'

'I'm not sure. She normally rings as they're leaving. Not before midday anyway.'

Jeff grinned. '*¡Excelente!* That'll give us plenty of time to get the wildcat home. Thanks for putting up with her tonight, guys.'

'She's really no trouble,' Gerald said. 'A few dropped consonants never 'urt no-one.'

Laughing, the boy from Canley Vale put a grateful hand on the city gent's shoulder. 'Cheers, sir. I know you don't mean that. It's like having a third kid who just doesn't get it. She's changing though, isn't she, angel? Slowly. But there's progress every time we see her.'

'Yes. Definitely,' Lynn affirmed. 'She's beginning to think a bit more widely. Less about herself. Stop worrying, baby bro'.'

'Worried? Who's worried? We just have to listen for our kids calling people dumb-asses and hopping about saying, "Effin' ribbit." Jesus!'

The reserved accountant gave his son's famous mate a look of horror. The parents turned and sighed to each other in frustration, not keen to relive the experience. Fortunately, Celia promised to fill her husband in on the fun he had missed earlier in the day.

'OK. Sleep well,' Jeff said to the Blakes, putting a flamboyant arm around his beautiful best friend. 'Enjoy that nice, comfortable bed, Celia, and you enjoy the couch, Gerald. I'm off to school now.'

Lynn rolled her eyes. 'Please! And we're worried about Lena's influence...'

***

'*Lena, es Jeff,*' the superstar said into the telephone speaker from his hotel room. '*¿Qué tal?*'

'Yeah. Hi, *chico*,' a cheerful voice responded. '*¿Qué pasa?*'

'He's dead,' he saw little point in dressing up his news. 'Dad died yesterday.'

The traveller was in Brussels attending a series of meetings at a summit for African peace and prosperity. The call from his management company had woken him early the previous morning. Parklea Prison's mental health counsellor had rung to inform him that his relative was close to passing away. The message hadn't been relayed to the busy negotiator for two hours, but as soon as he found out, he had jumped on the line with his fading father.

The estranged pair had struggled through a long, calm and determinative conversation, during which Paul Diamond apologised to his family for what he had put them through. Between agonising bouts of coughing, the compassionate son did his best to help his murderous nemesis find solace. The last fifteen minutes of this sobering interaction fast-forwarded through his head again while he spoke to his sister.

'Oh, fuck,' Jeff heard Madalena gasp. 'Why?'

'Why?' he repeated. 'That I can't answer. You OK?'

There was silence from the other end of the line, punctuated only by deep breathing. The woman was more shaken than her brother had expected, and he wished he could see her face, so that he might know better how to respond.

'Lena? Are you still there?'

'Yeah. I'm 'ere. I just don't know what to say. I dunno if I'm sad or not.'

'No. I know,' Jeff agreed. 'I was the same. I didn't know what to say when the prison rang this morning.'

'What did they say?'

'Are you OK to talk for a few minutes?' the songwriter checked. 'Are you sitting down at least?'

'Yeah.'

'Good. Cheers,' he continued. 'I'm in Europe. They rang a while ago. I had to go through this whole complex identification process to confirm I was me, which was ridiculous because I'd only spoken to them yesterday.'

'Why?' the Sydneysider asked again. 'Didn't they ring you?'

'Yeah. Nuts, huh?' he replied. 'They just needed to make sure they were giving the information to the right person, I s'pose. Anyway... Apparently, Dad had a huge coughing fit two days ago, and they put him in the sick bay. The doctor saw him and gave him some painkillers and a sedative, then left him to sleep for a couple of hours.'

'What's that?'

Her brother scoffed kindly. 'A sedative, or sleep?'

'Fuck off. I know what sleep is. The other one,' Madalena whined.

'Something to calm him down. To make him drowsy. Maybe he was panicking 'cause he couldn't stop coughing? I don't know.'

'So then what happened?'

'The next morning, he was transferred to Fairfield Hospital under armed guard, and they gave him a heart and lung scan which showed that the cancer had spread all over. They asked him if he wanted chemo', but he said no.'

'What will chemo' do?' his sister enquired again.

'Well, nothing now,' Jeff responded, chuckling at her bizarre choice of tense. 'He's dead.'

'¡*Ai!*' she shrieked. 'For Christ's sake, don't joke about it. Aren't you upset?'

'No. Are you?'

'Dunno. A bit. Shocked, right now.'

'Yeah, well... I was shocked in the beginning, but it didn't last long,' her brother replied. 'I talked to him for nearly an hour yesterday. He was ready to go. He knew he wasn't going to last much longer; told me the medics gave him morphine for the pain. Supposedly, the doc' told them to ring me yesterday morning, but somehow no-one got round to it. And then, while they weren't ringing me, he asked to see Chris Williams, the counsellor. D'you remember her?'

'The shrink woman?' Madalena confirmed. 'I didn't see 'er. That was before I got there.'

'Yep. That's right. I forgot. Well, she called me instead and put him on the line when I 'phoned back. Afterwards, it seems he asked her to write something in a letter to the two of us, which she did.'

'What's in it?'

Jeff chuckled. 'Don't know yet. The people I spoke to a few minutes ago didn't know what happened to the letter, so I guess it's coming in the post. Hopeless really. Comedy of errors, but it doesn't matter. Two hours later, he was dead.'

Another short period of silence followed, and the songwriter sat immersed in his own thoughts while he waited. Had he omitted anything?

'Wow!' the Sydneysider spoke, almost in a whisper. 'So that's it.'

'Yeah. That's it,' he laughed. 'We're finally orphans after so long feeling like one. How does it feel?'

'Weird,' Madalena confessed. 'Real bloody weird. I dunno what to think. Do Lynn and the kids know?'

'No. Not yet. They're at Benloch, the Dysons' farm. It's school holidays, so she's taken them up there for a long weekend. I rang but only got to leave a message.'

'Are you OK? I didn't know you hadn't talked to 'er.'

Jeff sighed and caught his breath, always surprised to hear his sister enquire after his wellbeing. 'Yeah. I will soon. I'm fine, Lena, thanks,' his voice cracked. 'It's nice to talk to you though. I needed to share it with you and test your reaction.'

The prostitute exhaled. 'So what next? What do we 'ave to do? Funeral?'

'Yep,' the superstar replied. 'I have to go up there again. I'm cutting short my trip and I'll probably fly back tomorrow. I'm in the middle of cancelling a few appointments. Luckily, I didn't have much on before the weekend. D'you want to come with me?'

'Where?'

Her brother laughed. 'To Parklea. Get with the program, woman!'

'Hey! Shut up, *culo*,' Madalena moaned. 'I don't know about these things.'

'I don't know about these things either,' Jeff assured her. 'I'm just following my gut. And right now it's telling me I'd like you to come with me to the prison, to sign the death certificate and collect his belongings. After that, we need to figure out if he's going to be buried or cremated, then book a funeral and lay him to rest finally.'

'Good riddance.'

'D'you really mean that?' Jeff asked. 'Was your initial reaction just surprise, like mine? Aren't you in the least bit sad?'

'Na. Not now anyways,' the prostitute answered. 'Maybe I will be later. Wonder what's in the letter...'

'OK. Yeah. So do I,' her brother agreed. 'I'm going to try and get hold of Chris, just to make sure it's been sent out. I don't want her to tell me what's in it though. I'd prefer to read it as if it were coming directly from Dad. She might be able to fax it to me.'

'Fax?' his sister asked again. 'What's fax?'

'Just some new-fangled machine that can send and receive stuff quickly. D'you want me to ring you when I get it?'

'When you comin' 'ere? I'll see it when you come.'

'OK. I'm going to see if I can get a flight home tonight or tomorrow morning. Can I stay at your place for a couple of nights, please, or will you be busy?' he asked, cringing at his pathetic euphemism.

'You can't stay at my place. It's a dump,' the woman whined. 'And I will be busy, unless I have to cancel 'em for you. Do I?'

Jeff smiled to himself. He couldn't blame her. What a pair they were! Neither in the least bit grief-stricken about the death of their father; one annoyed to be missing a bunch of appointments which stood to bring more grandstanding opportunities, and the other not affected sufficiently to stop humping strangers for money. Their very different worlds were equally bizarre!

'No. Don't cancel anything. I'll give Alberto a call later this morning. See if I can crash at his place.'

'At the club?' Madalena exclaimed. 'What's 'appened to you? Are you broke?'

The celebrity laughed aloud. 'No! I just don't fancy being there on my own, that's all.'

'Oh, right. Sorry, *chico*. If you can't stay at Alberto's then, come to my place.'

'It's fine, Lena. There's always Celia's spare room. Or she can roll out a sleeping bag for me on her lounge room floor.'

A screech burst through the telephone and into the millionnaire's ear. 'That's a joke! So when's the funeral going to be?'

'Who knows?' Jeff answered. 'I don't know how soon we can get everything arranged. I can't imagine there'll be a queue of people wanting to see him off.'

'Ha! I don't even wanna go,' his sister sneered. 'Do we 'ave to 'ave a funeral?'

'Yeah. Of course we do. We had one for Mamá, so we'll have one for Dad too. It's the respectful thing to do.'

'OK, boss. Whatever.'

'I wonder if he had a will...' the young man mused. 'We should wait 'til we read it, in case he had some special wishes about his funeral. Like he converted to Buddhism or something.'

'Buddhism? What difference does that make?' Madalena whined.

'I'm just kidding,' her brother whined back. 'We just need to make sure he didn't want to be cremated, if we decide to bury him. Or *vice versa*. We buried *Bubshka* and *Dziadek*, so I guess we do the same for Dad.'

'Did we?'

'Yes,' Jeff sighed, less annoyed at her lack of recall than at his own plight, having to arrange everything without any help. 'I'm not going to do all this on my own this time, Lena. You're older than me; his first. You should help out.'

'I'm no good at stuff like that,' his sister moaned.

'I'm no good at stuff like that either.'

'Yeah. But you always know what to do. I wouldn't 'ave a clue.'

Never a truer word spoken, the songwriter sniffed. 'OK. *No importa.* I don't want to fight about it. Are you going to tell *Abuela*?'

'Shit!' Madalena cried out. 'She's going to be dancing in the street.'

'Yeah. I'll bet,' the abandoned grandson's response was laced with sarcasm. 'Nasty old cow. Will you tell her, please?'

'Alright,' came a half-hearted promise.

'Hey, Lena. Don't forget, please. She wouldn't speak to me anyway. Look, I have to go. I'll ring you later, once I know what I'm doing.'

'OK, *chico*,' his sister said, sounding a little deflated. 'See ya.'

'Yeah. *Adiós.*'

Jeff sat back on the couch in the well-appointed meeting room he had been allocated at the European Law Courts, numbed by his own indifference. Why didn't he feel sorrow? In fact, he felt worse for not feeling anything. He recalled how emotional he had been on leaving his father only a week ago, right up until the parting salvo which had floored him.

There was no sign of this rekindled familial bond today, even to mourn his father's loss. Was finding out about another brother the reason? Or perhaps it was the old man's very brief association with his grandkids. Perhaps seeing them all thrust together into such an artificial sketch had cultivated some temporal feeling of connectedness then made redundant by the bolt of reality.

The telephone rang beside the bewildered celebrity, triggering a tug on the end of his invisible elastic connection. '¡*Olá, mi Regala!*' he sang into the receiver, which retained the previous call's heat.

'How did you know it was me?' Lynn's voice abounded with healing properties, educing a huge sigh of relief from somewhere deep within. 'Are you OK? What's up? Sorry not to call sooner. I've only just got your message.'

'No worries. I've been on the 'phone anyway. To Lena... Dad died,' Jeff's mood crashed, suddenly overcome with the sorrow that had previously eluded him. 'This morning.'

'Oh, no,' his wife whispered. 'I'm sorry. No wonder you're not OK. Did Parklea ring you?'

'Yeah. He just carked it,' the traveller confirmed, wiping the tears off his face. 'He was put into hospital the day before yesterday and only lasted another twenty-four hours.'

'Oh. That's sad. Sorry I wasn't here when you rang earlier. You'd better hurry up and get that cellular telephony thing happening.'

The venture capitalist chuckled. 'That's right. Jesus, you're such an angel,' he sighed. 'I already feel better.'

'Good,' Lynn said. 'I love you. Are you flying back? Do you want us to come home?'

'Yes, I do. But don't,' her husband's emphatic voice commanded. 'And I love you too. I'm going to get a flight to Sydney tonight or tomorrow morning. I've been talking to Lena for the last half-hour. Christ. She's a useless human being, baby. Totally bloody useless. I only asked her to do one thing, and that was to tell our *abuela*, but I can't be certain she'll even do that.'

'They don't need to know straightaway, do they?' Lynn sought to allay his fears. 'That can wait for a few days. What can I do?'

'Nothing, gorgeous,' Jeff said, composing himself. 'I've cancelled everything else in Brussels and asked Rae to postpone all my appointments for two weeks, so I'm clear to focus on this now. Apparently, he asked the counsellor... you know, Chris... to write a letter to Lena and me, so I'm going to try to get hold of her to find out what she did with it. And I need to know if he had a will, so I can arrange the right type of funeral.'

'I must be able to help with some of that,' the star's right-hand woman insisted. 'Please, Jeff?'

'Sure. Thanks. Once I know what needs to be done. Will you tell the kids for me, please? I don't think I could tell them over the 'phone. Too far away to share a cuddle.'

'That's fine,' his wife assured him. 'I'll ask them to save their cuddles up. Are you going to stay with the Blakes again.'

This time, the man's laughter contained a fair measure of bitterness. 'Na! You wouldn't believe it. Well, maybe you would...'

'Believe what? Is everything alright with them?'

'Oh, yeah. Well... I can't confirm that because I haven't spoken to them. I mean my sweetheart sister. I asked if I could crash at her place 'cause I didn't want to end up in an anonymous hotel room tomorrow night. But of course, she's entertaining.'

Lynn let out a soft, sympathetic chuckle. 'Life goes on.'

'*Exactement.* Dad should think himself bloody lucky she gave him two hours of her life last week. I assume she'll organise her appointments around the funeral. Or maybe she won't.'

'Oh, I'm sure she will,' the kind woman countered. 'The significance'll probably set in over the course of the day.'

'Hmm... You're right, I guess. I have to give her the benefit of the doubt. I hear ya, lady!'

'*Bueno, y te amo, Papá.* Are you sure you don't want some help with all this?' the master project manager reiterated. 'I can leave the kids with Mum and Dad for a few days and meet you in Sydney. They'd understand.'

'Yes, ma'am. I'd absolutely love that,' he responded, almost weakening, 'but I need to force Lena to share the responsibility, don't I? I'm learning, Lynn. Slowly.'

'You are!' she encouraged. 'And it hurts, I can tell. Now I feel like you do, wanting to take your pain away.'

Jeff felt a lump in his throat again, and tears stung in his eyes. 'Jesus, angel. Where did you come from?'

'You *regala*'d me, remember?' his dream girl's bright Melbourne Academy voice threw him back in time. 'Let me know what I can do. OK? Promise?'

'Sure thing. Go and hug the kids for me, and I'll ring again later with my plan of attack.'

'OK, gorgeous,' Lynn agreed. 'Good luck with Chris, and with Lena.'

'Thanks. I need it! Talk later. I love you.'

'Bye, Jeff. Safe journey home. I love you heaps.'

Feeling much stronger, the orphaned world-changer sprang off the couch and poured himself a second cup of coffee. He lifted the telephone again, this time to change his flight.

***

Stirring in three spoonfuls of sugar, Jeff took his mug and a banana into the office which gave over the atrium at the core of his five-star hotel in the area east of Brussels that had been designated for *la Cité Européene*, between the Royal Palace and the museums in *le Parc du Cinquantenaire*. Through the window, he could see various people going about their business, walking with purpose in all directions as if it were the marching band's very first rehearsal. He stood and watched the show while he ate, wondering what they were all doing in this brand new political arena.

He picked up the receiver, swallowing down his last mouthful. 'Hello. Is that Chris Williams?' he asked, hearing a woman's voice.

'Yes. This is Chris,' came the reply. 'Who's speaking?'

'Jeff Diamond.'

The celebrity heard the woman clear her throat, most likely trying to refresh her memory about what he did or didn't know about the prisoner's last hours. 'Yes. Good morning, Mister Diamond. How are you?'

'Jeff, please. Better than Dad,' he answered with a dry chuckle, 'if you don't mind the humour.'

The counsellor laughed. 'Good. So you know of his passing.'

'Yes, I do. The office rang me this morning,' the young man confirmed. 'They told me he asked to see you and that there may've been some sort of letter for me and my sister.'

'Yes. That's right. There is. I spent a couple of hours with your father. He was very close to death at that time and not always terribly coherent.'

'OK. Thanks,' Jeff relaxed a little. 'Do you happen to know if he had a will?'

'No, I don't,' Chris answered. 'The registrar'll have all that information for you. I can ask her to ring you, if you like.'

'No. Don't worry. I'm overseas at the moment, flying in the day after tomorrow. I'll sort all that out when I get there. I'd just like to know what happened to the letter, please.'

'I posted it that evening,' Chris said, with a hint of regret in her voice. 'I should've realised he was in danger of passing on soon.'

'Was he at peace with everything?'

'Yes. I believe he was. I won't pre-empt what the letter says, but your father was calm and expressed some very genuine wishes.'

'Excellent,' Jeff muttered, mainly to himself. 'You probably guessed, but we haven't had the greatest relationship, he and I.'

'Of course,' the counsellor said, ever professional. 'I've seen many fractured families over the years. It's a shame.'

The intellectual took a deep breath. 'D'you have a copy of the letter still, Chris? It'd be handy to know what's in it while I'm up there over the next few days, to help with the organisation. If he wanted anything particular by way of funeral, *et cetera.*'

'Yes, Jeff. I do have a copy,' she informed him. 'We're obliged to keep a record of all prisoner correspondence. But I can tell you now that it doesn't contain any practical requests. As I said, he wasn't fully aware of what he was saying towards the end of our session.'

'Fair enough. Thanks again. That's all I need to know really. I'll maybe see you the morning after next, if you're around. I don't even know what day it is. Tuesday?'

The woman in Sydney chuckled. 'Yes. Tuesday today. I'll be in the medical centre all day Thursday. I'll have coffee and your favourite biscuits here waiting.'

The superstar laughed. 'Does everyone know about my Monte Carlo fetish now?'

'I'm afraid so. News like that spreads like wildfire here, you know,' Chris answered. 'It's not every day we get a visit from a famous family. It's priceless information, you and your biscuits.'

His latest call to Parklea concluded, Jeff kept the receiver next to his ear while dialling Gerry's office number. He took a few more deep breaths as he waited for the line to connect. For a rotten old sod who had been all but forgotten, there was still a fair mess to tidy up. He could have done with his sexy planner *extraordinaire* sitting beside him after all.

'Paula, hi. It's Jeff,' he said to the flirty Blake & Partners executive assistant. 'Please could I speak to Gerry very quickly?'

'Morning, Jeff. Yes. Hold on,' the efficient woman must have cottoned on to the urgency in his voice.

'Mate!' his manager's usual boisterousness rang through the telephone and vibrated in the caller's ear, which was beginning to sting after having been attached to hot plastic all morning.

'G'day, mate. Listen… I just need to tell you something, and I don't want a long and drawn out conversation about it, if that's OK.'

'Oh. Right you are,' Gerry answered, curious. 'What's wrong? The lovely Lynn seen sense and dumped you?'

'No! You'd never get that lucky, mate. Nothing's wrong,' Jeff replied, shaking his head. 'My dad died yesterday.'

'Oh, shit!' the accountant exclaimed. 'You said nothing was wrong. I'm sorry, old boy.'

'Yeah. Thanks, mate,' his friend dismissed the sympathy as politely as he could. 'You know we didn't think much of each other, so it's no big deal. I'm just ringing to say that I'm flying to Sydney as soon as I can, to make whatever arrangements need making. I've cancelled all my appointments via Rae. Just so you know I'm back in Oz tomorrow night, that's all.'

'Christ, Jeff,' Gerry cursed, unable to grasp how his normally super-passionate friend could be so detached about his father's demise. 'Are you alright?'

'Yeah, mate. Don't worry about me. I'm on autopilot right now. I'll see you after the weekend.'

'Is Lynn going with you? Do you want some company?'

'No. All good. I'm going there straight from Brussels. No need for any pomp and circumstance. We'll all go to the funeral, I expect, but there's no sense in Lynn and the kids... or you or Cath... dragging around with me over the next few days.'

'Right you are, mate. Bloody mess,' Gerry said. 'Let me know if you need us to do anything from here.'

'Sure will,' Jeff acknowledged the magnanimous offer made on behalf of the man's many minions. 'Like kill my sister, for example. Cheers, mate. I might well take you up on that one.'

'I see. No worries then. *Bonne chance*, mate.'

The telephone line went dead. This time, the multi-millionnaire placed it back on the receiver, rubbing his burning right ear. Who was next? Flights or Alberto? He dialled Raelene at his management company to ask her to book the earliest flight to Sydney and then turned his attention to the ageing boxing club owner in Fairfield.

'Hello? Is Alberto there, please?' he asked the woman who answered the phone.

The voice hadn't belonged to Eva. Could the revitalised sports club afford a receptionist these days? After a few seconds' pause and some muffled words in the background, Jeff heard the familiar heavy Chilean accent.

'Who this?' the old man's tone conveyed considerable suspicion.

'*Olá, Alberto. Es bien. Soy Jeff Diamond en la línea,*' the former local announced. '*¿Qué tal, señor?*'

'*Olá, Jeff,*' the old man replied. '*¡Madre de Dios! Muy bien. ¿Y tú?*'

Even after all these years, the lost boy couldn't stop himself tensing up whenever he spoke to any of these voices from his past. Pleased to hear from his generous benefactor, the boxing club proprietor launched into a monologue describing the long list of events his coaches had organised since the latest injection of funds from the Diamond Celebration Foundation.

This was followed by news of Eva and his son, Felipe, who had recently returned from overseas. Business was going very well, and a few youngsters had even won medals in state bouts. The celebrity listened patiently, in no rush to pass on his own headline. In the end, the old man drew breath and remembered it had been Jeff who had initiated the call.

'*Perdóneme*, mate. *¿Por qué sonó?*' Alberto asked. '*¿Está todo OK? Lynn y los niños?*'

'*Sí, sí. Gracias. Somos fantásticos,*' the proud dad answered. '*¿Están Usted sentado?*'

'*¿Por qué, Jeff? ¿Qué ha pasado?*' the old man's voice turned fearful, sitting down as he had been advised.

'*Mi padre murió ayer,*' the star told him, once more in the numb zone. 'Lung cancer.'

'*¡Jesús Cristo!*' Alberto exclaimed. '*Mis condolencias, y a la Madalena.*'

'*Gracias, señor. Usted saben como estába con nosotros. Lo odiamos.*'

'*Sí. Ya lo se,*' the old man acknowledged. '*Esto es una cosa buena, en verdad.*'

'*¡Absolutamente!*' Jeff laughed. 'Hey, Alberto. *¿Por favor?*'

'*¿Sí, Jeff?*'

'*¿Podría yo quedarme en su lugar mañana por la noche?*' Australia's third richest citizen asked, thrown back to his teenage years, bumming a room off his neighbours when he couldn't face returning to the flat. '*Vuelo en Sydney esta noche para hacer preparativos, y no quiero quedarme en un hotel. ¿Es OK, por favor, señor?*'

'*Por supuesto. Muy, muy bueno. Es muy bienvenido, hombre,*' the old man sounded overjoyed. '*Conseguiré una botella muy buena de rioja.*'

'No way, *señor!*' Jeff objected. '*Esto será a mígo.*'

'OK. *Hasta luego. Tienes un vuelo seguro,*' Alberto signed off.

'*Adiós, señor.*'

***

The chapter on his father's last days almost complete, the author sat back and lit a cigarette, reaching down to tickle behind Indie's ears. An abiding image in his mind's eye of the deceased prisoner as a greying and decaying fifty-two-year-old had been reconstituted by a stiff-looking family portrait taken by the taciturn prison guard on that wintry day in nineteen-eighty-one.

No-one in the photograph had known how close the murderer was to death during that visit.

A recent picture of himself in a similar pose smiled up at the younger lookalike from the desk, deliberately selected by his caring teenagers for the purpose of comparison. Jeff pushed the computer keyboard away from the edge of the desk and sighed, clubbed squarely between the eyes once more by the futility of his own situation.

So why was the billionnaire tempted to attach so much significance to the old man's demise while writing his own lifestory? Nothing had changed for him on that August day. His own son had recently turned four, and he was busy scheming with Lynn's friends as to how best to celebrate her upcoming quarter-century.

Looking back over Act Two's table of contents, the grieving husband was baffled that an invisible man whom he had despised for as long as he remembered should warrant more than a couple of paragraphs, especially after he had documented an engagement in Edinburgh to the most beautiful woman in the world, a glorious wedding to the same and then the arrival of two priceless little jewels. And all this notwithstanding the countless professional accolades bestowed upon the mighty Dyson-Diamond partnership.

Indeed, by the time Jeff Diamond ascended the throne of his dubious dynasty, he already had everything he needed. Way before then, in fact. With the exception of world peace and equality among all humans, he might even have claimed he had everything he wanted too.

'Something must've changed inside me though, boy,' he explained to the dog while stroking his tummy with a socked foot.

The patient rented golden retriever hung off his master's every word, with doleful eyes and ears that pricked at the slightest hint of inbound affection. The faithful hound was by now a subject matter expert on the Diamond family, the calibre of which would have put him in high demand for pub trivia quizzes, had he been capable of sitting at a table without drooling.

'Because I did become a different man after his passing,' the forty-four-year-old added. 'The bastard neither earned it nor deserved it, but I can't deny that.'

Jeff thought back to those days in the early nineteen-eighties and to the many healthy relationships he enjoyed, both using and respecting: with his band members and other musical associates; the staff at his management company and at Blake & Partners; peacemakers the world over; and all the big-hearted, hard-working people dedicated to the various Diamond Celebration Foundation charities.

Only the previous week in fact, the humble celebrity had been reminded of an interview given by a very young Cathy Lane... probably while she was still Cathy Patterson... during which she had gone on record saying that her boss seldom pulled rank and was a lovely man to work for, but that she was never left in any doubt as to who called the shots.

Picking up another picture in the small batch that had been taken that morning at Parklea, the philosopher gazed at each smiling face in turn. He then held the snap next to one of himself and his dream girl from less than three years ago, to check the similarity between two Diamond men faced with the same looming destiny. The resemblance made him shudder, forced to refocus on Indie to quell the anxiety.

'We might've looked the same, boy,' he told his captive audience, 'but we weren't the same. We were opposites actually. One never stopped learning and changing; one never saw the point of either. One determined to succeed by pooling resources, and the other determined to fail by the fault of everyone else.'

The slim, stapled manuscript the superstar had left with his father had been the genesis of this very autobiography. Fifteen years later, the story he was so keen for the dying man to understand had since been shaped for a much wider readership. And ironically, it had taken another murdering bastard to render it as a finished article so soon.

Slapping his leg to encourage the Labrador to follow him, the widower fetched a glass of water from the kitchen and climbed the stairs. His heart skipped another beat when he looped his old leather jacket off the ornate, wooden post at the bottom of the hallway banister, feeling his "JL" tattoo give a sharp twinge. He lifted hopeful eyes to the landing, hoping to find Lynn's ghost there waiting for him.

The lady of the house had never allowed him or the children to leave anything on the staircase at Escondido. What had made him hang his coat there that evening? Bad habits were forming now that his guardian angel was no longer keeping him on the straight and narrow. Was he subconsciously rebelling against her? Surely not. Why? It showed a certain pathos to challenge someone who couldn't return fire.

Jeff opened the door to his son's bedroom in their temporary home near the northern bank of the Yarra River. Ryan had only seen it in photographs, and it contained all the possessions deemed unnecessary for university life. Harking back to the lad's tiny digs in Cambridge, with their low ceilings and cluttered mix of worn furniture, he slung the jacket onto the empty double bed.

'All yours, mate,' he said into the night air.

The proud father picked up an old cricket bat that was poking out of a battered Melbourne Academy sports bag and wielded it, fending off an imaginary fast bowler. Then, slumping down on the mattress, he delved further into the holdall and extracted a red, leather practice ball, still shiny on one hemisphere, and teased the eager canine by throwing it up in the air and catching it close to his chest.

Indie immediately jumped up and tried to grab the ball, but his master was too nimble, hiding it behind his back. The confused dog leaped up onto the bed, anxious to prove he was smarter than this. Sure enough, his keen nose soon found where the ball was tucked, requiring Jeff to struggle hard to keep both it and his fingers from being punctured by determined fangs. Who knew how many test players' wickets this ball had taken in the nets on its way to the Australian captaincy?

'Oh, no, you don't,' his master warned, showing the slobbering dog the palms of his empty hands. 'Bedtime. My fault, I'm sorry.'

Obediently, the retriever calmed down and allowed the ball to be tossed back into the bag, instead trying his luck at chewing one of the broken shoulder straps. Standing up to leave the room, the distracted author twisted the black jet-stone ring on his finger and kissed it, a discordant melody suddenly swirling in his head. Its volume was so loud that he was tempted to turn around.

'No? Not yet?'

Resolutely, the lonely man returned to fetch the leather jacket from the bed. His son would be home from university for Gerry's wedding in a few weeks' time. It was too soon to hand over this treasured heirloom in such an impersonal way. It would hurt the boy too much to find it here.

'You're an arsehole, Jeff Diamond,' the grieving husband cursed.

Lynn was reminding him that he was still prone to making outrageous statements, these days frequently as distasteful as his state of mind. Someone so decorated by the global human rights community ought to know better than to take his anger and resentment out on those around him. Full of self-loathing, the sickened world-changer pulled his son's bedroom door closed, traipsed halfway down the stairs again to sling the jacket back over the banister. His tattooed muscle began to sting as soon as he picked up the prized item, and neither did it stop when he exercised his rebellious right.

'Thanks, angel,' the contrite star whispered. 'You're right. Bad move.'

Jeff felt a little better having redressed this error of judgment. A more appropriate statement lay afoot, he was sure; a memorable way to pass on the old jacket to which his father had taken such a fancy. Just because he had committed this particular chapter to the annals of time, it didn't give him the right to ride roughshod over his precious boy's emotions.

Turning around and descending to the ground floor again, with Indie hot on his heels as ever, the songwriter let the dog into the garden. He diverted to the kitchen and opened the refrigerator, his stomach now hungry for the first time since last night's dinner. As he expected, the large appliance's contents were wholly unappetising. Groceries of any kind had been in short supply in Burnley South these last few weeks, and another day had gone by with neither dark-haired resident bothering to restock their empty cupboards.

The father chuckled to himself, opening a beer instead. The further Kierney delved into her fascinating research project at Melbourne University, the more mutinous she was becoming towards running the household. It was a passive rebellion, but he respected it wholeheartedly. At seventeen years of age, it was not her time for such mundane preoccupations.

***

'Are you OK?' Lynn asked, seeing a faraway look on her husband's face. 'I think your dad's on your mind more than you're admitting.'

Jeff had clung to his children like a limpet that evening, playing with them before dinner, then clowning around outside until it was too dark to see. In between, he had been unusually strict when Kierney hadn't wanted to finish her vegetables; bordering on unreasonable, the young woman had thought at the time.

And now here he was again, aggravated by something as yet not articulated. One of his contacts in Pretoria had rung with some urgent news while he had been reading to the kids, which normally would have resulted in a swift parental substitution. Tonight however, he had shouted down to his wife to take a message and hadn't bothered to return the man's call.

'Shit,' the twenty-nine-year-old groaned, unbuttoning his shirt, peeling it off and rolling his shoulders to relieve the tension. 'There's something I need to tell you. I don't know where the memory came from, but I'm a hundred percent sure I'm not making it up.'

'What sort of memory?' his concerned wife asked.

The man of her dreams stood naked in front of her, his muscular torso bathed in moonlight from the open shutters. Before climbing into bed, he raised both hands and gripped his temples as if attempting to squeeze a disturbing image from his mind. She knelt up on the mattress and held out her arms.

'Whoa! You look amazing,' Jeff whispered, drinking in the sight of her full breasts bouncing with the sudden movement and letting his eyes drop lower to feast his imagination on what lay between her clenched thighs. 'Can I talk you into opening those?'

Lynn's mouth widened into a smile, shyly covering her modesty with a magazine. There was nothing she would like more, but not until they had negotiated this new hurdle. Under normal conditions, her insatiable lover would have been sporting a full-on erection by the time he resorted to such blatant seduction. Whatever was currently eating him had also arrested his sex-drive, even though she knew he would be trying every trick in the book to ignite the passion.

'Tell me about this memory first,' the compassionate beauty helped him out. 'You can't leave me dangling like that.'

671

'What? Like this, you mean?' Jeff took hold of his flaccid penis and flicked the useless organ up in the air.

'Well, it's obviously serious. Unless you've used your quota for the month.'

The intellectual laughed. 'I'd never be that negligent,' he quipped. 'I'd bribe someone to hand over theirs rather than see you go without.'

Lynn giggled, leaning into his warm body as her comedian bedfellow pulled the quilt over himself. 'Good. I'm glad it's all about my satisfaction. Now, come on… What's going on in here?'

The troubled soul grasped his dream girl's fingers as they tapped his forehead. 'Christ, Lynn. It's disgusting. I don't really want to tell you.'

'What do you mean? Some kind of flashback about your sister or your mum with those men again?'

'No,' he shook his head. 'It was a flashback, yeah, but about me and Dad this time. I'd finished reading Kizzy's story and left her virtually *sparko*. Then I was on my way into Jet's room to read with him but decided to go for a pee first, so I poked my head round the door and told him I'd see him in a minute. As I turned round, I tripped over the pile of books on the floor by the desk, and it all came flooding back. Sound, vision, everything.'

Her husband's jawline was taut with stress, and his eyes shone in the moonlight. Lynn recognised these tell-tale signs of trauma revisited, wondering if they were in for a nightmare tonight. Violent dreams were so rare these days that she almost felt unprepared. Yet it wouldn't be beyond the realm of possibility, given his father's passing.

'Carry on,' she urged.

Jeff inhaled, closing his eyes. 'My dad pissed all over my books once. It definitely happened, angel. I remember hating him so fucking much for doing it. All my schoolbooks. They stank for weeks afterwards, and I had to get them out of my bag to air them overnight 'cause I didn't want anyone at school to smell it.'

'Oh, my God,' the shocked star gasped. 'That is disgusting. I'm so sorry. Why did he do it?'

'Drunk and bitter,' the lost boy sniffed back tears. 'Goes without saying, I guess. He never liked the fact I wanted to do well at school. Probably wanted to stop me going, or just to goad me into fighting back.'

'Nothing would've stopped you going to school.'

'No. I know. And Lena laughed so bloody hard, I remember. That bit didn't come back to me until Jet sniggered at something in his book. I nearly threw up all over him.'

'Really? Oh, God. Did he notice?' the young mother propped herself up on her elbow, desperate to see behind her husband's eyes.

'No,' Jeff chuckled. 'He was too engrossed in the story. Thank Christ.'

'So what happened after your dad did this?'

'Nothing. He flicked his cock so the stream flashed across my face before directing it down onto the bedcovers, then swang it in a wide arc towards Lena's bed, laughing his fucking head off. It didn't hit her, and she was still laughing too. Jesus! What a fucked-up memory, huh?'

Truly horrible, his wife agreed. How on Earth could a father do such a thing? She could never in a month of Sundays envisage her own dad behaving in such an uncivilised manner in front of his children. No wonder Jeff had appeared so shaken earlier, on top of the bewildering mix of emotions visited on him upon losing his remaining parent.

'That's so perverted,' she responded after a few seconds. 'Poor you. I bet your brain couldn't wait to block that out.'

She noticed the lines on her man's brow had smoothed a little, and the intensity had left his eyes. Something had changed during the course of this evening. Perhaps it had all hinged on this one last, hidden and abhorrent recollection making its way from the dark, stagnant crevices of his mind.

As if reading her thoughts, Jeff coughed. 'Being sprung by that cute, long-lost *memoir* has reinforced to me that I *am* glad he's dead. I don't like him. No... I hate him, angel.'

'That's fine. You're entitled. He doesn't deserve your love.'

Droplets of salty water massed in the corners of his eyes, but his voice remained steady. 'Yeah. I believe you. I've always hated him. I guess I just forgot for a while. No-one'll ever treat our kids that way on my watch. Or any kid, for that matter. And most definitely not me.'

'No. You won't,' his wife agreed, kissing his lips. 'You wouldn't anyway. It's out in the open now. Thanks for telling me.'

The relieved husband whistled a lungful of air through dry lips. 'Hey. You're welcome, angel. Not sure why you're thanking me, but I feel heaps better. Might even be able to get it up for you. How did I get this lucky?'

'Because you're an amazing man,' Lynn replied, kissing him and sending her tongue in search of his. 'We'll put you to the test in the morning. Go to sleep, and let's hope that's the last you see of that dreadful memory.'

Although both lovers knew this was the sensible thing to do under the circumstances, their mouths had decided otherwise. Jeff's hands fondled his wife's firm breasts with an insistence that was impossible to ignore. Love had infused their bodies, limbs wrapping themselves around each other like vines.

Lynn's hand worked its magic on his stiffened penis, and her thigh pressed tight against his balls. Words of devotion flowed from their hearts as the R-rated movie ran on after its unsavoury trailer, knowing their children were dreaming peacefully along the hallway.

Then without warning, Jeff turned away. 'Leave me alone, woman. Go to sleep. I'm not twenty anymore.'

His wife groaned, frustrated to have been left in the lurch. 'Oh, why? I'm not tired anymore either.'

'I'll handle it.'

'Are you sure?' she teased.

'Jesus! I don't know what I'm saying!'

Lynn giggled. 'But what if *I* want to handle it?'

'Oh, shut the fuck up! You don't need this tonight. I know you've got another full day tomorrow.'

'Yes. But it's not only about me.'

'It is, angel,' Jeff insisted. 'Go to sleep.'

The emotional man rolled onto his back and stared at the ceiling, while the strong fingers of an amorous tennis champion came to rest on top of his own, shielding the tattoo on his chest. How did he get this lucky? He would never know, yet he would always care.

He laughed quietly at the insistent drumming of deft fingertips on his skin. 'I'm warning you.'

'I'm sorry, Papá,' his beautiful best friend whispered, impersonating their dark-haired gipsy girl.

Jeff sighed. 'Don't let go, gorgeous. Ever.'

'I won't.'

The couple lay side-by-side in the silence of the Mornington Peninsula, talking casually about the future. They committed to fly to New York after Paul Diamond's funeral to find a suitable place to scatter a murderer's ashes. Their conversation drifted from The Good School to the latest venture capital deal, then to South Africa and back to their children's education, never once losing the physical connection which sustained them.

'*Je t'adore*, Jeff Diamond.'

'*Merci, Regala. Je t'adore aussi,*' her sleepy perfect stranger mumbled. 'Can I just say one thing?'

'Yes,' Lynn felt his grip tighten around her waist and his breathing accelerate again.

'Now you've taken care of these...' Jeff dragged her hand first to his forehead and then down to something warm and altogether too tempting, 'you can take care of this...'

End of Part Four

If you enjoyed reading this book, please take the time to tell your friends and leave a review on Amazon and Goodreads.

Book 5 in the series, "A Life Tested", was published in December 2015. Full details can be found at http://lorrainepestell.com.

The world was an enormous place; full of good and evil, beauty and ugliness, wonder and despair. Sometimes all seemed lost, returning from the latest round of negotiations and attempting to balance the surreal career of a chart-topping musician with the demands of an advocate for those discarded by mainstream society. With every problem the Diamonds worked to solve, a new one would be right around the corner.

All was not lost, however. Unity and liberty, the twin spirits living in two perfect beings waiting for him at home, were all Jeff needed to spur him on. They would one day inherit the world which he and his beautiful best friend were intent on changing for the better, along with the millions of others who wrote to the couple every day, seeking ever more of their energy, time and money.

The tired author kept reverting to the theme of reciprocity. We should never take more than we give. If only they could convince enough people of their byword... It was right that the struggle should never end. What would he do if it did? There was no room for self-satisfied fat cats in their life singular. What sort of example might that set for those who must follow?

Lynn had departed, the children were growing stronger now, and the widower heard the clock ticking night after night after night. Still with so many amazing experiences to recount, the lost boy knew his dream girl couldn't wait forever. He was grateful for this opportunity to set the record straight, but gratitude could only take him so far.